The Gift of a Cow

A Translation of the Classic Hindi Novel

Godaan

By

PREMCHAND ·

Translated by
Gordon C. Roadarmel

With a new introduction by
Vasudha Dalmia

INDIANA
University Press
Bloomington & Indianapolis

This book is a publication of

Indiana University Press
601 North Morton Street
Bloomington, Indiana 47404-3797 USA

http://iupress.indiana.edu

Telephone orders   800-842-6796
Fax orders   812-855-7931
Orders by e-mail   iuporder@indiana.edu

Premchand's *Godaan* was first published in India in 1936.
This English translation was first published
by Allen and Unwin (London)
and Indiana University Press (Bloomington) in 1968.
The present reprint edition has been published under an exclusive agreement
with UNESCO by Permanent Black, D-28 Oxford Apts,
11, IP Extension, Delhi 110092, India.

This edition is not for sale in South Asia.

Library of Congress Cataloging-in-Publication Data
Premacanda, 1881–1936.
    [Godana. English]
    The gift of a cow : a translation of the classic Hindi novel Godaan /
by Premchand; translated into English by Gordon C. Roadarmel ; with
a new introduction by Vasudha Dalmia.
        p. cm.
    ISBN 0-253-21567-6 (paper : alk. paper)
    I. Title.

PK2098.S7 G613 2002
891.4'335—dc21

                                                            2002023293

1   2   3   4   5   07   06   05   04   03   02

Godaan is an eminently political novel. It was written in 1936 by Premchand, the best-known Hindi writer of the twentieth century, who had gained a vast reputation for his gripping tales of social unrest and change, in a language measured but also polemical, elevated but also colloquial.[1] A nationalist at odds with the British, by the 1920s Premchand had come to subscribe almost entirely to the Gandhian ethos, and towards the end of his life he was formulating a more radical message. As he was to say in his now famous speech at the inaugural meeting of the Progressive Writers' Association in Lucknow in 1936:

> A litterateur or an artist is, by nature, progressive. He probably would not have been a litterateur if this were not his nature. He feels inadequacy inside as well as outside himself. He must remain restless in order to fulfill this deficiency. He does not perceive the individual and society in those conditions of happiness and freedom in which he wants to see them in his imagination. For this reason, he always feels dissatisfied with the present mental and social conditions. He wants to end these disgusting conditions so that the world become a better place to live in and die in.[2]

The individual and society in *Godaan* are set within two narrative frames which draw upon each other, namely the economics and social codes of village life in Awadh (on the eastern Gangetic plains in the heart of North India), and of the wider network of colonial and nationalist politics in the city of Lucknow, Awadh's capital.

At the apex of the village social pyramid is Rai Saheb, the local landowner. Himself exploited to some extent, he has inherited the mantle of exploitation. A Rajput, obliged to the British for

---

[1] The best and most easily accessible biography of Premchand is by Amrit Rai, *Premchand: A Life* (1982).

[2] As translated and cited by Coppola (1986: 26).

maintaining his position and power, he is now in the process of shifting his alliance to the Indian National Congress. He has been to jail for his part in the independence struggle and has thus gained another kind of moral authority in the eyes of his tenants. But the wide base which supports his existence is itself in disrepair. Over three-quarters of a century of British rule, the lot of the peasant has degenerated to the barely tolerable.

In his fiction, written over three decades in the early twentieth century, Premchand presented what academic scholarship was to face squarely only towards the close of that century. Colonial taxation policies, peasant unrest, and the failure of the nationalist leadership to respond to these issues were to be addressed from the peasant-subaltern viewpoint in the pioneering first volumes of the Subaltern Studies collective which appeared in the early 1980s. To respond to and participate in Premchand's literary language—itself stratified, generic, period-bound—and to comprehend in some measure its socio-ideological conceptual horizon (Bakhtin 1981: 272, 275), it is necessary to possess some understanding of the social and political history of the province of Awadh in Premchand's time, and for this purpose it is to some of the essays in the *Subaltern Studies* volumes that we turn. One of these essays tells us that—

> In 1856 Awadh was brought under direct British rule in order, it was said, to rescue the province from the effects of misrule and anarchy. The mutiny and civil rebellion of 1857–9, which brought some of the fiercest fighting and severest reprisals of the century, formed, from that point of view, an unfortunate interlude. After that the benefits of Pax Britannica flowed freely, towards some. Chief among the beneficiaries were the two hundred and eighty or so taluqdars who, for their part in the recent uprising, were now held up as the 'natural leaders' of the people. The taluqdars were mostly local rajas and heads of clans, officials and tax-farmers who had secured an independent position in the land before the British annexation, plus a handful of 'deserving chiefs' who were given estates confiscated from the most notorious of the rebels. On this motley crowd the new rulers formally conferred many of the rights of the landowning gentry of Britain. Three-fifths of the cultivated area of Awadh was settled with them in return for the regular payment of revenue and assistance in maintaining order in the countryside. And British policy was now directed towards ensuring the taluqdars the wealth, status and security necessary to fulfil this role (Pandey 1982: 144).

Village social life was entirely subordinate to the politics and interests of the *taluqdars* or *zamindars*. The intolerance of any kind of deviance from social norms began at the smallest unit of social control. The *biradari*, or brotherhood, of the *jati* or caste kept check and control over individual behavior, which was further kept in place by village heads who zealously guarded the complex hierarchical network of the various *biradaris* which constituted the village social order.

Premchand delineates these village heads, these "guardians of justice in the village," with masterly strokes in *Godaan*, and with the "parodic stylization"[3] he so excels in, which he reserves entirely for these dignitaries and their counterparts in the city:

> Pandit Nokheram, the agent of the zamindar's estate, was a very high caste brahman. His grandfather had held a high position with a local ruler but then had laid all his possessions at the feet of God and become an ascetic. His father had also spent his life singing praises to Rama and now Nokheram had inherited that same piety. By dawn he would be sitting at prayers, and until ten would go on writing the name of Rama. As soon as he left the presence of God, however, he would throw off all restraints and let loose venomous thoughts, words and deeds (157).

Another, more free-floating, authority was the Brahman Datadin:

> He was the village troublemaker, sticking his nose into everyone's business. He had never committed a theft—that was too dangerous. But when it came time for the loot to be divided up, he was always present. Somehow he always managed to get off unscathed. He'd not yet paid a single pice of rent to the zamindar. When the bailiff showed up, Datadin would threaten to throw himself in the well, leaving Nokheram helpless. Yet Datadin always managed to have money to loan out at interest to the tenants (154–5).

Then there is the local Rajput: "the biggest financier was Jhinguri Singh, who represented a rich moneylender in the city." He looked harmless enough:

[3] Bakhtin describes "parodic stylization" as one of a number of "internally dialogized interilluminations of languages" where "the intentions of the representing discourse are at odds with the intentions of the represented discourse," which fights against them, depicting "a real world of objects not by using the represented language as a productive point of view, but rather by using it as an exposé to destroy the represented language" (1981: 363–4).

Jhinguri Singh was sitting brushing his teeth with a twig. He looked like a clown—a short, fat, bald dark man with a long nose and a big moustache. And he was quite a joker as a matter of fact, calling the village the home of his in-laws and thereby assuming the right to make disparaging remarks about all the men as brothers-in-law or fathers-in-law, and about all the women as sisters-in-law or mothers-in-law . . . In business matters, however, he showed no mercy, extorting the last pice of interest and camping on people's doorsteps until they produced the money. (126)

And finally the village accountant:

Lala Patweshwari could also be benevolent at times. During the malaria season he acquired renown by distributing free government quinine and by showing concern for those laid up with fever. He would also arbitrate all kinds of petty quarrels. And for weddings he was the salvation of the poor, loaning out his palanquins and carpets, and letting them use his large canopy. He never missed an opportunity to make money, but he would also aid those he devoured. (155)

He was, he pointed out, answerable only to the very highest: " 'I'm not a servant of the zamindar or of a money lender. I serve the royal government ['*sarkar bhadur ka naukar*'], which rules the whole world and is the master of both your zamindar and your moneylender' " (228–9). As the protagonist of the novel—the small-time tenant Hori—acknowledges willingly: " 'The village council is the voice of God. Whatever they think fair must be accepted cheerfully' " (158).

But in the India of the early 1920s, even the sturdiest peasant could be driven to fury and revolt, though it took a lot to bring him to this point:

When a peasant rose in revolt at any time or place under the Raj, he did so necessarily and explicitly in violation of a series of codes which defined his very existence as a member of that colonial, and still largely semi-feudal society. For his subalternity was materialized by the structure of property, institutionalized by law, sanctified by religion and made tolerable—and even desirable—by tradition. To rebel was indeed to destroy many of those familiar signs which he had learned to read and manipulate in order to extract a meaning out of the harsh world around him and live with it. The risk in 'turning things upside down' under these conditions was indeed so great that he could hardly afford to engage in such a project in a state of absentmindedness (Guha 1983: 1).

Premchand's village is, at this stage, not in revolt, though deep discontent simmers below its surface. It is at all events far from representing the agricultural idyll, the stable unchanging village community conjured up by colonial officials early in the nineteenth century.[4] It pulses with life, with hope, disappointment, intrigues and love affairs, licit and illicit. In the years when there is a good harvest, Hori, with his small tract of land, produces just enough to feed himself, his wife Dhaniya, and their three children: the two girls, Sona and Rupa, and his son Gobar.

Amidst all the activity and movement in the village, it is Hori who is the focus of the narrative. He is endlessly compassionate, led by his own notion of *dharma* and *niti* (righteousness and morality). It is as if he carries the moral weight of this world, a weight which threatens to crush him at several points in the story. His utterance at the beginning of the novel, when he is departing to pay his respects to the landlord, is prophetic: " 'I'll never reach sixty, Dhaniya,' " he said, picking up his stick, " 'I'll be gone long before that' " (16). As he tells Bhola, the cowherd who will strike a deal with him and give him the cow he so longs to own: " 'My grain was all weighed out at the village barn. The master took his share and the moneylender his, leaving me just ten pounds. I carried off the straw and hid it during the night, or not a blade would have been left me' " (36). As Premchand noted in English in his diary entry of January 2, 1936:

Hori's debts at the opening

Mangru Shah	60 grown to 300/-
Dulari	100
Data Din	100
Rent	25
	25 + 80/-[5]

This debt never relinquishes its stranglehold on Hori and his family, even at the best of times. It is little consolation that Hori is not alone in this fate. The intensification of commodity production in this part of the Indian countryside meant, as Shahid Amin has pointed

[4]The one occasion when it does freeze into an idyll is when there is a visit from the city. It becomes then a picnic spot and the characters are reduced to the one-dimensional. On the changing British visions and views of the village and the policy changes accompanying it, see Dewey (1972).

[5] As cited in Goyanka (1981), Vol. 1, p. 214.

out, that "the reproduction of small peasant households came to be dependent on the cultivation of sugarcane for usurious dealers" (1982: 52). For one thing, there was the "want of congruence between the farm calendar and the routine of rent collection" (Amin 1982: 52).

> The rent is often received by the landlord in the autumn, some *six months before the cane is cut,* the time when the tenant receives the greater part of the advances on the crop from the manufacturer. In fact the rent is, for his own security, commonly paid by the manufacturer direct to the landlord and deducted from the advance to be paid to the cultivator; thus the landlord, though not necessarily himself a manufacturer, has an interest in encouraging the cultivation. By this custom the tenant has to borrow in order to pay rent six months before he can receive any return by sale of the produce.[6]

As another Settlement Officer pointed out in 1917, the peasant was deep in debt, usually to his own landlord. "He is in the habit of borrowing money for seed, for his rent, even for his subsistence. All these loans carry 25 per cent interest, and the interest forms the first charge on the ensuing crop" (as quoted in Amin 1982: 82).

According to this reckoning, the tenant ended up paying a more or less permanent enhancement of 25 per cent on his recorded rent. As if this was not enough, he was denied his legitimate share of the market price at each stage of production: "within a complex system of indebtedness and dependence, all avenues—market price, rate of interest, weights and measures and hire of implement of production—were manipulated by moneylending traders and refiners to flush out this important commodity at as low a price as possible" (Amin 1982: 72).

Hori, though so deeply entangled in this web of debt and social obligations, longs to own a cow. "For him the cow was not only an object of worship and devotion; it was also the living image of prosperity. He wanted it to beautify his door and to raise the prestige of his house. He wanted people to see the cow at his door and ask, 'Whose place is that?' " (53) When he does manage to negotiate a deal with Bhola the cowherd, and the cow arrives at his doorstep, "There was no stopping the hubbub. After all, the cow had not

[6] Report of a revenue official in 1870, as cited in Amin (1982: 81).

come hidden in a bridal palanquin. How could such a great event take place without causing a commotion? As soon as people heard, they dropped their work and ran to take a look. This was no ordinary local cow. She'd been bought from Bhola for eighty rupees!" (53) He arouses the envy and jealousy of the village and of his estranged brothers. Early in the story, the cow is poisoned by his brother and the downward slide of the family begins.

Is *Godaan* then primarily a story of unremitting suffering told with unrelenting sententiousness, both of which Premchand has been understood to represent? Is this what has made the novel a classic of modern Hindi literature? It seems to me that it is the immense tension within the novel, between the kind of *dharma* Hori tries to fulfill and the pulls—social and political—away from it, that fills the novel with a poignancy and a defiance to which readers through the decades have responded.

The novel can be read as containing, both in the sense of harbouring and of not allowing to ultimately step out of bounds, two kinds of rebellion—'*vidroh*' in Hindi—and Premchand uses the term. The first rebel is Hori's son Gobar, who falls in love with Jhuniya, who is of a lower, cowherd caste: she is Bhola's daughter. He leaves her pregnant at his parents' doorstep and runs away to the city because he cannot face his parents, but also because he cannot bear the yoke of eternal debt and humiliation. He enjoys the freedom which comes from earning money in the city but is eventually caught up in a new kind of exploitation, that of the industrial worker in an industrializing economy, with its own networks of exploitation. Working in a sugar mill, he looks back to the life of the village:

> Gobar had to start out early in the morning, and by the time he returned home at dusk after a full day's work, there was not a spark of life left in his body. In the village he'd been forced to work just as hard, but he had never felt the least bit tired. The work had been interspersed with laughter and conversation, and the open fields and broad skies had seemed to ease the strain. However hard his body worked there, his mind had remained free. Here, although his body was taxed less, the hubbub, the speed and the thundering noise weighed him down. There was also the constant apprehension of rebuke. The workers were all in the same boat and they drowned their physical fatigue and mental weariness in palm toddy or cheap liquor. Gobar took to drinking also. (339)

Filled with the headiness of his own early success, at one stage Gobar mocks his father: "'That's what comes of being too good'" (261–2); but by the end of the novel he has learnt to respect the dignity Hori has retained through all his trials. Gobar also sees that the traditions fostered in the village—even if he sees through them and can to some extent overcome them—are ultimately too strong for him to try and overcome on behalf of his father.

The second, more sustained but also more hopeless, rebellion is represented by Hori's wife Dhaniya. At the start of the novel she has turned thirty-six, yet she is already grey and aging. But she is full of insight and courage. This is how she is introduced: "Why bother with all this flattery for land that could not even provide food for their stomachs? Rebellion kept welling up in her heart—but then a few harsh words from her husband would jolt her back to reality" (16). She resists the agents of colonial 'law and order'; she refuses to pay the police officer who comes to investigate the killing of their cow and who promptly allies himself with the village headmen. The village is thrilled by her defiance. But the village is less thrilled with her resistance to caste laws, which forbid the alliance of her son with Jhuniya. Yet she chooses to take in the abandoned Jhuniya: "Suddenly Dhaniya put her arm around Hori's neck. 'Look,' she pleaded, 'swear to me you won't hit her. She's crying already. If fate weren't against her, she'd never have fallen into all this trouble'" (150). Not content with all the trouble this action will get them into, including the ruinous fines they will have to pay at the behest of the village council, she later takes in Siliya, another abandoned woman, this time of the Chamar (leatherworking) caste, who has been cast off by Matadin, a Brahman boy. The Chamars have risen against this caste oppression by having collectively defiled Matadin by forcing meat into his mouth, and he is so enraged that he now refuses to look at Siliya. Dhaniya has no pity for him, "'Men are all alike. No one was upset when Matadin defiled her. Now the same thing's happened to him, so what's wrong with that? Doesn't Siliya's virtue count as virtue? He takes a chamar woman and then makes out that he's so pious! Harkhu did just the right thing. That's exactly the punishment hoodlums like him deserve. You come home with me, Siliya.'" (310) The question is how far this kind of self-willed behavior will be allowed to go.

These village power structures are sustained in various ways by those of the city, and the characters in the city—mill owner, newspaper editor, banker turned industrialist, professor and medical doctor—who provide a counterpoint to the village dignitaries. For most of them, Premchand reserves the parodic stylization which he uses to achieve a certain distancing, often offering fictive solidarity with their hypocritical public posturing (Bakhtin 1981: 306) when speaking of their intents and concerns. Of others—those to whom he sets the task of seeking resolutions to these vast social problems—he offers idealized portraits. And in some senses they, who are materially better equipped to cope with the vicissitudes of life, provide much needed relief from the crushing misery and weight of village life. The most upright character, who almost never wavers from his beliefs, is the philosophy professor, Mr. Mehta. As he tells the vaguely philosophizing Rai Saheb, the zamindar, at the gathering at his county house, " 'I have no sympathy for people who talk like communists but live like princes in selfish luxury' " (72). He is paired with Miss Malti: "A practising physician who had studied medicine in England, she had frequent access to the mansions of the zamindars. She was the living image of modernity—expertly made up, delicate but full of life, lacking any trace of hesitation or shyness. . ." (76) She leaves her flighty social existence to become a model social reformer and eventually a partner in a Gandhian union (as against a partner in marriage). She has, as she tells Mr. Mehta,

. . . greater happiness in being friends than in being husband and wife. You love me, you believe in me, and I'm confident that, if the occasion arose, you would protect me with your life. I've found not only a guide but also a protector in you. I love you too, and I believe in you, and there's no sacrifice I couldn't make for you. And I humbly pray to God that he keep me firmly on this path the rest of my life. What more do we need for our fulfillment, for our self-development? If we set up our own household, shutting our souls in a little cage and restricting our joys and sorrows to each other, could we ever approach the Infinite? It would just put an obstacle in our path (412).

But the tale does not close with this Gandhian vow; rather it closes on a burning hot roadside, swept by the blazing wind which blows in from the desert. It is here that Hori, estranged from his patch of earth, labours to earn money enough to buy a cow which will provide milk for his grandson and it is here that he breathes his last. He does not know that a cow is on its way, sent by the daughter whom he has under extreme duress married to an elderly but kindly man, who fulfills all her wishes. The novel takes its title from the symbolic gesture of helplessness Dhaniya makes when asked to gift a cow to a brahman, signifying thereby, as I read it, the hollowness of such pious acts.

Writing in the wake of the great peasant movements of resistance in the early 1920s, it is this intricate web—of family history, village history as linked to the city, and from there to the prospective nation—that Premchand weaves with compassion and perspicuity. As he had pointed out in his 1936 speech to the Progressive Writers:

> Till now standards [of beauty] were based on those of wealth and luxury. Our artist wished to remain tied to the apron strings of the rich; his existence was dependent on their appreciation and the purpose of art was to describe their pleasures and sorrows, hopes and disappointments, their conflicts and competitions. . . . It was beyond the imagination of art to consider whether the villager also possessed a heart and hopes.[7]

★ ★ ★

The translation of a work as vibrant as *Godaan* poses a challenge to the best of translators. Though it has large stretches, veritable compact masses of authorial discourse—pathos-filled, moral-didactic, sentimental-elegiac and idyllic (Bakhtin 1981: 302)—many socially diverse speech types are represented here, sometimes juxtaposed, sometimes at extreme odds with each other. As Bakhtin points out, "at any given moment of its historical existence, language is heteroglot from top to bottom, it represents the co-existence of socio-ideological contradictions between the present and the past, between differing epochs of the past, between different socio-ideological groups in the present, between tendencies, schools, circles and so forth, all given a bodily form. These 'languages' of heteroglossia intersect each other in a variety of ways, forming new socially typifying 'languages' " (Bakhtin 1981: 291). With a novel as rich as this in speech types as well as the tensions between them, there are

[7] As translated and cited by Coppola (1986: 27).

more than the usual difficulties in translation. The differences are bound to be levelled out in translation, especially when the translator is trying to create a wide readership in the West by presenting the material and concerns at hand as neither too alien nor too remote. Gordon Roadarmel does not entirely escape this pitfall. If at a dramatic moment in her encounter with the police official Dhaniya speaks of the futility of trying to gain '*suraj*' as she calls it, that is, *svaraj* (self- or home-rule), on a moral basis as slim as that presented by the new leadership, Roadarmel elects to omit these few lines with their immediate reference to impending political disaster altogether. He also omits another telling sentence, in order perhaps not to belittle Hori, when Gobar calls his father a '*gau*' (cow)—that is, a man too simpleminded and submissive to survive village politics—linking him ironically to the very object he so desperately seeks to own. The cow has, in fact, positive connotations in Hori's culture, being revered precisely for her innocence and vulnerability.

These few problematic choices apart, Roadarmel managed to present what was widely seen as a fluent, readable and lively translation of a difficult novel at a time when modern Indian literature was practically unknown outside India. This reissue of *Godaan*, thirty years after Roadarmel's passing away, is a tribute to the durability of his work. As his successor in some senses, as an instructor of Hindi literature in the very department and the very university where he did most of his work, I should like to pay my personal tribute to him by recalling some details of his short life.

Gordon C. Roadarmel was born to missionary parents in 1932, in India. After graduating from Woodstock School in Mussoorie, he came to the United States, joining the College of Wooster in Ohio, where he received his B.A. in 1954. He took his M.A. degree in English and Asian Studies at the University of California in Berkeley, and his Ph.D. in Hindi literature in 1969 at the same institution, where he had been a member of the faculty and where, in 1966, he was cited for distinguished teaching. In 1970 he was elected to the South Asia Regional Council of the Association of Asian Studies and served as a member of its Library and Documentation Committee. Amongst other honors, he was given the Fulbright Research Grant for the study of Hindi literature at the University of Allahabad, 1962–4, and a Carnegie Internship at the University of Chicago. At the time of his death, he had just returned from India, where he had been continuing his research and his writing.

Roadarmel was a pioneer in introducing modern Hindi literature to the Western world. He wrote critical articles and translated the work of major figures of Hindi literature, such as Premchand, Jainendra Kumar, S.H.Vatsyayan 'Ajneya', and Mohan Rakesh. These articles, reviews and translations appeared widely in leading Indian and American journals. He worked closely with 'Ajneya', himself a leading figure in the world of Hindi letters in post-independence India, in the translation not only of *Godaan* but also of Ajneya's own existentialist novel *To Each His Stranger*. One of Roadarmel's most lasting contributions, however, was his analytical evaluation of the *nayi kahani* or 'new short story' movement in Hindi literature of the 1950s and 1960s, with its preoccupation with the newly nuclear family households in the cities and the vexed union of man and woman which formed their center. His doctoral dissertation, "The Theme of Alienation in the Modern Hindi Short Story," concerned itself with this topic. He did not live long enough to turn it into a book. But the short stories which he translated in the process were published in the fall of 1972 by the University of California Press, under the title *A Death in Delhi, Modern Hindi Short Stories*.

We seek to remember his work by continuing to carry it out.

Berkeley, March 2002   Vasudha Dalmia

REFERENCES

Amin, Shahid. 1982. "Small Peasant Commodity Production and Rural Indebtedness: The Culture of Sugarcane in Eastern U.P., *c.* 1880–1920," in *Subaltern Studies II: Writings on South Asian History and Society*. Delhi: Oxford University Press, pp. 39–87.

Bakhtin, M.M. 1981. *The Dialogic Imagination: Four Essays by M.M. Bakhtin*. Ed. Michael Holquist. Austin: University of Texas Press.

Coppola, Carlo. 1986. "Premchand's Address to the First Meeting of the All-India Progressive Writers Association: Some Speculations," in *Journal of South Asian Literature*, 21/2, Summer/Fall 1986, pp. 21–39.

Dewey, Clive. 1972. "Images of the Village Community: A Study in Anglo-Indian Ideology," in *Modern Asian Studies*, 6/3.

Goyanka, K. K. 1981. *Premchand Vishva Kosh.* 2 volumes. Delhi: Prabhat Prakashan.

Guha, Ranajit. 1983. "The Prose of Counter-insurgency," in *Subaltern Studies II: Writings on South Asian History and Society.* Delhi: Oxford University Press, pp. 1–40.

Pandey, Gyanendra. 1982. "Peasant Revolt and Indian Nationalism: The Peasant Movement in Awadh, 1919–22," in *Subaltern Studies I: Writings on South Asian History and Society.* Delhi: Oxford University Press, pp. 143–97.

Rai, Amrit. 1982. *Premchand: A Life.* Translated by Harish Trivedi. Delhi: People's Publishing House.

INTRODUCTION

The selection of Premchand's *Godaan* as one of the first Hindi novels to be translated into English and published in the West will come as no surprise to anyone familiar with Hindi literature, for Premchand is generally considered the greatest of Hindi fiction writers, and his last novel—*Godaan*, published in 1936, as his best or at least his most important work. These factors in themselves make it desirable that the book be accessible to English readers whose impressions of Indian literature, being based almost entirely on works written by Indians in English, are likely to be inaccurate.

At the beginning of the twentieth century, Hindi fiction, still in its infancy, was dominated by romantic treatments of Indian legend and history recounting the adventures of high-born heroes and heroines. Although twentieth-century developments in Hindi fiction can not be attributed solely to the influence of Premchand, there is no doubt that he played a very important part in shifting the focus of the novel to a contemporary social context in which individual characters, particularly those from the lower and middle levels of society, were developed.

The author's first book, a small collection of short stories in Urdu, was published in 1908 under the pseudonym 'Nawab Rai', but when the British government discovered that these 'inflammatory pieces' had been written by Dhanpat Rai, a teacher in a government school, all available copies of the book were burned and the author found it expedient to change his pen name. The name 'Premchand' appeared on his first major novel, *Sevasadan*, in 1918, and Dhanpat Rai was soon well known in Urdu and Hindi literary circles by that name. First an Urdu writer, Premchand soon found it easier to get his works published in Hindi translation, and he gradually shifted over to writing and publishing primarily in Hindi.

Premchand was born near Banaras in 1880, the son of a village postmaster of the *kayastha* caste. Educated first in Urdu and Persian, he later attended a Christian mission high school in Gorakhpur and then a high school in Banaras, a four-mile walk from his village home. Unsuccessful in gaining university admission because of deficiencies in mathematics, he taught in various small schools before being selected for teacher's training and being appointed as a sub-inspector of schools. At the age of thirty-nine, he completed a B.A., and within three years he was devoting himself almost entirely to literary and journalistic pursuits, rejecting government employment in Gandhian protest against foreign rule.

Premchand's mother had died when he was about eight years old. His father soon remarried. At fifteen, Premchand himself was married in accordance with his parents' wishes. His father died not long after. Quarrels between Premchand's stepmother and his wife led the wife to return to her family home some ten years after the marriage, but at the age of about twenty-nine, Premchand married again, choosing the daughter, widowed as a child, of an ardent Arya Samaj reformer. Satisfaction over the literary acclaim won in the years before his death in 1936 was somewhat dimmed by the author's chronic ill health and by the heavy debts and government restrictions which dogged his efforts to establish and run an independent press. Some of these financial and domestic tensions, Premchand's concern for political and social reform, and the conflicts aroused by his exposure to both village and city life, are reflected in the characters and themes of his novels and short stories.

In the preface in his first collection of short stories, Premchand noted that the tales revolve primarily around the theme of social reform and commented that 'such books are badly needed by the country in order to impress the stamp of patriotism on the coming generations'. Social reform had been a burning concern with many Indian intellectuals since the early nineteenth century, and the twentieth century brought rising demands for political reform also. Since Premchand's literary career took place during this time when most Indian intellectuals were involved in some sort of activist agitation, it is hardly surprising that he felt that his work should serve a definite social purpose, and the climate of literary criticism at the time can perhaps be seen in the comments of a reviewer of Premchand's short stories in 1919 who praised the moralistic conclusions of the stories, saying that 'for a popular writer these days to be able to teach his countrymen through the power of his pen is a matter of the deepest satisfaction and good fortune, not only for himself, but also for the country'.

Premchand's didactic intentions may intrude at times on contemporary literary sensibilities, but to the reader who views this novel not only as an isolated literary work but also as a kind of historical and social document, the occasional digressions, the moralizing and the romanticizing can be appreciated as a source of insight into the writer and his time. 'Idealism has to be there,' Premchand said in a lecture in Madras in 1934, 'even though it should not militate against realism and naturalness. Similarly it would be good for the realist not to forget idealism. We have to portray noble, idealistic aspirations. Otherwise, what would be the use of literature?' To Premchand, the alternative to this 'useful' literature seemed to be a literature intended only 'to entertain and to satisfy our lust for the amazing', the stories of magic, of fairies and ghosts, of princes pursuing their beloveds which were found in most of the early Hindi novels. Fortunately Premchand's view of 'usefulness' was tempered by a desire to depict characters 'according to the existing possibilities'. The writer could be expected 'to awaken us, and broaden our view and mental sphere', but he was to do so by presenting 'an honest critical view of life'.

In *Godaan*, the utopian solutions found in most of Premchand's earlier novels have been discarded. The area of conflict in this novel has become more complex, suggesting that there are no easy answers to the problems of either the village or the city, though there is the possibility of improvement and some hint that a better social order is likely to emerge. There seems to be a faith in basic human goodness which, if freed from external and internal pressures, could be the basis of a new society. Although Premchand seems to suggest that certain specific reforms are necessary such as the abolition of the *zamindari* system, this novel suggests that he believes the change of heart to be the most potent force for change.

The changes of heart in *Godaan* allow the author to end the novel on a hopeful note despite the tragic end of the protagonist. Khanna is changed by exposure to financial disaster and by the recognition of his wife's devotion, Mirza is changed by illness, Mehta is changed by philosophical investigation, and Malti is changed by her exposure to Mehta. Among the village characters, who are generally more convincing throughout, there are fewer of these drastic personality changes, but with Matadin and Gobar especially, one sees again a movement away from self-centredness toward self-sacrifice and humanitarian service.

Premchand is at his best in portraying the conflicts of Indian village life, and it is that picture of rural life which has made *Godaan* a classic in modern Hindi literature. Some of the forces operating in the village of this novel have been modified over the years in Indian villages, and some of the forces were especially characteristic of rural life in the section of north India known now as Uttar Pradesh, but the basic struggles depicted in *Godaan* can still be found in much of contemporary Indian rural life.

When Premchand turns to middle and upper class urban life, his portrait seems less convincing, although many of the ideological clashes continue to be live issues today. The reality of those clashes, however, does not negate the fact that the author's ideas and theories are not fully integrated into the narration, and that the city characters often seem to be delivering speeches rather than conversing. Such discussions would certainly be more likely in the city than in the village, but the settings for them are at times improbable, and one suspects that the characters are speaking more for the author than for themselves.

Critics have charged that Premchand did not understand the middle and upper classes as he did the peasants, and this may be true, but such a judgment must be weighed in terms of his literary intentions. However well he may have understood such people, it is possible that his desire to depict certain ideals and certain conflicts may have over-weighed the desire for more realistic characterization. The author did say that development of character counts above everything else in a novel, but he felt that such character development should serve a definite function, 'to bring finer and deeper emotions into play.'

In any case, the inclusion of both rural and urban life allows the author to present a total view of society that a concentration on either one would have eliminated. And the testimony to Premchand's artistic success would seem to be that, considering the novel as a whole, there does appear a wide range of vivid characters whose conflicts, though perhaps oversimplified at times, reflect a range of internal and external problems credible in the Indian setting. It is perhaps fortunate that Premchand did not fully resolve his own conflicting views about traditional and modern forces. Idealising the poor and the humble, he was nevertheless painfully aware that they bring on many of their own difficulties. And distrusting capitalism, he could still recognize that it offered an escape from some other forms of oppression. As a result, the human factor pushes through the political and social and economic statements, and Gobar finds hope not in some system but in recognizing that 'whatever one's situation, greed and selfishness would only make it worse.'

Readers unfamiliar with Indian life may feel at a loss in understanding some of the motivations, following parts of the narration, and picturing some of the settings. Novels in English dealing with India usually spell out the unfamiliar cultural details for the Western reader. One of the attractions, however, of novels written first in an Indian language is that one can explore the situation from within the local context, not feeling that the author is catering to the interests of English readers, that he is dealing not with the curious or the exotic but with matters of concern to those within the culture.

As a result, the reader or critic of a novel such as *Godaan* is challenged to share an experience within a distinctively though not exclusively Indian frame of reference. For example, the awareness of conservative Hindu views about the responsibilities of married women makes Malti's choice to remain unmarried so as to perform social service more credible than it might appear from a Western point of view. Similarly, Hori's attitude towards his rebellious brother reflects a traditional Indian view of family loyalty, honour and responsibility. And a number of the details—the touching of people's feet, the shoe beatings, the repeated references to women as goddesses, the apparent sentimentality about motherhood—need to be understood as natural for the Hindi reader and within the Indian context. By not adding explanatory notes in the text or in footnotes, the translator has accepted the fact that some readers may miss or misinterpret certain allusions, in the novel but this seems less offensive than intruding on the author's work and disturbing the pleasure of other readers.

Premchand wrote *Godaan* over a period of some three years, at a time when he was harassed by problems with his press, during which he went to Bombay for a while to write film scripts, and during which he was trying to establish a magazine reflecting the best literature being produced in all the Indian languages. His attention, then, was frequently diverted from the novel he was writing, and this may partially explain the looseness of structure and of detail. The fact that he died some four months after the initial publication of the novel may also help to explain why some of the inconsistencies in the plot were not corrected. Readers who compare this translation closely with the original will find that a few changes have been made to smooth over chronological and other inconsistencies. In general, however, the wording of the translation is intended to follow the original, so that the reader can judge both the strengths and the weaknesses of the author's work. A reader who carefully plots the time sequence and keeps in mind the details of the story will find a number of inconsistencies. When critics mentioned such matters in discussing earlier works by Premchand, the author passed them off usually as being irrelevant to his literary intentions. So if certain threads of the plots are left hanging, or if some of the comments and descriptions seem inappropriate, one can only accept these as reflecting a view of literature in which concise statement, tight plot structure and realism were not always given top priority, and appreciate the novel in the context of the author's intentions, his personal background, and the literary climate of the period in which the book was written.

Godaan can no longer be considered as representative of contemporary Indian or Hindi fiction, but there seems little doubt that it will always be considered as something of a classic in the development of Indian and Hindi fiction, and its portrayal of both village and urban society will undoubtedly continue to have relevance for the understanding of India for many generations.

THE TRANSLATION

A translator, consciously or unconsciously, works at least partly in terms of an abstract ideal of what he wishes to accomplish through his particular translation. That ideal leads to the formulation of principles within which to consider specific problems that arise in translating the text. In reviewing the final result, the inadequacy of principles and rules, and therefore the inconsistency of their application, becomes apparent. Nevertheless, the reader deserves to know something about the translator's intentions, so that the work can be seen at least partially within the context of those intentions, just as the novel itself needs to be seen at least partially within the context of the author's intentions.

If the enjoyment of the reader is the only consideration, a translator may be tempted to heighten that enjoyment by 'improving on the author'. Particularly in a work as well known as *Godaan*, however, the reader presented with such a translation could rightfully protest the presumption of the translator's view of both the original author and the reader. In order to allow *Godaan* to be considered from a variety of viewpoints—as an enjoyable novel, as a part of Hindi literary history, as a reflection of the social and intellectual concerns of its time—it has seemed wise to let Premchand speak for himself as much as possible, leaving him as the judge of what he wanted to say and how he wanted to say it.

This broad ideal has had to be modified, of course, since the translator has to rely in the end of his own intuition in trying to recreate for the English reader something of the experience of the Hindi reader. That attempt requires a consideration not only of equivalents of sense but also of levels of vocabulary and imagery, of syntactic emphasis, of sound patterns, and of cross-cultural intelligibility.

A few deliberate alterations have been made in the text to correct the most disturbing inconsistencies, particularly of chronology, in the original. If Premchand had lived to supervise a second edition of the novel, one can perhaps presume that he would have made at least these alterations. Some changes in style are necessitated by the differences between Hindi and English. Passive constructions are sometimes made active, rhetorical questions are sometimes turned into direct statements, short sentences are sometimes combined, and the direct thought and conversation characteristic of Hindi has sometimes been changed to indirect thought and conversation. In general such alterations have been allowed when the alternative would be a statement that would strike the English reader as peculiar in some way while the original seemed perfectly natural to the Hindi reader.

A similar problem arises in translating idioms and images. A Hindi phrase may have an English equivalent with a similar meaning, but which would in English be a cliché, and therefore produce an inappropriate response in the reader. If left closer to the original idiom or image, however, the phrase may have a startling freshness to the English reader that it did not have to the Hindi reader. Translators would inevitably differ in their judgment as to the nearest aesthetic and emotional equivalents in such cases, and justification for particular renderings could only be made in terms of having considered a variety of factors for each unit of text.

There has been a deliberate attempt to use as few Hindi terms as possible. Those that have been retained are italicized only when they first appear, and are explained in the glossary. Some readers may feel that too many terms have been translated, but their background will probably allow them to think immediately of the corresponding term anyway, so that they can substitute 'panchayat', for example, when they read 'village council'. The Indian coinage system has been retained, though the *pie* has been replaced by *pice* or *cowrie* to avoid confusion for some readers. Weights and measures have generally been given their approximate English equivalents, with *seers* changed to quarts, *bighas* to acres, *maunds* to bushels or pounds, and so on. Some of the terms of relationship which so commonly replace personal names in Hindi conversation have been retained, but they have been omitted in some places where they seemed particularly unnatural in English. Consistency in transliterating the Hindi terms has been sacrificed at times for more conventional spellings.

A manuscript by S. H. Vatsyayan was very helpful to me in translating the village section of this novel.

I would also like to express my deep appreciation to Mrs Saroj Kapadia, Mr G. Roy Chaudhury, Mr D. N. Sharma, Mr O. P. Jaiswal, and Mr V. B. Gupta, for their assistance in checking the translation, to Sripat Rai for his encouragement during the translation of his father's work, to Mr Daniel L. Milton and Mrs Bonnie Crown for several years of planning, negotiations and guidance towards making the publication of this work possible, to Mrs Florence Meyer for typing the manuscript, and to the United Nations Educational, Scientific and Cultural Organization (UNESCO), the United States Educational Foundation in India, the Asia Society in New York, the Centre for Indian Language and Area Studies at the University of Chicago, and the Department of Near Eastern Languages at Berkeley for helping to provide the time and money for this project. Readers interested in this novel and in the attitudes and techniques of translation may also wish to compare the present work with the version prepared by Mr P. Lal and Mr Jai Ratan, and published by Jaico in India.

Gordon C. Roadarmel.

PRINCIPAL CHARACTERS

In the village:

Hori Ram, a farmer living in Belari
Dhaniya, his wife
Gobar (Gobardhan), their son
Sona (Sonie), their elder daughter
Rupa (Rupiya), their younger daughter

Bhola, a herdsman living in an adjacent village
Kamta, his elder son
Jangi, his younger son
Jhuniya (Jhunni), his widowed daughter
Lallu (Chunnu), son of Jhuniya and Gobar
Mangal, second son of Jhuniya and Gobar
Nohri, Bhola's second wife

Shobha, Hori's younger brother
Hira, Hori's younger brother
Puniya (Punni), Hira's wife

Pandit Datadin, an elderly Brahman
Matadin (Matai), son of Datadin

Siliya (Sillo), a chamar girl, mistress of Matadin
Ramu, son of Siliya and Matadin
Harkhu, Siliya's father
Kalia, Siliya's mother

Dulari, a widowed shopkeeper and moneylender
Mangaru Shah, a moneylender
Lala Pateshwari, the patwari—government revenue
   official in the village; kayastha by caste
Jhinguri Singh, the village representative of a large
   urban moneylender; a thakur
Pandit Nokheram, the Rai Sahib's agent in the village
Bisesar Shah, a moneylender
Bindesari (Bhunesari), son of Lala Pateshwari
Damri, a cane-weaver
Girdhar, a farmer
Kodai, resident of a village between Belari and Lucknow

xxvi

Ganda Singh, regional police inspector
Mathura, a farmer in the village of Sonari
Gauri Ram, Mathura's father
Ramsevak, wealthy widower from another village

In the city:

The Rai Sahib (Amarpal Singh), zamindar whose
   lands include Belari; a resident of Semari
Rudrapal Singh, his eldest son
Minakshi, his daughter
Kunwar Digvijay Singh, a wealthy widower
Pandit Onkarnath, editor of *Lightning*
Gomti, his wife

Shyam Bihari Tankha, lawyer and 'broker'
Doctor Mehta, university professor of philosophy
Mr Chandra Prakash Khanna, bank manager and
   sugar mill managing director
Govindi (Kamini), his wife
Mirza Khurshed, Muslim businessman

Miss Malti, physician trained in England
Mr Kaul, her father
Saroj and Varda, her younger sisters

Raja Surya Pratap Singh, a member of the local
   aristocracy

Chuhia, seller of firewood; Gobar and Jhuniya's
   neighbour in the city
Aladin and Bhuri, ekka drivers

PUBLISHER'S NOTE ON THE TEXT AND
ITS PAGINATION

This new paperback edition comprises a photographic reproduction of the originally typeset text of the Roadarmel translation of *Godaan*, along with Roadarmel's original Introduction. The preliminary pages of that originally typeset text ran from page i to page xiv (Roman numerals). They were followed by the first page of the novel, which began on page 15 (Arabic numeral), thereby violating the modern publishing convention of numbering preliminary pages with Roman numbers and the main text, starting page 1, with Arabic numbers.

Vasudha Dalmia's new Introduction to this edition entailed an insertion within the preliminary pages. These preliminary pages, therefore, now conclude on this page, i.e. page xxviii. They are followed (unavoidably) by the first page of the text of the novel, page 15.

CHAPTER 1

————————

Hori Ram finished feeding his two bullocks and then turned to his wife Dhaniya. 'Send Gobar to hoe the sugar cane. I don't know when I'll be back. Just get me my stick.'

Dhaniya had been making fuel-cakes, so her hands were covered with dung. 'First eat something before you leave,' she said. 'What's the big hurry?'

A frown deepened the wrinkles on Hori's forehead. 'All you think about is food. But I have to worry that I may not even get to see the master if I reach there late. Once he starts his bathing and prayers I'll have to wait around for hours.'

'That's exactly why I'm suggesting you first have something to eat. And what harm would be done by not going at all today? You were there just two days ago.'

'Why do you go poking your nose into things you don't understand? Just hand me my stick and get on with your own work. It's thanks to all these visits of mine that we're still alive. God knows what would have become of us otherwise. You know how many people here in the village have been thrown off their land or had their property taken away. When someone's heel is on your neck, it's best to keep licking his feet.'

Dhaniya was less sophisticated in these matters. They ploughed the land of the *zamindar*,[1] so all he should care about was the rent. True, these twenty years of married life had taught her that however much she cut corners, skimped on food and clothes, and clung to every *cowrie*, it was still hard to pay the rent. But why should they have to flatter the landlord or lick his feet? She argued the question daily with her husband, refusing to admit defeat.

Only three of their six children were still alive—Gobar, a boy of about sixteen, and two girls—Sona, twelve, and Rupa, eight. Three sons had died in infancy. Dhaniya still believed that medicines would

[1]Hindi terms are only given in *italics* the first time they occur and are all explained in the Glossary at the end of this book.

15

have saved them, but she'd been unable to afford even a *pice* worth. She was not very old herself—just thirty-six—but her hair was completely grey and her face wrinkled. Her body had grown weak, the wheat complexion of her youth had turned dark brown, and her eyes had become dim—all because of the struggle for survival. Life had brought no joy—only a constant weariness which had worn away all concern for self-respect. Why bother with all this flattery for land that couldn't even provide food for their stomachs? Rebellion kept welling up in her heart—but then a few harsh words from her husband would jolt her back to reality.

Defeated again, she brought Hori's stick, jacket, turban, shoes and tobacco pouch and flung them down in front of him.

Hori glared at her. 'What's this outfit for? You think I'm going to your father's house? And even if I were, it's not as though you have some young sisters there that I should dress up for.' A trace of a smile softened his dark sunken features.

'I suppose you think that if some gorgeous young thing were there, she'd get a big thrill out of looking at you?'

Hori folded his tattered jacket carefully and placed it on the cot. 'So you consider me an old man, do you? I'm not even forty yet. And men are still lusty as bulls at sixty.'

'Not ones like you. Go look at your face in the mirror. Just how are you going to be lusty when you can't even get enough milk and butter to make a few drops of ointment for your eyes? It scares me to see the condition you're in—makes me wonder how we'll manage in our old age. Whose door will we beg at?'

Hori's momentary mellowness vanished as though consumed in the flames of reality. 'I'll never reach sixty, Dhaniya,' he said, picking up his stick. 'I'll be gone long before that.'

'All right now, that's enough!' Dhaniya snapped. 'Don't say such evil-omened things. Even when someone speaks nicely to you, you can't give a civil answer.'

Hori shouldered his stick and left the house. Dhaniya, standing in the doorway, watched him for a long time. His despairing words had shaken her already battered heart. Blessings for Hori welled up within her, inspired by all the devotion and self-sacrifice her womanhood could command. Her marriage was the one straw to which she clung in crossing the bottomless ocean of poverty. Hori's thoughtless remark, though close to the truth, had shaken her, threatening to tear even that one feeble straw from her grasp. In fact it was the very truthfulness of the statement that made it so disturbing. The taunt 'Hey One-eye!' hurts a one-eyed man more than it does a two-eyed one.

Hori hurried along. Looking over the green expanse of young sugar cane plants rippling on both sides of the footpath, he told himself that if God would just send enough rain for the crops to come up well, he'd certainly buy a cow . . . and not just one of those local ones, which give no milk and whose calves are no good except perhaps to turn the oilman's press. No, he would have a western cow, a Punjabi cow; and he'd take such good care of her that she'd give at least four or five quarts of milk. Gobar longed for milk. And if he couldn't be properly nourished now, when would he be? If Gobar could just get milk for a year, he'd be a boy worth looking at. Besides, the calves would become good bullocks, and a pair would bring a good two hundred *rupees*. What's more, it would be an excellent omen to have a cow tied by the front door where they could see it the first thing each morning. But there was no telling when this dream would be fulfilled, when that auspicious day would arrive.

Like all householders, Hori had for years nursed this longing for a cow. It was his life's ambition, his greatest dream, since any ideas of living off bank interest, of buying land or of building a mansion were too grandiose for his cramped mind to comprehend.

The June sun was rising over the mango grove, turning the red of dawn to brilliant silver, and the air was beginning to warm up. Farmers working in the fields beside the path greeted him respectfully and invited him to share a smoke with them. Hori had no time for such pleasantries, but they brought a glow of pride to his wrinkled face. It was only because he associated with the landlords that everyone showed him such respect. Otherwise who would pay any attention to a farmer with just three acres of land? As it was, though, even three and four-plough farmers greeted him—no small honour.

Leaving the path through the fields, he came to a hollow where so much rainwater collected during the monsoon that a little grass remained even in the height of summer. Cattle from the nearby villages came here to graze, and there was still a cool freshness in the air. Hori took several deep breaths and thought of sitting down for awhile, since he'd be dying of heat in the scorching loo wind the rest of the day. A number of farmers were eager to lease this bit of land and had offered a good price, but the Rai Sahib—God bless him— had plainly told them it was reserved for grazing and would not be relinquished at any price. If he'd been one of those selfish zamindars,

17

he'd have said the cattle could go to hell, that there was no reason for him to miss the chance to make a little money. But the Rai Sahib still held to the old values, feeling that any landlord who didn't look after his tenants was less than human.

Suddenly Hori saw Bhola, the milkman from the adjoining village, approaching with some cows. Bhola sold milk and butter, and sometimes, when he could get a good price, he would also sell cows to the villagers. Hori eyed the cows longingly. If only Bhola would let him have that first one! He'd pay for it in instalments. Hori knew that there was no money at home, that the land rent was still unpaid and that the loan from Bisesar Shah was still outstanding, with one *anna* to the rupee interest mounting on it monthly. But he was driven on by a boldness learned in poverty, a shamelessness that ignores demands, curses and even blows. Shaken by the yearning that had been disturbing his heart for years, he greeted the approaching milkman and said, 'How are things with you, brother Bhola? I hear you bought two new cows at the fair.'

'Yes, two cows and two calves,' Bhola answered casually, guessing Hori's intentions 'My old ones had all gone dry, and you can't make a living if there's no milk for the customers.'

Hori stroked the flank of the lead cow. 'Obviously a good milker. How much was she?'

Bhola began to show off. 'Prices are high these days. Eighty rupees I had to pay—and thirty for each calf as well. And yet my customers still demand four quarts to the rupee.'

'You people are really lion-hearted, brother. But then again, there's nothing like what you've got here in any of the villages around.'

Bhola swelled with pride. 'The Rai Sahib offered me a hundred for her—and fifty each for the calves. But I wouldn't sell. God willing, I should make a hundred rupees on her first calves.'

'No doubt about that. And how could the master afford them anyway? He'd probably take them as a gift of course. But only you people have the guts to trust to luck and risk handfuls of money that way. Ah to have the blessing of looking at this cow forever! How lucky you are, being able to spend your time serving cows. I can't even get their dung. It's shameful for a family man not to have even one cow. Year after year goes by without the sight of milk. My wife keeps pestering me to speak to you, and I tell her I will when we happen to run into each other. She thinks very highly of you—keeps saying she's never

18

seen such a man before, one who always keeps his eyes down when speaking to a woman.'

Bhola's pride swelled even more with this brimming cup of praise. 'A good man always treats others' daughters and daughters-in-law as though they were his own. Any villain who would stare at a woman deserves to be shot.'

'You're a hundred per cent right, brother. A gentleman is one who respects another man's honour as though it were his own.'

'When a man's wife dies, he's just as crippled as a woman when her husband dies. My home's a desert now, with no one to offer me even a cup of water.'

Bhola's wife had died of heatstroke the year before. Hori knew this, but he had not realized the passion that still coursed through Bola's decrepit, fifty-five-year-old frame. Now Bhola's eyes were glistening with longing for a wife, and Hori, his practical peasant shrewdness alerted, spotted his chance.

'There's truth in the old saying that a house without a woman is haunted by ghosts. Why don't you marry again?'

'I'm looking around, but no one's about to get trapped easily, even though I'm ready to shell out a hundred rupees or more. Well, it's in God's hands. . . .'

'I'll keep an eye out too. God willing, you'll soon have a home set up again.'

'Believe me, brother, that would be a big relief. By the grace of God there's plenty to eat in my house, and twenty quarts of milk a day. But what good does it do?'

'Well, there's a girl at my in-laws' place whose husband left her some three or four years ago and went off to Calcutta. Poor thing squeezes out a living grinding flour. No children . . . good-looking . . . talks nicely . . . a real goddess !'

The wrinkles vanished from Bhola's face. Wonderful the rejuvenating power of hope ! 'I'll count on you then. When you're free some time, let's go take a look at her.'

'I'll let you know when it's all settled. Rushing things is likely to spoil them.'

'Whenever you think best. There's no point in hurrying. And if you like that black and white cow, then take her.'

'I'm not worthy of such a cow, brother. And I don't want to put you to such a loss. It wouldn't be right for me to get a strangle-hold on a friend. I'll manage as I have in the past.'

19

'You talk as though we were strangers, Hori. Go ahead and take the cow, for whatever price you wish. Having her at your house will be no different than at mine. I paid eighty rupees. You can give me the same. Now go ahead.'

'But remember, brother, I don't have the cash.'

'So who's asking for cash?'

Hori's chest was bursting. Eighty rupees was not at all high for this cow—sturdy, able to give six or seven quarts of milk twice a day, so gentle that even a child could milk her. Each of her calves would be worth a hundred rupees. And how handsome his door would be with her tied there. He was already four hundred rupees in debt, but he looked on these loans as a kind of gift. Then too, if he could arrange another marriage for Bhola, that would keep him quiet for at least a year or two. And if no marriage worked out, it would still be no loss to Hori. At worst Bhola would come demanding the money, trying to start trouble and shouting curses. But it took more than that to shame Hori by this time. He'd become used to such things, thanks to his life as a peasant. Granted he was tricking Bhola, but that was only to be expected in his position, and he would have treated a written contract in the same way.

Hori was a God-fearing man, as far as that goes, constantly aware of the destructive side of God's nature, cowed by anxiety over the threat of drought or flood. He didn't consider this kind of deceit as deceit, however. It was just a matter of self-interest, and there was nothing wrong with that. He did it all the time. Though he had several rupees at home, he'd swear to the moneylender that he hadn't a pice. And it seemed only right to increase the weight of jute by soaking it, or of cotton by leaving seeds in it. Besides, this present situation involved more than profit—it was also good sport. An old man's lust is always amusing, and to make it pay something would surely be no crime.

Bhola handed the cow's halter to Hori. 'Take her. She'll remind you of me. As soon as she calves you'll start getting six quarts of milk. Come on—I'll lead her to your house. Otherwise, not knowing you, she might give some trouble on the way. And now I'll tell you the truth—the master was actually offering ninety for her. But what appreciation do those people have for cows? He'd have passed her on to some official, and what do they care about serving cows? All they know is how to suck blood. They'd keep her as long as she gave milk and then sell her to someone else. Who knows where she'd end up?

Money's not everything, brother. A man's sacred duty counts for something too. She'll do well at your place. You're not likely to eat and then go off to sleep leaving her hungry. You'll look after her and fuss over her. The cow will bring us blessings. And anyway, though I hate to admit it, there's not even a handful of straw in my house. The bazaar took all my money. I thought of borrowing a little from the moneylender for some straw, but I haven't yet paid back the last loan, so he refused. Trying to feed so many animals worries me to death. Even a handful each would add up to over a bushel a day. Only God can see me through....'

Hori sighed sympathetically. 'Why didn't you let me know earlier? I've just sold off a cartload of straw.'

Bhola beat his forehead and said, 'The reason I didn't tell you, brother, is that a man can't go around crying about his troubles to everyone. People aren't going to share them—they just make fun. I'm not worried about the cows that have gone dry—they can be kept alive on leaves and things. But this one can't go without proper fodder. What you might do is let me have ten or twenty rupees for some straw.'

Now it's true that a peasant is mercenary. It's hard to squeeze a bribe out of his purse. A shrewd bargainer, he'll haggle for hours with the moneylender to get the interest reduced one pice. And as long as he has a single doubt, he can't be inveigled into anything. But he also spends his whole life co-operating with nature. Trees produce fruit for men to eat. Fields produce grain which feeds the world. Cows produce milk—not for themselves, but for others to drink. Clouds produce rain which quenches the earth. In such a system there's no room for petty selfishness. As a farmer, Hori had been taught that one doesn't warm his hands on the flames of another man's burning house.

So, hearing Bhola's tale of woe, Hori's attitude changed. Handing back the halter, he said, "I don't have any money, brother, but there's a little straw left which you can have. Come and take it. If I were to accept a cow that you're selling just because you're out of fodder, I'd be inviting the punishment of God.'

'But won't your own bullocks starve?' Bhola asked. 'Surely you don't have that much straw to spare.'

'Not at all, brother. The crop was good this year.'

'It was wrong of me even to mention it to you.'

'If you'd said nothing and I found all this out later, I'd have been

21

very hurt that you treated me like an outsider. How could we get along if men didn't help their brothers in times of need?'

'Anyway, go ahead and take this cow.'

'Not now, brother. Some other time.'

'Then let me give you some milk to pay for the straw.'

'Why all this talk about payment?' Hori reproached him. 'If I ate a meal or two at your house, would you insist on my paying for it?'

'Your bullocks won't starve then?'

'God will open up a way. The rains are almost here—I'll grow another crop of something.'

'In any case, the cow is yours. Come get her whenever you want.'

'Taking the cow now would be as bad as buying my brother's bullocks at an auction.'

If Hori had been smart enough to realize the implications of this discussion, he'd have taken the cow home with no misgivings. Since Bhola had not demanded cash, he was obviously not selling her to buy fodder. But Hori was like a horse which hears a rustling in the leaves, stops abruptly, and, though whipped, refuses to take another step. Ingrained in him was the idea that taking anything from a person in trouble is a sin.

Bhola could hardly contain himself. 'Then should I send someone for the straw?'

'I'm on my way to the Rai Sahib's house right now,' Hori replied, 'but I should be back shortly. Send someone in a little while.'

Bhola's eye's filled with tears. 'Hori, brother, you've been my salvation. I now know that I'm not alone in the world, that even I have a friend.' He hesitated a moment and then added, 'Now don't forget that other matter.'

Hori set off in high spirits, his heart swelling with satisfaction. What if eight or ten bushels of straw have been lost, he thought. I've saved the poor fellow from having to sell his cow in a time of trouble. And as soon as I get some more fodder, I'll go collect the cow. God help me now to find a woman for him. Then there'll be no problem.

He turned and looked back. There was the spotted cow, tossing her head, flicking away flies with her tail, and sauntering along with the careless dignity of a queen in the midst of her slave-girls. What an auspicious day it would be when that giver of all blessings was tied up at his own door!

22

CHAPTER 2

BELARI and Semari are two villages in the province of Oudh. The name of the district is of no importance. Hori lived in Belari, the Rai Sahib in Semari, just five miles away. In the last civil disobedience campaign, the Rai Sahib had become quite a hero by resigning from the Provincial Council and going to jail. Ever since, he'd been held in great esteem by the tenants on his estate. Not that they had been shown any special concessions, or that the harsh fines and forced labour had been reduced, but now all these evils were blamed on his agents. The Rai Sahib was considered beyond reproach. After all, the poor fellow was just another slave to the established system, which would continue in the future, as it had in the past, unaffected by any benevolence on his part.

And so, though his income and authority had not diminished one iota, the Rai Sahib's prestige had grown considerably. He would talk and joke with his tenants—no small matter in itself. Of course a lion has to hunt; but if he can talk sweetly instead of growling and roaring, he can just stay home and catch what he wants instead of having to roam the jungle in search of it.

The Rai Sahib was a nationalist, but he also stayed on good terms with the government officials, presenting them with the usual baskets of fruit and things, and making the customary payments to lesser authorities. He was a lover of literature and music, a drama enthusiast, a fine speaker, a good writer and an excellent shot. Though his wife had been dead for ten years, he had not remarried, finding enough other diversions in his life as a widower.

Reaching the front gate, Hori found preparations in full swing for the *Dashahra* festival. All sorts of things were going up—a stage, a canopy, guest houses, and small shops for vendors. Despite the heat of the sun, the Rai Sahib himself was helping in the work. From his father he had inherited not only the property but also a devotion to *Rama*, and having put the ancient epic in dramatic form, he now sponsored a production of it every year, providing good entertainment for his friends and all the important people of the area. The festivities would last for two or three days.

The Rai Sahib had a huge family. About a hundred and fifty would be gathering here for the celebration, including a number of uncles, dozens of brothers and cousins, and a deluge of relatives by marriage. One uncle, a great devotee of *Radha*, had setttled permanently in Brindaban, writing great quantities of devotional poetry which he occasionally had printed and distributed to his friends. Another uncle, this one a faithful disciple of Rama, was translating the *Ramayana* into Persian. None of them had to work, living instead off stipends from the family estate.

Hori was standing under the canopy wondering how to announce his arrival when the Rai Sahib suddenly came over that way and spotted him. 'Well, Hori—so you've showed up. I was about to send for you. Look, you must take the part of *Raja* Janak's gardener. All right? You're to stand with a bouquet of flowers and hand it to Janak's daughter when she goes to the temple for worship. Now don't mess things up. And listen, urge all the tenants to show up with the proper donations. Come with me—I have something to say to you.'

The Rai Sahib walked through the house to the courtyard, Hori trailing along behind. The Rai Sahib seated himself on a chair in the shade of a large tree and motioned Hori to sit on the ground. 'You understand what I told you? My agent will do what he can, but the tenants won't pay as much attention to him as they will to another tenant. In the next week I have to scrape up twenty thousand rupees, and I'm not quite sure how to go about it. You're probably wondering why the master should be confiding his troubles in someone like you who has hardly two pice to his name. But to whom can I talk? For some reason I trust you. And at least I know you won't laugh at me. Even if you do, it won't bother me. It's the laughter of equals that's hard to tolerate, because it's so full of jealousy, sarcasm and bad feeling. And after all, why wouldn't they laugh at me? I have a good time making fun of their misfortunes and difficulties. You just don't find wealth going hand in hand with sympathy for others. Sure I make donations and perform acts of charity, but you know why? Just to show up those other people of my class. My generosity is a selfish matter, pure and simple. That's how it goes . . . if one of us loses a case or has his property confiscated or gets hauled in for not paying the revenue, or if his young son dies or his widowed daughter gets into trouble or his house catches fire or some prostitute makes a fool out of him or he's beaten up by his tenants, then the rest of us get a big kick out of it, as though all the good fortune in the world had fallen to us. When we happen to meet, of course, we're as full of love as though we'd give our last drops of blood for each other.

'But you don't have to look even that far away. All these uncles and aunts who have a fine time freeloading off the estate—writing and gambling, drinking and living it up—they're all jealous of me. If I were to drop dead today, they'd put the most expensive oil in their lamps and light them all in celebration. Not one of them will believe I'm ever unhappy—they figure I have no right to be. If I cry, I'm just making fun of sadness. If I'm sick, I'm enjoying it. If I don't drink, I'm stingy. If I do, I'm drinking the blood of my tenants. If I don't get married and fill the house with turmoil, I'm selfish. If I do get married, I'm lecherous. If I really were to be lecherous, Lord knows what they'd say. They've tried their best to lure me into dissipation, and they're still trying. Their one ambition is to get me so blind they can rob me. I'm not supposed to notice what they're doing even though it's perfectly obvious, and to keep making an ass of myself although I've caught on to the whole business.'

The Rai Sahib stuffed two rolls of betel in his mouth to sustain himself and then stared at Hori as though trying to read his mind.

Hori mustered up his courage. 'I knew this sort of thing went on with us poor people, but I take it there's plenty of it among the great also.'

'You consider us great?' the Rai Sahib mumbled, his mouth still full of betel. 'We have a big name but nothing to show for it. When there's jealousy or hatred among the poor, it's because of hunger or for self-defence. I consider that pardonable. If someone snatches the bread from our mouths we have the right to force our fingers down his throat and get it back. Only a saint would let him get away with it. The rich indulge in jealousy and hatred just for the fun of it, though. We've become so great that we find our chief satisfaction in meanness and cruelty, so godly that we laugh at the tears of others. That's no small accomplishment, you understand. In such a large family there's always someone ill. And great people also have to have great illnesses. How could one of us be a big shot and settle for some small ailment? If we have a slight fever, we're treated as though we're delirious. An ordinary pimple is considered a carbuncle.

Telegrams are sent calling the assistant surgeon, the surgeon and the chief surgeon. One man is sent to Delhi to fetch the most famous *hakim*, another to Calcutta for the most distinguished *vaidya*. Prayers to *Durga* are recited in the temple, horoscopes are studied by the astrologers, and *tantric* priests prepare their magic rituals. A race is on to rescue the raja sahib from the jaws of death.'

'So the vaidyas and the doctors wait breathlessly,' he continued, 'for the raja to have a headache, and the shower of gold to begin again. The payments, of course, are extracted from you and your brothers at the point of a dagger. I'm surprised that the blaze of your anger doesn't burn us to ashes. But no, there's no cause for surprise. It doesn't take long to be burned to ashes, and the agony would be short-lived. Instead we're being consumed slowly—knuckle by knuckle, joint by joint, finger by finger. We seek shelter from revenge with the police, the officials, the judges and the lawyers; and, like beautiful women, we become mere playthings in their hands. The world thinks us very happy—we have estates, mansions, carriages, servants, easy loans, prostitutes and what not. But a person without moral strength and self-respect is not a man, whatever else he may be. A person who can't sleep at night for fear of his enemies, who finds everyone laughing at his troubles and no one sympathizing, whose head is crushed under the feet of others, who's so drunk with dissipation that he completely forgets himself, who licks the feet of the officials and sucks the blood of his people—I don't call him happy. He's the most unfortunate creature in the world.'

'What's more,' the Rai Sahib added, 'when the British Sahib comes here on a tour or a hunt, it's my job to trail along after him. One frown from him and our blood runs cold. We zamindars would go to any lengths to please him. But if I were to tell you all the complications, you probably wouldn't even believe me. Presents and bribes are to be expected, but we don't even hesitate to prostrate ourselves before him. Our parasitic existence has crippled us. We've lost every spark of faith in ourselves, just wagging our tails before the officials and hoping to win enough favour to get their help in terrorizing our tenants. The flattery of our own hangers-on has made us so conceited and highhanded that we've lost all sense of decency, modesty and service. Sometimes I think the government would be doing us a big favour by confiscating our lands and making us work for a living. This much is sure though—the government won't keep on protecting us. They get no benefit from us. There's every indica-

26

tion that my class of people is about to be wiped out, and I for one am ready to welcome that day. May God bring it soon. It'll be a day of salvation for us. We've fallen prey to the system, a system that's completely destroying us. Until we're freed from the chains of wealth, this curse will keep hanging over our heads and we'll never reach those heights of manhood which are life's ultimate goal.'

The Rai Sahib took out the betel box and again filled his mouth with leaves. He was about to say something more when a servant appeared and announced, 'Sir, the men on forced labour have refused to work. They say they won't go on unless they're given food. When we threatened them, they quit their jobs and left.'

The Rai Sahib glowered at him. 'Come with me,' he declared, eyes bulging. 'I'll put those troublemakers in their place. They've never been given food in the past. Why this new demand today? They'll get the anna a day they always get, and they'll damn well do the work whether they like it or not.'

He turned to Hori. 'Run along now and make your arrangements. Keep in mind what I've told you. I expect at least five hundred rupees from your village.'

The Rai Sahib went off fuming. Hori was puzzled—all this talk about right and goodness, and then such a sudden outburst of anger.

The sun was directly overhead. Trees were shrivelling in the heat. Dust filled the air. The shimmering earth seemed to be trembling.

Hori picked up his stick and headed for home, tormented with worry as to where the money could be raised for this special occasion.

CHAPTER 3

NEARING his village, Hori saw Gobar still hoeing the sugar cane, the two girls working along with him. The burning wind was churning up great funnels of dust, and the earth blazed as though nature had mixed the air with fire. Why were they still out in the field? Did they want to kill themselves with work? 'Come on home, Gobar,' he shouted. 'Are you going to keep at it all day? Don't you know it's past noon?'

The three looked up, shouldered their hoes, and fell in behind him. Gobar, a tall, slim, swarthy young man, appeared to have no interest in the work. His face reflected no happiness—only discontent and defiance. He had kept working only to show his indifference towards food and drink. The older girl, Sona, was dark and shapely, modest, cheerful and vivacious. A coarse red *sari* turned up at the knees and tied at the waist filled out her slight body somewhat, giving it an adult look. Rupa, the youngest, was a girl of five or six—dirty, her hair like a bird's nest, wearing just a strip of cloth around her waist, stubborn, and easily moved to tears.

'Look, papa!' Rupa cried, clinging to her father's leg. 'I didn't leave a single lump of dirt. Sister told me to go sit under the tree. But if all the lumps aren't broken up, how can we make the ground flat?'

Hori picked her up in his arms and caressed her. 'You did very well, child. Come on, let's go home.'

Gobar had been controlling his anger but now he burst out. 'Why do you go flattering the master every day? His man still comes and curses us when the rent's not paid up. We're still made to do forced labour, and everyone gets fat off our gifts. So why should we go grovelling to them?'

Hori was wondering the same thing, but the boy's defiance had to be put down. 'And just where would we be without that grovelling? God made us slaves. There's nothing we can do about it. It's thanks to such bowing and scraping that no one objected when we built a hut against our wall. All Ghure did was drive a stake in the ground outside his door so as to tie up his cow, and the authorities fined him two rupees. Just think of all the dirt we've dug from the pond without the agent saying anything. Anyone else would have had to buy him off. I go and play up to them in order to get what I want. It's not as though Saturn's in my feet, forcing me to run around just for the fun of it. Nor do I get any great pleasure out of all this. I stand around for hours before the master is even informed, and then he sometimes comes out, but other times he just sends word that he can't be bothered.'

Gobar sneered. 'Well there must be some pleasure in being a yes-man for the authorities. Otherwise why would people run for office in the local elections?'

'Say what you please now, son. You'll see what it's like when the responsibilities fall on your shoulders. I used to talk that way myself, but I've found you can't be unbending or put on airs when someone's foot is crushing your neck.'

Gobar walked on in silence, feeling better after the outburst against his father. Sona, jealous at seeing her sister perched on Hori's arm, scolded, 'Why don't you get down and walk on your own two feet? Got a broken leg or something?'

'I won't get down, so there!' Rupa cried defiantly, throwing her arms around her father's neck. 'Papa, she makes fun of me all the time, saying her name means gold and mine just means silver. Give me some other name.'

Feigning a look of anger, Hori said, "Why do you tease her, Sonie? Gold is nice to look at, but we couldn't get along without silver. Tell me—just how could rupees be made if it weren't for silver?'

Sona rose to the defence—'And how would necklaces be made without gold? And where would nose-rings come from?'

Joining the fun, Gobar suggested to Rupa, 'Tell her that gold is yellow like dried leaves, while silver is pure white like the sun.'

'Brides always wear yellow saries at their weddings,' Sona retorted. 'No one wears white.'

Rupa was nonplussed. None of Hori and Gobar's arguments could match this one. She looked plaintively at her father.

Hori thought of a new line of attack. 'Gold is for the rich. For people like us there's only silver. It's just like men calling barley the king of grains and wheat the outcaste even though it's no longer true that the rich eat barley and we poor people only wheat.'

Sona had no answer to this powerful argument. 'You all ganged up on me,' she pouted. 'Otherwise I'd have made her cry.'

Rupa thumbed her nose. 'Sona is an outcaste. Sona is an outcaste.' Too delighted by the victory to remain in her father's arms, she jumped to the ground and began to prance up and down repeating, 'Rupa's a king—Sona's an outcaste! Rupa's a king—Sona's an outcaste!'

Reaching home, they found Dhaniya waiting at the door. 'Why so late today, Gobar?' she scolded. 'There's no need for anyone to kill himself working.' Then she turned angrily on her husband—'And you—after having such a profitable day, you had to go to the field also. Anyone would think that field was about to run off somewhere!'

Hori and Gobar each poured a jug of water over his head from the well next to the door. They bathed Rupa the same way and then went in to eat—*chapaties* of barley, but as white and smooth as though of wheat, and *dal* flavoured with green mango. Rupa sat and ate from her father's plate. Sona eyed her enviously as though to say 'Big deal! Father's pet!'

'What did you talk about with the master?' Dhaniya inquired.

'Oh just the revenue collections,' Hori replied, gulping down a jugful of water. 'What else did you expect? But you know something—although we think those rich people are happy, the truth is they're more miserable than we are. We have only our stomachs to worry about. They have thousands of worries plaguing them.' Hori had forgotten just what else the Rai Sahib had said, but this one impression clung in his memory.

'Then why doesn't he give his lands to us?' Gobar said sarcastically. 'We'd be perfectly willing to let him have our field, bullocks, plough, hoe—everything. Would he change places? All that talk is just hypocrisy—a pure fraud. People who are unhappy don't have dozens of cars or live in mansions or gorge themselves on rich food or loll around enjoying singing and dancing. They live like kings. That must make them very miserable!'

'It's no use arguing with you,' Hori said irritably. 'No one gives away his property. Why would he? Look at us ... What do we get out of our land? Not even an anna a day apiece. A servant making ten rupees a month eats and dresses better than we do. But we don't give up our field. How would we manage if we did? Where could we get jobs? And we still have our prestige to uphold. There's a kind of dignity in farming that isn't found in working for someone else.

Think of the situation of the zamindars in the same way. They're loaded down with hundreds of troubles too—feeding the officials and fawning over them, keeping the people under them happy ... And then if they don't pay the revenue on time they're likely to be arrested or have their property taken away. No one puts us in jail. All we get are a few threats and curses.'

'It's all very well to talk that way,' Gobar retorted, 'but we go without food, wear nothing but rags on our backs, slave in the fields until we're drenched head to foot with sweat, and we still can't make ends meet. And they? They lie around on their plush couches, with hundreds of servants and with thousands of people to order around. They may not save a lot of money, but they enjoy all the pleasures of life. Isn't that what people do when they get rich?'

'You expect our life to be like theirs?'

'Well, God created us all equal.'

'That's not so, son. God creates men great or small. Wealth is a reward for penance and devotion. Those rich people are enjoying happiness because of their good works in the last life. We built up no merit, so how can we expect pleasures now?'

'Those are just excuses. God creates all people equal. But when someone gets hold of a little power, he beats down the poor and becomes rich.'

'That's where you're wrong. Even now the master spends four hours a day singing hymns to God.'

'But whose labour supports that hymn-singing and charity-giving?'

'His own, of course.'

'Oh no—the work of the farmers and labourers. But he has trouble digesting that sinful money. That's why he has to give out charity and sing hymns to God. I'd like to see him naked and hungry and still singing hymns. If I could get two square meals a day I wouldn't mind reciting the names of God day and night myself. One day in the fields hoeing sugar cane and all his piety would be forgotten.'

Hori could argue no more. 'It's impossible to carry on a discussion with you, when you object even to the ways of God.'

When the lunch was over, Gobar took up his hoe and started out. 'Wait a minute, son,' Hori called, 'I'm coming too. But first set out a little straw. I told Bhola he could have some. Poor fellow's really hard up these days.'

Gobar eyed his father defiantly. 'We've no straw to sell.'

31

'I'm not selling it, son. I'm simply giving it to him. He's in trouble —we've got to help him.'

'He's never given us a cow.'

'Well he was going to give us one, but I wouldn't take it.'

Dhaniya shook her head sarcastically. 'Give a cow indeed! And especially to you! That man who wouldn't spare even a drop of milk for the eyes is now giving away a cow?'

'I swear by my youth,' Hori insisted. 'He offered me his best western cow. He's really in trouble and has no fodder stored up, so he wants to sell a cow to buy some straw. But how can anyone take a cow from a man when he's driven to the wall? So I'm giving him some straw, and then, when I scrape up a few rupees, I'll take the cow. I can pay the rest bit by bit. Eighty rupees ... but she's a real eye-catcher.'

'This piety of yours is going to be your downfall,' Gobar sneered. 'It's a perfectly simple matter. She's an eighty rupee cow, so let him take twenty rupees' worth of straw and give us the cow. We'll gradually pay off the remaining sixty.'

Hori smiled mysteriously. 'I've thought of a way to get the cow for nothing—just fix up a marriage somehow for Bhola, that's all. I'm giving these few bushels of straw just to get the upper hand.'

'Oh, so now you're going to run around arranging marriages for everyone!' Gobar jeered.

Dhaniya's eyes flashed. 'So that's all you can find to do, is it? Well listen here—we're not about to give straw to anyone. We don't owe Bhola a thing.'

Hori tried to justify himself. 'Just because my plan allows someone to make a home and settle down, what's so bad about that?'

Gobar, fed up with wrangling, picked up the *chilam* and went out for a light.

'The person who sets Bhola up in a new home shouldn't settle for any eighty-rupee cow,' Dhaniya snapped. 'A sack full of money would be more like it.'

'I know that,' Hori said soothingly. 'But remember what a gentleman he is. Whenever we meet he speaks so highly of you—"Such a goddess ... so well-mannered".'

Dhaniya's face softened a little. Trying not to show her pleasure, she said, 'I'm not hungry for praise from him. Let him keep it to himself.'

Hori smiled indulgently. 'I told him that you think so highly of yourself you won't even let a fly sit on your nose, and that you swear all the time. But he kept insisting you were a goddess, not a woman. Matter of fact, his own wife had a very sharp tongue. Poor fellow ran around scared to death of her. He says though that any morning he sees you—sure enough, that day he gets some money. I told him it must work only for him, since I see you every day and not a pice comes my way.'

'How can I help it if you have such bad luck?'

'He began telling me all the terrible things his wife used to do. She'd never give anything to beggars—chased them away with a broom. And she was so stingy that she'd go and beg even for salt from the neighbours.'

'One shouldn't speak evil of the dead—but she used to get jealous just looking at me.'

'Bhola had real patience, putting up with her. Anyone else would have taken poison. He must be a good ten years older than I, and yet he always gives the first greeting when we meet.'

'What was it he said happens on days when he sees me?'

'That God somehow or other always sends him something.'

'Well his daughters-in-law are certainly a greedy lot. Just recently they ate up two rupees' worth of melons they'd got on credit. As long as they can borrow, they never give a thought to paying anything back.'

'That's just what Bhola complains about.'

At that point Gobar came in and announced, 'Bhola has turned up. We have two or three bushels of straw. Give those to him and then go find him a wife.'

'There's a man at the door,' Dhaniya scolded, 'and instead of getting him a cot or something to sit on, you start grumbling. Learn some manners. Go fill the jug so he can wash his hands and face, and then serve him some juice or water. A man doesn't come begging for a handout unless he's in trouble.'

'There's no need for juice,' Hori said. 'It's not as though he's a guest.'

'Then what is a guest?' Dhaniya asked indignantly. 'Does he show up at the door every day? He must be thirsty, coming so far in the heat. Rupa, see if there's any tobacco in the box. No, there won't be any left with Gobar around. Run and get a pice worth from the woman at the shop.'

Bhola was entertained that day as never before. Gobar brought out a cot for him to sit on. Sona mixed up some sugar cane juice and brought it to him. Rupa filled the chilam with tobacco. And Dhaniya stood behind the door, anxious to hear his compliments with her own ears.

Bhola picked up the pipe and said, 'When a good wife enters a home it's like the goddess *Lakshmi* herself coming in. She knows how to respect both the high and the low.'

Dhaniya quivered with delight. These words were like a cool and tender touch to that soul beaten down with worry and despair and privation.

When Hori picked up Bhola's basket and went inside for the straw, Dhaniya followed him. 'Where could he have found such a huge basket?' Hori asked. 'He must have borrowed it from someone who gathers leaves. It'll take over a bushel to fill it. And that would mean losing about two bushels if I give him a second basketful.'

Dhaniya was bursting with happiness. She looked scornfully at Hori. 'Either don't invite guests or else satisfy them when you do. He didn't come here for a few flowers or leaves. So why should he have brought a small basket? If you're going to give anything, then make it three baskets full. Poor man, why didn't he bring his sons along? How can he carry all this home alone? It'll be the death of him.'

'I'm not about to fill up three baskets for him.'

'Oh, I suppose you're going to send him off with just one? Tell Gobar to fill his own basket and go along with Bhola.'

'Gobar's going to hoe the sugar cane.'

'The cane's not going to dry up if it's left for one day.'

'Well it was up to him to bring someone along. God's given him two sons.'

'They may not be home. They're probably off selling milk in the bazaar.'

'This is ridiculous. First I give him my stuff and then I have to get it home for him also. Give him the load, let him pile it on you, and then go along carrying it for him!'

'All right then, neither of you go. I'll carry it there myself. Serving one's elders is nothing to be ashamed of.'

'And what will our bullocks eat if we give him three baskets full?'

'You should have thought of that before making the offer. You and Gobar better both go along with him.'

34

'It's one thing to be generous, but that doesn't mean picking up your whole house and giving it to him.'

'Now if it were the zamindar's man who'd come, you'd load the straw on your own head and deliver it for him too—you, your son and your daughters—all of you. And you'd probably have to stay there and chop up a stack of wood in the bargain.'

'It's a different matter with the zamindar.'

'Sure, because he uses a big stick to get his work done. Isn't that right?'

'Don't we plough his land?'

'So we plough his land. Don't we pay rent for it?'

'All right, don't eat me alive. We'll both lend a hand. Like it or not. I did promise him the straw. But you ... always refusing to go along with things at all, or running away with them entirely.'

Three baskets were filled with straw. Gobar still disapproved. He had no faith in his father's business dealings, convinced that Hori managed to incur some loss for the family everywhere he went. Dhaniya was pleased. As for Hori, he was torn between duty and self-interest.

Hori and Gobar together carried out one basket. At once Bhola rolled his scarf into a head-pad, lifted the basket onto it, and said, 'I'll take this home and be right back for one more.'

'Not one,' Hori told him. 'There are two more ready and waiting. And you won't have to come back. Gobar and I will each carry one and go with you.'

Bhola was astounded. Hori seemed closer to him than his own brother, and this satisfaction refreshed his whole being.

The three of them set out with the straw and began talking on the way.

'Dashahra's almost here,' Bhola said. 'There must be a great hulla-baloo over at the master's place.'

'Yes, the tents and canopies have been set up. And this year I'm taking part in the show myself. The Rai Sahib told me I'm to play King Janak's gardener.'

'The master's evidently very pleased with you.'

'Oh, he's just being kind.'

Bhola was silent for a moment. 'But have you scraped up any money to present for the occasion? Just playing the gardener won't save your neck.'

Hori wiped the sweat from his face. 'I'm worried to death about that, brother. My grain was all weighed out at the village barn. The master took his share and the moneylender his, leaving me just ten pounds. I carried off the straw and hid it during the night, or not a blade would have been left me. There's only one zamindar of course, but there are three different moneylenders—that shopkeeper woman Dulari is one, Mangaru another, and Pandit Datadin a third. I've not yet paid off the interest to any of them, and there's still half the rent for the zamindar also. I had to borrow again from Dulari so as to get by. I've tried every way of cutting expenses, brother, but nothing helps. We people are born just to pour out our blood and make the rich still richer. I've paid double the amount of the loan in interest, but it hangs over my head just the same as before. People tell you to cut down the spending for weddings and funerals, for pilgrimages and vows. But no one sets an example. The Rai Sahib poured out twenty thousand on his son's wedding. No one spoke up about that. Mangaru spent five thousand on his father's funeral. No one asked him any questions. Those occasions mean just as much to us. . . .'

'But how can you put us on the same level with the rich, brother?' Bhola asked sympathetically.

'Well we're human too.'

'Who says we're human? What's human about us? A human being, a man, is someone with wealth and power and education. We're just bullocks born for the yoke. And what's more, we can't even get along with each other. We never unite on anything. If it wasn't that the farmers were ready to pounce on each other's fields, how could the landlords keep raising the rent? There's no love left in the world.'

Old men like nothing better than talking about the joys of the past, the sorrows of the present, and the inevitable calamities of the future. The two friends went on bemoaning their misfortunes, Bhola telling how his sons had behaved and Hori wailing about his brothers. Reaching a well, they put down their loads and sat down for a drink. Gobar borrowed a jug and began drawing some water.

'The separation must have been very hard on you,' Bhola commiserated. 'You'd brought up your brothers as though they were your own sons.'

'Don't talk about it, *dada*,' Hori replied in a choked voice. 'I wanted to go off and drown myself. That I should have lived to see all this! Those brothers for whom I slaved away my youth became my enemies. And what caused all the trouble? The question of why my wife didn't go work in the fields. Now I ask you, doesn't someone have to look after the house? Borrowing and lending, tidying up and keeping things in order—who's going to do all that? It's not as though she was just sitting around the house. What with sweeping and dusting, cooking, cleaning the pots and pans and taking care of the children—that's no small job. Could Shobha's wife have taken care of the house? Did Hira's wife even know how? Since the split-up they've been having only one meal a day in both those houses. Before, they used to be hungry four times a day. I'd like to see them eat four times a day now. Only I know the misery Gobar's mother had to put up with as head of the household. Poor woman had to go around in her sister-in-law's ragged old clothes. She'd go to bed hungry herself, but she had to make tea and snacks for the other women. She didn't have even a plain old thread to decorate herself with, and yet she had several pieces of jewellery made up for each of her sisters-in-law. Not gold, it's true, but silver anyway. They were just jealous that she had charge of the household. It was a good thing they moved away—takes a load off my shoulders.'

Bhola gulped down a jugful of water. 'It's that way in every family,' said, 'and not just with brothers. I can't get along with my sons, because I just can't keep my mouth shut when I see someone misbehaving. I tell them we can't afford to have them gambling and smoking *charas* and *ganja*; that if they want to spend, they'll first have to go out and earn. But neither of them wants to do that, though they'll spend with open hearts. When the older one, Kamta, takes supplies to the bazaar, half the proceeds disappear. When I question him, there's no answer. And the younger one, Jangi—he's mad about getting together with his friends and playing music. Every evening there he is—sitting down with his drum and cymbals. I don't say the get-togethers are bad. Music is no sin. But these are all things for one's spare time, not to be indulged in all day at the expense of the work around the place. Everything falls on my head. I feed and tend the cows. I milk them. I take the milk to the bazaar. This whole family business is a frustrating trap, like a gold nugget that can't be swallowed or thrown up. Then there's my daughter Jhuniya—also unlucky. You came to her wedding. Such a good match—her husband ran a milk shop in Bombay. But during the time of the Hindu-Muslim riots, someone stuck a knife in his belly. The family was ruined and she couldn't manage there any longer. I went and fetched her so as to marry her off again, but she's not willing. The two sisters-

37

in-law nag her day and night . . . A regular *Mahabharata* war keeps raging in our house. Her misfortunes drove her here, but there's no peace here either.'

These sad stories passed the time on the road. Bhola's village was small but flourishing. Most of its population were herdsmen, and generally their condition was somewhat better than that of the farmers. Bhola was the headman of the village. Ten or twelve cows and buffaloes stood eating from the large trough by his door. On the porch was a wooden cot so massive that ten men could scarcely have lifted it. A drum hung from one peg on the wall, cymbals from another. In a niche lay a book wrapped in cloth, probably the *Ramayana*. Both daughters-in-law were out front shaping dung cakes, and Jhuniya was standing in the doorway. Her eyes and the tip of her nose were red, apparently from weeping. Waves of youthful vigour seemed to be surging through her voluptuous limbs. Her mouth was large and full, her cheeks plump, and her eyes small and deep-set beneath a narrow forehead. But it was her swelling breasts and sensual body that caught the eye, and a rose-red printed sari gave that figure added allure.

Seeing Bhola, she sprang forward to help him set down the basket. Bhola assisted Gobar and Hori with theirs and then said to Jhuniya, "First get us a smoke and then make up a little juice. If there's no water, bring the pitcher and I'll draw some. You remember our friend Hori, don't you?'

He turned to Hori. 'It's not really a home without a wife, brother. There's an old saying that a daughter-in-law in the house is like a dwarf bullock in the field. How can a dwarf bullock plough a field or a daughter-in-law take care of a household? Ever since this girl's mother died, our house has fallen on bad days. Daughters-in-law can roll out flour, but what do they know about running a house? Of course they know all about running off at the mouth! The boys are probably hanging around some gambling place. They're all lazy, scared of work. As long as I'm alive, I slave for them. When I die, though, they'll put their hands to their heads and start howling. My daughter is no different—grumbling over every little chore she has to do. I put up with all this. If she had a husband around, he wouldn't stand for it.'

Jhuniya bustled towards them, chilam in one hand, juice in the other. Then, picking up the pitcher and rope, she started for the well.

Gobar put out his hand to take the pitcher from her and said timidly, 'Give it here. I'll fill it for you.'

Jhuniya kept hold of the pitcher. When they reached the edge of the well, she smiled and said, 'You're a guest. You'll say no one here gave you even a pot of water.'

'What makes me a guest? I'm just your neighbour.'

'A neighbour who doesn't show his face even once a year becomes a guest.'

'But if I showed up every day there wouldn't be any of this special attention.'

Jhuniya glanced over coyly and smiled. 'That's why I'm fussing over you this way. Come once a month. I'll give you cool water. Come twice a month, you'll be offered a smoke. Come once a week, I'll offer a seat. Come every day and you'll get nothing at all.'

'You'd give me at least a vision of yourself though?'

'For a vision one first has to worship.' But in saying this, her face dropped, as though something in her memory had been stirred. She was a widow. Previously, with her husband standing guard at the door of her heart, she had been carefree. Now that there was no guard at that door, she kept it shut all the time. Occasionally, tired of the emptiness within, she would open the door; but at the sight of anyone approaching, her courage would fail, and she would slam it shut.

Gobar filled the pitcher and drew it from the well. The father and son each had some juice, puffed on the pipe, and then started to leave. 'Come take the cow tomorrow, Gobar,' said Bhola. 'Right now she's having her feed.'

Gobar's eyes were fixed on the cow with secret delight. He had never imagined that she would be so beautiful and well-proportioned.

Hori struggled against his greed. 'I'll send for her,' he said. 'But what's the hurry?'

'Well you may not be in a hurry, but I am. Seeing her at the door will remind you of that other matter.'

'I've got that well in mind, brother.'

'Then do send Gobar tomorrow.'

The two picked up their baskets and set off, as pleased as though returning from their own weddings. Hori was delighted at the prospect of fulfilling his long-restrained desire, and at no expense. Gobar had found something even more valuable. Desire had been aroused in his heart. He looked back. Jhuniya was standing at the door, as tense and excited and restless as hope itself.

39

CHAPTER 4

─────────

THERE was no sleep for Hori that night. He lay on his bamboo
cot under the *neem* tree looking up at the stars. . . . A trough will
have to be dug for the cow, he thought. Hers had better be separate
from that of the bullocks. For the present she can stay outside at
night, but during the rainy season some other place must be fixed up
for her. Outside there, someone might put the evil eye on her or cast a
spell that would dry up her milk. Then she'd start kicking and refuse
to allow even a hand on her udder. No, keeping her outside will never
do. And besides, who would allow us to dig a trough outside? The
zamindar's agent would expect a pay-off . . . and I can't very well
petition the Rai Sahib over such a small matter. Anyway, who would
listen to me as against the agent? Besides, to say anything to the Rai
Sahib would just make an enemy of his agent. When you're living in
the water it's foolish to anger the crocodile. Better tie up the cow
inside. The courtyard is rather small, but by putting up a shed we
can manage. . . .

This will be her first calving—she'll give at least five quarts of
milk. Gobar alone needs a full quart. And Rupa eyes milk so hungrily.
Now she can get her fill. Once in a while I'll give a few quarts to the
master. The agent will have to be pacified too. And Bhola—he'd
better be paid in cash. Why dupe him with a promise of marriage?
It would be a dirty trick to cheat such a trusting fellow. He's giving
me an eighty-rupee cow on faith, and around here no one gives even
a pice that way. The hemp should bring something. And if I could
give even twenty-five rupees, that would be some consolation to
him. . . .

I shouldn't have told Dhaniya. If I'd just brought the cow secretly
and tied it up, she'd have been flabbergasted. 'Whose cow is it?' she'd
have asked. 'Where did you get it from?' After a good teasing, I'd
have told her. If only I could keep secrets from her. But even when
a little extra money comes in, I can't hide it from her. And perhaps
it's just as well. She runs the house, and if she found out I was keeping
money from her, she'd start fussing. If Gobar weren't so lazy, we

40

could take care of the cow in the style she deserves. Not that he's really lazy. Everyone takes things easy at that age. During my father's lifetime I used to loaf around a bit myself. The poor man used to start chopping fodder while it was still dark. Sometimes I'd still be sleeping while he was up sweeping the house or putting manure on the fields. The times when he did wake me up, I'd get angry and threaten to run away from home. Boys might as well enjoy life a bit while their parents are still around to look after them. It's not much fun once all the responsibility falls on their shoulders. And when my father died I took over the household, didn't I? The whole village said I'd ruin the family; but when the burden fell on me I turned over a new leaf and amazed everyone.

Shobha and Hira moved away. Otherwise the household would be very different. Three ploughs used to work side by side. Now they all go their separate ways. Well, that's how things are these days. Dhaniya surely can't be blamed. Poor woman hasn't had a moment's rest since she came to this house. From the time she stepped out of the bridal palanquin, she's taken everything upon herself. She had my mother twisted round her little finger. So when she, who was sacrificing herself for the sake of the family, asked my brothers' wives to help with the work, what was wrong with that? After all, she deserved a little rest and comfort too. But that comes only if it's written in your fate. In those days she slaved for her brothers-in-law; now she slaves for her children. If she weren't so innocent, honest and long-suffering, those brothers of mine who strut around twisting their moustaches would be beggars today. People are so selfish—the very man you've struggled to help becomes your deadly enemy.

Hori looked towards the eastern sky. Dawn must be approaching. Why would Gobar be stirring? No, that's right, he said last night he'd be off before it got light. I'd better go and dig the trough—but no, best not to do that until the cow is at the door. If Bhola should change his mind for some reason and not give us the cow, the whole village would make fun of me—'Oh, so he went to get a cow, did he? Big deal—he rushes out and digs a trough as though that were all it takes.' Bhola may be the head of his household, but how much weight does that carry now that his sons are grown up? If Kamta and Jangi get stubborn, could he still insist on giving me the cow? Never....

Gobar sat up and rubbed his eyes. 'Well! It's morning already. Have you dug the trough, father?'

Hori looked proudly at the boy's good physique and broad chest, thinking that with a little milk from somewhere he'd be a really husky young man. 'No, I've not dug it yet,' he said. 'I thought that there's no point in being laughed at in case we don't get her.'

Gobar bristled. 'Why wouldn't we get her?'

'Maybe he'll pull a fast one on us.'

'Fast one nothing—he has to give us the cow.' Saying no more, Gobar shouldered his stick and started off.

Hori's eyes followed him with satisfaction. . . . The boy's marriage ought to be arranged before long. He was going on seventeen. But how could they manage it? If only some money would turn up. The family reputation had been sinking ever since the three brothers parted. People had come to look at the boy, but when they saw the condition of the house they would turn their faces in disappointment and go away. One or two had been willing, but they wanted money. Two or three hundred would have to be collected for the price of a bride and an equal amount for other expenses. Then he could go and arrange a marriage. But where would all that money come from? The crops had been weighed up at the village barn and there was hardly enough left to feed themselves, what more pay for a marriage. And now Sona was at the age where a husband should be found for her. If a son's marriage doesn't take place, that's one thing. But for a daughter to remain unmarried would make them the laughing stock of the community. First they must settle things for her. After that, they'd see. . . .

Just then a man approached, greeted Hori, and asked if he had any bamboo in his cluster. Hori looked up. Standing before him was Damri the cane-weaver—short, dark and very fat, with a wide mouth, a huge moustache, red eyes, and a bamboo chopper stuck in his belt. Once or twice a year he came around and cut down bamboo to use for screens, chairs, stools, baskets and things.

Hori was delighted. Here was a chance to warm his hands with a little cash. He took Damri to see his three clumps of bamboo, bargained with him, and agreed to sell fifty poles at twenty-five rupees a hundred. Back at the house, Hori offered him a smoke and some refreshments and then whispered confidentially, 'My bamboo never goes for less than thirty rupees. But you're one of us. I can't bargain with you. By the way, that son of yours who got married the other day . . . has he gotten back yet?'

Damri took a puff and replied, coughing, 'That youngster's been

42

the ruin of me. With a young wife sitting at home, he gaily romps off with another woman from the community. After that, his wife ran away with someone too. A bad lot, women—never faithful to anyone. Time after time I told her she could eat and dress however she liked as long as she didn't disgrace me. But what did she care? Whatever else God gives a woman, he ought not to give her beauty or she becomes uncontrollable. I suppose the bamboo was divided among you three brothers?'

Hori looked up at the sky and, as though lifted to its heights, murmured distantly, 'Everything was divided up, Damri. After bringing them up like sons, they now have an equal share. Not that I want their share, mind you. The money I get from you I'll take right over and divide with them. When life's so short, why should we cheat anyone? But if I were to tell them the sale was for twenty rupees a hundred, how would they find out? You certainly wouldn't go tell them. I've always thought of you as a brother.'

With this hint of a proposition, Hori glanced over to see whether Damri would agree. His face wore the phony obsequious expression which a fat beggar puts on when asking for alms.

Having discovered Hori's weakness, Damri started exploiting it. "It's all very well to say we're brothers. But the point is that a man doesn't sell his honour unless there's some profit in it. Twenty rupees No, but I'll tell them fifteen, provided you give me the bamboo for twenty.'

Hori was annoyed. 'You're being unfair, Damri. Where can you get bamboo like this at twenty rupees a hundred?'

'What do you mean, "like this". I can get better for just ten rupees by going twenty miles west of here. The price is not for the bamboo, but because it's close to town. I figure I can earn several rupees in the time it would take to go there.'

The bargain was settled. Damri took off his jacket, hung it on the shed, and started cutting the bamboo.

The sugar cane was being irrigated, so Hira was at the well and his wife was taking lunch to him there. Seeing Damri, she pulled her sari over her face and called out, 'Who's that cutting the bamboo? Those are not to be chopped down.'

Damri paused for a moment. 'I've bought this bamboo—fifteen rupees a hundred in advance. I'm not getting it for nothing.'

Hira's wife was the mistress of her household. It was her intransigence that had led to the separation of the brothers. Having defeated

43

Dhaniya, she had turned into a regular tiger. Hira beat her now and then, and just recently he had hit her so hard that she'd been flat in bed for days, but she was not about to relinquish her authority. Hira might strike her in anger, but he still followed her orders, like a horse which kicks its master but still lets him ride on its back.

'We're not letting our bamboo go at that price,' she snapped, setting the lunch basket down off her head.

Damri considered it improper to argue the matter with a woman. 'Go send your husband to me. Let him come say whatever needs to be said.'

Hira's wife Punni, though the mother of only two children, looked faded already. She would have liked to repair the ravages of time with make-up, but where would she find money for that in a household where even food was a problem? Deprivation and frustration had dried up any kindness she once possessed, leaving her so dry and hard that even a pickaxe would have bounced off her.

Coming near, she tried to grab his hand, shouting, 'Why should I send my husband? You can tell me whatever you have to say. I've told you, my bamboo is not to be cut down.'

Damri freed his hand, but each time he did so Punni seized it again. This scuffling continued for a minute or so. Then Damri gave her a strong shove backwards. Punni lost her balance and fell over. Scrambling to her feet, she pulled off a sandal and struck him wildly again and again on the head and face and back. How dare he, a mere basket-weaver, push her! What an insult! She kept on hitting him, crying at the same time. Damri, having made the mistake of pushing her, having used force against a woman, could do nothing now but stand there and take it.

Hearing Punni's cries, Hori came running. Seeing him, she began shrieking still louder. Hori assumed that Damri had hit his sister-in-law. His family loyalties rose, breaking the dam created by the separation and releasing all his pent-up feelings. Giving Damri a swift kick, he shouted, 'If you know what's good for you, you'll get out of here—or they'll be carrying away your corpse. Just who do you think you are? How dare you raise a hand against my sister-in-law!'

Damri began swearing his innocence. His feelings of guilt had made him endure in silence the insult of the shoe-beating. But with this unjustified kick, tears began running down his puffy cheeks.

44

He hadn't even touched the woman. Was he such a boor as to strike a friend's wife?'

Hori was unconvinced. 'Don't try to throw dust in my eyes, Damri. I suppose you did nothing and she's just pretending to cry. If it's money that's made you hot-headed, I'll knock it out of you. Even if we are living apart, we're still of the same blood. If anyone starts giving her a bad time I'll gouge his eyes out.'

Punni now became as fierce as *Kali*. 'Oh, so you didn't shove me and knock me down?' she screamed. 'Go swear that on your son's head, you liar.'

Meanwhile Hira had also heard about the row—that Damri had pushed Puniya and she had struck him with a sandal. Leaving the well, he stalked to the scene with grim determination. Hira was notorious in the village for his temper. Short and stocky, his eyes now bulged like shells and the veins on his neck were stretched taut— but in anger at his wife, not at Damri. Why was she fighting with this fellow? Was she trying to drag their name in the dust? What possible excuse could she have for quarrelling with a basket-weaver? She should have come to him, Hira, and explained the difficulty. Then he could have done whatever seemed proper. There was no reason for her to go fight with him. If he had the power, he'd lock her up in the house. For her to open her mouth in front of an elder was intolerable. Hira expected Punni to be as tranquil as he himself was short-tempered. If his brother had made a deal for fifteen rupees, who was she to interfere?

Arriving on the scene, Hira grabbed Punni's hand, pulled her away, and began kicking her. 'You little bastard!' he shouted. 'Determined to ruin my reputation, aren't you? Running around fighting with these nobodies. Tell me, just whose turban is it gets dragged in the mud?' He kicked her again. 'There I am waiting for my food and you're here trying to pick a fight. What shamelessness! I've lost all respect for you. I'd like to dig a hole and bury you!'

Punni went on wailing and cursing—'May they carry away your corpse! May you get cholera! May Kali devour you with plague! May you suffer from flu! May God strike you with leprosy! May your hands and feet rot and fall off!'

Hira kept still during the other curses, but this last one was too much for him. Cholera and plague were not so bad—the fever strikes and you soon pass away. But leprosy! That horrible death and that even more horrible life! Blood boiling, he jumped up, gnashing his

45

teeth, and pounced on Puniya. Seizing her by the hair, he banged her head on the ground. 'And when my limbs rot and fall off, just where will that leave you? You think you could raise the children? Ha! You think you could run such a big house? No, you'd find another husband and start sponging off him.'

Damri's pity was aroused. 'Let her go, my friend,' he said, expansively, trying to calm Hira. 'She's had enough. What if she did hit me? It hasn't done me any harm. Thank God it was only your wife who struck me.'

'Shut up, Damri,' Hira snapped, 'or I'll get mad at you too, and then you'll be sorry. Women are always shooting off their mouths this way. Today she picks a fight with you; tomorrow it'll be with someone else. You're being big about it, laughing it off. The next person may not stand for it. Suppose he lets fly at her. What do you think my reputation would be worth then?'

The thought fanned his anger still more. He started for her again but Hori quickly caught him and pushed him back, saying, 'All right now, that's enough. Everyone has seen how tough you are. What more do you want—to grind her up and eat her?'

Hira still respected his elder brother and would not fight openly with him. He could easily have jerked himself free, but he couldn't bring himself to be disrespectful. Turning to Damri he said, 'What are you standing and gaping at? Go cut your bamboo. I've agreed—fifteen rupees a hundred. That's settled.'

At this Punni, who had been sitting there weeping, jumped up. 'Go ahead, set our house on fire!' she cried, beating her fists against her head. 'What do I care? It's my rotten fate to have fallen into the hands of a butcher like you. So burn down the house!'

She started for home, leaving the lunch basket behind. 'Where do you think you're going?' Hira roared. 'Go take that to the well or I'll drink your blood!"

Punni stopped in her tracks. She didn't want to start a second act in this drama. Sobbing quietly, she picked up the basket and headed for the well. Hira followed her.

'Don't get involved in this rough stuff again,' Hori shouted after him. 'It only makes women shameless.'

Dhaniya came to the door and called out, "What's the big show you're standing around watching over there? You think anyone's listening to you, passing out advice that way? Have you forgotten the day when that same girl called you names under cover of her

46

veil? Doesn't a newly married woman deserve to be punished if she fights with menfolk?'

Stepping up to the door Hori said mischievously, 'And if I were to beat you that way?'

'I suppose you never have? And that you've never wanted to?'

'If I beat you as cruelly as that, you'd leave the house and run away. Puniya puts up with a lot.'

'Oh ho, you're so considerate, are you? I've still got the marks from your beatings. Hira may beat her, but he gives her a lot of loving too. You've only learned how to beat a woman, not how to love her. I'm the only one who could ever put up with you.'

'All right, drop it. Don't start bragging about yourself now. It was you who started sulking and went running home to mother. I had to flatter you for months before you'd come back.'

'You only came to coax me when your own needs got too pressing, mister. It wasn't out of love for me.'

'I suppose that's why I'm always praising you to everyone?'

The dawn of married life is rosy with an intoxicating desire whose golden rays illumine the horizons of the soul. Then comes the scorching heat of noon, when whirlwinds blow and the earth begins to tremble. The golden shelter of desire melts away. Stark reality emerges. After that comes restful evening, cool and peaceful, when, like weary travellers, we discuss the day's journey with a detachment as though seated on some high mountain top removed from the clamour below.

Tears filled Dhaniya's eyes. 'Oh go on. Sing my praises indeed! Any little thing goes wrong and you're on my neck.'

'Hey, now you're being unfair to me,' Hori protested gently. 'Just ask Bhola what I say about you.'

Dhaniya changed the subject. 'Let's see whether Gobar comes back with the cow or returns empty-handed.'

At this point Damri turned up, drenched with sweat. 'Come count the bamboo. Tomorrow I'll bring a cart and haul it away.'

Hori thought it unnecessary to count the poles. Damri was not that kind of a man, and what difference did it make if he took an extra pole or two? Every day a few went for nothing, and during the marriage season people cut them by the dozens to build pavilions.

Damri took out seven and a half rupees and laid them in Hori's hand. Hori counted them and said, 'Give me the rest. According to our agreement there should be another two and a half.'

47

'Didn't we settle on fifteen rupees a hundred?' Damri replied coolly.

'No, not fifteen. It was twenty.'

'Right in your presence Hira said fifteen rupees. If you want, I'll call him.'

'The bargain was for twenty, Damri. Now you've got the upper hand, so you can say whatever you like. You still owe me two and a half. Make it just two.'

Damri was no novice at this game, however. He had nothing to fear now. Hori's lips were sealed and there was nothing he could do.

'That's a dirty trick, Damri,' Hori said, beating his forehead. 'And you're not going to get rich by swindling me out of two rupees.'

'I suppose you'd get rich if you swindled your brothers out of a little money?' retorted Damri harshly. 'You were selling your honour for two and a half rupees and now you give me advice! If I unveiled your little plot you'd look pretty small.'

It was as though a hundred shoes had fallen on Hori's head. Damri set the money on the ground in front of Hori and walked away. Then he sat for a long time under the neem tree, however, filled with remorse. He had discovered today just how greedy and selfish he was. He could have been perfectly happy now if he'd given Hori the two and a half rupees. He could have applauded his own cleverness in getting that two and a half for nothing. But only after a fall do we learn to watch our step.

Dhaniya had been inside. Coming out, she saw the coins on the ground, counted them, and demanded, 'Where's the rest? Weren't we supposed to get ten?'

Hori pulled a long face. 'Hira agreed on fifteen, so what could I do?'

'Hira can give his away for five, for all I care, but we're not letting ours go at this price.'

'A full-scale riot was going on over there. What could I do in the middle of it all?'

Hori kept his defeat to himself like a thief who climbs a tree to pick mangoes, falls down, and then, jumping up quickly, dusts himself off lest someone see him. A successful man can boast of his cunning. Success excuses everything. In defeat, however, one can only swallow his shame silently.

Dhaniya began to berate her husband—a rare opportunity, since Hori was usually more shrewd than she. Today she held the trump card, though. Gesturing sarcastically, she sneered, 'Why of course, when your brother said fifteen, how could you possibly interfere? My God, it would have crushed your darling brother's heart! And in the midst of such great calamity, when a knife was threatening your precious sister-in-law's throat, how could you possibly have spoken up? Someone could have robbed you of everything and you'd never have noticed!'

Hori listened without even a murmur. He was irritated and angry —his blood boiled, his eyes glared, his teeth gnashed—but he said nothing. Silently lifting his hoe, he started off.

Dhaniya caught hold of the hoe. 'You think it's morning, going to hoe the cane? The sun god is at his height. Go take your bath. The food's ready.'

'I'm not hungry,' Hori sulked.

Dhaniya poured salt on his wounds. 'Of course, why would you be hungry? Your brother has given you such a nice big feast! God should give everyone such loyal brothers.'

Hori's patience had reached the breaking point. 'Determined to get a beating today, aren't you?'

'How can I help it?' Dhaniya replied with affected meekness. 'I can't think straight, what with all your caresses.'

'Are you going to let me stay here in peace or not?'

'It's your house. You're the master. Who am I to throw you out?'

Hori was not up to Dhaniya today. His wits seemed blunted and he was defenceless against her scathing remarks. Slowly he set down the hoe, wrapped a cloth around his waist, and went off to take a bath. When he returned half an hour later, there was still no sign of Gobar. How could he go ahead and eat alone? The boy must be asleep on the job. Quite an exciting girl, that Jhuniya, over at Bhola's. He was probably flirting around with her. Even yesterday he was following her around. If they wouldn't give the cow, though, he should have come straight home. Did he think he could badger them into it?'

'What are you standing around for?' Dhaniya asked. 'He'll be back this evening.'

Hori said nothing lest Dhaniya start in on him again. He finished his meal and stretched out in the shade of the neem tree.

Rupa ran up in tears, just a cloth around her waist and her long tangled hair flying in all directions. She threw herself on her father's chest. 'Sona says she's going to make all the dung cakes when the cow comes. Why should she get to lord it over me? What makes her

49

any better than me? She may cook, but I scrub the pots and pans. She brings the water from the well, but don't I carry the rope there? She comes prancing back as soon as she's filled the bucket. I'm the one who winds up the rope and brings it home. We both make the dung cakes. Sona goes to hoe the fields, but don't I take the goats out to graze? Then why should she get to roll out the cowdung all by herself? It's not fair.'

Hori was touched by her innocence. 'Don't worry,' he assured her. 'You can make the dung cakes. If Sona goes near the cow, you chase her away.'

Rupa threw her arms around her father's neck. 'Can I milk the cow too?' she begged.

'Of course. If you don't milk her, who will?'

'She'll be my cow?'

'That's right, all yours.'

Thrilled, Rupa ran off to announce her glorious victory to Sona. 'The cow's going to be mine. I'm going to milk her. I'm going to make the cakes from her dung. You don't get to do anything.'

Sona was at an awkward age. Her body was that of a young woman, but her mind was still that of a child, as though adolescence were pulling her forward while childhood tried to hold her back. In some things she could have been a teacher; in others she was more ingenuous than most students. Her long face was plain but cheerful, her chin hung down, and her eyes reflected a kind of contentment. But the absence of oil in her hair, of kohl around her eyes, and of ornaments on her body suggested that household cares had stunted her development.

'Go ahead and make the dung cakes,' she retorted, tossing her head. 'After you've milked the cow, I'll drink it all up.'

'I'll lock up the milk pot.'

'I'll break the lock and get it out.'

With that, Sona went off toward the grove. The mangoes were beginning to ripen, and the wind sometimes knocked a few to the ground. Though dry and yellow from the hot summer wind, they were prized as though fully ripe by the children who constantly beseiged the garden. Rupa followed right behind her sister. Whatever Sona did, she had to do. There had been talk about Sona's marriage but none about hers, so Rupa speculated to herself about the possibilities—what her bridegroom would be like, what he would bring, how he would treat her and feed her and dress her. The image she built up was so extravagant that no young man hearing it would have ever agreed to marry her.

Evening was approaching. Hori felt too lazy to go hoe the sugar cane. So he led the bullocks to the trough, gave them their feed, and then sat down for a smoke.... Even though his whole crop had been weighed in at the barn, he still owed three hundred rupees, on top of which there was another hundred in interest. Five years ago he had borrowed sixty rupees from Mangaru Shah for a bullock. He had already paid sixty on it, but the principal remained unchanged. Then there was the thirty rupees he'd borrowed from Pandit Datadin so as to plant potatoes. Thieves had dug up the potatoes and made off with them, but the thirty rupee debt had swelled to a hundred in three years. As for Dulari, the widowed shopkeeper who sold salt, oil and tobacco to the village, he'd had to borrow forty rupees from her to give to his brothers at the time the property was divided. That amount had also grown to about a hundred, what with interest of one anna on the rupee every month. He also owed another twenty-five on the land rent, and he had to make some arrangement for a cash donation at the Dashahra function.

This money from the bamboo had come at a very opportune time. It might solve the problem of the donation, though one couldn't be sure, for as soon as anyone got a copper in hand, word spread through the village and creditors came clamouring from all sides. Well, whatever happened, he'd keep five rupees for the donation. Then again, though, two of his biggest responsibilities in life were pressing— Gobar's and Sona's marriages. Even if he cut corners as much as possible, they would cost at least three hundred rupees. Just where was that money to come from? How he wished there was no need to borrow a thing from anyone, that every pice could be paid back. But though they'd deprived themselves of everything imaginable, they were still caught by the neck. The interest would keep piling up until one day his whole place would be up for auction and his homeless children would have to turn to begging. ... *abject poverty*

Whenever Hori took a break from his work and sat down for a smoke, these worries rose up like a dark wall, hemming him in on all sides, with no route of escape. The only possible consolation was that these calamities were not falling on his head alone. Almost all the farmers were in the same predicament. In fact most of them were even worse off. Shobha and Hira had moved away only some three years ago, but each was now saddled with a debt of four hundred

51

rupees. Jhingur, who had a two-plough field, owed over a thousand. And even at Jiyawan's place, where they were so miserly that even a beggar couldn't get alms, there was no end to the debts. No one around had been spared.

Suddenly Sona and Rupa came running up shouting, 'Brother is bringing the cow. The cow's in front; he's behind.'

Rupa had been the first to see Gobar coming, so the honour of announcing the news was hers by right. She couldn't stand to let Sona share the glory. Pushing forward, she cried, 'I saw him first and started running. Sister saw him afterwards.'

'But you didn't recognize him,' Sona objected. 'You just said some cow was running this way. I was the one who said it was brother.'

They both raced off towards the grove to welcome the cow.

Dhaniya and Hori started making preparations to tie up the cow. 'Come on,' said Hori, 'let's quickly get a trough ready.'

Dhaniya's face sparkled with a youthful radiance. 'No, let's first mix up a plate of flour and sugar. Poor thing has been walking in the sun. She must be thirsty. You go dig the trough. I'll mix up the food.'

'There used to be a little bell around somewhere. We must find it and tie it around her neck.'

'Where's Sona gone? Send her to get a bit of black cord. Cows are easily struck by the evil eye.'

'Today my heart's greatest desire has been fulfilled.'

Dhaniya was trying to restrain her immense delight, for fear that such good fortune would bring calamity in its wake. Looking at the sky she said, 'The time to be happy over the cow's coming will be after we see what kind of luck she brings. Only God knows. . . .

It was as though Dhaniya were trying to put something over on a jealous God, to convince him that they were not so thrilled over the arrival of the cow that he need send some new misfortune to tilt the scales.

She was just preparing the flour when Gobar arrived at the door with the cow, a procession of children accompanying them. Hori ran and flung his arms around the creature's neck. Leaving the food, Dhaniya quickly tore the black border off an old sari and tied it around the cow's neck.

Hori stood gazing at the animal as reverently as though a goddess incarnate had just stepped into the house. At last God had brought the day when his house was being hallowed by the feet of a cow.

52

Whose deeds could have built up the merit to bring such good fortune?

'What are you standing around for?' Dhaniya said apprehensively. 'Go dig the trough in the courtyard.'

'In the courtyard? Where is there room?'

'There's plenty of room.'

'I'd better dig it outside.'

'Don't be crazy. How can you be so stupid when you know perfectly well what this village is like?'

'Well, and just where are you going to tie her in a courtyard the size of my hand?

'Don't start meddling in things you know nothing about. You weren't given all the brains in the world.'

Actually Hori was not in his usual form at the moment. For him the cow was not only an object of worship and devotion; it was also the living image of prosperity. He wanted it to beautify his door and to raise the prestige of his house. He wanted people to see the cow at his door and ask, 'Whose place is that?' 'Hori's,' the neighbours would answer. Then even the parents of eligible girls would be impressed by his affluence. If she were tied in the courtyard no one would even see her. Dhaniya, on the other hand, was suspicious. If she had her way, the cow would be kept hidden behind seven layers of curtains. If there were any way to keep the cow inside all day, she'd never let it out. Hori had always triumphed in matters like this insisting on his own way until Dhaniya was forced to give in. But this time he was no match for her. She was ready to fight; and even with Gobar, Sona and Rupa all taking Hori's side, she defeated them all. Today she was filled with amazing self-assurance and Hori with unusual submissiveness.

There was no stopping the hubbub. After all, the cow had not come hidden in a bridal palanquin. How could such a great event take place without causing a commotion? As soon as people heard, they dropped their work and ran to take a look. This was no ordinary local cow. She'd been bought from Bhola for eighty rupees! Hori give eighty rupees for a cow? He must have bought her for fifty or sixty. But even that price would be unprecedented in the history of the village. They sometimes bought bullocks for fifty, of course, or even a hundred, but how could a farmer possibly save up that much for a cow! She was more like a goddess! The curious and the critical

53

streamed to the spot and Hori dashed around greeting them all. He'd never been so cheerful, so gracious.

Datadin, the seventy-year-old *pandit*, came leaning on his stick and mumbled toothlessly, 'Where are you, Hori? Let's have a look at your cow. I hear she's a beauty.'

Hori ran and touched his feet in respect, and then, buoyed up with pride and joy, led the pandit with great ceremony into the courtyard. The old man's wise, experienced eyes scrutinized the cow, checking her horns, her udder and her rump. Then, the enthusiasm of youth shining from eyes almost hidden beneath his shaggy white brows, he pronounced her faultless. 'All the auspicious signs are there, my son. Everything is good. God willing, good fortune will bless you. Wah! What a perfect animal! Just don't skimp on her food. Each calf will be worth a hundred rupees.'

By this time Hori was wallowing in a sea of bliss. 'It's all due to your blessings, dada,' he gushed.

Datadin spat some tobacco juice. 'It's not my blessing, son. It's the kindness of God. This is all due to the kindness of the Lord. Did you pay cash?'

How could Hori ignore such an opportunity to make a show of prosperity, even though a creditor was present? When he could swagger over wearing a new cap worth two pice, or soar to the heavens over a brief ride in some borrowed vehicle, was it any wonder that his head was almost touching the clouds over this immense wealth? 'Bhola is not one for charity, *maharaj*,' he said. 'I counted out cash —every pice.'

This was a foolish boast in front of the moneylender, but Datadin's face showed no displeasure. The amount of truth in Hori's statement had not escaped those penetrating eyes, eyes in which the glow of experience remained though their radiance had disappeared.

'Well it's no loss, son, no loss,' the old man assured him cheerfully. 'God will give you every happiness. She's good for five quarts of milk over and above what the calf will need.'

'Oh no, maharaj,' Dhaniya quickly interrupted. 'How could there be that much milk? She's getting old. And besides, where would the feed come from?'

Datadin, appreciating her caution, gave her a knowing look as if to suggest that she was taking the right attitude for a housewife— that boasting should be left to the men. 'Let me just say this,' he whispered in a confidential tone. 'Don't tie her outside.'

Dhaniya shot a look of triumph at her husband as though to say 'There! Now will you listen to me?' Turning to Datadin, she said, 'Of course not, maharaj. Why should we tie her outside when, God willing, another three cows could fit in this courtyard?'

The whole village had come to see the cow—all except Shobha and Hira, Hori's own brothers. He still had a soft spot in his heart for them, and now if they would just come take a look and be pleased, his happiness would be complete. Evening came, and the two brothers, returning from the well, passed by the door. But they made no inquiries.

'Neither Shobha nor Hira has turned up,' Hori said timidly to Dhaniya. 'Could they have failed to hear about it?'

'So who's about to go call them?' Dhaniya said.

'You don't understand. You're always spoiling for a fight. Now that God has brought us this day, we should act with humility. A man hungers for some opinion, good or bad, from the mouths of his own people more than from outsiders. After all, a brother is still a brother, however bad he may be. Everyone fights for the share that belongs to him, but that doesn't cut the ties of blood. We ought to invite them over to see her. Otherwise they'll say we got a cow and didn't even inform them.'

Dhaniya sniffed. 'I've told you a hundred times not to throw your brothers' praises in my face. It makes me burn just to hear their names. The whole village has heard—I suppose they haven't? It's not as if they were living somewhere far away. The whole village came to see, but they're so busy sitting around looking pretty—how could they come? They must be boiling over our getting a cow. Their chests must be bursting with envy.'

It was time to light the lamps. Finding the oil bottle empty, Dhaniya went off to get some oil. If she'd had the money, she would have sent Rupa, but since she wanted it on credit, some flattery and cajolery would be necessary.

Hori called Rupa, set her lovingly on his lap, and said, 'Just go see if Uncle Hira is back yet or not. And find out about Uncle Shobha too. Tell them I've sent for them. If they don't want to come, take them by the hands and drag them here.'

'But the younger auntie picks on me,' Rupa whimpered.

'Then don't go near her. Uncle Shobha's wife loves you, doesn't she?'

'Uncle Shobha teases me. He says. . . . No, I won't say!'

'What does he say? Come on, tell me.'

'He just teases.'

'What does he says when he's teasing?'

'He says he's caught a mouse for me, and that I should cook it and eat it.'

Hori was amused. 'Why don't you tell him he should eat it first?'

'Anyway, mother has forbidden me. She says I'm not to go near those people's place.'

'Are you mother's girl or father's?'

Rupa put her arms around his neck. 'Mother's,' she said, breaking into a laugh.

'Then get down off my lap. And I won't let you eat off my plate today.'

There was only one fancy plate in the house, the *thali* off which Hori ate, and Rupa always sat next to him so as to have the privilege of sharing it. How could she give up that honour? After fussing a little she said, 'All right, I'm yours.'

'Now, will you follow my orders or mother's?'

'Yours.'

'Then go drag Hira and Shobha here.'

'And if mother gets mad?'

'Who's going to tell her?'

Rupa skipped off towards Hira's house. Only big fish get trapped in the net of jealousy. The small ones are either not caught at all or quickly free themselves. For them, that deadly snare is a plaything, not an object of fear. Rupa came and went freely between the houses even though Hori was not on speaking terms with his brothers. There could be no quarrel with children, after all.

Rupa was hardly out of the house, however, when she encountered her mother returning with the oil. 'And where are you off to at this time of evening?' Dhaniya demanded. 'Run along inside.'

Rupa paused, unable to resist the need to try and please her mother.

'Go into the house,' Dhaniya scolded. 'You're not to call anyone.'

Seizing Rupa by the hand, she led her inside and said to Hori, 'I've told you a thousand times you're not to send my children to anyone's house. If some harm came to them, what good would you be to me? If you love your brothers so much, why don't you go yourself? Evidently you haven't yet had a bellyful.'

Hori, working on the trough, gestured innocently with his mud-

56

smeared hands. 'What are you getting so worked up about? You're like a blind dog, barking at the wind over nothing.'

The lamps needed filling, so Dhaniya didn't want to start an argument just then. Rupa went off to join the other children.

The night grew late. The trough had been dug, and filled with wet chaff and oilcakes. But the cow sat there, as sad-eyed and depressed as a new bride at her father-in-law's home. She wouldn't go near the trough. Hori and Gobar finished eating and brought her some scraps of their food, but she wouldn't even sniff them. This was not surprising—a change of homes can be a sad experience for animals also.

When Hori sat down for a smoke on the cot outside, the thought of his brothers came up again. He just couldn't ignore them on such an auspicious day. The good fortune made him feel generous. Even if they had moved away, that didn't make them his enemies. If this cow had come just three years earlier, they'd have had equal rights to her. And if she were to start giving milk tomorrow, could he refuse to send milk and curds to their houses? That would be a violation of his sacred duty. Just because his brothers wished him ill was no reason for him to do the same. Each man has to answer for his own deeds. . . .

He leaned his chilam against the leg of the cot and set off for Hira's house. Shobha's place was right next to it. The two men were lounging on the ground outside their doors and talking to each other. In the darkness they were unaware of Hori's presence. He stopped, and began listening to their conversation. Who could resist the opportunity to eavesdrop on a conversation about himself?

'When we were together, he didn't even come up with a goat,' Hira was saying. 'Yet now he's able to buy a cow. Well, I've never yet seen anyone prosper by cheating his brothers of their due.'

'You're being unfair, Hira,' said Shobha. 'He accounted for every pice. I'll never believe that he hid any of our joint earnings.'

'Whether you believe it or not, this was money hidden from us.'

'You shouldn't accuse people falsely.'

'All right then, where did the money come from? Was there a shower of gold somewhere? Our fields are the same size as his. We have just as good crops. Then how is it that he appears with a new cow when we can't even afford a few cowries for a shroud?'

'He must have bought it on credit.'

'Bhola's not one to give credit.'

57

'Anyhow, the cow's a beautiful animal. I saw her on the road as Gobar was bringing her in.'

'Dishonest wealth goes the same way it comes. God willing, that cow won't be at his house for long.'

Hori could stand no more. Forgettting the past, he had come to his brothers with a heart full of friendship and affection; but this piercing attack drained him of all brotherly feelings. Stuffing the breach with rags could not check the flood now. Hori was boiling to answer the accusation then and there, but fear of heightening the quarrel kept him silent. No one could hurt him as long as his own conscience was clear. In the eyes of God he was blameless, so why should he worry about anyone else?

He turned and went home. Sitting down, he puffed on the chilam he'd left burning, but a kind of poison seemed to be seeping through his veins. He tried to sleep, but no sleep came. He went over to the bullocks and began rubbing them down, but the poison did not diminish. He filled another chilam, but that gave no satisfaction either. The poison seemed to have dulled his senses. His brain seemed intoxicated, running along a single track like a rush of water gathering speed as it flows on unchecked. Obsessed, he went back inside. The door was still open. On one side of the courtyard Dhaniya was stretched out on a mat with Sona massaging her, while Rupa, who usually went to sleep at sundown, stood stroking the cow's face. Hori untied the cow and led her towards the door. He had made up his mind to return her to Bhola immediately. He couldn't keep her any longer in the face of such shameful accusations. It would be impossible!

'Where are you taking her at this time of night?' Dhaniya inquired.

Hori took another step forward. 'I'm going back to Bhola's house. I'm giving her back.'

Dhaniya jumped up in astonishment and stood facing him. 'Why should you give her back? Was she brought here just to be returned?'

'Yes, we'll be better off returning her.'

'Why? What's the matter? You brought her here so enthusiastically and now you're going to give her back? Is Bhola demanding the money?'.

'No, he hasn't been around.'

'Then what's happened?'

'There's no use talking about it.'

58

Dhaniya rushed up and pulled the rope out of his hand. Her keen intuition had suddenly seized on the truth as though it were a bird flying overhead. 'If it's your brothers you're afraid of,' she said, 'then go fall at their feet. But I'm not afraid of anyone. If anyone's heart is bursting with jealousy over our good fortune, then let it burst. I don't care.'

'Quiet down, maharani!' Hori pleaded. 'People will overhear us and start talking about our fighting so late at night. You don't know what I've just heard with my own ears. Word is going around that I cheated my brothers when we split up, and put aside some money which is just now coming to light.'

'I suppose Hira's saying that?'

'Why blame only Hira? The whole village is saying it.'

'The whole village is saying nothing of the kind. It's Hira alone. I'll go there right now and ask him just how much money he thinks his father left when he died. We've wasted our lives for the sake of those good-for-nothings, grinding ourselves in the dust. And now that we've fed them and raised them to be strong as bulls, it's we who are dishonest. I'm telling you, if that cow steps out of this house, all hell is going to break loose. Sure we put money away. We buried it —right in the middle of the field we buried it! I'm announcing it to the beating of drums—I've hidden away a whole potful of pure gold coins! Let Hira and Shobha and the whole world do whatever they like about it. Why shouldn't we have some money set aside? Didn't we marry off those two oxes? Didn't we bring home brides for them?'

Hori stood flabbergasted as Dhaniya tied the cow to the post and started for the door. He wanted to stop her, but she was already out of the house. Hori sat down, his head in his hands, not wanting to stage a public spectacle by trying to catch her outside. He was well-acquainted with Dhaniya's anger. Once aroused she was like Kali herself. Beat her ... hurt her ... she still wouldn't listen. Hira also had a temper though, and if he were to let fly, there'd be absolute havoc. But no, Hira was not such a fool....

Stupid of me to have lit this fire, thought Hori, turning his anger against himself. If I'd kept my mouth shut, the trouble would never have started.

All at once his ears caught the harsh sound of Dhaniya's voice, followed by a roar from Hira and then shrieks from Punni. Suddenly reminded of Gobar, he dashed outside to check his bed. Gobar

59

was missing. He must have gone over there too. Now there'd be hell to pay. With his young blood, no telling what he might do. But Hori couldn't very well go himself. Hira would accuse him of sitting back quietly and sending that witch to fight his battles for him.

The uproar was getting more furious by the moment. The whole village had been aroused, and people began jumping out of bed and running for the spot as though to put out a fire.

Hori had been holding himself back all this time, but he could wait no longer. Anger at Dhaniya surged through him. Why had she flared up and gone to pick a fight? A man has the right to say anything he likes in his own house. Unless he insults you to your face, you should assume he's said nothing. Hori's peasant nature usually fled from quarrels, considering it better to swallow a little abuse than to get involved in a fight. A fracas only meant police and then jail ... getting locked up ... grovelling in front of everyone ... being dragged through the courts while the farm went to hell. He had no power over Hira, but he could at least haul Dhaniya away by force. The most she could do was swear at him and sulk for a day or two. At least there'd be no question of police or of jail.

Reaching Hira's place, he hid behind the far door, like a general wanting to size up the situation before taking the field. If his wife were winning, there'd be no need to say anything; if losing, he'd have to jump into the fray. He could see that quite a crowd had gathered already. Pandit Datadin, Lala Pateshwari, the two *thakurs* who ran the village ... they'd all come. The scales were tipping against Dhaniya, her ruthlessness having turned popular opinion against her. Unskilled in the rules of battle, she was talking so viciously that people had lost all sympathy.

'Why is it that just the sight of me burns you up?' she was shrieking. 'Why do you get jealous just seeing us? Is this the reward we get for bringing you up and making men out of you? If we hadn't raised you, you'd be off begging somewhere today with not even a tree to shade you.'

These words struck Hori as unnecessarily harsh. After all, it had been his duty to raise his brothers. Being in charge of their share in the property, he wouldn't have dared show his face in public if he'd refused to support them.

'You must take us for complete idiots,' Hira retorted. 'We were treated like dogs in your house—given one scrap of food and then expected to work all day. We never knew what it was to be young.

60

Day after day we spent gathering dry cowdung—and yet you never gave us even a bite of food without ten curses thrown in. Life was torture in the clutches of a hellcat like you!'

Dhaniya grew even more furious. 'Hold your tongue,' she shouted, 'or I'll pull it out. It's your wife who's the hellcat. Who do you think you are? You imagine you're going to cut my throat? You scavenger! You ungrateful bastard!'

'Why such bitter words, Dhaniya?' Datadin interrupted. 'It's a woman's duty to be long-suffering. He's just a boorish young fellow. Why egg him on?'

Lala Pateshwari, the revenue collector, nodded his agreement. 'You should answer statements with statements, not abuse. You did take care of him in childhood, but don't forget that his property was in your hands.'

Dhaniya felt that they were all ganging up to humiliate her, and braced herself for a war on all fronts. 'All right, Lala, now stop it! I know the lot of you. I've lived in this village for twenty years and I'm familiar with every hair on your heads. What if I am throwing curses? I suppose he's showering bouquets?'

'She's got a lot of cheek, that woman,' said Dulari, adding fuel to the fire. 'What a way to talk to a man. Only Hori could put up with her. No other man would tolerate her a single day.'

If Hira had softened a little at this point, the victory would have been his. But Dhaniya's invectives had driven him out of his mind, and seeing the others joining his side, he became ferocious as a tiger. 'Get out of here,' he shouted at the top of his lungs, 'or I'll start talking with my shoes. I'll grab your hair and pull it out. Cursing me . . . you witch! You think you can be conceited just because you have a son. I'll kill . . .'

He had overplayed his hand. The powder fuse had been lit. Hori came forward seething with rage. 'All right Hira, that's enough. Shut up now. I won't stand for any more of this. As for this woman, I don't know what to say to her. Every time I'm knocked in the dust it's because of her. I don't know why she can't hold her tongue.'

Now the shower started falling on Hira from all sides. Datadin called him shameless, Pateshwari pronounced him a hoodlum, Thakur Jhinguri Singh called him a devil, and Dulari declared him a disgraceful son. One word too much had tipped the balance against Dhaniya; another now put Hira in the wrong. And Hori's restrained speech had clinched the case.

61

Hira controlled himself. Furious though he was, he had sense enough to realize that with the whole village turning against him his wisest course now was to remain silent.

Dhaniya's courage revived. 'Open your ears now and listen to that!' she told Hori. 'You're still throwing your life away on these brothers. Well I hope I never see the face of a brother if that's what they're like. This one was about to hit me with his shoes—and after my having fed and nourished . . .'

'There's no need to start blabbering again!' Hori interrupted. 'Why don't you go on home?'

Dhaniya sat down on the ground and said in an injured tone, 'First let him beat me with his shoes and then I'll go. I want to see how brave he is. Where is that Gobar? When is he going to do something? Son! Are you going to stand by and watch while your mother gets a shoe-beating?'

This wailing revived Hori's anger as well as her own. She had fanned the fire into a roaring blaze. Hira fell back, recognizing defeat. Punni caught his hand and started pulling him homeward, but then Dhaniya suddenly leaped like a tigress and shoved him so hard that he fell right over. 'Where do you think you're going?' she yelled. 'Come on . . . hit me with your shoes. Hit me! I want to see what a man you are!'

Hori ran after her, grabbed her by the wrist, and dragged her home.

CHAPTER 5

MEANWHILE Gobar had finished dinner and gone to the cowherders' village. He'd had quite a talk with Jhuniya earlier that day, since she had walked halfway home with him when he was taking the cow. He couldn't very well have handled the animal alone. Being led away by a complete stranger, she would naturally have given trouble. After going some distance, Jhuniya had looked meaningfully at Gobar and said, 'I suppose you won't have any reason to be back this way again.'

Until the day before, Gobar had been just a boy. The young women in his village were either like sisters or like sisters-in-law to him. He couldn't very well flirt with sisters, and as for sisters-in-law, they teased him occasionally of course, but only in fun. In their eyes, the tree of his youth was just beginning to flower, and until some fruit appeared there was no point in throwing stones. So, lacking stimulus from anywhere, his manhood had remained dormant. But Jhuniya, whose frustrated desires had been heightened by the suggestive teasing and joking of her sisters-in-law, was attracted in spite of his immaturity. And at that point Gobar's manhood had suddenly awakened like a sleeping beast of prey at the sound of a crackling in the leaves.

'A beggar will stand at the door all day and all night if there's any hope of a handout,' Gobar declared with undisguised longing.

'So you're only after something for yourself?' Jhuniya said, throwing him a coy glance.

The blood pounded in Gobar's veins. 'If a hungry man puts out his hand to you, he should be forgiven.'

Jhuniya plunged still deeper. 'But how can a beggar fill his stomach without going to a dozen doors? I'm not interested in that kind of beggars. You find them in every alley. And what do they give in returned? Their blessings! No one's appetitite can be satisfied with blessings.'

Gobar was too slow-witted to understand what she was driving at. Ever since she was little, Jhuniya had been delivering milk to to people's houses. After her marriage she still had to make those rounds, and the job of selling curds still fell to her also. So she'd had experience with all kinds of men. Sometimes it brought in a few rupees and sometimes it was also amusing for a little while. But that was just borrowed pleasure, with no permanence, no commitment, no security. She wanted a love for which she could live and die, one to which she could surrender herself. It was not the glimmer of a firefly she wanted, but the steady glow of a lamp. Being the daughter of a householder, she had a longing for domesticity which remained uncrushed by these casual flirtations with passers-by.

'If a beggar can satisfy his hunger at just one house, why should he keep going from door to door?' Gobar asked, his face flushed with desire.

Jhuniya looked at him tenderly. How innocent he was—he had understood nothing. 'How can a beggar be satisfied at one place? He gets only a handful. You only receive everything when you have given everything.'

'But what have I to give, Jhuniya?'

'You think you have nothing? As I see it, you've got something even millionaires don't have. You don't need to come begging to me. You can buy me.'

Gobar stared at her in astonishment.

'And you know what price you'll have to pay?' Jhuniya went on. 'You'll have to be mine and stay mine. If I see you begging from anyone else, I'll throw you out of the house.'

Gobar was like a man groping in the dark who at last finds the thing he's been searching for. His body tingled with a wonderful and alarming delight. But how could this work out? How could he take her as a mistress and still live at home? And there was the problem of the other caste members—the whole village would start cackling. They'd all turn against him, and his mother wouldn't even let Jhuniya set foot in the house. But if she, a woman, was not afraid, then why should he, a man, have any fears? At worst, people could only ostracize him, and in that case he would live separately. Where was there another girl like Jhuniya in the village? Such wise things she said. She must realize he was not good enough for her, but nevertheless she loved him and was willing to put up with him. And if the village people did throw them out, well, weren't there other villages in the world? And why should they be forced to leave? Matadin

64

took on a *chamar* girl and no one did anything about that. His father Datadin ground his teeth for a while but he finally calmed down. Of course Matadin did the necessary things to preserve his religion. He still wouldn't take a drink of water until he'd had a bath and said his prayers. He even cooked his meals separately at first, though he no longer did that now, and father and son sat down and ate together again. . . . And then there was Jhinguri Singh. He took on a *brahman* girl, and who did anything about that? He was still as respected as ever—in fact more so. He was always hunting around for a job before. Now, with her money, he had become a moneylender. Of course he'd always had prestige as a thakur, but now he had the added prestige of being a moneylender as well. . . . But then Gobar began to wonder whether Jhuniya might only be playing with him. He would first have to be sure.

'Are you really serious, Jhuniya," he asked, "or are you just leading me on? I'm yours already—but will you really be mine?'

'You're mine already? How do I know?'

'I'm ready to give you my life if you want it.'

'Do you even know what giving your life means?'

'All right, you teach me.'

'Giving your life means living with me and getting along with me. Once you take my hand, it means you'll stay with me all your life, even if it means giving up parents, brothers, friends, home, everything. I've heard lots of people talk about giving their lives; but they sip the nectar from the flower and then fly away like bees. You won't fly away like that too?'

Gobar had the halter of the cow in one hand. With the other, he took hold of Jhuniya's hand. His body suddenly shook as though he'd touched a live wire. How soft and plump and smooth her hand was!

Jhuniya let his hand remain, as though this touch meant nothing special to her. But after a moment she said solemnly, 'Today you've taken my hand. Remember that.'

'I'll remember it well, Jhuniya, and be faithful to you until my dying breath.'

Jhuniya smiled sceptically. 'That's what they all say, Gobar, and even more sweetly and smoothly. If underneath all this you're just fooling me, come right out and say so. Then I'll be cautious. I can't give myself to men who are like that. A few laughs and some light conversation—that's the kind of relationship I have with them.

For years I've been taking milk and selling it in the bazaar. One after another the clerks, the shopkeepers, the thakurs, the lawyers and the officials of all sorts have declared their love and tried to seduce me. Some put their hands over their hearts and say, "Jhuniya, don't torture me." Some stare at me so lustfully you'd think love had driven them out of their senses. Some offer money, others jewellery. They're all ready to become my life-long slaves, and even in the next life. But I can see right through them. They're the kind who sip the honey and fly away. I egg them on, giving them coy glances and smiling at them. They make a fool of me, so I make asses out of them. If I should die, there'd be no tears in their eyes. And if they were to die, I'd say good riddance to the wretches. When I give myself to someone, it will be for a lifetime. I'll stick with him in happiness and in sorrow, in wealth and in poverty. I'm no whore running around flirting with everyone, nor am I hungry for money, jewels or clothes. All I want is a man who considers himself mine and whom I can think of as my own.'

'There's one pandit,' Jhuniya continued, 'who makes a big show of his caste markings. He takes half a quart of milk a day. One day his wife had gone out visiting. How was I to know? So I went inside to deliver the milk as usual. I called to her. There was no answer. Meanwhile I saw that the pandit had shut the outside door and was coming towards me. I realized he was up to no good and asked him sharply, "Why have you closed the door? Has your wife gone somewhere? Why is the house so quiet?" He said that she'd been invited out, and came a couple of steps closer. I said, "If you want the milk, then take it. Otherwise I'm leaving." Then he said, "Today you won't be able to get out of here, Jhuniya my queen. Day after day you stick a knife in my heart and then run away. Today you won't escape me." Believe me, Gobar—my hair stood on end!'

'If I get hold of that son of a bitch,' Gobar exclaimed, 'I'll bury him alive. I'll drink his blood. Just point him out to me.'

'Listen, I'm perfectly capable of handling things like that by myself. My heart began thumping. What would I do if he started trouble? A scream wouldn't be heard. So I made up my mind that I'd throw the whole pot of milk in his face if he laid a hand on me. It would be worth losing four or five quarts of milk to give that bastard something to remember. Summoning my courage I said, "Don't try anything sneaky, Panditji. I'm the daughter of a milkman, and I'll tear every hair out of your moustache. Is that what your sacred books tell you—to lock other people's wives and daughters in your house and disgrace them? Is that why you put on such a phony display of caste-marks?" At this he clasped his hands and fell to his knees begging, "Jhuniya, my queen, it's not going to hurt you to give in to such a lover. You should take pity on poor men occasionally or else God will say that although he gave you such beauty you wouldn't even do a favour for one brahman. What answer will you give then? Being a brahman, I get gifts of money every day. How about a gift of beauty today?" Just to test him, I said it would cost him fifty rupees. And this is no lie, Gobar—he went straight to his room and came out with five ten-rupee notes which he started putting in my hand. When I threw the money on the floor and headed for the door, he grabbed my hand. But I'd been ready for some time. I hit him right in the face with the milk pot. He was drenched from head to foot . . . hurt badly too. He sat down holding his head and moaning. When I saw he couldn't do anything, I gave him two kicks in the back, opened the door, and ran.'

'Very nicely done,' Gobar laughed. 'He must have had a good milk bath. And I suppose it washed away those caste-marks. You should have torn out his whiskers too.'

'The next day I went back to his house. His wife had returned. He was sitting in the living room, his head all bandaged up. I asked him if he wanted me to expose what he'd done the day before. He began pleading, so I said I'd let him go if he'd lick up his own spit. He cringed, with his head to the floor, and pleaded that his reputation was in my hands, that his wife would kill him if she found out. I couldn't help taking pity on him.'

'What did you do that for?' Gobar protested. 'Why didn't you go tell his wife? She'd have whacked him with a shoe. Hypocrites like that don't deserve pity. Just show me his face tomorrow and I'll really fix him.'

Jhuniya eyed his adolescent body and said, 'You'd never make it. He's a husky devil—gets his food free, after all.'

Gobar of course couldn't tolerate this disparagement of his manhood. 'So what if he is husky? I've got muscles of steel,' he bragged. 'I do three hundred push-ups a day. If it weren't for the fact that I get no milk or butter, my chest would be as big as this'—and he swelled out his chest for her to see.

Jhuniya gave him a look of reassurance. 'All right, some time I'll point him out. But they're all the same around here. How would you decide which ones to take care of? I don't know what it is about men—whenever they see a good-looking girl, they start staring and getting all excited. And the so-called big men are the most lecherous of all. And I'm no beauty. . . .'

'Rubbish!' Gobar protested. 'Every time I see you I want to pull you to me.'

Jhuniya punched him lightly on the back. 'Now you're beginning to flatter me just like the rest. I know what I'm like. But these people go for any woman who's young. All they want is a little amusement. They only look for character in the women they want to marry. I've heard and seen the strange things that go on in high society. There was a Kashmiri family named Gapru in the part of Bombay where I lived when I was married. Gapru had a high position—took five quarts of milk a day. He had three daughters, all in their early twenties and each more beautiful than the next. All three studied at the big college. One even did some teaching there, I think, making three hundred a month. They all played musical instruments and they all danced and sang. But none of them had married. God knows whether they didn't like any of the men or whether the men didn't like them. One time I asked the oldest one. She just laughed and said they didn't want to catch that disease. But on the sly they were having a gay old time. I always used to see them surrounded by three or four fellows. The oldest would wear coat and pants and go horse-riding with men. Their carrying-on was notorious all around town. Gapru Babu went around with his head bowed in shame. He tried persuasion and scolding with the girls, but they just told him openly that he had no right to interfere, that they were their own masters and would do whatever they pleased. What could the poor father do since the girls were all grown up? He couldn't very well beat them or lock them up or threaten them. No, these big people are above reproach. Anything they do is perfectly all right. They don't even have to fear the caste or the village council.'

'What I can't understand, though,' Jhuniya went on, 'is how men can keep changing their affections every day. Have they become more fickle than even cows or goats? Not that I'm calling anyone bad. A mind becomes whatever one makes it. We see some people who want rich food or sweets just once in a while, as a change of taste from their regular diets. Others almost get sick when they look at the plain food at home. But then there are some poor women who are perfectly satisfied with the same old simple meals, to whom

68

rich food and sweets mean nothing. And then look at my own sisters-in-law. It's not as though my brothers are one-eyed or hunchbacked. Not one man in ten can match them. But their wives aren't satisfied. They want men who'll buy them gold earrings and fine saries and special treats to eat every day. I like earrings and sweets as much as they do, but God help me if I start running around selling my honour for the sake of them. To go through life with one man, eating plain food and wearing coarse clothes—that's all I want. Of course it's often the men who lead their wives astray. If husbands start looking around every which way, their wives will do the same. If a man chases other women, his wife will run after other men. A husband's unfaithfulness hurts a woman just as much as hers would hurt him. You must realize that. I made it clear to my husband that if he went chasing around here and there, then I'd do whatever I liked also. To expect to do as you please and yet keep your wife under strict control by threatening to beat her—that just won't work. It just means that what you do openly, she'll do secretly. You can't keep making her jealous and still expect to live happily.'

This was all a new world for Gobar. Completely absorbed, he would come to a halt almost involuntarily and then, collecting himself, start walking again. Jhuniya had first charmed him with her beauty. Now she had captivated him with her wisdom and experience, and with her high regard for faithfulness. What a blessing it would be to own such a treasure-house of beauty, goodness and wisdom. Why should he be afraid of the village council or the caste?

When Jhuniya saw that she had succeeded in making a strong impression on him, she raised a hand to her breast, caught her tongue between her teeth, and said, 'Oh my, we're almost at your village. You're as tricky as Lord *Krishna* . . . didn't even tell me to go back.'

She turned to leave.

'Why not come along to my house for a moment?' Gobar urged. 'Then my mother can see you too.'

Jhuniya averted her eyes shyly. 'I can't go like this to your house. I'm surprised I even came this far. All right now, tell me—when will you be back again? There's going to be a good musical party at our place tonight. Come on over. I'll meet you behind the house.'

'And if you don't turn up?'

'Then go back home.'

'In that case I'm not coming.'

'You'll have to—or else. . . .'

69

'Promise you'll be there then?'

'I don't make promises.'

'Then I won't come.'

'I don't give a damn.'

Jhuniya made a defiant gesture with her thumb and walked away. Each had established his hold over the other. Jhuniya knew he would come . . . how could he help it? And Gobar knew she would meet him . . . how could she help it?

Gobar went on alone, driving the cow ahead of him and feeling as though he'd just tumbled out of heaven.

CHAPTER 6

THE roads and alleys of Semari had been sprayed with water, bringing a little coolness in the oppressive June evening. Potted plants and flowers adorned the pavilion on all sides and electric fans were spinning overhead, the power generated in the Rai Sahib's own workshop. His orderlies, in gold uniforms and blue turbans, roamed imperiously through the crowd, while servants in shining white *kurtas* and saffron turbans were greeting and looking after the guests.

A car pulled up to the main gate and three distinguished gentlemen stepped out. The one in a homespun kurta and sandals was Pandit Onkarnath, well-known editor of the daily paper *Lightning*, a man who had exhausted himself over the problems of the country. The second gentleman, in coat and pants, had once been a lawyer; but when he was unable to make a go of that profession, he had become a broker for an insurance company. By arranging loans for the zamindars from moneylenders and banks, he was now earning more than he could have in legal practice. His name was Shyam Bihari Tankha, while the third gentleman, dressed in a silk *achkan* and tight *pajamas*, was Mr B. Mehta, a philosophy professor at the university. These three were once schoolmates of the Rai Sahib and had of course been invited to attend the festivities.

The tenants on the estate would all be coming to make cash presentations on this auspicious occasion. Later that night there would be a feast for the guests, after which Rama's breaking of the bow would be enacted. Hori had already made his donation of five rupees. Now, dressed in a rose-coloured jacket with matching turban and knee-length loincloth, his face powdered and a trowel in hand, he had become the gardener of Raja Janak, and was swelling with pride as though the success of the whole function depended on his efforts.

The Rai Sahib welcomed the guests. He was a tall well-built man, and this evening his athletic body, radiant face, high forehead and fair complexion were enhanced by the cream-coloured silk shawl thrown over his shoulders.

71

'What play are you putting on this time?' asked Pandit Onkarnath. 'That's the only thing that interests me here.'

The Rai Sahib seated the three gentlemen on chairs in front of the portico. 'Well, first there'll be Rama's breaking of the bow and after that a comedy. I couldn't find a good play. Some were so long they'd have gone on for five hours, while others were so difficult that probably no one here would have understood what they meant. So I finally wrote a comedy myself which can be played in two hours.'

Pandit Onkarnath had serious doubts about the Rai Sahib's writing abilities, being convinced that brilliance sparkles only among the poor, just as lamps spread their light only in the dark. He turned and looked the other way, making no attempt to conceal his indifference.

Though Mr Tankha had not intended to get involved in this trivial conversation, he did want to show the Rai Sahib that he was qualified to comment on the subject. 'Any play can be good,' he declared, 'if it had good actors. And even the best play can be ruined in the hands of bad actors. Until educated women take to the stage there can be no renaissance of drama in our country. And by the way, the questions you raised in our recent council meetings had a great impact. I can testify to the fact that no other member made such a brilliant record.'

This praise was too much for the philosophy teacher, Mr Mehta. He was feeling resentful that the book he'd just completed after several years of work had received not even a hundredth of the acclaim he had anticipated. 'My friend,' he said, 'I'm not impressed by the ability to raise questions. I think it's more important to be able to act on one's principles. Now you're a supporter of the farmers, wanting to give them all kinds of concessions and to lessen the authority of the zamindars, whom you go so far as to call a curse on society. And yet you yourself are a zamindar, and no different from thousands of others. If you're convinced there should be peasant reforms, then start them yourself—write out deeds without having to be bribed into it by your tenants, abolish forced labour, eliminate rent increases and release land for grazing. I have no sympathy for people who talk like communists but live like princes in selfish luxury.'

The Rai Sahib looked shocked, the lawyer frowned, and the editor turned his head in embarrassment. Though he too was a devotee of equality, he had no desire to start a fire right here in this man's house.

Tankha took up the Rai Sahib's case. 'I happen to know that the Rai Sahib treats his tenants so well that if all zamindars were like him these questions wouldn't even arise.'

Mehta struck another blow—'I admit that you're very good to your tenants, but the question is whether selfish motives are involved or not. Maybe it's because food cooks better over a slow fire. Killing with sugar can be deadlier than killing with poison. All I know is this—either we are socialists or we're not. If we are, then we should act accordingly; if not, we should stop jabbering about it. I'm against hypocrisy. If you consider it all right to eat meat, then do so openly. If you think it wrong, then don't eat it. That's how I feel. But to think it right and yet eat it only in secret is something I can't understand. I call it both cowardice and deception, which actually amount to the same thing.'

The Rai Sahib was a sophisticated man, accustomed to responding patiently and generously to insults and attacks. He hesitated only briefly and then said, 'You're absolutely right, Mr Mehta. You know how much I respect your candour. But you forget that in the evolution of ideas, as in a journey, there are various stopping places. And you can't always leave one and move on to the next, as the history of human life clearly testifies. I was brought up in a tradition where the king was God and the zamindar God's minister. My late father was so benevolent that in times of frost or drought he would waive half or even the whole rent. He'd distribute grain from his own storehouse to the tenants and would sell the family jewellery to help with the marriage expenses of the village girls—but only as long as the people acknowledged him as both ruler and divine representative, and worshipped him as such. Taking care of the people was his religion, but he wouldn't surrender one particle of his authority. . . .

'That's the environment in which I was raised. But I'm proud to say that in all my dealings, in whatever I do, my attitudes have advanced even beyond those of my father. I've come to believe that the condition of farmers can not be improved by mere good will, but only by granting them concessions as their inherent right. It would be incongruous for us to give up our own interests voluntarily, though. However good my intentions, I can't ignore my own welfare. But I wish that either the government or the law would force us zamindars to surrender our selfish concerns. You may call this cowardice; I call it helplessness. I agree that no one has the right to grow fat off the labour of others. Exploiting them is absolutely shameful. Work is every man's moral obligation. This situation in society where a few people have it easy while the majority sweat and slave can never bring happiness. The sooner the fortress of wealth and education —which I consider as one form of wealth—is shattered, the better. . . .

'It's ridiculous and disgraceful that a few people can make thousands by governing and commanding those who can't get even a crust of bread. I know very well how dissolute, how immoral, how dependent and how shameless we zamindars have become in these circumstances. But these are not the reasons I oppose the situation. My feeling is that we can't even justify ourselves from the point of view of self-interest. In order to sustain such ostentation we have to destroy our consciences to such an extent that we're left without a trace of self-respect. We're forced to plunder our tenants. If we don't give expensive gifts to the officials, we're branded as traitors. If we don't live in luxury, we're called misers. At the slightest suggestion of progress, we start trembling and run to the authorities appealing for help. We no longer have any faith in ourselves or in our abilities. We're like spoon-fed babies—fat on the outside but weak inside, debilitated and impoverished.'

Mehta clapped his hands. 'Bravo!' he declared. 'If only your brain were half as brilliant as your tongue? Too bad that even though you admit all this, you don't put these ideas into practice.'

'One grain of popcorn can't blow the lid off the pan, Mr Mehta,' said Onkarnath. 'We have to go along with the times as well as trying to stay ahead of them. Cooperation is just as necessary for good works as for evil. How do you justify devouring eight hundred rupees a month when millions of our brothers get along on just eight rupees?'

Though inwardly pleased, the Rai Sahib frowned at the editor. 'Let's not get personal in our criticism,' he declared. 'We're discussing the condition of society in general.'

'No, no—I don't mind,' Mr Mehta said calmly. 'Society is made up of individuals, and we can't discuss any situation leaving out individuals. The reason I accept such a large salary is that I don't believe in the social set-up you've been describing.'

The editor looked surprised. 'You mean you support the present state of society?'

'I support the principle that there will always be rich and poor in the world and that this is as it should be. Eliminating those distinctions would lead to the destruction of the human race.'

74

With the contest entering this new phase, the Rai Sahib stepped aside and the editor climbed into the ring. 'You mean you still believe in the inequality between rich and poor even in this twentieth century?'

'I certainly do believe in it, and believe in it very strongly. After all, the doctrines you're upholding are nothing new. They date back to the first development of greed in man. Buddha and Plato and Jesus were all exponents of a collectivist society, and the civilizations of Greece and Rome and Syria all tried it, but being opposed to nature, such societies couldn't endure.'

'I'm surprised to hear you talk this way.'

'Surprise is another name for ignorance.'

'Perhaps you would write me a series of articles on the subject. You'd have my gratitude.'

'I'm not such a fool as to settle for that alone. But for a good price, I'd be delighted.'

'With principles like yours, you can easily hoodwink the public.'

'The only difference between us is that I practice what I believe whereas you people believe one thing and do another. By some unjust stratagem you might be able to get wealth distributed equally. But to distribute intelligence, character, beauty, talent and strength equally is beyond your power. The difference between the high and the low is not just one of wealth. I've seen millionaires bowing to beggars, and you have too. And kings will grovel in the dust at the door of some great beauty. Isn't that social inequality? You'll bring up the example of Russia, but the only difference there is that the mill owner has now become a government official. The intelligent were ruling in the past, they rule now, and they always will.'

A tray of refreshments appeared, and the Rai Sahib offered cardamom seeds and betel to the guests. 'If intelligence could be freed from selfishness,' he suggested, 'then there'd be nothing wrong with accepting its authority. That's the ideal of socialism. The reason we bow our heads before ascetics is that they have the strength of self-renunciation. That's why we want to turn over power, prestige and leadership, but not property, into the hands of the intelligent. A man's power and prestige die with him, but his property spreads out like a poison, growing in strength. Without intellect there can be no progress in society. But what we want to do is remove the sting from this scorpion.'

A second car drove up bringing Mr Khanna, the manager of a bank and managing director of a sugar mill. With him were two ladies whom the Rai Sahib helped from the car. The one wearing a homespun sari and looking very serious and thoughtful was Mr Khanna's wife, Kamini. The other, dressed in high heels and smiling brightly, was Miss Malti. A practising physician who had studied medicine in England, she had frequent access to the mansions of zamindars. She was the living image of modernity—expertly made up, delicate but full of life, lacking any trace of hesitation or shyness, a wizard at sharp repartee, an expert in male psychology, a connoisseur of the pleasures of life, and a master in the art of charm and enticement. In place of a conscience she had glitter; in place of a heart, coquetry. And she had put a strong block on her feelings that checked all desires and passions.

Shaking hands with Mr Mehta, she said, 'Honestly, your appearance alone makes it obvious that you're a philosopher. You've really unravelled the mysteries of metaphysics in that new book. But several times while reading it I wanted to come and argue with you. Why have human feelings disappeared among philosophers?'

Mehta blushed. He was unmarried, and usually sought protection against these modern young women. Though perfectly eloquent in the company of men, he became tongue-tied the moment a woman appeared. A lock seemed to snap on his mind, making him forget even the common courtesies due to ladies.

'What's so special about the appearance of a philosopher?' Mr Khanna asked.

Malti glanced sympathetically at Mehta. 'Well, if Mr Mehta won't get offended, I'll tell you.'

Khanna was one of Miss Malti's devotees. Everywhere she went, he had to go, hovering round her like a bee, trying constantly to talk to her, unable to take his eyes off her. Now, winking at her, he said, 'Nothing anyone says bothers the philosophers. That's their nature.'

'Then listen ... Philosophers are always lifeless souls. Whenever you see them, they're lost in thought. They stare at you but never see you. You speak to them but they never hear anything. It's as though they were floating around in a vacuum.'

Everyone burst out laughing. Mr Mehta wished that the earth would open and swallow him.

'My philosophy professor at Oxford was a Mr Husband,' Malti continued.

'What a funny name,' Khanna interrupted.

'Yes, and of course he was a bachelor. . . .'

'Mr Mehta's also a bachelor,' Khanna broke in.

'Well, all philosophers suffer from that disease.'

Mehta seized his opportunity. 'You've caught it too, though, haven't you?'

'Yes,' Miss Malti conceded, 'but I've sworn I'll marry a philososopher. They all panic at the mere mention of marriage. Just the sight of a woman and Mr Husband would go hide in his room. He had some girl students, and any time one of them would go to his office to ask something, he'd get as frightened as though a tiger were after him. We used to tease him a lot. He was a simple-hearted creature though. His salary was in the thousands, and yet I always saw him wearing the same suit. He had a widowed sister who kept house for him. Mr Husband never gave a thought to eating. Terrified of visitors, he'd lock the outside door to his room and just sit there studying. When it came time to eat, his sister would slip quietly in through the other door and snap his book shut. Then he'd realize it was the dinner hour. His sister would finally have to switch off the light. But one time when she tried to close his book, he grabbed it with both hands and a regular test of strength resulted. Finally the sister grabbed his chair and propelled him right into the dining room.'

'Mr Mehta's very good-natured and sociable, though,' said the Rai Sahib. 'Otherwise he'd never have stepped into this mob.'

'Then he must not be a philosopher,' Miss Malti declared. 'When our own worries are enough to start our heads aching, how can anyone enjoy taking the cares of the world on his shoulders?'

The editor, Pandit Onkarnath, was off to one side relating his financial difficulties to Mrs Khanna. 'So you see, an editor's life is one long tale of woe. When people hear about it, though, they clap their hands over their ears instead of feeling sympathetic. The poor editor can help neither himself nor anyone else. The public expects him to be at the forefront of every revolution, to go to jail, get beaten, have all his household possessions confiscated. . . . They consider all this his duty. But when it comes to his troubles, nobody can be bothered. Of course he must be everything—well-versed in every branch of learning and in all the arts—but he has no right to make a living for himself. By the way, you're not doing any writing these days. Why do you deprive me of one of my few pleasures—being of service to you?'

Mrs Khanna was fond of writing poems. Pandit Onkarnath

used to stop by occasionally to visit her in that connection, but household duties had kept her so busy that for some time she'd been unable to do any writing. The truth of the matter was that only his patronage let her pass as a poet. She possessed little real talent.

'I don't find anything to write about,' she said. 'Haven't you ever suggested to Miss Malti that she write something?'

'Her time is expensive, *Deviji*,' the editor replied contemptuously. 'And besides, in order to write, people must have some pain inside them—some passion, some love, some ideas. Those whose aim in life is wealth and pleasure ... what can they write?'

'But if you did get her to write something,' Kamini suggested with a mixture of amusement and envy, 'your circulation would double. There's not a lover in Lucknow who wouldn't become your subscriber.'

'If wealth had been my aim in life, I wouldn't be in such a sad state today. It's not that I don't know the art of making money. If I wanted, I could earn a fortune. But I've never cared anything for money. My life is devoted to the service of literature and will remain so.'

'Well, at least put my name down as a subscriber.'

'I'll put it down among the patrons, not the subscribers.'

'Save that for the *ranis* and maharanis. Just flatter them a little and you can turn your paper into a profitable enterprise.'

'You're my rani and maharani. Compared to you, none of them deserve those titles. My idea of a rani is someone with your kindness and keen intellect. And besides, I despise flattery.'

'And yet you're flattering me now, Mr Editor.'

Onkarnath's voice became serious and reverent. 'This is not flattery, Deviji. It's what I honestly feel in my heart.'

Just then the Rai Sahib called out, 'Onkarnath, could you come here for a moment? Miss Malti wants to tell you something.'

All the editor's proud dignity vanished. He went and stood before the Rai Sahib, the image of humility and modesty.

Malti turned to him, her eyes full of friendliness. 'I was just saying that nothing in the world frightens me more than editors. In a mere flash you people can destroy anyone you wish. The Chief Secretary said to me one time, "If I could just slap that bloody Onkarnath into jail, I'd count myself really fortunate".'

Onkarnath's huge moustache quivered and his eyes sparkled with pride. By nature he was very calm, but at the sound of a challenge his manhood was immediately aroused. 'I'm grateful to you for this

78

information,' he said stiffly. 'At least my name still comes up in the Council, whatever the circumstances. Please tell the Chief Secretary that Onkarnath is not one of those who can be intimidated by his threats—that my pen will not rest until the course of my life is completed—that I've taken on myself the duty of uprooting and destroying injustice and despotism.'

Miss Malti egged him on—'But I don't understand your policy. When just a little ordinary courtesy could get you the help of the authorities, why bypass them? If you would just reduce the amount of fire and poison in your editorials, I can promise you lots of government backing. You've seen what the public is like. You've appealed to them, flattered them, told them your troubles—but nothing has come of it. So why not give the authorities a try? If within three months you're not driving around in a car and being invited to all the official receptions, you can curse me all you like. All these rich people and nationalists who ignore you now—you'll have them hovering at your door.'

'Those are things I could never do, Deviji,' Onkarnath insisted haughtily. 'I've kept my ideals lofty and sacred and I intend to keep them that way as long as I live. Worshippers of money can be found in every alley. I stand among the worshippers of principle.'

'I call that arrogance.'

'Call it whatever you like.'

'You have no interest in money?'

'Not when it means violating my principles.'

'Then why do you carry advertisements for foreign goods in your paper? I've never seen as many in any other paper. You claim to be an idealist, a man of principle. Don't you have any regrets at helping to send our country's wealth abroad just so you can make a profit? You can't possibly justify that policy by any kind of logic.'

Onkarnath was at a complete loss for an answer. Seeing him looking around for some escape, the Rai Sahib came to the rescue. 'So what do you expect him to do? Either way he'd lose, and then how could he run the paper?'

Miss Malti had not learned to be charitable. 'If you can't run a paper, then close it down. You have no right to encourage foreign goods just to put out a paper. If there's no way out, then give up the façade of ideals. It burns me up to see these so-called high-principled newspapers. I'd like to set a match to all of them. If a person can't make his actions consistent with his statements, then he's not a man of principle, whatever else he may be.'

Mehta's face lit up. Only a short time before, he'd been propounding the same idea. He saw now that this young lady was not just a butterfly—that she held strong convictions. His reserve towards her disappeared. 'That's exactly what I was saying. A discrepancy between ideas and actions is pure hypocrisy and deceit.'

Miss Malti looked pleased. 'Then on this subject we agree, and I can claim to be a philosopher too.'

Khanna's tongue had been itching to say something. 'Of course ... every part of you is soaked in philosophy.'

Malti pulled in the reins on him. 'Well, so you're an authority on philosophy also. I thought you'd dumped all your philosophy in the Ganges long ago. Otherwise how could you have become a director of so many banks and companies?'

The Rai Sahib now stood up for Khanna. 'Do you feel then that all philosophers must settle for being destitute?'

'Yes I do. How can a man be a philosopher if he can't conquer worldly desires?'

'According to that standard, Mr Mehta probably isn't a philosopher either.'

Mehta, as though rolling up his sleeves for battle, declared, 'I've never claimed to be one, Rai Sahib. All I know is that a goldsmith doesn't use the same tools as a blacksmith. And you surely don't expect a mango tree to flourish in the same environment as an acacia or a toddy palm. For me, money just means that I can have the amenities necessary for leading a useful life. It's just a means towards that end, not something to raise my status or to provide luxuries. I have no desire to be rich. Just let me have enough to lead a useful life.'

Being a collectivist, Onkarnath couldn't very well accept this glorification of the individual. 'According to that argument,' he countered, 'every labourer could say he needs a thousand rupees a month in order to have the amenities for doing his job properly.'

'Well, if you felt your own work couldn't go on without that labourer, then you'd have to provide him with those amenities. But if another worker would do the same job for less, then there'd be no reason for you to pamper the first one.'

'If authority were in the hands of the workers,' Pandit Onkarnath declared, 'they'd consider women and liquor to be just as necessary amenities as do philosophers.'

'Believe me, I wouldn't be jealous of them.'

'Well, if a woman is so necessary for making life worthwhile, then why don't you get married?'

'Because, 'Mehta said without hesitation, 'I feel that free love is no hindrance to the development of the mind, whereas marriage locks you in a cage.'

'Imprisonment and punishment are outmoded theories,' Khanna agreed. 'Free love is the latest thing.'

Malti couldn't resist the opportunity. 'Then Mrs Khanna better be ready for a divorce.'

'Provided the divorce bill is passed. . . .'

'Maybe you can be the first to take advantage of it.'

Kamini threw a venomous look at Malti and then pursed her lips as though telling her she was welcome to Khanna.

Malti looked the other way. 'Mr Mehta, what's your opinion on this matter?'

Mehta grew serious. Whenever called on to express his views on any subject, he threw his whole heart and soul into it. 'I feel that marriage is a social contract and that neither the man nor the woman has a right to break it. Before making the contract, you're free. But once it's done, your hands are completely tied.'

'Then you're opposed to divorce.'

'Absolutely.'

'And the principle of free love?'

'That's for those who don't wish to marry.'

'But everyone wants his personality to develop as fully as possible. So why would anyone marry?'

'Because everyone wants salvation, but very few can free themselves from lust.'

'Which do you consider better—being married or being single?'

'From the point of view of society, being married; from the point of view of the individual, being single.'

The time for the performance was approaching. According to the programme, the scene from the *Ramayana* that night was to last from ten to one, and then the comedy from one to three. Meanwhile, preparations for the feast were underway. Separate rooms in the bungalow had been arranged for the guests. Two rooms had been reserved for the Khannas. A lot of other guests had arrived by this time and they all went to their rooms, changed for dinner, and then gathered in the dining room.

81

There was no question of untouchability here—people of all castes and subcastes sat down together for the meal. Only Onkarnath the editor remained aloof, having his special fruit diet served in his room. And Mrs Khanna had developed a headache, so she had declined dinner. Some twenty-five guests were in the dining room. Even alcohol and meat were being served. The Rai Sahib, under the pretext of making medicines, had managed to have the finest liquors distilled especially for the occasion. And the meat had been prepared in a variety of ways—curry balls, kababs and *palao*—and people could have whatever they liked—chicken, mutton, venison, partridge or peacock.

'Where's the editor?' Malti inquired, once the meal had begun. 'Rai Sahib, send someone to fetch him.'

'He's a strict vegatarian,' came the answer. 'Why call him here? Do you want the poor fellow to be polluted? He's very strict about these religious observances.'

'Well it would be great fun if nothing else.' Looking over at one of the gentlemen, she suddenly called out, 'Mirza Khurshed, so you're here too! This is a job for you. It'll be a real test of your abilities.' Muslim businessman

Mirza Khurshed was a light-complexioned man of Persian origin with a brown moustache, blue eyes, stocky build, and an absolutely bald head. He was wearing a showy achkan, tight pajamas, and a Muslim cap. At election time he had woken up and voted for the Nationalists. He'd made two pilgrimages to Mecca—but he drank heavily. He was a carefree soul, a great joker who was fond of saying that there's no point in sacrificing our lives for the sake of the poor as long as we don't obey any of God's other commandments.

Khurshed had started out as a contractor in Basra and made a fortune, but he ran into trouble when he started an affair with an English woman. A court case ensued. He was spared from jail but was ordered out of the country within twenty-four hours. So he fled, leaving behind everything except fifty thousand rupees. Having agents in Bombay, he figured that he could go over the accounts with them and collect enough to live on. But the agents swindled him and made off with that fifty thousand too. In despair he headed for Lucknow. On the train he met an ascetic who tricked him out of his watch, his rings and the rest of his cash. The poor fellow reached Lucknow with nothing but the clothes on his back. Fortunately he was an old acquaintance of the Rai Sahib, who along with some other friends helped him set up a shoe store, still the most popular one in Lucknow. He took in four or five hundred rupees a day, and soon people developed such confidence in him that he defeated a big Muslim zamindar and was elected to the Provincial Council.

'No, Miss Malti,' Khurshed replied, not moving from his seat. 'I don't interfere with anyone's religion. This is a job you should do yourself. It really would be fun if you could get him to take a drink. Here's a test of your charms.'

A chorus of approval rose from all sides—'Yes, yes, Miss Malti, show us your powers.'

'And my reward?' she challenged Mirza.

'A purse of a hundred rupees.'

'What? A hundred rupees? Only a hundred for spoiling a sacred honour worth thousands?'

'All right, name your own price.'

'A thousand—not a cowrie less.'

'It's a deal.'

'Oh no. First deposit the amount with Mr Mehta.'

Mirza immediately took a hundred-rupee note from his pocket. Displaying it to the crowd, he stood up and announced, 'Friends! The honour of us all is at stake here. If Miss Malti's demand is not met, we won't dare show our faces in public again. If I had the money, I'd sacrifice thousands to her charms. In ancient times a poet gave his sweetheart the provinces of Samarkand and Bokhara for the sake of the mole on your cheek. Today, gentlemen, your gallantry and devotion to beauty are being tested. Take out whatever money you have like true heroes and give it here. For the sake of your intelligence, for the sake of your beloveds, for the sake of your reputations, don't try to back out. Men! Riches will pass away, but honour endures forever. A fortune would be cheap for amusement like this.... See the queen of Lucknow beauties cast the spell of her loveliness on a victim!'

At the conclusion of his speech, Mirza began to search everyone's pockets. First was Khanna—his pocket turned up five rupees. Mirza pulled a long face. 'Shame, Khanna Sahib, shame! A big name but nothing to show for it. A director of so many companies, worth a fortune, and only five rupees in your pocket? Disgraceful! Mehta, where are you? Go and collect at least a hundred rupees from Mrs Khanna.'

Khanna looked embarrassed. 'Sir,' he spoke up, 'she probably hasn't even a pice on her. How was anyone to know you were going to start searching people here?'

'All right, don't get excited. We'll try our luck anyway.'

'Very well then,' Khanna said. 'I'll go and ask her.'

'Oh no. You stay where you are. Mr Mehta, you're the philosopher, the master of psychology. But be careful you don't make a fool of yourself.'

Mehta had become rather drunk on the wine, the result being that his philosophy had flown to the winds and his sense of humour had revived. He dashed off to find Mrs Khanna but was back five minutes later wearing a glum expression.

'What?' Mirza exclaimed. 'Empty-handed?'

The Rai Sahib chuckled. 'In the house of a judge even the rats are clever.'

'By God you're lucky, Khanna,' Mirza declared.

Mehta burst out laughing and pulled five hundred-rupee notes from his pocket. Mirza ran over and embraced him.

Shouts filled the air—'It's a miracle.' 'Now we admit your greatness.' 'Why not? He's a philosopher after all.'

Mirza eyed the notes lovingly. 'Brother Mehta, as of today I'm your disciple. Tell me, what magic did you use?'

'None at all,' Mehta bragged, gazing at the audience through bloodshot eyes. 'It was easy. I went and knocked on her door. She asked who it was and then told me to come in. I said to her, "They're playing bridge out there. You've seen that ring of Miss Malti's—worth at least a thousand rupees. Well if you have the cash you can buy it now for five hundred. You'll never get a chance like this again. If she can't raise the money, she'll be wiped out entirely. Malti probably staked the ring assuming no one would have five hundred on him." At that Mrs Khanna smiled and straightway pulled these five bills from her purse, saying she never went out without some cash, as you never know what emergency may arise.'

'If this is what professors are like,' Khanna snapped, 'then God help the universities.'

Khurshed poured salt on the wounds—'Come now, this isn't such a large sum that you should be getting so depressed. I'd be willing to swear it's only one day's income for you. Just pretend you've been sick for a day. And besides, it's going to Miss Malti, to the one who holds the cure for your heartache.'

84

Malti stamped her foot. 'Look here, Mr Mirza. A horse can't expect to live in a fine stable and still go around kicking people.'

'I pull my ears in apology, Deviji,' Mirza replied.

Mr Tankha was searched next, and ten rupees extracted with difficulty. Mehta's pocket produced only an eight-anna piece. Several gentlemen gave one or two rupees voluntarily. All this still left a deficit of about three hundred rupees, which the Rai Sahib generously contributed.

The editor had finished his meal of fruit and was just lying down for a moment when the Rai Sahib appeared and announced that Miss Malti was asking for him.

'Good heavens! Asking for me?' Onkarnath beamed with delight as he accompanied the Rai Sahib to the other room.

The servants were just clearing the tables. Miss Malti came forward to greet the pandit.

'Please sit down,' the editor said modestly. 'There's no need to be formal. I'm not that important.'

'You may think this a formality,' Malti purred. 'But I consider myself honoured to receive you. You may not think yourself important . . . that wouldn't be fitting for you. But all of us gathered here are well aware of your services to the nation and to literature. Some people may not yet recognize the value of the work that you've done in those fields, but the time is not far off—in fact I say the time has come—when streets and clubs in every town will be named after you and your picture hung in the town halls. What little awakening has already occurred is thanks to your great efforts alone. You'll be happy to know that you've already developed a following of people eager to lend a hand in your village uplift movement, and that their greatest desire is to see this work organized and a society for village uplift established with you as president.'

Never had Pandit Onkarnath been so highly honoured in a distinguished gathering. Of course he had given public speeches on occasion, and had been the secretary or joint-secretary of various societies, but until now he had been totally ignored by the intelligentsia. Unable to be one of them, he had criticized them in public lectures and denounced them in his paper as idle and selfish. People dismissed him as a mere noise-maker, however, since his pen was so cutting and his language so harsh that the result was more rant than honest criticism. But now to receive such respect from that same strata of society! Where now were those editors of *Independence*

and *Free India* and *The Hunter?* Let them come and witness his glory ! The gods were smiling on him at last. As the sages had said, 'Virtuous endeavour never goes unrewarded.' His opinion of himself soared. Overwhelmed with gratitude, he said, 'Deviji, you're dragging me onto thorny ground. Whatever service I've done for the people has been inspired only by a sense of duty. I consider this honour as a tribute not to myself but to the cause for which I have dedicated my life. I humbly request that some influential man be given the top position, however. I don't believe in high status. I'm a servant and I only wish to go on serving.'

Miss Malti wouldn't hear of it. Of course the pandit would have to be president. She knew no one else in town as influential as he. How could anyone with such magic in his pen, such magic in his tongue and such magic in his personality claim not to be influential? The time had passed in which influence was directly related to wealth. This was an age in which influence was related to intellect. Certainly the editor would have to accept the position. Miss Malti would be the secretary. A thousand rupees had already been raised for the organization, and there was still the whole town and the whole province to be tapped. Collecting half a million would be a simple matter. . . .

A kind of intoxication was beginning to grip Pandit Onkarnath. At first he had just been flattered, but now he saw the seriousness of his obligations. 'You must understand, Miss Malti, that this is a job involving great responsibility, and that you would have to devote a great deal of time to it. For my part, I give you my word that you'll always find me the first to arrive at the office of the organization.'

Mirza poured on the flattery. 'Not even your worst enemy could say you lag behind in fulfilling your moral obligations.'

Miss Malti, seeing that the wine of her praise was beginning to take effect, became still more solemn and said, 'If we people had not realized the importance of this task, we would not have formed this organization, nor established you as president. We could have given the position to some rich man or zamindar and raked in a lot of money, satisfying our own selfish interests on the pretext of service. But that's not our aim. Our sole ambition is to serve the people, and the best medium for doing that is your paper. We've decided that it should be distributed in every town and village, that the number of subscribers should reach twenty thousand as soon as possible. All the municipal and district board chairmen are our friends. In fact

86

several of them are here with us. If each of them would buy even five hundred copies, you'd be assured of success. In addition, the Rai Sahib and Mr Mirza have recommended that a resolution be placed before the Council that the government either subscribe to a copy of *Lightning* for each village in the province or give some annual assistance to the paper; and we have complete confidence that this resolution will be passed.'

By now Onkarnath was staggering as though thoroughly inebriated. 'We should send a deputation to the Governor also,' he declared.

'Of course, of course,' Mirza Khurshed agreed.

'And he should be told that it's a shame and a disgrace to any civilized government that the existence of *Lightning* is not even recognized although it's the only paper devoted to rural welfare.'

'Right, quite right,' Khurshed chimed in again.

'I'm not bragging. It's not yet time for that. But I swear that for the sake of village development, *Lightning* has made such efforts...'

'Not efforts, sir. You should say devotion.'

'Thank you, Mr Mehta. Yes, devotion is what it should be called —very arduous devotion. This devotion shown by *Lightning* has been unprecedented not only in the history of the province but also in the history of our nation.'

'Indeed, indeed,' said Mirza Khurshed.

Miss Malti poured out another glass of flattery—'Our group has also decided that you should stand for election to the next vacant seat in the Council. You have only to agree; we'll do the rest. You needn't worry about expenditures, propaganda or campaigning.'

Onkarnath's eyes shone still brighter. With proud condescension he declared, 'I am at your disposal. If you desire my services, they are yours.'

'That's just what we had hoped. Until now we've spent our time worshipping false gods, with no results. Now in you we've found a spiritual guide who can show us the true path. And in our happiness on this blessed occasion, we are of one mind in wishing to abandon all our conceit and all our hypocrisy. From this day on, we will no longer distinguish ourselves as high or low caste, as Hindu or Muslim, as rich or poor. We are all brothers, children of the same mother, who have played in the same lap and eaten from the same plate. There is no room in our organization for anyone who believes in discrimination, for anyone who worships segregation and bigotry. In a society which has as its president such an open-hearted man as the revered

87

Pandit Onkarnath, there can be no distinction between high and low, no segregation in eating or drinking, no division of caste or creed. Any who do not believe in the glorious oneness of humanity and of our nation may get up and leave.'

The Rai Sahib took exception. 'I don't think that unity means everyone must give up his beliefs about eating and drinking. I don't drink liquor—would I have to leave this organization?'

'Of course you would,' Malti insisted mercilessly. 'If you're going to remain in this gathering you can't cling to any prejudices.'

Mehta supported the Rai Sahib. 'I doubt that our president himself can accept integrated drinking and dining.'

Onkarnath turned pale. What an inopportune moment this scoundrel had chosen to sound such a note. The wretch! He'd better not start digging up that pile of corpses or all this good fortune would vanish like a dream into thin air.

Miss Malti eyed him quizzically. 'Your doubts, Mr Mehta, are unfounded,' she said firmly. 'Do you really believe that such an absolute worshipper of national unity, such a magnanimous gentleman, such a romantic poet would consider such shameful distinctions to be respectable? To harbour such suspicions is an insult to his patriotism....'

Onkarnath's face lit up with pleasure and satisfaction.

'And it's even more insulting to his manliness,' Malti continued. 'Where is the man who could refuse a glass of wine from the hands of a young lady? That would be an insult to womanhood—to all those women whose looks are the arrows men hope will pierce their hearts, to all those women for whose affections great kings have courted death. Please bring me a bottle and a glass, and pour another round of drinks. On this momentous occasion, any hesitation is nothing less than dangerous unpatriotism. First let us drink to the health of our president.'

The ice, liquor and soda had been ready for some time. Miss Malti offered Onkarnath a glass of the red poison with her own hands and gazed at him so bewitchingly that all his resolution, all his caste superiority, melted away. Religious observances depend on circumstances anyway, he told himself. If a man were poverty-stricken and saw some car stirring up dust, he might get angry enough to smash it with stones, but that wouldn't mean he didn't secretly long to own a car. Behaviour is just a matter of circumstance, nothing more. If his parents and grandparents didn't drink, they didn't, that was all. But did they even have the opportunity? Their livelihood depended on the sacred books. Where would they have bought liquor, and what would they have done if they had? They never travelled by train either, never drank tap water, and even considered the study of English a sin. But times had changed. If a person couldn't keep up with the times, they'd go on and leave him behind. If such a lovely lady were to offer even poison in those tender hands, one would have to accept it graciously. He was now facing an opportunity coveted by great kings. Could he throw it away?

Onkarnath took the glass, bowed his head in appreciation, drank down the liquor in one breath, and then looked up proudly as though saying that they now must have faith in him, that they could no longer think him just a foolish pandit, that no one would dare call him a hypocrite.

Indescribable uproar filled the hall, the laughter bursting out as though it had been sealed in a chest and just released. 'Congratulations, Deviji!' 'It's unbelievable!' 'A real wizard, that's what Miss Malti is, a wizard.' 'She's broken it ... broken the salt laws ... destroyed that bastion of holiness ... smashed that vat of orthodoxy.'

The liquor had hardly gone down Onkarnath's throat when his amorous feelings began to express themselves. With a broad smile, he announced, 'I have entrusted my soul into the tender hands of Miss Malti, and I have faith that she will protect it properly. I would willingly sacrifice a thousand souls at her lotus-like feet.'

The hall echoed with laughter.

The editor filled another glass. 'Here's to the health of Miss Malti,' he declared, face swollen and eyelids drooping. 'Everyone drink, and give her your blessings.'

The glasses were emptied again.

Mirza brought a garland, placed it around the editor's neck, and said, 'Gentlemen! Your humble servant, with your kind permission, will now recite an ode in praise of our president.'

'Yes, yes. Of course ... recite,' came the voices from all sides.

Onkarnath had frequently taken *bhang*, and was accustomed to its narcotic effects, but this was his first experience with liquor. The intoxication of bhang took effect slowly, spreading like a cloud and bringing on hallucinations, but leaving the sensibilities unaffected and leaving him aware that he had become talkative and that his imagination was more active. The intoxication of this liquor, however, sprang on him like a lion, subduing him completely. He intended to say one thing . . . something quite different came out. And he couldn't even remember what he was saying and doing. This was not some strange romantic dream, but the reverse: a disturbed awakening in which the world of forms became formless.

Somehow a notion leaped up in his inebriated mind that the recitation of an ode would be very improper. 'No, never!' he objected, pounding his fist on the table. 'There'll be no poems here . . . no poems. I'm the president and that's my order. I could tear this organization apart right now. I could tear it apart. I could throw you all out. No one can touch me. I'm the president. No one else is president.'

'But sir,' Mirza pleaded, 'this poem is full of your praises.'

'Why have you written praises about me?' said the editor, looking at Mirza with red glazed eyes. 'Why have you? Tell me, why have you written my praises? I'm no one's servant. I'm not the servant of anyone's father either, and I don't accept favours from any son of a bitch. I myself am the editor. I'm the editor of *Lightning*. I'll publish everyone's praises in that. Deviji, I won't praise you. I'm not some great man. I'm a slave to all. I'm the dust under your feet. Malti devi, you are my Lakshmi, my *Saraswati*, my Radha. . . .'

With that, he bowed towards her feet and fell flat on his face. Mirza Khurshed ran over, propped him up, pushed some chairs aside and then stretched him out on the floor. 'May your soul rest in peace,' Mirza whispered in his ear. 'Tell me—should we arrange your funeral procession?'

'You just wait and see how vicious he'll be tomorrow,' the Rai Sahib warned. 'He'll be denouncing all of us in his paper, and so violently that even you will take notice. He's a real tyrant—has no mercy on anyone. He has no equal as far as writing goes. The mystery is that such an ass can write so well.'

Some of the men picked up the editor and carried him to his room. Meanwhile, in the pavilion outside, the pageant of Rama and the bow had begun. A number of officials had arrived at the pavilion, and messengers had come several times to call these dinner guests. They were just getting ready to go out when an Afghan suddenly burst into the room. He was tall, fair, and broad chested, with a bushy moustache and wildly ferocious eyes, wearing a loose shirt and baggy pants, a gold embroidered vest and turban. A leather bag hung over one shoulder, a gun over the other, and a sword from his waist. Everyone wondered where he could have come from as he stood there and roared, 'Take care now. Don't anyone move from here. One of my men has been robbed. Whoever is your chief has robbed my man, and you'd better give back the money. I want every cowrie returned. Where is your chief? Call him here!'

The Rai Sahib came forward. 'What robbery? That's your people's profession. No one here is a robber. Speak up clearly—what is all this business?'

The Afghan averted his eyes, pounded the butt of his gun on the floor, and said, 'Oh you want to know what robbery, do you? Well either you're the robber, or some man of yours is a robber. I own a house here, a house with twenty-five young men in it. My men had been out collecting dues—a thousand rupees. That's what you've stolen, and you ask what robbery! We'll show you what kind of robbery it was. My men are on their way here right now, all twenty-five of them. We'll plunder your village. And none of you bastards will be able to do a thing about it, nothing at all.'

Khanna glanced quickly at the Afghan and then got up quietly and started to slip out. 'Where do you think you're going?' the *Khan* thundered. 'No one's to go anywhere, or I'll slaughter the lot of you. I'll shoot right here and now. There's nothing you can do about it. I'm not afraid of your police—they run when they see us. I have my own council. And by just writing a note I can go straight to the Viceroy. I'm not letting anyone out of here. You've stolen my thousand rupees and if I don't get it back, not one of you'll be left alive. You all go out robbing people and then sit around drinking like this with your women.'

Miss Malti, eluding his eyes, had just started to sneak out of the room when he swooped down like a hawk and blocked her way, threatening, 'Either you get the money back from these thieves or I'll carry you off with me and there'll be a big time at our house. I've fallen for your charms. Either you give me that thousand right now or you're coming with me. I'm not letting you go. I'm in love with you. My heart and soul are breaking. I have twenty-five men at my place and five hundred more working in this district. I'm the head of a clan which has ten thousand soldiers, strong enough to challenge the ruler of Kabul. And the English government pays us twenty thousand a year tribute. If you don't produce our money, we'll loot the village and carry off your women. Murder's just a game for us. We'll let loose a river of blood!'

Terror spread through the crowd. Miss Malti forgot her chirping. Khanna's legs were trembling. Poor soul was so afraid of being hurt that he lived in a one-storey bungalow. Climbing a staircase was as frightening to him as mounting the gallows. He didn't dare sleep outdoors even in summer. As for the Rai Sahib, he was proud to be a thakur and thought it ridiculous to fear an Afghan here on his own estate; but what could he do against that gun? Any commotion and it might go off. These were rough people, all of them, and deadly marksmen. If it weren't for that gun in the man's hand, the Rai Sahib would have been ready to lock antlers with him. Given their helplessness, the main problem now was that the brute wouldn't let anyone leave the room. Otherwise the entire village would appear in a flash and beat up this fellow's whole gang.

Summoning the courage at last to take his life in his hands, the Rai Sahib spoke up. 'We've told you that none of us here are thieves and robbers. I'm a member of the Provincial Council, and this lady is a very famous Lucknow doctor. We are all distinguished and reputable people here. We have no idea who robbed your man. Go report it to the police.'

The Afghan struck a fighting pose and took the gun from his shoulder. 'Don't start giving me that nonsense,' he thundered. 'I can grind a Council member under my feet just like that...' and he stamped his feet. 'My hands are strong, my heart is strong, and I fear no one but Almighty God. If you won't hand over our money, I'll butcher you right now,' he said, pointing to the Rai Sahib.

Seeing both barrels of the gun aimed in his direction, the Rai Sahib ducked down behind a table. What a crazy position to be trapped in, he thought. This devil insists that we've stolen his money. He won't listen to anyone, believe anyone, or let anyone in or out of the room. All my servants and soldiers are engrossed in the performance outside. Zamindars' servants are so lazy and scared of work anyway that they don't answer until you call them a dozen times— especially now, when they're absorbed in such an important function. To them this *Ramayana* show is more than just entertainment—it's the work of God himself. If even one of them had showed up here, the soldiers would have discovered what was happening and knocked all the toughness out of this hoodlum in no time. They'd have torn every hair from his beard. How ferocious he is! But then, all *Pathans* are assassins. They don't worry about the pains of death any more than they do about the joys of life.

Mr Mirza watched in dismay, wondering what to say, his mind

functioning only enough to think of the fun there would have been if he'd not left his pistol at home.

Khanna was on the verge of tears. 'Give him some money and get rid of the fiend,' he begged.

The Rai Sahib looked over at Miss Malti. 'What's your advice, Deviji?'

Malti was flushed with anger. 'What's going to happen? Here I am being disgraced and you all just sit around staring. Twenty men here, and yet one beastly Pathan goes on insulting me and your blood doesn't even get warm. Is life that precious to you? Why doesn't at least one man go out and sound the alarm? Why don't you all jump him and grab the gun out of his hand? The gun might go off? Well let it go off. One or two lives might be lost? Well let them be lost.'

The others were not convinced, though, that dying was so casual a matter. If someone got brave enough to run outside and the Pathan lost his temper and shot five or ten of them, then they'd all be wiped out. At most the police would hang him; and even that was not certain. He was a big chieftain, and even the government would think twice about hanging him. There'd be pressures from above. Where politics are concerned, who cares about justice? If a counter-charge were filed and the police forced to drop the case, it would be no surprise. They'd been having such a good time and would have been enjoying the drama by now. But then this fiend had to come and put them in a predicament which would probably cost several lives before it was over.

'But Deviji!' Khanna protested, 'You abuse us as though saving our lives was a sin. All human beings want to go on living, and if we do too, it's nothing to be ashamed of. I'm appalled to see how cheaply you value our lives. This is only a matter of a thousand rupees. You just collected a thousand for doing nothing. Why not give it to him and let him go away? When you're bringing disgrace on yourself, what fault is it of ours?'

'If he lays a hand on Miss Malti,' the Rai Sahib barked, 'I'll attack him even if it leaves me a wriggling corpse. He's only a man after all.'

Mirza shook his head in protest. 'Rai Sahib, you don't know what these fellows are like. If he starts shooting, there'll be no one left alive. He's got perfect aim.'

Poor Mr Tankha had come that evening so as to untangle some problems about the coming election, hoping to go home with a nice profit of five or ten thousand. Now his very life was in danger. 'The

93

simplest plan,' he suggested, 'is the one Khanna just mentioned. It's only a matter of a thousand rupees, and we've got the money here, so why all this debate?'

Miss Malti looked at him contemptuously. 'I never knew you people were such cowards.'

'And I never knew you were so crazy about money—especially when you got it free,' Tankha retorted.

'If you can just look on while I'm insulted, I imagine you'd do the same if it were happening to the women in your own families.'

'And I imagine you wouldn't hesitate to sacrifice the men in your family either for the sake of a little cash.'

All this time the Khan had been listening impatiently to their whispering. 'I won't stand for this any longer,' he bellowed. 'I've waited long enough for an answer.' He took a whistle from his pocket. 'I'm giving you one minute. If you don't produce the money, I'll blow this whistle and call in my twenty-five men. That's final.'

Eyes flashing with love, he turned to Miss Malti, 'You come with me, sweetheart. I'll be your slave. I'll lay my life at your feet. Lots of men may love you but none of them are real lovers. I'll show you what real love is. I'd even plunge a dagger into my chest to make you happy.'

'Deviji!' Mirza choked out. 'For God's sake give this barbarian the money.'

Tankha clasped his hands. 'Have mercy on us, Miss Malti.'

But the Rai Sahib stood erect and declared, 'Absolutely not! Whatever's going to happen, let it happen. Either we'll die or we'll teach these ruffians a lesson they'll never forget.'

'Going into a lion's den isn't courage,' Tankha protested. 'I call it idiocy.'

Miss Malti had a different attitude, however. The Khan's lust-filled eyes had bolstered her confidence, and she was beginning to enjoy the situation. Her heart longed to live with these Pathans for a while, to feel the thrill of their savage passions; and she was being drawn towards the wild love of this crude untamed tribesman as though she had just enjoyed some soft music and was now dashing outside to see a fight between mad elephants.

'You won't get any money,' she said, facing the Khan boldly.

He reached out his hand. 'Then I'll carry you away with me.'

'With all these men around, you couldn't carry me anywhere.'

'I could carry you away even if a thousand men were around.'

'You'd be courting death.'

'For the sake of your love, I'd let myself be skinned alive.'

Seizing Malti's hand, he pulled her towards him. Just then Hori stepped into the room. The villagers had been convulsed by his performance as Raja Janak's gardener, but he kept wondering why the master had not yet appeared. He should be there to see how well they were doing. And his good friends should be watching it too. But how could he call the master? Having been waiting for an opportunity, he had come running at the first free moment. Seeing what was happening, he stopped, stunned. People were huddled together in silence, trembling with fear, watching panic-stricken as the Khan pulled Malti towards him. Hori guessed what was happening.

'Hori!' the Rai Sahib called out. 'Run and call the soldiers. quickly!'

Hori turned to go, but the Khan was standing in front of him with the gun pointed. 'Where do you think you're going, you son of a pig? You want to get shot?'

Now Hori was a simple farmer, and the sight of a policeman's red turban was enough to frighten him to death. If he were locked up, who would get him out? Where would the money come from for a bribe? Who would take care of his family? Against an angry bull, however, he'd attack with only a stick. No coward, he knew how to kill and how to die and when his master shouted an order, Hori feared no one—he'd jump into the jaws of death itself.

Leaping on the Khan, Hori grabbed him by the waist and flipped him flat on the floor, where the man lay cursing in *Pushtoo*. Hori jumped on his chest and tugged at his beard. It came off in his hands. At once the Khan threw off his turban, knocked Hori aside, and stood up. It was Mr Mehta himself!

People swarmed around him on all sides, embracing him or slapping him on the back. But Mehta stood there as calmly as though nothing had happened, his face registering neither amusement nor pride.

Miss Malti tried to appear angry. 'Where did you learn that impersonation? My heart's still pounding.'

Mehta smiled. 'I was just testing the bravery of these gentlemen. Please forgive my rudeness....'

95

CHAPTER 7

By the time this drama had ended, the performance on the stage outside was over too, and preparations for the social comedy were underway. These guests were no longer interested, however. Only Mr
Mehta went to see it, staying from beginning to end and enjoying it
immensely. During the show, he encouraged the actors by clapping
and calling for lines to be repeated. In this comedy the Rai Sahib
was satirizing a village zamindar involved in a court case. A comedy
in name, it was also full of pathos. The hero's speeches were crammed
with legal quotations as he filed suit against his wife for a slight delay
in preparing his dinner. And then there were the extravagant demands of the lawyers and the cunning tricks of the village witnesses.
At first they were eager to testify, but at the time of the court hearing
they kept changing their minds and made fools of the prosecutor
with all kinds of new demands. These scenes had the audience doubled
up with laughter. In the funniest section, the lawyer was trying to
make the witnesses memorize his version of the affair; but they kept
forgetting, and the lawyer would get furious. He'd repeat the instructions in the village dialect, but when they finally reached the witness
box they again changed their story. All this was so vivid and realistic
that Mr Mehta jumped up when it was over, embraced the hero and
announced that there would be medals for all the actors. He felt a
new respect for the Rai Sahib, who had been directing the play from
back stage. Mehta ran to hug him and exclaimed affectionately, 'I
had no idea you possessed such insight.'

A hunt had been scheduled after breakfast the next day so that
the pleasures of rural life could be enjoyed. Lunch would be served
in a garden on the bank of some river, followed by swimming or
wading, and then the party would return to the house in the evening.
The guests with other things to do had already departed, leaving
only the Rai Sahib's closest friends.

Mrs Khanna still had a headache, so she couldn't go. And the
editor, angry at them all, was engrossed in thought, planning an

article denouncing them.... They're all expert thugs, making off with money by foul means and then sitting around preening themselves. What do they know of what's happening in the world? What do they care if their neighbours are dying? They're concerned only with their own selfish pleasures. This Mehta who runs around posing as a philosopher has only one passion—to get the most out of life. Just because he pockets a thousand rupees a month whether he works or not, he thinks he has the right to enjoy life to the full—or to the overflowing. But people who are crushed with worry over marrying off their sons or getting a doctor for a sick wife or finding money for the house rent—how are they to have full lives? Mehta runs around like a bull suddenly let loose, feeding off others' fields and thinking everyone in the world is happy. He won't come to his senses until there's a revolution and someone tells him, 'All right, you son of a bitch, go plough the fields.' Then he'll see how full life is!

As for that Malti, the pandit fumed, who still considers herself a 'Miss' even though she runs around all over the place, she says she's not going to marry—that it's just a trap in which one's personality doesn't get a chance to develop fully. Evidently she thinks that developing one's personality means going around robbing everyone and then wallowing in carefree dissipation. Tear away all restrictions, shoot down religion and society, don't let any of life's duties come near...and presto, you have a full life. What could be simpler? Provide no shelter for your parents—turn them out. Don't marry—it's a trap. Have children? That just ties you down. But why even pay taxes then? The law's a trap too, so why not break it? Let's face it—even the slightest disregard for the law puts you in chains. But she tears away only the chains that happen to interfere with her own enjoyment. Call a rope a snake; then you can avoid facing reality. Stay away from live snakes, though. One hiss and you'd be knocked flat. So if you see one coming, put your tail between your legs and run away. That's what she calls a full life!

The hunting party set off at eight. Khanna had never been on a hunt before—he trembled at the mere sound of a gun; but with Miss Malti going, he couldn't very well stay behind. Mr Tankha had not yet been able to discuss the election and thought there might be an opportunity on this trip. The Rai Sahib had not toured the area for a long time, so he wanted to see how things were going. By occasional visits he could make some contacts, consolidate his influence, and keep his agents and overseers alert. Mirza Khurshed was eager for new experiences, especially ones like this where some bravery might be displayed. And Miss Malti couldn't very well stay home alone—she needed to be surrounded by admirers. Only Mr Mehta was going hunting out of real love for the sport. The Rai Sahib wanted to take along food as well as a cook, men to skin the animals, and all kinds of other servants. But Mehta objected.

'Do we eat, then, or starve?' Khanna protested.

'Of course we'll eat,' Mehta replied, 'but we can fix our own food for once. Don't you think we can survive without servants? Miss Malti will cook for us. We can get clay pots and leaf plates in the villages, and there's no shortage of firewood. As for food, well we're on a hunt, after all.'

'You'll have to let me beg off,' Malti said. 'You gripped my wrist so hard last night that it still hurts.'

'We'll do the work. You just give the orders.'

'You can all just watch the fun,' said Mirza Khurshed. 'I'll make the arrangements. There's nothing to it. Searching for pots and pans in the jungle is foolishness. Let's just shoot a deer, cook and eat it, and then stretch out and snore in the shade of the trees there.'

The proposal was accepted. They left in two cars, Miss Malti driving one and the Rai Sahib the other. After some twenty or twenty-five miles they began winding through ranges of hills which ran along both sides of the road. After climbing for some distance, they suddenly came to a slope, and the cars started down. In the distance a river was visible, sluggish as a sick old man. Reaching the bank, they stopped the cars in the shade of a thick banyan tree and got out. It was suggested that they divide into groups of two for the hunt, returning to the spot at noon.

Miss Malti made ready to go with Mehta. Khanna suppressed his jealousy. His whole ambition in coming was deflated. If he'd known Malti would double-cross him, he'd have gone home. But although teaming up with the Rai Sahib was not as interesting as with her, it wouldn't be so bad, since Khanna had quite a few matters to discuss with him. That left Khurshed and Tankha together.

The three parties started off in different directions. After walking a little with Mehta over a rocky path, Miss Malti said, 'What's the rush? Let me catch my breath a moment.'

Mehta smiled. 'We've not come even a mile yet. Tired already?'

'Not tired—but why not take just a short breather?'

'We don't have the right to rest until we've shot something.'

98

'I didn't come to hunt.'

Mehta put on an innocent air. 'Oh, I didn't realize that. What did you come for then?'

'I can't very well say right now.'

A herd of grazing deer came into view. They both ducked behind a rock. Mehta took aim and fired. He missed, and the herd fled.

'Now what?' asked Malti.

'Nothing. Keep on going. We'll find some other game.'

They walked along silently for some time. Then Malti stopped. 'The sun's getting terrible,' she said. 'Come on, let's sit down under this tree.'

'Not now. If you want to sit, go ahead. I'm not going to rest yet.'

'You're really heartless, I swear.'

'I can't sit down until we've shot something.'

'Then you'll be the death of me. All right now, tell me, why did you give me such a bad time last night? I was really getting angry at you. Do you remember what you said? "Come away with me, sweetheart!" I never knew you were so evil. Now tell me the truth, would you really have carried me off?'

Mehta said nothing, acting as though he hadn't heard.

They kept walking for a while. But there was that June sunshine, and also the rocky path. . . . Malti, tired, sat down.

'That's all right, you get some rest,' Mehta said, remaining standing. 'I'll be back.'

'You're going to walk on and leave me alone?'

'I know you can protect yourself.'

'How do you know?'

'Girls these days have that ability. They don't want men to protect them. They want to walk shoulder to shoulder with them.'

Malti looked embarrassed. 'You're a philosopher through and through, Mehta. Honestly!'

Mehta took aim and fired at a peacock perched on a nearby tree. The bird flew away.

'Very good,' Malti gloated. 'My curse worked.'

'But more on you than on me,' Mehta replied, resting the gun on his shoulder. 'If I'd nabbed it, I'd have let you take a ten-minute rest. As it is, you'll have to start walking again right away.'

Getting up, Malti caught hold of Mehta's hand. 'Philosophers have no feelings. It's a good thing you never married. You'd just have

99

killed your poor wife. But I won't let go of you so easily. You can't run off and leave me.'

Mehta shook off her hand with one jerk and went on ahead.

'I'm warning you,' Malti shouted tearfully, 'don't go or I'll bash my head on this rock.'

Mehta quickened his pace. Malti stood watching. When he'd gone twenty steps she started running after him angrily. Resting alone was no fund.

Catching up, she said, 'I would never have thought you such a brute.'

'I'll present you with the skin of the deer I shoot.'

'To hell with the skin! I'm not talking to you any more.'

'Well, if we were to return emptyhanded while the others made a good haul, I'd be humiliated.'

A broad stream yawned in front of them, rocks scattered in it like teeth. The current was strong enough to produce waves. The sun had reached its height and its thirsty rays were playing over the water's surface.

'Now we'll have to go back,' Miss Malti said happily.

'Why? We'll cross over. That's where the game is.'

'But the current is so swift. I'll be swept away.'

'All right, you sit here. I'm going on.'

'Go right ahead. I'm not tired of living yet.'

Mehta stepped into the water and started wading cautiously across. He kept on, the water getting deeper and deeper until it was up to his chest.

Malti shook with a panic unfamiliar to her. 'The water's deep,' she screamed. 'Wait! I'm coming too.'

'No don't! You'll slip. The current's terrible.'

'That doesn't matter. I'm coming. Careful, don't move!'

She tucked up her sari and stepped into the stream. After just a few feet, she was already hip-deep.

Mehta waved her back with both hands, shouting, 'Don't come any farther, Malti! The water here is up to your neck.'

She took another step. 'I don't care. If you want me to die, I'll die next to you.'

She was up to her waist now, in a current so strong she seemed sure to lose her footing. Mehta waded back and caught her by the hand.

She looked at him indignantly. 'I've never seen a more cold-blooded man. Your heart must be made of stone. Well, you can torture me all you like today. Some day I'll get my chance.'

Her feet started slipping. She clung to him and he steadied his gun.

'I'll carry you on my shoulder,' Mehta reassured her. 'You can't keep your balance here.'

'Is it really so necessary to get to the other side?' she frowned.

Mehta said nothing. Tilting his chin to support the gun on his left shoulder, he lifted Malti with both hands and set her on his other shoulder.

'What if someone should see us?' Malti asked, trying to conceal her delight.

'He'd think it indecent.'

They advanced a couple of steps and then Malti whimpered, 'All right, tell me—if I should drown here, would you feel sad or not? I doubt you'd even care.'

'Do you think I'm not human?' Mehta protested in an injured tone.

'Why hide it? That's exactly what I think.'

'Is that the truth, Malti?'

'What do you think?'

'I? Some day I'll tell you.'

The water had reached Mehta's neck. Another step might put him over his head. Malti's heart was pounding. 'Mehta,' she cried, 'for God's sake don't go any farther or I'll jump into the water.'

At this critical moment the thought of God, usually a joking matter with her, crossed Malti's mind. She knew he was not sitting around somewhere waiting to come to her rescue, but there was nowhere else to turn for the support and strength she needed.

The water began to get shallower. 'Now you can put me down,' she said, relieved.

'Not yet. Just sit there quietly. We may hit some holes yet.'

'You must think I'm terribly selfish.'

'You can pay me for my labours.'

Malti was delighted. 'What will you take as payment?'

'Just this—that you call me if you're ever in a situation like this again.'

They reached the shore. Malti wrung out her sari on the sand, shook the water from her shoes, and then rinsed her face and hands. But her secret desires and Mehta's intriguing comments danced in front of her.

'I'll always remember this day,' she said exuberantly.

101

'Were you very scared?' Mehta asked.

'At first. But then I realized you were capable of taking care of both of us.'

Mehta looked at her with pride, his face flushed from his exertions and from her praise. 'Do you realize how happy it makes me to hear that?'

'How would I? You've never given me any reason to think so. Just the reverse—the way you've been dragging me into the jungle. And now we'll have to cross this stream again on the way back. What a mess you've landed us in. I wouldn't last a single day living with you.'

Mehta smiled, knowing full well the implications of what she was saying. 'You think I'm that bad? And if I told you I loved you? Would you marry me then?'

'Who would marry a man as unfeeling as a chunk of wood? Your constant tormenting would be the death of any wife.' But Malti looked at him tenderly, as though to say she knew full well he was smart enough to realize what she really meant.

'Is that the truth, Malti?' Mehta asked. 'I've never been very good at pleasing women. Whenever any girl who might be called pretty pretended to love me, I could see right through her, and then I'd lose interest.'

Malti started trembling. He was so honest! 'Tell me,' she asked, 'what kind of love would satisfy you?'

'One in which a woman says exactly what she feels in her heart, that's all. I value good looks, sex appeal and feminine wiles only for what they're worth. What I want is something to satisfy the soul. I don't need exciting or ephemeral things.'

'You're a shrewd one,' Malti said, pursing her lips and giving a sigh. 'No one's going to get the upper hand over you. Well tell me, what do you think of me?'

Mehta grinned mischievously. 'You're intelligent, shrewd, talented, kind, unpredictable, self-assured and capable of sacrifice. You can do everything—except love.'

Malti eyed him sharply. 'That's a lie, a downright lie. I think it's preposterous that you claim to understand the feelings of women.'

They were walking along the bank of the stream. It was past noon, but Malti no longer wanted to rest or turn back. She was finding a unique kind of pleasure in this discussion. She'd made fools of any number of learned and important men with just a smile, a stare or a sultry look, and had then dropped them, unable to build her life on those foundations of sand. But today she had found rugged, solid, rocky ground, the kind that gives off sparks when struck by a pickaxe. And its roughness became more and more fascinating.

A gun-shot resounded. Mehta had aimed and fired at a red-headed bird flying over the stream. The bird, wounded, fluttered some distance and then fell into the stream, where it began floating along with the current.

'What now?'

'I'm going to fetch it. It can't go far.'

With that, he ran across the sand, laid his gun on the bank, jumped into the water with a splash and started swimming downstream. But though he taxed all his strength, he had not yet caught up with the bird after half a mile. Though dead, it still seemed to be flying away from him.

All at once he saw a young woman emerge from a hut on the bank, spot the floating bird, tuck her sari above her knees, and jump into the water. In a flash she caught the bird and then, seeing Mehta, called to him to get out of the water, that she had his bird.

Mehta was charmed by her agility and courage. He swam straight to shore and in a couple of minutes was standing beside her. The girl was dark—very dark, in fact. Her clothes were extremely dirty and coarse, her hair was tangled, and her only ornaments were the two thick bangles on each arm. None of her features could have been called beautiful; but the fresh and pure surroundings had given her dark complexion such lustre, and being raised in the lap of nature had made her body so trim and shapely, that an artist seeking a model of ideal youth could have found no greater beauty. Her robust health seemed to radiate strength and energy to Mehta.

'You came at just the right time,' he thanked her. 'No telling how far I'd have had to swim otherwise.'

The girl smiled. 'I saw you swimming this way, so I ran. You must have been hunting.'

'Yes, we came on a hunt, but it's afternoon and the only thing I've shot is this bird.'

'If you want to kill a leopard, I'll show you where one is. It comes here to drink every night—and occasionally in the afternoon.' She lowered her head a little bashfully and then added, 'You'll have to give me the skin though. Come to my place over there in the shade of the *pipal* tree. You shouldn't stand in the sun like this, and your clothes are soaked too.'

103

Mehta looked at the wet sari clinging to her body. 'Well your clothes are also soaked.'

'That doesn't matter to us. We're jungle people. We go around all day in the sun and the rain—but you're not used to it.'

What an understanding girl—and yet completely uneducated. . . . 'What will you do with the skin?'

'My father sells them in the bazaar. That's what we do for a living.'

'But if I spend the afternoon here, what can you get me to eat?'

'There's nothing in our house suitable for you,' she apologized, 'but we do have some corn chapaties set aside. And I'll make up a curry with this bird if you'll tell me how to do it. There's also a little milk. Our cow was once attacked by a leopard, but she drove it off with her horns and managed to escape. Since then the leopard's been afraid of her.'

'I'm not alone though. There's a woman with me.'

'Your wife, I suppose?'

'No, just an acquaintance. I'm not married yet.'

'I'll run and call her. Go sit down in the shade.'

'No no, I'll go fetch her.'

'You must be tired. City people aren't used to the jungle. We belong here. She must be standing on the bank somewhere.'

Before Mehta could say a thing, the girl had vanished. He walked over to the pipal tree and sat down in its shade. Love for this free life welled up inside him. In front of him stretched a range of mountains, an inaccessible and unending as philosophical truth itself. They seemed to be proclaiming the wisdom of the ages, as though the soul were seeing wisdom, light and vastness manifested in their most splendid form. On a high peak in the distance was a small temple, as lofty and yet as lost in that vastness as his thoughts—like a bird which had perched there but was still looking for a resting place.

While Mehta was absorbed in these musings, the young woman returned with Miss Malti—the one blooming in the sunshine like a wild flower, the other drooping and fading like a potted plant.

'You must enjoy lying around here in the shade while others are dying of hunger,' Miss Malti said sarcastically.

The young woman picked up two large clay pitchers. 'You just sit here. I'll run and get some water. Then I'll light a fire and have some chapaties cooked for you in just a moment—that is if you don't mind food prepared by my hands. If you prefer, you can do the cooking

104

yourself. There's no wheat flour in the house, though, and no shop around here where I could get any.'

Malti was still angry at Mehta. 'Why did you stop here?' she demanded.

'You should find this kind of life rather pleasant for a day,' Mehta teased her. 'You'll find out how delicious corn-flour chapaties can be.'

'I can't eat them. Even if I forced myself to swallow them, I couldn't digest them. I regret having ever come with you. First you make me run all the way and then you bring me here and dump me.'

Mehta had taken off most of his clothes and was sitting around in just a pair of blue undershorts. Seeing the young woman lifting the pitchers, he took them from her and started for the well.

Even during his intensive study of philosophy, Mehta had taken care of his health, and the testimony to his efforts could be seen as he walked along carrying the pitchers—his muscular arms, broad chest and well-developed thighs looking like the husky limbs of some Greek statue. As he drew the water from the well, the young woman looked on with admiring eyes. He was no longer an object of pity but of reverence.

The well was very deep, some ninety feet, and the pots were heavy. Though Mehta was in good shape from regular exercise, he began tiring as he hauled up the first load. The girl ran over and took the rope from his hands, 'You'll never get it up. Go sit on the cot. I'll draw the water.'

Mehta couldn't tolerate such a slur on his manhood. Snatching back the rope, he pulled with all his might, and before long had filled both pitchers and carried them to the door of the hut. The girl quickly singed off the feathers of the bird, sliced it up, started a fire, and put the pot of meat and a pan of milk on the stove to boil.

Malti, her eyebrows drawn in a frown, was stretched out unhappily on the cot, looking as though she were about to be operated on.

Mehta stood at the door of the hut admiring the girl's domestic skill. 'Let me know what I can do to help,' he said. 'What would you like me to do?'

'There's nothing for you to do here,' she admonished him sweetly. 'Go sit by the lady. Poor thing's very hungry. You can give her some milk when it warms up.'

She took some flour from a clay pot and began kneading it. Mehta remained there, watching her sensuous limbs, and she occasionally paused in her work to glance provocatively at him also.

'What are you standing there for?' Malti called. 'I've got a splitting headache. My head's bursting as though half of it were about to drop off.'

Mehta walked over to her. 'It must be the heat,' he said.

'How did I know you were bringing me here to kill me?'

'Don't you even have any pills with you?'

'Why would I bring pills? Was I supposed to be coming to call on a patient? I have a box of medicines but I left it at Semari. Oof! My head is splitting.'

Mehta sat on the ground and began massaging her head slowly. Malti closed her eyes.

The young woman, hands smeared with flour, eyes red and watering from the smoke, her body so soaked with perspiration that the swelling breasts were clearly visible, came over and looked at Malti lying there with her eyes closed. 'What's the matter with the lady?' she inquired.

'She has a bad headache,' Mehta replied.

'The whole head or half of it?'

'Half, she says.'

'The right side or the left?'

'The left side.'

'I'll run and get something for that at once. Rub it on and she'll be all right.'

'Where are you going in this heat?'

But the girl didn't hear. She had dashed off and disappeared behind a hill. About a half hour later, Mehta saw her climbing high up on a tall peak, looking just like a doll at that distance. What a spirit of service and what great practical wisdom this jungle girl has, Mehta reflected, and she's climbing practically to the sky in all this heat.

Malti opened her eyes. 'Where has the black creature gone? How fantastically dark she is—like a chunk of ebony. Have her go to the Rai Sahib and tell him to send the car here. I'll suffocate in this heat.'

'She's gone for some medicine ... says it will relieve your headache very quickly.'

'Her remedies may do some good for people like herself, but not for me. You've really fallen for the brat. How despicable you are! Well, people are attracted by their own kind!'

Mehta had no qualms about speaking the truth, however unpleasant. 'If you had some of her qualities, you could be a real goddess.'

'She's welcome to her qualities. I have no desire to be a goddess.'

'I'll go bring the car if you want, though I can't promise that we can even get it here.'

'Why don't you send that black thing?'

'She's gone for the herbs, and after that she's going to cook the meal.'

'Obviously you're her guest today. I suppose you're planning to spend the night here too. The hunting would be better at night of course.'

Mehta was annoyed by her insinuations. 'With the kind of love and respect I feel for this girl, I hope I'm struck blind if I look at her lustfully. I wouldn't climb that steep hill in this heat even for my dearest friend. And we're only guests passing through for an hour or so. She knows that. But she'd have gone to all this trouble just as readily if you were some poor woman. All I can do is write essays and give speeches on universal love and brotherhood. She puts that love and sacrifice into practice. Talk's a lot easier than action . . . you know that as well as I do.'

'All right, all right, so she's a goddess,' Malti sneered sarcastically. 'I admit it. Her breasts are big, her buttocks are large—what more would a goddess need?'

Mehta bristled. Jumping up, he put on his clothes, which had dried out, picked up his gun and got ready to leave.

'You can't go and leave me here alone,' Malti hissed.

'Then who is to go?'

'That . . . that goddess of yours.'

Mehta stood there in a quandry. He was discovering for the first time how easily women can triumph over men.

The girl came back into view, running breathlessly towards them with a plant in her hand. When she got close and saw Mehta preparing to go somewhere, she said, 'I found the herbs. I'll make up a paste and rub it on. But where are you going? The meat must be ready. I'll just bake the chapaties. Do eat one or two. The lady can have some milk. You can leave later, when it's a bit cooler.'

With no self-consciousness, she began undoing the buttons on Mehta's achkan, and he had to restrain his desire to kiss the feet of this country girl.

'Forget about my medicine,' Malti said. 'Our car is waiting under the banyan tree on the bank of the river. There should be some other people there. Tell them to bring the car here. Go on now . . . run.'

Distressed, the girl turned to Mehta. Such ingratitude, he thought, and after all her trouble to get the plant. If she doesn't like the girl's remedy, that's all right; but she could at least try a little, just to make the girl happy.

'The fire will go out if I leave,' the young woman said, putting the plant on the ground. 'Would it be all right if I bake the chapaties first? The gentleman can have some food, you can drink some milk, and then you both can relax while I go for the car.'

She walked into the hut and fanned the dying fire. She looked at the meat and found it done—some of it had burned, in fact. She quickly put on the chapaties, let the milk cool, and then took it to Malti in a small bowl. Malti made a face when she saw the crude container, but she was too hungry to refuse the milk. Mehta sat down by the door of the house and began eating the meat and chapaties off a thali. The girl stood fanning him.

'Let him eat,' Malti scolded. 'He's not going to run away. Go and get the car.'

The girl glanced briefly at Malti, wondering just what she wanted. Malti's face showed none of the humility, gratitude or anxiety found in sick women. It reflected only pride and deceit. The uneducated girl was a shrewd judge of character. 'I'm nobody's slave,' she spoke up. 'You may be rich, but only in your own house. I haven't come begging to you for anything. I won't go for the car.'

'Very well,' Malti glowered, 'so you're going to be insolent, are you? Tell me—whose estate is this?'

'It belongs to the Rai Sahib.'

'Then I'll see to it that the Rai Sahib himself gives you a good caning.'

'If having me beaten will make you happy, then go ahead. I'm no rani or maharani . . . he won't have to send an army.'

Mehta had just swallowed a couple of mouthfuls when he heard what Malti was saying. The food stuck in his throat. Quickly rinsing his hands, he said, 'She's not to go. I'm going.'

Malti jumped to her feet. 'She'll have to go.'

Mehta addressed her in English. 'You won't gain any respect by insulting her, Malti.'

'Men go for these sluts,' Malti retorted, 'who, whether they have any other abilities or not, run gaily around fawning over them and

108

delighting in the good fortune of having a man to order them about. They're goddesses all right—glorious and powerful ones. I thought there was one male quality you'd been spared, but underneath all that sophistication you're evidently just as barbaric as the rest of them.'

Mehta was a teacher of psychology and understood Malti's real motives. He'd never before seen such a perfect example of jealousy. What a furious blaze of envy for a woman who was ordinarily so gentle, so generous and so cheerful!

'Say what you like,' Mehta insisted. 'I won't let her go. I'm not about to lower myself by rewarding her hospitality in that fashion.'

Mehta's tone was so cutting that Malti slowly stood up and prepared the leave. 'All right then,' she said angrily, 'I'll go myself. You can come later, once you've worshipped at her feet.'

When Malti had started on her way, Mehta turned to the young woman. 'Let me take leave of you now, sister. I'll always remember your affection and unselfish hospitality.'

The girl's eyes filled with tears. Folding her hands respectfully, she bowed and then disappeared into the hut.

The Rai Sahib and Khanna made up the second party. The Rai Sahib was dressed in his best silk shirt and scarf, while Khanna had stuffed himself into a hunting outfit, probably ordered just for this occasion since he was usually too busy hunting down clients to take time out for hunting animals. He was a short, slim, good-looking man, with a light complexion, large eyes, a pock-marked face, and a gift for conversation.

Ever since the previous day, Khanna's brain had been obsessed by Mr Mehta as though by a demon. Now, after walking awhile, he said in a derogatory tone, 'Queer fellow, that Mehta. I think he's a fake.'

The Rai Sahib respected Mehta, considering him honest and straightforward; but being a peace-loving man, and having business dealings with Khanna, he didn't want to contradict him. 'I just find him amusing,' he ventured. 'I never get into arguments with him. Even if I wanted to, I'm not smart enough. But I do get amused when someone with no practical experience of life starts expounding new theories about it. He cheerfully pockets a thousand rupees a month and has no wife or any other worries. Who could be in a better position to sit around philosophizing? Leading a nice carefree existence, he dreams about the full life. How can you argue with a man like that?'

'I've heard he doesn't have a very good character.'

'How can a man have a good character when he's leading such an irresponsible life? Let him live in society awhile and try to follow its rules and regulations. Then he'll find out!'

'I can't understand what Malti sees in him that makes her so crazy about him.'

'I think she's just trying to make you jealous.'

'Make me jealous? Why the poor girl's nothing but a plaything as far as I'm concerned.'

'Don't tell me that, Mr Khanna. You'd give your life for her.'

'I could accuse you of the same thing.'

'But I really do see her as just a plaything. You idolize her.'

There was nothing funny in this, but Khanna burst into a roar of laughter. 'If I can get my prayers answered by offering just a jug of water to the goddess, what's wrong with that?'

Now it was the Rai Sahib who burst out laughing for no apparent reason. 'Then you don't understand this particular goddess,' he said. 'The more you worship her, the more she'll run away from you. But the more you ignore her, the more she'll chase after you.'

'In that case it's you she should be chasing.'

'Me! I'm not part of that love-sick bunch, Mr Khanna, I assure you. Whatever brains and energy I possess are spent taking care of my estate. All the people at my house are preoccupied with their own pursuits, some indulging their souls, others their bodies. It's my job, my duty, to feed all those parasites. Many of my fellow zamindars wallow in luxury and dissipation—I'm perfectly aware of that. They squander their money and have a fine time. Their debts pile up and they're always being hauled into court. They're notorious everywhere for never returning anything they borrow. I'd rather die, though, than live like that. I don't know which of my previous births left me with this conscience that forces me to serve my country and my fellowmen. When the civil disobedience movement began, the other zamindars were all intoxicated with wine, women and song. But I had no alternative—I went to jail, lost thousands of rupees, and am still paying the price for it. I have no regrets, however—none at all. I'm proud of it. A man's not a man in my estimation unless he works for the welfare of the country and of society, unless he's willing to make sacrifices. Do you think I enjoy sucking the blood of half-dead farmers in order to satisfy the desires of my relatives? But what can I do? Although I despise the system in which I grew up and in which I live, I can't give it up. I'm caught in a vicious circle where I still have a regard for position but can't get rid of my feelings of guilt. A man like me couldn't run after any girl, much less Miss Malti. And if he did, it would be his downfall. Of course a little fun now and then is another matter.'

Mr Khanna was also brave in battle and had never known defeat. He'd been to jail twice. Though he had never adopted the homespun dress of the nationalists, and used to drink French wines, he could endure great hardships when the occasion demanded. In jail he never even touched liquor, and though he could have had all kinds of special privileges as an 'A' class prisoner, he'd gotten along on a 'C' class diet. Even a war chariot can't roll down the battlefield without an occasional oiling, however. His life needed a bit of romance now and then.

'You're able to lead an ascetic life,' Khanna said, 'but I'm not. As I see it, a man who's not something of a libertine can't plunge whole-heartedly into battle either. If a man can't love a woman, I have little faith in his love for his country.'

The Rai Sahib smiled. 'Now you're beginning to make insinuations about me.'

'It's not a matter of insinuation but of fact.'

'Perhaps so.'

'If you search your heart, you'll realize I'm right.'

'I have searched my heart, and I assure you—whatever faults I may have, lust is not one of them.'

'Then I feel sorry for you. It's that self-denial which makes you so unhappy and depressed and worried. I'm going to keep on playing this drama even if it has a tragic ending. She's been trying to fool me, pretending not to care, but I'm not one to lose heart. Until now I hadn't understood her temperament. I couldn't decide just where the target was located.'

'But you may still not have the secret. Mehta will probably run away with the prize first.'

They spotted a black buck with massive antlers grazing in the distance. The Rai Sahib took aim. Khanna tried to stop him. 'Why kill it? Let the poor thing go on grazing. It's getting hot. Come on, let's sit down somewhere. I have some things to discuss with you.'

The Rai Sahib fired but the deer ran away. 'The first game we've seen, and I missed it,' he said.

'That's one murder you've been spared,' Khanna remarked. 'By the way, do you raise sugar cane on your estate?'

'Lots of it.'

'Then why don't you affiliate with our sugar mill? The shares are selling like crazy. Why don't you buy up at least a thousand of them?'

'Good heavens! Where would I get that kind of money?'

'Don't tell me a big zamindar like you is short of money! The whole lot would only come to fifty thousand. And you'd only have to pay twenty-five per cent of that now.'

'Sorry, brother. I can't afford a thing right now.'

'I can let you have all the money you want. My bank is at your disposal. Which reminds me—you probably haven't insured your life yet. Why don't you take out a good policy from my company? You can easily afford one or two hundred rupees a month, and you'll get back a nice lump sum—forty or fifty thousand. You couldn't make any better provision for your children. Take a look at our terms. We work on the principle of full partnership. Not a pice of profit goes into anyone's pocket except for office expenses and salaries. You're probably surprised that a company can run on that basis. I'd advise you to go in for a bit of speculation also. The hundreds of men who are millionaires today all got that way through speculation. Get some shares in any of the corporations—cotton, sugar, wheat or rubber. In a matter of minutes you can make a fortune. Of course the stock market's a complicated business and a lot of people get fooled—but only the stupid ones. For experienced, educated and far-sighted people like yourself, there's no better way to make big profits. The ups and downs of the market are no accident. Predicting them is a regular science. Just study it carefully and you'll never be hoodwinked.'

The Rai Sahib had no confidence in companies, having had a few bitter experiences with them. But he'd watched Mr Khanna prosper with his own eyes and had developed a faith in his business acumen. This man, a bank clerk just ten years ago, had worked his way up by sheer diligence, energy and intelligence, until now the whole town worshipped him. His advice could not be ignored. With Khanna as his guide, he should be able to achieve considerable success. Why let such an opportunity pass by? The Rai Sahib questioned him closely on the details. . . .

Just then a villager approached, carrying a large basket of roots, leaves and flowers.

'Say, what are you selling?' Khanna inquired.

The villager hesitated, afraid he might be pressed into forced labour for them. 'Nothing much, master,' he said. 'Just some grass and leaves.'

'What are you going to do with them?'

'Sell them, sir. They're medicinal plants.'

'Show us what you've got.'

The villager opened up shop and displayed the contents. They were ordinary plants which the jungle people dug up and took to the city where they sold them to the druggists for a few annas—such things as solanum, thorn-apple seeds and swallow-wort flowers. He exhibited each item, rattling off a stock list of its qualities. 'This is a kind of solanum, sir. One dose will bring relief from fever, indigestion, enlarged spleen, heart palpitations, rheumatism and coughs. And these are thorn-apple seeds, sir, for gout, aches....'

Khanna asked their price. Eight annas for the lot, the man said. Khanna tossed him a rupee, instructing him to deliver the whole load to his car. The poor villager blessed them for paying double the price and went on down the road.

'What will you do with all that trash?' the Rai Sahib asked.

Khanna smiled. 'Turn it into pure gold. I'm an alchemist—perhaps you didn't know.'

'All right, my friend, then teach me the spells.'

'With pleasure. You can become my disciple, but first make your offering of two and a half pounds of sweets. Then I'll explain the system to you. Actually the point is that I have dealings with all kinds of people, some of whom would stake their lives on medicinal herbs. All you have to tell them is that these plants have come from some saint and they'll start flattering you and begging you for them. And if you give them some, they're indebted to you for life. It's not a bad bargain if you can make ten or twenty fools obligated to you for one rupee. By capitalizing on that bit of gratitude, you can get all kinds of big favours.'

The Rai Sahib's curiosity was aroused. 'But how do you remember the properties of all these plants?'

Khanna laughed. 'Not you too, Rai Sahib! Don't be silly. You just ascribe any properties you wish to the plant. It all depends on how clever you are. In any rupee's worth of good health, eight annas of it is nothing more than faith. Those big officials you see, and those learned men with all the degrees after their names, and those rich men—they all accept things on blind faith. I know botany professors who don't know the names of even half these things. Swamiji, my spiritual adviser, loves to make fun of those great intellects. You probably haven't met him. Next time you're over, I'll introduce you. Ever since he moved into our garden, there's been a constant stream of visitors. He's beyond all worldly desires—takes only some milk once a day. I've never known such a learned saint. For years he meditated and did penance high in the Himalayas. He's found complete salvation. You really must let him initiate you. I'm sure all those problems of yours would vanish. Just looking at you, he'll reveal your past and your future. And he's so cheerful that just seeing him is a delight to the heart. The amazing thing is that, although he's such a saint himself, he says that renunciation and sacrifice, temples and monasteries, religious sects and orders are all a big fraud. He says they're all humbug, and tells people to liberate themselves from useless conventions and become human beings rather than trying to turn into gods. When you turn into a god, you no longer remain human.'

The Rai Sahib considered all this very suspicious. He had as much respect for holy men as do most people in positions of power and he coveted the peace that unhappy souls could obtain by inner reflection. When depressed by financial difficulties, he would consider renouncing the world, retiring into solitude, and reflecting there on the emancipation of the soul. He held the common belief that worldly attachments obstruct the path of spiritual progress, and his goal in life was to detach himself from all such mundane desires. But how could these obstacles be removed except by renunciation and sacrifice?

'But if he calls renunciation a fraud,' the Rai Sahib said, 'then why has he renounced the world himself?'

'He doesn't claim to have renounced the world. What he says is that a person should keep on performing his duties. The essence of his message is mental emancipation.'

'I'm not understanding any of this. What's meant by mental emancipation?'

'I don't understand it myself, I'm afraid. Come over some time and perhaps we can discuss it with him. He says love is the fundamental truth in life. And he explains it so beautifully that you can't help being captivated.'

'Have you introduced Miss Malti to him?'

'Don't be funny. What good would it do Malti to . . .'

Before he'd finished his sentence, Khanna heard a rustling in the bushes and jumped behind the Rai Sahib for protection. A leopard emerged from the bushes and stalked slowly down the path in front of them.

The Rai Sahib raised his gun and was about to fire when Khanna whispered, 'What do you think you're doing? You'll just upset him unnecessarily. What if he turns around and comes after us?'

'No chance of that. He'll be done for right where he is.'

'Well let me climb that ridge over there first. I'm not much of a hunting enthusiast.'

'Then why did you come along?'

'Fate was against me, that's all.'

The Rai Sahib lowered his gun. 'We just lost a superb animal. Opportunities like that are few and far between.'

'I can't stay here any longer. This place is too dangerous.'

'Just let me shoot one or two animals. I'd be ashamed to return emptyhanded.'

'Please . . . just get me back to the car. Then you can hunt anything you like—leopards or panthers or whatever.'

'You're a terrible coward, Mr Khanna, I swear.'

'Bravery doesn't mean risking your life foolishly.'

'All right then, you're welcome to go back.'

'Alone?'

'The path's perfectly safe.'

'Oh no. You'll have to come with me.'

The Rai Sahib tried to reassure him but Khanna wouldn't hear of it. His face had turned pale with fear; and if even a squirrel had come out of the bushes just then, he'd have fallen to the ground screaming. Every inch of his body was trembling and he was drenched with perspiration. The Rai Sahib had no choice but to return with him.

Once they were well out of the jungle, Khanna began to revive. 'I'm not afraid of danger,' he said, 'but sticking your finger in the jaws of danger is idiotic.'

'Oh go on. Just the sight of a leopard and you almost died.'

'I think hunting is a carry-over from the days when man himself was just a beast. Civilization has made great strides since then.'

'I'm going to expose you to Miss Malti.'

'I don't think belief in nonviolence is anything to be ashamed of.'

'Wonderful! So you were just demonstrating your nonviolence. Bully for you!'

'That's right,' Khanna said smugly. 'I was practising what I believe. You're full of talk about Buddha and *Shiva* and yet you go around killing animals. You're the one who should feel ashamed, not I.'

They walked in silence for some distance. Then Khanna spoke up again. 'So when will you be coming over? I'd like you to fill out the forms for a policy today, and for some shares of sugar too. I happen to have both forms with me.'

'Let me think it over a little,' the Rai Sahib said hesitantly.

'There's no need to think it over.'

Mirza Khurshed and Mr Tankha comprised the third group. To Mirza Khurshed the past and the future were like blank sheets of paper. He lived in the present, with no regrets about the past and no worries about the future. He applied himself to whatever was at hand. In the company of friends, he was the image of good fun; but in the Council, no one was more conscientious. Whenever problems came up, he kept after the ministers relentlessly, showing no partiality to anyone, and yet he could still joke around. After all, he was alive today; tomorrow, who could say? Once aroused, though, he was ready to fight. He respected politeness, but would display no mercy if someone began showing off. He remembered neither his favours to others nor theirs to him. Having given away his heart long ago, women now were only an amusing pastime. Poetry and wine were his only passions.

Mr Tankha was a shrewd manipulator—an expert in business deals, in untangling disputes, in tripping people up, in squeezing oil out of gravel, in applying strangleholds, and in sneaking out quietly at the opportune moment. Just ask him, and he would float a boat on dry land or grow grass on top of rocks. Arranging loans from the moneylenders for zamindars, starting new companies, backing candidates for elections—these were his means of livelihood.

His fortunes shone brightest at election times, when he would back a powerful candidate, campaign diligently for him, and make himself ten or twenty thousand rupees. When the Congress party was strongest, he supported Congress candidates. When the communal party was in favour, he campaigned for the Hindu Mahasabha. But he used such clever arguments to justify his about-faces that no one could point an accusing finger at him. He kept on good terms with all the officials and wealthy people in town. Even if people secretly disliked his manipulations, they couldn't come out and say anything, since he displayed such humility and politeness.

Mirza Khurshed took out a handkerchief and wiped the perspiration from his brow. 'This is no day for hunting. We should have had a poetry recital instead.'

'You're right,' the lawyer agreed. 'That would have been delightful, especially there in the Rai Sahib's garden.' Tankha waited a moment and then got down to business. 'There's going to be a lot of mudslinging in the coming election. It's going to be tough even for you.'

'I'm not even going to run this time,' Mirza said indifferently.

'Why not?' asked Tankha.

'Who wants to go around raving and ranting needlessly? What good does it do? I've lost faith in this democracy. Months of wrangling and almost nothing gets done. Sure, it's a good front for throwing dust in the eyes of the people. But we'd do better to have only a governor—whether Indian or British makes little difference. Even the joint efforts of ten thousand men can't pull a train as fast as one engine, which can easily haul it thousands of miles. After seeing the whole farce, I'm fed up with the Council. If I had my way, I'd make a bonfire of the whole business. What we call democracy is actually nothing but the rule of big businessmen and landlords. Only those with money win out in elections. Everything's rigged nicely for them because of their wealth. The big Hindu and Muslim religious leaders, the best writers and speakers, who can use their pens and their tongues to push the public in any direction they please— they all bow down at the feet of the god of gold. I've made up my mind to steer clear of elections. My campaigning from now on is going to be aimed against the whole idea of democracy.'

Mirza Khurshed quoted from the *Koran* to show what high ideals the emperors held in ancient times. 'Today we can't even look at such heights—our eyes would be too dazzled. Those emperors weren't allowed to spend even a cowrie from the treasury for their personal use. They earned a living putting out books, stitching clothes and teaching young men.' He recited a long list of model rulers. 'Those emperors cared for their subjects, whereas nowadays the ministers expect monthly salaries of five, six, seven or even eight thousand. Is this democracy or is it organized robbery?'

A herd of grazing deer came in sight. Mirza's face lit up with the excitement of the hunt. Steadying his gun, he took aim and fired. A black deer dropped. 'Got it,' Mirza shouted, and ran forward impetuously, prancing and springing and clapping his hands like a child.

A man cutting branches in a nearby tree immediately slid down and ran forward also. The deer, shot in the neck, lay with its legs quivering, its eyes like stone.

'That was a fine animal,' the woodcutter said, looking sadly at the deer. 'Must weigh a good eighty pounds at least. Would you like me to carry it somewhere for you?'

Mirza gazed in silence at the pathetic pain-filled eyes of the animal. Just a moment ago, he thought, it was full of life, standing there with its friends and family, eating the God-given grass. At the slightest rustling of leaves, it would have pricked up its ears and bolted for safety. Yet now it lay motionless. Skin it, slice it, chop it up—the deer would never know. What was left in this lifeless corpse of the charm and joy of that carefree life? What a beautiful body ... what beautiful eyes ... what a glossy skin. The beat of the deer's hooves bounding along once radiated waves of delight, quickening the heartbeat of onlookers. It spread life wherever it went, like a flower spreadings its fragrance. But now ... Mirza was filled with remorse.

'Where shall I take it, master?' the woodcutter asked again. 'You can just give me a few annas for the job.'

Mirza was startled out of his reverie. 'All right, pick it up. But where will you take it?'

'Wherever you say, master.'

'Take it anywhere you wish. I'm giving it to you.'

The woodcutter, unable to believe his ears, stared curiously at Mirza. 'Oh no, master. You shot it. Why should I be the one to eat it?'

'Not at all. I'm happy to let you have it. How far is your house from here?'

'About a mile, master.'

'Then I'll come along. I'd like to see how happy this makes your family.'

'I can't take it this way, sir. How can I just walk off with it when you've come from so far away to hunt in this terrific heat?'

'Pick it up, pick it up. Stop wasting time. I realize you're a deserving man.'

With fear and hesitation, keeping a cautious eye on Mirza to make sure he wasn't getting angry, the woodcutter started lifting the deer.

Then suddenly he let go of it, declaring, 'Now I understand, master! You didn't follow the Muslim ritual in killing it.'

Mirza chuckled. 'All right—now you know. So pick it up and take it home.'

Actually Mirza had no such religious scruples. He'd not said his prayers for ten years, and he fasted completely only once every two months. But he didn't want to spoil the satisfaction the woodcutter got in thinking that Mirza couldn't eat the deer for religious reasons. His conscience eased, the woodcutter hoisted the animal onto his shoulders and started for home. Tankha had been standing indifferently under a nearby tree. Why bother stepping out in the sun just to go see the deer? He had no idea of what had transpired. Seeing the woodcutter head in the opposite direction, however, he caught up with Mirza and said, 'Why are you going over there? Have you forgotten the way?'

Mirza gave a guilty smile. 'I've donated the animal to this poor man. I'm just going to his house for a moment. Why don't you come along?'

Tankha stared at him in astonishment. 'Are you out of your mind or something?'

'I can't say. I really don't know.'

'But why did you give him the animal?'

'Because he'll get a lot more pleasure out of it than either you or I would.'

'Very well then, go to his place,' Tankha grumbled. 'I thought we were going to gorge ourselves on mounds of kababs, but now you've spoiled all the fun. Oh well, the Rai Sahib and Mehta should turn up with something. No hard feelings. By the way, I have a little favour to ask you regarding this election. If you don't want to run—all right, that's your privilege. But what would you think of our getting a good price from the candidates while we're at it? I only ask you not to let anyone know you aren't running. Please do just that much for me. Khwaja Jamal Tahir is going to be a candidate from this constituency. The rich people will vote for him a hundred percent and the officials will also support him. Your influence over the general public, though, gives you an edge on him. If you're agreeable, you can make an easy ten or twenty thousand just by letting him know you'll throw your support towards him. Or let me do it for you. You don't have to do anything. Just relax and don't worry about a thing. I'll issue a statement on your behalf, and that very evening you can collect ten thousand rupees from me in cash.'

Mr Mirza looked at him contemptuously. 'You can go to hell, and that money too.'

Mr Tankha, not offended in the least, ignored the outburst. 'Curse me all you want. But cursing the money is only going to hurt yourself.'

'I consider that kind of money tainted.'

'Come off it ... you're not that strict in following your religion.'

'One doesn't have to be strict about his religion to believe that extortion money is tainted.'

'Then you won't reconsider your decision in this matter?'

'No.'

'Very well then, forget it. But you don't have any objection to being made director of an insurance company, do you? You won't have to buy even a single share in the company. Just give me permission to use your name.'

'Sorry, I can't agree to that either. I used to be a director of several companies, managing agent for others, and chairman of still others. I was wallowing in wealth. I'm fully aware of how much comfort and prestige money can buy. But I'm also aware of how much selfishness it brings—and how much love of luxury, deceit and indifference towards others.'

The lawyer didn't dare make any further proposals. By this time he had little faith left in Mirza's intelligence and influence. For him, money was everything, and he couldn't respect a man like this who'd kick the goddess of wealth herself.

The woodcutter bounded along with the deer on his shoulders. Mirza had also quickened his pace, while Tankha trailed sluggishly in the rear.

'Wait a minute, Mirza,' he called. 'You're practically running.'

'If this poor man can walk so fast with the load he's carrying,' Mirza replied without slowing down, 'shouldn't we be able to keep up with him when we're carrying only our own bodies?'

The woodcutter rested the deer on a stump and stopped to catch his breath.

'Tired?' Mirza asked.

'It's very heavy, sir,' the woodcutter apologized.

'Give it here then. I'll carry it awhile.'

The woodcutter laughed. Mirza reacted as though to a whiplash.

After all, he was considerably taller and brawnier than this scrawny fellow who was laughing at him. 'What's so funny? You think I can't lift it?'

'Sir, carrying loads is a job for common labourers like me, not for big men like yourselves.'

'I'm twice your size.'

'That makes no difference, master.'

Mirza could tolerate no further insult to his manhood. Stepping forward, he heaved the deer on his shoulders and started walking, but he had hardly gone fifty paces when he felt as though his neck were breaking. His legs began wobbling and butterflies seemed to be flitting in front of his eyes. With grim determination he covered another twenty paces. The carcass seemed filled with lead. It would be fun to dump it on Tankha's neck for a while. That fellow walking around puffed up like a bagpipe should be given a chance to share in the sport. But how could he set the load down so soon? Both of them would think he'd only been trying to display his strength. Fifty steps—and already calling it quits.

The woodcutter smiled. 'How are you doing, sir? Very light, isn't it?'

Mirza felt as though the load had eased a bit. 'I'll carry it as far as you did,' he insisted.

'You'll have a sore neck for days, master.'

'What do you think I am—a helpless weakling?'

'No sir, not any more. But please don't bother any further. Just set it down on that rock over there.'

'I can carry it at least this far again.'

'But I don't like walking along empty-handed this way while you're loaded down.'

Mr Mirza lowered the deer onto the rock. The lawyer meanwhile caught up with them and Mirza threw out the bait—'Now it's up to you to carry it a little way, my friend.'

Tankha had lost all respect for Mirza by this time. 'You'll have to excuse me,' he said. 'I make no claims to athletic ability.'

'It's not very heavy, honestly.'

'A likely story.'

'Look, if you'll carry it a hundred yards, I promise to accept all those proposals you were making.'

'I'm not going to get caught by your tricks.'

'I'm not trying to trick you. I'll stand for election in any constituency you say and withdraw whenever you say. I'll become a director, member, accountant or canvasser for any company you name. Just carry this a hundred yards. My friends must be able to rise to the demands of any occasion that arises.'

Tankha felt a tingle of excitement. Mirza would keep his word—no doubt about that. And the deer couldn't be so very heavy. After all, Mirza had carried it this far and he didn't seem terribly tired. To refuse might mean letting a golden opportunity slip through his fingers. And it wasn't as though this were a mountain or something. At most it might weigh twenty or twenty-five pounds. It would only mean a sore neck for three or four days, and with all that money in his pocket, a little discomfort would be a pleasure.

'Only a hundred yards?'

'That's right—a hundred yards. I'll come along and keep count.'

'You won't back out of the agreement?'

'A curse on me if I do.'

Tankha retied his shoelaces, handed his coat to the woodcutter, rolled up his pant-legs and wiped his face with a handkerchief. He eyed the deer as apprehensively as though it were a grindstone under which he was about to place his head. Then he took hold of the deer and tried to lift it onto his shoulders.

After straining two or three times, he got the carcass on his shoulders, but then he was unable to raise his neck. Bent over at the waist and gasping for breath, he was about to let it fall to the ground when Mirza propped him up and got him started forward.

Tankha took one step, his feet dragging as though stuck in a swamp. 'Congratulations!' Mirza urged him on. 'Well done, my lion!'

Tankha took a second step. He felt as though his neck were about to snap.

'Now you're winning. Keep going, tough guy.'

Tankha took two more steps. His eyes were bulging.

'Just dig in once more, my friend. Forget the agreement of a hundred yards. Make it only fifty.'

The lawyer was in bad shape, with the dead deer crushing him like a tiger sucking away his life blood. He summoned all his strength. Greed was the one thing supporting him, like an iron beam holding up a roof. The stakes were high—anywhere up to twenty-five thousand rupees. But in the end the beam failed him—even the power of greed was insufficient. Darkness enveloped his eyes. His head reeled and he fell to the ground, the carcass still on his shoulders.

Mirza immediately helped him up and then, fanning him with a handkerchief, thumped him on the back. 'You did your best, buddy,' he said, 'but fate must have been against you.'

Gasping for breath, Tankha sighed and said, 'You've nearly killed me today. The damn thing must weigh a good hundred and fifty pounds.'

Mirza laughed. 'But after all, old pal, I carried it this far myself.'

The lawyer began playing up to him. 'Well, I had to obey your request. You wanted some fun, so I obliged you. Now you must keep your promise.'

'Since when did you complete your part of the bargain?'

'I almost killed myself trying.'

'That's beside the point.'

The woodcutter picked up the deer again and set off at a fast pace, to show these people they were no match for him even if they did carry it, moaning and groaning, for a few paces. Despite his frailty, he was far ahead of them in this field, however good they might be at paper work or at arranging phony court cases.

They came to a shallow stream, on the far bank of which was a small settlement with five or six houses. A few children were playing under a tamarind tree. They ran to greet the woodcutter and began plying him with questions—'Who killed it, father?' 'How was it shot?' 'Where did it happen?' 'How did the bullet hit?' 'Where did it hit?' 'Why was only this one hit and none of the others?' The man mumbled a few brief answers as he set down the deer near the tamarind tree. Then he ran to a hut to get a cot for the two distinguished visitors. A swarm of children assumed charge of the animal, while some others tried to chase them away.

'It's ours,' said the smallest boy.

His big sister, some fourteen or fifteen years old, looked over at the guests. 'Shut up,' she scolded, 'or these people will grab you and carry you away.'

'It's ours, not yours,' Mirza teased the boy.

'But papa brought it,' the boy said, establishing his claim to the deer by sitting on it.

'Tell them it's theirs,' the sister instructed him.

The children's mother had been out gathering leaves for the goats. Seeing two unfamiliar gentlemen, she drew her veil slightly, embarrassed that her sari was so dirty, so ragged, and so haphazardly tied. She wondered how she could appear before these guests in such an outfit. Yet how could she avoid it? Water and things would have to be offered.

It was almost noon, but Mirza decided to spend the afternoon there. The villagers gathered. Liquor, *ghee* and flour were ordered from a nearby village market, the deer was cooked, and a feast was given for the entire village. Everyone joined in the festivities. The men drank a lot and went on singing happily until evening. As for Mirza, he became childish with the children, drunk with the drinkers, old with the elderly, and youthful with the young people. In his short stay there, he became as well acquainted with all the villagers as though this were his home. The boys climbed all over him, one trying on his tasselled cap, another strutting around with the rifle on his shoulder, and a third undoing his watch and strapping it on his own wrist. Mirza drank freely of the country liquor and swayed back and forth singing with these simple people.

At sunset, when the two men took leave, the villagers accompanied them for a long way. Several were crying. Never in their destitute lives had they been so fortunate as to be feasted by a hunter. He must be some kind of king ... who else would be so generous? And they'd probably never see him again.

After going some distance, Mirza looked around and said, 'How happy the poor things were. I wish to God there were such opportunities every day. This was really a wonderful day.'

'Wonderful for you, maybe,' Tankha responded unenthusiastically, 'but it was a miserable day for me. Nothing of any value was accomplished—just slogging across jungles and hills all day and then returning with nothing to show for it.'

'I have no sympathy for you,' Mirza said harshly.

By the time the two men reached the banyan tree, the other groups had already returned. Mehta looked unhappy. Malti, pouting, sat apart from the others—something unusual for her. The Rai Sahib and Khanna were still hungry, and speaking to no one. Tankha was upset because Mirza had made a fool of him. Only Mirza was happy, glowing with a kind of ethereal delight.

CHAPTER 8

EVER since the arrival of the cow, Hori's place had taken on a new air of prosperity. Dhaniya could hardly contain her pride, and talked about the animal all the time.

The supply of straw was almost exhausted, however. Some fodder which had been sown in with the sugar cane was being chopped up and fed to the cattle. Anxious eyes watched the sky, waiting for the rain that would make the grass grow again. It was the end of June and still no rain had fallen.

Then one day the clouds suddenly gathered, and burst into the first downpour of the season. The farmers had just gone out with their ploughs to sow the fall crop when word came from the Rai Sahib's agent that no one would be allowed to start ploughing his fields until all debts were paid. The announcement hit the villagers like a bolt of lightning. Never before had there been such unreasonable demands. Why this order now? No one was going to run away from the village. And if the land couldn't be ploughed, where was the money to come from? It could only come from the fields. Joining together, they went to plead with the agent, a man named Pandit Nokheram. He was not a bad man, but he said those were the master's orders and there was nothing he could do.

Just the other day the Rai Sahib had been expressing such generous and noble sentiments to Hori, and yet now he was treating his tenants so ruthlessly. Hori thought of going to see him, but then he realized that once the Rai Sahib had given his agent this order, he would be unlikely to withdraw it. So why incriminate himself by becoming the ringleader? If no one else was protesting, why should be jump into the fire? They were all in the same boat, and he'd manage somehow like the rest of them.

Panic seized the farmers and they ran to the village moneylenders for loans. Mangaru was especially popular. He'd made a good profit that year from hemp and had also done well in wheat and linseed. Pandit Datadin and the shopkeeper Dulari also made loans. But the biggest financier was Jhinguri Singh, who represented a rich money-lender in the city. He had several men under him who went around the neighbouring villages making loans. There were also a number of lesser moneylenders who dispensed money with no written contracts, at interest rates of two annas on the rupee per month. As a matter of fact, the villagers were so fond of borrowing money that anyone who collected ten or twenty rupees could set himself up as a moneylender. Hori had once done that himself. As a result, people asssumed he must still have money hidden away. Where else could it have gone? After all, none had appeared when the family split up, and he'd made no pilgrimages, taken no vows and given no feasts. So if the money was exhausted, where had it been spent? A man's shoes may be gone, but he still has the corns on his feet to testify that they were once there.

The villagers rushed to appease these god-like benefactors, some agreeing to interest of one anna on the rupee, others to two annas. Not having lost all self-respect, Hori couldn't bring himself to face his old creditors. That left him only Jhinguri Singh, who would insist on having proper documents drawn up and would charge a commission, an additional gratuity, and a fee for preparing the document. On top of that, the first year's interest would be deducted in advance. So out of a bond for twenty-five rupees, he'd be lucky to get his hands on seventeen. But what alternative was there at such a desperate time? If it weren't for the heavy hand of the Rai Sahib, there'd be no need to beg from anyone.

Jhinguri Singh was sitting brushing his teeth with a twig. He looked like a clown—a short, fat, bald dark man with a long nose and a big moustache. And he *was* quite a joker as a matter of fact, calling the village the home of his in-laws and thereby assuming the right to make disparaging remarks about all the men as brothers-in-law or fathers-in-law, and about all the women as sisters-in-law or mothers-in-law. 'Oh, Panditji, let us touch your feet!' children would taunt him on the street. And Jhinguri Singh would shout back his blessing—'May you go blind! May your knees break! May you get epilepsy! May your house catch fire!' and so forth, delighting the children no end. In business matters, however, he showed no mercy, extorting the last pice of interest and camping on people's doorsteps until they produced the money.

Hori salaamed and recited his tale of woe.

126

Jhinguri Singh smiled. 'What have you done with that fortune you used to have?'

'If I had a fortune, thakur, would my neck still be in the clutches of the moneylenders? Or do you think people like to pay interest?'

'You probably wouldn't dig up your buried treasure no matter how much interest you were having to pay. That's the way you people are.'

'Just where would I have buried treasure, sahib? I don't even have anything to eat. My boy's grown up now and we can't even afford to get him married. My older girl should be getting married too. If I had money, why would I be keeping it buried?'

Jhinguri Singh had been itching to get his hands on the cow ever since he saw her at Hori's door. Her size and good health indicated that she'd give at least five quarts of milk a day, and he had decided there and then that he must somehow get Hori in a tight spot and make off with the cow. Now he saw his chance.

'All right, brother,' he said, 'I believe you—you don't have a thing. You can have all the money you want. But I'm telling you for your own good—if you have jewellery or anything, you'd be wise to mortgage it. If you sign for a formal loan, the interest will pile up and you'll find yourself in trouble.'

Hori swore they hadn't even a plain piece of thread for an ornament. Dhaniya did have a couple of bangles, but they weren't real gold.

Jhinguri Singh assumed a sympathetic look. 'Well then,' he said, 'here's what you can do—sell me that cow you just bought. Save yourself all the bother of interest and legal papers. Get some villagers to set a price and I'll pay it. I know you bought it for your own pleasure and naturally you don't want to sell it. But you've got to find some way out of your difficulties.'

Hori first laughed at the suggestion, unwilling to take it seriously. But the thakur was so persuasive, and portrayed the tactics of the moneylending business in such a terrifying way, that this alternate proposal began to take root in his mind. What the thakur said was true—he could buy back the cow when he got some money. Otherwise, if he signed a paper for thirty rupees, he'd get only about twenty-five, and if that wasn't paid up in three or four years, the sum would have grown to a full hundred. He knew from experience that debt is a guest who, having once arrived, stays on forever.

'I'd better go home and discuss it,' he said. 'I'll let you know.'

'There's no need for discussion. Just tell them there's no other way to get the money without ruining yourselves.'

'I see what you mean, thakur. I'll be back with an answer right away.'

But when Hori got home, a storm of protest greeted the proposal. Dhaniya didn't say much, but the two girls acted as though it were the end of the world. No matter how the money had to be obtained, they were not going to give up their cow. Sona went so far as to declare that she'd rather they sold her . . . and she'd bring more than the cow too!'

Both girls were ready to give their lives for the cow. Rupa used to hang on its neck; and she never took a bite of food without first giving some to the animal. It would lick her hand so lovingly, and look at her with such tender eyes. And how beautiful the calf would be. It had already been given a name—Matru. Rupa had announced that it was going to sleep with her. The sisters had already quarrelled several times, each insisting that the cow loved her more. The question was not yet settled, so both claims still stood.

But Hori explained the situation backward and forward until at last Dhaniya consented reluctantly. To borrow a cow from a friend and then sell it was rather sneaky, but in a crisis people had even been known to violate their religions. So what was so terrible about this? Crisis was bound to involve things like this, or people wouldn't fear it so much. Gobar raised no great objections, being absorbed in other matters these days. It was decided that the cow should be taken to Jhinguri Singh as soon as the girls fell asleep that night.

The day dragged to a close. Evening came. About eight, the two girls had their dinner and went to bed. Gobar had run off somewhere to avoid the pitiful sight. How could he stay and watch the cow being taken away? How could he hold back his tears? Hori appeared composed, but his heart was greatly disturbed too. There was nothing else to be done, though, since no one around would be kind enough to loan him twenty-five rupees even if he agreed to pay back fifty. Standing in front of the cow, he thought he could see her expressive dark eyes filling with tears as though to say he'd promised not to sell her as long as he lived. . . . 'Are you tired of me already after only four days? I've never complained about anything, eating contentedly whatever scraps you gave me. What do you have to say?'

'The girls are asleep now,' Dhaniya said. 'You'd better take her and go. If she has to be sold, then let's get it over with.'

'I can't bring myself to do it, Dhaniya,' Hori said, his voice trembling. 'Don't you see her face? Let her stay. I'll take the loan, interest and all. God willing, we'll pay off the whole thing. What's three or four hundred, after all, once the sugar cane crop comes up?'

Dhaniya looked at him with loving pride. 'You're doing the right thing. We've sacrificed so much to get a cow . . . how could we sell it? Take a loan tomorrow. We can pay off the debt the same way we do the others.'

It was stifling inside the house. Outside, there was not a breath of wind; not a leaf was stirring. Clouds had gathered but there was no sign of rain. Hori took the cow and tied her outside. 'Where are you taking her?' Dhaniya protested.

Hori brushed her aside. 'I'm tying her outdoors where there's a little air. She'll be more comfortable there. After all, she has feelings too.'

Having tethered the cow, Hori went off to see his brother Shobha, who'd been suffering from asthma for several months and could not afford treatment. Since he had to keep toiling in order to eat, his health was deteriorating daily. Shobha was a tolerant sort of man who avoided quarrels, minding his own business and not worrying about anyone else. Hori liked him, and he in turn respected Hori. They began to discuss financial matters, the focus of concern being the Rai Sahib's recent edict.

Hori returned about eleven o'clock, and was just going inside when he thought he saw someone standing near the cow. 'Who's that over there?' he asked.

'Just me, brother,' Hira answered. 'I came to get a light from your fire.'

So Hira, his youngest brother, had come for a light from his fire! To Hori, this little gesture was a sign of their bond as brothers. There were plenty of other fires in the village—he could have lit his chilam from any of them. His coming to this fire showed that he thought of it as his own. True, the whole village came here to start their fires, since Hori's house had the best fire-pit around; but Hira's coming was a different matter, especially after that fight the other day. Hira never holds a grudge, thought Hori. However hot-tempered he may be, he's a good man at heart.

'Do you have tobacco or shall I bring you some?' Hori asked in a friendly tone.

'No, I have tobacco, dada.'

'Shobha's in real bad shape today.'

'What does he expect when he won't take any medicine? According to him all vaidyas, doctors and hakims are quacks. He thinks God gave all the wisdom in the world to him and his wife.'

'That's just the trouble with him,' Hori said anxiously. 'He pays no attention to anyone. And of course we all get irritated easily when we're sick. Do you remember when you had the flu? You picked up the medicine and threw it out. I used to grab your hands while my wife forced the medicine down your throat, and then you'd curse her in a thousand ways.'

'Yes, dada, how could I ever forget that? If you hadn't done all that for me, I'd never have been spared to fight with you now.'

It seemed to Hori that Hira's voice was choked with emotion, and he felt a lump rising in his own throat. 'Fighting and quarrelling are a natural part of life, brother. They shouldn't make strangers of one's own people. When a family lives together there are bound to be arguments. If a man had no relatives, he'd have no one to fight with.'

They shared a smoke. Then Hira went home and Hori went inside to have his dinner.

'Do you realize how your son is carrying on?' Dhaniya stormed. 'At this hour of the night he's still out roaming around. I know all about it. I found out the whole story. You know that slut Jhuniya, the widowed daughter of Bhola? Well he's falling into her clutches.'

Rumours of this had already reached Hori's ears, but he'd dismissed them. What would poor Gobar know of such things?

'Who told you that?' Hori demanded.

Dhaniya snorted. 'I suppose you know nothing about it even though the whole village is discussing it. He's a dumbbell, while she's an old hand at this sort of thing. She has him dancing on her fingers and he thinks she can't live without him. You'd better straighten him out or something bad is likely to happen and then where'll you be?'

Hori was in a good mood and thought he would tease her. 'Jhuniya's not bad looking, you know. He ought to marry her. Where else could we get him such a cheap wife?'

This joking struck Dhaniya like an arrow. 'If Jhuniya sets foot in this house I'll scald her face, the whore! If he's so crazy about her, let him take her and live wherever he likes.'

'And if he brings her here?'

'Then who'd ever marry our two daughters? The caste people would have nothing to do with you. No one would even come near our door.'

'What would he care?'

'I'm not going to give up my boy that easily. I kill myself raising him and then Jhuniya thinks she can come and start lording it over me. That widow! I'll throw hot coals in her mouth!'

Just then Gobar rushed in, a worried look on his face. 'Father! What's happened to Sundariya? Has she been bitten by a cobra? She's lying out there rolling in agony.'

Hori pushed aside the thali from which he'd been eating. 'What's that awful thing you're saying? I just saw her on my way in. She was lying down.'

Taking a lamp, the three of them went out to see what had happened. Foam was coming from Sundariya's mouth. Her eyes were glazed, her belly was bloated, and her legs were spread out stiffly. Dhaniya began tearing her hair in despair. Hori ran for Pandit Datadin, the village veterinary expert. The pandit was sleeping, but he roused himself and came running. In a flash the whole village had gathered. Someone had fed the cow something. It was obvious from the symptoms that she'd been poisoned. But who could be the culprit? The village had never known such an outrage. But what outsider could have come in? Hori had no enemies who could be suspected. There had been a bit of a row with Hira, but that was just a family spat. And Hira was acting more upset than anyone else, threatening that if he got hold of the killer he'd drink his blood. Hira was terribly hot-headed, but he couldn't possibly stoop to such a vile act.

The crowd hung around until midnight, sympathizing with Hori's affliction and cursing the unknown killer. If he'd been caught then, it would have been too bad for him. As it was, no one dared tie his animals outside now. Previously the cattle had always been left out overnight and no one had thought anything about it. Now they were faced with a new menace. And what a cow this had been—you couldn't take your eyes off her. She deserved to be worshipped. Gave no less than five quarts of milk. Each calf would have been worth a hundred. Such a short time she had been here and now this blow had struck.

When all the villagers had gone home, Dhaniya turned on Hori. 'You think you're so smart, always doing just what you please. I kept warning you not to take the cow outside, even when you were leading her out of the courtyard. I told you these are bad times for us, that anything might happen. But no, it would be too warm for her inside. Well she's cool enough now, and your heart should be well chilled too. The thakur wanted her. If you'd given her to him, it would have meant a load off our shoulders and he'd have been obligated to us besides. This blow would never have fallen. When something bad's about to happen, men lose all their good sense. All this time the cow had been tied up inside perfectly happily, not feeling the heat or the cold. She'd come to recognize us all so quickly that she didn't seem like a newcomer at all. The children would play with her horns and she wouldn't even toss her head. Whatever was put in her trough, she'd lick it clean. She was like Lakshmi herself. How could she be expected to stay on in such an unlucky house!'

Gobar and the two girls finally cried themselves to sleep. Hori lay down also. When Dhaniya came to set a pot of water by the head of his bed, Hori whispered, 'You can't keep anything to yourself. Anything you happen to hear, you rush around announcing to the whole village.'

'Now tell me,' Dhaniya protested. 'Just what have I been spreading around, for you to accuse me this way?'

'All right then. Do you suspect anyone?'

'I don't suspect anyone. It must have been an outsider.'

'You won't tell anybody?'

'If I don't keep telling tales,' she retorted sarcastically, 'then the villagers will stop having ornaments made for me!'

'If you tell anyone, I'll kill you.'

'Killing me isn't going to make you happy. You'd never get another wife. As long as I'm around, your house will be kept in order. The day I die, you'll start weeping and wailing. Right now you think I'm all bad, but you'll be sorry then.'

'Hira's the one I suspect.'

'You're wrong, dead wrong. Hira's not as low as all that. He just has a foul mouth.'

'I saw him with my own eyes. I swear it by your head.'

'You saw him with your own eyes? When?'

'Right after I came back from seeing Shobha. He was standing near Sundariya's trough. I asked who was there and he said it was just he, Hira, come to get a light from our fire. He stayed and talked to me for a while. Gave me his chilam to smoke. He went off, I came inside, and then Gobar started shouting. Seems to me that he must have come and fed her something after I'd tied her up and gone to Shobha's house. He probably came back again to see if she was dead yet.'

Dhaniya sucked in her breath. 'So that's the kind of brothers you have—men who don't even hesitate to cut their own brother's throat. So Hira's heart is as black as all that, is that? And to think I was the one who fed and raised the bastard!'

'All right, now go get some sleep. But don't forget and go mentioning this to anyone.'

'Who, me? If I don't drag him to the police station the first thing in the morning then I'm not my father's daughter. That murderer isn't fit to be called a brother. He's an enemy, an out and out enemy —and the sin is to spare an enemy, not to kill one.'

'I'm telling you, Dhaniya,' Hori threatened, 'there'll just be trouble.'

'Trouble hell!' Dhaniya raged. 'There's going to be more than trouble. I won't rest until I've had him sent to jail. I'll have him turning the grindstone for three years ... three years. And when he gets out, he'll be branded a murderer. He'll have to take a pilgrimage and give a feast. He's not going to get away with this atrocity. And I'll get you to swear on your son's head that you were an eyewitness.'

She went in and slammed the door. Hori lay there cursing himself. If he hadn't been able to keep this to himself, how could he expect Dhaniya to? That witch wouldn't think of listening to him any longer. Now that her mind was made up, she wouldn't listen to anyone. He had just made the biggest mistake of his life. ...

The dark night was wrapped in stillness, broken only by an occasional tinkling from the little bells on the necks of the two bullocks. Ten steps away lay the dead cow. Hori tossed restlessly, wretched with remorse. No ray of light relieved the darkness.

CHAPTER 9

By sunrise Hori's house was in a complete uproar. Hori was beating Dhaniya. Dhaniya was cursing him. The two girls were clinging to their father's legs and screaming. Gobar was trying to protect his mother. Time after time he would grab Hori's hand and push him back, but as soon as Dhaniya let fly another curse, Hori would free his hands and give her a few more kicks and blows. Anger seemed to have tapped some hidden source of strength in his old body.

The commotion aroused the whole village. People came to watch the fun on the pretext of trying to reason with Hori. Shobha appeared, leaning on his stick. 'What's all this, Hori?' Datadin scolded. 'Have you gone mad or something? Lifting your hand that way against the Lakshmi of your own home! You weren't like this before—have you caught the disease from Hira?'

Hori touched the pandit's feet and said, 'Maharaj, please don't say anything just now. I'm going to break her of this bad habit today, once and for all. Then I'll let her alone. The more I give in to her, the more insolent she becomes.'

Dhaniya spoke up through angry tears—'You be the witness, maharaj. I won't rest until I've sent him and his murderous brother to jail. His brother poisoned our cow. I was just going to report him to the police when this fiend started beating me. This is the reward he gives me for devoting my life to him.'

Hori glared at her. 'There you go saying it again. Did you see Hira give the cow poison?'

'All right then—can you swear you didn't see Hira standing near the cow's trough?'

'I didn't see him, I swear.'

'Put your hand on your son's head and swear it.'

Hori placed a trembling hand on Gobar's head and said in a quavering voice, 'I swear on my son's life that I didn't see Hira near the cow's trough.'

Dhaniya spat on the ground. 'You're a damn liar. You told me yourself that Hira was standing like a thief near the trough. And now you're lying to protect your brother. Damn you! If harm comes to even a hair on my son's head because of your lies, I'll burn the house down. God! To think that a man would say something and then deny it so shamelessly!'

Hori slammed his foot down. 'Don't get me angry, Dhaniya, or there'll be trouble.'

'You're already beating me. Keep it up all you like. If you're your father's son, you won't rest until the job is finished. The brute has already beaten me to a pulp and still he's not satisfied. He thinks beating me makes him a big hero. But in front of his brothers he's like a bedraggled cat. Sinner! Murderer!'

She burst into tears and began a wailing recital of all the woes she'd endured since coming to his house—how she'd skimped and starved—how she had slaved over every scrap of clothing—how she had hoarded every pice as though it were life itself—how she had fed the whole family and then gone to bed after having only a drink of water herself. . . . And this was the reward for all those sacrifices! That God who had left Paradise and come running to save *Draupadi* and even an elephant—why was he lost in sleep now?

The spectators' sympathies gradually veered towards Dhaniya. No one doubted any longer that it was Hira who had poisoned the cow. They were all convinced that Hori had sworn a false oath. Even Gobar turned against his father, fearing the disastrous consequences of that treacherous curse. On top of this there was Datadin's condemnation. Hori was utterly defeated. He quietly went inside. Truth had been victorious.

'Do you know anything about what happened, Shobha?' Datadin inquired.

Shobha was stretched out on the ground, resting. 'I, maharaj? I've not been out of the house for eight days. My brother Hori has been coming to see me from time to time—I get by on whatever he brings. He came to my place last night too. But if anyone did anything, I know nothing about it. Wait a minute though—Hira did come over last evening to borrow a trowel. Said he wanted to dig up a small root. But I've not seen him since.'

Seizing this bit of corroboration, Dhaniya declared, 'You see, Panditji—it was obviously Hira's doing. He borrowed that trowel from Shobha, dug up a root of some kind and fed it to the cow.

He's been waiting for revenge ever since that fight we had the other night.'

'If this charge can be proved, he'll have to bear the full consequences of the sin of cowslaughter. Whether the police do anything or not, the moral law demands his punishment. Rupa, go call Hira and bring him here. Tell him the pandit has sent for him. If he's innocent of the crime, then let him take some Ganges water and make an oath on it at the temple altar.'

'But maharaj,' protested Dhaniya, 'his oath can't be trusted. He'll swear to his innocence easily enough. When my husband here, who's so religious, has sworn a false oath, why should we trust Hira?'

Now Gobar spoke up. 'Let him swear falsely. Let the family come to an end. Let the old people go on living. What do the young people have to live for?'

Rupa was back in a moment. 'Uncle isn't at home, Pandit dada! Auntie says he's gone away somewhere.'

'Didn't you ask her where he'd gone?' Datadin inquired, stroking his long beard. 'Maybe he's hiding in the house. You go look, Sona —and make sure he's not inside somewhere.'

'Don't send her, dada,' Dhaniya interrupted. 'Hira's in a mood for murder. No telling what he might do.'

Datadin himself hobbled off on his stick and brought back word that Hira had indeed disappeared. 'Punni said he left, taking his sacred thread, pot, stick—everything. She asked where he was going but he wouldn't say. The five rupees she'd been keeping in a niche in the wall are gone. He must have taken them also.'

'He blackened his name, so now he's run off somewhere,' Dhaniya said bitterly.

'Where could he run to?' Shobha said. 'Maybe he's gone to bathe in the Ganges.'

Dhaniya disagreed. 'Why would he have taken the money if he were going to the Ganges? And besides, there's no festival on right now.'

The suspicion could not be dispelled. Belief in Hira's guilt was firmly established.

No food was cooked in Hori's house that day, nor did anyone tend the bullocks. The whole village buzzed with excitement. Small groups gathered, discussing the matter. Hira certainly must have run away somewhere. He evidently realized that his crime had been exposed, that he would be sent to jail and that he would also have to suffer the moral consequences of his sin. So he had run off, disappeared without a word, leaving Punni behind, weeping.

The only touch still lacking was supplied that evening by the arrival of the regional police inspector. The village watchman had reported the incident, as was his duty. The Inspector was not one to shirk his duties either. Now it was up to the villagers to do their duty by providing him with a proper reception. Datadin, Jhinguri Singh, Mangaru and Lala Pateshwari, Nokheram and his four men—all of them came and stood with folded hands before the Inspector. Hori was summoned. This was his first appearance before the police, and he was as frightened as though being led to the gallows. While beating Dhaniya that morning, his limbs had swelled with excitement, but in the presence of the Inspector, they shrank up like the legs of a turtle. The Inspector's critical look penetrated all the way to his heart. The Inspector was highly experienced in evaluating men's nerve, an expert in practical psychology though he knew nothing of the subject academically. One glance at Hori and he was sure this would be one of his good days. Hori's face showed that one threat would be sufficient.

'Whom do you suspect?' asked the Inspector.

Hori touched the ground, folded his hands respectfully and said, 'I don't suspect anyone, your honour. The cow died of her own accord. She was getting old.'

Dhaniya had come along with Hori and was standing behind him. 'The cow was killed,' she interjected, 'and by your brother Hira. This gentleman is not so foolish as to believe whatever you tell him. He's come here to investigate.'

'Who is this woman?' the Inspector asked.

Answers tumbled in from all sides, everyone being eager to have the good fortune of exchanging a few words with the Inspector. By all speaking at once, each satisfied himself that he had spoken first— 'This is Hori's wife, your honour.'

'Well, call her here. I'll take down her story first. Where is this Hira?'

'He's been away ever since morning, sir,' the village elders chorused.

'I must have his house searched.'

A search! Hori's heart sank. His brother Hira's house to be searched while he was away! Well, any such search would be over Hori's dead body! And as of now he was through with Dhaniya.

She could go wherever she liked, but he couldn't have her living in his house after she had deliberately disgraced him this way. Maybe she'd get wise if she had to stumble around through the alleys for a while.

The village leaders began to whisper among themselves, looking for a way to avert this great calamity.

'It's all just a trick to get some money,' Datadin said, shaking his bald head. 'Everyone knows there's nothing to be found in Hira's house.'

Pateshwari Lal, no fool despite his great height, made his long dark face even longer. 'Well what do you think he came here for? And now that he's come, do you think he's going to leave without a little something to show for it?'

Jhinguri Singh called Hori over and whispered in his ear, 'You'd better give him whatever you have to. Otherwise you'll never get your neck out of this....'

'I'm going to search Hira's house,' the Inspector growled again.

Hori's face turned as pale as though all his blood had dried up. It was all the same thing whether his brother's house or his own were searched. Hira had separated from him, that was true, but the world knew they were still brothers. But he was helpless now. If he had any money, he'd have brought fifty rupees and laid it at the Inspector's feet, saying, 'Sir, my honour is in your hands.' But he didn't even have a pice to buy poison for himself. Dhaniya might have three or four rupees laid away somewhere but the witch certainly wouldn't part with it. Hori stood there silently, enduring the agony of this public humiliation, his head bowed like that of a man being sentenced to death.

'Nothing's going to be accomplished by your standing around this way, Hori,' Datadin warned. 'Find a way to give him some money.'

'What can I do, maharaj,' Hori replied abjectly. 'I'm already so weighed down with old debts—who can I borrow anything more from? Please save me from this disaster. I'll pay back every cowrie as sure as I'm alive. And if I should die, there'd still be Gobar to repay you.'

The elders went into consultation again to decide how much the Inspector should be offered. Datadin proposed fifty rupees. Jhinguri Singh felt the matter couldn't be settled for less than a hundred. Nokheram also argued for a hundred. As for Hori, it made no difference to him whether it took fifty or a hundred, as long as the

138

catastrophe of a search could be averted. Whatever the cost, one must make offerings to the gods. It makes no difference to a corpse whether he's cremated with a hundred pounds of wood or a thousand.

Pateshwari couldn't bear to see such injustice, however. It was not as though Hori had committed a robbery or a murder after all. The police were only going to conduct a search. Twenty rupees was plenty for that.

The others were contemptuous. 'All right then, you go talk with the Inspector. We'll stay out of it. We don't want to get on his black list.'

Hori touched his forehead to Pateshwari's feet. 'Save me, my brother. I'll be your slave the rest of my life.'

Summoning all the strength of his broad chest and even broader belly, the Inspector bellowed—'Where is that Hira's house? I'm going to search it.'

Pateshwari stepped forward and whispered in the Inspector's ear, 'What would you get out of a search, sir? The man's brother is here at your service.'

The two men moved away from the crowd and began to confer.

'What kind of man is he?'

'Extremely poor, your honour. He can't even scrape up enough for a decent meal.'

'Is that the truth?'

'Yes, sir. I'm telling you honestly.'

'Can't he produce even a miserable fifty rupees?'

'Not a chance, your honour! To get ten from him would be like getting a thousand. It would take him fifty lifetimes to collect fifty rupees—and even then, only if some moneylender advanced the money.'

The Inspector reflected a moment. 'Well, there's no use in hounding him then. I'm not one to harass people who are already dying.'

Pateshwari realized that he had overshot his mark. 'Oh now don't look at it that way, sir. Where would that leave us? This sort of thing is our only source of income.'

'What are you talking about? You're the revenue clerk for this region, aren't you?'

'Yes, but it's only when opportunities like this arise that, thanks to your kindness, we're able to make something too. At other times, who cares about a *patwari*?'

'All right then, get me thirty rupees—twenty for me, ten for you.'

'Oh please, there are four of us to consider. . . .'

'Very well, make it half and half. Be quick about it. I'm late already.'

Pateshwari spoke to Jhinguri, who beckoned Hori to follow him to his house. He counted out thirty rupees, handed it to Hori and, impressing him with the obligation involved, said, 'You can sign the paper later today. I'm giving you the money on faith because I can tell by looking at you that you're an honest man.'

Beaming happily, Hori tied up the money in a corner of his scarf and went back to give it to the Inspector.

Suddenly Dhaniya sprang in front of him and with a lunge snatched the scarf from his hand. The loose knot jerked open and the money fell to the ground. Dhaniya hissed like a cobra. 'Where do you think you're taking this money? Speak up. I'm warning you—if you know what's good for you, you'll return it all right now. Here we are starving at home, longing for just a grain of food, with nothing to wear, and you go around tossing out handfuls of money just to save your honour. You think you have that much honour left to be saved? I suppose you call a house filled with rats honourable! The Inspector is only going to make a search. Let him search all he wants. Here we've lost a cow worth a hundred rupees, and yet you're trying to put us still further in debt. To hell with your honour!'

Hori swallowed his anger and kept still. The whole crowd trembled before her. The leaders hung their heads. The Inspector cringed—he'd never before been dealt such an insult.

Hori just stood there, stunned. This was the first time that Dhaniya had defeated him in a public arena—right there in the open with everyone watching. How could he ever hold up his head again?

But the Inspector was not one to give up so easily. 'It appears to me,' he snapped angrily, 'that this sister of the devil poisoned the cow herself just to get Hori in trouble.'

'Sure I did,' Dhaniya retorted, gesturing defiantly. 'But it was my own cow I killed. At least I don't go around poisoning other people's cattle. If that's what your investigation shows, go ahead and write it down. Slap the handcuffs on me. I've seen what your justice is like —and your brains too. Cutting the throats of the poor is easy enough. But separating milk from water, running an honest investigation, is something else again.'

Hori, eyes blazing, rushed at Dhaniya, but Gobar jumped between then and said sternly, 'All right, father, that's enough. Get back or I

warn you—you'll never see me again. I won't lift a hand at
you—I'm not such a bad son as all that. But I'll hang mysel
here in your presence.'

Hori stepped back, and Dhaniya, becoming a tigress again, shouted,
'You keep out of this, Gobar. I want to see just how far he'll go. Let
the Inspector here be a witness. Let's see how brave he is. He's going to
lose face by allowing that house to be searched, but not by kicking
his own wife right here in front of everyone! So that's what it takes
to be a hero! If you're really brave, go fight with a man. You can't
be called brave just for beating up the wife you took by the arm and
brought home to cherish. You must think you can do whatever you
like, just because you feed and clothe me. Well from now on you can
take care of the house yourself. I'll stay right here in the village and
shame you—just wait and see. And I'll be better fed and dressed than
ever before. See if I'm not!'

Hori was defeated, realizing the weakness and helplessness of a
man when confronted by a woman.

The village leaders meanwhile had gathered up the coins and were
beckoning the Inspector to come away. Dhaniya gave them a parting
kick—'Go on, take the money and give it back to whomever it belongs. We're not borrowing from anyone. If someone thinks he has
to pay, let him do so himself. I won't give up a single pice even if
you drag me into court. When we wanted twenty-five rupees to pay
the rent, no one would loan it to us. Today you're giving out whole
handfuls of jingling coins. I know what's going on. You're all full of
sweetness now that you're each going to get a cut. Murderers and
blood-suckers, that's what you village headmen are. Interest rates
of twenty-five and fifty per cent, tips and donations, bribes and graft
—rob the poor any way you can!'

The village elders looked as though their faces had been smeared
with tar, and the Inspector as though his had been beaten with a
broom. To preserve their dignity, they turned and marched off towards Hira's house.

'That woman certainly has guts,' the Inspector conceded when
they were on their way.

'Guts, your honour?' Pateshwari said. 'A brazen slut, that's what
she is. Women like that should be shot.'

'Well, she certainly put you all in a bad spot. If it hadn't been for
her, you'd each have pocketed four rupees.'

'Your fifteen rupees disappeared too though, sir.'

'Mine hasn't disappeared anywhere. If he doesn't pay it, then the heads of the village will—and fifty, rather than fifteen rupees! You people better hurry up and take care of the matter.'

Pateshwari Lal chuckled. 'You have a great sense of humour, your honour.'

'That's a sign of greatness,' Datadin added. 'And great men are so rare these days.'

'Save your flattery,' the Inspector barked. 'Get me that fifty rupees right now—and in cash. And get this straight—if you dawdle around, I'll have all your houses searched. You probably cooked up this whole plot just to incriminate Hira and Hori and squeeze fifty or a hundred out of them.'

They still thought the Inspector must be joking. Jhinguri Singh winked at Pateshwari and said, 'All right, Patwari, out with fifty rupees!'

'That's right,' Nokheram agreed. 'The patwari should take care of your hospitality—it's his district.'

By this time they had reached the entrance to Pandit Nokheram's house. Seating himself on a cot, the Inspector said, 'Well, what have you all decided? Are you going to produce the money or do you want your houses searched?'

'But your honour....' Datadin protested.

'I don't want to hear any if's or but's.'

Jhinguri Singh mustered his courage. 'Sir, this is absolutely....'

'I'm giving you fifteen minutes. If I don't have the full fifty rupees in that time, you four will have your houses searched. And you know me—Ganda Singh! After I beat someone he's in no condition even to beg for water.'

'Go ahead and search our houses—that's your privilege,' Pateshwari Lal snapped. 'Big joke! One person commits a crime and someone else gets the blame.'

'You realize I've been with the police for twenty-five years?'

'But we've never been treated so ruthlessly before....'

'You don't even know what ruthlessness is, but I'll be happy to show you if you want. I'll have each of you sent up for five years—I could do that with just my left hand. I could have the whole village deported to the Andaman Islands for gang robbery. Don't fool yourselves about that!'

The four men scurried inside to talk over the matter. What

happened next, nobody knows—but soon the Inspector was beaming happily, while the four gentlemen looked thoroughly cowed.

When the Inspector mounted his horse and started off, the four leaders ran alongside. But then the horse galloped off and they turned back, looking as stricken as though returning from the cremation of some dear friend.

'If my curse doesn't fall on him, I'll never show my face again,' Datadin muttered.

Nokheram. nodded. 'I've never seen that kind of wealth pay off in the long run.'

'What's earned by extortion will be lost the same way,' Pateshwari prophesied.

Jhinguri Singh expressed doubts about the justice of God. How could the Almighty witness such tyranny and not punish the offenders!

The looks on their faces would have delighted an artist.

CHAPTER 10

———

Days passed with no news of Hira. Hori searched around for him as best he could, but finally gave it up as hopeless. Besides, he had to pay some attention to his fields—and even more to those of Punni. Anyway, what could one man do? Punni had become more irascible than ever now that she was alone, and Hori had to spend his time pacifying her. When Hira had been there, he'd kept a firm hand on her, but there was no check on her now that he was away.

Hori and Hira owned some land jointly. Punni was helpless—how could she fight for her rights? Being familiar with Hori's personality, she exploited his good nature. Fortunately the agent had not pressed her for the balance of the land rent. An occasional gift kept him quiet. If necessary, however, Hori was ready to take a loan for settling her debts as well as his own. In late July there was such a rush to transplant the rice that workers were unobtainable and Hori couldn't get his own fields planted; but he couldn't very well neglect Punni's fields and he worked day and night transplanting her rice. After all, he was now her only protector, and the world would mock him if any trouble came to her. The result was that Hori harvested only a meagre autumn crop, whereas Punni's barn was filled to overflowing.

The feud between Hori and Dhaniya continued unabated, and Gobar and Hori were not on speaking terms either. The mother and son seemed to have teamed up to ostracize him. Hori had become a stranger in his own home, suffering the unfortunate consequences of a man trying to ride in two boats at the same time. Where Hori's prestige in the village had declined, however, Dhaniya by her courage had won the respect not only of the village women but even of the men. For months the incident with the Inspector was the talk of the whole region—so much so that supernatural elements were added to the story. 'Dhaniya's the woman's name,' people would say. 'She's blessed by the goddess *Bhavani*. The moment the Inspector slapped the handcuffs on her husband, she called on Bhavani and the goddess

144

entered her head. Such strength filled her body that she immediately snapped the handcuffs, tore the whiskers out of the Inspector's moustache, and then sat on his chest. Only after a lot of pleading did she let him go.'

For some time people came to be blessed by a glimpse of Dhaniya. After a while the excitement died down, but her esteem in the village remained very high. She was said to have fantastic courage and to be capable of silencing any man who dared oppose her.

A change gradually came over Dhaniya, however. Even when she watched Hori devoting himself to Punni's fields she said nothing, not because she was indifferent about him but because she too had begun to feel sorry for Punni. Her desire for revenge had been sufficiently appeased by Hira's desertion.

Then Hori came down with a fever brought on by the change of weather, and he suffered in full for having escaped such fevers the last several years. For a month he was confined to bed. The disease crushed Hori, of course, but it also subdued Dhaniya completely. How could she be angry at her husband when he lay dying? At such times even enemies can't cling to their hatred—and this was her own husband. However bad he might be, she'd spent twenty-five years of her life with him, sharing times of sorrow and of happiness. And whether he be good or bad, he was hers. The old wretch had beaten her in front of everyone, but he'd been so ashamed ever since that he wouldn't even look her in the eye, coming in to eat and going through the meal with his head bowed for fear of provoking her. By the time Hori had recovered, the husband and wife were reconciled.

'How could you have gotten so angry?' Dhaniya asked one day. 'No matter how furious I get, I could never raise a hand against you.'

'Don't bring that up again, Dhaniya,' Hori said apologetically. 'Some demon must have taken hold of me. You can't imagine how I've suffered for it since.'

'And if I'd drowned myself in desperation?'

'You think I'd have stayed behind to mourn? My corpse would have joined yours on the funeral pyre.'

'That's enough now. Don't talk so lightly about such evil-omened things.'

'Well, if the cow's gone, she's gone. But she certainly left misfortune on my head. This worry about Punni is killing me.'

'That's why people say the eldest son in a family is not created by

God. No one blames the younger ones for anything, but the eldest is held responsible for whatever happens, good or bad.'

It was the month of Magh, damp and cold. The heavy clouds and January rain deepened the gloom of the dark winter night. A silence like that of death enveloped the land. Nothing was visible in the darkness. After eating dinner, Hori had gone and stretched out in a small hut at the edge of Punni's pea field. He was trying to forget the cold and get some sleep, but his blanket was tattered, his jacket torn, and his bed of straw damp. Faced with such resistance sleep lacked the courage to approach him. And today he hadn't even been able to get a little tobacco to divert his mind. The smouldering dung cake he'd brought along had been extinguished by the damp cold.

Curling his calloused knees against his stomach, burying his hands between his thighs, and pulling the blanket up over his head, Hori tried to warm himself with his own breath. The jacket had been made five years ago. Dhaniya had practically forced him to get the material that time when the Afghan peddler had come around selling cloth. What trouble it had brought on, and what curses they'd had to suffer from him on account of the debt! As for the blanket, it was even older than Hori. As a child, he had slept under it huddled next to his father. As a young man, he'd shared it with Gobar during the winter months. And now, in old age, that same ancient blanket was still his companion, although, like a decayed and painful tooth, it was no longer of much use.

Hori couldn't recall a single day when there had been anything left over after paying the rent and the moneylenders. And now, through no fault of his own, he was caught up in still another mess. If he did nothing for Punni, everyone would sneer at him. But even when he did help her, there was some doubt as to what people were saying. They all thought he was swindling her, filling his barn with her grain. Instead of gratitude, he was earning only slander and disgrace.

And then there was Bhola, who kept reminding him over and over that no progress was being made on finding him a wife. And Shobha had informed him several times that Punni was harbouring ill feeling towards him. There was nothing he could do about it. He'd still have to take care of her household, whether it brought happiness or tears.

Even Dhaniya had not entirely forgiven him—something was still upsetting her. He shouldn't have beaten her in front of all those people. It was despicable of him to strike her, the woman with whom he'd spent twenty-five years, in front of the whole village; but she'd done her best to humiliate him also. She had ignored him as though they were total strangers, using Sona or Rupa as messengers when there was something to be communicated.

He had noticed that Dhaniya's sari was in shreds. When she finally mentioned the subject, however, it was with regard to a sari for Sona —not a word about one for herself. Actually, Sona's sari, with a bit of mending, would do for another month or so, whereas her own had been mended so often that it was nothing but a mass of patches.

He hadn't been giving her much affection, though. It probably would have done no harm to say a few kind words to her. She could only have turned nasty, and a few unpleasant words from her wouldn't have hurt him. But he'd become a silly fool in his old age. In fact, if the illness hadn't aroused her sympathies for him, she might have gone on sulking indefinitely.

The words that had passed between them that day were like food to the starving. She had spoken from her heart, and Hori was completely overwhelmed. He had felt like touching his head to her feet and saying, 'I struck you—Now look, I'm bowing my head before you. Hit me as much as you like; curse me all you want.'

In the midst of these thoughts, Hori suddenly heard a jingling of bracelets in front of the hut. He strained his ears. Yes, someone was there. It must be the patwari's daughter, or perhaps the pandit's wife, come to steal some peas. Why in the world were these people so dishonest? They were the best dressed and best fed people in the village. They had thousands of rupees buried in their houses; they loaned out money at twenty-five and fifty percent interest; they got bribes and commissions; and they ground down everyone they could get hold of. Yet still they behaved this way! Like father, like off-spring.... And then instead of coming themselves, they sent their womenfolk. If he were to get up and catch hold of this woman now, he'd be breaking caste rules. Low people were actually low only in name—it was the upper classes who were really low-minded. But he couldn't just go seize a woman. All he could do was look on, and swallow his pride as though it were a fly. Go ahead—tear up the plants to your heart's content! If the rich people had no sense of shame, the poor folk would have to bear the shame for them.

But no—it was Dhaniya! She was calling him—'Are you asleep or awake?'

Hori jumped to his feet and came out of the hut. Evidently his goddess was pleased today and had come to bestow a favour on him. But then he had misgivings about her coming so late at night and in this chilly winter dampness. Something must have happened. . . .

'How could anyone sleep in this miserable cold?' Hori said. 'What brings you here in such weather? Is everything all right?'

'Yes, everything's fine.'

'Why didn't you send Gobar to call me?'

Dhaniya gave no answer. Coming in the hut, she sat down and then said, 'Don't talk about Gobar and his doings. He's blackened our name. What I feared has happened.'

'What's happened? Has he been in a fight with someone?'

'How would I know? Go ask that cursed widow.'

'What widow? What are you talking about? Have you gone crazy?'

'Why shouldn't I go crazy? I suppose I should swell with pride over what's happened!'

A thin ray of light illuminated Hori's mind. 'Why don't you speak up plainly? Who's this woman you're talking about?'

'That Jhuniya—who else?'

'Well what is it? Has she come to our place?'

'Where else could she go? Who else cares about her?'

'Isn't Gobar at home?'

'There's no sign of Gobar. He's run off somewhere. She's five months pregnant.'

Hori put everything together at last. He'd been getting a little suspicious about Gobar's frequent trips to the cowherds' village, but he'd not realized the boy was playing this kind of game. It was nothing new for a young man to be having a little fun; but not even a god could have guessed that the little fluff of cotton which he had watched with a smile being tossed by the wind in the blue sky, would turn into a threatening cloud filling the heavens and obscuring the path. To think that the simple country boy he'd thought a mere child could be such a lecher! Hori wasn't worried about the feast of penance he would have to give; nor was he afraid of the village council, nor even about how Jhuniya would live in the house. He was concerned only about Gobar. The boy was so sensitive, so simpleminded, so proud—he might do something foolish.

148

'Didn't Jhuniya say anything about where Gobar went?' he asked anxiously. 'He must have told her something before leaving.'

'Is your head stuffed with grass?' Jhuniya snapped. 'With his sweetheart here, why would he run away? He must be hiding somewhere nearby. He's not a baby who'd get lost. What I'm worried about is what to do with this cursed Jhuniya. I won't let her stay in the house for a minute. They've been carrying on ever since the day he went to get the cow. If it weren't for her belly, the secret still wouldn't be known, but she started getting worried when she found out she was pregnant. She began suggesting they run away somewhere, but Gobar kept putting her off. Where could he take the woman? There was no place. Finally, when she threatened suicide today unless he took her away somewhere, he told her to come stay with us—that no one would say anything and that he'd explain the situation to me. So that ass Jhuniya set off with him. He was walking ahead of her for some time, and then he slipped away God knows where. She stood there calling him. But when night came and he hadn't returned, she came dashing to our place. I told her she could damn well enjoy the consequences of what she'd done. The witch! She's ruined my boy! She's been sitting there crying ever since. She won't get up —says she can't show her face at home. If God would only make girls like that barren, it would be a good thing. The whole village will be buzzing by dawn. I feel like taking poison. I'm warning you, I won't have her in my house. If Gobar wants to take care of her, that's his responsibility, but there's no room in my house for a sneaky whore like her. And if you try to interfere, then either you can leave or I will.'

'You've handled this all wrong,' Hori said. 'You should never have allowed her in the house in the first place.'

'She paid no attention to anything I said. Wouldn't budge—just sat down right there.'

'All right, come on. We'll see whether she budges or not. I'll drag her right out.'

'That miserable Bhola knew about it all along, but he just kept nice and quiet. What a shameless father!'

'How could he know what those two were cooking up between themselves?'

'Why wouldn't he know? Gobar was hanging around day and night—was he blind or something? He should have realized why the boy was running over there.'

149

'Come on. I have some things to ask Jhuniya.'

They left the hut and started for the village. 'It must be after midnight,' Hori said.

'It certainly is,' Dhaniya replied, 'and everyone's sleeping so soundly a thief could come and rob the whole village.'

'Thieves don't come to villages like this. They go to rich people's houses . . . and to ours!'

All at once Dhaniya stopped and caught hold of Hori's hand. 'Look, don't make a big racket or the whole village will wake up and start spreading the news.'

'I don't care,' Hori declared. 'I'm going to grab her by the hand and drag her out—all the way out of the village. The news is bound to get out some time—it might as well be today. Why did she come to my house anyway? Let her go wherever Gobar is. Did she ask our permission when she was sinning with him?'

Dhaniya seized his hand again and said softly, 'If you grab her, she'll scream.'

'Then let her scream.'

'But where could she go, all alone in the dark and so late at night? Take that into consideration.'

'She can go to her relatives. There's no reason for her to stay at our house.'

'Yes, but it wouldn't be right to throw her out of the house at this hour of the night. After all, she's carrying a child, and if she got frightened, there'd be even worse trouble. Given the situation, there's nothing we can do.'

'What business is it of ours whether she lives or dies? Let her go where she wants. Why should we bring disgrace on ourselves? I intend to throw Gobar out too.'

'It's too late now to worry about disgrace,' Dhaniya said gravely. 'We can't rid ourselves of it now as long as we live. Gobar has sunk the boat.'

'She was the one who sank it, not Gobar. He's just a child who fell into her clutches.'

'Well, whoever's responsible, it's too late now.'

They approached the door. Suddenly Dhaniya put her arm around Hori's neck. 'Look,' she pleaded, 'swear to me you won't hit her. She's crying already. If fate weren't against her, she'd never have fallen into all this trouble.'

Hori's eyes mellowed. Even in the darkness, Dhaniya's motherly affection shone forth like a lamp, dispelling the worried expression on his face. It was as though a long-lost youth were reviving in their hearts. In this aging woman Hori recognized the tender-hearted girl who had entered his life twenty-five years ago. There was such great affection in her embrace that it swept away all the ugliness, all the barriers and all the misunderstandings between them.

They peeked through the cracks in the door. By the glow of a small oil lamp, they could see Jhuniya sitting with her head resting on her knees, and her face turned toward the door—as though searching in the darkness for the happiness which had given her just a glimpse of its beauty and then vanished. Battered by misfortune, wounded by mocking voices, beaten down by life, she had been searching for some shady spot and had found one place at last that seemed to offer security and happiness. But today that haven had vanished like Aladdin's palace, taking with it all her glorious happiness, and leaving her to confront a future that loomed like some terrible demon waiting to devour her.

When Jhuniya saw the door suddenly open and Hori walk in, she jumped up, trembling with fear, and fell sobbing at his feet. 'Dada, I have no other place to go. Hit me or kill me if you like, but don't drive me away from your door.'

Hori bent down and patted her gently on the back. 'Don't be afraid, daughter,' he assured her lovingly. 'Don't be afraid. This is your home and we are your people. You can live here in comfort. You're now my daughter as much as you are Bhola's. As long as we're alive, you have nothing to worry about. While we're here, no one will be able to give you even a dirty look. And we'll take care of whatever feast has to be given for penance—you can rest assured of that.'

Somewhat consoled, Jhuniya clung even more tightly to Hori's feet. 'Dada, now you are my father, and Amma, you are my mother. I have no one. Please give me shelter—or my father and brothers will eat me alive.'

Dhaniya could no longer restrain her pity. 'Come sit down now,' she said. 'You're to stay with us. I'll see to your father and your brothers. They don't rule the world. The most they can do is take your jewellery. Pull it off and throw it at them!'

Only a short while before, Dhaniya had been angrily calling Jhuniya a whore, a sinner, a bringer of bad luck, and God knows what else. She was going to chase her out of the house with a broom. Now,

151

hearing these words of love, forgiveness and reassurance, Jhuniya let go of Hori's feet and clung to Dhaniya's. And that good woman, who herself had never looked at any man but her husband, put her arms around the offender's neck and wiped away her tears, calming the girl's frightened heart with tender words, like a bird sheltering its young under its wing.

Hori motioned his wife to get the girl some food and then asked, 'Daughter, do you have any idea where Gobar has gone?'

'He told me nothing,' she sobbed. 'And now, because of me, you're burdened....' Her voice was lost in a flood of tears.

Hori could not conceal his anxiety. 'Did he seem worried when you saw him today?'

'He was talking cheerfully enough, but God knows what he was thinking.'

'Well, what's your opinion? Is he still in the village or has he gone away somewhere?'

'I suspect he's gone away somewhere.'

'That's what I think too. What a stupid thing to do. We're not his enemies. What's done is done—we have to make the best of it. By running away like this, he's only making life miserable for us.'

Dhaniya took Jhuniya by the hand and led her inside, 'What a coward! Once involved with you, he should have stood by you instead of disgracing himself by running away. If he comes back now, I won't let him in the house.'

Hori returned to the field and lay down again in the hut there. Where could Gobar have gone? The question fluttered through his heart like a bird fluttering through the sky.

CHAPTER 11

THIS extraordinary event naturally aroused a furor in the village, and the excitement lasted for months. Jhuniya's brothers, armed with sticks, went around hunting for Gobar. Bhola swore he would never again look at Jhuniya, nor set foot in the village where she was now living. The talks with Hori about arranging a marriage were broken off. And he now wanted cash for the cow. Any delay about that and he would file suit and have Hori's house and property put up for auction. The members of Hori's caste excommunicated him. No one would share a smoke with him or have a drink of water at his house. There was some talk of banning him from the village well; but when Dhaniya became as ferocious as Kali, no one dared carry out the proposal. Faced with this challenge, the threats melted away.

Most unhappy of all was Jhuniya, who had brought on all the trouble, and she became more and more miserable with the absence of news about Gobar. All day she hid herself in the house. To go out would mean risking her life in a torrent of ridicule and abuse. So she stayed around the house doing chores during the day; and when she found time to spare, she wept. Heart pounding, she trembled in constant fear lest Dhaniya start complaining again. Jhuniya couldn't do the cooking, since no one would eat food touched by her hands, but she took all the other chores on herself. Meanwhile, whenever any of the village people got together, Jhuniya became the target of their contempt.

One day Dhaniya was returning from the market when she ran into Pandit Datadin. She bowed her head, hoping to slink by, but the pandit was not going to miss the opportunity of taunting her. 'Any news of Gobar, Dhaniya?' he called out maliciously. 'What a rotten son he turned out to be, ruining your whole family name.'

Dhaniya often felt this way herself. 'When evil days come, men lose their senses,' she muttered sadly. 'What more can I say?'

'You shouldn't have taken that wicked girl into your house,' Datadin declared. 'If a fly falls in the milk, men pluck it out and throw it away before taking a drink. Just think how you're being sneered at and ridiculed. Nothing would have happened if that whore weren't living in your house. Boys often make mistakes like that. But now there's no way to improve things until you give a feast for the whole caste and feed the brahmans. If you'd not taken her in, none of this would have happened. Hori's a fool, of course, but how did you get tricked?'

Datadin's son Matadin had become involved with a low-caste chamar girl, as the whole village knew. But he put a caste mark on his forehead, read the holy books, recited from the scriptures, did penance for his sins by bathing frequently in the Ganges, and observed all the other religious rites. So his reputation hadn't suffered at all.

Dhaniya knew that all the trouble had started when they gave refuge to Jhuniya. She wondered why she had felt so sorry for the girl. If it hadn't been for that, she could have driven Jhuniya away and avoided all this slander. But she'd feared that the girl, finding no shelter, would throw herself in the river or the well. And how could she protect her own reputation at the cost of a life—or rather, of two lives? Besides, the child Jhuniya was carrying was part of Dhaniya's own flesh and blood. How could she take its life just because she feared ridicule? Then too, the girl's quiet humility was disarming. Dhaniya would come home seething with rage, but somehow the anger would melt away when Jhuniya brought her a pot of water to drink and began massaging her feet. The poor girl was already crushed with shame and misery. What more was one to do—kick the corpse?

'We don't value our family name so highly, maharaj, that we would kill someone for the sake of preserving it,' she replied sharply. 'She's not married to our son, that's true, but he's responsible for her nevertheless. How could I throw her out? Rich people do the same thing and no one says anything to them. It doesn't affect their standing. It's only when the poor do something that their reputations are ruined. The rich may prefer to save face even at the cost of others' lives, but we don't.'

Datadin was not one to accept defeat. He was the village trouble-maker, sticking his nose into everyone's business. He had never committed a theft—that was too dangerous. But when it came time for the loot to be divided up, he was always present. Somehow he always managed to get off unscathed. He'd not yet paid a single pice of rent to the zamindar. When the bailiff showed up, Datadin would threaten to throw himself in the well, leaving Nokheram helpless. Yet Datadin always managed to have money to loan out at interest to the tenants. And whenever a woman wanted some jewellery made up, he was always there to oblige. Arranging marriages brought him great satisfaction ... it also brought him prestige and financial rewards. In cases of sickness, he dispensed medicines—or hocus pocus, depending on which the patient preferred. A shrewd judge of human nature, he could be young with the young and old with the old. He could play friend to both thieves and their victims. No one in the village trusted him, but he was such a shrewd talker that even those who'd just been deceived walked right back into his trap.

Datadin nodded his head sagely. 'What you say is right, Dhaniya,' he conceded, 'and it's fine for people whose souls are dedicated to righteousness. But most of us have to go along with the conventions of society.'

Another day, Lala Pateshwari provoked Hori in a similar way. Pateshwari was well known in the village for his piety, going every full moon to hear the story of *Vishnu* recited. In his role as revenue clerk, though, he would conscript workers without pay to plough and irrigate his fields, and he would play off the farmers against each other so as to make a profit for himself. The whole village trembled before him. By loaning five or ten rupees at a time to the poor, he had built up a fortune of thousands. Taking produce from the farmers, he would present it to the court officials and police, thereby building up a great reputation throughout the region. The only one who had not gone along with his game was Ganda Singh the Inspector, a newcomer to the area.

Lala Pateshwari could also be benevolent at times. During the malaria season he acquired renown by distributing free government quinine and by showing concern for those laid up with fever. He would also arbitrate all kinds of petty quarrels. And for weddings he was the salvation of the poor, loaning out his palanquins and carpets, and letting them use his large canopy. He never missed an opportunity to make money, but he would also aid those he devoured.

'What's all this trouble you've brought on yourself, Hori?' he called.

Hori turned around. 'What's that you said, Lala? I didn't quite hear you.'

Pateshwari caught up with him. 'I was just asking whether you'd lost your senses the way Dhaniya has. Why don't you send Jhuniya back to her father? You're needlessly making yourself the laughing-stock of the village. No telling whose child she's carrying, and yet you take her into your house. You've got two daughters to marry off still. You'd better think about how you're going to cross that river!'

Hori was tired of hearing this kind of criticism and solicitude. 'I know all that, Lala,' he said wearily. 'But tell me, what am I supposed to do? If I threw Jhuniya out, would Bhola take her back? I'd send her home today if he were agreeable. If you can persuade him to take her in, I'll be eternally grateful to you. But how can I turn her out when her brothers are out for blood? She's already had one no-good man make promises and then desert her. And if I were to throw her out in her present condition, she couldn't make a living anywhere. Who'd get the blame if she drowned herself? As for the girls' marriages—well, that's in the hands of God. Something or other is sure to open up when the time comes. No girl of our community has stayed unmarried yet. I can't commit murder just out of fear of the community.'

Hori was mild by nature, deferring to others and swallowing the insults that came his way. No one in the village except Hira wished him ill. But society could not tolerate such impropriety. And just look at his obstinacy—refusing to listen to reason. This husband and wife seemed to be daring society to take action against them. Well, society would prove that those who violate its rules can not be left to sleep in peace.

That very night the guardians of justice in the village met to discuss the problem.

'I'm not the kind of person who finds fault with others,' Datadin declared. 'All kinds of evil go on in the world, and it's no concern of mine. But that bitch Dhaniya is determined to pick a fight with me. Having acquired some money by pocketing part of the brothers' share of the property ... well, what can you expect of her now except wickedness? These low-caste people—once they get a stomach full of food, they become even more devious. That's why the holy books say it's good to kick them.'

Pateshwari sucked on the coconut pipe. 'The trouble with them,' he agreed, 'is that as soon as they get a little money they start putting on airs. Today Hori was so rude that I was left speechless. I don't know who he thinks he is. Just think what the effect of such insolence will be on the village. Won't the other widows in the village start following Jhuniya's example? Today this has happened in Bhola's house; tomorrow it may happen in yours and mine too. After all, society is based on fear. If it loses that weapon, imagine what chaos would be let loose in the world.'

Jhinguri Singh had two wives currently. His first had died, leaving five children, when he was about forty-five, so he had married again. When the second wife produced no children, he married a third time. Now fifty, he had two young wives at home. All kinds of stories were whispered around concerning them, but people were too scared of the Thakur Sahib to say anything openly, and there was no opportunity for open scandal anyway. With the husband as a front, the women could get away with all kinds of things. Only those with no such protection have a problem. The Thakur Sahib ruled his wives with an iron hand, and prided himself that no outsider had seen even their veils—but he knew nothing of what was going on behind those veils.

'A woman like that should have her head chopped off!' he pronounced. 'By taking this whore into his house, Hori is spreading poison in our society. Letting a man like that live here pollutes the whole village. The Rai Sahib should be notified. He should be plainly informed that if this kind of wickedness is tolerated in the village, no one's honour will be safe.'

Pandit Nokheram, the agent of the zamindar's estate, was a very high caste brahman. His grandfather had held a high position with a local ruler but then had laid all his possessions at the feet of God and become an ascetic. His father had also spent his life singing praises to Rama and now Nokheram had inherited that same piety. By dawn he would be sitting at prayers, and until ten would go on writing the name of Rama. As soon as he left the presence of God, however, he would throw off all restraints and let loose venomous thoughts words and deeds.

Nokheram considered Jhinguri Singh's proposal an affront to his authority. 'Why should the Rai Sahib get involved in this?' he protested, his eyes peering angrily through slits in his puffy cheeks. 'I have the authority to do anything I please. Let's fine him a hundred rupees. That'll drive him out of the village. Meanwhile I'll start eviction proceedings against him.'

'But hasn't he paid his land rent?' Pateshwari asked.

'That's right,' Jhinguri Singh said. 'He borrowed thirty rupees from me to pay it.'

'But he has no receipt yet,' Nokheram exulted. 'What proof does he have that he's paid the rent?'

It was decided unanimously that Hori should be fined a hundred rupees. All that was necessary to complete the farce was enough time to gather the men of the village and get their approval. This might have delayed matters by five or ten days—but that very night Jhuniya gave birth to a son.

The village council met the next day. Hori and Dhaniya were summoned to hear the verdict on their fate. The meeting place was so crowded that not even a sesame seed could have been squeezed in. The council announced its decision—Hori was to be fined a hundred rupees in cash and four bushels of grain.

Dhaniya addressed the group, her voice choked with emotion—'Judges, no good will come to you by harassing the poor. That much you should realize. We may perish ... we may keep on living in the village or we may not ... no one knows. But one thing's dead certain—my curse will fall on you. We're being given such a harsh fine just because I'm letting my daughter-in-law stay in the house. Why didn't I drive her out and let her beg in the streets, you ask. Is that what you call justice?'

'She's not your daughter-in-law,' Pateshwari retorted. 'She's a common adulteress.'

'Why are you arguing, Dhaniya?' Hori rebuked her. 'The village council is the voice of God. Whatever they think fair must be accepted cheerfully. If it's God's will that we leave the village, there's nothing we can do about it. Judges, everything we own is in the village barn. Not a single grain has reached our house. Take as much as you want. If you want it all, then take it all. God will look after us. To make up whatever we still owe, take both our bullocks.'

'I won't give up one bit of grain or a single cowrie as a fine,' Dhaniya insisted. 'If one of you thinks he's brave enough, let him come and take it from me. Big joke this is! I suppose you think you can take away all our property on the excuse of collecting a fine, and then give it away to someone who'll pay you a bribe for it. Sell our fields and gardens and then live in luxury yourselves! Not while Dhaniya is alive, you won't! Your greed won't get a chance to express itself. We don't have to stay in the caste—staying in the caste won't bring us salvation. We're living by our own sweat now, and we'll keep doing so even if you outcaste us.'

Hori turned and faced her, his hands folded imploringly. 'Dhaniya,

I beg at your feet—please keep quiet. We're all bound to the caste, and we can't break away from it. We must bow to whatever punishment they give. It would be better to hang ourselves than to live so shamelessly. If we were to die today, the people of our caste would carry our bodies to the pyre. Our salvation depends completely on the caste. Judges, may I never see my young son again if I own anything other than the grain that's in the barn. I wouldn't try to cheat my own community. If you feel any pity for my children, then arrange some support for them. If not, I can only submit to your demands.'

Dhaniya stormed off in a rage, while Hori worked late into the night carrying his grain sack by sack from the barn and stacking it at Jhinguri Singh's place. There were forty bushels of barley, ten of wheat, an equal quantity of peas, a little gram and some oilseeds. He was singlehandedly bearing the burden for two families now. What little food there was had been due to Dhaniya's labours. She and the two daughters had slaved in the fields while Jhuniya took care of all the housework. They had planned to use the wheat and oilseeds to pay an instalment on the land rent and, if possible, a little toward the interest on the loans. They would then live on the barley, scraping by for five or six months until the millet and rice crops were ready. Now all these hopes had been crushed in the dust. The grain was gone, and another hundred rupees had been added to the burden of debt on their heads. There was nowhere to turn for food.

And God knows what had become of Gobar. Not a word or a sign from him. If he was so fainthearted, why had he done what he did? But who can alter fate? Fear of the caste was so strong that Hori was carrying away his grain on his own head, as though digging his grave with his own hands. Zamindar, moneylender, government—none of them could have inspired such awe. He was sick with worry as to where his children's next meal would come from, but fear of the caste community kept goading him like a demon. Life outside the caste was unthinkable. The marriage sacrament, tonsure and ear-piercing rites, birth and death ceremonies—all were in the hands of the caste. His life was like a tree rooted in the caste, bound to it heart and soul. Outcasting would throw his life into complete chaos—he would be utterly shattered.

Only a bushel or two of barley was left in the barn when Dhaniya rushed up, grabbed his hand and said, 'All right—that's enough now. You've done enough to satisfy the caste. Are you going to give it all to them? Aren't you going to save anything for the children? I can't win with you. What a fate to be stuck with such an idiot!'

Freeing his hand, Hori scooped the rest of the grain into the basket. 'It would be a sin to keep back even one grain. We can't do that, Dhaniya. I'm going to haul every bit of it over there. Then, if they feel any pity, maybe they'll give some back for the children. If not, well God is our keeper.'

Dhaniya bristled. 'Those aren't judges—they're devils, absolute devils. They just want to grab our land and possessions for themselves. Calling it punishment is just camouflage. I keep explaining that to you, but you refuse to open your eyes. You expect pity from those fiends? You think they're going to give back ten or twenty bushels? Fat chance of that!'

When Hori, still turning a deaf ear, loaded the basket on his head, Dhaniya took hold of the basket with both hands and held on with all her might. 'I won't let you take it,' she cried. 'If you do, it'll be over my dead body. Have we been just about killing ourselves, irrigating the crop and keeping guard on it late into the night, just so these men can sit back twirling their moustaches and enjoying the harvest while our children starve for just a few grains? You're not the only one who's worked. The girls and I have sacrificed ourselves too. Put the basket down right now or I'm through with you forever —and that's final!'

Hori was forced to reconsider. There was some truth in what Dhaniya had said. After all, what right did he have to take away what his family had earned, in order to pay a fine? As head of the family he was supposed to care for them all, not to snatch away their earnings so as to look respectable in the eyes of the community. The basket dropped from his hands. 'What you say is true, Dhaniya,' he admitted slowly. 'I have no right to give away the share that doesn't belong to me. Take what's left. I'll go speak to the judges.'

Dhaniya set the basket of grain inside the house. Then she joined with her daughters and began singing songs of welcome for the newly born grandchild so loudly that the whole village could hear. This was the first time that no other women of the community were present on such an auspicious occasion. Jhuniya had sent word from her confinement that the customary songs were unnecessary. But since when had Dhaniya ever listened to anyone? If the other women in the community didn't care about her, why should she care about them?

Meanwhile Hori was in the process of mortgaging his house to

Jhinguri Singh for eighty rupees. There was no other way to raise the money for the fine. The oilseeds, peas and wheat had brought twenty rupees. To collect the balance, he was forced to sign away his house. Nokheram wanted the bullocks sold too, but Pateshwari and Datadin objected—if the bullocks were sold, how could Hori work the fields? Let the money come from his property, but not to the extent that he be forced out of the village. As a result of this stand, the bullocks were spared.

It was about eleven o'clock when Hori, having signed the mortgage deed, arrived home. 'What kept you so long?' Dhaniya demanded immediately.

Frustrated, Hori turned his anger on his own house. 'What else was there to do except finish up what our troublemaking son began? That damned boy lit the fire and then ran away leaving the sparks untended. I'm the one who had to put out the fire. I was forced to mortgage the house for eighty rupees. What else could I do? Now we're back in the fold and I can share a smoke with any man. The caste leaders have forgiven us.'

Dhaniya bit her lip angrily. 'What harm would it have done if they'd not taken us back? For four or five months now no one shared a smoke with you anyway—and are you any the worse for it? I ask you now—why do you have to be such an idiot? In front of me you pretend to be so smart. Why don't you use your head when you're away from home? All we had to remember our ancestors by was the house, and now you've done away even with that. I suppose tomorrow you'll go and mortgage off these few acres of land too and then we can go begging from door to door. What's the matter, don't you have a tongue in your head? Couldn't you have asked them just who they think they are, passing out punishments to people? You should have told them that they're the ones who are sinners—that just the sight of their faces pollutes us.'

'Shut up,' Hori scolded her. 'Don't talk so big. We've not been in any real trouble with the caste yet or you wouldn't be talking this way.'

Dhaniya grew more excited. 'What sin have we committed that we should be afraid of the caste? Have we robbed someone? Have we swindled anyone out of his possessions? It's no sin to keep a woman— the sin is in leaving her. Being too good can also be wrong ... then even the swine start trampling on you. I suppose everyone's complimenting you now on obeying the decision of the judges. It's my rotten luck to have gotten mixed up with you in the first place. I've never had even a crumb of happiness.'

'Did I fall at your father's feet and beg for you? It was he that hung you around my neck.'

'He must have had rocks in his head, that's all I can say. I can't imagine what he saw in you that charmed him so much. It's not as though you were handsome or anything.'

The argument had finally reached a level of good-humoured banter. If eighty rupees was gone, then it was gone. They still had a child worth millions, and no one could snatch him away. If Gobar would only come back, Dhaniya would be happy even if she had to live alone in a separate hut.

'Who does the baby look like?' Hori asked.

Dhaniya smiled. 'Just like Gobar. Honestly!'

'And healthy?'

'Yes, he's a fine child.'

———

On the night Gobar had taken Jhuniya from her home, he had been trembling as though taking a move that would disgrace him completely. His feet faltered as he thought of the outrage that would sweep through the village when Jhuniya was seen there. There'd be cries of horror and protest on all sides. And how Dhaniya would curse! He was not afraid of Hori—he would roar once and then calm down. It was Dhaniya he was afraid of—she might even take poison or set the house on fire. No, he couldn't go home with Jhuniya as yet.

But what if Dhaniya refused to allow her in the house and drove her away with a broom? Where would the poor girl go? She couldn't go back to her own house. What if she were to jump in a well or hang herself? Gobar sighed deeply, wondering where to turn for refuge.

Then he reassured himself with the thought that his mother surely wouldn't be so heartless as to beat Jhuniya and send her away. She might abuse her angrily for a while; but when Jhuniya fell at her feet and started crying, she'd surely take pity on her. Until then, he'd hide out somewhere. After the storm had died down, he'd sneak back one day and make peace with his mother. Meanwhile, if he could get some work so as to return home with a few rupees, she'd have to hold her tongue.

'My heart's pounding,' Jhuniya said. 'How was I to know you were going to get me into trouble like this? It was an evil hour when I first saw you. If you'd not come for the cow, none of this would have happened. You lead the way and say whatever has to be said. I'll come afterwards.'

'Oh no,' Gobar protested. 'You go first. Say that you were on your way home from selling milk in the bazaar, but that it got dark and you couldn't very well go on. Then I'll show up.'

'Your mother has a terrible temper,' Jhuniya said apprehensively. 'I'm losing my nerve. What'll I do if she starts beating me?'

'She's not that kind of a person,' Gobar assured her. 'She's never laid a hand on any of us—why would she beat you? Anything she has to say, she'll say to me. She won't take it out on you.'

They were nearing the village. Gobar suddenly stopped and said, 'Now you go ahead.'

'Don't be long, then,' Jhuniya begged.

'No, no—I'll be coming in just a moment. You go on now.'

'For some reason I feel angry at you.'

'What are you so afraid of? I'll be right behind you.'

'Maybe we'd have done better to run off somewhere else.'

'When we have a home, why run some place else? You're worrying for no reason at all.'

'You will come soon, won't you?'

'Yes, yes—I'll be there in just a minute.'

'You're not tricking me? You're not planning to send me to your house and then desert me?'

'I'm not as low as all that, Jhuniya. Now that I've committed myself to you, I'll stick with you to my dying breath.'

Jhuniya started walking toward the house. Gobar stood there undecided for a moment. Then the shame which had been hovering in the back of his mind rose before him in all its horror. What if his mother did rush out and beat her? His feet seemed rooted to the ground. Only a small mango orchard lay between him and the house. He could see Jhuniya's dark shadow moving slowly ahead. His senses on edge, he suddenly heard a faint noise that sounded like his mother cursing Jhuniya. The blood froze in his veins and he felt as though an axe were about to drop on his head. A moment later, he thought he saw Dhaniya coming out of the house. She must be looking for Hori, heading for the pea field where he'd gone after dinner to keep guard.

Gobar started running in that direction also, trampling the barley and wheat as though someone were chasing him. Spotting his father's hut, he slowed down. Tiptoeing around behind the hut, he crouched down. His guess had been correct. No sooner had he reached the spot than he heard Dhaniya's voice.

I'm ruined, he thought to himself. How cruel my mother is! Not a drop of mercy even for a poor homeless girl. It would really puncture her pride if I were to face her and say she had no right to talk that way to Jhuniya. And now ... even father is getting angry. When it comes to cutting a banana, even a chunk of broken pot thinks itself sharp! This is my reward for all the respect I've shown him. And now he's heading for the house too. I won't put up with it if he hits her. God, everything is in your hands now! I had no idea I was involving myself in such a mess. What a sneak and a coward Jhuniya must be thinking me. But surely they won't beat her; and how could they throw her out of the house either? After all, don't I have a share in the house? Anyway, if anyone lifts a hand against her, there'll be another *Mahabharata* war. A father and mother are only father and mother as long as they care for their children. If they no longer love them at all, how can they still be called parents?

Gobar had been following Hori slowly and stealthily ever since he left the door of the hut, but he stopped when he saw the light shining from the door of the house, unable to step into that ring of light. Courage failing, he flattened himself against the wall in the shadows. His mother and father were pouring out their fury on poor innocent Jhuniya and there was nothing he could do about it. He'd never dreamed that the spark which he'd tossed carelessly aside would burn down the whole barn. And now he lacked the courage to come forward and tell them that he was the one who had started the whole thing. All the props sustaining him had been knocked away in this earthquake, and his dwelling had utterly collapsed. He turned away .... how could he face Jhuniya now?

Gobar walked for some distance feeling like a soldier deserting the battlefield. All his love for Jhuniya and his promises of marriage began coming to mind. He thrilled to the memory of those secret assignations when, heart pounding and eyes glazed with intoxicating rapture, he had offered his life at her feet. Previously, Jhuniya had been leading a solitary life in her little nest, like a bird deserted by its mate, with no delirious male urgings, no fiery rapture, no tender chirping of young ones. But there had been no hunter's wily snare either. Who could say whether Gobar's entering that lonely nest had brought her happiness or not? This much was certain though—he had gotten her into trouble. Pulling himself together, Gobar suddenly turned back, like a fleeing soldier on hearing the encouraging voice of a comrade.

When he again reached the house, Gobar found the door closed, a few rays of light shining out through the chinks. Peering through a crack in the door, he saw that Dhaniya and Jhuniya were standing up and that Hori was sitting. Jhuniya was sobbing and Dhaniya was consoling her—'You're to stay with us. I'll see to your father and your brothers. As long as we're alive, you have nothing to worry about. No one will be able to give you even a dirty look.'

Gobar was elated. Were he able, he'd have showered them with gold and told them they no longer needed to do anything but take it easy and enjoy themselves and give away all they wanted to charity. Gone was his anxiety for Jhuniya. She had found the refuge he'd hoped to provide for her. If she thought he was betraying her, that was her problem. He'd return home only when he had enough money to silence the tongues of the village. And then his mother would realize that he was not a blemish on the family name but rather its crowning glory.

The more severe the shock to one's system, the more intense the reaction. This dishonour and shame had cut into Gobar's inner being and uncovered a jewel hitherto concealed. For the first time he realized his responsibility and felt the determination necessary to fulfil it. Until now he had considered it his right to work as little and eat as much as possible. It had never occurred to him that he also had a duty to his family. Now his parents' generous forgiveness had enlightened him. When Jhuniya and Dhaniya disappeared into an inside room, he walked back to Hori's hut in the pea field and sat down to start working out his future plans.

He had heard that labourers in the city were earning five or six annas a day. If he could make six annas a day and live on one anna, he'd be saving five, which would add up to ten rupees a month, or a hundred and a quarter in a year. If he came back with a purseful like that, no one would dare say anything against him. Those Datadins and Pateshwaris would fawn over him, and Jhuniya would burst with pride. If he kept earning that kind of money for three or four years, the family poverty could be wiped out entirely. Right now the entire family was not making a hundred and a quarter, and here he would earn that much all by himself. Of course people in the village would sneer at him for doing common labour. Let them sneer. That kind of work was no sin. And it wasn't as though he'd always be earning only six annas a day. As he got more skilled, his wages would go up too. Then he could tell his father to sit home and relax and spend his time singing praises to God. This farming was nothing but a waste of a man's life. First of all he'd buy a good western cow, one that gave four or five quarts of milk a day; and then he'd tell his father to look after her, bringing the old man happiness both in this world and the next.

He could easily live on one anna a day. He wouldn't need a house —he could sleep on someone's porch, or there were those hundreds of temples with free rest-houses for pilgrims. And after all, wouldn't his employer give him a place to live? Of course a rupee would buy only twenty pounds of wheat flour. That meant an anna would buy only a little more than a pound, and in a day he'd eat that much flour alone. Where would he get wood, dal, salt, greens and all that? Two meals a day would require a good two pounds of flour. But why all this worry about food? People can make do with just a handful of gram or they can live on sweets and delicacies, depending on what they're able to afford. He could manage perfectly well on a single pound of flour. Dung cakes picked up here and there would do just as well as firewood. Once in a while he could spend a pice on dal or potatoes . . . baked potatoes were easy to prepare. After all, it was a question of getting by, not of living in luxury. Knead the dough on a leaf, bake it over a dung fire, cook a potato, eat your fill and then go to sleep content. Even at home they didn't have chapaties for both meals—at one there was only gram. He could do the same in the city.

He hesitated. . . . What would he do if he didn't get work? But why wouldn't he? If he put his whole heart into it, a hundred employers would ask for his services. What they really wanted was work, not good looks. Besides, here in the village people had to face droughts and frost, termites in the sugar cane, and blight on the barley and mustard seeds. If he got night work too, he'd accept that also. He could do manual labour all day and then serve as a watchman at night. If the night job brought in two annas more, he'd really be in luck. He'd come back with saries for all of them, along with a bracelet made especially for Jhuniya and a turban for his father.

Revelling in these delightful fancies, he dozed off—but it was too cold for real sleep. He managed somehow to pass the night and at the crack of dawn started down the road to Lucknow. It was only forty miles away, and he'd reach there by nightfall. The village people didn't use this road, and he wouldn't divulge his address in any case. If he did he'd have his father on his head the very next day. His only regret was in not having told Jhuniya the plain truth—that she should go to his home and that he'd be back after some time, when he'd made some money. But then she wouldn't have gone there at all. She'd have insisted on coming along and he'd have been too tied down to get any work done.

The day wore on, and having eaten nothing the previous night, he got so hungry that he started staggering slightly. He felt like sitting down to catch his breath. He couldn't keep walking without something in his stomach, but he hadn't even a pice. Beside the road were some bushes though, from which he picked berries to distract his stomach as he walked along. On reaching a village where he caught the rich aroma of boiling molasses, though, he was unable to restrain himself. Going to the cane mill, he borrowed a rope and a jug and drew some water from the well. As he sat down to drink it, a farmer spoke up—'What? Drinking just plain water? Have a bit of something sweet. So far we've been able to crush our own cane this way and make coarse sugar, but next year the power mill will be working so we'll sell all the cane while it's still standing in the fields. Who'd buy our coarse brown sugar and molasses when good white sugar can be had for the same price?' He brought several lumps of sticky molasses candy and offered them to Gobar, who ate them and then drank the water. 'You smoke?' the farmer asked.

'Thanks, but I've not taken up smoking.' Gobar thought it best not to admit the truth.

'You're on the right track,' the old man said, pleased. 'It's a bad habit. Once it gets hold of you, you can't stop.'

Stoked up with fuel and water, Gobar quickened his pace. With it being winter, he hardly noticed that it was noon already. Up the road he saw a young woman sitting under a tree offering passive resistance to a man, evidently her husband, who stood there trying to pacify her. Gobar joined the passersby who had stopped to watch the fun. Nothing in life is more amusing than a husband trying to pacify his wife.

The woman glared at her husband. 'I won't go—I won't—I won't!'

'Oh, so you're not going!' the man answered as though giving an ultimatum.

'No I won't go.'

'You won't?'

'I won't.'

The man seized her by the hair and started dragging her along. She lay down on the ground. He was at a loss. 'I'm telling you once more —get up and come along.'

The woman was as defiant as before. 'I won't go to your house. Never . . . not even in my next seven rebirths . . . not even if you hack me to bits.'

'I'll cut your throat.'

'Then you'll be hanged.'

Letting go of her hair, the man sat down by the road, his head in his hands. All his manly resources had been exhausted—there was nothing more he could do. A moment later he got up again and said resignedly. 'All right. What is it you want?'

The young woman sat up and said calmly, 'I just want you to go away and leave me alone.'

'But tell me—what's the matter?'

'Why should I have to listen to someone abusing my father and brothers?'

'Who abused your father and brothers?'

'Go home and you'll find out.'

'How can I, unless you come with me?'

'As though you'd speak up anyway! You don't have the guts. Run along—bury your head in your mother's lap and go to sleep. She's your mother, not mine. You go listen to her cursing if you want. Why should I? For every chapati I eat, I do four chapaties' worth of work. Why should I put up with bullying from anyone? And as for you, you've given me nothing—not even a brass ring.'

This quarrel was as entertaining as any stage play for the spectators but there seemed no hope of its reaching a conclusion, and the travellers couldn't afford to hang around indefinitely. One by one they began drifting away. Gobar disliked the man's unnecessary harshness, but he'd been unable to say anything in front of the crowd. Now that the field was clear, though, he spoke up. 'I realize no one has the right to interfere with a man and his wife, but cruelty like this is no good either.'

'And just who are you?' The husband's eyes bulged with anger.

'That's beside the point,' Gobar said calmly. 'No one likes to see bad things going on.'

'It's easy to see you're not married,' the man retorted, shaking his head emphatically. 'That's why you sympathize with her so much. Just wait!'

'Well when I do have a wife, I won't pull her around by the hair.'

'All right, now go mind your own business. This is my woman and I'll beat her or cut her to bits if I want. Who are you to say anything? Get moving now—quit standing around.'

The fire in Gobar's veins blazed up still more. Why should he leave? This was a public road—did this fellow think he owned it or something? He could stand there as long as he liked, and no one had the right to order him off.

The man bit his lip. 'Oh, so you insist on staying? Do I have to come and force you on your way?'

Gobar tied his scarf around his waist and prepared for battle. 'That's up to you. I'll go when I feel like going.'

'Then you may be going with a broken arm or leg.'

'I wouldn't be so sure whose arm or leg gets broken.'

'Then you're not going?'

'No.'

Fists clenched, the man was about to pounce on Gobar when the young woman caught hold of her husband's *dhoti* and pulled him back. Then she turned on Gobar. 'Why are you so set on fighting? Why don't you just move on? You think we're putting on a public show or something? This argument is strictly our own affair. Sometimes he hits me; sometimes I tell him off. What business is it of yours?'

At this reproach, Gobar started off, telling himself that the woman deserved to be beaten.

Before he had gone very far, the woman began berating her husband again. 'Why do you have to pick fights with everyone? What was so bad in what he said that you should take offence? If you misbehave, people are bound to criticize. And he seems to come from a good family—our own caste too. Why don't you consider him as a possible husband for your sister?'

'You think it likely that he's still unmarried?' the husband asked dubiously.

'Well why not at least ask him and find out?'

The man began to run after Gobar, shouting and signalling to him to stop. Gobar thought the devil must have seized him again and that this was another challenge. Evidently he wouldn't be satisfied until he'd been given a good licking. Even a dog can be a tiger in his own village. Oh well, let him come!

But the expression on the man's face seemed to invite friendship rather than battle. He asked Gobar his village, his name and his caste. Gobar answered truthfully, and found out the man's name was Kodai.

'We narrowly escaped a fight,' Kodai said with a smile, 'but as you were walking away, I got to thinking that what you said was perfectly true. I had no reason to get all excited. Your family owns some land, I suppose?'

Gobar told him that the family property amounted to about three acres and that they worked it with one plough.

'Please forgive the rude things I said to you, brother. Anger makes us blind. Actually my wife has all the virtues of a goddess, but at times a kind of evil spirit seems to get hold of her. You tell me now—how can I be expected to control my mother? It was she who gave me birth and who brought me up. When a quarrel arises and I have something to say it's my wife I must say it to. I can lay down the law to her. If you think about it, you'll realize I'm right. True, I didn't have to drag her by the hair, but women are uncontrollable unless they're given a bit of rough treatment. She wants me to go live apart from my mother. Just imagine! How could I move away—and especially from the very mother who gave me birth. I'll never do that, not even if my wife leaves me.'

Gobar was forced to alter his position. 'All of us are morally obliged to respect our mothers,' he conceded. 'How can anyone fully repay the debt he owes his mother?'

Kodai thereupon invited Gobar home with him. There was no way for him to reach Lucknow that day anyway. He could hardly make two or three miles before dark, and then he'd have to stop somewhere for the night.

'Has your wife given in?' Gobar asked jokingly.

'What choice does she have?'

'Such a scolding she gave me—it really made me feel ashamed.'

'She's sorry about that. Come along and explain things for me to my mother. I can't tell her anything. She ought to think over this business of abusing her daughter-in-law's family. I have a sister who'll be getting married soon, and how would she like it if her new mother-in-law started abusing us? My wife isn't the only one at fault. Mother is also in the wrong. She always takes my sister's side in everything, which I don't like of course. And this much I give my wife credit for—she may leave home and sulk when she's abused, but she doesn't answer back.'

Gobar needed some place to spend the night, so he went along with Kodai. When they got back to where the woman was sitting, they found she had assumed the modest demeanour of a housewife, her sari pulled shyly over her face.

'At first he wasn't going to come,' Kodai smiled. 'Said he couldn't very well go home with us after getting such a tongue-lashing.'

The wife peeked at Gobar from behind her veil. 'Frightened of a little rebuke like that? Where will you run to when you have a wife of your own?'

They were soon in the village. Actually it could hardly be called a village—just a cluster of ten or twelve little houses, some thatched and some tiled. When they reached his place, Kodai got out a rope cot, spread a cover over it, ordered some sugar-water to drink, and filled a chilam for them to smoke. The young wife quickly appeared with the drink and playfully flicked a drop on Gobar as though to make up for her earlier harshness. Besides, since this young man was going to marry her sister-in-law, she might as well start to give him the customary teasing.

CHAPTER 13

It was still dark the next morning when Gobar got up and took leave of Kodai. Since everyone had soon realized that Gobar already had a woman, no mention had been made of the marriage proposal. Nevertheless, his courteous manners had charmed them all, and in advising Kodai's mother he had used such sweet words and showed such respect for motherhood that she was thoroughly delighted and had even given him her blessing.

'You hold an exalted position, mother,' he had told her, 'a position worthy of worship. A son can never repay his debt to his mother, not in a hundred rebirths, nor in a thousand, nor even in a million.'

The prospect of such unending veneration had thrilled the old lady. After that, Gobar could say nothing wrong as far as she was concerned. A patient will take even poison cheerfully from a doctor who has once cured him.

'Now consider the way your daughter-in-law left home sulking today,' Gobar had continued. 'Whose reputation would be hurt by that? No one cares about the girl, or about whose daughter or granddaughter she is. Her father might well be a mere grass-cutter....'

'That's exactly what he is, my son,' the old woman declared emphatically. 'Nothing more than a grass-cutter, plain and simple. Just the sight of his face in the morning is such bad luck that a person can't get even a drink of water the rest of the day.'

'Exactly!' Gobar replied. 'So how could a man like that be hurt by ridicule? It's you and your husband that people would laugh at. They'd want to know whose daughter-in-law she was. And after all she's still just a girl—ignorant and immature. You can't expect much of someone who comes from such a low-class family. It's you who must now teach an old parrot to repeat the name of God! Beatings won't do any good, but she might learn something from simple kindness. Punish her when necessary, but avoid getting into squabbles. It's only you who'd be disgraced, not she.'

When Gobar was leaving, the old woman gave him a mixture of

gram flour and molasses to eat on the journey. Several other men from the village were going to the city in search of work, and the miles passed quickly in conversation with them. It was just nine o'clock when they reached the Aminabad Bazaar in Lucknow.

Gobar, bewildered, wondered where so many people could have come from. They seemed to be falling all over each other. There were at least four or five hundred labourers in the bazaar waiting to be hired for the day—masons and carpenters, blacksmiths and ditch-diggers, cot-stringers, basket-carrying porters and stone-cutters. At the sight of the crowd, Gobar lost heart. How could all these people get work? And here he was without even a tool in his hand. No one would even know the kind of work he could do, much less hire him. Without a tool, who'd even notice him?

One by one the workers were being taken on. Some others, giving up hope, returned home. Those who were left, ignored by the employers, were mostly the old and the useless—and among them was Gobar. At least he had a day's food with him, though, so there was no immediate cause for anxiety.

All at once Mirza Khurshed appeared in the midst of the crowd and called out in a booming voice, 'All those willing to do a day's work for six annas, come with me. Six annas apiece. You'll be through at five o'clock.'

All except a half dozen masons and carpenters were willing to accompany him, and soon a great army of four hundred ragged down-and-outers was on the march. In front walked Mirza Khurshed, a heavy cane over his shoulder. Behind, like a flock of sheep, straggled the long column of half-starved men.

'What kind of work will we be doing?' asked one old man.

Mirza's answer astounded them all—they were to play kabaddi. What sort of man could this be who would pay people six annas a day just to play games? He must be some kind of nut—probably one of those people whose minds get unbalanced by too much wealth or too much studying. Some of them began wondering whether this were a kind of practical joke. If he took them all the way to his place and then announced that there was no work, there'd be nothing any of them could do about it. Of course if he paid in advance, they'd play kabaddi or hide-and-seek or anything. But how else could one trust such a screwball?

'Master,' Gobar ventured timidly, 'I don't have anything to eat

174

with me. If you could let me have some money in advance, I'd get some food.'

Mirza immediately thrust six annas into Gobar's hand and called out, 'You'll all be paid in advance. Don't worry about that.'

Mirza owned a little land outside the city. When the workers arrived there, they found a large enclosure containing only a small thatched hut. In it were three or four chairs, and a table on which lay a few books. The flowering vines covering the hut added a certain charm to the place. The enclosure itself was uncultivated, except for some mango, lemon and guava saplings on one side and some flowers on the other.

Lining up the workers, Mirza paid their wages in advance. Now they were all sure the man must be crazy.

Gobar, having been paid earlier, was assigned the job of watering the plants. He felt somewhat cheated at not getting to play kabaddi, as he could have taken on these old men and trounced them soundly. But why fret about that? He'd played the game plenty of times before, and after all, he'd received the full wages.

It had been ages, though, since the oldsters had been given a chance to play kabaddi. In fact most of them could hardly remember whether they had ever played the game or not. All day they slaved in the city, only to come home late at night, eat what dry scraps of food were available, and then sleep. At dawn the same cycle would begin again. Life had become only this fixed routine, with no flavour or relish.

But the opportunity being provided that day made even the elderly once again young. The half-dead old men, little more than skeletons, their gums and their bellies equally empty, hitched up their garments, slapped their thighs in challenge, and leaped around as though their ancient bones had been rejuvenated. In no time the field was lined off, two captains appointed, and teams chosen. When the game began it was just noon—an ideal time for outdoor games, what with the winter sunshine being so mild.

Mirza was standing at the gate of the enclosure selling tickets to the spectacle. He was always up to some sort of crazy scheme like this to take money from the rich and give it to the poor. The old men's kabaddi match had been advertised for several days on huge posters and in handbills: 'This game will be absolutely unique— completely unprecedented! Come see with your own eyes the strength still possessed by the old men of India! Those who miss the fun will be sorry! This is the opportunity of a lifetime!'

Tickets were selling from two annas to ten rupees. By three o'clock, cars and horse carriages were lined up outside and a crowd of at least two thousand had packed the enclosure. For the wealthy, there were chairs and benches; for the common people, seats on the good clean ground.

Miss Malti, Mehta, Khanna, Tankha and the Rai Sahib had all graced the festivities with their presence.

As the game got underway, Mirza turned to Mehta. 'Come on, Doctor, let's you and I have a crack at it also.'

Miss Malti intervened. 'The only match for a philosopher is another philosopher.'

'Oh, so you think I'm not a philosopher?' Mirza retorted, twirling his moustache. 'I don't have a tail of degrees, but I'm a philosopher all right. You can put me to the test, Dr Mehta.'

'Very well,' said Miss Malti, 'then tell me, are you an idealist or a materialist?'

'Both.'

'How can that be?'

'Very simple. I change myself to suit the situation.'

'Then you have no definite convictions of your own?'

'How can I hold definite convictions about questions for which there are still no fixed answers and never will be? I've just stumbled on this conclusion which others arrived at only after lapping up endless books and ruining their eyes. Can you name one thing a philosopher has done other than involve himself in intellectual gymnastics?'

'Come on then,' Dr Mehta said, unbuttoning his coat. 'I'll take you on. Whether anyone else agrees or not, I consider you a philosopher.'

Mirza turned to Khanna. 'Shall I fix up a match for you too?'

'Yes, yes,' Miss Malti urged. 'Take him along and pit him against Mr Tankha.'

'No,' Khanna protested, blushing. 'Please leave me out of this.'

'What about you then?' Mirza asked the Rai Sahib.

'Onkarnath is the right opponent for me,' the Rai Sahib replied, 'but he hasn't showed up today.'

Mirza and Mehta, stripped to their shorts, went out on the field, one joining each side.

The spectators were enjoying the sight of the aged contestants immensely. They laughed and clapped, called them names, urged them on, laid bets on the results, and kept up a barrage of comment ... Wonderful! Just look at that old fellow, strutting along as though he's going to smear them all before going back to his side ...Yes, but that looks like his older brother coming out from the other side ... Notice the way they're making passes at each other ... Plenty of life left in those bones ... These people have been fed more butter than we've had water ... People say India's getting richer, and that may be true, but it would be hard to find the guts in today's young men that we're seeing in these old codgers ... There—that old man over there has grabbed him. Look at how the poor fellow's struggling to get loose ... You'll never get away now, kid! Three men have just jumped him....

So it went, as the viewers gave vent to their enthusiasm, their full attention riveted on the playing field—on the attacks and counterattacks, the leaping and prancing, the grabbing and tackling, being knocked out and then reentering the fray. Occasionally guffaws would ring out from all sides, or the spectators would spot some foul play and fill the air with a roar of protests. Some people got so excited that they dashed out towards the field.

But the handful of gentry, those who'd bought the expensive tickets and were seated under a canopy, were not getting much pleasure out of the game. They were discussing more important matters....

Khanna drank down his glass of ginger, lit a cigar, and then said to the Rai Sahib, 'As I told you, the bank won't settle for any lower rate of interest. I'm already making a special concession for you because you're like one of the family.'

The Rai Sahib's smile was almost hidden behind his moustache as he said, 'Your policy is to use a blunt knife to hack the throats of family members only?'

'What's that you're saying?'

'I'm just telling the truth. You charged Surya Pratap Singh seven per cent. From me you're asking nine, and claiming to be doing me a big favour. But then, why not?'

Khanna burst out laughing as though this were a good joke. 'I'll charge you the same interest, but on the same conditions. I have a mortgage on his property, and chances are he'll never lay hands on that again.'

'I'm willing to give up some of my property. Better to get rid of some useless holdings than to pay nine per cent. You get the Jackson Road house sold and you can take a commission.'

'It would be rather hard to make anything on that house. You know how far out of town it is. Anyway, I'll see what I can do. What do you estimate it to be worth?'

The Rai Sahib suggested a hundred and twenty-five thousand, pointing out that ten acres of land went with the place.

Khanna was taken aback. 'You must be dreaming of the prices fifteen years ago, Rai Sahib,' he protested. 'Surely you realize that property values have dropped fifty per cent since then.'

'That's not true,' the Rai Sahib retorted, offended. 'Fifteen years ago it was worth a hundred and fifty thousand.'

'Well I'll keep an eye out for a buyer. But my commission will be five per cent—from you.'

'I suppose you get ten per cent from other people! What are you going to do with all the money you're making?'

'All right—pay me anything you like. That should satisfy you. By the way, you've not yet bought any shares in the sugar mill. There are only a few left. If you miss the chance, you'll regret it later. And you've not taken out an insurance policy either. You have a bad habit of procrastinating. When you put things off like this even where your own interests are involved, how can other people expect any help from you? That's why they say an estate makes a man soft in the head. If I had the power, I'd confiscate all these hereditary estates.'

Mr Tankha, meanwhile, was casting his net at Malti. She had clearly stated that she had no desire to get involved in all the bother of an election, but Tankha was not one to give up so easily. Coming over, he propped his elbows on the table and urged her to reconsider. 'I'm telling you, you may never get such a good opportunity again. The Rani Chanda hasn't even a one-anna-to-the-rupee chance against you. I only want the people going into the Council to be ones who've had some experience and who've been of some service to the people. There's no room in the Council for a woman who only knows how to have a good time and live in luxury, to whom people are nothing but fuel for her car, whose greatest service has been giving parties for governors and secretaries. In the new Council the members will have quite a lot of power, and I don't want to see that power getting into the wrong hands.'

'My dear sir,' Malti protested, trying to shake him off. 'I don't have ten or twelve thousand to spend on an election campaign. The Rani, of course, can easily put out several hundred thousand. What's more, I make about a thousand rupees a year from her, and I'd lose that income if I were to run against her.'

'First tell me this—do you want to get on the Council or not?'

'I'd like to—but only with a free pass.'

'Leave that to me. You'll get your free pass.'

'No thanks. Please excuse me. I don't want to risk the disgrace of being defeated. When the Rani opens up her purse and there's a gold sovereign going for every vote, even you'll give her your support.'

'You think elections can only be won with money?'

'Oh no, the individual also counts for something. But what service have I done the people, other than having gone to jail once? And to tell you the truth, I did even that for the sake of my own interests—as did Khanna and the Rai Sahib. The new social order is based on wealth. Education and service and family and caste count nothing in comparison. Granted, there have been times in history when the rich were overthrown by revolution, but those have been the exceptions. Take my own case—if some poor woman comes to my clinic, she may not even be called for hours. But if a lady shows up in a car, I go greet her at the door and wait on her as though some goddess had appeared. I'm no match for the Rani. For the kind of councils being set up these days, she's much more suitable.'

Out on the field, Mehta's team was losing steadily. More than half his side were already out. Mehta had never played kabaddi before, whereas Mirza was a past master of the game. Mehta devoted his vacations to acting in dramas, where his skill surprised even the experts. Mirza, on the other hand, was interested only in arenas—both of wrestlers and of beautiful women.

Malti's attention was focussed on the game. Going over to the Rai Sahib, she said, 'Mehta's side is certainly getting badly beaten.'

The Rai Sahib and Khanna were still discussing insurance, but the Rai Sahib, tired of the topic, saw Malti as a good avenue of escape. 'Yes indeed,' he said, rising. 'They really are taking a beating. Mirza's a first-class player.'

'What possessed Mehta, anyway?' Khanna put in. 'He's just making a fool of himself needlessly.'

'What's so foolish about it?' Malti snapped. 'It's all in fun.'

'Well, everyone from Mehta's side who crosses the line is done for.'

'Isn't there any half-time in this game?' Malti asked after a moment.

Khanna saw the chance for a bit of devilry. 'It was he who wanted to take Mirza on. Probably thought this would be as simple as philosophy.'

'What I'm asking is whether there isn't a half-time in the game.'

'The game's practically over,' Khanna teased her again. 'The fun's going to start when Mirza tackles Mehta, throws him to the ground, and makes him squeal "give up".'

'I wasn't talking to you. I'm asking the Rai Sahib.'

'A half-time in this game?' the Rai Sahib said. 'The men only go into action one at a time.'

'All right. Well, there goes another of Mehta's men dead.'

'Just watch,' Khanna gloated. 'They'll all be finished off that way and it'll be Mehta's turn.'

Malti flared up. 'You didn't even have the courage to go out on the field.'

'I don't play such boorish games. Tennis is for me.'

'Yes, and I've beaten you hundreds of times at tennis.'

'Have I ever denied that?'

'Well if you do, I'm ready to challenge you.'

With that retort, Malti returned to her seat. Nobody was sympathizing with Mehta. Nobody was asking that the game be stopped right now. And Mehta himself—what a silly fool he was being. Why didn't he cheat a little and end the game? But no, he was determined to show that he respected the rules. In just a moment he'd be coming back trounced, with everyone clapping and making fun of him. How delighted people were getting, seeing only about twenty of his men left in the game.

As the end drew near, the crowd grew impatient and surged towards the field. The rope barricades were torn down. Volunteers tried to hold people back, but they were helpless against the wild excitement of the crowd. The flood tide of the game had at last swept within reach of its main target. Mehta had one advantage—being the last man left on his side, he would not have to hold his breath while he attacked. Everything depended on him now. If he could make his sortie into enemy territory and return unscathed, his side would be saved. As many of the enemy as he tagged before coming back across the centre line would be dead, and an equal number of his own men would come back in the game. If he failed, all the blame and shame of the defeat would fall on him.

All eyes were on Mehta. He started to move. The crowd had surrounded the field. Tension was at its height. How calmly he was
advancing towards the enemy. Each movement he made was reflected in the spectators, who were craning their necks and leaning
forward in their seats. The charged atmosphere was nearing the
combustion point. Mehta entered hostile territory. The enemy moved
back, their strategy so clever that Mehta's attempts to catch or touch
any of them were proving futile, disappointing those who'd hoped
he could win back at least six or eight men.

All at once Mirza leaped forward and seized him around the waist.
Mehta, struggling furiously to get free, began pulling Mirza towards
the centre line. The crowd went wild, and it was hard to distinguish
players from spectators in the confusion. It was a bout between Mirza
and Mehta—but then several of Mirza's old men sprang at Mehta and
clung to him also. He lay quietly, pinned to the ground. If only he
could somehow drag himself to the centre line, just two feet away, fifty
of his men would be resurrected. But he couldn't move an inch—
Mirza was sitting on his shoulders. Mehta's face was turning purple,
his eyes were red as an insect's, and he was dripping with perspiration; but Mirza kept pressing down on his back with the full weight
of his massive body.

Malti pushed her way forward and cried out sharply, 'Mirza
Khurshed! That's not fair! The game is a tie.'

Khurshed squeezed down on Mehta's neck. 'I'll never let go unless
he says "give up": There's nothing stopping him.'

Malti stepped closer. 'You can't use force like that just to get him
to say "give up".'

'I certainly can,' Mirza insisted, increasing the pressure on Mehta's
back. 'Tell him to say it and I'll get off right now.'

Mehta tried once more to rise, but Mirza pushed down on his neck.

'This is no game; it's a fight,' Malti protested, seizing Mirza's hand
and trying to pull him away.

'So what if it is?'

'You mean you won't let go?'

Just then a kind of earthquake took place. Mirza lay sprawled on
on the ground, Mehta was racing toward the line, and thousands
of people seemed to have suddenly gone mad and were tossing their
hats, turbans and sticks in the air. No one knew just how the upset
had occurred.

Mirza picked Mehta up and carried him to the pavilion. Every mouth seemed to be crying out that the Doctor Sahib had won the game, praising his courage and tenacity, and exclaiming over the way the tables had been turned.

Oranges had been provided for the hired players. They were each given one and then told they could leave. For the special guests, refreshments were being served in the pavilion. Mirza and Mehta sat down opposite each other at the same table, and Malti took a seat next to Mehta.

'I've had a new experience today,' Mehta said, 'discovering that a woman's sympathy can turn defeat into victory.'

'So that was it!' Mirza declared, glancing at Malti. 'I was wondering how you suddenly managed to flip me that way.'

Malti blushed. 'I never knew until today what a heartless man you are, Mirzaji.'

'It was his own fault. Why didn't he give up?'

'I wouldn't have done that even if you'd killed me,' said Mehta.

The clusters of friends stayed there chatting for some time. Then, after expressing thanks and congratulations, the guests took leave. Malti had a call to make, so she left also. Only Mehta and Mirza remained, since they were covered with dirt and would have to wash up before getting dressed. Gobar drew some water from the well and the two friends started their baths.

'When's the wedding to be?' Mirza inquired.

'Whose?' Mehta asked, surprised.

'Yours.'

'My wedding? With whom?'

'Come now! You act as though it were something to hide.'

'Not at all. I'm telling you the truth—I know absolutely nothing about it. Is a marriage being arranged for me?'

'You think Miss Malti will settle for being just a companion?'

Mehta became serious. 'Your guess is all wrong. Listen, Mirza—Miss Malti is beautiful and good-natured and understanding and broadminded, and she has lots of other virtues. But she doesn't have, and probably can't have, what I want in a life partner. I expect a wife to be a model of devotion and selflessness, someone who by her silent submission, by her self-sacrifice, by her complete self-effacement becomes an integral part of her husband's inner being. The body remains that of the man, but the soul becomes that of the woman. You'll ask why the man shouldn't be self-effacing too—why all this is expected only of the woman. But a man just isn't capable of it. If he were to efface himself, he'd become a nothing. He'd go sit in a cave and dream of merging with the Supreme Being. A man is dynamic and he takes pride in thinking himself a paragon of wisdom. So he'd immediately imagine himself becoming one with God. But a woman is like the earth—patient, peaceful and forbearing. When a man takes on feminine qualities, he becomes a saint. When a woman takes on masculine qualities, she turns into a slut. Men are attracted to a woman who's entirely a woman. Malti hasn't yet attracted me. How can I explain my concept of a woman to you? The embodiment of all that's beautiful in the world—that's what I call a woman. I expect her to have no desire to retaliate even if I try to kill her, to feel no jealousy even if I make love to another woman before her very eyes. If I ever find such a woman, I'll fall at her feet and offer myself to her.'

'You'll probably never find a woman like that in this world,' Mirza said, shaking his head.

'Not one, but thousands,' Mehta insisted. 'Otherwise the world would be utterly desolate by now.'

'Give me just one example.'

'Take Mrs Khanna.'

'But what about Mr Khanna?'

'Khanna is one of those unfortunates who gets hold of a diamond and thinks it a mere piece of glass. Just think how unselfish she is and at the same time how loving. But Khanna's heart is so set on physical attractions that it probably has no room for her. If some calamity were to strike him today, though, she'd lay down her life for him. Even if he went blind or got leprosy, it would make no difference in her devotion to him. He can't appreciate her worth yet, but you watch—one day this same Khanna will consider it an honour to drink the water with which he's washed her feet. I don't want the kind of wife with whom I can discuss Einstein's theories or who'll proofread my books. I want the kind of woman whose love and sacrifice will make my life bright and pure.'

Khurshed stroked his beard thoughtfully, as though recalling something from the distant past. 'Your ideas are perfectly sound, Mehta. If a woman like that were to be found anywhere, I'd get married myself. But I don't have any such hopes.'

Mehta laughed. 'Well, you keep searching and I will too. Maybe some day we'll be in luck.'

'But Miss Malti's not about to let go of you. I'd be willing to put that in writing.'

'Well, I can only amuse myself with a woman like her. I couldn't marry her. Marriage means self-surrender.'

'If marriage is self-surrender, then what's love?'

'When love takes the form of self-surrender, then it leads to marriage. Until then it's just indulgence.'

Mehta finished dressing and said goodbye. It was evening. As Mirza started to leave he saw that Gobar was still watering the plants. 'Go on, you're free now,' he said, pleased. 'Will you come back tomorrow?'

'I'm looking for some kind of job, sir,' Gobar ventured timidly.

'Well if it's a job you want, then I'll take you on.'

'How much will I make, sir?'

'Whatever you say.'

'Who am I to say? Give me whatever you wish.'

'I'll pay you fifteen rupees and expect good hard work.'

Gobar was not afraid of work. As long as he got paid for it, he was prepared to slave day and night. For fifteen rupees, there was no question about it—he'd work himself to death if necessary.

'If I could get a shack of some kind, I'd stay right here,' he said.

'Yes, yes, I'll arrange a place for you. In fact you can use a corner of this hut.'

CHAPTER 14

HORI'S entire crop had gone to pay the fine. They somehow struggled through May, but by the beginning of June not a grain was left in the house. Five mouths to feed and the food supply utterly exhausted. Even if two meals a day were not possible, there had to be at least one. If stomachs couldn't be filled, they must at least be half filled. After all, how many days could one live without food? They'd have to borrow, but from whom? Even now he didn't dare show his face to any of the people who loaned money in the village. He could hire himself out as a labourer, but to whom? And in June his own work piled up. But a man couldn't very well work on an empty stomach.

It was evening. The baby was wailing. How could a mother's breasts supply milk though, when she was getting nothing to eat? Sona was resigned to the situation, but Rupa didn't understand and kept crying for something to eat. During the day she distracted her hunger by nibbling on green mangoes; now she wanted something more substantial.

Hori went to Dulari to borrow some grain, but she had closed the shop and gone to market. Mangaru not only turned him down but scolded him also. 'So you've come begging for a loan! In three years you've not paid even half a pice interest on the last one and now you expect another. You'll pay it back in the next world, I suppose. A person with evil intentions is bound to end up in your predicament. God himself won't put up with such wickedness. How is it that you cough up the money without a murmur when the overseer threatens? I suppose my rupees weren't really rupees? Besides, that woman of yours treats me like dirt.'

Hori, close to tears, returned home and sat dejectedly on the doorstep. Just then his brother's wife showed up to get a light for her fire. Reaching the door of the kitchen, she saw that the room was in darkness. 'Aren't you cooking today or what, sister?' she asked. 'It's past the time.'

Punni had reestablished a speaking relationship with Dhaniya after Gobar ran away, and she had even begun feeling grateful to Hori. Cursing Hira, she would say, 'That killer! Murdering a cow and then running away. He blackens the family name and then deserts us. If he ever tries to come back, I won't let him set foot in the house. Even killing a cow doesn't shame him. It would have been a good thing if the police had caught him and put him on hard labour turning the grindstone.'

'How can I cook when there's not a grain of food in the house?' Dhaniya said, unable to think of an excuse. 'That brother-in-law you're so fond of paid the fine and filled the bellies of the village elders, but he doesn't care whether our children live or die. And now the caste just ignores us.'

Puniya realized that Hori's tireless labours had been responsible for the success of her crop. They'd never had such a good harvest when Hira was doing the work.

'Why haven't you sent to my place for some grain?' she said. 'Whatever we have is thanks to your good husband and no one else. When times are good, we can afford to quarrel, but when times are bad, we can only get by if we share each other's troubles. I'm not so blind that I can't recognize a kind heart. Where would I be today if that good man hadn't looked after me?'

She turned and started for home, taking Sona with her. In no time they were back with two baskets of grain, which were set in the courtyard. There was a good three bushels of barley. Before Dhaniya could say a word, Puniya was off again, and a moment later she reappeared with a big basket of dal and offered to help start the fire.

Dhaniya now saw that there was a small basket containining eight or ten pounds of wheat flour on top of the barley. For the first time in her life she was completely overcome. 'You've brought so much,' she said with tears of love and gratitude filling her eyes. 'Have you kept anything for yourself? One would think it was about to run away or something.'

The baby lay crying on a cot in the courtyard. Puniya took him in her arms and caressed him. 'Thanks to you, sister, there's still plenty more. There were twenty bushels of barley and twelve of wheat, and over six of peas too. . . . I've nothing to hide from you. It's enough for both our families. And in two or three months the corn will be in too. After that, we're in the hands of God.'

Jhuniya came forward and touched Punni's feet with the edge of her sari, receiving her blessing. Sona went to light the fire and Rupa took the jug to fetch water. The wheels started rolling again. Choked with obstructions, the river had been swirling and foaming and roaring. Now, with the obstructions cleared away, it began slowly surging forward again in a quiet, smooth flow.

'Why was your husband in such a hurry to pay the fine?' Puniya asked.

'How else could he get back in the good graces of the community?' Dhaniya said sarcastically.

'You won't be offended if I tell you something, sister?'

'Of course not. Why should I be offended?'

'No, I'd better not say. It might make you angry.'

'I won't mind, I assure you. Go ahead and tell me.'

'You shouldn't have taken Jhuniya into your house.'

'What else could I have done? She'd have drowned herself.'

'You could have sent her to my house. Then nobody would have said a thing.'

'That's what you say now. If I'd sent her then, you'd have chased her off with a broom.'

'You could have paid for Gobar's wedding with what you've spent.'

'One can't stand in the way of fate, my dear. And despite all that, we've still not saved our necks yet. Bhola is demanding payment now for the cow. He gave it to us with the understanding that we'd find him a wife. Now he says he's not going to get married—that all he wants is his money. His two sons have been coming around with big sticks. We don't have anyone to put up a fight against them. That damned cow has been the ruin of our family.'

After a little more talk, Puniya took a light from the fire and went away. Hori, sitting outside, had been observing everything. Coming in, he said, 'Puniya's really a good woman at heart.'

'I suppose you think Hira was good at heart too,' Dhaniya retorted. Although she accepted the grain, she had felt ashamed and disgraced at having to do so. A twist of fortune had thrown her into this humiliating position.

'You're never grateful to anyone—that's one bad thing about you.'

'Why should I feel grateful? Hasn't my husband been slaving his life away over her fields? And it's not as though I've taken this from her as a gift. I'll pay back every grain.'

Puniya realized how her sister-in-law felt, but she still wanted to show her appreciation to Hori. When this grain was exhausted, she'd sent over another two or three bushels.

But when July arrived and there was still no rain, the problem became more acute. Then came August, and hot winds began to whirl, drying up the wells and scorching the sugar cane. There was still a little water in the river, but the farmers brandished big sticks and fought for access to it. Finally the river gave up the struggle and ran dry too. Thefts began occurring, and then armed robberies. The whole province was in an uproar.

At last, late in August, the blessed rain came, and the farmers' spirits revived. What rejoicing there was that day ! It seemed as though the thirsty earth would never be satiated, and the farmers danced around as excitedly as though it were raining gold sovereigns which were theirs for the taking. Ploughs began to move in the fields where hot whirlwinds had been blowing. Children ran out to inspect the tanks and ponds and puddles. 'Aha, the tank's half full already,' they shouted, and ran from there to check the puddles.

No matter how much rain fell now, however, the sugar cane was ruined. The stalks would grow to a height of one foot, but no more, and the corn and millet and rye wouldn't even pay the rent, much less satisfy the appetites of the moneylenders. At least, though, there would be fodder for the cattle, and the people would survive.

When January had passed and Bhola had still not received his money, he lost his patience and stormed over to Hori's house. 'So this is how you keep your word,' he raged. 'Didn't you promise with your own mouth to pay me once the cane had been crushed? Now it's been crushed, so come on—hand over the money.'

Hori explained his predicament, pleading in every possible way, but without success. Bhola refused to budge from the door. At last Hori became exasperated. 'I've told you—I have no money now and I can't get a loan from anyone. Just where am I to get it? There's hardly a grain of food in the house. If you don't believe me, come inside and see for yourself. You're welcome to take anything you find.'

'Why should I search your house?' Bhola said relentlessly. 'I'm not asking whether you have money or not. You told me you'd pay once the cane was pressed. That's been done. Now give me my money.'

'You tell me how, and I'll do it.'

'How am I to say?'

'That's up to you.'

'Very well, I'll unhitch your two bullocks and take them.'

Hori stared at him in astonishment, unable to believe his ears. Then, crushed, his head drooped. Did Bhola want to leave him a beggar? Giving up those bullocks would be like having his own hands cut off.

'I'll be ruined if you take the bullocks,' he murmured abjectly, 'But if your *dharma* says so—if you think it's the only right thing to do—then go ahead and take them.'

'It's no concern of mine whether you're helped or whether you're hurt. What I want is my money.'

'And if I claim I've already paid you?'

Bhola was speechless. Now it was his turn to doubt his ears. Surely Hori couldn't be as dishonest as all that. 'All right,' he declared angrily, 'if you'll take Ganges water in your hands and swear you've paid me, I won't push the matter any further.'

'I'm tempted to take that oath. A starving man will do anything. I won't do it, though.'

'You couldn't even if you wanted to.'

'That's right, brother, I couldn't. I was only joking.' Hori hesitated a moment and then added, 'Why do you hold such a grudge against me, Bhola? Do you think it's been heaven for me having Jhuniya in the house? Not only did my son run away, but I had to pay a two-hundred rupee fine as well. I've been left with nothing. And now you come to dig up the roots. God knows, I had no idea what my boy was doing. I thought he was going over to your place to listen to the singing. I only discovered the truth when Jhuniya showed up here late that night. And if I hadn't taken her in, where could she have gone? Tell me—to whom could she have turned?'

Jhuniya had been standing behind the door to the porch, listening to all this. As far as she was concerned, Bhola was now an enemy, not a father. Afraid that Hori might surrender the bullocks, she told Rupa to run and tell Dhaniya to come at once, that it was very important.

Dhaniya was out spreading manure on the field. Hearing the message, she hurried back immediately. 'Why did you send for me, daughter? Your message had me worried.'

'You saw my father, didn't you?'

'I saw him all right—sitting at the door looking like a butcher. I didn't bother to speak to him.'

'He's asking dada for the two bullocks.'

Dhaniya felt as though a sudden cramp had hit her stomach. 'He's asking for the bullocks!'

'Yes. Says either we produce the money or he'll take them.'

'And what did your dada say?'

'He told him to take them if his dharma said it was the right thing to do.'

'Then let him take them. But if he doesn't end up as a beggar at this very door, you can spit on my name. If our blood is the only thing that will make him happy, then let him have it.'

She stormed out of the house and addressed Hori—'If this man's asking for the bullocks, why don't you give them to him? Let him fill up his belly. God will look after us. After all, he's not cutting off our hands, is he? So far we've worked for ourselves; now we'll work for others. If God wills it, we'll own bullocks again some day. If not, if we have to go on being hired labourers—well, what's so bad about that? At least we won't be weighed down with worry about floods and droughts and rents. I didn't realize this man was our enemy or I'd never have accepted that cow and all the misery that came with her. Our house has been a complete wreck ever since the day that cursed creature appeared on the scene.'

This was Bhola's chance to pull out the weapon he'd been concealing. Seeing that the bullocks were their only means of support, he was sure they would do anything to save them. Like an expert marksman, he aimed at the heart—'If you think you can pile disgrace on me and then sit back in comfort, you're sadly mistaken. You cry over your two hundred rupees. Well I've had a reputation worth millions ruined. There's only one way you can improve matters—turn Jhuniya out of your house the same way you took her in. Then I won't ask either for your bullocks or for the price of the cow. That girl's given our family a bloody nose—now I want to see her get kicked around too. I can't bear to see her sitting around here like a queen while our faces get tarred with shame and we're made to weep instead of her. True, she's my daughter. I rocked her in my own arms, and, as God is my witness, I loved her no less than my sons. But if I were to see her today begging from door to door and picking over garbage heaps, it would warm my heart. Just think how badly I must have been hurt in order to feel so hard-hearted towards my own daughter. The witch has torn down a reputation built up by seven generations of our family. If that's not a slap in the face, I'd like to know what is.'

Dhaniya spoke up with a force that could have cut into rock. 'All right. Now you listen to what I have to say. What you're hoping for is not going to happen—not now and not in a hundred rebirths. Jhuniya's a part of our flesh and blood now. You say you'll take the bullocks? Then take them. If that's going to heal the bloody nose of family, then heal it. If that will save the honour of your ancestors, then save it. Jhuniya did wrong, that's true. That day she set foot in our house I was all ready to drive her out with a broom. But when the tears started pouring from her eyes, I took pity on her. You're an old man now, Bhola, and yet you're still in hot pursuit of another wife. And here she's still just a child. . . .'

Bhola gave Hori a pleading look. 'You hear how she talks, Hori. Now don't blame me. I won't leave without the bullocks.'

'Take them,' Hori declared.

'Then don't start crying later that I've gone and taken your bullocks.'

'I won't.'

Bhola was just loosening the halters on the animals when Jhuniya came out of the house, wearing an old patched sari and carrying the baby in her arms. 'All right, father,' she declared, 'I'm leaving this house. I'll fill my stomach and the baby's by begging, just as you want. And if begging doesn't work, I'll drown myself somewhere.'

'Get out of my sight,' Bhola snarled. 'God spare me from ever having to see your face again. Depraved hag! Disgrace to the family! Drowning is just what you deserve.'

Jhuniya didn't even glance in his direction. The anger consuming her was aimed at self-destruction rather than violence. If the earth had opened up and swallowed her, she'd have thought herself blessed. She started walking.

But she'd not gone two steps when Dhaniya ran and caught hold of her. 'Where are you going, daughter?' she said with fierce affection. 'Go back in the house. This is your home as long as we're alive and even when we're dead. The person who deserves to drown is the one who can hate his own child. Any decent man would be ashamed to say such things. That lowdown creature—trying to threaten me!' She turned to Bhola. 'Take the bullocks, and go drink their blood.'

'Mother,' Jhuniya sobbed, 'when even my own father condemns me, you should let me go drown myself. My evil fate has brought you nothing but misery. You've been dragged in the mud ever since I came. And all the while, you've given me more love than even my own mother would have. All I pray is that you be my mother if God grants me another birth.'

Jhuniya followed her mother-in-law into the house. Outside, Bhola untethered the bullocks and started home, huffing and puffing, and looking as though he were coming from a feast where he'd been attacked with shoes rather than fed rich pastries. 'Well,' he consoled himself, 'now let's see them plough their fields and play their flutes! Trying to humiliate me, the whole lot of them. No telling how long they'd been nursing that hatred. But what respectable man would keep such a girl in his house! Absolutely shameless, all of them. No wonder they couldn't find a wife for that no-good son. And look at the nerve of that slut Jhuniya—coming and standing right in front of me. Any other girl would have been ashamed to show her face. But there's not even a tear in her eyes. They're all crooks—and fools too, thinking Jhuniya is theirs now. They don't realize that any girl who would leave her own father's house won't stay long in anyone else's. If these weren't such bad times, I'd grab that bitch Dhaniya by the hair and drag her through the middle of the bazaar. The foul things she said about me!'

Bhola looked over the bullocks again. A fine pair of animals, and in good shape. He could easily sell them for a hundred rupees. He'd get his eighty rupees back all right.

Before he was even out of the village, however, Bhola spotted Datadin, Pateshwari, Shobha and some fifteen or twenty others coming after him. His blood ran cold. Now there'd be a battle royal. They'd snatch away the bullocks and beat him up besides. He stopped and tightened up his dhoti. If he had to die, he'd die fighting.

'Hey Bhola!' Datadin shouted as he came running up. 'What sort of dirty work have you been up to? You think you're a big lion just because he couldn't stop you from taking his bullocks? We were all too busy with our work to realize what was happening. If Hori had given the slightest sign, we'd have torn every hair from your head. You'll take those bullocks right now, if you know what's good for you. What an inhuman thing to do!'

'It's all because Hori's so gentle,' Pateshwari said. 'If you have some money coming from him, then go file a suit with the proper authorities and get a decree. What right have you to make off with the bullocks? He could file a complaint and have you locked up in no time.'

'But sir,' Bhola replied meekly, 'I didn't take them by force. Hori gave them to me himself.'

Pateshwari turned to Hori's younger brother. 'Shobha, you take the bullocks back. What farmer would give away his own bullocks?'

'We're taking the animals. You go file a suit if you want your money. After all, did you give him cash? First you dump a curse-ridden cow on his head and now you want to take his bullocks in exchange. We ought to knock you down and beat the life out of you.'

Bhola didn't move, standing in front of the bullocks as quietly and firmly as though they'd have to kill him before he'd step aside. He certainly couldn't hope to win by arguing with a patwari.

Datadin took a step forward, straightened his bent back, and called out, 'What are you all standing around staring for? Beat him up and chase him out of here. Running off with bullocks from our village!'

Banshi, a sturdy young man, gave Bhola a hard push. Losing his balance, Bhola fell to the ground, and when he tried to get up, Banshi punched him again.

Just then they saw Hori running towards them. Bhola dashed out to meet him. 'Swear on your honour, Hori—did I take the bullocks by force?'

Datadin felt some explanation was necessary. 'He says you gave him the bullocks of your own free will. He's trying to make asses out of us.'

Hori hesitated. 'He told me that either we had to throw Jhuniya out or give him his money. Otherwise he'd take the bullocks. I told him I wouldn't turn out my daughter-in-law and that I had no money ... so if his dharma said it was the right thing to do, he should take the bullocks. That was all—I left it to his dharma, and he took them.'

Pateshwari looked glum. 'If you left it to his dharma, then there's no question of force. His dharma said to take them. Go ahead, brother, the bullocks are all yours.'

'That's right,' Datadin agreed. 'When it becomes a matter of dharma, there's nothing anyone can say.'

They glanced contemptuously at Hori and then, the battle lost, headed homeward, while Bhola, his head held high in triumph, led the bullocks away.

G

CHAPTER 15

———————

OUTWARDLY, Malti was a butterfly; inwardly, she was a bee. Her life was not just laughter and gaiety. After all, one can't live on sweets alone—and even if he could, it would not be a very pleasant life. Malti was gay, but because she knew the price for gaiety. Her twittering and glittering did not mean she thought life to be all fun or the world intended only for her enjoyment. On the contrary, her lightheartedness was an attempt to ease the burden of her responsibilities a little.

Her father was one of those amazing people whose gift of speech alone brings money rolling in by the thousands. He made his entire living from zamindars and other rich people—handling sales of their property, arranging loans for them, and getting problems settled for them with the help of his influential contacts. In other words, he was a middleman or broker. People of this gifted class of people take up any job that promises a profit and manage somehow or other to make it succeed. They'll arrange a marriage between a raja and a princess and knock off ten or twenty thousand for themselves in the process. When these middlemen deal in minor affairs, they are known as touts and universally despised. But when those touts operate on a larger scale, they end up on hunting trips with rajas and at the tea tables of governors. Mr Kaul was among these fortunate ones.

Kaul's only children were three daughters, whom he hoped to send to England so as to assure them a brilliant education. Like many other well-to-do men, he believed that an English education somehow transforms people. Perhaps the climate there had some power to sharpen the intellect. Only a third of his desire had been fulfilled, however. While Malti was in England, he had been incapacitated by a paralytic stroke. He could just barely get in and out of a chair even with the help of two men, and he had completely lost the power of speech. When his voice stopped, his income stopped also. All that he owned had been earned by that voice, that eloquence, and he'd not been in the habit of putting aside any savings. His income had been irregular and his expenses unrestrained. As a result, they'd been in very tight straits for the last several years.

The full responsibility fell on Malti. They couldn't exactly live in ease and luxury on her income of four or five hundred a month, but at least her sisters were still getting an education, and they managed to lead a respectable life. Malti rushed around from early morning until late night. She wanted her father to lead an austere and simple life, but he was hopelessly addicted to meat and alcohol. When no money was available, he'd go to a certain moneylender, make out a promissory note against his house, and collect a thousand rupees or so. The moneylender was an old friend who'd earned a fortune through Mr Kaul's manipulations, so he couldn't very well refuse. The debt had mounted to twenty-five thousand rupees, and the moneylender could have had the property put up for auction any time he wished. But the obligations of friendship prevailed, even though Kaul developed all the shamelessness that comes to self-centred people and paid no attention to requests for payment. Malti would get upset at his extravagance; but her mother—a goddess incarnate who even in this day and age felt that a woman's chief reason for existence was to serve her husband—kept pacifying her, and this prevented an open battle from breaking out in the family.

It was evening. The air was still warm and the sky was overshadowed with haze. Malti and her two sisters were seated on the lawn in front of the house. The grass there, unwatered, had dried up, exposing bare patches of dirt.

'Doesn't the gardener ever water the lawn?' Malti asked.

'That pig—he does nothing but sleep,' replied Saroj, the second sister. 'When we say anything, he starts dragging out a dozen excuses.'

Saroj was studying for her B.A. A rather slim, tall, pale, harsh and bitter girl, she was always finding fault with others, since nothing anyone said was to her liking. Doctors had advised her to take it easy and go live in the hills, but the family situation was such that they couldn't afford to send her.

Varda, the youngest, was jealous of the way the family seemed to pamper Saroj. She wished that she could get some illness that would arouse equal sympathy. Fair, poised and robust, she had sparkling eyes and the glow of intelligence on her face. She loved everything in creation except Saroj, and automatically opposed everything Saroj said. 'Father keeps sending him to the bazaar all day,' she said.

'When would he have time for anything else? He doesn't even get time off to die—and you say he sleeps all the time.'

'That's a lie,' Saroj snapped back. 'When has father ever sent him to the bazaar?'

'Every day—every single day. Just today he sent him. You want me to send for him and have him questioned?'

'You want me to send for him and ask him myself?'

Malti, afraid that the evening would be spoiled if the two got any more embroiled, changed the subject. 'Let's drop the matter for now. Saroj, did Dr Mehta give a lecture at your school today?'

Saroj wrinkled her nose. 'Yes, he gave it all right. Nobody enjoyed it though. He started saying that the role of women in the world is completely different from that of men, and that women's encroachment on male territory is the disgrace of our times. All the girls started clapping and whistling. The poor fellow got embarrassed and sat down. He seems like a strange sort of man—also said that love is just something dreamed up by poets, that there's no evidence of it in real life. Lady Hukku really made fun of him.'

'Lady Hukku!' Malti sneered. 'What nerve she has even to open her mouth on the subject! You should have paid attention to Dr Mehta's speech from beginning to end. What an impression he must have of you girls!'

'Who would have the patience to listen to him give a whole lecture? That would just be pouring salt on the wounds.'

'Then why was he even invited? And after all, he's not a woman-hater. We all express our own ideas as to what is true. He's not one of those people who just say what they think the ladies want to hear. And besides, who knows whether the path women want to take is the right one or not? It's quite possible that after trying it for a while, we'll be forced to change our course.' Malti went on to describe the ideals held by French, German and Italian women, and then mentioned that Mehta would be addressing the Women's League some time soon.

Saroj was intrigued. 'But even you say that women should have equal rights with men.'

'I still say so, but we must listen to the other side too. It's possible that we're in the wrong.'

The Women's League had recently been organized, largely due to Malti's efforts. All the educated ladies in town had become members. That evening when Mehta spoke, he arrived at the League

196

hall and found it packed to the bursting point. He felt proud—such enthusiasm to hear his speech! And the enthusiasm was reflected not only in their faces and eyes—the ladies were all loaded down with silks and gold as though taking part in a wedding. They were determined to use every possible means to defeat Mehta, and no one can deny that dazzling splendour is a powerful weapon. Malti had selected her most fashionable sari, bought a blouse of the latest cut, and decked herself out with make-up and flowers as though her marriage were being celebrated. The Women's League had never before attracted such a huge gathering. Though Dr Mehta was the sole opposition, the women's hearts were trembling. One spark of truth can reduce a mountain of falsehood to ashes.

Mirza, Khanna and the Editor were also gracing the occasion with their presence, sitting in the very last row. The Rai Sahib arrived after the lecture had begun and stood behind them.

'Come join us,' Mirza said. 'You won't want to keep standing for long.'

'No thanks,' the Rai Sahib replied. 'At least there's room to breathe here.'

'I'll stand up and you take my seat.'

Mirza started to rise but the Rai Sahib put a hand on his shoulder. 'No formality ... please keep your seat. If I get tired, I'll sit down and let you stand awhile. Well, so Miss Malti's presiding over the meeting. Khanna, this must be a treat for you.'

Khanna pulled a long face. 'She has eyes only for Mr Mehta now. I've been displaced.'

Mehta began his speech:

'Devijis—When I address you this way as "goddesses", none of you find it surprising. You consider such homage to be your natural right. But have you ever heard a woman address a man as *devta*? If you were to call him a god that way, he'd think you were making fun of him. You have sympathy, devotion and sacrifice to offer. What does a man have to offer? He's not a god, a giver; he's a taker. In order to acquire power he commits violence, he gets into quarrels, he fights battles. . . .'

Applause broke out.

'He really knows how to please the women,' commented the Rai Sahib.

The editor of *Lightning* was unimpressed. 'He's said nothing new. I've said the same thing countless times.'

Mehta continued—'That is why, when I see our enlightened ladies becoming dissatisfied with a life of sympathy, devotion and sacrifice, and running after a life of discord, violence and battle, thinking they'll find heavenly bliss there, I can't congratulate them.'

Mrs Khanna's eyes flashed with pride as she glanced over at Malti. Malti lowered her head.

'Now what do you have to say?' Khurshed asked the Editor. 'Mehta's a brave man—speaks the truth, and right to your face.'

Onkarnath grimaced. 'The days are gone when women could be taken in by such simple tricks—usurping their rights and telling them it's because they're goddesses, they're Lakshmis, they're mothers.'

Mehta went on speaking. 'To see a woman looking like a man and doing a man's job pains me just as much as to see a man looking and acting like a woman. I'm sure none of you would consider such a man worthy of your trust and love. And I assure you, a woman like that can't expect a man's love and devotion either.'

Khanna beamed with delight.

'You're looking very happy, Khannaji,' the Rai Sahib needled him.

'When I meet Malti, I must find out what she says now about all this.'

'I believe,' Mehta went on, 'that women have reached a higher stage in the evolutionary process than men, just as I believe love, sacrifice and devotion are superior to violence, warfare and discord. If our devijis want to leave their sacred temples of child-bearing and family-rearing and go out on the fiendish battlefields of violence and discord, no good will come to society. Of that I'm convinced. Men in their arrogance have attached great importance to their devilish fame. By usurping the rights and shedding the blood of their brothers, they think they've won a great victory. Men consider themselves heroes when, with bombs and machine-guns and armoured tanks, they hunt down the children whom women have created and nurtured with their own blood. And when a man's own mother puts a saffron mark on his forehead and sends him to the battlefield with the armour of her blessings, it's astonishing that he can still believe that destruction alone will save the world. Day by day his destructive tendencies have increased until today we find this ungodliness in all its fury—crushing the whole world, trampling out lives, burning up rich green fields and desolating once-flourishing cities. Ladies, I ask you—do you want to take part in this dance of the devil? Do you think you can benefit the world by descending into that field of conflict? I beseech you—let the forces of destruction do their work alone. Devote yourselves to the nurture of your own sacred duties.'

'Malti hasn't even raised her eyes,' Khanna remarked.

The Rai Sahib nodded. 'What Mehta says is perfectly true.'

'But he's still saying nothing new,' the Editor growled. 'All the opponents of the feminist movement resort to this same jargon and gibberish. I don't agree at all that the world has progressed through love and sacrifice. The world has progressed because of manliness, bravery, brainpower and vigour.'

'All right, all right,' Khurshed broke in. 'Are you going to let us listen to the speech or do you intend to keep on sounding off?'

Mehta's lecture continued—'Ladies, I'm not one of those people who say that men and women have the same powers and instincts and that there's no difference between them. I can't imagine a more ghastly falsehood. It's this falsehood that is attempting to blot out the accumulated experience of the ages, like a cloud blotting out the sun. I warn you not to get caught in that trap. Women are as superior to men as light is to darkness. The highest ideals of the human race are forgiveness, sacrifice and nonviolence. Women have already attained that ideal. Men, on the other hand, have been struggling for centuries to reach that goal, supporting themselves with spirituality and a sense of duty and the help of the sages. But they've not been able to succeed. I tell you—put all men's spirituality and religious discipline on one side of the scale and it will be outweighed by the sacrifice of women on the other.'

Applause rocked the hall. The Rai Sahib was delighted. 'Mehta's only saying what he honestly feels in his heart,' he declared.

'Nothing but ancient arguments,' Onkarnath said. 'All rot!'

'But even ancient arguments become new if they're spoken with deep conviction.'

'Anyone who pulls in a thousand rupees a month and throws it around on luxuries doesn't have any deep convictions. He only knows how to please those who are old-fashioned and conservative.'

Khanna glanced over at Malti. 'Why is she looking so happy? She ought to be feeling ashamed.'

Khurshed spurred him on—'Now you must give a speech too, Khanna, or Mehta will knock you right out of the arena. He's already won half the battle.'

'Leave me alone!' Khanna said testily. 'I've caught plenty of sparrows like her before and then set them free.'

The Rai Sahib winked at Khurshed. 'But you're a regular visitor at the Women's League these days. Tell us the truth now—how much have you donated to them?'

Khanna flushed. 'I don't contribute to organizations like this that promote immorality behind a façade of artistic activities.'

Mehta was still speaking—'Men say that they've made all the scientific discoveries, that all the great philosophers and saints have been men, that all the warriors, the statesmen, the best navigators, the best in all fields have been men. But put all these great men together and what have you got? What have they accomplished? What have the saints and founders of religions done except start rivers of blood and whip up flames of hatred? And what's remembered of the great warriors except that they slaughtered their own brothers? What's left to mark the statesmen except the ruins of vanished empires? And what problems have been solved by the inventors and scientists? All they've done is make men slaves to machines. Where do we find peace in this man-made culture? Where do we find brother-hood and cooperation?'

Onkarnath got up and was about to walk out. 'It burns me up to hear such high-flown talk from people who care only about pleasure.'

Khurshed caught hold of his hand and sat him down again. 'Don't be such a fool. Calm down. This is the way of the world—men blurt out whatever happens to come into their heads. Some people listen and applaud. But that's the end of the matter. Countless of these Mehtas will come and go, but the world will move along in the same old way. What's there to get excited about?'

'I can't stand listening to lies.'

The Rai Sahib egged him on. 'Who wouldn't get heated up at hearing the words of a devoted wife coming from the mouth of a loose woman?'

Onkarnath settled back in his seat again as Mehta went on with the speech—'I ask you, would it be fitting for a swan, after watching a hawk in action, to forsake the pleasant peacefulness of Lake Mansarovar and start hunting down sparrows? And if it did manage to become a bird of prey, would you congratulate it? A swan doesn't have such swift wings, anyway, nor such a sharp beak, nor such sharp claws, nor such sharp eyes, nor such a sharp thirst for blood. It would take centuries for a swan to accumulate these weapons, and there's considerable doubt whether it could become a hawk even then. But whether it became a hawk or not, it would no longer be a swan—a swan that feeds on pearls.'

'Those are the arguments of a poet,' Khurshed remarked. 'A female hawk hunts just like a male hawk does.'

Onkarnath smiled. 'And yet he still pretends to be a philosopher on the basis of just that kind of reasoning.'

Khanna's resentment burst out. 'He's nothing but the hind end of a philosopher. A philosopher is one who. . . .'

'One who doesn't deviate even a hair from the truth,' Onkarnath said, completing the sentence.

Khanna objected to the interruption. 'I don't know anything about truth and all that. I call a person a philosopher who really is a philosopher.'

Khurshed congratulated him. 'What a perfect definition you've given of a philosopher! God, that's superb! A philosopher is one who's a philosopher. No denying that!'

'I'm not saying women don't need education,' Mehta continued. 'They do, and more than men. I don't say women don't need strength. They do, and more than men—but not the education and strength with which men have converted the world into a field for violence. If you ladies also go in for that sort of education and strength, then the world will turn into a desert. Your intelligence and strength finds expression in creation and nourishment, not in violence and destruction. Do you believe that mankind can be redeemed either by the vote or by the wagging of tongues and scribbling of pens in offices and courts? For the sake of those spurious, unnatural, destructive rights, do you want to give up the rights which nature has bestowed on you?'

Thus far, Saroj had been restraining herself out of deference to her older sister, but she could tolerate it no longer. 'We want the vote, the same as men!' she shouted.

Several other young women took up the cry—'The vote! The vote!'

Onkarnath stood up and bellowed, 'Shame on the enemies of women's rights!'

Malti pounded on the table. 'Order, order! Those who want to speak on either side of the question will have a full opportunity to do so later.'

Mehta proceeded with his speech—'The vote is a delusion of the modern age—a mirage, a disgrace, a fraud. If you get caught up in

G*

that spiral, you'll end up neither here nor there. Who says your sphere is too narrow, that you don't get a chance to express yourselves? We're all human beings first and anything else later. Our lives depend on our homes. That's where we're born, where we're raised and where we spend our lives. If that sphere is limited, then what sphere is unlimited? The sphere of conflict where there's just organized looting? Do you want to leave the workshop where man and his destiny are shaped, and move to the factories where man is ground into dust, where the blood is squeezed out of him?'

'It's the tyranny of men which has aroused this spirit of revolt in women,' Mirza shouted.

'That's true,' Mehta agreed. 'Men have been guilty of injustice. But this attitude of women is no solution. Destroy injustice, but don't destroy yourself in the process.'

'The reason women want rights,' Malti interrupted, 'is so they can make proper use of them and stop men from abusing their power.'

'The greatest power in the world,' Mehta replied, 'comes from service and sacrifice, and you already have that power. Compared with that power, the vote is nothing. It saddens me to see our sisters adopting the ideals of the West, where women have surrendered their rightful position as mistresses of the home and have fallen to a level where they are mere sensual playthings. The Western woman wants independence so as to indulge herself fully in worldly pleasures. A life of pleasure was never the ideal of *our* mothers. It's because of women's selfless service that they have been given the right to direct and manage the household. Take from the West those things which are good . . . culture involves constant give and take. But blind imitation is a sign of mental weakness. The Western woman doesn't want to remain a housewife. The keen desire for sensual pleasure has robbed her of all restraint. She is sacrificing the modesty and dignity which is her crowning glory on the altar of frivolity and amusement. When I see educated Western girls making a display of their charms—their shapely limbs, their nakedness—I feel sorry for them. Their passions have conquered them so fully that they can't even protect their own modesty. And what greater degradation can exist for a woman?'

The Rai Sahib began clapping, and applause resounded through the hall like a volley of firecrackers.

'Even you have no answer for that argument,' Mirza told the Editor.

'That's the only valid point he's made in the whole lecture,' Onkarnath conceded drily.

'Well that makes you one of Mehta's disciples too.'

'Oh no, I'm not a disciple of anyone. I'll search out an answer to him—you'll see it in *Lightning*.'

'In other words, you aren't searching for truth—you just want to fight for your own prejudices.'

The Rai Sahib decided to give him a hard time too. 'And yet you brag about your love for truth?'

The Editor was unperturbed. 'An advocate's job is to look after the welfare of his clients, not to sort out truth from untruth.'

'Then you should just say that you're an advocate for women.'

'I'm an advocate for all those who are weak, who are defenceless, who are oppressed.'

'You really are incorrigible.'

'Actually,' Mehta was saying, 'it's men who are behind this plot to pull women down from their exalted position to the same level as themselves . . . those men who are cowards; who can't handle the responsibilities of married life, who want to gratify their despicable passion in a sea of sexual licence like bulls running wild through lush new pastures. In the West, this conspiracy has been successful and women have become mere butterflies. And now in India too, I'm ashamed to say—in this land of sacrifice and austerity—that same wind has begun to blow. Our educated sisters especially are falling under the spell of that plot, surrendering their ideal of domesticity and turning themselves into gaudy butterflies.'

'We're not asking men for advice,' Saroj burst out. 'If they have the right to be free, then so do women. Girls today don't want to make marriage their career. They'll get married only on the basis of love.'

There was enthusiastic applause, especially from the front rows where the ladies were sitting.

'What you call love is a fraud,' Mehta replied, 'a distorted form of inflamed passion, just as ascetic renunciation is only a refined form of begging. If there's a deficiency of love in married life, then there's a complete absence of it in unrestrained sensuality. True happiness and true peace are found only in selfless service. That alone is the fountainhead of rights; that alone is the source of power. Service is the only cement that can bind husband and wife together in a lifelong love and companionship that is impervious to even the strongest of blows. Where service is lacking, one finds divorce, desertion and distrust. And the responsibility rests largely on you, since you are the helmsmen in the boat of men's lives. If you wish, you can steer that boat through wind and storm. But if you get careless, the boat will sink and drag you down with it.'

The lecture was over. Several ladies asked permission to present the other side of this controversial subject. It was already late, however, so Malti adjourned the meeting with thanks to Dr Mehta, announcing that on the following Sunday several ladies would present their ideas on the subject.

'I liked your speech very much, Mr Mehta,' the Rai Sahib congratulated him. 'I agree with every word you said.'

Malti laughed. 'Of course you congratulate him—there's no disagreement among thieves. But why should all this advice be dumped only on the heads of women? Why should they have to carry the full burden of preserving ideals, respecting traditions and making sacrifices?'

'Because they understand these things,' Mehta replied.

Khanna's big eyes were staring at Malti as though trying to read her mind. 'It seems to me,' he ventured, 'that the Doctor Sahib's views are about a hundred years behind the times.'

'Which views?' Malti asked curtly.

'All this service and duty and stuff.'

'Oh, so you think those ideas are a century behind the times! Then please do tell us your fresh new ideas. You have some brand new prescription for marital happiness?'

Khanna winced. He'd only been trying to please her, and instead she had become more irritated with him. 'Mehta Sahib must know that prescription,' he said.

'But the doctor has already explained his remedy, and you declared it out of date by a hundred years. So you're the one who must provide a new solution. Aren't you aware that many things in the world never go out of date? Problems like this keep coming up in society and will continue to do so.'

Mrs Khanna had gone out on the veranda. Mehta went over, greeted her respectfully and asked, 'How did you like what I said in the lecture?'

Mrs Khanna lowered her eyes. 'It was good—very good. But it's because you're not yet married that you can still talk of women as goddesses, as superior creatures, as helmsmen. Get married though and then tell me what women are like. And you'll have to get married now, after saying that men who try to avoid marriage are cowards.'

Mehta smiled. 'That's exactly why I'm preparing the ground.'

'Miss Malti's a good match for you, too.'

'On one condition—that she first sit at your feet for a while and learn the duties of a woman.'

'That's your male selfishness again. Have you ever learned the duties of a man?'

'The only problem is to find a teacher.'

'Mr Khanna could teach you very well.'

Mehta laughed. 'No, I'd rather learn from you—even about the duties of men.'

'Very well then, I'll be your teacher. The first thing you must learn is this—forget that business about the superiority of women and the responsibility they must bear as a result. Men are superior, and it's they who support the household. It's men who inspire all that service and self-control and sense of duty in women. If men lack these qualities, their women will lack them also. The reason women are rebelling these days is that men have lost those virtues.'

Mirza came up and lifted Mehta off the ground with a great hug. 'Congratulations!'

Mehta eyed him quizzically. 'You liked my speech?'

'The speech was ... well ... so-so. But it was a smashing success. You've bewitched even that elusive pixie. You can thank your good fortune—that woman who until today never paid much attention to anyone is now singing your praises.'

'Wait and see if the intoxication lasts before you say that,' Mrs Khanna murmured.

'What woman's going to be attracted to a bookworm like me, Deviji?' Mehta asked in a detached tone of voice. 'I'm just a thorough idealist.'

Mrs Khanna saw her husband heading for the car, and went off to join him. Mirza left too. Mehta had just picked up his cane and started for the door when Malti caught his hand. 'You can't go yet,' she said, her eyes pleading. 'Come home, let me introduce you to my father, and then have dinner with us.'

Mehta clapped his hands over his ears in feigned horror. 'Oh no, you'll have to excuse me. That Saroj would eat my head off. I'm really scared of girls like that.'

'No, please. I'll see to it that she doesn't even open her mouth.'

'All right. You go on ahead. I'll be along after a little while.'

'I'm sorry—Saroj has gone off with my car. I'll have to ask you for a lift home.'

They got into Mehta's car and drove away. 'I've heard that Mr Khanna beats his wife regularly,' Mehta said after a moment. 'Ever since then, I've hated the very sight of him. I can't consider someone a man who's as cruel as that. And yet he pretends to have great respect for women. Haven't you ever given him a talking to?'

'You forget that it takes two people to make a fight,' Malti retorted.

'I can't imagine anything that would justify a man's beating his wife.'

'No matter how foul-mouthed she were?'

'Even then.'

'Then you're some new species of man.'

'If a person has an unpleasant disposition, would you say he automatically deserves to be whipped?'

'Men can't forgive as readily as women can. You admitted that yourself in your speech.'

'So is that all the reward a woman gets for her forbearance? I think that you're just encouraging Khanna by being so friendly with him. With all the respect and adoration he has for you, you could easily straighten him out. But by defending him, you become a partner in his crime.'

'You should never have brought up this subject,' Malti said sharply. 'I don't like to speak badly of anyone. But you don't really know his wife Govindi. You assume from her innocent and calm appearance that she must be an angel. I wouldn't give her such an exalted position. If I were to tell you all the ways she's tried to hurt me and give me a bad name, you'd be shocked, but then you'd realize the treatment she's getting is just what women like that deserve.'

'There must be some reason, though, behind her disliking you so much.'

'You'll have to ask her about that. How do I know what's going on in someone else's heart?'

'I can guess the trouble without even asking, and it goes like this. . . . If any man dared come between me and my wife, I'd shoot him dead. If I couldn't kill him, then I'd shoot myself. Similarly, if I were to try to put another woman between my wife and myself, my wife would have the right to do everything possible to prevent it. There could be no compromise in that situation. It's a basic human reaction, inherited from our jungle ancestors. Maybe it's unscientific, and some people today might call it uncivilized and antisocial, but I've not yet been able to suppress that instinct . . . nor would I want to. I don't care what the law says in the matter. In my home, I am the law.'

'And just what makes you assume,' Malti said sharply, 'that I want—as you put it—to come between Khanna and Govindi? That assumption is an insult to me. I care more for the toe of my shoe than I do for Khanna.'

Mehta looked sceptical. 'You're just saying that, Miss Malti. Do you think everyone in the world is a fool? I can't blame Mrs Khanna for believing the same thing that everyone else does.'

'People take great delight in tearing others down,' Malti said resentfully. 'That's the way they are, and I can't change human nature. But this is just plain slander. True, I'm not so heartless as to drive him away every time he comes around. In my kind of work I have to greet everyone and be gracious to them. If someone wants to give some other interpretation to it, then . . . he . . .'

Malti's voice caught in her throat. She turned her face and dabbed her eyes with a handkerchief. 'And you—' she sniffed after a moment, 'just like all the others . . . that's what really hurts . . . I hadn't expected it from you.'

Then, perhaps regretting this show of weakness, she burst out angrily, 'You have no right to accuse me. If you're one of those people who can't see a man and a woman together without pointing an accusing finger, then go ahead and point all you like. I couldn't care less. If some woman were to keep coming to you on one excuse or the other, treating you like a god, taking your advice about everything, laying herself at your feet, ready to jump into the fire if you gave even the slightest hint, I'd be willing to swear that you wouldn't ignore her. If you could just kick her aside, then you're completely inhuman. I don't believe you could do it, no matter how much logic and evidence you present to claim that you could. I'm telling you—far from ignoring her, not to speak of kicking her aside, you'd be drinking the water with which you'd washed her feet; and before many days had passed, she'd have won your heart completely. I beg you with folded hands, don't ever again mention Khanna's name in front of me.'

As though warming his hands over this blaze, Mehta said, 'On one condition—that I never see Khanna with you again.'

'I'm only human. If he comes around, I can't drive him away.'

'Tell him to go display all that gallantry to his own wife.'

'I don't think it's proper to meddle in other people's personal affairs. Nor do I have the right.'

'Then you can't stop people from talking.'

They had reached Malti's bungalow. The car stopped. Malti got out and walked off without shaking hands. She even forgot that she'd invited Mehta for dinner. All she wanted was to get off by herself and have a good cry. This was not the first time that Govindi had hurt her feelings, but the blow which that woman had just struck through Mehta had been the hardest, the cruelest and the most penetrating.

CHAPTER 16

WHEN the Rai Sahib got word that there'd been a dispute in one of his villages and that the elders had collected a fine from Hori, he immediately sent for Nokheram and demanded an explanation. Why had he not been informed? There was no place in his service for such a double-crossing traitor.

Nokerham became hot with indignation at having to swallow such a diatribe. 'It's not as though I was the only one,' he protested. 'The other leaders were all in on it. What could I have done?'

The Rai Sahib levelled a piercing gaze at the man's protruding belly. 'Don't talk nonsense. You should have forbidden them to collect the fine until I had been notified. What right does the village council have to come between me and my tenants? The only income I get from my villages comes from these fines and penalties. The rent that's collected goes to the government, and the tenants make off with everything else. So where does that leave me? What am I supposed to eat—your head? The yearly expenses run into hundreds of thousands of rupees, and where's that money to come from? It's pitiful that you still have to be told all this when your family has been working for me for two generations. How much money was collected from Hori?'

Nokheram hesitated. 'Eighty rupees,' he said apprehensively.

'In cash?'

'Where would he get cash, sir? He gave some grain and mortgaged his house for the rest.'

The Rai Sahib dropped the question of his own interests and came to the defence of Hori. 'Oh, so you and that bunch of hypocrites have ganged up and ruined a faithful tenant of mine! Answer me this— what right did you all have to collect a fine from a tenant on my estate without even informing me? I could easily have you all slapped in jail for seven years for this—you and that fraud of a patwari and that sly pandit. You think you're the rulers of this estate. Well let me tell you something—either the whole amount of that fine reaches me by this evening or there'll be real trouble. I'll have every one of you turning the grindstone in the jail. Get out now. Oh, one more thing—send Hori and his son to me.'

'His son ran away from the village,' Nokheram muttered timidly. 'He ran away that same night the trouble started.'

'Stop lying!' the Rai Sahib shouted furiously. 'You know I can't stand lies. Who ever heard of a boy getting his girlfriend to elope with him and then running away from her? If he were going to run away, why would he have bothered taking her to his home? This is undoubtedly some more of your villainy. Even if you drowned yourself in the Ganges to prove your innocence, I wouldn't believe you. You people must have bullied him for violating the blessed conventions of your society. The poor fellow had no choice but to run away.'

Nokheram dared not argue. He couldn't even suggest that the Rai Sahib go and check the truth for himself. The master is always right. The anger of these big men demands complete surrender— they can't tolerate even a word of protest.

When the village elders heard the Rai Sahib's decision, their smugness melted away. The grain was still there, but the money had long since vanished. Hori's house was mortgaged, but who would buy a house way out there in the village? Just as a Hindu wife, the royal mistress of the household, becomes suddenly worthless if her husband deserts her, so Hori's house, worth a fortune to him, was of no value to anyone else. But the Rai Sahib would settle for nothing less than the money. That Hori must have gone crying to him! Pateshwari Lal was the most frightened of all, since he was in danger of losing his job. The four men racked their brains, but no one came up with any bright ideas. Each blamed the others, and soon they were quarrelling bitterly.

'I warned you that we should leave Hori alone,' Pateshwari declared, shaking his long neck in dismay. 'We've already paid a fine over that cow business, and this time it's likely to take more than a fine to save our necks. It might cost us our jobs. But all you people cared about was the money. Well, there's still one hope—take out twenty rupees, each of you. Remember that we'll all be locked up if the Rai Sahib should decide to report the matter.'

Datadin put on a display of brahmanic power. 'I don't have even twenty pice, let alone twenty rupees! There was that feast for the brahmans, and the special sacrifices that were performed. . . . I suppose nothing was spent for all that! Let the Rai Sahib put me in jail if he dares. I'll become a brahman phantom and wipe out his whole family line. He's evidently never tangled with a brahman before.'

Jhinguri Singh spoke up in much the same way. He was not employed by the Rai Sahib, and besides, they'd not beaten Hori nor used force of any kind. If Hori wanted to do penance and they'd given him the opportunity, no one could condemn them for that.'

It was not quite so easy for Nokheram to wriggle loose, though. It was he who sat in comfort at a desk and ruled the village. His pay was only ten rupees a month, but he took in another thousand a year on the side. He had authority over hundreds of people, four errand boys awaited his commands, all his work was done by forced labour, and even the police inspector offered him a chair. Where else could he find such a soft life?

As for Pateshwari, it was only his job that had enabled him to set himself up as a moneylender. What was to be done? For two or three days he struggled to find some way out of the predicament, and an idea came to him at last. He had occasionally seen copies of the daily paper *Lightning*. If they sent an anonymous letter to the editor describing how the Rai Sahib squeezed fines from his tenants, the tables might really be turned. Nokheram agreed to the proposal, and the two of them got together and drafted a letter which they then sent off by registered mail.

Onkarnath was always on the lookout for such letters. As soon as this one arrived, he sent word to the Rai Sahib that he'd received some information which he was not inclined to believe. The amount of evidence supplied by the correspondent made it impossible just to ignore the allegations, however. Was it true that the Rai Sahib had collected an eighty-rupee fine from one of his tenants just because the man's son had started living with a widow? His duty as an editor compelled him to investigate the matter, and to publish the letter as a public service. Of course anything the Rai Sahib wished to say in the matter would also be published. The editor sincerely hoped that the information was false; but if there was any truth in it at all, he would have to bring it to light. Friendship could not shake him from the path of duty.

When the Rai Sahib received this notice, he clasped his hands to his head. His first impulse was to give the editor a good fifty lashes with a whip and tell him to go report that in the paper along with the letter. But then, reflecting on the consequences, he controlled himself and set out to meet the man. Any delay might mean the letter would be printed, blackening his entire reputation.

Onkarnath returned after a stroll and sat down to work out his editorial for the day, but his mind was fluttering around like a bird. His wife had made some remarks to him the night before which were still pricking him like thorns. He wouldn't have minded in the least if she had called him poor or unfortunate or stupid. But to be told he had no manliness—that was insufferable. And what right had his wife, of all people, to say that? It was she who was supposed to silence anyone who tried to say things against him. It was true, of course, that he never printed news or comments that might bring trouble on his head, and that he took each step cautiously. But what else could one do in these days of black laws? And why was it he didn't put his hand into the snake's hole? Only to save his family from hardship. And then this was the reward for his forbearance. What injustice! How could he buy Banaras saries for her when he had no money? How could he help it if the wives of Doctor Seth and Professor Bhatiya and heavens knows who else wore brocade saries? Why didn't his wife shame them all by wearing homespun ones? His own practice was to wear the coarsest homespun when visiting any important person, and to be ready with a devastating reply for anyone who dared criticize his dress. Why didn't his wife have that same self-confidence, instead of getting all upset at seeing the other ladies in their flashy finery. She ought to understand that she was the wife of a dedicated patriot . . . and a patriot has no assets other than his devotion.

Thinking that this might be a good topic for the day's editorial, his thoughts drifted back to the matter involving the Rai Sahib. He'd have to wait and see how the Rai Sahib replied. If he could successfully establish his innocence, that would be the end of the matter. But if he thought that Onkarnath could be bullied, threatened or cajoled into neglecting his duty, then he was sadly mistaken. The Editor's only reward for all his self-denial and dedication was an occasional chance like this to expose these legalized bandits. He was well aware that the Rai Sahib was a very powerful man. He was a member of the Council and had a lot of influence with the authorities. He could easily get the Editor hauled into court on some false charge, or have him beaten up on the road somewhere by hired thugs. But Onkarnath was not afraid of that sort of thing. As long as a breath of life remained in his body, he would continue to expose these tyrants.

The sound of a motor car suddenly roused him. Snatching a piece of paper, he began writing his article. A moment later, the Rai Sahib stepped into the office.

Onkarnath neither greeted him nor asked about his health nor offered him a seat. Instead, he just surveyed the Rai Sahib as a judge might look over a prisoner just produced in court. 'You got my note?' he asked in an imperious tone. 'I was under no obligation to write to you that way. My only duty was to investigate the matter myself. But one must sometimes sacrifice principles a little out of consideration for friends. Was there any truth in that accusation?'

The Rai Sahib could have flatly denied taking the money, since he'd not received any of it yet. But he wanted to see what the Editor had in mind. So he admitted that the report was true.

Onkarnath tried to sound regretful. 'Then I'm afraid the only course open to me is to publish the letter. I'm very sorry to be forced to criticize such a good friend, but personal feelings must not stand in the way of duty. What right does a man have to be an editor if he can't fulfil the duties of the position?'

The Rai Sahib pulled up a chair, filled his mouth with betel, and said, 'I think you'll find this detrimental to your own interests. Whatever may happen to me will happen some time in the future. But you'll suffer immediately. If you don't care at all about friends, well then I'll play the same game.'

Onkarnath assumed the air of a martyr. 'I've never been afraid of threats. The day I accepted the burden of editing a paper, I took my life in my hands. And for me, the most glorious death of all would be to lay down my life defending truth and justice.'

'All right then, I accept your challenge. Until now, I've thought of you as a friend; but since you insist on a fight, then a fight it shall be. After all, why do you suppose I pay five times the regular subscription price to your paper? For only one reason—to keep it under some kind of obligation to me. It was God who made me a rich man. I give you seventy-five rupees just so you'll keep your mouth shut. Hardly three months go by without your crying about deficits and appealing for help, and I'm the one who comes to your aid. Why? At festival times—on Diwali, Dashahra and Holi—I send you sweets and things, and every other week I invite you to dinner. Why? You can't combine both bribes and duty.'

'I've never taken a bribe,' Onkarnath protested hotly.

'If those things aren't bribery, then just what is?' the Rai Sahib retorted contemptuously. 'Do you think everyone in the world except you is a complete ass? That people make up your deficits without any selfish motives? Take out your ledger and tell me how much you've made so far from my estate. It must add up to thousands. And if you're not ashamed to print advertisements of foreign medicines and things while you keep shouting "Buy local products", then why should I be ashamed about imposing punishments, penalties and fines on my tenants? Don't try to tell me that you're the only one taking up the sword on behalf of the peasants. My fortunes rise and fall with the peasants. Nobody could be more concerned about their welfare than I. But I do have to make a living, after all. How else can I give those banquets for the officials, and make donations to the government, and take care of the needs of hundreds of relatives? You surely know how high the expenses are at my house. You think we grow money on trees? It all has to come from the tenants. You probably think zamindars are the happiest people on earth. Well, you have no idea about the actual state of affairs. If we tried to be absolutely virtuous, we'd have trouble even staying alive. If we didn't give presents to the officials, they'd soon have us in jail. We're not scorpions, rushing around stinging people for the fun of it. Throttling the poor is no great pleasure. But we do have to maintain a certain position. You expect to profit from my wealth—and everyone else also considers a zamindar to be the goose that lays the golden eggs. Just come to my bungalow and I'll show you how I'm hounded from morning till night. One person comes with shawls from Kashmir, another keeps pestering me to buy a gramophone, another is an agent for perfumes and tobacco, another for books and magazines, another for life insurance, and so on. Everyone has something to sell. And then there are the countless people collecting donations. Am I to sit down and recite my tale of woe to each of them? They're certainly not coming to tell me their troubles. They come to fleece me, to play me for a sucker. If I were to drop all appearances, they'd start making fun of me. And if I stopped making gifts to the officials, I'd be considered a rebel. And you wouldn't be writing articles to defend me if that happened. I once joined the Congress party, and I'm still paying the price. My name's on the black list. And have you ever cared to find out how loaded down with debts I am? If all the moneylenders got decrees against me, everything down to this ring on my finger would have to be sold off. You'll say there's no need for me to keep up all this show. It's easy to say that—but I can't just toss away a tradition built up by seven generations of ancestors. It's impossible for me to give up everything and go become a grass-cutter. You can afford to be fearless—you have no lands, no property, no hereditary position to maintain. And yet even you sit cowering with your tail between your legs. Have you any idea of how much bribery goes on in the courts, of how many poor people are being wiped out, of how many innocent girls are being defiled? Do you have the guts to write about that? I'll give you the material, and with it the full evidence.'

Onkarnath softened a little. 'Whenever such occasions arise, I always step forward to accept them.'

The Rai Sahib had mellowed somewhat also. 'Yes, I admit that on one or two occasions you've shown some manliness, but always with an eye to your own interests, not the public welfare. Now don't start looking shocked and angry. Every campaign you've fought has had the same opportune results—the enhancement of your own prestige and power and income. If you're playing that old game against me now, then all right, I'm willing to go along with you somewhat. I won't give you money—that would be a bribe. But I'll have some piece of jewellery made up for your wife. Would that do? And now I'll tell you the truth—the information you received was false. I admit that, like all zamindars, I collect fines and levies which add up to a few thousand a year. But if you try to snatch that nice morsel away from me, you'll be the loser. Look—you want to lead a good life and so do I. What's the point of putting up a big show of justice and duty when it would only damage both of us? Let's speak frankly. I'm not your enemy. Many's the time we've sat down and eaten together on the kitchen floor or at the same table. And I realize that you have troubles too. Perhaps you're in worse shape than I am. But of course if you've sworn to play Harishchandra, to sacrifice everything for the sake of virtue, that's your privilege. I'd better be going.'

The Rai Sahib stood up. Onkarnath caught his hand and said with a conciliatory air, 'No, no, do sit down. Let me clarify my position. I'm very grateful to you for the favours you've done me. It's just that this is a matter of principle, and you know that principles are more precious to me than life itself.'

'All right, my friend,' the Rai Sahib said with a smile as he sat down again. 'Write whatever you wish. I don't want to damage your principles. After all, it'll only mean a little notoriety, and there are limits to what one can do in trying to keep a spotless reputation. All

215

the big landlords harass their tenants to some degree or other. A dog can't eat his bone and guard it too. All I can do is make sure you get no more complaints like this in the future. If you believe in me at all, then please forget the matter this once. With any other editor, I wouldn't be playing up to him this way. I'd be having him whipped in public. But you're a friend, so I have to restrain myself. This is the age of newspapers. Even governments are afraid of them ... what more a mere individual like myself. You can make or break anyone you wish. Anyway, let's consider the matter closed. Tell me, how's the paper doing these days? Any increase in circulation?'

'We manage somehow or other,' Onkarnath said, unhappy with the direction the conversation was taking. 'And under the present circumstances, that's all I expect. I didn't go into this business for the sake of money or pleasure, so I'm not complaining. I wanted to serve the people, and I'm doing that to the best of my ability. My only desire is that the nation prosper. A single individual's happiness or unhappiness is inconsequential.'

The Rai Sahib nodded even more understandingly. 'That's all quite true, my dear fellow,' he said, 'but one has to make a living before he can start serving. You can't concentrate on service if you're preoccupied with financial worries. Isn't your circulation increasing at all?'

'The problem is this—that I don't want to lower the standards of my paper. I could attract more subscribers by publishing pictures and articles about film stars, but that's not my policy. There are any number of such devices by which papers can make money, but I consider them reprehensible.'

'That's why you're so respected today. I'd like to make a proposal. ... I don't know whether you'll agree to it or not. Add a hundred people to your list of subscribers. I'll pay the charges.'

Onkarnath bowed his head in gratitude. 'I accept your donation with thanks. It's a pity that people are so indifferent about the press. There's no lack of funds for schools and colleges and temples, but as yet not a single benefactor has appeared with money for the advancement of newspapers, even though the goal of educating the public could be achieved at less expense through newspapers than through any other means. If newspapers could be supported by endowments as educational institutions are, there'd be no need to waste so much time and space on advertisements. I'm very grateful to you.'

The Rai Sahib left. Onkarnath's face was not exactly sparkling with delight. The Rai Sahib had imposed no conditions or restrictions of any kind, but it was humiliating to be unable to refuse his charity after getting such a tongue-lashing. Things had reached a point, however, where Onkarnath was desperate for help. The workers at the press had not been paid for three months, and he owed the paper-supplier over a thousand rupees. At least he had the satisfaction though, of not having begged the Rai Sahib for charity.

Just then Onkarnath's wife Gomti appeared. 'Don't you think it's time to eat yet?' she complained. 'Or is there some rule that you have to sit here until one o'clock? How long am I expected to go on tending the fire?'

Onkarnath looked up, his eyes full of misery, and Gomti's defiance evaporated. She knew the difficulties he faced. Rebellious thoughts sometimes flared up in her mind when she saw other women in their finery and jewels, and she would lash out momentarily at her husband. Actually, though, that anger was directed not at him but at her own unlucky fate. In the process, however, a little of its heat unavoidably spread as far as Onkarnath. His austere life aroused both resentment and sympathy in her. He was just a bit eccentric, that was all. Seeing how depressed he looked, she asked, 'Why so unhappy? Is your stomach upset or something?'

Onkarnath forced a smile. 'Who's unhappy? I? I'm even happier today than I was the day I was married. The first transaction this morning brought in fifteen hundred rupees. I must have seen an auspicious face when I first woke up.'

'Where would you get fifteen hundred?' Gomti said. 'That couldn't be true. If you say fifteen, I might believe you.'

'No, I swear by your head—I knocked off fifteen hundred. The Rai Sahib was just here. He promised to cover the cost of a hundred new subscriptions.'

Gomti's face fell. 'And you expect to get the money?'

'Of course. The Rai Sahib always keeps his word.'

'I've never yet seen a zamindar keep his word. My father worked for one. He'd go all year without getting paid. So he quit and went to work for another zamindar. That one didn't give him a pice for two years, and when Father finally protested, he was beaten up and chased away. The promises of those people don't mean a thing.'

'I'll send him a bill today.'

'Go ahead and send it. He'll tell you to come tomorrow. Tomorrow he'll be off on a tour of his estate and won't be back for three months.'

Onkarnath began feeling some misgivings. It was quite true that there'd be nothing he could do if the Rai Sahib went back on his word. But he steeled his heart and declared, 'That's impossible. The Rai Sahib is one person I don't think could be such a double-crosser. He's always made good on his promises.'

Gomti was as sceptical as before. 'That's why I call you such an idiot. If someone shows just the least bit of sympathy, you get all puffed up. These fat rich men have room in their bellies to swallow up any number of promises like that. If they started making good on all their promises, they'd soon be out begging on the streets. The zamindar in my village would go for two and three years at a time without settling his bills with the shopkeepers. He made only nominal payments to the servants, and if one of them, after a full year's work, asked for his wages, he'd be thrashed and thrown out. The names of his sons were struck from the school rolls a number of times because their fees had not been paid. Finally he took the boys out of school and kept them at home. Once he even asked for a railway ticket on credit! This Rai Sahib belongs to the same fraternity. Go eat your dinner—and keep turning the grindstone that fate has allotted you. You should consider it a blessing if these big men keep finding fault with you. For every pice they give you, they extort four times that amount from their tenants. As of now you're free to write whatever you like about them. Otherwise you'd be forced to say only what they want to hear.'

Panditji was eating his dinner, but he was having trouble swallowing. At last he couldn't go on without unburdening his heart somewhat. 'If he doesn't pay up, I'll give him a lesson he'll never forget. I've got him by the throat. Those villagers wouldn't have sent me a false report. When they're scared to death even to pass on true information, it's not likely they'd dare make false charges. I've received a report making accusations against the Rai Sahib. If I were to publish it, he wouldn't dare show his face in public. He's not giving me anything out of charity. It's the only way he can get out of a desperate situation. At first he tried threats, but when he saw that wouldn't work, he threw this bait to me. I thought I might as well accept the gift, since my setting this one man right was not going to wipe out injustice in the country. True, I've lowered my ideals. If on top of that the Rai Sahib cheats me, I won't hesitate to use underhanded methods myself. It wouldn't take much to soothe my conscience about robbing a person who steals from the poor.'

CHAPTER 17

WORD swept through the village that the Rai Sahib had summoned the members of the village council, given them a good scolding, and made them cough up all the money they had collected. He'd been about to send them to jail; but they'd fallen at his feet and licked up their own spit, so he'd let them off. Dhaniya, her heart warmed by the news, went around the village trying to shame the five judges— 'Human beings may not hear the cries of the poor, but God certainly does. Those men thought they could just fine us and then sit back gorging themselves on fried cakes. Well, God gave them such a whack that the cakes fell right out of their mouths. They had to pay double what they'd taken from us. Now let's see them take my house and lick their lips !'

But how could the fields be cultivated without bullocks? The sowing season had begun in the village. For a farmer to be without bullocks in October was like having both hands cut off. Hori was helpless. In everyone else's fields, ploughs were moving and seeds were being sown, and occasional snatches of song could be heard. But Hori's fields lay as desolate as the house of a destitute widow. Puniya had a pair of bullocks and so did Shobha, but they couldn't very well find time to do Hori's work on top of all their own. All day Hori wandered aimlessly from field to field. In some of them, he would just sit idly by, but in others he helped with the sowing and got a little grain in return. Dhaniya, Rupa and Sona were all doing the same. As long as the sowing season lasted, there was no special problem in getting something to fill their stomachs. There was mental suffering, of course, but at least there was enough to eat. Every night, though, little quarrels would break out between the husband and wife.

As November wore on, work became scarce in the village. Everything depended now on the sugar cane which was standing in the fields.

It was night, and bitterly cold. There was nothing to eat in Hori's house. They'd gotten hold of a few cooked peas during the day but now there was no reason to start the fire. Rupa, overwhelmed by hunger, sat by the door and sobbed. With not a grain of food in the house, there was no point in her asking for anything to eat.

When the hunger became unbearable, she went off to Puniya's house on the excuse of getting a light. Puniya was making millet chapaties and cooking up some greens. The aroma made Rupa's mouth water.

'Hasn't the fire been lit yet at your house?' Puniya asked.

'There's no food in the house today,' Rupa said meekly, 'so why start a fire?'

'Then why have you come asking for a light?'

'So father can smoke.'

Puniya tossed a smouldering dung cake towards her, but Rupa let it lie there and moved in closer. 'Your bread sure smells good, auntie. I love millet chapaties.'

Puniya smiled. 'Will you have some?'

'Mother will scold me.'

'Who's going to tell her?'

Rupa ate her fill and then ran home without even rinsing out her mouth.

Hori was sitting dejectedly inside the house when he heard Pandit Datadin calling him. His heart began thumping. Was some new disaster about to strike? Going outside, he touched the pandit's feet and pulled over a stool for him.

Datadin sat down and said benevolently, 'Your fields are still lying fallow, Hori. If you'd only said something to one of us, Bhola would never have dared to take away your bullocks. He'd have been killed right then and there. And Hori—I swear on my sacred thread, it wasn't I who imposed that fine on you. Dhaniya has been going around accusing me unfairly. It was the conniving of Lala Pateshwari and Jhinguri Singh. I only sat in on the meeting because people insisted. The others were going to set a heavier fine. I spoke up and had it reduced. Now all of them are weeping and wailing though. They thought this was their kingdom, forgetting that someone else rules the village. Anyway, what arrangements are you making to get your fields planted?'

'What's there to say, maharaj?' Hori answered pathetically. 'They'll just lie fallow.'

'Lie fallow! That would be a great pity.'

'What can I do if it's God's will?'

'How can I sit by and let your fields remain unplanted? I'll have the sowing done tomorrow. The soil is still moist. The crop will be ten days late but otherwise there's no harm done. We'll each take a half share. That way neither of us will lose out. I was just thinking about this today, and feeling very sad that good ploughed land was going to waste.'

Hori was in a quandary. For four months during the rainy season he'd manured and ploughed the fields, and now he'd have to give away half the crop just to get the sowing done... and he was supposed to consider that a favour. But at least it would be better than letting the land lie fallow. If nothing else, he'd at least make enough to pay the land rent. If he didn't pay up this time, his land would be confiscated for sure. So he accepted the proposal.

'Come on then,' Datadin said happily. 'I'll weigh out the seeds now, so you won't have to bother with that in the morning. You've had your dinner, haven't you?'

With some embarrassment, Hori narrated the story of how their fire had remained unlit all that day.

'What!' Datadin chided him gently, 'Nothing to eat in the house and you didn't even tell me? It's not as if I were your enemy. This is what provokes me about you. My dear fellow, what's there to be embarrassed or ashamed about? We're all one, after all. What if you are a *shudra* and I a brahman? We're all one family. All of us have our ups and downs. For all I know, some disaster may strike me tomorrow, and who could I turn to if I couldn't tell my troubles to you? Well, what's past is past. Come on—in addition to the seeds I'll weigh out a bushel or two of grain for you to eat.'

Half an hour later, Hori returned carrying a bushel of barley in a basket on his head, and the grindstone in the house began to turn again. Dhaniya wept as she ground the barley. What sin was God punishing her for this time?

The next day the sowing began. Hori's whole family pitched in as wholeheartedly as though the whole crop were to be theirs. A few days later the irrigating was done with equal zeal. Datadin was getting all this work done for nothing. And now his son Matadin began stopping by Hori's house. A sweet-talking, lusty young man, he was addicted to bhang, on which he spent whatever money Datadin managed to rake in. He had been having an affair with a low-caste chamar girl, so he had not yet married. The affair was still going on; but although the whole village knew about it, no one could say

221

anything. Piety is judged by the observance of rules about eating. If those rules are followed meticulously, a person's piety can not be questioned. Food habits become a shield protecting us against any accusation of unrighteousness.

Because of the farming partnership, Matadin began finding occasions to talk with Jhuniya. On one pretext or another he managed to show up at times when no one but Jhuniya was at home. Jhuniya might not be beautiful, but she was young, and better looking than his chamar mistress. Besides, having lived for some time in the city, she knew how to dress and how to conduct herself, at the same time retaining that modesty which is a woman's greatest attraction. Matadin would sometimes take her baby in his arms and caress it, and this delighted Jhuniya.

'What did you see in Gobar that made you run off with him, Jhunni?' he asked her one day.

'I was drawn by fate, maharaj,' Jhuniya said shyly. 'What else can I say?'

'Unfaithful wretch, that's what he is,' Matadin commisserated. 'Deserting a Lakshmi like you and wandering off God knows where. He's completely irresponsible. I wouldn't be surprised if he's carrying on with someone else by now. Men like that ought to be shot. It's a man's sacred duty to support a woman once he's taken her as his wife. What's this business of ruining the life of one person and then looking around for other victims?'

The young woman began to cry. Matadin glanced furtively around and then took hold of her hand. 'Why do you bother about him? He's gone . . . so let him go. You won't be left in need. Anything you want—money, clothes, jewellery—you can get from me.'

Jhuniya slowly drew her hand away and stepped back. 'That's very kind of you, maharaj. I don't belong anywhere now. I left home to come here, and now there's nothing here for me either. I've lost out on both counts. I was innocent about the ways of the world, so I listened to his sweet talk and walked right into the trap.'

Matadin began maligning Gobar. 'He's just a dissolute loafer, a complete good-for-nothing. Whenever he got hold of a little money, he'd gamble it all away. And he smoked charas and ganja as though his life depended on it. Loitering around with his friends and giving the girls a bad time—that was his main occupation. The police inspector was about to have him arrested, but we pleaded for him and had him spared. He used to steal grain from other people's fields and

222

barns. Several times I caught him myself, but we let him off, figuring that after all he was part of the village family.'

Just then Sona came out of the house. 'Sister,' she said, 'Mother wants you to to take out the grain and let it dry in the sun for a little while. Otherwise we'll lose a lot in the grinding. The pandit must have soaked the grain beforehand to make·it weigh more.'

'You talk as though your house had escaped the rain,' Matadin said defensively. 'In the monsoons even the firewood gets damp, what more the grain.'

With that, he walked off. Sona's arrival had spoiled his game.

'What did Matadin come for?' Sona asked.

Jhuniya frowned. 'He wanted to borrow a tether. I told him we didn't have one.'

'That's nothing but an excuse. He's a very·bad man.'

'He strikes me as a very nice man. What's bad about him?'

'You don't know? He's living with that chamar woman Siliya.'

'And that makes him a bad man?'

'Why else do people call someone bad?'

'In that case, your brother brought me here. Is he bad too?'

Sona evaded the question. 'If that man ever comes here again, I'll tell him to get out.'

'And if your marriage is arranged with him?'

Sona blushed. 'Now you're being nasty, sister.'

'Why? What's so nasty about that?'

'If he even speaks to me, I'll scorch his face.'

'You expect to marry some kind of god? Isn't he the most handsome young man in the village?'

'Then you go off with him. You're a thousand times better than Siliya.'

'Why would I want him? I've already got a man, good or bad.'

'Well, whoever I'm married to, good or bad, I'll stick with him too.'

'And if you're married to some old man?'

Sona laughed. 'Then I'll make soft chapaties for him, I'll prepare his medicines—pounding and straining the herbs, I'll give him a hand when he's trying to stand up, and when he dies I'll cover my face and cry.'

'And if it's a young man?'

'Then . . . oh stop it. Now you're just being silly.'

'All right, tell me—do you prefer them old or young?'

'A man is young if he loves me, old if he doesn't.'

'If only fate would marry you off to some old man—then we'd see how much you loved him. You'd be praying for the miserable creature to die so you could latch on to some young man.'

'Not at all. I'd feel sorry for the old man.'

That year a sugar mill had been opened nearby, and its agents were going from village to village buying up the standing crops of cane from the farmers. This was the same mill which Mr Khanna had started. One day an agent arrived in Hori's village. The farmers who discussed terms with him found that there would be no advantage in making molasses from their cane. Why go to all the trouble of crushing it when the price would be the same? All the villagers were willing to sell their standing crops. Even if they made a little less they wouldn't mind, since they'd be getting immediate payment. Some had bullocks to buy, others had to pay off the rent, and some wanted to get out of the clutches of the moneylenders. Since the cane crop that year was not very good, there had been some doubt as to what it would bring. And no one would buy molasses when mill sugar was available at the same price. They all accepted advances on their crops.

Hori needed a pair of bullocks. He was hoping to make at least a hundred rupees, which would be enough for an ordinary pair of bullocks. But what would he do about the moneylenders? Datadin, Mangaru, Dulari and Jhinguri Singh were all badgering him, but if he started paying them off, the money wouldn't even cover the interest on his debts. He couldn't think of any way to get paid for the cane without people finding out. Once he'd actually bought the bullocks, no one could do anything. But meanwhile the whole village would see the cane when it was loaded on a cart, and everyone would know how much he had been paid once it was weighed. In fact Mangaru and Datadin would probably shadow him the whole time. One moment he'd be getting the money; the next moment they'd have him by the throat.

One evening Girdhar asked him, 'When will your cane be going, Hori?'

'Nothing definite has been settled yet, brother,' Hori replied evasively. 'When will you be taking yours?'

Girdhar was also evasive. 'There's nothing definite about mine either.'

224

Other people were being equally vague. No one trusted anybody. They were all in debt to Jhinguri Singh, and their chief concern was to keep the money from falling into his hands. Otherwise it would all be gobbled up, and the next day the tenants would have to go asking for money again—which would mean new papers, new fees and new gratuities.

The following day Shobha came and said to Hori, 'Can't you find some way to make Jhinguri Singh get cholera? That would finish him off for good.'

Hori smiled. 'How can you say that? He has a family, doesn't he?'

'Should we worry about his family or our own? He keeps two wives in luxury while we don't have even dry bread for one. He'll take everything we make on the cane. He won't let us bring home even a pice of it.'

'My situation's even worse, brother. If this money slips through my fingers, I'm ruined. I can't go on without bullocks.'

'It'll take two or three days to carry the cane to the mill. As soon as that's done, let's offer the foreman a commission if he'll weigh up the cane right away but give us the money later. Then we'll tell Jhinguri Singh that we've not been paid yet.'

Hori thought a moment and then said, 'Jhinguri Singh is twice as clever as you and I together, Shobha. He'll go and get the money straight from the cashier and we'll be left gaping. That Khanna who owns the mill is the same Khanna who has a money-lending business. He and Jhinguri are in the same racket.'

'I wonder if we'll ever get out of the clutches of these money-lenders,' Shobha said dejectedly.

'No hope of that in this life, brother,' Hori said. 'We don't expect to become rulers, and we're not asking for a life of luxury. All we want is just some coarse cloth to wear and some coarse food to eat and a life with some dignity—but even that is impossible.'

'Well, brother,' Shobha said craftily, 'I'm going to fool all of them this time. I'll give something to the man in charge and get him to agree to make me chase around for the money. Jhinguri can't keep running after me indefinitely.'

Hori laughed. 'That won't work. The best thing would be to go beg at Jhinguri Singh's feet. We're caught in a net, and the more we struggle, the more entangled we'll get.'

'You're talking like an old man. Sitting trapped in a cage is just cowardice. What if the noose does get tighter? We'll have to use force

225

H

to get free. If worst comes to worst and Jhinguri has the house auctioned off, let him auction it! I wish that no one would lend us money—that they'd let us starve and be kicked around but not loan us a single pice. But if people with money didn't give loans, then they couldn't collect interest. When one of them sues us, another makes loans at a slightly lower rate of interest and catches us in his net. I won't go to get my money until a day when Jhinguri Singh has gone away somewhere.'

'Yes, that's a good idea,' Hori said, shifting his position.

'We'll have the cane weighed, and then collect the money when we find just the right moment.'

'All right. That's the way we'll work it.'

The next morning several villagers began cutting their sugar cane. Hori, sickle in hand, went to his field also. Shobha came to help, as did Puniya, Jhuniya, Dhaniya and Sona. Some chopped the cane, others stripped the leaves, and others tied it in bundles. When the moneylenders saw the cane being cut, their appetites sharpened as though mice were gnawing at their stomachs. Dulari came running from one direction, Mangaru from another, and Matadin, Pateshwari and the henchmen of Jhinguri Singh from a third.

Old Dulari came painted up and decked out like a young girl, with heavy silver bracelets and anklets, gold pendants dangling from her ears, and her eyes darkened with kohl. 'First give me my money,' she cried out, 'or I won't let you cut the cane. The more lenient I am, the bolder you get. For two years you've not paid even half a pice, and the interest alone comes to fifty rupees.'

'Let us cut the cane, sister, 'Hori pleaded. 'When I get the money, I'll give you as much as I can. I'm not going to run away from the village, nor am I about to die as yet. Is the cane going to bring in any money by just standing in the field?'

Dulari snatched the sickle from his hand. 'You people have such evil intentions . . . it's no wonder you don't prosper.'

Five years before, Hori had borrowed thirty rupees from Dulari. In three years the loan had reached a hundred, and then an official note had been signed. In the next two years the interest had grown to fifty rupees.

'I've never had any evil intentions,' Hori protested, 'and God willing, I'll pay back every pice. The fact is that things are a little tight just at present. Say whatever you like—there's nothing I can do.'

Dulari had no sooner left than Mangaru arrived—dark com-

plexioned, his pot-belly sagging, and his two large front teeth protruding as though ready to bite someone. He wore a cap on his head
and a shawl around his shoulders, and, though not more than fifty
years old, he walked with the help of a long stick. He suffered from
gout and from a bad cough. 'First give me my money, Hori,' he demanded, leaning on his stick. 'Then you can cut your cane. The
money I gave you was a loan, not charity. Three years have gone by
with no payment on the interest, but don't think you can get away
with gobbling up my money. I'll collect it even if it's from your
corpse.'

Shobha was quite a joker. 'In that case,' he said, 'what are you
worried about? Collect it from his corpse. Or better still—since you'll
reach heaven within a year or two of each other, you can settle the
account right there in the presence of God.'

Mangaru burst into a torrent of abuse—'Swindler! Cheat! When
it comes to borrowing, you come wagging your tail, but when it's time
to pay up, you start growling. I'll have your house sold and your
bullocks auctioned off.'

'All right,' Shobha taunted him further, 'tell me honestly how
much money you loaned that now adds up to three hundred rupees.'

'When you don't pay any interest year after year, it's bound to
mount up.'

'But how much was it you first gave? A mere fifty rupees.'

'Yes, but look at how long ago that was.'

'Five or six years it must have been.'

'It's been a full ten years—this is the eleventh.'

'Don't you feel even slightly ashamed at demanding three hundred
rupees in return for fifty?'

'Why should I feel ashamed? I gave you the money. I'm not asking
for charity.'

Hori grovelled and pleaded and got him to leave also. As for
Datadin, he now had a joint interest in Hori's farm, getting half the
yield in return for having provided the seed. So it would have been
unwise for him to provoke trouble with Hori as yet. Jhinguri Singh
had already settled everything with the manager of the mill. His
men were supervising the loading of the cane into carts, and accompanying the carts to a boat on the river half a mile from the village.
A cart could have made only seven or eight trips in a day, whereas
the boat could carry fifty cartloads at a time. By providing this eco-

nomical transportation, Jhinguri Singh had indebted the whole area to him.

As soon as the weighing began, Jhinguri Singh stationed himself at the gate of the mill. He got each person's cane weighed, took the payment slip, collected the money from the cashier, and then deducted what was owed him before giving the balance to the farmer. No matter how much the tenants cried and shrieked, he paid no attention. These were his master's orders. What could he do?

Hori received a hundred and twenty rupees. Jhinguri Singh deducted his full dues with interest and turned over some twenty-five rupees. Hori eyed the money sadly. 'What good will it do me to take this, thakur? You might as well keep it too. I'll get plenty of work as a labourer.'

Jhinguri flung the twenty-five rupees on the ground. 'Keep it or throw it away—that's up to you. It was because of you that the master took me to task, and the Rai Sahib's still hounding me for the money collected as a fine. I'm giving you this much out of pity for your miserable poverty. Otherwise you wouldn't get even half a pice. If the Rai Sahib cracks down, the money will have to come out of my own pocket.'

Hori picked up the money slowly and was just leaving when he was accosted by Nokheram. Hori handed him the twenty-five rupees and, without a word, walked quickly away. His head was reeling.

Shobha received a similar amount. As he came out he was cornered by Pateshwari. Shobha reacted differently. 'I have no money,' he declared. 'You can do what you like about it.'

'Did you or did you not sell the cane?' Pateshwari asked angrily.

'Yes, I sold it.'

'And didn't you promise to pay me when you'd sold the cane?'

'Yes, I did.'

'Then why aren't you paying up? You've paid all the others, haven't you?'

'Yes, I have.'

'Then why aren't you paying me?'

'What I have left now is for my family.'

'You'll pay that money, Shobha,' Pateshwari snarled, 'and this very day—and with folded hands. Act up all you like right now. I'll send in a report and have you put away for six months—a full six months, not a day less. That report's going to take care of all that gambling of yours. I'm not a servant of the zamindar or of a money lender. I serve the royal government, which rules the whole world and is the master of both your zamindar and your moneylender.'

Pateshwari stalked off. Shobha and Hori walked some distance in silence, as though knocked senseless by the onslaught. Then Hori said, 'Give him the money, Shobha. Just look at it as though a fire had burned up the sugar cane. That's how I've consoled myself.'

'Yes, I'll pay him, brother,' Shobha replied in a pained tone. 'How can I avoid it?'

Girdhar, intoxicated on toddy, was weaving down the road toward them. Seeing the two of them, he said, 'Jhinguri took it all, brother. Not even a pice left for a bit of parched gram. The rotten murderer! I cried and begged, but the brute showed no mercy.'

'You've been drinking toddy,' Shobha said, 'and yet you say he didn't leave you a pice.'

Girdhar pointed to his stomach. 'It's evening, and not even a drop of water has touched my throat all day. May I eat beef if I'm telling a lie. I hid a one-anna piece in my mouth. That's what paid for the toddy. After sweating for a whole year, I thought I deserved to drink toddy on one day. But I'm not really drunk. How could anyone get drunk on one anna? I know I'm staggering—that's so people will think I've had a lot to drink. A wonderful thing happened though —my debt is gone. I borrowed twenty and paid back a hundred and sixty. Isn't that the limit?'

As soon as Hori reached home, Rupa came running with water, Sona brought the chilam all ready to smoke, and Dhaniya set some parched gram and salt in front of him. Then they all stood staring at him expectantly. Even Jhuniya came and stood in the doorway. Hori sat down dejectedly. How could he wash up, or eat the gram? He felt as ashamed and guilty as though he'd just committed a murder.

'How much did it weigh?' Dhaniya asked.

'It came to a hundred and twenty rupees. But it was all stolen from me right then and there. Not even a half-pice was left.'

Dhaniya was on fire from head to foot. In the fury of the moment she wanted to tear her hair and scratch her face. 'If I ever come face to face with the Almighty,' she said, 'I'd like to ask him why he created a man as halfwitted as you. My whole life has been hell because of you. And God won't even let me die to escape this misery. So you just handed over all the money to those—those brothers-in-law of yours! Now where will we get the money to buy bullocks?

Are you going to hitch me to the plough, or pull it yourself? You've lived a long time . . . I ask you now, why didn't you at least have the sense to save out enough money for a pair of bullocks? They couldn't have just grabbed it out of your hands. Here it is the cold of December and not a rag to cover any one of us. Go drown us all in the river. A quick death would be better than this slow torture. How long can we go on crawling under the straw at night to keep warm? And even if we do crawl under the straw, we can't keep ourselves alive by eating it. You go ahead and eat grass if that's what you want. The rest of us can't do it.'

Even as she was saying this, though, Dhaniya couldn't restrain a smile. While talking, she'd begun to realize that there's no way of escape when the moneylenders are on a poor man's neck and he has some money and the moneylenders know he has some money.

Hori, head bowed, was bemoaning his fate and didn't notice Dhaniya's smile. 'We'll get work,' he muttered. 'We'll make enough that way to feed ourselves.'

'Where are we to find work in this village?' Dhaniya asked. 'And could you bring yourself to do menial labour when you're known as a respectable farmer?'

Hori took several puffs on the chilam. 'Working for pay is no sin. And if the worker does well, he can become a farmer. If that kind of work weren't written in my fate, then why would all these troubles have come? Why would the cow have died? Why would our son have turned out to be worthless?'

Dhaniya turned to the girls. 'What are you all standing around for? Go tend to your chores. Some other kind of man would have come back from the market with three or four annas' worth of something for his family. But this man must have been too stingy to get change for a rupee, not wanting there to be one less rupee. That's why his earnings aren't very good. People who spend money make money. Why should people get money who don't know how to eat well or dress well? To bury it in the ground?'

Hori chuckled. 'Where is all that buried wealth?'

'It must be right where you put it. The crying shame is that you'd die rather than spend anything even though you know all this. If you'd brought some four-pice thing for the children it wouldn't have sunk you. If you'd told Jhinguri that you wouldn't give him anything unless he let you have one rupee—that he could go to court over it—he'd certainly have given it to you.'

Hori felt ashamed. What could Nokheram have done if he'd not panicked and given him the twenty-five rupees? At most he could have added three or four annas interest to the balance. But now the mistake had been made.

Jhuniya went inside and said to Sona, 'I feel very sorry for dada. Poor man comes home tired after a hard day and mother starts scolding him. What could the poor fellow do when the moneylenders were at his throat?'

'But where will we get the bullocks?'

'The moneylender wants his money. What does he care about people's troubles?'

'If mother had been there, she'd have taken care of those damned moneylenders. They'd have been left weeping and wailing.'

'Well, there's no need for us to be short of money,' Jhiuniya teased. 'You just smile and speak to the moneylender and then see if he doesn't write off the whole debt. Believe me, that would solve all dada's troubles.'

Sona clapped her hands over Jhuniya's mouth. 'That's enough now. Shut up, I'm warning you. You'll have something to cry about if I go to mother and tell all about you and Matadin.'

'What could you say to her? There's nothing to tell. When he finds some excuse to come to the house, am I to tell him to get out? It's not as though he gets anything from me. He only gives something of his own. He can't get anything from Jhuniya except a few sweet words. And I know how to get a good price for those sweet words. I'm not such a simpleton as to fall into anyone's trap. Of course if I find out your brother has some other woman, then I can't say what I'll do. If that happens, no one will have any hold over me. For the present, though, I have faith that he's mine and that he's knocking around from alley to alley for my sake. There's nothing wrong with a little joking around, but I'm not about to betray him. A girl who can't stick to one man ends up with no one at all.'

Shobha came by, called Hori, and handed him the money for Pateshwari. 'You go pay him, brother. I don't know what came over me then.'

Hori took the money and had just stood up when he heard the sound of a conch shell being blown. At the other end of the village lived a thakur named Dhyan Singh. After ten years in the army, he had come home on leave a few days before. Baghdad, Aden, Singapore, Burma—he'd travelled all over. Now he was anxious to

231

get married, so he was holding ceremonies to try to please the brahmans.

'The last chapter of the scripture reading must be finished. The *aarti* ceremony is going on.'

'It seems so,' Shobha said. 'Let's go get some of the blessing.'

'You go,' Hori said thoughtfully. 'I'll come after a little while.'

The day Dhyan Singh returned, he'd sent two pounds of sweets to each family in the village. Whenever he met Hori on the street, he would ask how he was getting along. To go to the ceremony at his house without taking anything would be an insult.

Dhyan Singh himself would pass around the aarti tray. How could Hori take a blessing from it without making an offering? It would be better not to go at all. With so many people around, he wouldn't notice that Hori was not there. It wasn't as if someone were making a list of who had come and who had not. He went and stretched out on his cot.

But something seemed to be churning inside him. He didn't have even a pice—not a single copper. The importance and the sanctity of the ceremony didn't concern him at all. It was strictly a question of doing the proper thing. He could accept the thakur's aarti and offer merely his devotion in return. But how could he go against tradition that way and lower himself in everyone's eyes?

Suddenly he sat up. Why should he be a slave to tradition? Why give up the sacred blessing for the sake of prestige? If people laughed at him, let them laugh. He didn't care. All he wanted was for God to keep him from doing wrong.

Hori set out for the thakur's house.

CHAPTER 18

KHANNA and Govindi weren't getting along. Why they weren't getting along is hard to say. Astrology would suggest that their stars must have been in conflict, though at the time of their marriage all the heavenly bodies had been shown to be in perfect harmony. The ancient texts on sex might have suggested some other secret behind the discord; and psychologists could search for still other explanations. All that was evident was that they weren't getting along.

Khanna was rich, amorous, sociable, handsome and well educated —one of the distinguished men of the town. Govindi may not have been a raving beauty, but she was certainly good-looking—with a wheat-coloured complexion, modest eyes which would look up just once and then remain lowered, cheeks which if not pink were at least smooth, a delicate body, shapely limbs, soft arms, and an air of indifference mixed with just a glimmer of disdain—as though she attached little value to wordly affairs. Khanna had more than enough resources for leading a life of luxury—the finest type of bungalow, the finest type of furniture, the finest type of car and an infinite amount of money.

Govindi seemed to set no store by these things, however. In this salty ocean of luxury, her thirst remained unquenched. She devoted all her energies to looking after the children and taking care of household details, keeping too busy with these things to give any thought to sensual pleasures. She never paid any attention to the nature of charm or how it can be created. She was not some man's plaything, or an object for his indulgence, so why should she try to make herself charming? If a man had no eyes for her genuine beauty and chased around after sexy women, that was his tough luck. She went on treating her husband with a love and devotion as detached as though she had overcome any feelings of either jealousy or passion. Their vast possessions seemed to be crushing her soul, and her heart longed to escape from all this ostentation and affectation, dreaming of how happy she could be in leading a simple and natural life. Why then did Malti have to come and obstruct her path? Why should a person have to put up with the singing and dancing of prostitutes? Why was the road of life made thorny with all this distrust and pretence and unpleasantness?

Long ago, as a child in school, she had become addicted to poetry, in which suffering and sorrow were the real essence of life, while riches and sensuality, because they led men to untruth and unrest, were to be burned up like a festival bonfire. She still made up poetry occasionally, but to whom could she recite it? Her poems were more than mere flights of fancy. Each word was filled with the anguish of her life and with her warm tears—with her yearning to go some place far away from all this affectation and indulgence where she could live in a little hut and enjoy simple pleasures. When Khanna saw her poems, however, he made fun of them, sometimes even tearing them up and throwing them away.

The barrier of riches grew higher every day, driving the couple farther and farther apart. At home Khanna was as rude and hot-tempered as he was sweet and gentle at the office. To him, politeness was not a quality of the heart but an instrument with which to hoodwink the world. Often he would lash out angrily at Govindi. On such occasions, she would retreat to her own room and spend the night weeping, while Khanna sat in the living-room listening to the music of prostitutes, or went out drinking to the club. In spite of all this, however, Khanna was still her lord and master. Though trampled and insulted, she was still his slave. She might fight with him, get angry at him and weep over him, but she still belonged to him alone. She couldn't imagine a life apart from him.

On this particular day, Khanna must have seen a bad omen when he first woke up. Opening the morning paper, he found that a number of his stocks had dropped, meaning a loss of several thousand for him. The workers at the sugar mill had gone on strike and were bent on violence. The price of silver, which he'd bought expecting to make a good profit, had dropped still further. The deal he was making with the Rai Sahib, hoping to make a killing, appeared stalled for some time. In addition, the night's heavy drinking had brought on a splitting headache and an aching body. Then his chauffeur reported some trouble with the engine of the car, and he got word that a case had been filed in the civil courts against his bank in Lahore. He was sitting there fuming over all this when Govindi appeared and an-

234

nounced that Bhisham's fever was still not down and they'd better call a doctor.

Bhisham was their youngest son. Sickly ever since birth, he seemed to have something or other wrong with him all the time. One day it would be a cough, the next a fever; sometimes he'd start having chest pains, other times it would be diarrhoea. Ten months old now, he looked only five or six months. Khanna had become indifferent toward the boy, convinced he wouldn't live anyway. But Govindi for that very·reason cared more about the baby than about any of the other children.

Khanna assumed an air of fatherly concern. 'It's not good to get babies in the habit of taking drugs, and you have a fetish for doling out medicines. You call the doctor at the slightest excuse. This is only the third day. Wait another day. The fever'll probably drop all by itself today.'

'It hasn't come down for three days,' Govindi persisted. 'All the home remedies have failed.'

'All right then, I'll make a call. Whom should I send for?'

'Call Dr Naag.'

'Very well, I'll get him, but remember that a big name doesn't mean the man's a good doctor. Despite the high fees he collects, I've never seen his treatment cure anyone. He's notorious for dispatching his patients to heaven.'

'Then call anyone you like. I only suggested Dr Naag because he's been here several times.'

'Why don't I send for Miss Malti? Her fees are lower, and a lady doctor knows more about children than any man could.'

Govindi flared up. 'I don't consider Miss Malti a doctor.'

Khanna glared back at her. 'I suppose she was in England digging ditches. Besides, thousands of people owe their lives to her today. Doesn't that mean anything?'

'Maybe so, but I have no faith in her. She may have the remedy for men's ailing hearts, but she can't cure anything else.'

That did it. Khanna began to thunder, and Govindi let loose a torrent. Malti's name was like a declaration of war between them.

Khanna flung all his papers on the floor. 'Life with you has really gone sour,' he declared.

'Then go ahead and marry Malti,' Govindi snapped back in a shrill voice. 'There's nothing stopping you—that is if she can stomach it.'

'What kind of an opinion do you have of me anyway?'

'It's just that Malti keeps people like you as slaves, but not as husbands.'

'You think I'm as contemptible as all that, do you?' He then started citing evidence to prove her wrong—Malti showed more respect for him than for anyone else. She didn't even care about the Rai Sahib and the Raja Sahib, whereas she complained if she didn't see him for even a day. . . .

Govindi scattered all this proof with a single blast—'That's only because she realizes you're blind—that she couldn't make fools of the others so easily.'

'I could marry Malti today if I wanted,' Khanna boasted. 'This very day—right now. . . .'

Govindi was completely unconvinced. 'She wouldn't marry you even if you spent seven lifetimes rubbing your nose on the ground. You're like a pony to her. She'll feed you grass, and occasionally stroke your face or pat your rump—but only so she can keep riding you. She has a thousand old fools like you in her pocket.'

Govindi was pushing things rather far today, as though she had come prepared for battle. Calling a doctor was obviously just an excuse. Khanna couldn't tolerate such an aspersion on his worth, his abilities and his manliness. 'You think I'm so stupid and idiotic—well then why do I have thousands of people bowing and scraping at my door? There's not a prince or a zamindar who doesn't prostrate himself before me. I've made monkeys of them by the hundreds and then dismissed them.'

'That's Miss Malti's speciality—taking a person who skins others with a sharp knife, and then skinning him with the blunt edge.'

'However much you slander Malti, you're not equal even to the dust of her feet.'

'In my opinion she's even worse than the prostitutes, because she does her hunting under cover.'

Both of them had fired their most fiery darts. Govindi wouldn't have minded any other harsh words from Khanna, but his odious comparison of her with Malti was more than she could tolerate. And Khanna wouldn't have become so heated over anything she said if she'd not insulted Malti. Each knew the other's tender spots. Both hit their targets and both blazed up. Jumping to his feet, Khanna caught hold of her ears, twisted them sharply, and slapped her several times. Sobbing, Govindi left the room.

A short while later, Dr Naag arrived—and the Civil Surgeon Mr

Todd arrived—and the Ayurvedic practitioner Nilkanth Shastri arrived. Govindi just kept sitting in her room holding the baby, however, and had no idea who said what or what diagnosis was made. The calamity she had been envisioning had fallen on her head today, and she felt as though Khanna had severed relations with her, driven her out of the house, and slammed the door. Was she going to let herself be indirectly ruled by that woman who had set up shop to market her beauty, that woman whose shadow she didn't even want to fall on her? Never! Khanna was her husband, and he had the right to argue with her and all that. She could even respect him if he beat her. But to be ruled by Malti? Impossible! As long as the baby's fever didn't calm down, though, she couldn't move. Even self-respect must bow before the demands of duty.

The next day the child's temperature had come down. Govindi sent for a *tonga* and left the house. She could no longer stay in a place where she was held in such contempt. The blow was so harsh that it had even snapped her attachment to the children. She had fulfilled her duties toward them. The rest was now up to Khanna. True, she couldn't leave behind the babe in arms. He was a part of her very life, and she would leave this house taking only her life. She owned nothing else, and Khanna thought she was completely dependent on him. She would show this man that she could stay alive even if she left his protection. Three of the children had gone off to play. Govindi was tempted to hug them just once more, but she was not running away, after all. If the children loved her, they'd come to see her and play at her place. And when she felt it necessary, she'd come to see the children. It was only dependence on Khanna that she wanted to cast aside.

It was evening, and the park was buzzing with activity. People sprawled on the grass drinking in the fresh air. Govindi passed through Hazratganj, the shopping district, and had just turned in the direction of the zoo when she spotted Malti and Khanna coming towards her in a car. She thought that Khanna pointed to her and said something to Malti that made her smile. No, she must be imagining things. Khanna wouldn't ridicule her in front of Malti. But the woman was so shameless. Govindi had heard that she had a good medical practice and belonged to a well-to-do family, but despite that, here she was running around like a huckster. No telling why she didn't get married—except who would marry her? No, that wasn't it. There were plenty of the sort of men who would think themselves lucky to get her. Malti herself would first have to fall for someone, though. And after all, what happiness was there in marriage? A girl was doing the right thing not to marry. Then everyone could be her slave. Otherwise she'd get stuck as a slave to one man. Malti was playing it quite right. At the moment, even this bigshot was licking her feet. If she were somehow to marry him, he'd start lording it over her. But why would she marry him anyway? It was a good thing to have a few women like Malti around all the time—they kept the men squirming.

Govindi now felt very sympathetic towards Malti. She was being unjust in denouncing the woman. The sight of her own condition must have been an eye-opener to Malti. Who could blame her if, having seen the misery of marriage, she had decided not to get caught in the same trap?

The zoo was shrouded in silence. Govindi told the tonga driver to stop and headed for the green lawn; but after just a few steps, her sandals began to get wet. The lawn had just been sprinkled, and water was flowing across the ground under the grass. Instead of turning back, she quickly took another step forward, only to find her foot stuck in the mud. She looked at her feet and wondered where she could find water to wash them off. All her previous worries vanished with this new concern about getting her feet clean. Her train of thought was broken, and as long as her feet were not clean, she couldn't think about anything else. Suddenly she spotted a long pipe hidden in the grass, with water flowing from it. Going over, she washed her feet, then her sandals, and then her face and hands. Cupping her palms, she took a drink, and then walked over to the dry ground on the other side of the pipe and sat down.

In times of despair the thought of death quickly arises. What if she were somehow to die, sitting right there? The tonga driver would go straight to Khanna and give him the news. Khanna would brighten up as soon as he got the word, though he'd put a handkerchief to his eyes for the sake of appearances. As for the children, toys and fun meant more to them than a mother. That was all her life added up to—with no one even to shed a few tears over its departure. She remembered the days when her mother-in-law was still living and Khanna was not yet carousing around. In those days she got upset about the way her mother-in-law nagged her about everything, but now she realized that the woman's anger had been mixed with affection. In those days, when she began sulking, the old lady would start to soothe and caress her. Now she could go on sulking for months without anybody caring. Suddenly her thoughts took wing and flew to her own mother. Oh if only her mother were alive, she'd not be in this miserable state. If nothing else, her mother had a lap filled with love, where she could bury her head and cry. But no, she wouldn't cry—she didn't want to upset that angel in heaven, who had done everything possible for her, and who had no control over what happened to her now as a result of the deeds in past lives. And why should she cry? She was no longer dependent on anyone. She could earn her own living. First thing in the morning she'd buy some things from the Gandhi Ashram and start peddling them. What was there to be ashamed of? At most, people would point and say 'There goes Khanna's wife.' Why even stay in this city though? Why not go somewhere else, where no one even knew her? What was so hard about earning ten or fifteen rupees? She'd live off the sweat of her own brow and then no one could lord it over her. The only reason this bigshot could be so arrogant was that he supported her. Now she would support herself.

Just then she saw Mehta coming in her direction and felt disconcerted. She had wanted to be completely alone, and didn't feel like talking to anyone, but even here she couldn't get away from these men. And then the baby had begun to cry too.

'What brought you here at this hour?' Mehta came up and asked in surprise.

'The same thing that brought you,' Govindi said, trying to quiet the child.

Mehta smiled. 'With me it's different. I'm like the washerman's dog, belonging neither at the stream where he works nor at the house where he lives. Hand me the baby. I'll quiet him down.'

'Since when have you learned that art?'

'I need the practice. The day of testing may come....'

'So! Is the day close at hand?'

'That depends on my preparation. When I'm ready, I'll sit for the test. We wear out our eyes studying for trivial little degrees. This is the test of a lifetime.'

'That's true,' she said, handing him the child. 'I'll be interested to see what grade you get on it.'

Mehta tossed the baby lightly in the air a few times and the crying stopped. 'You see how my magic formula quieted him down?' Mehta boasted boyishly. 'I must get myself a baby from somewhere.'

'Just a baby, or its mother too?' Govindi teased.

Mehta shook his head in mock despair. 'Women like that simply aren't to be found.'

'There's Miss Malti, isn't there? Beautiful, educated, talented, captivating. What more do you want?'

'Miss Malti doesn't have a single one of the qualities I'm looking for in a wife.'

'What's wrong with her?' Govindi said, pleased at this criticism. 'Admirers buzz around her all the time like bees. I hear that's just the type of woman men go for these days.'

'My wife's going to be different,' Mehta said, trying to keep the baby's hands away from his moustache. 'She's going to be the kind I can worship.'

Govindi couldn't help laughing. 'Then what you want is an idol, not a woman. You're not likely to find a woman like that anywhere.'

'I disagree. There's one right here in this city.'

'Really? I'd like to meet her, and try to become like her.'

'You know her very well. She's the wife of a millionaire, but one to whom sensuality means nothing—one who never neglects her duties even though she's treated with indifference and disrespect, who sacrifices herself on the altar of motherhood, who considers sacrifice a great privilege, and who deserves to be made into an idol and worshipped.'

Govindi felt a shiver of delight. Pretending not to understand, she said, 'You praise that kind of woman, but I think she deserves to be pitied. You're speaking of an ideal woman, and if she's able to be an ideal woman, she should be able to be an ideal wife also.'

Mehta, taken by surprise, protested, 'You're insulting her.'

'Well, that ideal doesn't belong to this day and age.'

'It's an unchanging eternal ideal. By destroying it, men are bringing on their own destruction.'

Govindi lit up inwardly with a rapture she'd never before known. Of all the men she knew, she thought most highly of Mehta, and to hear this encouragement from his own lips was intoxicating.

'Come on, then. Please introduce me to her.'

Mehta hid his face, his lips pressed to the baby's cheek. 'She's sitting right here.'

'Where? I don't see her.'

'I am talking to her.'

Govindi burst out laughing. 'You've been making fun of me, haven't you?'

'Deviji,' Mehta said reverently, 'you're being unfair to me, and even more unfair to yourself. There are very few people in the world for whom I feel devout respect. One of them is you. Your patience and sacrifice and modesty and love are second to none. I can imagine no greater happiness in life than to be a servant at the feet of a woman like you. You're the living image of what I consider ideal womanhood.'

Tears of happiness came to her eyes. Armoured with a faith such as this, she could face up to any difficulty. Every pore in her body seemed to sing with joy.

'Why did you become a philosopher, Mehtaji?' she said, trying not to display her delight. 'You should have been a poet.'

With an easy smile, Mehta said, 'You think someone can become a poet without being a philosopher? Philosophy is only a middle stage.'

'Now you're on the way to becoming a poet, but are you aware that there's no happiness for a poet in this world?'

'What the world calls sadness is happiness for the poet. Wealth and power, beauty and strength, knowledge and learning—no matter how these values captivate the world, they hold no attraction for the poet. What pleases and attracts him are crushed hopes, lost memories, and the tears of broken hearts. When he no longer cares about these things, he's no longer a poet. Philosophy only makes fun of these mysteries of life, whereas a poet is immersed in them. I've read two or three of your poems, and only I know how much feeling, how much sensitivity, how much tender anguish, how much touching passion they contain. Nature has treated me very unjustly in not creating another woman like you.'

'No, Mehtaji,' Govindi said regretfully, 'that's where you're mistaken. You'll find such women down every alley, and they leave me way behind. What kind of woman is someone who can't keep her husband happy, who can't win a place in his heart? Sometimes I think I should take lessons in that art from Malti. Where I'm a failure, she's a success. I can't even win over those who belong to me, while she wins over outsiders also. Isn't that a credit to her?'

Mehta made a face. 'Just because wine makes people crazy, does that mean it's better than water—which quenches thirst, gives life, and brings peace and tranquillity?'

Taking refuge in sarcasm, Govindi answered, 'Be that as it may, I notice that water flows freely all over the place, whereas people sell off houses and possessions for the sake of wine. And the stronger and more intoxicating it is, the better! Didn't I hear that you too are one of its devotees?'

Govindi had reached the level of despair where people begin to have doubts even about truth and righteousness. Mehta was unaware of that, however. His attention was caught by the last part of her statement. It made him feel more ashamed and disturbed at his fondness for drinking than lengthy sermons on the subject had done in the past. He was good at answering such arguments with shattering repartee, but he had no answer for this mild jab. He regretted having ever brought up the subject of liquor. It was he who had first compared Malti with wine, but the analogy had boomeranged back on his own head.

'Yes, I admit I have that weakness,' he said, somewhat embarrassed. 'I won't rationalize by explaining my need for it or by testifying to its intellectually stimulating effects. That would be worse than the sin itself. But I hereby swear in your presence that I'll never let another drop touch my throat.'

Govindi was stunned. 'What have you gone and done, Mehtaji! I swear to God, that wasn't my intention. I'm sorry about it.'

'Not at all. You should be pleased that you've saved someone.'

'Did I save you? And here I was about to beg you to save me!'

'Me? What good fortune!'

'Yes,' she said in a pained voice. 'You're the only one I can think of to whom I can tell my story. And listen—I don't really need to remind you, but please keep all this to yourself. My life has become intolerable. So far I've put up with whatever mortification came along, but I can't stand it any longer. Malti is out to destroy me. I don't have any weapon capable of defeating her. You have some influence on her. She respects you more than anyone else. If you can somehow free me from her claws, I'll be indebted to you for life. She's gradually stealing away my happiness and good fortune. Please protect me if you can. I left home today determined never to go back. I tried as hard as I could to break off all ties of affection, but a woman is very weak-hearted, Mehtaji. Love is the breath of life for her. As long as she's alive, it's impossible for her to break away from love. Until today, I've kept my distress to myself, but now I'm stretching out my hands like a beggar to plead for your charity. Please save me from Malti. I'm being destroyed in the hands of that sorceress.'

She burst into tears, and the sobbing drowned out her voice.

Mehta had never before felt so important, not even when the French Academy had applauded his work as the greatest achievement of the century. The idol whom he had reverently worshipped, whom he had inwardly adored, and on whom he'd rested his hope of finding an ideal to lead him through the darkness and obscurity of life, was today begging him for help. Suddenly he felt a strength that could have torn apart mountains or swum across oceans, and he was as intoxicated as a little boy riding a wooden horse who thinks he is flying through the air. The impossibility of the task was forgotten. And the extent to which his own principles would be violated in the process never entered his mind.

He spoke up reassuringly. 'I didn't realize that this was making you so unhappy. My intelligence, my eyes and my imagination are defective. How else can I explain it? Otherwise how could I have let you suffer such misery?'

'But remember,—snatching the prey away from a lioness is no simple matter,' she said dubiously.

'A woman's heart is like soil,' Mehta declared, 'which can produce sweetness or bitterness, depending on the kind of seeds which fall into it.'

'You must be regretting that you even met me today.'

'You probably wouldn't believe me if I were to tell you that only today have I found the most genuine happiness in life.'

'But I've put such a heavy burden on your shoulders.'

'Now you're embarrassing me, Deviji,' Mehta replied, his voice full of tender devotion. 'I've told you that I'm at your service. Even if I were to lose my life for your sake, I'd consider myself fortunate. And don't think this is poetic exaggeration; it's the truest thing in my life. I can't resist the temptation to tell you what I value most highly in life. I'm a worshipper of nature, and I want to see man in his natural form : laughing when he's happy, crying when he's sad, and violent when he's angry. I don't have anything in common with those who suppress their happiness and sadness, who consider crying to be a weakness and take laughter lightly. To me, life is a pleasant game, simple and free, in which there's no room for faultfinding or jealousy or spite. I don't worry about the past; I'm not concerned about the future. To me, the present is all that counts. Worry about the future makes cowards of us; the burden of the past breaks our backs. There's so little strength in our lives that it would be exhausted if we were to spread it out over the past and the future. By loading ourselves down with needless burdens, we get buried under the debris of conventions and beliefs and traditions. There's no question of raising ourselves up. We no longer even have the strength to do so. The strength and energy which should have been used to fulfill our human obligations through cooperation and brotherhood has been spent avenging old grudges and settling the debts of our fathers and grandfathers. And these gyrations about God and salvation make me laugh. All that concern for worship and salvation represents the height of egotism and destroys our humanity. Where there's life, where there's fun, where there's love—that's where God is. And making life happy is the only worship, the only salvation. Sages say—"Let no smile come to your lips; let no tears come to your eyes", but I say that if you're unable to laugh and unable to cry, then you're not a human being, you're a stone. The learning which crushes our humanity is not really learning—it's a grindstone. But forgive me, I've gone and delivered a whole speech. It's getting late. Come along, I'll see you home. The baby's gone to sleep in my arms.'

'I have a tonga waiting.'

'I'll send it away.'

'But where are you going to take me?' Govindi asked when Mehta returned from paying off the driver.

Mehta looked surprised. 'What do you mean? I'll take you to your home.'

'That's not my home, Mehtaji.'

'What is it then? Mr Khanna's?'

'Is there any doubt about that? It's no longer home for me. I can't call a place home, or even think of it as home, where I'm insulted and abused.'

Mehta's voice was filled with pain, each syllable coming from the bottom of his heart. 'No, Deviji, that home is yours and it always will be. You created it and you brought life into it, and life is what sparks the body. When life is gone, what's left of the body? Motherhood is the most exalted position in life, Deviji, and in such an exalted position there are bound to be insults and abuses and reproach. A mother's job is to bestow the gift of life. With such matchless power in her hands, why should she worry about those who seem displeased or annoyed? But just as the body can't exist without life, so the body is the most appropriate place for life to exist. What can I teach you, though, about virtue and sacrifice? You're the living embodiment of those qualities. All I can say is. . . .'

'But I'm not just a mother,' Govindi interrupted impatiently, 'I'm also a woman.'

Mehta was silent for a while and then said, 'You are, that's true, but as I see it, a woman is only a mother. Anything else she may be is purely incidental. Motherhood is the greatest accomplishment in the world—involving the greatest self-denial, the greatest sacrifice, the greatest victory. In short, I'd say that it encompasses everything—life, human personality and womanhood. As for Mr Khanna, you should just figure that he's not in his right mind. Everything he says and does reflects a kind of drunken state; but before long that will wear off and he'll be idolizing you.'

Giving no reply, Govindi walked slowly toward the car. Mehta stepped forward and opened the door. She got in and the car started off, but they both remained silent.

When the car reached her house and Govindi got out, Mehta saw by the light that there were tears in her eyes.

The children came running from the house calling, 'Mama! Mama!' and clung to her. Govindi's face lit up with motherly pride.

'Many thanks for all your trouble,' she said to Mehta, and then lowered her eyes. A tear rolled down her cheek.

Mehta's eyes were moist too. What sadness that womanly heart had known, even in the midst of such wealth and luxury!

CHAPTER 19

————

Mïrza Khurshed's yard served as a club, a gymnasium and a court of law. All day long it was crowded with people. Since there was no place in the neighbourhood to hold wrestling matches, Mirza had set up a thatched arena here. Fifty or more contestants were almost always gathered around, and sometimes Mirza himself joined in. The neighbourhood councils also met there in the yard, settling quarrels between brother and brother, between husband and wife, or between mother and daughter-in-law. It was the centre for neighbourhood social life and political activity. Almost every day, meetings were being held, volunteers given lodging, programmes planned, and the political affairs of the town directed. At the last meeting, Malti had been elected chairman of the City Congress Committee, and since then the place had become even more renowned.

Gobar had been living there for a year now. No longer a simple country boy, he had seen something of the world and had begun to understand its ways. At heart he was still a villager, keeping his teeth clamped on every pice, looking out constantly for his own interests, putting his heart in his work and keeping his spirits high. The city air, however, had also gotten to him. The first month he'd lived on his wages as a labourer, only half-filling his stomach and saving up a few rupees. Then he became a hawker, selling spiced potatoes, peas, and curd delicacies. Finding this more profitable, he gave up his other job. In the summer he opened a stand for cold drinks and ice, and soon established a reputation because of his fair dealing. When winter came, he substituted hot tea for the cold drinks. He was now making at least two or three rupees a day. He had his hair cut in the English style, took to wearing a finespun dhoti and shiny leather shoes, bought a red woollen shawl, and began smoking cigarettes and chewing betel.

By getting in on the meetings, he also came to know something about politics and began to understand the concepts of nation and social class. He no longer had much respect for social conventions nor much fear of public criticism. Attending the council meetings almost daily had built up his self-confidence. The thing which had made him hide out in this place far from home—or rather much worse things—went on all the time here, and no one ran away. So why should he be afraid and hide his face?

All this time he'd not sent home even a single pice, figuring that his parents were not very shrewd in money matters, that the moment they got a little money, they'd start throwing it around. His father would immediately be anxious to make a pilgrimage to Gaya, and his mother to have some jewellery made. He had no money to spare for such trivial things. He had now become something of a money-lender too, loaning money on interest to the neighbourhood hack drivers, cart-men and washermen. In these ten or twelve months he had established himself by hard work, thrift and enterprise, and now he was thinking of bringing Jhuniya there to live with him.

It was mid-afternoon. Gobar had taken a bath at the roadside tap and was just boiling some potatoes for his evening meal when Mirza Khurshed appeared at the door. Though no longer working for him, Gobar still respected the man as highly as before and would have laid down his life for him. 'Can I be of service, sir?' he asked, going to the door.

Mirza came straight to the point. 'If you have any money, please let me have it. I finished off my last bottle three days ago, and I'm getting awfully tense.'

Gobar had loaned money to Mirza two or three times before, but so far he'd been unable to recover any of it. He was too timid to press the issue, and Mirza was not in the habit of returning borrowed money. Not that money stayed in his hands—one moment it was there and the next moment it was gone. Gobar couldn't say that he had no money or that he wouldn't part with it, so he began attacking liquor. 'Why don't you give it up, sir? Does drinking that stuff do any good?'

Mirza stepped inside and sat down on the cot. 'You think I don't want to give it up? That I drink for the pleasure of it? I can't live without it, that's all. Don't worry about your money. I'll pay back every cowrie.'

Gobar stood his ground. 'I'm telling you the truth, master. If I had the money on me, would I refuse you?'

'You can't even let me have two rupees?'

'I don't have it just now.'

247

'Take my ring as security.'

Gobar was tempted, but he couldn't very well change his story now. 'What are you talking about, master? If I had the money I'd give it to you. Why bring the ring into the picture?'

'I'll never beg you for money again, Gobar,' Mirza persisted, in the meekest tone he could muster. 'I'm getting so I can't even stand up straight. Thanks to drinking, I've wasted a fortune and turned into a beggar, but I've become so set in my ways now that I won't give it up even if I have to beg for it.'

When Gobar still turned him down, Mirza gave up in despair and went away. He had thousands of friends in the city, many of whom he'd helped in times of trouble and many of whom owed their prosperity to him, but he didn't like to turn to them. He knew any number of tricks which he'd used at various times to raise stacks of money. Money itself meant nothing to him, however. It just seemed to scorch his hands, and he was only content when he'd found some excuse to scatter it to the winds.

Gobar began peeling the potatoes. It was astonishing that in less than a year he'd become so shrewd, so clever at building up his assets. The room he lived in had been given him by Mirza Sahib. The room and its veranda could easily have rented for five rupees a month. Gobar had lived there for almost a year, but Mirza had never asked for any rent and Gobar had never offered any. It probably never even occurred to Mirza that the room could have brought in some rent.

A little later, an *ekka* driver came asking for a loan. Aladin was his name, a one-eyed man with a shaved head and speckled beard. He was desperately in need of five rupees because his daughter was going away to her in-laws' house. Gobar loaned him the money, at interest of one anna on the rupee monthly.

Aladin thanked him and said, 'You ought to send for your family now, brother. How long are you going to keep doing all your own cooking?'

Gobar started bemoaning the high cost of living in the city. How could a family get along on such a small income?

Aladin lit up a *biri*. 'God will provide for your needs, brother. Just think how much easier it would be for you. And I tell you, a whole family could manage on the amount you're spending on yourself. A woman's touch brings prosperity. I swear to God, when I was living here alone, things stayed just the same no matter how much I earned. There wasn't even money left over for tobacco. It was really disturbing, coming home worn out and then having to feed the horse and walk it, and then rushing out for a bite to eat at the Afghan's shop. I got fed up. Since my wife has joined me, though, the same amount of money covers her food also, and I get some rest and comfort besides. After all, the whole point of earning is to get a little comfort in life. If you work yourself to death and don't even get that, then life is worthless. And I'm telling you, brother, your income may even go up. In the time spent boiling potatoes and peas, you could be selling three or four cups of tea. Nowadays there's a demand for tea all the year round. And when you lie down at night, your wife will massage your legs. All your weariness will melt away.'

These remarks hit home; Gobar suddenly felt lonely. He would have to bring Jhuniya. Forgetting the potatoes he'd put on the fire, he started making preparations to return home. Then he remembered that the *Holi* festival was approaching and he should take along presents for the occasion. The emotion that makes misers spend lavishly on festivals welled up in him. After all, this was the day for which he'd been saving every cowrie. He'd take pairs of saries for his mother, his sisters and Jhuniya, and a dhoti and a wrap for Hori. For Sona he'd buy a bottle of hair oil and a pair of sandals, for Rupa some Japanese dolls, for Jhuniya a wicker beauty-kit containing oil, vermilion and a mirror, and for the baby a dress and bonnet of the ready-made kind sold in the market. He took out the money and headed for the bazaar.

By noon the next day he had bought everything and finished packing. The neighbours had heard that he was going home, and several came to see him off. Entrusting his house to them, he said, 'I'm leaving everything in your care. God willing, I'll be back the second day of Holi.'

'Don't return without a wife,' smiled a young woman, 'or we won't let you back in the house.'

'That's right,' an older lady insisted. 'You've been blowing on that fire and doing your own cooking for months. Settle down and start getting some regular meals.'

Gobar bade farewell to them all. There were Hindus and Muslims, all friendly with each other, sharing in each other's trials and tribulations. The Muslims fasted during the month of Ramzan, the Hindus on the eleventh day of the moon. Occasionally they would tease each other in fun. Gobar would call Aladin's prayer-ritual mere calisthenics, while Aladin would refer to the assorted Shiva lingams under the holy pipal tree as a bunch of weights. There was no trace of communal hatred, however. Now Gobar was going home, and they all wanted to give him a warm send-off.

Meanwhile Bhure had appeared, driving his ekka. He'd just returned home after a hard day's rushing around; but when he heard that Gobar was going home, he immediately headed the carriage towards Gobar's place. The horse balked and got several whiplashings. Gobar set his bundles in the ekka, and it started up. He followed behind with the well-wishers as far as the turn in the road before saying goodbye once again and jumping up on the ekka.

The horse galloped down the street. Gobar was drunk with joy at going home, and Bhure with the pleasure of seeing him off. The horse, brave and spirited, raced along. In no time they were at the station.

Delighted, Gobar took out a rupee and offered it to Bhure. 'Take it and buy some sweets for your wife.'

Bhure's look of gratitude was mixed with injured pride. 'You're treating me like a stranger, brother. I'd be willing to bleed rather than let you sweat. Would I take a reward just because you had a little ride in the ekka? I'm not as small-hearted as that—and if I were to take it, my wife would skin me alive.'

Gobar said nothing more. Abashed, he unloaded his things and went off to buy a ticket.

CHAPTER 20

FEBRUARY had arrived, bringing with it the rich promise of new life. Mango trees were flinging out the fragrance of their blossoms, while a cuckoo poured out a secret gift of song from its hiding-place in the branches.

In the countryside, the sugar cane planting had begun. The sun was not yet up, but Hori was already in the field. Dhaniya, Sona and Rupa were taking the well-soaked bundles of cane from the pond and carrying them to the field, while Hori was chopping the stalks into smaller pieces. He was now working for Datadin—no longer a farmer, but just a hired man. The relationship was no longer one of family priest and household patron, but of employer and employee.

Datadin arrived on the scene. 'Move those hands faster, Hori!' he scolded. 'At this rate you won't even get through the cutting today.'

'I'm working right along,' Hori said with hurt pride. 'It's not as though I'm sitting down on the job.'

Datadin expected such backbreaking work from his employees that none of them stayed with him for long. Hori was well aware of this, but he had no alternative.

The pandit strode up to him and shouted, 'There are ways and ways of swinging a chopper. A person can finish up the work in half an hour, or he can drag it out all day and not even get through cutting one bundle of cane.'

Hori swallowed hard and began chopping faster. For months he'd not had a filling meal. Generally one meal a day consisted of just parched grain, while the other only half-filled his stomach. Sometimes he had to fast completely. However much he wanted to swing his arms more quickly, they refused to perform. Moreover, Datadin kept standing over him. If he could have had just a moment to catch his breath, he might have found some fresh energy, but what could he do? He was afraid of another scolding.

Dhaniya and the three girls, their saries soaking wet and smeared with mud, came carrying the bundles of cane. Dropping their loads, they were just pausing for breath when Datadin shouted—'You think you're here to watch some kind of show, Dhaniya? Get on with your work. You're not being paid to do nothing. You've taken hours to bring a single load. At this rate you won't have all the cane carried here even in a whole day.'

Dhaniya's eyes flashed. 'Aren't you even going to let us breathe, maharaj? We're human beings too, after all. Just because we're working for you doesn't make us bullocks. Try carrying a load on your own head—then you'll know what it's like.'

Datadin flew into a rage. 'I'm paying you to work, not to rest. If you have to take a breather, go take it at home.'

Dhaniya was about to speak up again, but Hori cut her off. 'Why don't you go, Dhaniya? What are you arguing for?'

Dhaniya picked up her basket. 'Well I am going, but there's no need to whack a bullock when it's already moving.'

'Evidently you're still on your high horse,' glowered Datadin, 'even though you're living on crumbs.'

Dhaniya couldn't let that pass in silence. 'At least I don't come begging at your door.'

'Well if you keep on this way,' Datadin said sharply, 'you will end up begging.'

Dhaniya had an answer ready, but Sona pulled her away in the direction of the pond, to keep things from getting worse. Once out of earshot, however, Dhaniya's anger exploded. 'Go begging yourself! You're the one who belongs to the beggar caste. We're workers, and we work for what money we get.'

'Let it be, mama,' Sona protested. 'You don't stop to realize these are bad times for us. You keep picking fights at the slightest excuse.'

Hori kept frenziedly swinging the chopper up and down, piling up the chunks of cane. A fire seemed to be raging within him, filling him with superhuman energy. It was as though the strength of his ancestors had filled his veins, providing the steam whose blind force drove him on like a machine. Darkness began enveloping his eyes. His head was reeling. Sweat poured from his body, saliva oozed from his mouth, and pounding filled his head; but still his hands rose and fell mechanically—untiring and unceasing, as though some demon were riding him.

Suddenly utter darkness engulfed him and he felt as though he were sinking into the earth. Trying to regain control, his fingers clutched at the air. The chopper dropped from his hands and he fell face-down on the ground, unconscious.

Dhaniya, approaching with another load of cane, saw a group of men clustered over Hori. A ploughman was telling Datadin, 'You shouldn't say things that hurt people, master. Self-respect takes a long time to die, and you can't expect to change him overnight.'

Dropping the bundle of cane, Dhaniya ran like a madwoman towards Hori. Placing his head on her lap, she wailed, 'How can you go off and leave me? Hey Sona, run and get some water. And go tell Shobha your father's in a bad way. Oh God, what's to become of me now? Who can I turn to? Who'll be left to call me by my first name?'

Lala Pateshwari came running and said with gentle firmness, 'What are you talking about, Dhaniya? Pull yourself together. Nothing's happened to Hori. He just fainted from the heat. He'll come around any moment now. Your being so fainthearted won't accomplish anything.'

Dhaniya clung to Pateshwari's feet and wept. 'What am I to do, Lala? I can't help it. God has taken everything away and I've borne it patiently, but now my endurance has run out. Oh, my precious jewel!'

Sona brought the water and Pateshwari sprinkled it over Hori's face while several people fanned him with their shoulder cloths. Hori's body had turned cold. Pateshwari became anxious too, but he kept trying to hearten Dhaniya.

She panicked again. 'This has never happened before, Lala—never!'

'Did he have anything to eat last night?' Pateshwari inquired.

'Yes, I made chapaties. But you surely know—it's no secret—how things have been going for us lately. There's not been a full meal for months. Time and again I've told him to take it easy when he works, but rest and comfort are not in our fate.'

Suddenly Hori opened his eyes and gazed blankly around. Dhaniya seemed to spring back to life. Throwing her arms frantically around his neck, she asked, 'How are you feeling now? You scared the life out of me.'

'I'm all right,' Hori said weakly. 'I don't know what came over me.'

'Your body just doesn't have the strength, and yet you work yourself to death,' she chided him lovingly. 'Luck must be with your children. With you gone, they'd be sunk.'

Pateshwari chuckled. 'Dhaniya was sobbing and beating her breast.'

'Honestly? You were crying, Dhaniya?' Hori asked with concern.

'*He* should talk!' she answered, giving Pateshwari a shove. 'Ask him why he dropped his papers and came running.'

'She was crying and calling you her jewel,' Pateshwari taunted. 'Now she's denying it out of embarrassment. She was beating her breast.'

There were tears in Hori's eyes as he looked over at Dhaniya. 'She's a little crazy, that's all. I don't know what happiness she's anxious to keep me alive for.'

Two men helped Hori to his feet and then took him home and put him to bed.

Datadin was annoyed over the delay in the planting, but Matadin was less callous. He hurried home and brought some warm milk and a bottle of rosewater. The milk seemed to revive Hori.

At that moment Gobar appeared in the distance, followed by a porter carrying his things on his head.

At first the village dogs rushed barking towards him, but then they began wagging their tails. 'Brother has come,' Rupa cried out, and ran towards him clapping her hands. Sona took a few steps forward too, but then she restrained her excitement. That one year of growth towards womanhood had made her more reserved. Jhuniya pulled her sari modestly over her face and stood at the door.

Gobar touched the feet of his mother and father and then took Rupa in his arms and hugged her. Dhaniya gave him her blessing and pressed his head to her bosom, as though her motherhood was now fully rewarded. Her heart was bursting with pride. Today she was a queen. Even in those sorry circumstances she was a queen, as one could tell by observing her eyes, her face, her heart and her bearing. In fact she would have humbled any queen. How big Gobar had grown, and what a gentleman he looked in those clothes! She had never had any doubts about him—her heart had kept assuring her that he was well and happy. Seeing him now with her own eyes was like finding a jewel she had lost in the dust and confusion of her life; but Hori turned his face away.

'What's the matter with father?' Gobar asked.

Dhaniya didn't want to trouble him by describing their present condition. 'It's nothing, son,' she said. 'Just a slight headache. Go change your clothes and get washed up. Where have you been all this time? Is it right for anyone to run away from home that way?

And you didn't even write once. Now, a whole year later, you've remembered us. My eyes have almost burst, what with looking and looking for you, hoping against hope that the day would come when I'd see you again. Some people said you'd run off to Mauritius, and others that you were with the convicts in the Andamans. The life in me withered away just listening to them. Where were you living all this time?'

Gobar looked ashamed. 'I didn't go far, mother. I was just in Lucknow.'

'So close and yet you never wrote a single letter.'

Sona and Rupa had opened up Gobar's bundles and were sorting and distributing the things. Jhuniya stood at a distance, however, a flush of resentment on her face. It was time to pay Gobar back for the way he had treated her. When a moneylender finds a missing debtor, he gets anxious to recover his money even though he'd written it off as a bad debt. The baby was struggling to reach the bright new things and put them all in his mouth, but Jhuniya wouldn't let him out of her arms.

Sona turned to her sister-in-law. 'He's brought you a comb and mirror.'

'What do I want with a comb and mirror?' Jhuniya said indifferently. 'Let him keep them himself.'

Rupa pulled out the bright bonnet. 'Oh ho! Here's a cap for Chunnu,' she cried, putting it on the baby's head.

Jhuniya pulled off the bonnet and flung it aside. Then, seeing Gobar enter the room, she took the baby and went off to the other part of the house. Gobar looked at all the things scattered around. What he most wanted to do was go to Jhuniya and ask her forgiveness, but he didn't dare follow her to the inner room. So he sat down instead and began handing out the gifts to everyone. Rupa sulked, though, because he'd brought no sandals for her, and Sona began teasing her—'What would you do with sandals? Go play with your dolls. I don't cry when I look at your doll; why should you cry over my sandals?'

Dhaniya took on the responsibility of dividing up the sweets. Her boy had come home safely after all this time. She would send sweets to everyone in the village. But for Rupa one *gulabjamun* was like a cumin seed in a camel's mouth. She wanted the whole pot set in front of her where she could dance around and eat her fill!

The box was then opened and the saries taken out. They all had borders like the ones worn in Lala Pateshwari's house, but they were so delicate. Such fine saries certainly wouldn't last very long! Rich people could wear saries as fine as they wanted. Their womenfolk had nothing to do but sit around or sleep. Here, though, the fields and the barn were what counted. Ah, there was a scarf as well as a dhoti for Hori.

'That was a wonderful thing for you to do, son,' Dhaniya said happily. 'His scarf is down to its last threads.'

By this time Gobar had realized the condition of the family. Dhaniya's sari was all patched and Sona's had a hole in the head-part through which her hair showed. Rupa's dhoti hung down in shreds on all sides like a fringe. Their faces were rough and their skin had lost its sheen. Misery and destitution reigned everywhere.

While the girls were still busily absorbed in the saries, Dhaniya began worrying about a meal for Gobar. There was a little barley flour that had been set aside for the evening meal. At midday they usually got by on a bit of parched grain. But this was no longer the Gobar of old—could he even eat barley flour? No telling what he'd become used to eating while he was away. Going to Dulari's shop, she got wheat flour, rice and ghee on credit. For months the shopkeeper had not given them even one pice worth of food on credit, but now she didn't even ask when she would be paid. 'Gobar's come back rich, hasn't he?' Dulari inquired.

'So far he's not said anything, sister,' Dhaniya replied, 'and I've not felt it proper to ask him as yet. He did bring saries with borders for all of us though. Thanks to your blessings, he's returned safe and sound, which is all that matters to me.'

'God grant him the best of everything wherever he lives,' Dulari said. 'What more could parents hope for? He's a smart boy, not a spendthrift like most young punks. If you can't pay back all the money yet, let me have at least the interest. That burden just keeps getting heavier and heavier, you know.'

At home, meanwhile, Sona had dressed Chunnu in his frock, bonnet and shoes, making a regular prince out of him. The child, of course, would rather have kept the things in his hands to play with. In the inner room, a little scene was underway, with Gobar trying to pacify Jhuniya.

Jhiuniya looked at him contemptuously. 'You brought me here and dumped me, running off somewhere. And then no attempt to find out what had happened to me—as to whether I was dead or alive. Now, a whole year later, you've suddenly woken up. What a double-crosser you are! There I was, thinking you were right behind me, and you just disappeared for a whole year. How can men be trusted? You probably had your eye on someone else, figuring that with one girl at home, you might as well have another in the city.'

'Jhuniya!' Gobar protested. 'I swear to God I've never even looked at another woman. I ran away from home out of shame and fear, that's true, but you were never out of my thoughts even for a moment. Now I've decided to come and take you back with me. That's why I'm here. Your family was furious, I suppose?'

'Papa was out to kill me.'

'Honestly?'

'The three of them came storming over here, but your mother gave them such a telling-off that it shut them up. They did take away both our bullocks, though.'

'As cruel as that? And father just kept his mouth closed?'

'How could he put up a fight all by himself? The villagers weren't going to let them get away with the animals, but what could they do when your father himself gave in so easily?'

'Then how are you doing the field-work now?'

'The fields are ruined. One of them's being worked in partnership with Pandit Datadin. No sugar cane has been planted this season.'

Gobar was carrying two hundred rupees in his waistband. That in itself made him hot with power, and on hearing this state of affairs a fire blazed up in him.

'Then the first thing I must do is go settle with them. What nerve they have, taking the bullocks away from my door! This is robbery —plain and simple robbery. They'll be locked up for three years each. If they don't hand the animals right over, I'll get them back through the courts, and smash all that conceit of theirs in the process.'

Still fuming, he turned to leave, but Jhuniya caught hold of him and said, 'Do go there—but what's the rush? Take a little rest and have something to eat. You have the whole day ahead of you. The village council had a big meeting here and levied a fine of eighty rupees—and four bushels of grain besides. That was what ruined us.'

Sona brought in the little boy, dressed up in his new clothes. He really did look like a prince in that outfit. Gobar took the child in his arms, but hugging him didn't bring much pleasure just then. His blood was boiling, and the money in his waistband was only making him more heated. He'd have it out with every one of them. What right had the council to impose a fine on him? Who did they think they were, meddling in his affairs? If he was keeping a woman, what harm was it doing them? If he were to swear out a complaint at the criminal court, those men would be slapped into handcuffs. The whole household had gone to rack and ruin. Just what did they take him to be?

The child in his arms smiled a little and then let out a scream as though he'd seen something terrifying.

'Go and have your bath,' Jhuniya said, taking the baby from him. 'Why get upset? If you start fighting all of them at once, you won't last a day. Whoever has money is the big man around here—only he is respected. A person without money is at the mercy of everyone.'

'I was an ass to run away from home. I'd like to have seen them fine us even half a pice if I'd been here.'

'It's only now, since you've breathed the city air, that you feel that way. Why would you have run away otherwise?'

'I feel like taking my stick and knocking down all those bastards like Pateshwari, Datadin and Jhinguri and ripping the money out of their bellies.'

'You must have a lot of money to get so violent. Come on—take it out. Let me see what you've saved up in all these months.'

She reached for Gobar's waist. Standing up, he said, 'My savings are nothing as yet. If you go with me now, though, I'll really start earning. It's taken me a whole year to get acquainted with the ways of the city.'

'If mother would let me go. . . .'

'Why wouldn't she? What business is it of hers?'

'Well, I'm not going without her permission. After all, you went off and deserted me. And whom did that leave me with? Where would I have gone if she hadn't taken me in? I'll sing her praises as long as I live. And you—are you planning to go on living away from home forever?'

'What would I do sitting around here? Work and die—what else is there to do here? Anyone who has a little brains and is not afraid of work will never starve in the city. But brains are no use at all here. Why is papa sore at me?'

'Thank your lucky stars that he's letting you off so easily. If he were as angry as he deserves to be for all the trouble you've caused, he'd beat the daylights out of you.'

'He must have really abused you then.'

'Never, not even in an off moment. Your mother was angry in the beginning, but father never said a thing. Whenever he spoke to me, it was with lots of affection. He worried even when I got a slight headache. I consider him a god compared to my own father. He's always telling mother not to say anything bad to me. Countless times he got angry at you though, for dumping me at home and going off heavens-knows-where. These days the money is tight though. The income from the cane crop vanished before it even reached home. Now he's working as a hired labourer. Today the poor man fainted in the field. We were all weeping and wailing. He's been lying down ever since.'

After washing up and combing his hair fastidiously, Gobar set out to conquer the village. He went and paid his respects at both uncles' houses and then went around visiting friends. The village hadn't changed especially, except that Pateshwari had built a new living-room, and Jhinguri Singh had put in a well near his door. Gobar's heart pounded with even more defiance and anger. Everyone he met treated him with respect, and the young men lionized him and were ready to accompany him to Lucknow. How he had changed in just a year!

All at once he ran into Jhinguri Singh taking a bath at his well. Gobar walked by without a word, giving no sign of recognition. He wanted to show the thakur that he considered him of no importance.

It was Jhinguri Singh who spoke up—'When did you get back, Gobar? Things went well for you? You worked as a servant somewhere in Lucknow?'

'I didn't go to Lucknow to become a slave,' Gobar snapped. 'A servant is nothing but a slave. I was in business.'

The thakur looked him up and down with new interest. 'How much did you earn a day?'

Gobar seized the opportunity to make his small stock of ammunition look like an arsenal. 'Oh, I was making some two and a half or three rupees a day. At times when I got a real break, maybe four. Not more than that.'

Jhinguri, however much he snatched and plundered, could never earn more than twenty-five or thirty a month. And here this stupid yokel was making a hundred. His face fell. What basis was there to lord it over this fellow now? Jhinguri's caste was higher, of course, but who paid any attention to caste? This was no time to antagonize the boy. Something might be gained by playing up to him instead.

'That's no small sum you're earning, son, and you'll need wisdom

259

in spending it. In the village we don't get even three annas a day. If you could find some sort of work any place for my son Bhavaniya, I'd send him there. He never studies, and he's always up to mischief of one kind or another. Do let me know if a clerk's job opens up anywhere. Or better yet, take him along with you. After all, he's a friend of yours. If the salary's small, that's no problem, as long as there's a little income to be made on the side.'

Gobar laughed scornfully. 'That greed for earnings on the side is what corrupts men, thakur. But we've sunk so low that we're not satisfied until we can indulge in something dishonest. Clerks' jobs are available in Lucknow, but all the shopkeepers want a man who's honest and wide-awake. I could palm Bhavani off on someone, but if he later became light-fingered or something, they'd be at my throat. What counts in the world is not knowledge, but honesty.'

With that slap in the face, Gobar walked on. Jhinguri was left writhing. How self-righteously the brat spoke, as though he were virtue incarnate or something!

Gobar was equally rough on Datadin, whom he met heading home for dinner. The pandit looked pleased to see him. 'Things been going well, Gobar? I hear you found a good job there. How about wangling something for Matadin too? He does nothing but lie around and drink bhang.'

Gobar played along—'How could there be a shortage of anything in your house, maharaj? As a family priest, you can go to anyone's door and come back with something in hand. You people get something whenever there's a birth, whenever there's a death, whenever there's a marriage, whenever there's a funeral. You work the fields. You lend out money. You act as brokers. And if anyone makes a mistake, you set a fine and ransack his place. With all that money, your bellies still aren't full? What good would it do you to pile up still more? Or have you worked out some way of taking it with you to the next world?'

Datadin gaped at Gobar's audacity. He seemed to have forgotten all about politeness and deference. Perhaps the boy didn't know that his father was now little more than his slave. How true that a shallow river soon overflows. Datadin let no shadow cross his face, however. Like old men who laugh even when children yank at their whiskers, he took this berating in good humour and said lightly, 'That Lucknow air has really made you clever, Gobar! Come on now, how much money have you brought back? What about some for me? Believe me,

Gobar, I thought of you often. You're going to stay a while now, aren't you?'

'Yes, I'll be staying a while. I have to file suit against those village elders who gobbled up a hundred and fifty rupees of ours by making out that it was a fine. I want to see who's going to cut off connections with me, and how they're going to throw me out of the caste.'

With that threat, he moved on. His boldness had completely over-awed his train of young admirers.

'Go ahead and file a complaint, Gobar,' one said. 'The old man's a cobra. There's no charm to cure his bite. You told him off nicely. Warm up the ears of that patwari Pateshwari too. He's a sneaky one —setting fathers against sons, and brothers against brothers. He teams up with the zamindar's man and cuts the throats of the tenants. They can plough their own fields later; first they have to plough his. They can do their own irrigating later; first they have to do his.'

Gobar twirled his moustache. 'You don't have to tell me, my friends. In one year I've certainly not forgotten. I'm not going to be living here, or I'd make every one of them dance before I got through. Let's celebrate Holi with a bang this year and put on a show for the occasion that will really smash all of them.'

They began making plans for the festival. There would have to be lots of bhang, both sweet and salty, and some black paint should be mixed up along with the other colours. Only black would be used on the faces of the village elders. Nobody could object during Holi. Then they'd take out a procession lampooning the headmen. Money was no problem. Good old Gobar had come back with his pile of earnings.

After his meal, Gobar went to see Bhola. He couldn't relax until he'd retrieved those two bullocks and tied them by his own door. He was ready to fight to the finish.

'Don't make the quarrel worse, son,' Hori said nervously. 'Bhola took the animals. Let God see to him. After all, he did have some money coming to him.'

Gobar flared up. 'Don't you meddle in this, father. His cow was worth fifty rupees. Our bullocks cost us a hundred and fifty. We'd used them for three years, but they were still worth a hundred. He could have sued us for the money or sworn out a warrant or what-ever he wished, but he had no right to undo the bullocks and lead them away. And as for you—what can I say? First you lose the bullocks and then you pay a hundred and fifty rupee fine. That's what comes of being too good. I'd like to have seen them take the animals if I'd been here. I'd have flattened all three of them, right here on the ground. And I wouldn't have had a thing to do with the village council. Then we'd have seen who would dare turn me out of the caste. But you just sat back and watched!'

Hori bowed his head like a convict, but Dhaniya couldn't put up with disrespect. 'You're in the wrong too, son. How could we have lived in the village if people had cut us off completely? And there's our grown-up daughter too. She has to be settled someplace also, doesn't she? Whether people are living or dying, the caste. . . .'

'We were in good standing in the caste and respected in the community,' Gobar broke in. 'So why couldn't I be married? Tell me. Simply because we couldn't afford even food in the house. If you have money, there's no problem about caste or social approval. Money's what runs the world. No one cares about caste-standing.'

Dhaniya heard the child crying and went inside. Gobar started out the door. Hori was sitting and thinking. The boy was speaking so senselessly—he'd evidently lost his head. Nevertheless Gobar's wisdom and common sense had won out over his father's standards of justice and virtue.

'Shall I come along too?' Hori asked suddenly.

'I'm not going there to fight, father. Don't worry. The law is on my side. Why should I start a fight?'

'Would it do any harm if I went too?'

'Yes, lots of harm. You'd foul up my plan.'

Hori fell silent and Gobar set off.

Hardly five minutes had passed when Dhaniya came out carrying the baby. 'Has Gobar gone alone? I ask you now, isn't God ever going to give you any sense? Is Bhola about to part with the bullocks just like that? The three of them will pounce on him like hawks. God help him. Whom can I ask now to run and stop him? You're hopeless.'

Hori picked up his staff from the corner and ran after Gobar. Once outside the village, he looked all around. Only a tiny speck was visible on the horizon. How could Gobar have gone so far in such a short time? Why hadn't he stopped the boy, he reproached himself. If he'd opposed him firmly, telling him not to go to Bhola's house, Gobar never would have gone. To run after him now was no use—he hadn't the strength to catch up. Acknowledging defeat, he sat down and began to pray 'O Hanuman, protect him.'

Reaching the next village, Gobar saw a group of men gambling under a banyan tree. Thinking him a policeman, they grabbed up their cowrie shells and were just running off when Jangi suddenly recognized him. 'Oh, it's just Gobardhan.'

Gobar saw Jangi peering out from behind the tree. 'Don't be scared, brother. It's me. Greetings! I just arrived today and thought I'd come visit you all. No telling when I'll get back this way again. Thanks to your good wishes, things went very well for me while I was away. The raja I'm working for told me to bring back one or two others if possible, to work as watchmen. I told him I'd get men who'd stick to their posts even if it cost them their lives. Come along with me if you're interested. It's a good job.'

Jangi was already awed by Gobar's splendid appearance. He himself had never been able to afford even rawhide sandals, and here was Gobar wearing shiny leather shoes. He'd become a regular gentleman, what with a clean striped shirt and neatly parted hair. This immaculate figure was very different from the poor and ragged Gobar he'd known. Jangi's violent hostility had already been somewhat pacified with the passing of time, and the remainder now melted away. Addicted to both gambling and ganja, he had trouble getting any money at home. Now his mouth was watering. 'Of course I'll go with you. Why not? All I do here is sit around swatting flies. How much will I make?'

'Don't worry about it,' Gobar said with great confidence. 'All that's in my hands. You'll get what you want. I figured there was no point in looking around outside when there were men right here at home.'

'What kind of work will it be?' Jangi asked eagerly.

'You might be a watchman, or you might collect rents. Rent-collecting is the best deal. You make a bargain with the tenant and then go tell the master he wasn't at home. You can make eight annas or more a day that way, if you want.'

'Would I get a place to live too?'

'No problem about that. The whole palace is practically empty. Running water and electricity—there's nothing at all lacking. Is Kamta around or has he gone somewhere?'

'He's gone to sell the milk. No one lets me go to the bazaar. They say I'll just spend the money on ganja. I smoke very little of it now, brother, but I do need two pice worth a day. Don't say anything to Kamta. I'll go with you.'

'That's fine. Sure, come along. We'll leave after Holi.'

'That's settled then.'

Still talking, the two of them had reached Bhola's house. Bhola was sitting by the door twisting hemp into rope. Gomar sprang forward and touched his feet. This time his voice was filled with genuine emotion. 'Please forgive me, uncle, for whatever wrong I've done.'

Bhola set the hemp aside. 'For what you did, Gobar,' he said, his voice hard as flint, 'it would have been no sin for me to have cut off your head. But what can I say now that you've come to my door? Very well, God will take care of the punishment for what you did to me. When did you get back?'

Gobar gave a highly embroidered account of his rising fortunes and asked permission to take Jangi back with him. This came as an unsolicited boon for Bhola. Jangi was always stirring up some kind of trouble at home. If he went away, he'd at least be earning a little something. Even if he kept it all himself, they'd at least be freed from the burden of supporting him, anyway.

'God willing,' Gobar added, 'and if he sticks with it, uncle, he'll be a real man within a year or two.'

'Yes, if he can stick with it.'

'People straighten themselves out once they're on their own.'

'So when are you thinking of returning?'

'I'll leave after Holi. If I can get our farm and all running properly again, I can go away without worrying.'

'Tell Hori he should sit back now and spend his time in prayer.'

'That's what I tell him, but since when has he been willing to sit back?'

'You must know some doctor there. This cough's giving me a lot of trouble. Do send some medicine if you can.'

'There's a famous doctor right in my neighbourhood. I'll describe your condition to him, get some medicine made up, and have it sent to you. Is the cough worse during the day or at night?'

'At night, son. I can't sleep a wink. In fact, if there's any way, I might go live there too. Business doesn't pay at all here.'

'What fun is there in business here compared with it there, uncle? Even at ten quarts to the rupee, no one wants milk here. You have to force it down the throats of the sweet-sellers, whereas there you can sell dozens of gallons of milk any old time at five or six quarts to the rupee.'

Jangi had gone to mix up some sweetened milk for Gobar. Bhola, seeing that they were alone, said, 'Besides brother, I'm fed up with this mess here. You see for yourself how things are with Jangi. As for Kamta, he does take the milk to market. But feeding and watering the cows, letting them out and tying them up—I have to do all of that. What I want now is just to have one square meal a day and then sit back and take it easy. How long can I go on shouting after everyone? Every day it's just fighting and wrangling, and I can't go on indefinitely pacifying the people he's quarrelled with. Then at night the cough comes on, and I haven't the strength to get up; but no one would think of fetching me a jug of water. A tether has broken, but no one's going to mend it. It'll only get fixed when I do it.'

'You come to Lucknow, uncle,' Gobar assured him warmly. 'Sell your milk at five quarts to the rupee—cash. I'm acquainted with any number of rich men. I guarantee the sale of at least ten gallons a day. I have my own tea-shop too, so I'll take ten quarts a day myself. You'll have no trouble at all.'

Jangi brought the milk and Gobar drank a glass. 'Even if you just sit in the shop mornings and evenings, uncle, you can easily make a rupee a day.'

After a moment, Bhola said hesitantly. 'Anger makes a man blind, son. I made off with your bullocks. Take them with you when you go. There's no farming to be done here anyway.'

'I've arranged to get another pair, uncle.'

'Nonsense. Why should you buy new bullocks? Take these ones.'

'Well, I'll see that you get your money.'

'It's not as though the money's with some outsider, son. It's all in the family. Other than the foolishness about caste, what difference is there between you and me? If you want to know the truth, I should have been happy that Jhuniya found a good home and is comfortably settled. And there I was, thirsty for her blood!'

At dusk, when Gobar started back from there, the bullocks went along with him, and Jangi followed behind carrying two pots of curds.

I*

CHAPTER 21

SIX months of every year, Indian villages resound to the beating of drums and the clashing of cymbals in celebration of some festival or other. Beginning a month before Holi and continuing a month after it, songs of spring fill the air. When summer sets in, there are heroic ballads; and during July and August, the songs of the rainy season festival. After that, the chanting of the *Ramayana* begins.

The village of Belari was no exception. Neither the threats of the moneylenders nor the curses of the agent could restrain these celebrations. Nor did it matter if there was no grain in the house, no clothes on one's back, and no money in one's purse. The instinctive joy of life could not be suppressed. To live without laughter would have been impossible.

Most of the Holi festivities usually took place in front of Nokheram's house. It was there that the bhang was prepared and the colour thrown and the dancing carried on. The agent spent five or ten rupees for the festival. Who else could have afforded to put on the entertainment?

This time, however, Gobar had drawn all the young people of the village to his door, and Nokheram's place was deserted. In front of Gobar's house they were crushing bhang, rolling betel leaves and mixing coloured powders. Matting was spread out, and the singing had begun. Nokheram's courtyard was silent. The bhang was there, but who would grind it? The drums and cymbals were on hand, but who would play and sing? People were flocking from all directions towards Gobar's place—'The drinks there are really a delight, what with rosewater, saffron and almonds mixed in along with the bhang ... That's right. Gobar brought two full pounds of almonds himself ... One drink and you're starry-eyed, in another world ... And he bought special perfumed tobacco too ... He's even scented the colouring ... He knows how to earn money and how to spend it too ... What good does it do to dig a hole and bury it? That's the real beauty of wealth ... And it's not just the bhang. All the singers are invited

266

to dinner—and there's no dearth of them in the village, nor of dancers, nor of actors for that matter. Shobha himself does an imitation of a lame man that beats anything you've ever seen, and no one is better at imitating voices. Ask him and he'll mimic any voice—of an animal or a person. Lawyers and patwaris, the police chief, his peon and the moneylender—he can do take-offs on them all. He doesn't own all the stuff for putting on that kind of show, but this time Gobar's ordered everything, and the performance should really be something to see. . . .'

There had been so much talk of all this that people started gathering to watch the fun long before dark. Crowds of spectators poured in from the neighbouring villages also. By ten o'clock, three or four thousand people had assembled, and not even standing room was left by the time Girdhar and his cohorts made their grand entrance. Girdhar was made up as Jhinguri Singh—that same bald head, those same long whiskers, that same pot belly!

The scene opened with the thakur seated at dinner, his senior wife sitting nearby fanning him. He looked at her lovingly and said, 'You're still so beautiful that the sight of you would make any young man's heart flutter.'

The wife puffed up with pride. 'I suppose that's why you went out and got a new bride.'

'I only brought her to be your servant. How could she begin to compare with you?'

The younger wife overheard this and went off pouting.

In the second scene, the thakur was lying on his cot and the younger wife sat on the ground, her face averted. He tried over and over to get her to look toward him. 'Why are you mad at me, my darling?'

'Go find your darling wherever she is. I'm just a servant girl, brought here to wait on others.'

'You're my queen. That old woman is here only to wait on you.'

The first wife heard this and burst in holding a broom with which she whacked him several times. The old man fled for his life.

In the second skit, the thakur signed a loan agreement for ten rupees and handed over five rupees. The rest had been withheld for commission, gratuity and service charges.

The scene opened with the farmer coming and falling weeping at the master's feet. The thakur very reluctantly agreed to make the loan. After the document had been prepared, he handed over five rupees. The farmer was taken aback and said, 'But this is only five, master.'

'That's not five. It's ten. Go home and count it.'

'No, your honour, it's five.'

'One rupee goes for my tip, right?'

'Yes, your honour.'

'And one for writing up the note?'

'Yes, your honour.'

'And one for the official form?'

'Yes, your honour.'

'And one for commission?'

'Yes, your honour.'

'And one for the interest?'

'Yes, your honour.'

'Plus five in cash. Does that make ten or doesn't it?'

'Yes, your honour. Now please keep the other five also.'

'Are you crazy?'

'No, your honour. One rupee is a donation to your younger wife, and one rupee is for your senior wife. One rupee is to buy betel leaves for your younger wife to chew, and one is to buy them for your senior wife. That leaves only one rupee—and it can go for your funeral arrangements.'

So it went, with Nokheram and Pateshwari and Datadin, one by one, each getting the treatment. Although the jokes were nothing new and the caricatures were familiar, Girdhar's acting was so amusing and the audience so unsophisticated that they laughed at anything. The show kept going all night, allowing oppressed hearts to feel cheered with vicarious revenge. By the time the last impersonation ended, it was dawn and crows were cawing overhead.

The night's songs and jokes were on everyone's lips that morning. The elders had been made the laughing-stock of the village. Wherever they appeared, three or four little boys would trail behind repeating the jibes of the previous night. Jhinguri Singh had a good sense of humour and took it all in fun, but Pateshwari was habitually irritable, and Pandit Datadin was so quick-tempered that he was ready to fight everyone. He was accustomed to deference from everyone, and not only the agent but even the Rai Sahib himself would bow when they met. To be ridiculed this way—and in his own village at that—was insufferable. If he had possessed the full power of brahmanic fury, he'd have burned these villains to a crisp. His curses would have reduced them all to ashes. But in this evil age even those curses had lost their power, so he would have to resort to the conventional weapons of the time. Striding up to Hori's door, he demanded angrily, 'Aren't you going to work today either, Hori? You've recovered now. Don't you realize what a loss I've been taking?'

Gobar had slept late and had just gotten up. He was heading outside, rubbing his eyes, when Datadin's voice reached his ears. Far from touching the pandit's feet in the usual respectful greeting, he spoke up rudely, 'He won't be working for you any more. We have our own sugar cane to plant.'

Datadin popped a pinch of tobacco into his mouth. 'What do you mean he won't work? He can't quit in the middle of the season. In June he can stop or keep working, whichever he wants, but he can't quit before that.'

Gobar yawned. 'He didn't sign up as your slave. He worked for you while he felt like it. Now he doesn't feel like it, so he won't. No one can force him into it.'

'So Hori won't work?'

'No!'

'Then give me my money as well as the interest. The interest for three years comes to a hundred rupees. That's two hundred all together. I was figuring on subtracting three rupees a month from the interest, but if you don't want that, then don't take it. Give me my money. If you're going to play the rich man, then act like one.'

'I've never denied you my services, maharaj,' Hori put in, 'but our cane does have to be planted too.'

'What kind of services? And whose services?' Gobar snapped at his father. 'No one here is anyone's servant. We're all equals. Very funny —lending someone a hundred rupees and getting him to work off the interest for the rest of his life while the principal stays exactly the same! That's not moneylending—it's bloodsucking.'

'Then just give me the money, brother. There's no need to fight. I usually collect interest of one anna on the rupee. I had cut it by a half, figuring you were one of the village family.'

'We'll give you one per cent a month, not a cowrie more. If that suits you, you can have it. Otherwise, take the matter to court. One per cent interest every month is plenty.'

'Money seems to have given you a swollen head.'

'The people with swollen heads are those who expect ten rupees for every one they give out. We are workers, and our pride comes from sweating for what we earn. I remember your giving us thirty rupees to buy a bullock. Then it became a hundred, and now the hundred has become two hundred. That's how you people rob the farmers and turn them into hired hands while you take over control of their land. How long has it been, father?'

'Must be about eight or nine years,' Hori muttered timidly.

Gobar put his hand to his heart. 'From thirty rupees to two hundred in nine years! How much would it be at the rate of one per cent?' He made some calculations on the ground with a chunk of pottery. 'In ten years it comes to thirty-six rupees. Added to the principal, that makes sixty-six. We'll let you have seventy. I won't pay a cowrie more than that.'

Datadin turned to Hori. 'You hear his verdict? Either I forget the two hundred, and take seventy, or else I take it to court. How long could the world last if business were conducted that way? And you just sit back quietly. Well take it from me—I'm a brahman, and there'll be no peace for you if you swindle away my money. Very well, I'll write off the seventy also, and I won't even go to court. Let it go. As sure as I'm a brahman, I'll get that full two hundred rupees. You'll see! And you'll come to my door with folded hands begging me to take it.'

Datadin turned and stalked off. Gobar held his ground, but a surge of conscience swept through Hori's heart. If it had been the money of some lower caste landowner or merchant, he wouldn't have worried much, but a brahman's money! Hold back even one pice and it would have to be paid back in blood. God forbid that anyone fall victim to a brahman's fury. The whole family would be wiped out, leaving no one to light even a single lamp or offer even a drink of water in the home. His duty-ridden heart panicking at the thought, Hori ran after Datadin and clutched his feet. 'Maharaj,' he moaned, 'as long as I'm alive I'll pay back every pice of your money. Pay no attention to what the boy says. The matter is between you and me. He has nothing to do with it.'

Datadin mellowed a little. 'What nerve! Just think—telling me either to take seventy rupees for two hundred or else make a court case out of it. He only says that because he's never had a taste of the courts. Some time he's going to tangle with the law and then he'll lose that cockiness. Thinks he's a king, just because he's lived a few days in the city.'

'I'm telling you, maharaj, I'll pay back every pice.'

'Then you'll have to come and work my field starting tomorrow.'

'I'd be happy to, if my sugar cane didn't have to be planted.'

When Datadin had gone, Gobar looked at his father contemptuously. 'So you went to appease your god ! It's people like you who've spoiled them. He gave us thirty rupees. So now he'll collect two hundred, and on top of that give you a telling-off, get you to work for him, and keep you slaving away until he's killed you.'

Hori defended the rightness of his position. 'We mustn't lose our integrity, son. Every man's responsible for his own actions. We must pay whatever interest was agreed upon when we took the money. What's more, he's a brahman. Only they can consume that kind of money—it would stick in our throats.'

Gobar raised his eybrows. 'Who's saying we should lose our integrity? No one's suggesting that we swindle money from brahmans. All I'm saying is we won't pay all that interest. The banks charge twelve annas interest. You'll be letting him have one rupee interest. How much more does he want to rob us?'

'Won't he be offended?'

'Let him. Why should we dig our own graves for fear he might feel offended?'

'Son, let me do things my own way while I'm alive. When I'm dead and gone, you can do anything you like.'

'Well then you'll have to pay him yourself. I'm not going to take an axe and chop off my own legs. I was an ass to try to intervene. You took the money—you pay it back. Why should I sacrifice my life?'

With that, Gobar went in the house.

'How come you got in a row with your father the first thing in the morning?' Jhuniya asked.

Gobar related the whole incident and then said, 'The weight of his debt is going to keep getting heavier and heavier this way. Am I supposed to keep paying it off forever? All his earnings have gone to fill other people's houses. Why should I fall into the pit he's dug for himself? They weren't for my benefit. I'm not responsible for them.'

Meanwhile the village elders were hatching a plot to humiliate Gobar. If they didn't clamp down on this rascal, he'd spread wickedness all through the village. When a pawn turns into a bishop, he's bound to go crooked. Lord knows where he had learned so much law. Saying he wouldn't pay more than one per cent a month interest, and to accept it or go to court ! And what an indecent show he'd put on last night with all those good-for-nothing village boys he collected.

There was no lack of jealousy between the elders themselves, however, and each had enjoyed the lampooning of the others. Pateshwari and Nokheram were discussing the matter—

'They know down to the last detail what goes on in everyone's house,' said Pateshwari. 'The way they went after Jhinguri Singh was perfect. People almost died laughing when they heard that business about the two wives.'

'The impersonation was so realistic too,' Nokheram guffawed. 'I've seen his young queen several times myself, standing at the door and joking with the village boys.'

'And the old empress keeps trying to look young by putting makeup around her eyes and decorating her feet.'

'The two of them are at odds day and night. Jhinguri has absolutely no shame though. Anyone else would have gone crazy.'

'I hear they did a very crude take-off of you too, showing you being locked up and beaten in the house of a low-caste cobbler woman.'

'I'll fix that brat by filing a suit for the back land rent. This is going to be one bout he'll never forget.'

'But he's paid the rent, hasn't he?'

'I didn't give him a receipt, though. What proof is there that he's paid? Besides, who ever checks the account books around here? I'm going to send a man for him right now.'

Hori and Gobar were irrigating the field for the cane planting. There had been no hope of growing a cane crop this season, so the land had been lying fallow, but now that the bullocks were back, there was no reason not to plant the cane.

The two men were at loggerheads, however. They didn't even glance at each other or exchange any words. Hori was driving the bullocks while Gobar handled the leather bucket. Sona and Rupa, who were directing the flow of the water, soon began quarrelling. The point in question was whether Jhinguri Singh's younger wife fed herself first and then served her husband's meal, or whether she fed him first and then herself. Sona said that she fed herself first, whereas Rupa insisted on the opposite.

'If she eats first,' Rupa argued, 'then why isn't she fat rather than her husband? If he ever fell on top of her, she'd be crushed to bits.'

'You think good food makes people fat?' Sona retorted. 'It makes

272

them strong, not fat. Fatness comes from eating stuff like grass and leaves.'

'You mean then that she's stronger than he is?'

'Of course. Just the other day the two of them were fighting and she gave him such a shove that he skinned his knees.'

'Then will you eat first too, before feeding your husband?'

'Naturally.'

'But mama serves papa first.'

'That's why he's always bawling her out. I'm going to grow strong and keep my man in his place, but your husband will beat you and break your bones.'

Rupa was on the verge of tears. 'Why would he beat me? I won't do anything to bring that on.'

'He won't listen to anything you say. The moment you open your mouth he'll start beating you—whacking your skin right off!'

Frustrated, Rupa took Sona's sari between her teeth and tried to rip it. When that didn't work, she began pinching her.

Sona just teased her still more. 'He'll cut off your nose too.'

At that, Rupa bit her sister on the arm, which started bleeding. Sona gave her a hard push. She fell over and then got up crying. Sona looked at the teeth marks and began crying too.

Hearing their howling, Gobar lost his temper and slapped them each twice, at which the girls set off for home, crying all the more. The irrigating came to a standstill, and this brought on a squabble between father and son.

'Who's going to channel the water now?' Hori demanded. 'What do you mean—rushing over and chasing them both away. Why don't you go make up with them and bring them back?'

'It's you who's spoiled them.'

'Hitting them that way will just make them even more shameless.'

'Cut off their food for a day and they'll straighten themselves out.'

'I'm their father, not a butcher.'

Stub a toe once and somehow it keeps on getting struck—and sometimes it gets infected and gives trouble for months. The harmony between father and son had been injured that morning, and the sore spot had now been struck for the third time.

Gobar went home and brought Jhuniya back with him to water the field. She carried the baby with her, while Dhaniya and the two daughters looked on. The mother also resented Gobar's highhandedness. If he'd slapped only Rupa, she wouldn't have minded, but to strike a grown girl was unforgivable.

Gobar made up his mind to go back to Lucknow that very evening. Staying here was impossible now. Why should he hang around if nobody cared about him? He was given no say in the money matters, and when he barely touched the girls, people lost their heads as though he were some stranger. Well then, he wouldn't stay on in this cheap inn!

The two men had just finished their evening meal and stepped out-side when Nokheram's man appeared. 'Come on. The agent has sent for you.'

'Why's he sending for me at this time of night?' Hori asked indignantly. 'I've paid up my accounts.'

'My orders were just to fetch you. If you have some petition to make, go there and present it.'

Hori didn't feel like going, but he had no choice. Gobar stayed behind, apparently indifferent. Half an hour later Hori returned and settled down for a smoke. Gobar could no longer restrain himself. 'Why did he send for you?'

Hori's voice was full of anguish. 'I paid every pice of the rent. Now he says I still owe for the last two years. Just the other day I sold the sugar cane and gave him twenty-five rupees on the spot. And now he comes out with the story of two years' unpaid dues. I told him I won't pay a copper.'

'You must have the receipt, don't you?' Gobar asked.

'Since when has he ever given receipts?'

'Then why haven't you refused to pay him until you get a receipt?'

'How did I know those people would be so dishonest? This is all the result of your doings. You made fun of them last night and this is the punishment. When you live in the water, you can't offend the crocodile. After adding in the interest, he's come up with a claim for seventy rupees. Where can I find that much money?'

'If you'd taken a receipt,' Gobar defended himself, 'he couldn't have touched a hair on your head even if I'd made a complete ass out of him. I just can't understand why you're so careless in these money matters. If he doesn't give receipts, then send the sum by mail. It might mean a rupee or so in fees, but there'd be none of this foul play.'

'If you hadn't lit the fuse, nothing would have happened. Now all the headmen are up in arms. They're threatening to evict us. God knows how we'll ride out this storm.'

'I'm going over there to ask him a thing or two.'

'You'll just go and add more fuel to the fire.'

'If a fire is necessary, then I'll start one. If he wants to evict us, just let him try. I'll make him swear an oath in court with his hand on the holy water of the Ganges. You can stay here with your tail between your legs, but I'm going to fight him to the finish. I don't intend to cheat anyone out of a single pice nor do I intend to be cheated out of a single pice myself.'

He got up and went directly to Nokheram's place, where he found all the elders meeting in full session. At the sight of Gobar, they stiffened. The air was thick with conspiracy.

'Sir,' Gobar demanded sharply, 'how is it that my father paid up all the back rent and now you claim he still owes you for two years? What sort of racket is this?'

Nokheram leaned back against a bolster. 'As long as Hori's alive,' he declared imperiously, 'I don't wish to discuss financial matters with you.'

'I count for nothing in the family, is that it?' Gobar asked in an injured tone of voice.

'You may count for everything in your own family, but here you're a nobody.'

'Very well, go file a suit to evict us. When you've sworn in court on the water of .the Ganges, I'll pay the money. But I'll produce a hundred witnesses from this very village to testify that you don't give receipts. Just because they're simple farmers who don't talk back, you assume they're all nincompoops. I live in the same town as the Rai Sahib. All the village people may think he's an ogre, but I don't. I'll tell him every bit of what's happened, and then we'll see how you're going to collect from us a second time.'

His words had the strength of truth. In a coward, even truth remains dumb. Cover brick with cement and it becomes like stone, but put that same cement on a mud wall and all you have is mud. Gobar's fearless candour pierced the armour of injustice with which Nokheram had tried to fortify his feeble soul.

As though he'd just remembered something, Nokheram said, 'Why are you getting so worked up? There's no need to get mad. If Hori paid the money, it must be noted down somewhere or other. I'll look through my papers tomorrow. I seem to vaguely recall now that

Hori may have made some payment. Rest assured—if the money's been paid, it can't have gone astray. I'm sure you wouldn't lie over such a paltry sum of money, and it certainly isn't going to make a rich man out of me.'

When Gobar got home he lit into Hori so heatedly that the poor old man was almost in tears. 'You're worse than a baby who hears a cat meow and starts screaming. How long do I have to run around defending you? I'm leaving you seventy rupees. If Datadin accepts it, then pay him off and get a receipt. If you pay even one pice more than that, you'll never get another thing from me. I've not taken up life in a strange city just so you can keep letting yourself be robbed and paying for it out of my earnings. I'm going away tomorrow. All I'm telling you is this—don't borrow another pice from anyone and don't pay another thing. Mangaru, Dulari, Datadin—they'll all have to accept the one per cent a month interest rate.'

Dhaniya finished her meal and joined them outside. 'Why leave so soon, son? Stay three or four more days. Get the sugar cane planted and these debts straightened out properly and then go.'

Gobar began showing off. 'You might stop to realize that I'm losing two or three rupees a day here. The most I can earn here is four annas a day. And this time I'll take Jhuniya with me too. Fixing meals and all that is a lot of trouble.'

'As you wish,' Dhaniya said timidly. 'But how can she manage the house and look after the baby all by herself?'

'Should I care first about the baby or about my own welfare? I can't fuss around with cooking meals myself.'

'I'm not stopping you from taking them, but think of how tough it will be—living among strangers, with a family to take care of and no responsible person around to help.'

'Now mother! People do find friends even in a foreign country. Besides, the world is a selfish place, and you can get a friend by just forgiving some four-pice debt. If you're flat broke, even your mother and father don't care about you.'

Dhaniya felt the barb. A wave of resentment swept through her. 'So you consider even your parents among those who love you for your money?'

'My eyes see it that way.'

'You're not looking, then. Parents aren't that heartless. It's the children who turn their backs on their parents as soon as they start making a little money. I can give you not just one or two but scores of examples from this very village. Parents take on debts. What for? For their own enjoyment or for the sake of their sons and daughters?'

'Goodness knows why you've borrowed money. Not a pice of it ever reached me.'

'You grew up without any nourishment, I suppose?'

'What did that nourishment cost you? When I was a baby, I drank your milk. Later I was turned loose like an orphan. I ate what everyone else was eating. It wasn't as though you ordered milk or butter for me. And now you and father both expect me to settle all your debts, pay the rent and take care of the girls' marriages. It's as though I'm living only to finance your payments. Don't I have a family too?'

Dhaniya was stunned. In one brief moment, the fond dreams of a lifetime seemed shattered. Until now she had been happy in the thought that at last all her sorrows were at an end. Ever since Gobar had come home, her face had sparkled with delight. A new tenderness filled her voice and a new generosity marked her behaviour. God had been merciful to her, and she should show her gratitude through modesty and humility. The inward peace expressed itself in outward compassion. Gobar's words were like burning sand on her heart, and her hopes, like gram, were scorched by the touch. All her pride crumbled to dust. The boat she had hoped would carry her across the sea of life had been shattered. There was nothing left to live for.

But no, her Gobar couldn't be so selfish. He had never talked back to his mother, and he'd never been obstinate about anything, swallowing whatever dry crumbs fell his way. Why was that image of gentle kindness and simplicity now talking in this heartbreaking way? No one had said anything counter to his wishes. She and his father both looked to him for guidance. He himself had brought up the idea of repayment. None of them would have suggested he pay off his parent's debts. For a mother and father it was satisfying enough that he was making a decent living and leading a respectable life. If it was possible for him to help his parents, well and good. If not, they weren't going to put the squeeze on him. If he wanted to take Jhuniya with him, he could take her with pleasure. When she'd said that to take Jhuniya along might create more problems than it solved, she was only thinking of his own welfare. There was no reason for him to get all upset about it.

Obviously Jhuniya must be behind all this trouble—sitting back and poisoning his mind. She was getting no chance here to deck herself out and lead a gay life, and there was always some work to be done around the house. There, she'd have money, and she could enjoy herself, eating in style, dressing in style, and going to sleep without a care in the world. Cooking for two people was simple enough—and in the city money was the only thing necessary. It was said that in the bazaar there one could buy food already cooked. Yes, this whole disturbance must be her doing. Jhuniya herself had once lived in a city for a while, and she must have developed a taste for that sort of life. No one had been taking any notice of her around here until she met this simple-minded boy and hooked him. She was meowing like a bedraggled cat the day she came here five months gone. If they'd not given her shelter, she'd be out begging today. And this was the reward for their kindness! It was all because of this hellcat that they'd had to pay the fine, that their reputation in the community had been spoiled, that their lands had been ruined and that all the other calamities had taken place. And now the bitch was knocking holes in the plate off which she'd been fed. The sight of money had gone to her head—she'd been swaggering around ever since. After all, wasn't her young man earning a little money now? All these months when there was no word from him, she had run around getting oil to massage her mother-in-law's feet, and going out of her way to humour her, whereas now the witch wanted to snatch away her life's treasure.

'Who's putting these ideas in your head, son?' she asked sadly. 'You didn't used to be like this. We're your own mother and father, the girls are your own sisters, and the home is your very own too. No one's an outsider here. And our days are numbered. If you keep up the prestige of the family, it'll be to your own advantage. A man earns for the sake of his family, doesn't he, rather than for anyone else? Even a pig can fill its own belly, after all. I hadn't thought that Jhuniya would turn into a snake and bite back at us.'

'Mother,' Gobar said sharply, 'I'm no child that Jhuniya would be dictating to me. You've been cursing her for no reason at all. I can't take on the burden of your entire household. I'll do whatever I can to help you, but I can't chain myself down.'

Jhuniya emerged from the inner room and declared, 'Don't turn your anger on an innocent scapegoat, mother. He's no baby. I couldn't just tear him away from you. Each person knows what's good for him and what's bad. Men aren't born to spend their lives depriving themselves and then dying emptyhanded some day. Everyone wants a little happiness out of life. Everyone longs to get hold of a little money.'

'All right, Jhuniya,' Dhaniya said, grinding her teeth. 'Don't try to show off how smart you are. Suddenly you've become able to realize what's good and bad for you. Where was all that wisdom the day you showed up here, weeping and wailing and putting your head to my feet? If we had started thinking then of what was good for us, Lord knows where you'd be today.'

At this, the battle began in earnest. Insinuations and accusations, abuses and curses, charges and countercharges—no words were spared. Every so often Gobar added his sting also. Hori sat on the porch listening while Sona and Rupa cowered in the courtyard. Dulari, Puniya and a number of other women appeared as mediators. The thunder was punctuated by showers too. Both women were weeping, bemoaning their fates, reproaching God, and protesting their innocence. Jhuniya was unearthing old skeletons. She had suddenly become especially sympathetic towards Hira and Shobha, whom Dhaniya had treated so shabbily. Dhaniya had never gotten along with anybody, so how could she have taken to Jhuniya? Dhaniya was trying to clear herself, but general opinion favoured Jhuniya for some reason, perhaps because Jhuniya never lost her self-control whereas Dhaniya got completely carried away. Or perhaps it was because Jhuniya was now the wife of a man making good money and it might be more profitable to play up to her.

At last Hori came into the courtyard. 'I beg you, Dhaniya—keep quiet before you disgrace me completely. Haven't you heard your fill yet?'

Dhaniya snorted and turned on him. 'So you're going to jump on the winning team too! I'm the only one at fault. I suppose she's showering bouquets on me!'

The field of battle shifted.

'Fighting with inferiors only shows one's own inferiority.'

But Dhaniya could see no logic for considering Jhuniya an inferior.

'All right then, she's not below you. She's above you,' Hori declared in a troubled voice. 'But if someone doesn't want to stay, are you going to tie him up and hang onto him? The duty of parents is to raise their children to be adults. We've done that. They can fend for themselves now. What more do you expect—that they should provide for you? Parents have a sixteen-anna duty to their children, but children don't have even a one-anna duty to their parents. If someone's going to leave, let him leave with your blessing. God is our protector. We'll undergo whatever we're fated to undergo. Forty-

279

seven years of this sort of struggle have passed. Only five years or so are left, and they'll pass somehow too.'

Meanwhile Gobar was preparing for the departure. Even a drink of water in this house would be polluting for him now. If his own mother could say such things, then he didn't ever want to see her face again.

The packing was finished in no time. Jhuniya was dressed up to leave, and Chunnu looked like a prince in the frock and bonnet.

'Son,' Hori choked out, 'I'm in no position to say anything to you, but my heart compels me. Would it be too much to ask you to go touch your poor mother's feet before you leave? Couldn't you do at least that for the mother who gave you birth and who poured out her life's blood to nourish you?'

Gobar turned away. 'I don't consider her my mother.'

Hori's eyes filled with tears. 'As you wish. May you be happy wherever you are.'

Jhuniya went over and touched her mother-in-law's feet with the end of her sari. Not a word of blessing came from Dhaniya's mouth, and she didn't even raise her eyes to look at the girl.

Gobar had taken the child in his arms and gone ahead. Jhuniya followed, the bundle of possessions under her arm. A chamar boy carried their trunk. A number of men and women walked to the edge of the village to see them off.

Meanwhile Dhaniya sat down and cried as though someone were slicing her heart out. The mother in her was like a house burned to ashes, with no place left even to sit and weep.

CHAPTER 22

NEGOTIATIONS for the marriage of the Rai Sahib's daughter had been going on for some time. Elections were also near at hand. Even more urgent, though, was a lawsuit the Rai Sahib had to initiate which would require fifty thousand in court fees alone, not to mention the other expenses.

The brother-in-law of the Rai Sahib, sole owner of a large estate, had died in the prime of youth as the result of a car crash, so the Rai Sahib was trying to get legal support in claiming the estate on behalf of his young son. A cousin of the Rai Sahib's wife had already taken possession of the estate, however, and was unwilling to give the Rai Sahib any share in it. The Rai Sahib had hoped very much that an agreement could be reached amongst themselves whereby the other relative would step aside in return for a suitable annuity. He was even prepared to give up half the income from the estate, but the man had refused to accept any compromise and had begun collecting rents backed purely by the force of the stick. The only course open to the Rai Sahib was to seek the help of the courts. The case would cost several hundred thousand rupees, but the estate was worth a couple of million.

Lawyers had assured him that the decision would definitely be in his favour, so the opportunity was too good to miss. The only problem was that all three of these matters had come up simultaneously and there was no way to postpone any of them. His daughter was already eighteen years old, and her marriage had been delayed this long only because ready cash was not available. It would cost an estimated hundred thousand rupees. Most of those who had been approached as prospective grooms had made exorbitant demands, but recently a very good opportunity had appeared. The wife of Kunwar Digvijay Singh had succumbed to tuberculosis, and he was now anxious to restore his desolated home. An economical bargain had been struck, and, lest the prey escape, it was imperative to hold the ceremony during the current auspicious season for marriages.

The Kunwar Sahib was a treasurehouse of vices. Liquor, ganja, opium, charas—he refrained from none of the intoxicants. After all, indulgence was what distinguished men of means. How could a person call himself rich and not lead a somewhat dissolute life? And what better way was there to enjoy one's wealth? Despite all these vices, however, he was so gifted that even great scholars held him in great esteem. He was unrivalled in music, drama, astrology, yoga, stick-fighting, wrestling and marksmanship. He was also known for his courage and daring. He had contributed unstintingly to the nationalist movement—though secretly, of course. This was no secret to the authorities, but he was respected highly nevertheless, and even the Governor himself was his guest once or twice a year. Besides, the man was no more than thirty or thirty-two and so healthy that he could polish off a whole goat by himself in one sitting.

Here was a windfall for the Rai Sahib. The Kunwar Sahib had not even completed the mourning ceremonies when the Rai Sahib started negotiations. For the Kunwar Sahib, marriage was only a means of expanding his power and influence. After all, the Rai Sahib was a member of the Council and a prestigious figure in his own right. The self-sacrifice he had displayed in the national struggle had also made him an object of veneration. There could be no possible objection to the marriage. So the matter was settled.

That left the election, a gold nugget which could neither be gulped down nor thrown up. The Rai Sahib had been elected twice now, and each campaign had set him back a hundred thousand rupees. This time, however, a raja was also running in this constituency, and had publicly announced that he would keep the Rai Sahib Amarpal Singh out of the Council even if it meant paying each voter a thousand rupees—even if his five million rupee estate crumbled to dust. What's more, the authorities had assured him of their support. The Rai Sahib was intelligent and shrewd enough to realize the odds, but he belonged to the clan of fighting Rajputs and was descended from a long line of wealthy aristocrats. How could he desert the field of battle after being openly challenged? Of course if Raja Surya Pratap Singh had come and requested politely that the Rai Sahib, having served two terms already, should let him be elected this time, the suggestion might well have been welcomed. He was no longer enamoured of the Council. But in the face of this challenge, there was no choice but to put up his fists.

There had been one other alternative. Mr Tankha had assured

him that if he stood for office, the Raja Sahib would hand over a hundred thousand rupees on a platter to get him to drop out of the race. Tankha went so far as to say that he'd already discussed the matter with the Raja and found him eager to make such a pay-off. Recently, though, it had become known that the Raja did not wish to forego the distinction of defeating the Rai Sahib, primarily because of the marriage plans between the Rai Sahib's daughter and the Kunwar Sahib. He felt that the union of these two influential families would be detrimental to his own prestige. Another thorn in the Raja's side was the in-laws' estate which the Rai Sahib hoped to inherit. If the Rai Sahib somehow succeeded—and the law obviously favoured him—then he would become a formidable rival. It would be a good thing therefore to stamp down the Rai Sahib and crush his prestige in the dust.

The poor Rai Sahib was in a real quandary. He began suspecting that Mr Tankha had doublecrossed him to further his own selfish interests. He heard reports that Tankha was now supporting the Raja Sahib, which added salt to the wounds. He'd sent for Tankha several times, but either he was not to be found at home or he'd promise to come and then forget all about it.

At last the Rai Sahib determined to confront him personally. Tankha was at home, fortunately, but the Rai Sahib was kept waiting for a full hour. That Mr Tankha who used to show up once a day at the Rai Sahib's door had certainly become arrogant! The Rai Sahib sat there fuming. When Mr Tankha, freshly bathed and dressed, a cigar clamped in his mouth, sauntered into the room and held out his hand, the Rai Sahib blew up—'I've been sitting here a full hour and now at last you decide to emerge. I take this as a personal insult.'

Mr Tankha sat down on the sofa, deliberately blew out a cloud of smoke and said, 'I'm sorry about that. I was involved in some very urgent business. You should have phoned and made an appointment with me.'

Fuel was being added to the fire, but the Rai Sahib restrained his anger. He'd not come to fight, and the insult would have to be swallowed this time. 'Yes, it was my fault. You evidently have very little free time these days.'

'That's right—very little. Otherwise I'd certainly have come to see you.'

'I've come to ask you about that certain matter. There appears to be no chance of a settlement. Battle preparations are in full swing over there.'

'You know what the Raja Sahib's like. He's a bit of a nut— completely unpredictable, always getting carried away by some whim or other. Right now he's determined to show you up, and when he's obsessed with some idea, he listens to no one, whatever loss may be involved for himself. He's already carrying a debt of four million, but he's as brash as ever, throwing his money around. Money means nothing to him. He's not paid his servants' salaries for six months and yet he's building a jewel of a palace. The floor is of marble, and the mosaic work so dazzling you can hardly look at it. Gift baskets are despatched every day to the officials, and I hear he's about to take on an Englishman as a manager.'

'Then how come you claimed you would work out an understanding with him?'

'I've done all I could. What more could I have done? If a man's determined to blow away a fortune, what power do I have?'

The Rai Sahib couldn't restrain his anger any longer. 'Especially when you expect to lay hands on a good share of that fortune!'

Tankha saw no reason to take this lying down. 'Don't force me to spell it out, Rai Sahib. I'm no saint and neither are you. All of us are out to earn a little something or other. You're searching for filthy-rich fools just as much as I am. I suggested that you run for office, and you did so because you were greedy for a hundred thousand rupees. If your stars had been right, you'd now be in possession of a hundred thousand rupees. In addition, without having spent a pice, you'd also be allied with the Kunwar Sahib and have that suit filed in court. It's just your bad luck that the plot has fizzled out. When you yourself have been stranded high and dry, what would I get out of it? Finally I got a bright idea and caught hold of the Raja's tail. I had to get across the river of hell somehow or other.'

The Rai Sahib was so furious he could have shot this villain. The scoundrel had lured him into the race with a tempting bait and now was trying to clear himself by wriggling around so that none of the blame could attach itself to him. Given the situation, however, there was not much he could say.

'Then there's nothing you can do now?'

'You might as well look at it that way.'

'I'm prepared to settle for even fifty thousand.'

'The Raja Sahib would never agree.'

'He'd agree to twenty-five thousand, wouldn't he?'

'There's no hope of it. He's stated his position clearly.'

'He stated it or you're stating it?'

'You think I'm a liar?'

'I don't think you're a liar,' the Rai Sahib said politely, 'but this much I certainly do believe—that the matter could be worked out if you wanted it to.'

'Then you think I've prevented a settlement?'

'No, that's not what I was implying. All I'm trying to say is that, if you'd wanted, things would have worked out so that I wouldn't have landed in this mess.'

Mr Tankha glanced at his watch. 'Very well, Rai Sahib, if you want me to be perfectly frank, then listen. If you had put a ten thousand rupee check in my hand, you would undoubtedly have that hundred thousand today. You probably hoped to get the money from the Raja Sahib and then pass a thousand or two on to me. Well I'm not as new at the game as all that. Tell me, if you'd taken the money from him, locked it in your safe and left me in the lurch, what could I have done about it? It's not as though I could have gone to court or something.'

The Rai Sahib looked hurt. 'You think me as dishonest as all that?'

'Who says it's dishonesty?' Tankha declared, rising from his chair. 'Nowadays that's just cleverness. The best policy these days is to find ways of making asses out of people. And you're a past master at that.'

The Rai Sahib clenched his fist. 'I?'

'Yes, you. In the first election, I campaigned for you tooth and nail. After much moaning and groaning, you finally gave me five hundred rupees. In the second election you let yourself off the hook by giving me an old broken-down car. Once scalded by milk, a man blows even on buttermilk.'

The Rai Sahib was boiling. There was surely some limit to discourtesy! First he'd been kept waiting for a full hour and now he was being ejected from the house. If he'd thought it possible to knock Tankha flat, he wouldn't have hesitated, but Tankha was a quarter again as big as he was. Hearing the horn on Tankha's car, the Rai Sahib jumped into his own car and drove straight to Mr Khanna's place.

It was almost nine, but Khanna was still enjoying sweet slumber. Since he never went to bed before two in the morning, sleeping until nine was perfectly natural. Here too the Rai Sahib was forced to

285

wait, so when Mr Khanna emerged smiling at nine-thirty, the Rai Sahib snapped—'Well! So his lordship has awakened, at half-past nine. You must have a lot of money hoarded up in order to be so carefree. If you were just a zamindar like me, you'd be waiting at someone's door too. All this sitting around makes my head spin.'

Mr Khanna offered a cigarette from his case and said with a smile, 'I got to bed very late last night. Where are you coming from?'

The Rai Sahib briefly described all his troubles. On the surface, he was playing up to Khanna, but inwardly he was cursing this man who, though once a classmate, was always figuring out ways to rob him.

Khanna assumed an air of great concern. 'My advice is that you write off this election and file that suit for your brother-in-law's estate. As for the marriage, that's just a matter of a three-day celebration. There's no need to bankrupt yourself over it. The Kunwar Sahib is a friend of mine—so there'll be no question of your going into debt.'

'You forget, Mr Khanna,' the Rai Sahib said sarcastically, 'that I'm a zamindar, not a banker. God's given you everything. As for me, though, even if the Kunwar Sahib doesn't ask for a dowry, this is my only daughter, you know, and her mother is dead. Were she alive today, she'd probably mortgage house and home and still not be satisfied. In such circumstances I might have held her back and given advice on the spending. As it is, though, I'm now the girl's mother as well as her father. Even if I have to bleed myself dry, I'll do it gladly. In this sad widower's life, only love and devotion to the children satisfies the hunger of my soul. My marriage vows have been maintained only through my love for the two children. It's impossible for me not to be as lavish as my heart desires on this blessed occasion. I can certainly argue with myself, but I can't argue with what I feel to be my wife's wishes. And to run out on the election contest is also impossible for me. I know I'll lose. I'm no match for the Raja Sahib. But at least I want to show him that Amarpal Singh is no man of straw.'

'And the court case is absolutely essential too, of course?'

'That's what everything else depends on. Now tell me, what help can you give me?'

'You realize, of course, the orders of my directors in the matter. And the Raja Sahib is one of our directors too, as you know. They keep urging us to get all the outstanding debts paid up. There's little possibility of any new loans.'

The Rai Sahib pulled a long face. 'You're sinking my boat, Mr Khanna.'

'Whatever I possess personally is yours, but on bank matters I'm forced to obey the instructions of my superiors.'

'If that estate comes to me, and I'm completely confident that it will, I'll pay back every pice.'

'Can you tell me how deeply in debt you are at the moment?'

The Rai Sahib hesitated. 'Figure about five or six hundred thousand. Probably a little less.'

'Either you don't remember,' Khanna said sceptically, 'or you're trying to conceal the truth.'

'No,' the Rai Sahib insisted, 'I've not forgotten and I'm not concealing anything. My property at present is worth at least five million, and that of my in-laws is no smaller. Against an estate like that, carrying a million or so is next to nothing.'

'But how do you know there aren't debts against your in-laws' property too?'

'As far as I know, that estate is in the clear.'

'And I've been notified that it's carrying a debt of at least a million. Nothing more can be had against that estate, and I think your estate owes at least a million too. Moreover it's worth not five million, but barely two and a half. Under these circumstances, no bank can make you a loan. You should realize that you're standing on the mouth of a volcano. The slightest tremor and you could be swallowed right up. You should proceed with the utmost caution at this point.'

'I'm perfectly aware of all that, my dear friend,' the Rai Sahib said, gripping Khanna by the arm, 'but the tragedy of life is just this— that the thing you don't want to do is the very thing you're forced to do. What you must do for me now is arrange for me to borrow two hundred thousand at least.'

Khanna let out a deep sigh. 'My God! Two hundred thousand? Impossible, absolutely impossible.'

'I'll bash my head against your door and kill myself, Khanna, and you'd better believe it. I've made all these plans counting on your support. If you disappoint me, I guess I'll have to poison myself. I can't kneel in front of Surya Pratap Singh. The girl's marriage can be postponed two or three months longer, and there's plenty of time to file that suit, but the election is on my head right now. That's my biggest worry.'

'Then you're going to put two hundred thousand towards the election?' Khanna asked in amazement.

'It's not a question of the election, brother. It's a question of reputation and prestige. Do you think my reputation isn't worth even two hundred thousand? I don't care if my entire estate has to be sold, but I won't let Surya Pratap Singh win an easy victory over me.'

Khanna puffed on his cigarette for a minute and then said, 'I've already outlined the bank's position to you. In a way, the bank has stopped giving loans. I'll try to work out a special concession in your case, but business is business—you know that. What would my commission be? I'll have to make special recommendations on your behalf, and you know how much influence the Raja Sahib holds over the other directors. I'll have to organize an opposition. As you can see, I'll have to accept full responsibility for the affair.'

The Rai Sahib's face dropped. Khanna was one of his most intimate friends. They'd been in school together and had stuck together later. Yet now he was being so heartless as to expect a commission. If all his flattery of Khanna meant nothing now, then it never would. When fruit appeared in the garden, or vegetables came up, he sent a basket over to Khanna first of all. When there was some festival or some function, he first of all sent an invitation to Khanna. Was this to be his reward? 'Whatever you wish,' he said dejectedly, 'but I had thought of you as a brother.'

'That's very kind of you,' Khanna said gratefully. 'I've always thought of you as my older brother too, and I still do. I've never kept anything from you, but business is something else again. Here no one is a friend or a brother to anyone else. Just as I can't ask you to pay more commission than others do because you're a brother, so you shouldn't urge me to make concessions in my commission. I assure you, I'll make whatever concessions I can. Come over tomorrow during office hours and we'll draw up the papers. So much for business. Have you heard the other news? Mehta is completely taken with Malti these days. All his philosophy has disappeared. He calls on her at least once or twice a day, and they often go out together in the evening for walks. At least I had the dignity never to go fawning at her door. She seems to be making up for that omission of mine now. There was a time when all that counted was Mr Khanna. If there was anything to be done, she came running to me. When she needed money, she'd send a note to me. Yet now she sees me and turns her face away. I ordered a watch from France just for her and took it to

288

her eagerly, but she wouldn't accept it. Just yesterday I sent over a basket of fruit ordered from Kashmir, and she returned it. I'm amazed at how much a person can change in so short a time.'

At heart, the Rai Sahib was pleased at Khanna's rebuff, but he expressed only sympathy. 'Even granted that she's in love with Mehta, there's still no reason for her to break off relations with you.'

'That's what hurts, brother,' Khanna whimpered. 'I knew from the start that she was out of my reach. I'm telling you the truth—I never deluded myself that Malti loved me. I never had the slightest hope of getting anything like love from her. I only worshipped her beauty. Even though we know a snake is poisonous, we still feed it milk. There's nothing more unfeeling than a parrot, but people make a pet of it and keep it in a golden cage just because they're enchanted by its beauty and its voice. To me, Malti was like one of those parrots. I'm only sorry I didn't come to my senses earlier. I've wasted thousands of rupees on her. When her message would arrive, I'd send over money right away. She's using my car this very day. I've destroyed my home because of her. Everything in my heart poured out in such a rush on that barren soil that the garden on the other side was left to dry up. It's been years since I even talked freely with Govindi. I had become as indifferent to her service and love and sacrifice as a man suffering from indigestion is to sweets. Malti had me dancing like a trained monkey and I was happy to dance. She'd insult me and I'd laugh with delight. She would lay down the law and I'd bow my head submissively. True, she never gave me any encouragement, but I was nevertheless like a moth sacrificing myself at the flame of her beauty. And now she doesn't even show me common courtesy. But brother, I give you my word that Khanna is not a man to sit back and say nothing. Her notes are all carefully preserved in my possession. I'll get back every single pice from her, and I won't rest until I've driven Mehta out of Lucknow. I'll make it impossible for him to stay here.'

Just then a horn sounded, and a moment later Mr Mehta walked in. With his fair complexion, the glow of health on his cheeks, a long achkan over his tight pajamas, and his gold-rimmed glasses, he was the very image of gentility.

Khanna stood up and offered his hand. 'Come in, Mr Mehta. We were just talking about you.'

Mehta shook hands with both men. 'I must have left home at a very auspicious moment, finding both you gentlemen at the same place. You've no doubt read in the papers that a gymnasium for women is being planned here. The cost has been estimated at about two hundred thousand rupees. You know better than I do how necessary it is. I'd like your names to be at the very head of the list. Miss Malti was coming to see you herself, but her father's not well today so she couldn't make it.'

He handed the list of donors to the Rai Sahib. The first name was Raja Surya Pratap Singh, and in front of it was written the sum of five thousand rupees. Next came Kunwar Digvijay Singh with three thousand rupees. Following that were several other contributions of an equal amount or slightly less. Malti had given five hundred rupees and Dr Mehta a thousand.

'You've snagged a good forty thousand,' the Rai Sahib murmured weakly.

'All thanks to the kindness of you people,' Mehta said with pride, 'and this is the result of just three hours' work. Raja Surya Pratap Singh has seldom taken part in any community projects, but today he wrote out a cheque without a word. There's a new awakening in the country. People are willing to assist any good cause. All they need is assurance that their contributions will be used wisely. I have great expectations of you, Mr Khanna.'

'I steer clear of these worthless projects,' Khanna said coolly. 'No telling how far you people are willing to go in this slavish attachment to the West. Women are already losing interest in their homes. If they get caught up in a craze for athletics, they'll be ruined for good. A woman who does her housework needs no other exercise, and I feel it's wrong to contribute so as to provide exercise for women who don't do any housework and care only for a life of sensual indulgence.'

Mehta was not discouraged in the least. 'In that case I won't ask you for anything. When you don't believe in something, it would certainly be wrong to give any assistance to it. But Rai Sahib— you're not going to take the same stand as Mr Khanna, are you?'

The Rai Sahib was lost in grave concern. Surya Pratap's five thousand rupees had thrown him into a depression. He looked up with a start. 'You asked me something?'

'I was saying that surely you don't consider it wrong to assist in this venture.'

'I don't concern myself about the rights and wrongs of anything that has your backing.'

'I'd like you to reflect on this yourself. If you feel the project will benefit society, then please help support it. I was very pleased with Mr Khanna's adherence to his principles.'

'I'm very frank,' Khanna said, 'and I've become notorious as a result.'

The Rai Sahib smiled weakly. 'I just don't have the ability to evaluate these things. I consider it my duty merely to follow the lead of other good people.'

'Then please write down some good amount.'

'I'll put whatever you say.'

'It's up to you.'

'No, I'll write whatever you tell me to.'

'Well then, you'd want to make it two thousand anyway.'

The Rai Sahib looked offended. 'Is that all you think I'm worth?' Picking up the pen, he signed his name and then wrote in front of it—five thousand rupees.

Mehta took back the list, so ashamed that he even forgot to thank the Rai Sahib. His conscience was troubling him for having been so unkind as to show the list of donors to the Rai Sahib.

Khanna eyed the Rai Sahib with pity and contempt, as though telling him what an ass he was.

Suddenly Mehta threw his arms around the Rai Sahib and shouted —'Three cheers for you—hip, hip, hooray!'

Khanna snickered uncomfortably. 'These people are the kings around here. If they don't contribute, who would?'

'I consider you a king of kings,' Mehta responded. 'You rule over them. Their property rests mostly in your hands.'

The Rai Sahib looked pleased. 'You really hit it on the nose that time, Mr Mehta. We're rulers in name, but our bankers are the real rajas.'

Mehta switched over to flattering Khanna—'I have no complaint against you, Khannaji. At present you don't care to support this effort. That's all right—you'll come around some time or other. It's only thanks to you people who control the wealth that our great institutions keep going. And who has been sponsoring the independence movement so magnificently the last two or three years? Who's putting up all the pilgrim lodges and schools? Bankers have the ruling hand in the world today. Governments are just puppets in their hands. I'm not disappointed in you. Spending three or four thousand is no big thing for a man who's willing to go to jail for his country. We've decided to have the foundation stone of the building laid by Govindi Devi. We'll be meeting with the Governor very soon, and I'm sure we'll receive his support. You know how devoted Lady Wilson is to the cause of women. The Raja Sahib and some other gentlemen proposed that Lady Wilson lay the cornerstone, but it was finally decided that the auspicious task should be entrusted to one of our own sisters. You'll at least attend that function certainly?'

'Yes, indeed,' Khanna said sarcastically. 'When Lord Wilson is coming, it's terribly important that I be there. You'll rope in a lot of rich people that way. You folks know all the tricks, and our rich people are deserving targets. Make fools out of them and then you can skin them nicely.'

'When an excess of wealth accumulates, it seeks an outlet. Lacking a better channel, it flows into gambling, into horse-racing, into brick and stone or into debauchery.'

It was eleven o'clock, time for Khanna to go to the office. Mehta left, and the Rai Sahib also got up to go. 'No, please wait a minute,' Khanna said, taking his arm and seating him again. 'You realize that Mehta has me so badly trapped that there's no way out. Govindi is to lay the foundation stone. Under those circumstances I'd look ridiculous not to attend, wouldn't I? What made Govindi agree to it is beyond my comprehension. And what made Malti tolerate it is even harder to understand. What do you think? Isn't there some mystery behind all this?'

'In such matters a wife should always ask the advice of her husband,' the Rai Sahib declared earnestly.

Khanna gave him a grateful look. 'It's times like these when Govindi really burns me up, and then I'm the one people blame. Tell me, what have I to do with these quarrels? The ones who should get involved are those with spare cash, spare time, and a thirst for publicity. All it means is that they'll name a few celebrities as secretary and under-secretary, president and vice-president; then they'll ingratiate themselves with the officials by holding dinners for them; and they they'll call in some wenches from the university and have a little fun. Exercise is just a front. It's always that way in these organizations and it always will be, while the ones who get rooked are you and I and our friends—those who are said to be wealthy. And all this because of Govindi.'

He rose from his chair and then sat down again, growing more and more angry at his wife. Putting his hands to his head, he declared, 'I don't know what I should do.'

'Don't do anything,' the Rai Sahib humoured him. 'Just tell Govindi plainly to write Mehta a note declining the offer. That's all there is to it. I got trapped by the competition involved, but there's no need for you to get hooked.'

Khanna considered the suggestion for a moment. 'Consider how complicated the matter is, though. Lady Wilson must have been notified already. The news has spread all over town and it'll probably come out in today's paper. This is all Malti's deviltry. She's come up with this as a way of checkmating me.'

'Yes, it does look that way.'

'She wants to humiliate me.'

'You might go out of town the day before the foundation stone is laid.'

'It's not that simple, Rai Sahib. I'd be ashamed to show my face again. Even if I'm suffering from cholera, I'll have to attend.'

The Rai Sahib, saying he'd try to drop in the next day, had no sooner left than Khanna went inside and turned on Govindi. 'Why did you agree to lay the foundation stone of that gymnasium?'

How could Govindi explain the pleasure she had felt at receiving the honour, the careful thought with which she was writing her speech for the occasion, and the brilliance of the poem she had composed? She had thought that accepting the invitation would please Khanna. Any honour awarded her was really an honour to her husband. The thought had never even crossed her mind that it might offend him in any way, and her spirits had risen as she noticed him mellowing somewhat in the last few days. She had been dreaming of captivating people with her speech and her poetry.

Now, hearing his question and seeing the expression on his face, her heart began pounding. 'Dr Mehta insisted,' she said guiltily, 'so I agreed.'

'If Dr Mehta told you to jump in a well, you probably wouldn't have been quite so willing.'

Govindi was silent.

'Since God didn't give you any intelligence, why didn't you ask me? Those two, Mehta and Malti, hatched this plot figuring they could squeeze three or four thousand out of me. Well I'm determined not to give them a single cowrie. Write a note refusing the invitation this very day.'

Govindi thought for a moment. 'Why don't you write it?'

'Why should I write it? You started the matter; now I'm supposed to write!'

'If Doctor Sahib asks the reason, what'll I say?'

'Say any damn thing. I don't intend to give one copper to that den of iniquity.'

'Well nobody says you have to give.'

Khanna bit his lip. 'What kind of stupid talk is that? What will everyone say if you lay the foundation stone and don't contribute anything?'

As though at bayonet-point, Govindi said, 'Very well, I'll write it.'

'It must be written today.'

'I've told you I'll write.'

Khanna went out and began looking through the mail, which the peon brought to the house whenever he was late going to the office. Sugar was up. Khanna's face lit up. He opened the second letter. The committee appointed to set the rate for sugar cane had decided that no such controls were possible. Well hell, that's exactly what he had been saying earlier, but that Agnihotri had made a big fuss and forced a committee to be formed. Well, that fellow had finally been slapped in the face. This was a matter between the mill owners and the cultivators. Why should the government meddle in it?

Just then a car drove up and Miss Malti got out. Blooming like a lotus and shining like a light, she was the image of gaiety and enthusiasm, as dauntless and carefree as though she believed all the world's doors were flung open for her pleasure and honour. Khanna came out on the veranda and greeted her.

'Has Mehta been here?' she asked.

'Yes, he was here.'

'Did he say anything about where he was going?'

'He said nothing about that.'

'Where in the world has he disappeared? I've been hunting for him everywhere. How much did you give for the gymnasium?'

'I couldn't even understand the matter,' Khanna said guiltily.

Malti looked at him wide-eyed, as though debating whether to show pity or indignation. 'What's there to understand? You could understand it later—the present question is one of giving. I pushed Mehta into coming here. Poor fellow was afraid of how you might respond. Do you realize what the effect of your miserliness will be? We'll get nothing from the business community here. Evidently you've decided to humiliate me. Everyone felt that Lady Wilson should lay the foundation stone. I nominated Govindi and fought for her until they all agreed, and now you proclaim that you still have to understand the matter. You understand all the intricacies of banking, but you can't figure out something as obvious as this. The only possible explanation is that you want to embarrass me. Isn't that right?'

Malti's face was flushed. Khanna was worried, and his arrogance was crumbling away; but he also realized that, though he might be in a sticky situation, Malti was caught in a real quagmire. His pocketbook might be in danger, but Malti had something more valuable than a pocketbook at stake—her reputation. So he might as well enjoy her predicament. He had put her on the spot, and though he'd lost the courage to make her angry, he didn't want to miss this chance to speak his mind a little, and he also wanted to show that he was not a complete fool. Blocking her exit, he said, 'I'm surprised that you're being so good to me, Malti.'

Malti raised her eyebrows. 'I don't understand what you mean.'

'Is this the way you were behaving toward me before?'

'I don't see that there's any difference.'

'Well I see a world of difference.'

'All right, suppose your guess is correct. So what? I've come to ask your assistance in a worthy cause, not to be cross-examined about my actions. And if you think that giving a donation is going to get you anything other than gratitude and recognition, you're sadly mistaken.'

Khanna was vanquished. He'd been squeezed into such a tight corner that there was no longer any room to move. How could he dare to complain about being thus rewarded for the thousands of rupees he'd showered on her in the past? He seemed to be withering away in embarrassment. 'That wasn't what I meant, Malti,' he said, blushing. 'You completely misunderstood me.'

'I hope that I misunderstood you,' she said contemptuously, 'because otherwise I'd run even from your shadow. I'm an attractive woman, and you're one of my many admirers. I showed you my favour in that, whereas I turned away gifts from other people, I accepted even the most trivial things from you with gratitude. And in times of need I even asked you for loans. If, in your obsession over money, you took it to mean something else, I'll forgive you. That's only human nature. But understand this—money has never yet won a woman's heart and it never will.'

With each word, Khanna felt as though he were sinking a yard lower. He no longer had the strength to endure any more blows. 'Don't humiliate me any further, Malti, I beg of you. And let's at least continue to be friends.'

He took the cheque-book from the drawer, wrote down the sum of one thousand rupees, and held it out timidly to Malti.

Malti took the check and sneered, 'Is this the price of my behaviour or a contribution for the gymnasium?'

'Spare me now, Malti. Why are you blackening my face?'

Malti burst out laughing. 'Look, I've reprimanded you and collected a thousand rupees in the bargain. Now, will you ever behave so badly again?'

'Never. Not so long as I live.'

'Swear it.'

'I swear it. But now take pity and leave me to myself, to think and to cry. You've taken away all my pleasure in life today and . . .'

Malti laughed still louder. 'Look, Khanna, you're insulting me, and you know beauty can't stand insults. I've done you a favour and you take it as an injury.'

Khanna glared at her. 'Have you done me a favour or have you cut my throat with the blunt edge of a knife?'

'What do you mean? I've been robbing you and making myself rich. Now you're spared that plundering.'

'Why are you rubbing salt in the wound, Malti? I'm also human.'

Malti looked at him as though trying to decide whether he was human or not. 'So far I don't see any signs of it.'

'One thing has been proved today—that you're a complete enigma.'

'Yes, I'm an enigma as far as you're concerned, and I always will be.'

With that she flew off like a bird. Khanna put his head in his hands and tried to decide whether this had all been a game or whether she had been showing her true colours.

CHAPTER 23

WITH Gobar and Jhuniya gone, the house seemed desolate. Dhaniya kept remembering Chunnu. Jhuniya was the child's mother, of course, but Dhaniya had really taken care of him. It was she who gave him oil rub-downs, applied kohl to his eyes, lulled him to sleep, and, whenever she found time from her work, fondled him. The intoxication of this motherly affection had kept her mind off her troubles. Seeing his innocent, butter-soft face, she would forget all her worries and her heart would swell with loving pride. That prop was now gone from her life. Stripped of the armour which had protected her from anxiety, she would burst into tears at the sight of his empty cradle. Over and over she asked herself what wrong she had done to Jhuniya to deserve this punishment. The witch had come and smashed her mansion of gold into the dust, while Gobar never even answered back to the woman. That wretched widow had won him over and taken him away. No telling what tune she'd have him dancing to there. Even here she'd not paid much attention to the child. Decorating her own teeth and eyes, and fixing her hair left her no time. How could she take care of the child now? Poor thing was probably lying neglected and crying on the floor. That pitiful child couldn't spend a single day in real happiness and comfort. Either there'd be a cough or diarrhoea or something else. Thinking of it, she became angry at Jhuniya. She still felt the same affection for Gobar, but that hellion had given him some potion and caught him in her power. How could she have cast such a spell unless she were a sorceress? No one had cared about her. She'd been kicked around by her sisters-in-law. Having got hold of this dolt, however, she now acted like a queen.

Hori became irritated. 'Every time I turn around, you're putting all the blame on Jhuniya. Don't you realize the goldsmith is not to blame if the gold you give him is counterfeit? If Gobar hadn't taken her away, would she have gone on her own? Coming in contact with the city has changed the boy's outlook. Why don't you realize that?'

K*

'All right, shut up,' Dhaniya roared. 'It was you who gave that bitch such a swelled head. Otherwise I'd have chased her away with a broom that very first day.'

The harvest had been gathered and Hori was setting out with the bullocks to thresh the grain. Looking back, he said, 'And even if the girl did lure Gobar away, why are you so worked up? He's only doing what the whole world does. He has his own family now. Why should he bring misery on himself for our sake? Why should he take our burdens on his head? '

'You're at the root of this mess.'

'Then throw me out too. Here, take the bullocks and go thresh the grain. I'm going to have a smoke.'

'If you'll come turn the grindstone, I'll thresh the grain.'

The unpleasantness vanished in the face of the sovereign remedy —humour. Dhaniya, smiling, sat down to untangle and braid Rupa's snarled hair, while Hori headed for the barn.

Spring was flinging out fragrance and joy and the glory of life with open hands and heart. The sweet, soul-stirring song of the koel hidden in the branches of mango trees was awakening hopes and longings. Flocks of mynahs had gathered like marriage parties among the blossoms on the mahua trees. The fragrance of the neem, acacia and karaunda trees seemed strangely intoxicating. When Hori walked into the mango grove, where star-like blossoms were scattered beneath the trees, even his troubled and despairing heart was inspired by the pervasive splendour, and he began to sing—

'My heart, night and day, keeps burning with desire.

The koel sings on the mango branch.

I get no rest at all.'

Dulari the shopkeeper was coming towards him, dressed in a pink sari, with heavy silver anklets on her feet and a heavy gold ornament around her neck. Her face had dried up with age, but her heart was still young and luxuriant. There was a time when Hori would tease her in the fields or the barn. By village custom she was his sister-in-law, so they could joke with each other. After her husband died, though, Dulari stopped going out so freely. All day she sat in the shop, keeping track from there of all that was happening in the village. If a quarrel broke out anywhere, she'd always show up to mediate. She never loaned money at less than one anna interest per rupee. And her rate of interest remained just the same, even though her greed for interest sometimes made her lose even the principal—

on people who would take the money, gobble it up, and then just sit back. How could the poor woman force payment? Unable to resort to the courts and unable to go to the police, she was left with only the power of her tongue, and though the tongue had grown sharper over the years, its cutting power kept diminishing. People now laughed at her abuses, saying 'What do you want money for now, auntie? You can't take even a pice with you. You'd better get all the merit you can by feeding the poor. That's all that counts in the next world.' And Dulari would get furious at the mention of the next world.

'You really look young today, sister,' Hori teased.

Dulari was pleased. 'Today is Tuesday. Don't put the evil eye on me. That's why I don't get dressed up at all. Whenever I leave the house, people start staring as though they've never seen a woman before. That Pateshwari, for example, still hasn't dropped his old habits.'

Hori slowed to a halt at the mention of this delightful topic. The bullocks went on ahead.

'He's turned very religious lately, though. Haven't you seen the way he listens to the sacred recitations every full moon and visits the temple both morning and evening?'

'All those rakes become religious when they get old. They have to atone for their wicked deeds after all. But I'm an old woman now, you know. Why should they tease me?'

'What do you mean you're an old woman, *bhaabi*? To me you're still. . . .'

'All right, hold your tongue or I'll let loose a hundred and fifty curses on you. Your boy has begun earning a living in the city and you've not even once invited me over for a feast. You're prepared to call me a sister-in-law as long as it doesn't cost anything.'

'I swear to you, bhaabi, I've not touched even a pice of his earnings. I haven't the slightest idea how much he brought or where it was spent. All I got from him were a couple of dhoties and a turban.'

'Well anyway, he's started earning, and sooner or later he'll straighten out the family affairs. God grant him happiness. Meanwhile you ought to start paying back my money little by little. The interest just keeps growing, you know.'

'I'll pay you every last pice. Only let me get hold of some money. And even if it's all just swallowed up, it's not as though I'm some stranger. I'm your own kin.'

Such lighthearted flattery always disarmed Dulari. She smiled and went on her way. Hori hurried to catch up with the bullocks. Leading them to the threshing-floor, he started driving them in a circle, trampling out the grain.

The whole village used this one barnyard. Some people were separating corn, others were winnowing grain, and still others were weighing up their crops. The barbers, leaf-plate makers, carpenters, blacksmiths, priests, bards and beggars were all gathered there to receive their customary share. On a cot in the shade sat Jhinguri Singh, collecting with interest on his seed-grain loans. Several merchants stood around haggling over the crop prices. The whole area was as lively as a wholesale marketplace. A woman was hawking sour plums and a vendor roamed about with his basket of sweets fried in oil. Pandit Datadin had showed up also, to get his share of Hori's grain, and he sat on the cot next to Jhinguri Singh.

Shaping a pellet of tobacco in the palm of his hand, he said, 'Have you heard? The government is telling the moneylenders to cut their rate of interest or their claims won't be accepted in court.'

Jhinguri tossed some tobacco into his mouth and replied, 'I know only one thing, pandit. When people are in need, they'll come to me a hundred times for a loan, and I'll charge any interest I please. As long as the government doesn't work out some system of providing loans to the farmers, the law won't have any effect on us. We'll write down a lower interest rate, but from every hundred rupees we'll deduct twenty-five in advance. What can the government do about that?'

'That's all very well, but the government is very wise to that sort of thing too. You wait and see—they'll find some way to prevent it also.'

'But there is no way to prevent it.'

'Well, what if they stipulate that a document is invalid unless it's signed by the village elders or the zamindar's agent? What would you do then?'

'If a farmer is badly in need, he'll go on bended knee and get the elders to sign. In any case we'd deduct twenty-five per cent.'

'And if you got caught? You'd get put away for fourteen years for keeping false accounts.'

Jinguri Singh laughed boisterously. 'What are you talking about, pandit? You expect the world to be changed suddenly? Law and justice belong to those who have money. It's already the law that a moneylender can't be too severe with a debtor and that no zamindar can use violence against a tenant. But what actually happens? You see it every day—the zamindar has them beaten with their hands tied behind their backs, and the moneylender does his talking with kicks and shoes. Neither the zamindar nor the moneylender does anything to the farmer who's well-to-do, though. We join with those people and get their help in crushing the necks of the others. You yourself owe the Rai Sahib five hundred rupees, but would Nokheram have the nerve to make a fuss about repayment? He knows that his own well-being depends on staying in good with you. What peasant has the wherewithal to be running to the courts every day? The whole business will go on operating exactly as it does now. The courts are on the side of those who have money. We people have nothing to worry about.'

With that he got up and made a round of the barnyard. Then, seating himself again on the cot, he said, 'By the way, what about Matai's marriage? I'd advise you to get that taken care of right away. He's getting a terrible reputation.

Datadin winced as though a wasp had just stung him. He knew all too well what this criticism referred to. 'There's nothing I can do about people talking behind our backs,' he said heatedly, 'but if anyone says anything to my face, I'll yank out his whiskers. Name one person who follows all the sacred rules the way we do. So many of the people I know never say their daily prayers, care nothing about either faith or practice, and ignore both the sacred recitations and the holy texts. Yet they call themselves brahmans. How dare they jeer at us, who've never missed even a single monthly fast and who never take even a drop of water until we've done our morning prayers and ablutions. Following all the rituals is difficult. If anyone can say that we've ever eaten anything in the bazaar or taken water offered by a non-brahman, I'll become his devoted slave. Siliya has never once crossed the threshold of our house, not to speak of touching the pots and pans. I'm not saying that Matai is behaving properly, but once a thing has happened, it would be wicked to just leave the woman. I say it right out in the open—there's nothing to hide. Women are sacred.'

Datadin had been quite a profligate in his own youth, but he'd never neglected his religious rites and duties. Matadin, like a worthy son, was following in his father's footsteps. The crucial elements of religion were ritual worship, fasts and scripture lessons, and the observance of taboos about cooking and eating. When both father and son held tight to these crucial elements, how could anyone have the gall to call them wayward?

Jhinguri Singh was convinced. 'I was only passing on to you what I'd heard.'

Datadin reeled off a long list of instances from the *Mahabharata* and the *Puranas* in which brahmans had taken women of other castes. He then explained that their offspring had been considered brahmans, and claimed that the brahmans of today were the offspring of their offspring. This practice had been going on since time immemorial, and it was nothing to be ashamed of.

Jhinguri Singh was impressed by Datadin's learning but went on to ask, 'Then why do people today set so much store by their brahman subcaste distinctions, bragging about being Bajpeyis and Shuklas?'

'Customs vary with the times, that's all. It just depends on how much spiritual strength you have. If a man eats poison, he needs the strength to digest it. All those things took place in the golden age of truth, and they passed away along with that age. In this dark age you can only survive by sticking to your caste. But what am I supposed to do when no one even shows up with a suitable girl? I've asked you, and I've asked other people too, but no one pays any attention. So am I supposed to manufacture a girl?'

'Don't tell lies now, pandit,' Jhinguri protested. 'I've snared two prospects for you, but you began making exorbitant demands and they both got leery and fled. After all, what grounds do you have for asking five hundred to a thousand rupees? What do you have except some six acres of land and the charity you get from the village?'

His pride hurt, Datadin stroked his beard and said, 'I have nothing, that's true, and I just beg for charity. Nevertheless, I've spent five hundred for each of my daughter's marriages, so why shouldn't I demand five hundred for my son? If someone had married my daughters free of dowry, I'd marry the boy off gratis also. As for my status, maybe you think of the patronage system as begging, but I consider it as good as landowning or a bank. Property may be wiped out and banks may fail, but the patronage of priests will last forever. As long as there are Hindus there'll be brahmans and there'll be payments to them. During the marriage season we can easily rake in two or three hundred just sitting at home; and with a real lucky break, I've knocked off four or five hundred at times—and that's not counting the clothes and kitchenware and feasts. There's always something coming up at one home or another. Even when there's nothing going on, I still get offerings of a few annas and a meal or two a day. Neither property nor moneylending offers that kind of security. Besides, what brahman girl could be as providential as that Siliya of ours? A brahman would just play the bride and sit around all the time. At most she'd do the cooking, whereas Siliya here does the work of three people all by herself. And I give her what? Just her food, and maybe one sari a year.'

Datadin's own grain was being threshed under another tree. Four bullocks were walking in a circle, driven by Dhanna the chamar. Siliya was gathering the grain from under their feet and winnowing it, while Matadin sat on the sidelines rubbing a staff with oil.

Siliya was a dark, provocative, lively young thing, attractive though perhaps not beautiful. There was joyful abandon in her laugh, in her glances and in her sensuous limbs, as though every part of her were dancing. Covered head to foot with bits of straw, drenched with perspiration, hair half undone, she ran around doing the winnowing as though it were some absorbing game.

'Siliya,' Maradin called out, 'that job ought to be finished up by evening. Are you tired? Shall I take over?'

'Why should you take over, pandit?' she smiled. 'I'll have it all done by evening.'

'All right, then I'll start carrying in the grain. You can't handle everything alone.'

'What are you worrying about? I'll do the winnowing and carry it in too. By dark there won't be a single grain left here.'

Dulari was going around collecting on her debts. During the Holi festival, Siliya had taken two pice worth of rose colouring from the store and had not paid for it yet. Coming over, she said, 'Look here, Siliya, it's been a whole month since you took that colour and you still haven't paid for it. When I ask, you just bat your eyes and walk away. Today I won't leave until I get the money.'

Matadin had slipped away quietly. Although he'd taken possession of Siliya, body and soul, he didn't want to give anything in return. As far as he was concerned, she was now nothing more than a machine to serve him, and he manipulated her devotion to him with great dexterity.

Siliya looked up and found Matadin gone. 'Don't shout,' she said. 'Here, take this—four pice worth of grain instead of two pice. What more do you want—my life? After all, I wasn't about to die on you!'

She took some two pounds of grain from the pile and poured it into the outstretched border of the woman's sari. Just then Matadin stormed out from behind the tree and caught hold of Dulari's sari. 'Put that grain right back. It's not here to be looted.' Eyes flashing, he turned to Siliya. 'Why did you hand over the grain? Who gave you permission? Who are you to be giving away my grain?'

Dulari poured the grain back on the pile while Siliya looked at Matadin in bewilderment, feeling as though the branch where she had been confidently sitting had snapped, hurling her helplessly into an abyss. With a frustrated look and with tears in her eyes, she said to Dulari, 'I'll pay you another day. Have mercy on me this time.'

Dulari's eyes filled with pity. Throwing Matadin a look of contempt, she walked away.

Going back to her winnowing, Siliya asked in an injured tone, 'Don't I have any right to the things you own?'

'No, you have no right,' Matadin retorted angrily. 'You work and you get fed. If you expect to eat and also to squander my possessions, you're sadly mistaken. If you're not satisfied here, go work somewhere else. There's no shortage of hired help. It's not as though we're expecting free labour. We give you food and clothes.'

Siliya gazed at Matadin with anguish and accusation, like a bird whose master has clipped her wings and then turned her out of the cage. Like that bird, however, her heart fluttered helplessly around. Lacking the strength to soar to the freedom of some lofty branch, she longed to get back in the cage, even if it meant dying from hunger or from thirst or from beating her head against the bars. Siliya could think of no other place to go. Though not actually married, she was a married woman now in her beliefs, her actions and her attitudes; and she had no other refuge, no other shelter, even if Matadin were to attack her or kill her. She recalled the days, not even two years ago, when this same Matadin would caress her feet; when he swore by his sacred threat that he would treat her as a wife as long as there was breath in his body; when, consumed with desire, he chased her like a madman through the fields and the groves and along the riverbank . . . and now this brutal treatment, humiliating her over a handful of grain.

She kept silent. A lump of salt seemed to have risen in her throat, and with a heavy heart and drooping hands she went back to work.

Just then her mother, father, both brothers and several other chamars appeared out of nowhere and surrounded Matadin. Siliya's mother snatched the basket of grain from her hands and threw it aside, shouting, 'You slut! If all you wanted was to be a common labourer, there was no need for you to leave the work at home and come here. If you're living with a brahman, then live like a brahman. If after shaming our whole community you're still just a chamar, then what big fat gain is that? Why don't you go find a cupful of water and drown yourself?'

Jhinguri Singh and Datadin came running over, but on seeing the menacing expression of the chamars, they adopted a conciliatory tone. 'What's the matter?' Jhinguri asked Siliya's father. 'What's all the trouble about?'

Siliya's father Harkhu was an old man of sixty, dark and thin, wrinkled as a dried pepper and just as biting. 'There's no trouble, thakur. Today we'll either make a chamar out of Matadin or shed his blood along with our own. Siliya is a woman, and she has to go live with some man or other. We have no objection to that, but whoever takes her must become one of us. You can't make brahmans out of us, but we can make chamars out of you. If you're willing to make us brahmans, our whole community is agreeable. As long as that's not possible, then become chamars. Eat with us, drink with us and live with us. If you're going to take away our honour, then give us your caste.'

Datadin raised his stick. 'Control your tongue, Harkhu. Your girl's over there. Take her anywhere you please. We haven't tied her down. She worked and she got paid. There's no shortage of labourers around here.'

Siliya's mother shook her finger at him. 'Bully for you, pandit! You're being terribly fair! I'd like to see you talk that way if your daughter had run off with a chamar. We're chamars, though, so of course we don't have any honour! We're not taking Siliya away alone. We're taking Matadin with her—the one who ruined her. You're so pious—you'll sleep with her, but you won't drink water from her hands. No one but this bitch would tolerate all that. I'd have poisoned such a man.'

'Didn't you hear what these people are saying?' Harkhu challenged the group with him. 'What are you standing there gaping for?'

At this, two of the chamars sprang forward and grabbed Matadin's hands while a third tore off his sacred thread. Before Datadin and Jhinguri Singh could wield their sticks, two chamars had stuffed a big piece of bone in Matadin's mouth. Matadin clenched his teeth but the abominable thing caught between his lips all the same. Overcome by nausea, he opened his mouth involuntarily—and the bone slipped inside.

All the men in the vicinity had gathered around by this time, but no one, surprisingly, came forward to prevent this sacrilege. They had all disliked Matadin's behaviour, the way he made eyes at all the young women, so they were inwardly pleased at his predicament. Outwardly, of course, they had to assert their superiority over the chamars.

'All right, Harkhu, that's enough now,' Hori insisted. 'If you know what's good for you, you'll clear out.'

'Don't forget you have daughters too, Hori,' Harkhu replied fearlessly. 'Once the good name of the village starts being ruined like this, no one's reputation will be spared.'

Having completed their speedy triumph over the enemy, the assailants thought it wise to disappear. Public opinion doesn't take long to change, and the only thing to do was to stay clear of it.

Matadin was vomiting. Datadin patted him gently on the back, saying, 'Just wait. I'll get each one of them sent to jail for five years. They'll go on hard labour and turn the grindstone for five years.'

'That doesn't worry us,' Harkhu retorted defiantly. 'None of us sit around the way you do anyway. We'll get our bellies half filled no matter where we work.'

The vomiting over, Matadin stretched out almost lifeless on the ground as though his back were broken, as though he only wanted a cupful of water in which to drown himself. The ritual propriety which had allowed him to flaunt his passion and his pride had been wiped out. That piece of bone had polluted not only his mouth but also his soul. His religion depended on absolute purity in eating and drinking; now that righteousness had been cut off at the root. Performing thousands of penances—eating cowdung and drinking Ganges water, giving alms or going on pilgrimages—could not restore his virtue. If it had been a private matter, it could have been hushed up, but he had been defiled in front of everyone. He could never again hold up his head. From now on he would be considered an untouchable even in his own home. Even his own loving mother would despise him. And to think that piety had vanished so completely from the world that all those people just stood there and watched the show. No one had even let cut a peep. The people who a moment ago fell at his feet in reverence would now turn away in contempt. He couldn't even enter a temple or touch anyone's cooking utensils—and all because of this cursed Siliya.

Siliya was still standing in the spot where she had been winnowing, her head bowed as though she were the one being humiliated. Suddenly her mother went over and hissed, 'Don't just stand there gawking. Go straight home or I'll hack you to pieces. What a blaze of glory you've brought to the family name! What more do you intend to do?'

Siliya just stood like a statue, anger welling up against her parents and her brothers. Why had they come meddling in her affairs? She was living the way she wanted. What business was it of theirs? They claimed she was being insulted, but how could any brahman be expected to eat her cooking or drink water from her hands? Only a short while ago she had been resenting Matadin's callous behaviour, but this offence by her own family and caste had changed that resentment to fierce loyalty.

'I'm not going anywhere,' she announced defiantly. 'Can't you even let me live my own life?'

'You won't leave?' the old woman demanded threateningly.

'No.'

'Get going right now.'

'I'm not going.'

The two brothers caught hold of her hands and began dragging her away. Siliya sat down on the ground, but her brothers still didn't let go and kept dragging her along. Her sari was torn and her body was scraped, but she refused to surrender.

'All right, let her go,' Harkhu called to the boys. 'We'll consider her dead. But if she ever appears at my door, I'll drink her blood.'

'If I ever show up at your place again you're welcome to drink my blood,' Siliya said recklessly.

In a fit of rage, the old woman started kicking Siliya, and if Harkhu had not intervened, she might have kept at it as long as there was life left in the girl.

When the old woman leaped forward again, Harkhu shoved her aside, saying, 'You're a regular murderess, Kalia! Do you want to kill her?'

Siliya clung to her father's feet. 'Kill me, father. All of you join in and kill me. Oh mother, how can you be so cruel? Is this why you raised me? Why didn't you strangle me as soon as I was born?

And you've polluted the pandit himself on my account. Just what have you gained by defiling him? Now he won't care for me either. I'm staying with him though, whether he cares or not. I won't leave him even if he starves me and kills me. How could I desert him after bringing all this trouble on him? I'd rather die than act like a common prostitute. I gave him my hand once; now I'm his forever.'

Kalia bit her lip angrily. 'Let the bitch go. She thinks he'll provide for her. Well if he doesn't beat her and drive her out this very day, I'll never show my face in public again.'

The brothers also relented and let go of Siliya. Everyone left. Moaning with pain, she slowly picked herself up, limped to the barn and sat down. Burying her face in the end of her sari, she began to weep.

Datadin took out his anger on her. 'Why didn't you go with them, Siliya? What more are you bent on doing? Aren't you even satisfied now that you've had me destroyed?'

Siliya raised her head resolutely, her eyes flashing despite the tears. 'Why should I go with them? Whoever chose me, I'll stick with him.'

'If you set foot in my house, I'll kick you right out,' the pandit threatened.

'I'll stay anywhere he puts me,' Siliya insisted defiantly, 'whether it's in a palace or with only a tree over my head.'

Matadin was still sitting there in a stupor. It was almost noon, and the sun's rays, filtered through the leaves overhead, were beating down on his face. Perspiration dripped from his brow, but he sat there mute and motionless. All at once, as though regaining consciousness, he asked, 'What do you advise me to do now father?'

Datadin placed his hand on the boy's head, trying to reassure him. 'What can I tell you as yet, son? Go have a bath and eat. Then we'll do whatever the pandits prescribe. One thing though—you'll have to give up Siliya.'

Matadin glared at Siliya, his eyes bloodshot with anger. 'I'll never look at her again. But will this penance leave me free of all guilt?'

'Once penance has been done, no guilt or sin remains.'

'Then go see the pandits right away.'

'I'll go this very day, son.'

'But what if the pandits say there's no way to atone for it?'

'That's up to them.'

'In that case, would you turn me out of the house?'

Overwhelmed with fatherly affection, Datadin said, 'How could that ever happen, son? I'd give up my wealth, my religion and my prestige, but I couldn't give you up.'

Matadin picked up his stick and started following his father home. Siliya got up too and limped after him.

Matadin turned and said harshly, 'Stop following me. I have no connection with you any more. Isn't your belly satisfied with all the suffering you've caused?'

Siliya seized his hand boldly and said, 'How can you have no connection with me? There are richer, more handsome, more respectable men than you in the village. Why don't I go live with them? After all, what brought on this tragedy today? However much you wish it, you can't get rid of the rope that's around your neck. Nor will I go off somewhere and leave you. I'll do common labour or I'll beg, but I won't leave you.'

She let go of his hand and went back to the barn to resume her winnowing. Hori was still threshing his grain there, and Dhaniya had come to call him for the noon meal. Hori led the bullocks out of the straw, tied them to a tree, and then said to Siliya, 'You better go get something to eat too, Siliya. Dhaniya will keep an eye on things here. Oh, the back of your sari is covered with blood. Don't let the injuries get infected. Your folks are really cruel.'

Siliya looked at him sadly. 'Who isn't cruel around here? I've not found anyone who's kind.'

'What did the pandit say?'

'He says he'll have nothing to do with me.'

'Well! So that's how he's talking!'

'He must figure he can save face this way, but how can something be hidden which the whole world knows? If my food is a burden, he needn't give me any. What's that to me? I work now anyway, and I can go on working. And if I have to beg you for a tiny place to sleep, I know you'd give it to me.'

Dhaniya felt sorry for her. 'There's no shortage of space, daughter. Come and stay at our place.'

'It's all very well inviting her,' Hori said nervously, 'but don't you realize what the pandit is like?'

Dhaniya was undismayed. 'If he gets mad, so what? Let him take it out on his food or something. We're not his underlings. He's taken her honour, forced her out of her community, and now he says he'll have nothing to do with her. Is he a man or a butcher? He got his just desserts today for those evil intentions. Why didn't he think of these things at the beginning? First, he just goes on having a good time; now he says she's not his concern.'

Hori felt that Dhaniya was making a mistake. Siliya's people had done wrong to defile Matadin that way. They could have taken Siliya away either by coaxing her or by beating her. She was their daughter, after all. There had been no reason for them to pollute Matadin.

'That's enough now,' Dhaniya retorted. 'How righteous you've suddenly become! Men are all alike. No one was upset when Matadin defiled her. Now the same thing's happened to him, so what's wrong with that? Doesn't Siliya's virtue count as virtue? He takes a chamar woman and then makes out that he's so pious! Harkhu did just the right thing. That's exactly the punishment hoodlums like him deserve. You come home with me, Siliya. What kind of hardhearted parents they must be, bloodying the poor girl's whole back. You go and send Sona. I'll bring Siliya along with me.'

Hori headed home. Siliya fell at Dhaniya's feet and started sobbing.

CHAPTER 24

SONA was going on seventeen, so it was imperative to get her married that year. Hori had been anxious about this for the last two years, but being emptyhanded, he'd been powerless. This year, however, she would have to be married off somehow, even if it meant taking another loan or mortgaging the land. Actually, if Hori could have had his way, the marriage would have taken place two years before. He had wanted to do it economically, but Dhaniya had said that no matter how they held back on expenses, it would still cost at least two hundred and fifty rupees. Jhuniya's arrival had lowered their family position in the caste community so that they couldn't get a groom from any good family without a dowry of one or two hundred. The summer crop the previous year had brought in nothing. They were equal partners with Pandit Datadin, but the pandit had presented the accounts for seed and hired labour in such a way that Hori was left with only a quarter of the produce. He'd had to pay the whole land rent also and then the sugar cane and hemp crops had been ruined—the hemp from too much rain and the cane by white ants.

This year, though, the summer crop was fine, and the sugar cane was doing well too. There was food enough for a wedding. Now if he could lay his hands on two hundred rupees as well, he could fulfil his duty to the girl. If Gobar would help out with a hundred, he could easily get hold of the other hundred. Jhinguri Singh and Mangaru had both softened a little, since their loans had some security now that Gobar was earning money in the city.

One day Hori suggested going to visit Gobar for two or three days. Dhaniya had not forgotten the boy's brutal words, though. She had no intention of taking even a pice from Gobar, no matter what the circumstances.

'Then tell me,' Hori sputtered, 'how are we to manage?'

Dhaniya shook her head. 'Just decide what you would have done if Gobar had never gone to the city, and then do that.'

Hori was nonplussed for a moment and then said, 'I'm asking you.'

Dhaniya evaded the issue. 'You men are responsible for figuring out these things.'

Hori had his answer ready. 'Just decide what you would do if I weren't around and you were living all alone—and then do that.'

Dhaniya threw him a withering look. 'In that case I could give her away without any dowry and no one would make fun of me.'

Hori could have done that too, and it would have been a blessing, but how could he give up the family prestige that way? At each of his sisters' weddings, they'd entertained three hundred men in the groom's party, and a good dowry was given besides. Dancers, bands, horses and elephants—the celebrations had included everything. People were still talking about them. His prestige could also be seen in his good contacts with ten villages. How could he show his face if he gave his daughter with only sacred grass for a dowry? It would be better to die. And why should he pass her off that way? He had his trees, his land, and even a little credit. By selling even half an acre, he could get a hundred rupees. To a peasant, though, land is dearer than life, dearer even than family prestige; and that would be a third of all the land he owned. If he were to sell off that much, how could he live off the land?

This vacillation went on for days. Hori just couldn't make a decision. The Dashahra holidays arrived and the sons of Jhinguri, Pateshwari and Nokheram came home on vacation. All of them were studying in an English school. Though they were all over twenty, there were no prospects of their moving on to college, since they spent two or three years in each class. All three were married, and Pateshwari's worthy son Bindesari had even become the father of a baby boy.

All day the three of them played cards, drank bhang, and paraded around in their city finery. Several times a day they would pass by Hori's door, and by some strange coincidence Sona would be standing in the door doing something or other at just those times. Those days she was wearing the sari that Gobar had brought her. Watching all this sport, Hori's blood ran cold, as though ominous hail-bearing clouds had massed and were about to devastate his field.

One day the three of them came to bathe at the well from which Hori was irrigating his sugar cane. Sona was handling the leather bucket. Hori's blood began to boil. That evening he went to see Dulari. Woman are naturally sympathetic, he thought, and perhaps she would relent and give him a loan at lower interest. Dulari had her own tale of woe, however. She had money coming to her from every family in the village. Even Jhinguri Singh owed her twenty rupees. Yet no one gave the slightest hint of paying her back. Poor thing— where was she to get any cash for another loan?'

'You'll build up a lot of merit, bhaabi,' Hori pleaded. 'You won't be giving me money; you'll be undoing the noose around my neck. Jhinguri and Pateshwari have their hearts set on my fields. As I see it, this land is the one thing my ancestors have left me. Lose that and I'd have nowhere to go. A worthy son increases the family holdings. Could I be so unworthy as to sweep away what my forefathers have earned?'

'Hori, I swear at the feet of Shiva, I have nothing at present. When the people who've borrowed don't pay up, what am I to do? It's not as though you're some stranger. Sona is just like a daughter to me. But tell me, what am I to do? Take your own brother Hira. He borrowed fifty rupees for a bullock. Now he's nowhere to be found, and when I ask his wife, she starts spoiling for a fight. And Shobha— he looks very honest and straightforward, but he doesn't know how to pay his debts either. The simple fact is that no one has any money, so how can they pay? I see the condition everyone's in and let things ride. It's all people can do to keep body and soul together somehow. I wouldn't advise you to sell the land, though. It gives you some status, if nothing else.'

Then she whispered in his ear, 'Pateshwari's son hovers around your house a lot. All three of them do, in fact. Watch out for them. They've become city boys—what do they care about the conventions of the village? There are other boys in the village, but they still have some sense of propriety, some respect, some fear. Those three, though, are just bulls on the rampage. My Kausalya came from her father-in-law's house for a visit, but when I saw the way these boys were behaving, I sent her right back. One can't keep guard all the time!'

Noticing a smile on Hori's face, she protested coyly—'If you think it's funny, Hori, then let me tell you something—you used to be as much a rascal as anyone. Twenty-five times a day you'd find some excuse to come to my shop, but I never even looked at you.'

'Now you're telling lies, bhaabi,' Hori teased. 'I would hardly have kept coming if there'd been no reward. The first time a sparrow shows up, it sizes up the situation. The next time, it flies into the house.'

'Oh, you liar!'

313

'You may not have raised your eyes to look at me, but your heart was watching. In fact it was calling me.'

'So now you're the almighty and all-knowing one! Come off it. I just felt sorry for you, seeing you hovering around all the time. It wasn't as though you were such a gorgeous thing as a young man, after all.'

Husaini showed up to buy a pice worth of salt, and the banter broke off. When he had left with the salt, Dulari turned to Hori again. 'Why don't you go to see Gobar? You can find out how he's getting along, and you might get something too.'

'He won't give anything,' Hori said dejectedly. 'As soon as sons start earning a few pice, they turn their backs. I'm willing to swallow my pride and go to him, but Dhaniya won't agree. And if I left without her approval, she'd make life impossible for me. You know what she's like.'

Dulari gave him a sly look. 'You've become a regular slave to your wife.'

'You didn't want me, so what could I do?'

'If you'd offered to be my slave, I'd have signed you up. No lie!'

'It's still not too late. Why not sign me up now? I'll do it for two hundred rupees. At that price I'm a pretty good bargain.'

'You won't tell Dhaniya?'

'I won't. You want me to swear it?'

'And if you do?'

'Then cut off my tongue.'

'Very well, go fix up a good match. I'll give you the money.'

His eyes brimming, Hori clasped her feet. He was too moved to speak.

The woman drew her feet away. 'Now that's just the sort of nonsense I don't like. I'll get back my money and the full interest within a year even if I have to grab you by the ears to do it. You're not very reliable when it comes to business, but I have confidence in Dhaniya. I hear the pandit is furious at you. He's saying that he'll drive you out of the village as sure as he's a brahman. Why don't you turn Siliya out? You're just asking for trouble.'

'Dhaniya took her in. What can I do?'

'I hear the pandit has been to Banaras, where there's a very famous and learned brahman. He wants five hundred rupees to arrange the penance and absolution. Have you ever heard of anything so stupid? Once you're completely defiled, what good would even a thousand penances do? No one will drink water from his hands, no matter how much penance he does.'

When Hori started home, his heart was dancing with joy. Life had never before seemed so good. On the way, he stopped off at Shobha's place and asked him to come help arrange the betrothal. The two of them went to consult Datadin about the auspicious time for the ceremony. From there they went to Hori's house and sat on the doorstep discussing preparations for the occasion.

Dhaniya came out and said, 'It's getting late. Isn't it time you had your dinner? First eat—then come back and sit down. You have the whole night to gossip.'

Hori invited her to join in the deliberations. 'The auspicious day has been set in this very marriage season. Tell me, what all needs to be bought? I don't know anything about these matters.'

'If you don't know anything, then what have you been sitting around discussing? Has the money actually appeared, though, or are you just licking your lips over imaginary sweets?'

'That's none of your business,' Hori said haughtily. 'You just tell me what things are needed.'

'Well I don't indulge in such fanciful pastimes.'

'Just tell me what all was bought for our sisters' weddings.'

'First tell me—did you get the money?'

'Of course I got it. What do you think—that I've been taking bhang?'

'Well first go eat and then we'll talk.'

When she learned that the matter had been negotiated through Dulari, however, she made a face and said, 'No one's yet been able to clear a debt with her. The witch charges such fantastic interest.'

'But what choice is there? Who else would even make a loan?'

'Why don't you admit you just used this excuse to go flirt with her? You've grown old but you've not changed your ways.'

'Sometimes you talk like a child, Dhaniya. Would she flirt with a good-for-nothing wreck like me? She doesn't even speak to me with a civil tongue.'

'Whom could she get other than someone like you?'

'What do you know about it, Dhaniya? The best people go to her on bended knee. She has money.'

'She probably just gave some slight hint of agreeing and you run all around proclaiming the good news.'

'She didn't just agree. She made a firm promise.'

When Hori went inside to eat and Shobha left for his place, Sona stepped outside with Siliya. She had been standing inside behind the door, listening to the whole conversation. The thought that two hundred rupees was being borrowed from Dulari for her marriage made her insides churn like quicklime dropped in water. A little clay lamp was burning in a niche by the door, the wall above blackened by its smoke. By the dim light, the girls could see the two bullocks eating at the trough and a dog sitting on the ground nearby hoping for some scraps of food. The two girls walked over by the trough.

'Did you hear that?' Sona asked. 'Father is borrowing two hundred rupees from the shopkeeper for my marriage.'

Siliya knew every detail of the family situation. 'What choice had he, with no money in the house?'

Sona stared out at the dark trees. 'I don't want my parents to be put further in debt. Tell me, how will they ever pay it back? They're already staggering under their debts. If they take on another two hundred, the burden's bound to be even heavier, isn't it?'

'With respectable people, marriage always means a good dowry, silly. Without a dowry, all you'd get would be some doddering old man. You want to marry an old man?'

'Why should I have to marry an old man? Was my brother an old man when he brought Jhuniya here? Who paid him anything as a dowry?'

'That gives the family a bad name, though.'

'I'll tell those people in Sonari that if they take even one pice as dowry, I won't go through with the marriage.'

Sona's marriage had been settled with the son of a well-to-do farmer in Sonari.

'What if he says there's nothing he can do, that your father gave the money and his father took it—and he has no control over the matter?'

The weapon which Sona had thought to be as invincible as the arrow of Rama now appeared to be only a bamboo cane. In despair she said, 'I intend to tell him anyway and see what happens. If he says he has no control over the matter, well, the Gomti River isn't far from here. I'll go drown myself. My mother and father have just about killed themselves raising me. Am I to repay them by loading still more debt on them as I leave? Parents who've been blessed by God can give their daughters as much as they like. I have no objection. But when they're in such tight straits that the moneylender could file suit this very day and have their belongings auctioned off, so tomorrow they'd be forced to work as hired hands, then it's a daughter's sacred duty to go drown herself. The family land would be saved and the supply of food would continue. My parents would weep over me for a few days and then calm down. At least they wouldn't have to weep the rest of their lives because of my marriage. That two hundred would double in three or four years. Where would father ever get the money to pay it off?'

Siliya felt as though she were seeing everything in a new light. She hugged Sona in a sudden burst of emotion and said, 'Where did you get so much wisdom, Sona? You look so innocent.'

'What's so wise about this, you little devil? Don't I have eyes? Or am I crazy? They borrow two hundred for my wedding. It doubles in three or four years. Then they borrow another two hundred for Rupa's wedding. All the land and property is auctioned off and they're left to beg from door to door. Right? Surely it would be better for me to sacrifice my life. Go to Sonari before it gets light and send him here. But no, there's no use sending for him. I'd be embarrassed to talk to him. You give him the message yourself from me. See what answer he gives. It's not far—just across the river. He sometimes comes over to this side with his cattle. One time his buffalo got into our field and I gave him a good cursing. He started begging for mercy. By the way, tell me, haven't you seen Matai since you've been here? I hear the brahmans aren't letting him back into the caste.'

'They'll take him back all right,' Siliya said contemptuously. 'It's just that the old man doesn't want to spend the money. If there were money in it for him, he'd even swear a false oath on the water of the Ganges. His son cooks the meals for himself outside on the porch these days.'

'Why don't you give him up? Settle down with someone of your own caste and live in peace and comfort. At least he wouldn't insult you.'

'Why not? Indeed! I should leave him now, after all the misfortune he's suffered on my account? Whether he becomes a brahman or even a god, to me he'll still be the same Matai who used to coax and flatter me. Even if he becomes a brahman and marries a brahman girl, I've served him better than any brahman girl ever could. Right now he might throw me aside for the sake of his dignity and prestige, but wait and see—he'll come running back again.'

317

'That's all in the past. If he got hold of you he'd skin you alive.'

'Well no one's asking him to come. Each of us is responsible for his own dharma. Just because he violates his doesn't mean I should violate mine.'

Early the next morning Siliya was just leaving for Sonari when Hori stopped her. Dhaniya had a headache, so Siliya was needed to take her place directing the water in the fields. Siliya couldn't refuse, but at the noon break she set off for Sonari.

In mid-afternoon, when Hori was ready to return to the well, Siliya was nowhere to be found. 'Where has Siliya disappeared?' he said angrily. 'Sometimes she's here, sometimes she's there, and where she goes, nobody knows. She doesn't seem to have her heart in any of the work. Sona, do you know where she's gone?'

Sona looked for an excuse. 'I don't know anything. She spoke of getting some clothes from the washerwoman. That must be where she went.'

'Come on,' Dhaniya said, getting up from the bed, 'I'll take care of the irrigating. She's not being paid to work, so why should you get mad at her?'

'She lives in our house, doesn't she? Aren't we getting a bad name in the whole village on account of her?'

'Come now! You want her to pay rent for taking up one little corner?'

'She's not taking up one corner. She's occupying a whole room.'

'And that room would rent for fifty rupees a month, I suppose!'

'Even if the rent were one pice, she lives in our house and she should ask permission before going anywhere. I'll settle with her when she comes back.'

The irrigating started up again. Hori had not allowed Dhaniya to come. Rupa cut the channels for the water while Sona handled the bucket—but Rupa was making fire-places and cooking pots out of the wet clay, and Sona kept looking anxiously in the direction of Sonari. She was doubtful and hopeful—but there was more doubt than hope. Why would those people part with the money they were being given? Those who have money are always eager for more, and Gauri Mahto was singularly greedy. Mathura was kind and he was good, but he'd have to go along with whatever his father wanted. Anyway, Sona could still give the boy a telling-off he'd never forget. She'd tell him plainly to go marry some rich girl—that she couldn't put up with a man like him. If Gauri were somehow to agree, however, she'd worship him like a god and drink the water poured over his feet! She'd serve him with more devotion than she showed even her own father—and she'd give Siliya her fill of sweets. She still had the rupee Gobar had given her. The thought of this brought a sparkle to her eyes and a touch of colour to her cheeks.

But why hadn't Siliya returned? It was no great distance. Maybe they hadn't let her come back. Ah, there she was—but coming so slowly. Sona's heart sank. The wretches must not have agreed. Otherwise Siliya would come running. Well, that was the end of the marriage prospects as far as she was concerned.

Siliya did return, but instead of coming to the well, she started work on the water-channels in the field. She was afraid, wondering how she could answer Hori if he asked where she'd been. Sona endured the next two hours with great difficulty. As soon as the work stopped, she rushed over to Siliya.

'Did you die there or something? My eyes just about burst, watching for you.'

'You think I was sleeping there?' Siliya protested. 'One doesn't just come right out and talk about such matters. You have to wait for the right moment. Mathura had gone over near the river to graze the cattle. After hunting around, I finally found him and gave him your message. I can't tell you how delighted he was. He fell at my feet and said, "Sillo, ever since I heard that Sona was going to marry me, I've not been able to get a wink of sleep. That abuse she once gave me has become a blessing. But what am I to do about my father? He turns a deaf ear to everyone...."'

'Then let him be deaf,' Sona interrupted. 'I'm stubborn too. I'll show that I meant what I said—and he'll be left wringing his hands.'

'He left the cattle right there and straightway took me along with him to see Gauri Mahto. Mahto has his own well, and four pairs of bullocks to draw water. He's got six acres of sugar cane. But I had to laugh when I saw him. He looked like some grass-cutter. Anyway, his luck has been good. Well, there was a big squabble between the father and son. Gauri Mahto said it was none of the boy's business whether he accepted anything or not—that the boy had no say in the matter. Mathura said, "If it's a business transaction for you, then don't arrange the marriage. I'll take care of my own marriage as I please." The quarrel grew hotter and Gauri Mahto took off his shoe and gave Mathura a terrific beating. A thrashing like that would have made any other boy furious. And if Mathura had given just one blow, the old man would have been knocked flat for good. But the poor boy just let the shoe whack him dozens of times and said nothing. He looked at me like some beggar, his eyes full of tears, and walked away. Then Mahto began getting mad at me, calling me hundreds of dirty names. But there was no reason for me to put up with that. I had no need to be scared of him. I told him plain and simple—"Mahto, two or three hundred rupees is no great fortune. It won't buy out Hori and it won't make you rich. It'll just be wasted on having a good time, and you'll never find another daughter-in-law like Sona." '

'Mahto beat him just because of that?' Sona asked, her eyes moist.

Siliya had held back something, not wanting such an insult to reach Sona's ears, but she could no longer restrain herself. 'It was really over brother Gobar. Mahto said people only eat polluted food if it's sweet—that a stain is washed away only by silver. At that, Mathura asked what family was completely free of stain, saying it was just that some had been exposed while others remained hidden. Gauri was once involved with a chamar girl himself. He even has two sons by her. When Mathura came out with that, it was as though a devil took hold of the old man. He's as bad tempered as he is greedy. He'll never agree unless he gets a dowry.'

The two girls started home. Sona bore the great weight of the leather bucket and the rope and the yoke on her head, but it felt lighter than a flower to her now. A spring of gaiety and happiness seemed to have burst loose within her. It was as though she had taken the brave and noble image of Mathura and enshrined it in her heart, bathing its feet with her tears. She felt as though heavenly goddesses had raised her in their arms and were carrying her through the glowing sunset sky.

That night Sona developed a high fever.

Three days later Gauri dispatched a letter through the village barber:

'In the name of God, Gauri Ram sends greetings to Shri Hori Mahto, worthy of all praise. I have soberly reconsidered the matter of the dowry on which we previously agreed, and have come to the conclusion that such transactions are injurious to the families of both bride and groom. Having entered into this relationship with each other, we should act in a way that gives trouble to no one. We therefore give you our oath that you need have no concern regarding a dowry. Serve the wedding party any sort of simple fare. We won't even insist on that, and have made our own arrangements for food. Of course any hospitality you provide out of the goodness of your heart, we will accept with humble gratitude.'

Hori read the letter and then rushed inside to read it to Dhaniya. He was dancing around with delight, but Dhaniya remained seated, deep in thought. After a moment she said, 'This is very good of Gauri Mahto, but we also have our position to maintain. What would people say? Money is just dirt on one's hands. The family reputation shouldn't be sacrificed for the sake of it. We'll give whatever we can and Gauri Mahto will have to accept it. Write that to him in your answer. Does a daughter have no claim on her parent's earnings? No, wait—there's no need to write. I'll tell the barber what to say.'

Hori stood dumbfounded in the courtyard while Dhaniya, her generosity aroused by Gauri's chivalrous offer, was delivering the message. After serving the barber a drink, she dismissed him with the customary gift.

'What have you gone and done, Dhaniya?' Hori protested after the messenger had left. 'To this day I can't figure you out. You walk backward and forward at the same time! First you shout not to borrow a pice from anyone, that there's no need to give anything, and then when God takes hold of Gauri and inspires him to write this letter, you start this song and dance about family prestige. God only knows what's in your heart.'

'You have to see someone before you know what to serve him,' Dhaniya replied. 'Don't you realize that? At first Gauri was putting on airs. Now he's behaving like a gentleman. If someone tosses a brick, you can throw back a rock, but if he bows politely, you don't answer with a curse.'

Hori puckered up his nose. 'All right, show how courteous you are. Let's see where you get the money.'

Dhaniya's eyes flashed. 'Getting the money is your job, not mine.'

'I'll just get it from Dulari.'

'Then go get it from her. Everyone charges interest. When you have to drown, what difference does it make whether it's in a pond or in the Ganges?'

Hori went outside for a smoke. How beautifully his neck could be spared if only Dhaniya would leave him free to do things his own way. She always had to take the opposite path, as if some devil were driving her. She refused to open her eyes even with the present state of the family staring her in the face.

321

CHAPTER 25

BHOLA had at last found a second wife. Life had lost its flavour without a woman. While Jhuniya was around, she had taken care of him, preparing his hookah and serving his meals at regular times, but ever since then the poor fellow had been neglected. The daughters-in-law were too busy with household chores to devote themselves to his needs so a second marriage had become absolutely necessary. Luckily he'd come across a young widow whose husband had died only three months previously and who had a son too. Mouth watering, Bhola immediately pounced on the prey and kept after her until she consented.

Until now, the daughters-in-law had had full charge of the house, running it as they wished and living as they pleased. And ever since Jangi had gone off to Lucknow with his wife, Kamta's wife had been the sole mistress of the house. In just five or six months she'd managed to pocket thirty or forty rupees by occasionally selling a quart or so of milk or yogurt on the sly.

Now her husband's stepmother was mistress of the house. The girl objected to being restrained, and such endless bickering went on between the two women that Bhola and Kamta also began quarrelling. The feud finally became so intense that a breakup of the family was imminent. The ancient tradition requiring blows at the time of such a separation was faithfully observed. Kamta was a sturdy young man, and Bhola's only source of power had been his position as a father. By remarrying, though, he had forfeited any claim to a son's respect—at least Kamta didn't accept any such claim. He knocked Bhola down, kicked him, and turned him out of the house empty-handed.

None of the villagers sided with Bhola. He had made an ass of himself by remarrying at his age. He spent the night under a tree and then at daybreak appeared at Nokheram's door where he recited his tale of woe. Bhola's village lay within Nokheram's territory, and what authority there was over the region lay in his hands. Nokheram felt no particular sympathy for Bhola, but when he saw the vivacious and attractive young woman with him, he agreed to provide them with shelter, letting them stay in a little room off the cow-shed. Suddenly feeling the need for an experienced man to look after the animals and take care of the fodder, he hired Bhola for three rupees a month and two pounds of grain a day.

Nokheram was short, fat and dark, with a bald head, a long nose and small beady eyes. He wore a massive turban, a long loose shirt and, in winter, a quilt thrown around his shoulders when he went outside. Because of his great fondness for oil massages, his clothes were always greasy and dirty. He had a huge family, with seven brothers and their families completely dependent on him. In addition, his own son was in the ninth class of an English school, and supporting the boy's fancy city tastes was no easy job. The Rai Sahib paid him a monthly salary of only twelve rupees, while his expenses were not a pice less than a hundred. As a result, when a tenant happened to fall into his clutches, Nokheram held on to him until he'd been sucked dry. Formerly, when he'd been getting a salary of six rupees, he had been easier on the tenants, but with the increased income his greed had also increased so the Rai Sahib withheld any further raises.

Everyone in the village acknowledged Nokheram's authority in one way or another, and even Datadin and Jhinguri Singh played up to him. Pateshwari alone stood constantly ready to challenge him. If Nokheram prided himself on being a brahman and making the *kayasthas* dance on his little finger, Pateshwari could also boast—of being a kayastha, sovereigns of the pen and the account book, a field in which no one could outmanoeuvre them. Besides, he was not employed by the zamindar but by the government, on whose empire the sun never set. If Nokheram observed the monthly day of fasting and gave a feast for five brahmans, Pateshwari would arrange a recitation of the scriptures every full moon and give a feast for ten brahmans. Ever since Pateshwari's older son had found a government job, Nokheram was just waiting for his boy to get through the tenth class somehow so as to get him a job as a court copyist. With that in mind, he regularly paid his humble respects to the officials, offering produce from the harvest of each season. In one other respect, however, Pateshwari still had an edge on him—it was generally believed that Pateshwari was having an affair with the *kahar* widow who worked for him. Nokheram now saw his chance to get even by winning similar distinction.

'Make yourself comfortable here, Bhola. There's nothing to worry about. If you need anything, just let me know. As for your wife, there'll be some sort of work for her too. What with carrying grain to and from the silo, and cleaning and airing it, there's plenty to do around here.'

'Sir,' Bhola urged, 'send for Kamta at least once and ask him if this is any way for a son to treat his father. I built the house and bought the cows and buffaloes. Now he's grabbed everything and thrown me out. If that's not injustice, then what is? You're our only protector, the tribunal from which there should be some ruling in the matter.'

Nokheram tried to pacify him. 'You won't win by fighting him, Bhola. God will punish him for what he's done. Has anyone ever yet prospered by dishonesty? If there weren't injustice in the world, why would people call it hell? Who pays any attention to goodness and justice here? But God sees everything. He knows every little thing that goes on in the world. He even knows what's in your mind this very moment. That's why he's called the omniscient one. Where could anyone go to escape him? Just wait patiently. God willing, you'll be as well off here as you were before.'

Bhola went off to Hori's place and poured out his misfortunes. Hori responded with his own sad story and concluded, 'Sons are impossible nowadays, brother. You practically kill yourself raising them, and when they grow up they turn into enemies. Look at my own son Gobar. He quarrelled with his mother and left, and there's been not a word from him for ages. We could be dead for all he cares. My daughter's marriage is about to hit, but that doesn't concern him in the least. We've received two hundred rupees by mortgaging the land. Prestige must be maintained somehow, after all.'

Though it was Kamta who had thrown his father out, he soon began to realize how hardworking the old man had been. Starting early in the morning, he now had to feed and water the cattle, do the milking, take the milk to market, come back and feed the cattle again, and then milk the cows a second time. A fortnight of this and he was in bad shape. Quarrelling broke out between the husband and wife.

'I didn't marry you and come here just to kill myself working,' his wife protested. 'If feeding me is a burden to you, I'll go back home.'

Kamta was afraid that she might carry out her threat and leave him with the additional job of doing his own cooking. He finally hired a servant, but that didn't work out. The man started stealing and selling the cattle-feed, so they had to fire him. Quarrelling broke out again and the wife went sulking off to her father's house. Kamta, at a complete loss, finally came crawling to Bhola. 'Forgive me for whatever I've done wrong, father. Come back and take over the house. Any way you set things up will be all right with me.'

Life as a common labourer had been galling for Bhola. The consideration shown to him in the first month or two had come to an end. At times he was even told to do such menial jobs as filling Nokheram's pipe or making his bed. On those occasions Bhola had no choice but to swallow the bitter pill. In his own home there might be fighting and squabbling, but at least he wouldn't be forced to wait on anyone hand and foot.

When his wife Nohri heard the proposal, she retorted, 'So you intend going back to the place where you were kicked right out? Don't you have any shame?'

'Well it's not as though I've been set on a throne here either.'

Nohri shrugged. 'You can go if you like. I'm not going.'

Bhola had expected her to protest, and he knew something—in fact he'd been seeing something—of why she would object. This was one reason he was anxious that they get away. No one paid any attention to him here, but Nohri was treated with great respect. Even Nokheram's henchmen treated her with deference. Her refusal infuriated Bhola, but there was little he could do. If he'd had the courage to go off and leave her, Nohri would probably have had to follow. Nokheram would not have the nerve to keep her there alone, being one of those who hunt only from behind some shelter. Nohri knew full well how to deal with Bhola, however.

'Look here, Nohri,' Bhola begged, 'don't be difficult. There's not even a daughter-in-law there any more. You'll have complete charge over everything. Just think of what a bad name we're getting in our community by working here as common labourers.'

Waving her thumb in a gesture of contempt, Nohri flatly refused. 'If you're going, then go. I'm not stopping you. You must love being kicked around by your sons. I don't. I'm perfectly content to work here.'

So Bhola was forced to stay, and Kamta managed to coax his wife into returning. Meanwhile the whispers about Nohri went on circulating—'Today she's wearing a red sari.'—'So what? If she wanted, she could wear a new sari every day now.'—'When your lover's a police chief, what's there to be afraid of?'—'Has Bhola gone blind or something?'

Shobha had a great sense of humour, but though he played the part of the village joker he was also a good troublemaker and tracked down everything going on in the village. Finding Nohri alone in her house one day, he began joking with her. Nohri complained to Nokheram, who called Shobha on the carpet and gave him a scolding he'd never forget.

Another day it was Lala Pateshwari who got into trouble. It was summer, and he was sitting in the mango grove supervising the picking when Nohri showed up in all her finery. 'Nohri my queen!' he called out. 'Come here and have a few mangoes. They're delicious.'

Nohri was under the illusion that he was making fun of her. She'd developed quite a pride and expected people to treat her as though she was a zamindar's wife. Vain people tend to be suspicious anyway, and a guilty conscience makes them even more suspicious. Why had he looked at her and laughed? Why did everyone get jealous when they saw her? She didn't go around begging people for anything. As if they were so pure! Let them get in her way and she'd show them a thing or two. Nohri had been there long enough to find out all the secret scandal in the village. This Lala himself was having an affair with a kahar woman and he had the nerve to laugh at her! Nobody would accuse him—he was a bigshot. But she was poor and low caste, so everyone ridiculed her. And like father, like son—that Rameshwari of his chased around madly after Siliya. They pounced like vultures on those chamar girls and then proclaimed themselves to be superior.

Stopping in her tracks, she said, 'Since when have you become so generous, Lala? You'd steal the bread off someone's plate if you had the chance. Now you've become a big man in mangoes. In future you'd better leave me alone or you'll be sorry, I'm warning you.'

Well! The nerve of that cowherd girl! Thinking she ruled the world because she'd bagged Nokheram. 'The way you're all worked up, Nohri,' he said, 'one would think you were going to drive us all out of the village. In future watch your tongue before you speak, and don't forget your position.'

'Did I ever come begging at your door?'

'If Nokheram hadn't given you shelter, you would be begging.'

Stung as though by a red hot pepper, Nohri started shouting 'Shamefaced wretch! Lecher!' and everything else that came to mind.

Storming to her room, she began gathering up her belongings and piling them outside.

When word reached Nokheram, he rushed over anxiously and asked, 'What's this you're doing, Nohri? Why are you putting all your clothes and stuff outside? Did someone say something or what?'

Nohri knew how to make men dance. That was the one art she had fully mastered. Nokheram was an educated man. Well-versed in law, he had read a lot of the sacred texts and he'd licked the boots of great lawyers and barristers, but he had become a mere puppet in the hands of this untutored woman. Nohri frowned and said, 'Fate was against me the day I came here, but I don't intend to lose my honour.'

The brahman in Nokheram was aroused. Twirling his moustache, he declared, 'If anyone dares look at you, I'll tear out his eyes.'

Finding the iron red-hot, Nohri applied the sledge-hammer. 'Lala Pateshwari is always making unnecessary remarks to me. I'm no prostitute, that anyone should flaunt his money at me. The village is full of women, but no one bothers them. I'm the one who always gets picked on.'

A demon seized hold of Nokheram. Picking up his heavy staff, he rushed to the orchard and began bellowing, 'Come on out if you're such a big man. I'll tear out your whiskers. I'll bury you alive. Come out and face me. If you ever annoy Nohri again, I'll drink your blood. I'll knock all that patwari stuffing out of you. You must think everyone else is as rotten as yourself. Just who do you think you are?'

Lala Pateshwari stood there petrified, head bowed and hardly daring to breathe. To say even a word would only make things worse. Never in his life had he been so insulted. One time he had been ambushed near the village pond at night and badly beaten, but no one in the village had heard about it—or at least no one had any proof. Today, however, he had been humiliated in front of the whole village. That woman who only yesterday was going around begging for shelter now had the whole village terrorized. Who had the courage to cross her now? Who could do anything when Pateshwari himself was helpless?

Nohri was now queen of the village. Seeing her coming, farmers would step off the path. It was an open secret that buttering her up could get one a lot of concessions from Nokheram. No one wanting property partitioned or a deferment of land rent or a plot to build a house could ever succeed without first propitiating Nohri. At times she would berate even the wealthiest tenants, and not only the tenants but even the agent, Nokheram himself, was now in her power.

Bhola had no desire to be dependent on her. Nothing seemed to him more degrading than to live off the earnings of a woman. He made just three rupees a month, but before he could lay his hands even on that sum, Nohri would make off with it. He couldn't get even a half pice of tobacco, while she chewed two annas worth of betel a day. Moreover, everyone ordered him around. Nokheram's men had him preparing their chilams and chopping wood for them. After a heavy day's work, the poor man would drop exhausted on his dilapidated cot under a tree outside. There was no one to bring him even a drink of water. At night he had to eat chapaties left over from the morning meal, accompanied only by a little salt or by salt and water.

Eventually he made up his mind to go back and live with Kamta. That was his home, after all, and at least he'd get a decent meal there.

'I'm not about to go there and become a slave to anyone,' Nohri declared.

Bhola mustered his courage. 'I'm not asking you to go. I'm only speaking for myself.'

'You'd go off and leave me? Aren't you ashamed even to suggest such a thing?'

'I've swallowed all my sense of shame.'

'Well I've not swallowed mine. You can't go off and leave me.'

'You're your own boss, but there's no reason for me to be a slave to you.'

'I'll summon the village council and blacken your face in public, I'm warning you.'

'Is it any less black already? Do you still want to keep up this pretence with me?'

'You're acting as high and mighty as though you were having jewels made for me every day. Well this is one woman who doesn't have to put up with that highhandedness.'

Exasperated, Bhola picked up his stick and rose to leave, but Nohri sprang forward and caught him by the wrist. Unable to shake off her powerful grip, Bhola sat down as meekly as though he were a prisoner. There was a time when he'd had women dancing to his tune, but today he was held captive by a woman and could find no escape. He didn't feel like pulling free and starting an argument that would bring everything into the open. Realizing the limits of his strength, he nevertheless wished he had the courage to come right out and say that she was of no use to him and that he was leaving her. She had threatened to summon the village council, but that was certainly no dragon. If she wasn't afraid of the council, why should he be?

But he lacked the courage to give words to these thoughts. It was as though Nohri had cast a spell over him.

L*

CHAPTER 26

LALA PATESHWARI was a living example of all the virtues of that class of men known as patwaris. He couldn't bear to see a peasant encroach even an inch on someone else's land, nor could he bear to see a peasant hold back on repaying a debt to a moneylender. It was his sacred responsibility to look after the welfare of everyone in the village. He had no faith in compromise or mutual conciliation. They only indicated a lack of spirit. He was a worshipper of conflict, which reflected vitality. As a result, he was always trying to inspire a life of conflict, setting off fireworks of one kind or another.

Lala's benevolent eye was especially focused on Mangaru Shah at this particular time. Although Mangaru was the wealthiest man in the village, he took absolutely no interest in local politics and had no desire for power or prestige. He had even located his house outside the village, where he had put in an orchard and a well and a small temple to Shiva. Being childless, he had now reduced his moneylending business and spent most of his time in worship and meditation. Any number of peasants had made off with his money but he had never taken anyone to court. Hori alone owed about a hundred and fifty rupees, counting interest and everything, but Mangaru seemed no more concerned to collect the debt than Hori was to pay it. He had pressed Hori for the money two or three times and even made threats, but on realizing Hori's condition, he had let the matter drop.

This season, however, Hori's sugar cane crop happened to be the best in the village. People figured it would bring in a good two hundred or two hundred and fifty rupees. Pateshwari suggested to Mangaru that he seize this opportunity to file suit at a time when all the money could be realized. Mangaru was not so much generous as he was lazy, wanting to avoid all that bother, but when Pateshwari guaranteed that he wouldn't have to spend even one day in court or go to any other trouble, that he could sit back and let the case take care of itself, Mangaru gave permission to start proceedings and made a payment toward court costs.

Hori had no idea of what was brewing. He never knew when the suit was filed or the decree granted, and found out only when a court officer arrived to auction off his cane. The whole village gathered at the edge of the field. Hori ran to Mangaru Shah while Dhaniya started cursing Pateshwari, knowing intuitively that this was one of his tricks. Mangaru was busy with his prayers, though, so Hori couldn't see him, and Dhaniya's shower of abuse left Pateshwari unscathed. Meanwhile the cane had been auctioned for a hundred and fifty rupees, the bidder having been named as Mangaru Shah. No one else dared make an offer. Even Datadin lacked the courage to make himself the target of Dhaniya's curses.

Dhaniya tried to arouse Hori. 'What are you sitting around for? Why don't you go ask the patwari if this is any way to treat people of his own village?'

'They must have heard your curses,' Hori answered meekly. 'How could we show our faces now?'

'Anyone who does things that deserve cursing is bound to get cursed.'

'And you shout abuses and then expect him to treat you as a sister?'

'I'd just like to see anyone come near my field.'

'If the men from the sugar mill come and chop it down, what can you or I do about it? Of course you can shout curses so as to help stop the itching in your tongue.'

'Someone's going to carry away my crop while I'm alive and breathing?'

'Yes, while you and I are both alive and breathing. The whole village put together couldn't stop them. It's no longer ours. It belongs to Mangaru Shah.'

'Was it Mangaru Shah who killed himself watering and hoeing in the heat of the day during May and June?'

'That was all your doing, but now it belongs to Mangaru Shah. Aren't we in debt to him?'

The sugar cane went, but its going only brought on a new problem. Dulari had agreed to loan the money on the strength of this crop alone. Now what security was there? Hori already owed her two hundred rupees, but she had planned to collect that old debt out of the cane and then start up a fresh account. In her eyes, Hori's credit was good up to two hundred rupees. Giving more than that would be too risky. The marriage season was fast approaching and the date had been set. Gauri Mahto must have made all the preparations, and postponing the wedding now would be impossible. Hori was so furious he could have strangled Dulari. He did everything in his power to coax and cajole her, but that goddess of stone wouldn't relent in the least. He finally folded his hands in supplication and said, 'Dulari, I'm not going to run away with your money, nor am I about to die so soon. With my land, my trees, a house and a grown son, your money won't be lost. My honour is at stake. Please help me save it.'

Dulari did not believe in mixing charity with business, however. If charity were her business, she'd be taking no risk, but she had not been taught to do business that way.

Hori returned home. 'What now, Dhaniya?'

Dhaniya took out her frustration on him. 'This is exactly what you wanted.'

Hori looked at her in pain. 'So it's all my fault?'

'Whoever's fault it was, it turned out the way you wanted.'

'You'd like me to mortgage the land?'

'What would you do if you mortgaged the land?'

'Paid labour.'

The land was equally dear to them both, though. On it depended their prestige and their honour. To be without land was to be a mere labourer.

Getting no answer, Hori asked again, 'So what do you suggest?'

'What's there to say?' Dhaniya murmured in distress. 'Gauri will come with the marriage party. Give them one meal and send the girl off with them the next morning. Let the world laugh if it wants to. If it's God's will that we be disgraced and humilated, there's nothing we can do about it.'

Just then they saw Nohri approaching, a colourful shawl thrown over her shoulders. Seeing Hori, she drew her sari down a little over her face, treating him with the modesty befitting the father-in-law of one's daughter.

The two women had already met. 'Where are you going, sister?' Dhaniya called out. 'Come sit down for a while.'

Nohri had completed her conquest and was now trying to rally public opinion in her favour. She walked over and remained standing.

Dhaniya surveyed her critically from head to foot and then said, 'How did you happen to come this way today?'

'Oh I just thought I'd come see you folks,' Nohri said casually. 'When's the girl's wedding?'

'That depends on the will of God,' Dhaniya said dubiously.

'I hear it's to take place this marriage season. The date's been set?'

'Yes, a date has been set.'

'Don't forget to send me an invitation.'

'Why would you need an invitation? You should think of her as your own daughter.'

'You must have bought the things for the dowry. May I have a look?'

Dhaniya was at a loss for an answer but Hori came to her rescue. 'We've not bought anything yet. In fact there's nothing to buy. We're giving her without dowry.'

Nohri stared at them in disbelief. 'How can you do that? She's your first daughter. You must do everything lavishly.'

Hori gave a hollow laugh as though to say that she might be living in green pastures but that they'd been hit by drought. Aloud he said, 'We're short of money, so there's no question of being lavish. There's no need to hide anything from you.'

'You're short on money even though you and your son are both earning? Who's to believe that?'

'If my son had turned out well, there'd be no problem. He doesn't even send a letter, much less any money. It's been over a year with no word from him.'

Meanwhile Sona showed up carrying a bundle of green fodder on her head. Drawing the sari over her young breasts with childlike artlessness, she came up, threw down the bundle, and went in the house.

'The girl has certainly grown up a lot,' Nohri remarked.

'Girls shoot up suddenly like castor-oil trees. She's still just a child.'

'You've settled on a groom, haven't you?'

'Oh yes, the groom is perfectly all right. If the money can be arranged, we'll hold the wedding this very month.'

Nohri's motives were rather selfish. The money she'd saved recently was gnawing at her insides. What glory it would bring her to spend some of the money on Sona's wedding. The whole village would talk about her, saying in amazement that she must be a real goddess to give away so much money. Hori and Dhaniya would go around singing her praises to everyone and she'd gain all kinds of new honour and respect. That would shut the mouths of those who'd been point-

333

ing their fingers at her. And who would then have the nerve to make sarcastic remarks or to jeer at her? Right now the whole village was against her; then, the whole village would uphold her. Her face lit up at the thought.

'If a small sum will do the job, I'd be happy to let you have it. You can pay me back at your convenience.'

Both Hori and Dhaniya gaped. No, she was not joking. Their eyes reflected amazement and gratitude, hesitation and embarrassment. Obviously Nohri was not as bad as people had been thinking.

'Your reputation is like my own,' Nohri continued. 'If you're ridiculed, doesn't it mean I'm ridiculed too? No matter how it happened, we're related now by marriage.'

'Your money is here in the family where we can draw on it whenever the need arises,' Hori said hesitantly. 'A man can always depend on his own people, but why touch their money if arrangements can be made elsewhere?'

'That's right,' Dhaniya nodded.

'When there's money in the family,' Nohri insisted, 'why beg for help from outsiders? Besides, after courting their favour with all kinds of flattery, you'd have to pay interest, make out a bond, get witnesses, and pay a commission. Of course if my money's contaminated, then that's a different matter.'

'It's not that, Nohri,' Hori assured her. 'It's true that there's no need to go out begging when things can be taken care of within the family, but there are obligations in any family matter also. The crops are rather unreliable, and if you should need the money at a time when we couldn't scrape it together, you'd think badly of us and we'd be upset too. That's why we hesitated, but the girl is of course your daughter just as much as she's ours.'

'All right then, we'll borrow it from you. After all, why should some outsider enjoy the pleasure and the merit that comes with giving a girl in marriage?'

'How much money do you need?'

'How much could you spare?'

'Would a hundred do?'

Hori's appetite began growing. As long as God was raining down the money, why not take all he could get?

'That all depends. We could make do with a hundred. We could also do with five hundred.'

334

'I have some two hundred rupees. I'll let you have it all.'

'With that much we can manage things nicely. We have enough grain already. I must confess, I never realized you were such a goddess. In this evil age, who gives help to anyone? Who could afford to? You've really saved me from going under.'

It was time to light the lamps and a chill was setting in. The earth had wrapped itself in a mantle of blue haze. Dhaniya brought a brazier from inside and they began to warm themselves. In the light of the straw fire, that adulterous wench Nohri seemed as bright and beautiful as a blessing from the gods. Such sympathy now filled her eyes, such modesty tinged her cheeks, and such goodwill was on her lips!

After chatting casually for awhile, Nohri got up to leave, saying, 'It's getting late. Come get the money tomorrow, Mahto.'

'Come on, I'll see you home.'

'No, no, don't bother. I can go alone.'

'Nonsense. If I had my way, I'd carry you there on my shoulders.'

Nokheram's house was at the other end of the village, and the best way to get there was by skirting the village. Setting out by that path they were soon surrounded by silence.

'I wish you'd say a few words to my husband,' Nohri said, 'and explain that there's no point in quarrelling with everyone. When you have to live with other people, you should behave in such a way as to become one of them. What he does is pick fights with everyone. Since he can't afford to keep me in seclusion at home and I'm forced to go out and earn a living, how can he expect me not to talk or joke with anyone? And how can he expect that no one will look at me or smile at me? That works only when women are kept in purdah, completely out of sight. Tell me—what am I supposed to do if someone stares or makes eyes at me? I can't very well tear out his eyes. Besides, by being amiable you can get men to do all kinds of things for you. I try to tell him that actions must be adapted to the situation at hand. The fact that he was once rich enough to have an elephant by his door is no help to him now that he's just a hired hand at three rupees a month. We kept buffaloes at my house, after all, but now I'm just a common labourer. He refuses to understand anything, though. One moment he's thinking of moving back in with his sons; the next, he's planning to go live in Lucknow. He's plaguing the life out of me.'

335

Hori tried to humour her. 'That's utterly stupid of Bhola. He's old enough to have more sense. I'll explain things to him.'

'Come in the morning, then, and I'll give you the money.'

'Is there anything to be signed?'

'I know you're not going to make off with my money.'

They had reached her house. Nohri went inside and Hori headed back home.

CHAPTER 27

WHEN Gobar returned to the city, he found that another vendor had set up shop at the place where he had been doing business and the customers had forgotten him. That room of his seemed like a cage now too. Jhuniya spent most of her time sitting there alone and crying. The child had been accustomed to playing all day in the courtyard or in front of the door. Here there was no place for him to play. The alley in front of the door was barely a yard wide and filled with a constant stench. In the heat of summer there was nowhere outdoors to sleep or even to sit. The boy wouldn't leave his mother for even a moment. When there was no place to play, what was there for him to do but eat and drink milk? At home Dhaniya would play with him sometimes and other times Rupa, Sona, Hori or Puniya. Here there was only Jhuniya, and she had all the household chores to do.

As for Gobar, he was intoxicated with the passion of youth, eager to drown his pent-up desires in a sea of sexual pleasure. He couldn't keep his mind on any work. He'd set out to peddle his wares and return in just an hour. There was no other recreation available. The workmen and ekka drivers in the neighbourhood played cards and gambled all night. Previously he had played a lot too, but now the only thing that interested him was making love to Jhuniya. She very soon tired of this kind of life, longing for a place where she could go off by herself and sleep completely undisturbed. There was no such solitude to be found, however, so she would get angry at Gobar. Such a lovely picture he had painted of life in the city, and here there was nothing but this grim dungeon. The child irritated her also, and at times she would spank him, set him outdoors, and then lock the door from inside. The boy would whimper and cry until he wore himself out.

A year went by. To add to her misery, Jhuniya was expecting again, and with not a soul around to look after her. She kept getting headaches, lost all interest in food, and got so lethargic that she just wanted to lie silently in some corner where no one would speak to her or disturb her. But Gobar's unrelenting affections kept pounding at the door, demanding recognition. Her milk had practically dried up but Lallu, as the boy was now called, kept after her breasts. Jhuniya's will had grown weak along with her body, and what little resistance remained broke down under the least bit of pressure. While she was lying down Lallu would come, force his way onto her chest, take a nipple in his mouth and begin chewing on it. He was two years old now and his teeth were very sharp. When no milk came, he'd get angry and sink his teeth into her breast, but Jhuniya no longer had even the strength to push him away. Death seemed to be standing constantly in front of her. She felt no love for either the child or his father. All people cared about was their own interests. During the rainy season, when Lallu came down with diarrhoea and stopped nursing, Jhuniya was conscious only that one of her afflictions had been relieved. A week later, however, when the boy died, his memory stirred her to tears.

When Gobar began making demands on her again just a week after the child's death, she flared up with rage. 'What a beast you are!'

Lallu's memory was now more dear to Jhuniya than the child had ever been. While he was alive, any joy he brought had been overweighed by the trouble he caused; but the child in her mind now was calm, quiet, well-behaved and cheerful. This image gave her a melancholy pleasure unmarred by any dark shadow of actuality, since the boy turned into a mere reflection of the child in her imagination. With his false erratic representation removed, his true form took shape within her, created of her hopes and wishes. Instead of milk, she was nourishing him now with her blood. She seemed oblivious to the cramped room, the pervading stench, and the acrid smoke of the cooking fire, as though she found strength in her world of memories. The one who in life had been only a burden had by dying permeated her whole being; and as her concerns turned inward, she became indifferent to everything outside. She no longer cared whether Gobar got back early or late, whether he enjoyed his meals or not, and whether he was happy or sad. Nor did she care what he earned or how he spent it. Her life, such as it was, went on within. Outwardly she was only an unfeeling machine.

Had Gobar shared in her sorrow and penetrated her inner recesses, he might have drawn closer to her and become a part of her life.

Instead, he stopped short at the arid banks of her external existence and turned away with unquenched thirst.

He finally spoke up harshly—'How long are you going to keep crying over Lallu? It's been four or five months now.'

Jhuniya sighed. 'You wouldn't understand my sadness. Go take care of your own affairs and leave me alone,.just the way I am.'

'You think your crying will bring Lallu back?'

Jhuniya had never realized that Gobar could be so hardhearted. Unable to reply, she went over and put a pan of potatoes on to boil.

This lack of sympathy made her cling even tighter to her mental image of Lallu. He was hers alone, to be shared with no one. Until now, a part of him had remained outside her, having a place in Gobar's heart. Now he was entirely her own.

Discouraged about selling, Gobar had taken a job in a sugar mill. Mr Khanna, inspired by the success of his first mill, had recently set up this second one. Gobar had to start out early in the morning, and by the time he returned home at dusk after a full day's work, there was not a spark of life left in his body. In the village he'd been forced to work just as hard, but he had never felt the least bit tired. The work had been interspersed with laughter and conversation, and the open fields and broad skies had seemed to ease the strain. However hard his body worked there, his mind had remained free. Here, although his body was taxed less, the hubbub, the speed and the thundering noise weighed him down. There was also the constant apprehension of rebuke. The workers were all in the same boat and they drowned their physical fatigue and mental weariness in palm toddy or cheap liquor. Gobar took to drinking also. By the time he reached home, the night would be late and he would be staggering drunk. Finding some excuse or other, he would swear at Jhuniya, threaten to throw her out of the house, and sometimes even beat her.

Jhuniya began to suspect that she was being abused this way just because she was a kept woman. Gobar would never have had the nerve to treat a wife that way—the caste would have punished and probably even excommunicated him. What a terrible mistake it had been to run away from home with this rotter. The whole world had ridiculed her and then she had gained nothing to compensate for it. She began to consider Gobar an enemy, paying no attention to his meals or to her own. When he hit her, she would get so furious she could have cut his throat.

As her pregnancy advanced, her anxiety also increased. To have the baby in this house would mean certain death. Who was there to take care of her, and who would handle the delivery? And if Gobar kept beating her this way, life would be absolute hell.

One day when she'd gone to the public tap for water, a neighbour woman asked her, 'How many months along are you?'

'I don't know, sister,' Jhuniya replied bashfully. 'I haven't kept count.'

She was a short, fat woman, dark and ugly, with huge breasts. Her husband drove an ekka, while she ran a place that sold firewood. Jhuniya had bought wood there a number of times, but that was the extent of their acquaintance.

The woman smiled. 'It seems to me your time is up. Probably to-morrow, or even today. Have you arranged for a midwife and all that?'

'I don't know anyone around here,' Jhuniya said, her voice trembling with fright.

'What a no-good man you must have, sitting around as though he's deaf and dumb.'

'He doesn't care about me.'

'That's obvious enough, but while you're in confinement you'll need someone to look after things. What about your mother-in-law or a sister-in-law or somebody? You should have sent for someone.'

'They're all dead as far as I'm concerned.'

When she returned with the water and began scrubbing the pots and pans, her heart was pounding with fear over the delivery. Oh God, what was going to happen? Well, she would die, that was all, and a good thing too—she'd be freed from all her miseries.

That evening the pains began, and she realized that the hour of agony had arrived. Drenched with perspiration, one hand clutching her belly, she lit the fire, put the rice and dal mixture on to boil, and then lay down in a daze there on the bare floor.

About ten o'clock that night Gobar showed up reeking of toddy. Tripping drunkenly over his words, he began babbling—'I don't give a damn about anyone. Those who want me will have to come begging a hundred times. Otherwise they can look elsewhere. I can't stand anyone nagging me. I didn't put up with it from the mother and father who gave me birth, so why should I put up with it from anyone else? The foreman gave me a dirty look. Well I'm not about to be bullied by anyone. If people hadn't grabbed me, I'd have drunk his blood—yes his blood! I'll fix him tomorrow. So they'll hang me.

I'll show them how a real man dies. Laughing and swaggering and twirling my moustache as I step up the gallows, that's how. As for women—what an unfaithful breed they are. She puts some rice on to cook and then sprawls there asleep. Doesn't care whether anyone eats or not. Gobbles up all sorts of goodies herself and then mixes up a little plain rice and dal for me. Torment me all you like. God takes care of justice—you'll get your torment from him.'

Without rousing Jhuniya or even speaking to her, he poured the food onto a plate, gulped down a few bites and then lay down outside on the veranda. In the early hours of the morning he felt cold. Coming inside for a blanket, he heard Jhuniya moaning. The effects of the toddy had worn off.

'How do you feel, Jhuniya?' he asked. 'You have a pain or something?'

'Yes, my belly's hurting terribly.'

'Why didn't you say something earlier? Where am I to go at this time of night?'

'Who could I have told?'

'Was I dead or something?'

'What do you care whether I live or die?'

Gobar wondered anxiously where he could find a midwife. And would one even come at this hour? There wasn't even any money in the house. If the bitch had told him earlier, he'd have borrowed two or three rupees from someone. He always used to keep a hundred rupees or so on hand, and people would come around and play up to him. Ever since this cursed woman had arrived, though, the goddess of wealth seemed angry at him and he was always flat broke.

'Is that your wife moaning?' someone suddenly called out. 'Have the pains begun?'

It was the same stout woman who had been talking to Jhuniya previously. She had gotten up to feed their horse, and hearing Jhuniya's groans, had come to inquire.

Gobar went out on the veranda and said, 'Yes, she has a pain in her belly. She's tossing around. Can we get a midwife around here?'

'I guessed as much the moment I saw her this morning. There's a midwife living in Kacchi Serai. Go quickly and call her. Tell her to hurry. I'll stay here in the meantime.'

'I don't know where Kacchi Serai is. Which way is it?'

'All right, you stay here and fan her. I'll go get her. Just like they say, a stupid man messes up everything. Here she's about to deliver and you don't even know where the midwife lives.'

With that she started off. To her face, people called the woman by her proper name, Chuhia, but behind her back they called her Fatso. Anyone she overheard would have had his family cursed for seven generations back.

Gobar had hardly waited ten minutes before she returned and declared, 'How in the world are poor people to manage? The slut says she wants five rupees before she'll come—and then eight annas a day, and a sari on the twelfth day. I told her to go to hell, that I'd take care of it myself. I didn't become the mother of twelve children just like that. You go outside, Gobardhan, I'll see to everything. Any decent human being helps others when the need arises. Delivers three or four babies and thinks that makes her a midwife!'

She sat down, rested Jhuniya's head on her lap, and gently massaged her abdomen. 'I knew it as soon as I saw you today. To tell you the truth. I couldn't get to sleep, worrying about you here with none of your family to look after you.'

Jhuniya gritted her teeth, gasping with pain. 'I won't pull through this time, sister. Hai! It's not as though I prayed to God for a child. I raised one and he snatched it away, so why should he send another? If I die, mother, take pity on the baby and bring it up. God will bless you.'

Chuhia stroked her hair affectionately and said, 'Be brave, child, be brave. The pain'll be over in just a moment now. You were being so secretive about everything. It's nothing to be ashamed of. If you'd told me, I'd have brought you an amulet from the *maulvi* sahib, that Mirzaji who lives in this block.'

Jhuniya lost consciousness at that point. At nine in the morning, she awoke to find herself lying there in a fresh sari and Chuhia seated nearby holding the baby. She felt as weak as though not a drop of blood remained in her body.

Chuhia came every morning to cook up special preparations for Jhuniya and then returned several times during the day to massage the baby boy with oil and give him cow's milk. It was the fourth day and there was still no milk in Jhuniya's breasts. The child cried his eyes out, unable to keep the cow's milk down. To stop the incessant crying, Chuhia would put her own breast in his mouth. The baby would suck for a moment and then start screaming again when no milk came. When the fourth evening came and Jhuniya still had no milk, Chuhia

342

became alarmed. The baby was growing weaker and weaker. Remembering a retired doctor who lived near the cattle market, Chuhia went and brought him to the house.

The doctor examined Jhuniya. 'How could she produce any milk,' he exclaimed, 'when there's no blood left in her?' The problem was a complex one. She would need months of tonics to build up her blood before any milk could start, and by that time this little bundle of flesh would have breathed its last.

The night was late. Gobar, drunk with toddy, lay on the veranda. Chuhia was trying to quiet the baby with her breasts when suddenly she felt them fill with milk. 'Look Jhuniya,' she cried out in delight, 'your baby's going to live now. My milk has started.'

'Yours?' Jhuniya gasped in astonishment. 'You're getting milk?'

'Honest I am.'

'I can't believe it.'

'Well look !' She squeezed her breast and a thin stream of milk shot out.

'But your youngest girl must be at least eight, isn't she?' Jhuniya asked.

'Yes, going on eight, but I used to have lots of milk.'

'You've had no children since then?'

'She was the last. My breasts had dried up completely. It must be an act of God, that's all.'

After that, Chuhia came four or five times a day to nurse the baby, and despite his frailty at birth he gradually picked up strength from her milk. One morning Chuhia went to the river to bathe and the baby started whimpering with hunger. When Chuhia returned at ten, Jhuniya was rocking the baby but he was still crying. Chuhia reached out to take the child, intending to nurse him.

'Leave him alone,' Jhuniya said sharply. 'If the unlucky creature dies, so much the better. At least we won't be under the obligation of taking charity from anyone.'

Chuhia began pleading with her, and after a lot of soothing and coaxing, Jhuniya finally handed over the baby.

Jhuniya and Gobar were still not getting along. She was convinced that this man was utterly selfish and unfeeling, that he thought of her only as a source of physical pleasure. She could be dying for all he cared, as long as she satisfied his desires. He probably was hoping she would die so he could get another woman. Well he'd better just cool off. Only she was naive and dumb enough to fall into his trap.

343

In those days he'd laid himself at her feet, but the moment they reached the city, he seemed to have changed into a different person for some reason.

Winter had set in but there were no warm clothes or bedding. What little money was not spent on their skimpy meals went for toddy. There was just one old quilt. They both slept under it, but as though separated by a hundred miles, spending the night in one position to avoid touching each other. Gobar longed to cuddle the baby in his arms and would sometimes get up during the night to gaze lovingly at the child's face. With Jhuniya, though, he felt only estrangement. As for Jhuniya, she wouldn't speak to him or do anything for him, and the unpleasantness between them, like a patch of rust, kept growing harder and deeper. They would deliberately misconstrue each other's statements, as though to fan the flames of resentment between them, and bitterly nurse every remark for days, like bloodthirsty hunting dogs ready to snap at each other at the slightest provocation.

Meanwhile, at the factory where Gobar worked, some disturbance or other kept boiling up almost every day. The new budget had imposed a tax on sugar, giving the mill owners a good excuse to cut wages. For every five rupee loss from the tax, there was now a gain of ten rupees from the reduced wages. For months the controversy had been raging in the mill. The labour union was prepared to strike. Reduce the wages and they'd all walk out. Even a half-pice cut was unacceptable. When there had not been even a half-pice raise during these tough times, why should they now go along with this loss?

Mirza Khurshed was the president of the union and Pandit Onkarnath, editor of *Lightning*, its secretary. In their determination to have a strike that the mill owners would long remember, they completely overlooked the fact that the strike would also bring distress to the workers, depriving thousands of people of even their daily bread. Gobar was at the forefront of the agitators for a strike. Fiery by nature, he needed only a challenge, and, once aroused, he had no hesitation about killing or being killed.

One day Jhuniya mustered the courage to protest, 'You're a family man. It's not right for you to go leaping into a fire this way.'

Gobar immediately took offence. 'Who are you to meddle in my affairs? I didn't ask for your advice.'

The quarrel became more heated and Gobar ended up giving Jhuniya a thorough beating. Chuhia came to her rescue and started

344

rebuking Gobar. A devilish fury seized him. Eyes flashing, he shouted, 'Don't ever come back to my house again, *Chuha*. You have no business here.'

'If I didn't come to your house,' she replied sarcastically, 'how could I possibly survive? I only live on the warmed-up scraps that I beg from you. If it hadn't been for me, mister, this wife of yours wouldn't even be around for you to kick.'

Gobar shook his fist. 'I'm warning you—stay away from my house. You're the one who's made this witch so high and mighty.'

'Oh shut your mouth, Gobar,' Chuhia said, holding her ground fearlessly. 'You've not done anything manly or heroic by beating up a poor woman still half-dead from childbirth. What have you done for her that she should put up with blows from you? You feed her a few crumbs, is that it? Thank your stars that you got such a simple woman. Any other wife would have hit you in the face with a broom and left you.'

The people of the neighbourhood had gathered around and rebukes started raining down on Gobar from all sides. Men who at home beat their wives daily now presented themselves as models of justice and kindness. Chuhia grew more ferocious—'The bastard tells me to stay away from his house. He poses as a family man without even knowing that it takes real guts to raise a family. Ask him where this baby, as lively as a calf, would be today if it hadn't been for me. Shows off his strength and courage by beating a woman ! You're lucky I'm not your wife or I'd have taken off this shoe and swatted you right in the face. Then I'd have slammed the door on you and locked it from the outside so you could starve there.'

Fuming, Gobar left for work. If Chuhia had been a man, he would have fixed her good. But what could one do to a woman?

Clouds of discontent were massing in the mill. Workers went around with copies of *Lightning* in their pockets, huddling together in little groups to read it whenever they found a free moment. The paper's sales were mounting rapidly. The labour leaders would meet at the *Lightning* office and work half the night drawing up plans for the strike, and when the news was announced in bold headlines the following morning, such a scramble would ensue that copies would sell for two and three times the regular price.

Meanwhile the directors of the company sat biding their time. A strike would be to their advantage. There was no shortage of labourers, after all. Unemployment had risen and men could easily be hired at half the present wages. Production costs could be cut in half just like that. Five or six working days would be lost, but that was no problem. At last it was decided to announce the wage reduction to the employees. The day and hour were set and the police informed. The workers knew nothing about this. They had their own plot, intending to call the strike at a time when there was very little stock left in the warehouse and the demand was keen.

Suddenly one evening when the mill was letting out, the directors' announcement was broadcast. Police moved in simultaneously. The workers were forced to strike at a time when the warehouse was so fully stocked that supplies could not be exhausted in less than six months, however great the demand.

Mirza Khurshed smiled when he heard the news, like a clever fighter appreciating the tactical skill of his enemy. After a moment's thought he said, 'Very well. If that's what the directors want, that's the way it'll be. Circumstances are in their favour but the force of justice is on our side. They intend to hire new men to carry on the work. What we must do is try and prevent them from getting even a single new employee. That's the only way we can win.'

An emergency meeting was held at the *Lightning* office, a committee for action was organized, and officers were elected. At eight that night, workers marched through the streets in a long procession. By ten, plans for the next day had been settled and a warning given to avoid violence of any kind.

The whole attempt proved futile, however. As soon as the strikers saw new men swarming like locusts around the entrance to the mill their violent feelings burst out of control. They had expected new hands to show up in batches of fifty or a hundred a day, and had planned to drive them away by persuasion or threats. The sheer number of strikers would be enough to scare the newcomers. Now the whole picture had changed, though. If all these men were employed, there'd be no hope of any compromise with the strikers. They decided to prevent the new recruits from entering the premises, and this could only be done with the use of force. The job-seekers were also prepared to battle to the death, most of them being so starved that they were not about to let anything deprive them of this opportunity. It would be far better to go down struggling than to starve to death or watch their wives and children starve to death.

Fighting broke out. The *Lightning* editor beat a hasty retreat, but poor Mirza was beaten up, and Gobar, trying to protect him, was

346

seriously injured. Mirza was built like a wrestler and adept at self-defence, so he had warded off any dangerous blows. Gobar was a novice, however. He knew all about attacking with sticks and clubs, but he was unfamiliar with defence, which in battle is more important than offence. Bruised all over from countless blows, an arm broken and his head bleeding, every part of him smashed to pieces, Gobar finally collapsed in a heap on the ground. Seeing him fall, most of the strikers fled. Only ten or twelve stalwarts still stood firm around Mirza. The new workers entered the mill in triumph while the defeated strikers began picking up their wounded and carrying them to the hospital. The hospital had no room for so many casualties. Mirza was admitted but Gobar was treated, bandaged up and then sent home.

The sight of Gobar's limp corpse aroused the woman in Jhuniya. Until now she had seen him only as a man of strength who ordered her around, berated her and beat her. Now he was a piteous, helpless cripple. Eyes brimming with tears, she leaned over the cot and gazed at him. Then anger and bitterness welled up in her as she realized their predicament. Gobar knew there was not a pice in the house. Despite that, and despite her repeated warnings, he had brought this calamity on himself. Time and again she had told him to stay out of the fight, that the instigators would start the fire and then stand aside and let the poor people bear the brunt of it. But since when had he ever listened to her? She was an enemy. His friends were those people riding merrily around in their cars now. Her anger was mixed with the kind of satisfaction one feels on seeing a child fall off a chair after repeated warnings not to stand on it. 'Nice going. That's very good. Why didn't you split your head open while you were at it?'

The very next moment, though, when she heard Gobar moan in anguish, trembling seized her and a cry of distress broke from her lips—'Oh God! His whole body has been mangled. No one showed even a speck of mercy.'

She stood for a long time gazing at his face that way, searching with dwindling hope for some sign of life. With each moment her courage sank lower, like the setting sun, and the darkness of the future gradually engulfed her.

All at once Chuhia showed up and called, 'How is Gobar, daughter? I just heard the news and came running from the shop.'

The tears Jhuniya had been restraining suddenly broke loose. Unable to speak, she turned to Chuhia with frightened eyes.

Chuhia examined Gobar's face, felt his heartbeat and then said reassuringly, 'Don't worry. He'll be all right in four days. You're very lucky. The stars of your married life must be very auspicious. A number of men were killed in that fight. Do you have any money on hand?'

Ashamed, Jhuniya shook her head.

'I'll bring some. Get a little milk and warm it up for him.'

Jhuniya clasped Chuhia's feet. 'You're my real mother. I have no other family.'

The gloomy winter twilight seemed ever more bleak than usual that evening. Jhuniya lighted the fire and put the milk on to boil. Chuhia was taking care of the baby out on the veranda.

Suddenly Jhuniya choked out—'I'm an unlucky, ill-omened woman, sister. I have a feeling that I brought all this on him. Inner resentment leads to unhappiness and then to swearing and even to cursing. Who knows but what my curses. . . .' She was unable to go on, her voice lost in a flood of tears.

Chuhia took a corner of her sari and wiped Jhuniya's tears. 'How can you think such things, daughter? The merit of your devotion is what saved him. It is true though that one shouldn't nurse a grudge no matter what's been said during a quarrel. Once a seed takes hold, it's bound to sprout up.'

'What am I to do now, sister?' Jhuniya asked, her voice trembling.

'Nothing at all, my child,' Chuhia assured her. 'Put your trust in God. Only he comes to the aid of the poor.'

Just then Gobar opened his eyes. Seeing Jhuniya standing in front of him, he muttered weakly, 'I got hurt badly today, Jhuniya. I didn't do a thing to anyone. They just beat me up for no reason at all. Forgive me for treating you so badly. I've given you a bad time and this is my punishment for it. I'm not long for this world. There's no hope for me now. The pain's tearing my whole body apart.'

Chuhia came inside and said, 'Lie still and don't talk. You have my guarantee—you're not going to die.'

A ray of hope flashed across Gobar's face. 'You're telling the truth? I'm not going to die?'

'No, you're not going to die. Nothing much happened to you, after all. Just a little cut on the head and a broken arm. Those things happen to people all the time. No one dies from them.'

348

'I'll never strike Jhuniya again.'

'Afraid she might hit you back?'

'I won't do a thing even if she hits me.'

'You'll forget all that once you're well.'

'No, sister, I'll never forget.'

Gobar would lapse into baby-talk and then lose consciousness for five or ten minutes, his mind wandering all over the place. Sometimes he saw himself drowning in a river and Jhuniya wading in to save him. Other times he saw a demon sitting on his chest and a goddess who looked like Jhuniya coming to the rescue. Periodically he would awake with a start and ask, 'You're sure I won't die, Jhuniya?'

He was in this condition for three days, with Jhuniya lying awake at night and watching over him during the day, as though protecting him from death. Chuhia took care of the baby. On the fourth day, Jhuniya hired an ekka and Gobar was taken to the hospital for a check-up. By the time he returned, Gobar was convinced that he would indeed recover.

'Forgive me, Jhuniya,' he said, with tears in his eyes.

They had spent three or four rupees of Chuhia's money during those four days and Jhuniya was reluctant to accept any more from her. Chuhia wasn't rich either, after all. She was giving them the money earned by selling firewood. Finally Jhuniya made up her mind to go to work. It would be months before Gobar was well, and meanwhile they would need money not only for food but also for medicines and things. She could at least make enough to feed the family. Since childhood she had known how to tend cows and to cut grass. There were no cows around here, but she could certainly cut grass. Lots of men and women from that neighbourhood went outside the city to cut grass and earned eight or ten annas a day.

Early in the morning she would help Gobar wash himself and then set off for work, leaving the baby in his care. Ignoring hunger and thirst, she would cut grass until mid-afternoon and then go sell it in the market, reaching home late in the evening. At night she would sleep when Gobar slept and stay awake when he was awake.

Despite all the hard work, Jhuniya was as happy as though she were spending the days singing and rocking on a swing. On the way to work, she would laugh and joke with the other grasscutters, and the banter continued even while they were at work. There was no wailing about fate or fretting about troubles. The joy of leading a useful life, of service voluntarily undertaken, of sacrificing for those she loved, made every part of her sparkle. She felt as though she were a child standing for the first time on its own two feet and clapping with glee, as though some spring of happiness had burst forth within her. And with such mental well-being, physical well-being was bound to follow. Within a month, she seemed completely rejuvenated. Gone was the lethargy in her limbs, the pallor on her cheeks. In their place were vigour and buoyancy and the pink glow of health, as though the youthfulness which had been stifled with insults and acrimony in the confines of that small room had suddenly bloomed as it found light and fresh air. Nothing made her angry any more, and the woman who once got irritated at the slightest whimper of the child now seemed to have endless patience and affection.

Gobar, on the other hand, remained rather morose even though he was getting better. When the onslaught of calamity suddenly makes a man agonizingly aware of his cruelty to a loved one, the awakening of heart and soul makes him eager to atone for his wrongdoing. This desire to make amends was troubling Gobar. He would completely alter his life so that kindness would replace bitterness and humility would replace pride. He realized now that the opportunity to be of service was a great privilege, and he would never again neglect such an opportunity.

CHAPTER 28

———————

MR KHANNA felt that the strike had been completely unjustified. He had always tried to stay in touch with the common people and considered himself one of them. During the last national uprising he had displayed great zeal. The most active leader in the district, he had gone to jail twice and incurred losses amounting to several thousand rupees. He was still prepared to listen to the workers' grievances, but of course he couldn't allow the welfare of the shareholders in the sugar mill to be neglected. He might have been willing to sacrifice his own interests if his lofty ideals had been tapped, but it would be sinful for him not to protect the interests of the shareholders. After all, this was a business, not some charitable institution which should distribute everything to the workers. The shareholders had invested their money with the assurance that it would bring a fifteen or twenty per cent profit. If they failed to get even ten per cent, they would consider the directors—and Mr Khanna in particular—to be swindlers. Compared to directors of other companies, he had already set a low salary for himself—only a thousand a month. He made a little on commissions as well, but those earnings were only fair, since he was running the plant. The labourers worked only with their hands, whereas the director had to use his intelligence, his learning, his genius and his influence. Obviously the two sets of skills could not be priced equally.

The workers should be content to realize that these were slack times and that the growing unemployment everywhere had made labour cheap. Even if their earnings dropped by a quarter, they should still be content. And if the truth were known, of course, they were content. The fault was not theirs. They were just stupid, a bunch of dumb sheep. Onkarnath and Mirza Khurshed were the real villains. It was those people, caught up in their greed for a measly bit of wealth and fame, who were making these poor fools dance like puppets, not stopping to realize how many families would be ruined by their fun.

If sales of Onkarnath's paper were poor, what did Khanna have to do with that? If the circulation hit a hundred thousand today and Onkarnath began making a profit of half a million, would he take just enough to live on and divide the rest among his employees? Fat chance! And that self-sacrificing Mirza Khurshed had once been a millionaire himself, with thousands of men working for him. So did he take just a living wage and distribute the remainder to his employees? On that living wage he had caroused around with European wenches, thrown banquets on every important occasion, drunk up thousands of rupees of liquor a month, and whipped off to France and Switzerland every year. Yet now his heart was breaking over the plight of the workers!

Khanna had lost all sympathy for those two outstanding citizens in his skepticism about their motives. Nor did he care much for the Rai Sahib, who seconded whatever he said and supported whatever he did. Among his acquaintances, the only person he fully trusted to give an unbiased judgment was Dr Mehta. But Khanna's respect for him had been failing considerably as Mehta became more and more friendly with Malti. For years Khanna had thought of Malti as his sweetheart, but he had always looked on her as a kind of plaything. There was no doubt that he was very fond of this plaything, and if it were lost or broken or stolen, he would have wept bitterly. And he had wept, but she was still only a plaything. He had never put much faith in Malti, having been unable to break through the veneer of flippancy and reach her heart. If she herself had proposed marriage to Khanna, he wouldn't have accepted. He'd have found some excuse to stall. Like so many people, Khanna enjoyed—or suffered—a kind of double life. On the one hand he was devoted to sacrifice and public service and benevolence, while on the other, to self-interest and indulgence and status. It would be hard to say which was his true face. Perhaps his higher self was composed of kindness and service while his lower self was made up of selfishness and indulgence. There was constant conflict between the two parts, with the aggressiveness and persistence of the lower self usually overshadowing the gentility and peacefulness of the higher self. The lower leaned toward Malti, the higher toward Mehta, but now the two had coalesced. How an idealist like Mehta could fall for a flighty pleasure-loving doll like Malti was more than he could understand. However hard he tried, he couldn't peg Mehta as a prey to passion, though, which made him wonder if there might be a different side of Malti

352

which he had never discovered—or which he lacked the capacity to discover.

Having considered all the pros and cons, he came to the conclusion that only Mehta could shed some light on the situation.

Dr Mehta had an obsession for work. He'd go to bed at midnight and be up again before daybreak. Somehow or other he found time for everything that came along. Whether it was a hockey game or a university debate, a village aid project or a marriage celebration, he had both the interest and the time. He also wrote for the papers and had almost completed a large book on philosophy which he'd been working on for several years.

Currently he was engaged in a scientific experiment and was busy in the garden testing the effect of electricity on plants. At a recent meeting of scientists, he had shown that with the application of electricity, plants could be made to grow much faster, they could be made to grow larger, and barren plants could even be made productive. These days he was spending two or three hours every morning making these experiments.

On hearing Mr Khanna's report, his face hardened. 'Was it necessary to lower the workers' wages because taxes were imposed? You should have complained to the government. If the government won't listen, does that mean the workers should be punished for it? Do you think they make so much that a quarter cut wouldn't hurt them? Your workers are living in holes—in filthy, stinking holes where you couldn't last even a minute without retching. You wouldn't even wipe your shoes with what they wear for clothes. You wouldn't even feed your dog what they eat. I've been close to them and seen the way they live. You want to snatch away their food and fill the bellies of your shareholders.'

'But all our shareholders aren't rich,' Khanna said impatiently. 'Lots of them have invested everything they possess in this mill and have no means of support other than the profits from it.'

Mehta was unimpressed. 'No one who buys shares in a business is so poverty-stricken that his life can be said to depend on those profits alone. If he makes less profit, he might have to let one servant go, or reduce his butter or fruit bill, but he's not going to starve or go naked. Those who invest their lives have a greater claim than those who spend only their money.'

This was just what Pandit Onkarnath had said, and Mirza Khurshed had also given the same advice. In fact even Govindi herself

M

had sided with the workers. Khanna hadn't cared about those people, but the same thing coming from Mehta's mouth made a strong impression on him. He considered Onkarnath selfish, Mirza Khurshed irresponsible and Govindi unqualified to judge, but Mehta's words were backed by integrity, learning and unselfishness.

'Have you asked your wife her views in the matter?' Mehta inquired suddenly.

Khanna looked embarrassed. 'Yes, I asked her.'

'What was her opinion?'

'The same as yours.'

'That's what I expected. And you probably considered the good woman incapable of judging.'

Malti turned up just then. Seeing Khanna, she said, 'Well, so this is where you are! I've arranged a dinner for Mehtaji today. I've done all the cooking myself. I'm inviting you too. I'll see to it that Govindi forgives you.'

Khanna was intrigued. Had Malti taken to cooking with her own hands—that same Malti who never even put on her shoes by herself, whose life was so easygoing that she never so much as turned off a light herself? 'If you did the cooking,' Khanna said with a smile, 'I'll certainly come and eat. I never dreamed that you were also talented in the culinary arts.'

'This man browbeat me into becoming an expert,' she said without hesitation. 'How could I turn down his commands? Men are gods, after all.'

Khanna winked at Mehta in amusement. 'You didn't used to think men deserved such respect.'

Malti was unabashed by the implication and declared with conviction, 'Well I do now, the reason being that he displays a more attractive image of manhood than I ever saw in my previous circle of acquaintances. A man so attractive, so kind-hearted......'

'Come off it, Malti,' Mehta interrupted with a look of distress. 'Have pity on me or I'll run away from here.'

Malti subjected everyone she met those days to extravagant praise of Mehta, like a new convert going around beating the drum for her new beliefs. Whether it was in good taste was of no concern to her, and poor Mehta had to suffer the consequences. He would listen with pleasure to severe criticism, but listening to his own praises made him look like a fool and he would cringe as though being laughed at. Malti was not a woman to keep things to herself, though. Now, as before, she had to be frank and open both in thought and deed, not knowing how to hold anything back. Just as the possession of a new sari made her anxious to wear it, so the possession of a pleasant emotion made her restless until she could display it.

Stepping closer, Malti put her hand on his back protectively and said, 'All right, don't run away. I won't say anything more. You seem to prefer criticism. All right then, I'll criticize—Khannaji, this gentleman has thrown his net of love over me.'

The chimney of the sugar mill was clearly visible from there. Khanna gazed towards it, his eyes glowing with pride. That chimney rising in the sky was like a tower proclaiming his renown. It was time for him to go to his office. An urgent meeting of the directors must be called so he could explain the situation to them and outline a way of solving the problem.

But what was that smoke rising near the chimney? As he watched, the sky filled with great balloons of smoke. They all gazed apprehensively in that direction. Wasn't that a fire burning? It must be a fire.

Soon they saw thousands of people running toward the mill. 'Where are you people running?' Khanna shouted.

One man stopped and said, 'The sugar mill is on fire, sir. Can't you see?'

Khanna looked at Mehta and Mehta at Khanna. This was no time for sympathy or criticism. No one said a word. In times of crisis, men restrain their emotions. Khanna's car was standing there, so the three anxiously jumped in and raced toward the mill. At the intersection, the whole city seemed to be rushing in that direction. Fire has the magic to draw people. The car could go no further.

'You have fire insurance, don't you?' Mehta asked.

'How could I, brother?' Khanna sighed. 'The papers were just being drawn up. How did I know this disaster was about to strike?'

Abandoning the car, the three of them pushed through the crowd to the mill. A sea of fire was pouring into the sky. Boiling waves pounded one on top of the other, and tongues of flame lashed out as though to devour the sky. Below that blazing ocean billowed smoke so dense it seemed as though pitch-black monsoon clouds had descended. Through the clouds rose towering Himalayan peaks of quivering, seething flame. A crowd of thousands had gathered on the premises, along with the police, the fire brigade, and the service society volunteers, but they were all frozen in the face of the holocaust. The jets shooting up from the fire engines seemed suddenly extinguished when

355

they hit that sea of fire. Bricks were blazing, steel girders were blazing, and streams of molten sugar flowed in all directions. Flames even seemed to be bursting from the ground.

Watching from a distance, Mehta and Khanna were amazed to see so many people standing around observing the spectacle instead of helping to put out the fire, but then they realized that there was nothing to do but watch. To get within fifty yards of the mill would mean risking one's life. Chunks of brick and stone were crashing down, and occasional shifts of wind sent the crowd stampeding back.

Malti, Mehta and Khana stood in the rear of the crowd, unable to decide what to do. How had the fire started? And how had it spread so fast? Had no one seen it earlier? Or had they seen it and not tried to put it out? Questions such as these rose in all their minds, but there was no one to ask. The mill staff must be around, but locating them in that mob would be difficult.

Suddenly there was such a blast of wind that the flames shot downward and leaped out toward the crowd like a tidal wave. People fled in panic, pushing and falling all over each other as though some lion were springing at them. The flames lashed out with renewed vigour like a thousand-headed cobra spitting fire. Countless people were trampled in the confusion. Khanna was knocked flat on his face and Malti was able to keep from falling only by clinging to Mehta with both hands. The three finally took shelter under a tamarind tree near the wall around the factory yard, and Khanna stood staring at the chimney of the mill in a kind of dazed fascination.

'Were you hurt much?' Mehta asked.

Khanna gave no answer and kept staring ahead, his eyes as vacant as a madman's.

Mehta took hold of his hand and spoke up again—'There's no point in our hanging around here. I'm afraid you have been hurt badly. Come on, let's go back.'

Khanna turned to him and began raving, 'I know full well who's behind this deviltry. If this is what makes them happy, then God bless them. I don't care at all, not at all. I don't care at all! If I wanted, I could put up a new mill today. That's right, I could put up a brand new mill. What do those people think I am? The mill didn't make me; I made the mill. And I can build it again. But I'll smash those people who did it to dust. I know all about it. I know every bit of it.'

Disturbed by the look on his face, Mehta said, 'Come on, I'll take you home. You're not well.'

Khanna burst into raucous laughter. 'I'm not well? Just because the mill has burned down? I can open a mill like this in no time. My name is Khanna, Chandra Prakash Khanna! I invested everything I had in this mill. The first mill was bringing me a twenty per cent profit so I was encouraged to open this second one. Half the money in this one was mine. I borrowed two hundred thousand from the bank for it. Not even an hour ago—a half hour ago, I was worth a million rupees. That's right—a million. But now I'm a penniless joker—I'm bankrupt. Two hundred thousand I owe the bank. The house I'm living in is no longer mine. I no longer own even the plates off which I eat. I'll be thrown out of the bank. The Khanna that people used to look at and envy—that Khanna is now smeared in the dust. I no longer have any place in society. I'm no longer an object of confidence to my friends but an object of pity. My enemies will laugh at me instead of envying me. You have no idea, Mr Mehta, how I've sacrificed my principles—how many bribes were given, how many bribes were taken, the kind of men I hired to weigh the farmers' sugar cane, the false weights that were used. But why bother to tell you everything—there's nothing you can do about it. But why should I go on living now that I've brought this misfortune on myself? Whatever's going to happen, let it happen. The world can laugh all it wants; friends can be as sorry as they please; people can curse all they like. Khanna will no longer be alive to see it with his eyes and hear it with his ears. I still have some shame, some decency.' At that he began beating his head with both fists and burst out sobbing.

Mehta put his arm around him. 'Buck up a little, Khannaji. You're smart enough not to take such a narrow view of things. The respect a man gets for being wealthy is only respect for the wealth, not for the man. Even if you're poor, friends can still have faith in you— and enemies too. In fact you won't have any enemies left. Come, let's go home. You'll feel better after a little rest.'

Khanna made no reply. The three of them reached the intersection where the car was waiting and within ten minutes they were at Khanna's house.

Khanna got out and said calmly, 'Please take the car with you. I have no need for it now.'

Mehta and Malti got out also. 'You go lie down and rest,' she said. 'We'll sit here and chat. We're in no hurry to get home.'

Khanna looked at her gratefully and said in a pathetic voice, 'For-

357

give me for the wrong I've done, Malti. You and Mehta are all I have in the world. I only hope you don't lose all respect for me. In five or six days I'll probably have to give up this house too. What a dirty trick fate has played.'

'I'm telling you the truth, Khannaji,' Mehta said. 'I have more respect for you today than ever before.'

The three of them walked in the house. Govindi came into the room as soon as she heard the door. 'Are you all coming from there? The cook brought me the terrible news.'

Khanna's heart was stormed by a longing to fall at her feet and bathe them with tears. 'Yes, dear,' he said thickly, 'we've been ruined.'

His lifeless, despairing, injured soul pined for consolation—for consolation steeped in affection, like an invalid on the brink of death who nevertheless gazes at the doctor with eyes full of hope. The same Govindi whom he had always bullied, whom he had continually insulted, to whom he had been constantly disloyal, whom he had considered a great burden, whose death he had kept longing for, now seemed to be approaching with offerings of courage and hope and blessing. He felt as though paradise lay at her feet, as though the mere touch of her hand on his unlucky head would start the blood circulating again in his lifeless veins. In his feeble state of mind, in his terrible distress, she seemed to be standing there waiting to take him in her arms. When a boat is sinking we cling to the same rocks which earlier looked like treacherous obstacles that must be dislodged and pushed aside.

Govindi had him sit down on a sofa and said tenderly, 'Why are you so disheartened? Because of wealth, the root of all evil? What happiness did that wealth bring us? Just one problem after another from morning till night—ruining our lives. The children dying to talk to you and you getting not even time to drop a line to your relatives. Was there any great honour involved? Yes there was, since the world still goes on worshipping wealth, but it had nothing to do with you. As long as you have money, tails wag in front of you. The next day just as many devotees prostrate themselves at someone else's door without even a glance in your direction. The good man does not bow down to wealth. He looks to see what you are. If you're honest and just, unselfish and diligent, he'll be devoted to you. If not, he'll turn away and become an enemy instead, considering you a plunderer of society. I'm not wrong am I, Mehtaji?'

'Wrong?' Mehta said, as though breaking out of a reverie. 'You're saying just what the world's greatest men have said after experiencing the greatest truths of life. It's the only true basis of existence.'

'Nobody cares who's wealthy,' Govindi said to Mehta. 'Anyone who has the talent to make fools out of everyone.'...'

'No, Govindi,' Mehta interrupted, 'it takes more than talent to make money. It takes inner strength to earn a fortune, and it also takes sacrifice and discipline. The amount of devotion involved would probably be enough to win salvation. Wealth denotes a perfect balance of all our spiritual and intellectual and physical capacities.'

Without opposing Mehta, Govindi took a somewhat milder position. 'I grant that it takes more than a little self-sacrifice to get rich, but it's still not as important a thing in life as we make it out to be. I'm glad this weight is off your head. Now your sons will have a chance to become real men, rather than just models of selfishness and pride. Happiness comes in making others happy, not in looting them. Please don't take it badly if I say that until now your life has been based on self-interest, indulgence and pleasure. God has frustrated those ambitions and opened a way to a higher and purer life. If the process involves some hardship, then welcome it. Why consider it a tragedy? Why not see it as a chance to fight injustice? To my mind it's far better to suffer than to cause suffering. If we can find our souls by losing our fortune, that's not too high a price to pay. Have you forgotten so soon the pride and excitement of battling for justice?'

Govindi's pale parched face glowed with a strange new strength, as though all her quiet devotion was being rewarded. Mehta was eyeing her with reverence. Khanna, head bowed, was trying to think of her as a divine inspiration. And Malti was feeling ashamed of herself. How lofty Govindi's thoughts were, how bighearted she was, and how radiant her life was!

CHAPTER 29

NOHRI was not a woman to practice virtue and let it be ignored. Having done a good deed, she would strain every nerve to drum up all possible credit—and then keep trying for still more. Such people usually end up with a bad reputation instead. There's no disgrace in not doing a good deed. It may lie beyond our interests or abilities, and no one can blame us for that. But to do a good deed and then demand grateful recognition destroys any gratitude and turns the beneficiary into an enemy. Virtue is only virtue when the doer keeps it to himself. Once displayed, it becomes an offence.

Nohri went all around proclaiming, 'That poor Hori was in real trouble. He was about to mortgage his land to pay for his daughter's marriage. I was touched by his predicament. Dhaniya makes me sick. The bitch is so proud she doesn't think her feet should touch the ground. But Hori was wasting away with anxiety. I figured I could be of help. People must look out for their fellowmen after all. And Hori's no outsider. Like it or not, he's related to me now. So I gave him the money. Otherwise the girl would still be left in the lurch.'

This condescension was too much for Dhaniya. 'Was the money charity? Such generosity! The moneylender would have charged interest, and so did she. Big favour! If she had loaned the money to anyone else, they would make off with the interest and with the principal as well. With our taking it, she'll get it back as soon as we make some money. It was we who took the poison from that house and swallowed it without a murmur. No one else would even let her darken their door. We've given her an appearance of respectability.'

It was ten o'clock at night and black August storm clouds wrapped the village in darkness. Hori had finished his after-dinner smoke and was about to go to bed when Bhola appeared at the door.

'What are you doing out, Bhola Mahto?' Hori inquired. 'Since you have to live in this village, why don't you go ahead and build a little house of your own here? Or do you enjoy the ugly tales people are spreading? Don't take me wrong. It's only that we're related now,

360

so I can't stand to see you getting a bad name. Otherwise it would be none of my business.'

Dhaniya came out just then with a pot of water to leave by Hori's bed. After listening a moment, she said, 'Any other man would have chopped the woman's head off.'

'Don't talk nonsense,' Hori protested. 'Set down the water and clear out. If you were suddenly to start misbehaving, would I cut off your head? Would you let me?'

Dhaniya flicked a drop of water at him. 'Let your sisters misbehave. Why should I? I just made a simple statement and you start throwing abuse at me. Well maybe your tongue will be a little more civil now. Anyway, I still don't consider anyone a man who sits around gawking while his wife does whatever she pleases.'

Hori was embarrassed. Bhola had obviously come to pour out his troubles and here she was tearing into him. 'Listen here,' he said heatedly, 'you're no one to talk. All day long you do what your heart desires and there's nothing I can do about it. If I say anything, you fly into a rage.'

Dhaniya had not learned to mince words. 'If a woman knocks over the pot of ghee or even sets the house on fire, a man will put up with her, but no man will tolerate her misbehaving.'

'What you say is quite right, Dhaniya,' Bhola said glumly. 'No doubt I should have chopped off her head, but I don't have that much manhood left. You go talk to her. I've tried everything. Now I've just given up.'

'If you didn't have the strength to keep a woman under control, why did you go and get married? Just so you could be disgraced this way? Did you expect her just to come rub your feet and fill the chilam with tobacco for you and wait on you when you got sick? A woman will do that only if she has shared the joys of youth with you. What I can't understand is how you fell for her at first sight. You might at least have checked to see what she was like, instead of just pouncing on her like a starved jackal. It's your sacred duty now to take an axe and cut off her head. You'll be hanged of course, but hanging would be better than this disgrace.'

Bhola's blood began to stir. 'That's your only advice, then?'

'Yes, that's my advice,' Dhaniya said. 'It's not as though you'll live to be a hundred and fifty anyway. Consider yourself destined to live only this long.'

'Shut up,' Hori burst out. 'You think you're so smart and virtuous.

361

Even a sparrow can't be forced to live in a cage—what more a human being. Just give her up, Bhola. Consider her as dead and go live in peace and comfort with your children. Eat your two meals a day and say your prayers to God. The joys of youth are gone now. With that fickle woman all you'll get is jealousy and disgrace.'

Give up Nohri? Impossible! Even now he could see her eyes flashing at him in fury. But then again—yes, he would leave her. Let her enjoy the fruits of her actions.

Tears came to Bhola's eyes. 'Hori my brother, only I know what misery I've suffered because of this woman. It was on her account that I had the fight with Kamta. And now this humiliation too has fallen on me in old age. She's always taunting me that my daughter ran off. My daughter did run off, but at least she has stuck with her man, sharing his joys and sorrows. As for Nohri, I've never seen a woman like her. With other people she's all smiles; at the sight of me she starts pouting. I'm a poor man, working for three or four annas a day. How can I provide her with milk and curds, meat and fish, sweets and cream?'

Bhola went home vowing that he had let himself be pushed around long enough—he would go live with his sons. The next morning, however, Hori spotted him buying tobacco at Dulari's shop.

Hori thought it best not to call to him. An infatuated man is no longer his own master. Returning home, he said to Dhaniya, 'Bhola's still in the village, right where he was before. Nohri must really have cast some spell over him.'

Dhaniya turned up her nose. 'He's just as shameless as she is. Men like that should go find a puddle and drown themselves. Where has all that blood and thunder disappeared to? When Jhuniya came here, he was chasing around after her with a big stick. His honour had been destroyed. What's become of that honour now?'

Hori was feeling sorry for Bhola. The poor wretch had fallen into the clutches of that slut and was ruining his life, but how could he walk out on her even if he tried? Leaving a woman that way is no simple matter. The witch wouldn't let him rest in peace even if he went back to his sons. She'd sue him for maintenance. So far only the village folks knew about it and no one dared say anything except in whispers, whereas then the whole world would lay the blame on Bhola. What could the helpless woman do, they'd say, when her husband deserted her? When a man's bad, he can only cut his woman's throat. When a woman's bad, she can blacken a man's honour and reputation.

Two months later, word spread in the village one day that Nohri had given Bhola such a shoe-beating that not a hair was left on his head!

The rains were over and preparations were underway for putting in a new crop. With Hori's sugar cane having been auctioned, he had no money for fresh cuttings, so no cane had been planted. On top of that, one of the bullocks had given out, and no work could be done without a new one. One of Puniya's bullocks had been killed by falling into a ditch, which made matters still worse. Puniya's and Hori's fields had to be ploughed on alternate days, and the work naturally suffered.

Hori was in the field behind the plough, but he was worrying about Bhola. In all his life he'd never heard of a wife giving her husband a shoe-beating. In fact, he couldn't recall even a case of a slap or a blow much less a shoe-beating, the supreme humiliation. And here Nohri had beaten Bhola with a shoe while everyone stood around watching the spectacle. That unlucky wretch would never be able to get free of that woman. Now he could only go drown himself somewhere. When life holds nothing but shame and humiliation, a man's better off dead. There was no one to mourn over him. The sons might perform the last rites, but only to avoid public censure. There'd be no tears in anyone's eyes. Well, that just went to show how a man could wreck his life by falling victim to his passions. And why should one be eager for life or afraid of death when there was no one to shed even a tear?

On the one hand there was Nohri and on the other the chamar girl Siliya. Siliya was a thousand times more attractive. If she chose, she could turn on the charm, make enough to feed two people, and have a gay time. Instead, she starved herself doing manual labour and stayed true to Matai while he just ignored her completely. If Dhaniya had died, who knows but what Hori might have been in the same plight as Bhola. The very thought of her dying set Hori's hair on end.

Dhaniya's image rose up in his mind's eye—the heavenly embodiment of service and sacrifice, sharp of tongue but with a heart soft as wax, staking her life on every pice but ready to sacrifice her all to defend the family honour. In her youth she'd been no mean beauty. Nohri was nothing by comparison. Dhaniya had walked like a queen, and once a person saw her he couldn't take his eyes off her. Pateshwari and Jhinguri had been young then. Overcome at the mere sight of her, the two would put their hands on their hearts and hang around outside the door all the time. Hori kept a sharp eye on them, but he had never found any excuse to tell them off. They had really been hard up for food in those days. Frost had struck and the fields had not even produced straw. People were living on wild berries. Hori was forced to work at the famine camp at six pice a day. Dhaniya stayed home all alone, but no one ever saw her even glance at one of those village loafers. One time Pateshwari had teased her a little and he'd still not forgotten the tongue-lashing she gave him in return.

All at once Hori saw Matadin approaching. That butcher! Displaying his caste-marks as though he were God's truest devotee. The painted jackal! Who'd touch the feet of a brahman like that?

Matadin came up and said, 'Your right-hand bullock has grown old, Hori. He'll never last through the irrigating this season. It must be about five years since you bought him.'

Hori patted the bullock's back. 'What do you mean five? It's going on eight years now. I'd like to pension him off, but farmers and farmers' bullocks only get a pension when the god of death provides it. Putting the yoke on his neck breaks my heart. Poor thing must think he'll never get a rest, that I'll even yoke up his skeleton. But I have no choice. How are you doing? You're in good shape now?'

Matadin had been laid up with malaria for the last month. One day his pulse had nearly stopped and he'd been lowered from the bed to the ground as though the end were at hand. Ever since, he had been haunted by the conviction that he was being punished for his cruelty to Siliya. She'd been pregnant when he turned her out of the house. He had shown not the least sympathy, and she had kept working right up to the end of her time. If Dhaniya had not taken pity on her, she'd surely have died. It was a wonder she was still alive after all that suffering. She still wasn't fit to go back to work. Now, full of sympathy and shame, Matadin had come to give Hori two rupees to pass on to her. He'd be deeply grateful if Hori would give her the money.

'Why don't you go give it to her yourself?' Hori said.

'Please don't make me go to her, Hori,' Matadin pleaded. 'How could I face her? And I'm afraid she'd burst into a rage at the sight of me. Just show me this much mercy. I still can hardly walk, but I raced a good mile to get this money from a patron. I've already suffered the consequences of my wrongdoings. This burden of being a brahman has become unbearable. By acting on the sly, one can get away with murder and no one says a word. But do anything in the open and it's a blot on the family name. Please explain to her that she should forgive me. These ties of religion and caste are terribly rigid. We're forced to uphold the traditions of the society in which we're born and raised. In any other caste, a breach of the rules is not particularly serious, but a brahman loses everything if his dharma is violated. It's the one legacy passed on to him by his forefathers. It's the one thing that earns him a living. We've already thrown away three hundred rupees on this purification business. Since I'm still considered polluted by the caste, I might as well do everything openly. A man may have a sacred duty as a member of society but he also has a duty as a human being. Fulfilling one's duty to society brings approval from the community, but fulfilling one's duty to his fellow man is pleasing to God himself.'

When Hori timidly handed the money to Siliya that evening, she acted as though it were a boon rewarding her penance. She had been able to carry the weight of suffering alone, but the weight of happiness now was more than she could bear by herself. To whom could she report the good news? She couldn't discuss her innermost feelings with Dhaniya, and no one else in the village was an intimate friend. Siliya's stomach was churning. Sona had been her one confidante, and she was dying to go see her. She couldn't wait a whole night. A kind of storm was lashing her mind. She was no longer forsaken and homeless. Matadin had again claimed her as his own. The horrible dark chasm yawning ahead had disappeared and in its place was a flowering green meadow in which brooks were singing and deer were frolicking. Her repressed affection now burst forth in a frenzy. How she had inwardly cursed Matadin for all her suffering! Now she would beg his forgiveness. It had been very wrong of her to disgrace him in front of the whole village. She was only a chamar woman and had little to lose. She could be taken back into the caste at any time by just spending ten or twenty rupees on a dinner for its members, whereas poor Matadin's honour had been ruined forever. He could never regain his status or prestige. Rage had blinded her so completely that she'd gone around broadcasting their love affair to everyone. It was not surprising that he'd become angry, what with his dharma defiled, but there had been no reason for her to get angry. It wouldn't have hurt her to return to her own home that day. No one would have tied her up there. People respected Matadin purely because he was so faithful in observing his sacred duties, his dharma. When that dharma was violated, he had every reason to thirst for her blood.

Shortly before, she had been considering Matadin completely at fault, but now she put all the blame on herself. Sympathy had created sympathy. Hugging the baby to her bosom, she covered him with caresses. The sight of him no longer brought shame and remorse. No longer just an object of compassion, he had every right to her full maternal love and pride.

The shimmering October moonlight spread over the earth like sweet music. Siliya stepped out of the house. She would go at once to Sona and pass on the good news. She could no longer hold herself back. The night was still young and there'd be a boat she could catch.

She hurried toward the river, only to find that the boat was on the other side and the boatman nowhere in sight. The moonlight seemed to be dissolving in the river and floating away. She stood there debating for a moment and then waded into the water. The river couldn't be very deep, certainly, and what was this little stream compared to the ocean of happiness surging within her. At first the water reached her knees, then her waist, and finally her neck. She hesitated, afraid lest she hit a hole and drown, but then, taking her life in her hands, she stepped forward. She was out in midstream now, with death dancing ahead of her, but she was not afraid. As a young girl she had often come paddling in this river, and once she had even waded across. Her heart was pounding nevertheless—but then the water began getting shallower. Now there was nothing to worry about. She quickly made it to shore, wrung out her clothes, and proceeded, shivering, on her way. The night was silent and still, broken not even by the cry of jackals. The prospect of seeing Sona gave wings to her feet.

On reaching the village, however, she began having qualms about appearing at Sona's house. What would Mathura say? And what about the rest of the family? Even Sona might be annoyed at her coming so late at night. Village farmers, worn out from a long day's work, go to sleep early. The whole village seemed to have fallen asleep. The door to Mathura's house was closed and she couldn't bring herself to make them open up again. What would people say to see her in such disarray?

The embers of a fire were still glowing out far from the door. Siliya began drying out her clothes. All at once the door opened and Mathura stepped out, calling 'Hey! Who's sitting there by the fire?'

Siliya quickly covered her head and stepped forward. 'It's me, Siliya.'

'Siliya! What are you doing here at this hour? Things are all right at home, aren't they?'

'Yes, everything's fine. I was just feeling restless and thought I'd come see you all. I can't get away during the day.'

'And you waded the river to get here?'

'How else? It wasn't exactly shallow, either.'

Mathura led her inside. The passageway was dark. He caught her hand and pulled her toward him. Siliya snatched away her hand and said indignantly, 'Look here, Mathura, if you get funny I'll tell Sona. You're my younger sister's husband—remember that. One would think you weren't on good terms with Sona.'

Mathura put his arm around her waist. 'You're awfully cruel, Sillo. No one can see us here.'

'Am I prettier than Sona? You should thank your stars for getting such a rare beauty, and here you're letting your mind wander like a bee buzzing off to new pastures. If I were to tell her, she'd refuse to set eyes on you again.'

Mathura was no lecher and he loved Sona, but the darkness and the solitude and Siliya's youthful charm had aroused him for a moment. Her rebuke brought him to his senses. Letting go of her, he said, 'Don't say anything to her, Sillo, I beg of you. Give me any other punishment you wish.'

Siliya felt sorry for him. Slapping him gently on the face, she said, 'Your punishment is this—that you never get fresh with me again, nor with anyone else. Otherwise you'll lose Sona.'

'I swear it'll never happen again, Sillo.'

The pleading in his voice stirred Siliya's heart deeply. 'And if it does.

'Then do whatever you like.'

Siliya's face was close to his, and their breaths and voices and bodies were trembling. Suddenly Sona called out, 'Who are you talking to out there?'

Siliya drew back. Mathura stepped into the courtyard and said, 'Sillo is here, from your village.'

Siliya had trailed him into the courtyard and saw now the com-

367

fort in which Sona was living. On the porch was a cot, covered with a soft mattress just like the one on Matadin's bed. There was a pillow too, and a quilt. Beneath the bed was a jug of water. The moonlight lit up the courtyard like a mirror. In one corner there was a small platform holding a tulsi plant. On the other side, bundles of millet were stacked against the wall. In the middle of the courtyard, straw was stacked and nearby was a hand mortar with the husked rice piled alongside. A lauki vine climbed up over the tile roof on which a number of gourds glistened in the moonlight.

A cow was tethered on the porch across the courtyard. This must be the area where Mathura and Sona slept, Siliya decided, and the rest of the family in some other part of the house. What a happy life Sona must lead.

Meanwhile Sona got up and came out in the courtyard, but she did not rush forward to embrace Siliya. Maybe she felt hesitant with her husband standing there, Siliya thought, or perhaps she'd become too proud now to put her arms around a chamar girl. Siliya's excitement and enthusiasm melted away. This meeting had brought only envy instead of delight.

Sona's complexion had brightened so, and her skin shone like pure gold. Her figure had filled out too, while her face reflected the dignity of a housewife along with the happy radiance of a young girl. Siliya stood for a moment staring as though in a trance. This was that same Sona with the skinny body who used to run all around covered only by rags and tatters, her dishevelled hair untouched by oil for months. Today she was queen of her own household, with a necklace and chain around her neck, gold ornaments in her ears and silver bracelets on her wrists. Her eyelids were darkened with kohl and the part in her hair was marked with vermilion. This was the paradise of Siliya's dreams, and it was not especially pleasing to find that Sona had attained it. And how haughty she was—wouldn't even look at her, where once she would walk with her arm around her as they went to cut grass. She had expected Sona to fall on her neck and cry a little, respectfully offer a seat, give her something to eat, ask thousands of questions about her village and family, and describe the experiences and adventures of her new life from the wedding night on down. Sona's mouth appeared to be sealed, however. Siliya regretted having come at all.

Sona spoke up at last. 'What are you doing out so late at night, Sillo?' she asked gruffly.

368

Siliya struggled to hold back her tears. 'My heart was aching to see you. It's been so long—I thought I'd come pay a visit.'

Sona's voice became still more harsh. 'But when people go to visit someone, they do it during the day, not at this hour.'

Sona obviously resented her coming. Night was her time for the delights of love, and for Siliya to interrupt was like snatching a plate of food from in front of her.

Siliya stared in a daze at the ground below. Why couldn't the earth open up and just swallow her? Such humiliation! In these few years she had already suffered many misfortunes and endured plenty of humiliation, but nothing before had ever cut so deeply into her soul. Raw sugar sealed in a pot inside the house is unharmed no matter how hard the rain pours down, but when it's been spread outside to dry, a single drop of water is enough to ruin it. Siliya had bared her soul, exposing her most tender feelings in the expectation that nectar would rain down from the skies. What rained down was not nectar but poison, penetrating every inch of her being and convulsing her like the sting of a cobra. To go without eating in one's own home is one thing, but better to die than to be thrown out of a public feast. Every moment Siliya remained was as unbearable as though someone were strangling her. Unable to ask any questions, she began to guess what was on Sona's mind, and she longed to escape before that snake lurking in its hole darted out. But how could she escape? What excuse could she give? If only she could fall over dead!

Mathura picked up the key to the store-room so as to get some refreshments for Siliya, but then stood still, wondering whether his duty was to go ahead or to stay with his wife. Meanwhile Siliya hardly dared breathe, as though a sword were dangling over her head.

In Sona's eyes the greatest of all sins was for a man to eye someone's wife or a woman to eye someone's husband. Such an offence was unforgiveable. Other crimes—theft, murder, fraud—were not so horrible. She didn't mind a little joking around if it were done in the open, but even that, she felt, was bad if done on the sly. Since early childhood she had learned to recognize and to evaluate these moral distinctions. When Hori would be late getting home from the market and Dhaniya found out that he'd stopped at Dulari's shop, even if it were just to buy tobacco, she wouldn't speak to him or do her housework for days. On one of those occasions she had even run home to her father's house.

In Sona's case, those feelings had been sharpened still further. They had not been so strong before she was married, but later she had taken them on as though they involved a sacred principle. She'd have felt no pity for such men and women even if they were skinned alive. For her, there was no room for love outside of the marital relationship. Love was what a husband and wife owed to each other, nothing more. Besides, Siliya was related to her as a sister. She had loved and trusted her. And now that same Sillo was betraying her. There must have been some connection between Mathura and her before the marriage. He must have been meeting her on the riverbank or in the fields. That was why she had crossed the river so late at night. If she had not heard them talking, she'd never have known. Evidently he'd figured this was the best time for a rendezvous, when the house was all quiet. She was anxious to find out everything— to know the whole secret so as to figure out some way of protecting herself. Why was Mathura just standing there? Was he trying to prevent her from speaking up?

'Why don't you go outside?' she said sharply. 'Or do you intend to keep standing guard over us?'

Mathura left without a word, terrified lest Sillo divulge everything. And Sillo stood there terrified that the sword hanging overhead was about to fall.

'Look here, Sillo,' Sona said somberly, 'you'd better come clean now or I'll slash my throat right here in front of you with that sickle. Then you can become his second wife and reign supreme. The sickle's right over there—look and see. A single sheath can't hold two swords.'

Dashing into the courtyard, she picked up the sickle and said, 'Don't think this is just an empty threat. When I'm angry there's no telling what I might do. Let's have the full truth now.'

Siliya began quaking. Every word of the conversation rolled out as though a phonograph were playing. With that grim, bloodthirsty determination playing across Sona's face, she could hold nothing back.

Sona's eyes pierced like spears and her voice had the thrust of a dagger. 'You're telling it straight?'

'Absolutely. I swear by my child.'

'You've not hidden anything?'

'May I be struck blind if I've hidden the least detail.'

'Why didn't you give that wretch a good kick? Why didn't you bite him and drink his blood? Why didn't you scream?'

Siliya had no answer.

Sona was like a madwoman, her eyes flashing like red-hot coals. 'Why don't you speak up? Why didn't you bite off his nose? Why didn't you strangle him with both hands? Then I'd have bowed my head to your feet. As it is, you're just a prostitute in my eyes—a common whore. If you were going to do this, why did you go and blacken Matadin's name? Why didn't you get someone to keep you? Why didn't you go back to your own home that day? That was what your family wanted. You could have kept on selling dungcakes and grass in the bazaar and brought back money so your father could sit back and spend it on toddy. But why cause the brahman to be insulted and his honour ruined, while you put on an act of being so pure and noble? If you can't live alone, why don't you get married —or go drown yourself somewhere? Why do you have to go poisoning other people's lives? I'm warning you—if this sort of thing happens again and I find out about it, not one of us three will be left alive. That's all I have to say. Now take your filthy face and get out. As of today, any connection between you and me is finished.'

Siliya rose slowly to her feet and steadied herself. She felt as though her back were broken. She tried to summon her courage, but could find no words to clear herself. Her eyes were shrouded in darkness, her head was reeling, and her throat had gone dry. Her whole body was as numb as though life itself were escaping from every pore. Setting one foot before the other as hesitantly as though on the brink of a pit, she went outside and headed toward the river.

Mathura was standing at the door. 'Where are you going at this hour, Sillo?'

She gave no answer and Mathura asked nothing more.

The same silvery moonlight covered the earth, its rays still bathing in the ripples on the river. And Siliya, wading across, was like a shadow in a dream, distraught and broken.

371

CHAPTER 30

THE mill had burned down almost completely, but Mr. Khanna applied all his energies to having it rebuilt. Although the strike was still in effect, the mill owners were no longer incurring any particular loss on account of it. New employees had been hired at lower wages and were working their heads off, since all of them had suffered the distress of unemployment and were anxious now to avoid anything that might jeopardize their livelihood. No matter how heavy the work or how long the hours, they made no complaints, working along with their heads bowed as meekly as bullocks. Threats, curses, even beatings aroused no resentment, and the previous workers now had no alternative but to come grovelling to Khanna and beg for work at the reduced rates.

They no longer had an ounce of confidence in Pandit Onkarnath. If they could have encountered him alone, they would probably have given him a good going-over, but the pandit kept out of their way. He never stirred out of his office after dark, and he began buttering up the police officials. Mirza Khurshed's standing with the workers was as high as before, but he could see no way of easing their misery. Although he was concerned to get them all reinstated, he was also aware of the new employees' difficulties, and those seeking advice were told to do whatever they felt best.

Observing the strikers' eagerness to return to work, Mr Khanna became more arrogant than ever, though he secretly hoped to get back the oldtimers at the new rates. However hard the new men slaved, they could not work as well as the experienced hands. Most of the older men had worked in the mill ever since childhood and were highly skilled. Most of the new recruits were peasants in trouble who had come in from the villages. Used to working with primitive wooden tools in the open fields and fresh air, they felt suffocated in a factory and were afraid of the fast-moving machines.

Once the strikers were thoroughly subdued and helpless, Khanna finally agreed to take them back. However, the new men were now prepared to work for even less money, so the directors had to decide whether to reinstate the old workers or retain the new. Half the directors favoured retaining the newcomers at reduced wages, while the other half wanted to hire back the oldtimers at the current rates. True, it would cost a little more, but that would be overweighed by the increased production.

Khanna was the nucleus of the mill, a kind of lord of lords with the directors mere puppets in his hands. The decision lay with him alone, but he sought advice in the matter from both enemies and friends. The first person he consulted was Govindi. Ever since Khanna had lost hope with Malti, and once Govindi had become aware of the respect in which she was held by a man as learned, experienced and wise as Mehta, and aware of the kind of faith he had in her resources, love had revived between the husband and wife. Perhaps love is not quite the right word, but certainly there was companionship now. The mutual jealousy and antagonism were gone and the wall between them had given way.

Malti's behaviour had undergone a drastic change also as a result of Mehta's influence. Until now Mehta had spent most of his time in study and meditation. After trying everything and carefully investigating various schools of philosophy, he had concluded that the path of service, lying between those of activity and inactivity, was the only thing that could make life meaningful, that could elevate and ennoble it. He did not believe in any omniscient God, but he made no display of that disbelief since he felt himself unable to hold any conclusive position in the matter. He had become firmly convinced, however, that birth and death, happiness and sorrow, sin and virtue were not ordained by God. He believed that man in his conceit had given himself such airs as to attribute the inspiration for everything he did to God. By that kind of reasoning, even locusts could place the responsibility on God when their path led into the sea and they were destroyed by the billions. But if the ordinances of God were so incomprehensible as to be beyond the understanding of man, then what satisfaction could men get by professing faith in them? The only reason Mehta could accept for a belief in God was the oneness of mankind. He viewed belief in a single soul or in an all-pervading soul or in non-violence from an earthly rather than a spiritual point of view. Although these views had never been supreme at any time in history, they had nevertheless played a very significant part in man's cultural development.

Mehta did not feel that his firm faith in the oneness of humanity necessitated a belief in God. His love for man was not based on the existence of a soul only in living beings. As for dualism and non-dualism, he saw these as useless concepts unless they had practical significance, and for him that practical significance meant bringing human beings closer to one another, destroying their prejudices and strengthening their sense of brotherhood. This oneness, this insepar-ability, was so firmly rooted in him that he felt it unnecessary to create any spiritual support for his position.

Having once discovered this truth, he could no longer rest in peace. It had become necessary for him to act without self-interest as much as possible. Otherwise his mind could not be at ease. Feelings of glory, of greed, or of fulfilling obligations never entered his head. Their meanness was enough to save him from them. Service itself was becoming a matter of self-interest to him, and these benevolent instincts of his were unwittingly having an effect even on Malti.

All the men she had met previously had encouraged her sensual instincts, and any inclination to service and sacrifice had been wasting away until it was revived by the contact with Mehta. This feeling remains hidden in the human consciousness until, touched by light, it suddenly sparkles to the surface. If a man is caught up with wealth and fame, one can assume that he has not yet come in contact with any pure soul. Malti would often make sick-calls in poor families without charging fees now, and there was a new tenderness in her behaviour toward patients. True, she could not yet fully turn her mind away from frills and gaiety—to give up powder and rouge seemed more difficult for her than inner transformation.

The two of them would sometimes go out in the country and visit with the villagers, spending the evening in their huts, eating their type of food, and considering themselves blessed. One day they reached Semari, and then in wandering around happened to pass through Belari.

Hori was sitting in his doorway having a smoke when Malti and Mehta walked up. Mehta recognized Hori immediately and said, 'Is this your village? Remember, we came to the Rai Sahib's place and you were acting as the gardener in the play about Rama's breaking the bow.'

Hori placed them immediately and was about to go get some chairs from Pateshwari's house.

'There's no need for chairs,' Mehta said. 'We'll sit here on the cot.

374

We've not come to sit around on chairs but to learn something from you.'

The two sat down on the cot while Hori stood there dumbfounded, wondering how he could entertain these people properly. They were highclass folks, and he had nothing suitable to offer them.

'Can I at least get you some water?' he asked finally.

'Fine,' Mehta said. 'We are a bit thirsty.'

'May I bring something sweet too?'

'All right, if you happen to have something on hand.'

Hori disappeared into the house, at which point the children of the village clustered around the newcomers and began staring as though these were strange creatures escaped from a zoo.

Siliya, carrying the baby, was heading off on an errand, but on seeing these guests, she stopped in her tracks, overcome with curiosity.

Malti took the child in her arms and began fondling it. 'How old is he?'

Siliya was not sure, but another woman spoke up. 'Must be about a year, isn't he?'

Siliya nodded.

'He's a lovely baby,' Malti said and then added playfully, 'May I have him?'

Siliya swelled with pride. 'He's all yours.'

'Then shall I take him with me?'

'Go ahead. He'll become a fine man if you bring him up.'

Some other women of the village had appeared, and they took Malti inside Hori's house since they were not free to talk with her in front of the men. Malti saw that a cot had been set out, covered with a cotton pad borrowed from Pateshwari's house. Seating herself there, she got to talking about baby care and child raising, while the women listened attentively.

'How can we have all that cleanliness and discipline here, ma'am?' Dhaniya inquired. 'There's not even any provision for food.'

Malti explained that cleanliness cost only a little effort and ingenuity.

'How do you know about all these things, ma'am?' Dulari asked. 'You're not even married yet.'

Malti smiled. 'How did you know I'm not married?'

The women hid their faces and giggled.

'As if that's any secret. Miss,' Dhaniya said. 'Just a look at your face gives it away.'

Malti blushed. 'I've remained unmarried in order to be of service to you people.'

'Bless you, bless you,' the women chorused.

Siliya began massaging Malti's feet. 'You must be tired, ma'am, having come such a long way.'

Malti drew back her foot. 'No, please, I'm not tired. I came here by car. I'd like you to bring your children so I can look at them and let you know how to keep them strong and healthy.'

In no time some twenty children had arrived and Malti began examining them. Several had inflamed eyes, which she treated with drops. Most of them were weak, being born of undernourished parents. Malti was surprised to discover that few families got any milk and that years went by without even the sight of ghee.

Malti explained the importance of diet as she did in all the villages. She felt disturbed and angry at the villagers for not eating decent food. Were they born only to work themselves to death and yet be unable to eat what they'd grown themselves? When there was food for a pair of bullocks or two, why wasn't there straw enough for cows or buffaloes? Why did they think of food only as a physical necessity and not as the most crucial thing in life? Why didn't they ask the government for loans at nominal interest rates and escape the exorbitant clutches of the moneylenders? Everyone she talked to said that most of his earnings went to pay off debts to the moneylenders. The disease of splitting land holdings was also on the increase. There was so much mutual animosity that brothers were seldom able to live together. Narrow-mindedness and selfishness accounted for a great deal of this misery of theirs.

Malti went on discussing these matters with the women, and their concern strengthened her desire to be of service. In comparison with this life of dedication, that life of indulgence seemed empty and artificial, and she began feeling embarrassed about her perfumed body, her powdered face, and her silk clothes with their gold embroidery. The gold watch on her wrist seemed to be staring at her with unblinking eyes, and the jewel-studded necklace glittering at her throat seemed to be choking her. Confronted by these devoted and selfless women, she felt herself to be petty and small. She knew a lot more than these villagers, being more aware of what was happening in the world, but she wondered whether she could live for even a day under the conditions in which these poor women were making a meaningful life for themselves. With no trace of pride, they worked all day, went without food, wept, and still looked so cheerful. They had made others so much a part of themselves as to lose all awareness of their own existence except as it was found in their children, their husbands and their relatives. Nurturing such sentiments—enlarging the scope of such sentiments—would create an ideal of womanhood in the future. Considering the self-centredness which had replaced such feelings in the awakened women—everything for one's self and one's own enjoyment—they'd have done better just to remain asleep. Men were heartless, granted; but they were the sons of those mothers. Why was it that women didn't teach their sons to show reverence for mothers and for all women? Was it because the mothers had completely effaced themselves, losing all individuality, and didn't know how to give such instruction?

No, self-negation was not the answer. In order to benefit society, women would have to defend their rights in the same way that these farmers had to sacrifice some of their saintliness to defend their lives.

It was evening, but the women still crowded around Malti as though they could never be satiated with her words. Some of them urged her to spend the night there, and Malti was so touched by their open affection that she accepted the invitation. After dark the women would sing their village songs for her. Meanwhile she made good use of her time by visiting each family and acquainting herself with its circumstances. To the simple village women, her sincerity and sympathy appeared as nothing less than the blessing of a goddess.

Meanwhile, Mehta was settled on the cot watching the village men wrestling, and regretting that he'd not brought Mirza along to join in a bout. It seemed surprising to him that educated people could be so cruel toward these innocent overgrown children. The learned man, like the ignorant, is simple and guileless, a dreamer of golden dreams, having a faith in humanity so firm, so vital, that he considers behaviour directed against humanity as inhuman. He forgets that the wolf has always answered the innocence of the lamb with teeth and claws. Having created his own ideal world, he populates it with ideal people and becomes absorbed in it. Reality is so inaccessible, so incomprehensible, so unnatural, that it becomes difficult for him to think about it. Sitting there in the midst of these simple peasants, Mehta was trying to solve the problem of why their condition was so pitiful. He hadn't the heart to face up to the fact that their saintliness itself was responsible for their misery. Would that they were less saintly and more human, so they wouldn't be kicked around

377

so. No matter what happened in the country—even revolution itself —they remained unconcerned, willing to bow before any faction that came on the scene backed by force. Their meekness had reached a point of inertia from which only some great shock could arouse them to action. It was as though their souls had lost all hope, leaving them inwardly broken—as though their awareness of existence itself had dissolved.

Now that it was evening, the people who had been working in the fields were also hurrying home. Mehta saw Malti holding a baby in her lap, as involved with the village women as though she were one of them. His heart pounded with delight. In a way she had dedicated herself to him. He no longer had any doubts about that, but Malti had not yet aroused the intense emotions in him without which a proposal of marriage would be ridiculous. She had come and stood at his door like an uninvited guest and he had welcomed her gladly. It was not a question of love but simply of human decency. If Malti thought him worthy of her favour, he could hardly refuse it. Besides, he wanted to get her out of Govindi's way and knew she would not take a second step until her first foot was firmly established. He knew that he was revealing his own baseness by leading her on, and his conscience constantly reproached him.

The more he saw of Malti, however, the more he felt attracted to her. Only virtue, not beauty, could be attractive enough to affect him. He knew that true love could develop only after people were bound in marriage. Any prior love was only infatuation with beauty, having no permanence. But he first had to make sure that the stone which he hoped to put on the lathe and carve into a companion had the necessary potential. Not all stones can be shaped into beautiful statues. Malti had been pouring her rays into the various parts of his being, but previously they had not focused enough to burst into a blaze engulfing his whole being. Today, however, Malti's mixing with the village women and trying to erase their prejudices seemed to have brought those rays into focus, and today for the first time Mehta felt completely at one with her.

As soon as Malti returned from her tour of the village, he suggested a walk over by the river. It was decided that they would stay over-night. Malti didn't know why her heart was pounding so, but she detected a strange new radiance and interest in Mehta's face.

A carpet of moonlight was spread over the river bank, and the jewel-studded river sang softly as it danced before the branches which, heavy with sleep, bowed with their heads toward the moon and stars. Mehta became almost intoxicated under the stimulation of this natural splendour. It was as though his childhood had returned with all its delights. Suddenly he somersaulted on the sand and then ran into the water up to his knees.

'Don't stand there in the water,' Malti said. 'You wouldn't want to catch cold.'

'I feel like swimming over to the other side,' Mehta replied, splashing the water around.

'No, please, come out of the water. I won't allow you to go.'

'Won't you come with me—to the deserted place where dreams hold sway?'

'I don't know how to swim.'

'All right, come on—we'll build a boat and sail over.'

He came out of the water. A forest of tamarisk trees stretched far into the distance. Mehta took a knife from his pocket and cut a stack of small branches. Climbing a nearby ridge, he cut down a bunch of reeds and then sat on the carpet of sand and began braiding a rope out of them, as happy as though preparing for an ascent to heaven. His fingers were soon cut and bleeding. Malti, upset, kept urging that they return to the village, but he paid no attention, being as enthusiastic, unconcerned and stubborn as a child. All his philosophy and learning had been swept away in the stream.

The rope was ready. A sizeable platform was constructed of branches and bound at both ends with the reeds. The holes were stuffed with twigs to keep out the water, and the raft was ready. The night had become even more dreamlike.

Mehta pushed the raft into the water and caught hold of Malti's hand. 'Come sit down.'

'Will it hold two people?' she asked dubiously.

Mehta smiled philosophically. 'Is the boat we're taking through life any more substantial than this? Are you afraid?'

'What's there to be afraid of when you're along?'

'You really mean that?'

'So far I've conquered all obstacles without anyone's help, but now I'm teamed up with you.'

They sat on the raft and Mehta pushed off with a long pole. Rocking from side to side, the raft started down the river.

To distract her mind from the danger, Malti asked, 'How come you're so familiar with village life when you've always lived in the city? I could never have made a boat like this.'

Mehta looked at her lovingly. 'Maybe I inherited it from a previous birth. Contact with nature gives me new life. Every vein starts throbbing. Each bird, each animal seems to be inviting me to share its happiness, as though reminding me of some forgotten joys. Nothing else could give me this kind of pleasure, Malti—neither the mournful tones of music nor the lofty flights of philosophy. It's like finding myself again, like a bird returning to its nest.'

The raft bobbed along, sometimes going straight, sometimes sideways, sometimes in a circle.

'And don't I ever play a part in your life?' Malti asked timidly.

Mehta took her hand. 'You certainly do. You come into it again and again—like a fragrant breeze, like the shadow of a thought which then vanishes. I rush to catch you in my snare, but you disappear leaving me empty-handed.'

'Have you ever considered the reason for that?' Malti said passionately. 'Have you tried to understand?'

'Yes, Malti. I've thought about it a lot. Over and over I've thought about it.'

'Well, what did you discover?'

'Only that the foundation on which I want to build the house of my life is a shaky one. It's no great mansion—just a peaceful little cottage—but even that needs a firm foundation.'

Acting indignant, Malti snatched away her hand. 'That's a false insinuation. You've always viewed me with the eyes of an examiner, never with the eyes of a lover. Don't you even know that a woman wants to be loved, not tested? A test can turn virtues into vices and beauty into ugliness. Love turns vices into virtues and ugliness into beauty. I loved you, and I could never have dreamed that you had any faults; but you've been testing me, and having concluded that I'm unstable, fickle and goodness knows what else, you've kept your distance. No, let me finish what I want to say. Why am I unstable and fickle? Because I've not had the love to make me stable and steadfast. If you had given me the kind of dedication which I've given you, you wouldn't be making those insinuations about me now.'

Capitalizing on her indignation, Mehta said, 'Haven't you ever tested me? Tell me the truth.'

'Never.'

'Then that was your mistake.'

380

'I don't care if it was.'

'Now don't get sentimental, Malti. Before giving our love, we all test each other, and you did too, even if it was done subconsciously. To be frank—I first looked at you as I look at thousands of women, with a desire only for amusement, and unless I'm mistaken, you considered me just a new toy for your diversion too.'

'That's not true,' she interrupted. 'I never looked at you that way. I made you my idol that very first day, and my heart. . . .'

'There's that sentimentality again,' Mehta broke in. 'I don't like sentimentality in matters of such importance. If you thought me worthy of such favour the very first day, it could only have been because I'm more clever than you at putting on an appearance. Insofar as I've seen what women are like, they carefully scrutinize anything involving love. Even in the old days, women tested their suitors in *swayamvara* contests, didn't they? The same mentality exists today, even if its form has changed. Ever since our meeting I've tried to reveal myself to you completely and come close to you in spirit. And as I've reached down into your inner depths, I've found only pure jewels. I came only to be amused but I became a devotee. What you found in me, I have no idea.'

They had reached the far shore. Getting out, they sat on the sand and Mehta took up where he had left off. 'So that's what I brought you here to ask.'

Malti's voice was trembling. 'Do you have to ask me that right now?'

'Yes, because I'm going to show you a side of myself today that you may not have seen since I've been keeping it hidden. All right— what if I were to marry you and then turn around and be unfaithful? How would you punish me?'

Malti gave him a puzzled look. 'What makes you ask a question like that?'

'It's of great importance to me.'

'I don't believe a situation like that would be possible.'

'In this world nothing's impossible. The greatest saints may suddenly become corrupt.'

'I'd look for the cause and eliminate it.'

'Suppose I couldn't break the habit.'

'Then I can't say what I'd do. Maybe I'd take poison.'

'If you were to ask me that question, I'd give you a different answer.'

Malti looked dubious. 'Tell me.'

'First I'd kill you and then myself,' Mehta said firmly.

Malti let out a roar of laughter which covered the shiver that suddenly ran through her.

'Why do you laugh?' Mehta asked.

'Because you don't strike me as being that violent.'

'No, Malti, in this matter I'm a pure animal, and I see no reason to be ashamed of it. Spiritual love and sacrificial love and selfless love, where a man effaces himself and lives only for his beloved—happy only in her happiness, laying himself at her feet—are absurd as far as I'm concerned. I've read love stories where a man gives up his life because his sweetheart has some new lover, but I could only call that devotion or dedication. I could never call it love. Love's not a meek and gentle cow. It's a ferocious lion, which lets nothing set eye on its prey.'

'If love's a ferocious lion,' Malti said, looking him in the eye, 'then I'll keep my distance from it. I've always thought of it as a cow. I consider love to be above suspicion—a thing of the spirit, not the body. It has no room for the least suspicion, and violence is just a result of suspicion. Love means complete self-surrender. You can obtain blessings in its temple only by becoming a worshipper, not an inspector.'

She got up and walked quickly toward the river, as though having just found the path that she had lost. Never had she felt such a flood of emotion. Even in the independence of her life she had felt a certain vulnerability which kept making her restless and disturbed. Her heart seemed to have been searching for some refuge with the strength to support her and enable her to face the world. She had found no such strength within herself. Seeing the power of intelligence and character had made her mouth water, but she was like a liquid having no shape of its own and assuming the form of one container after another.

Until now her mentality had been that of a student preparing for examinations. A student may love books, but he concentrates mostly on the sections which might appear on the test. His primary concern is to pass the examination; the acquisition of knowledge is secondary. If he finds out that the examiner is very lenient, or blind, and passes all the students automatically, he may never even glance at a book. All Malti's actions had been aimed at pleasing Mehta, in the hope of winning his confidence and his love and becoming the queen of his heart's domain. Like a student, however, she would first have to convince him that she was deserving. She lacked the confidence that the examiner would be automatically satisfied when her merits came to light.

Today it was as though Mehta had given her a swift kick and aroused her latent strength. She had been attracted to Mehta ever since she first saw him. Of all her acquaintances, he seemed to have the most depth, leading a pure life in which the sparkle of intelligence and the strength of conviction predominated. Wealth and glory meant no more to him than the toys which a child plays with and then carelessly discards. Even beauty had no particular attraction for him, although he hated ugliness. Only strength of mind could win over this man whose support could awaken her self-confidence, stimulate her development, instill strength in her, and give meaning to her life. Mehta's inner strength and lustre had put its stamp on her, and this was her passport to a better life. She had received the inspiration she needed, and in a subconscious way it had been giving her strength and momentum. She had been trying to draw the new ideal closer to herself, and feeling a sense of success, had been dreaming of the day when she and Mehta would become one—a dream which had been making her still more dedicated and resolute.

Today, however, when Mehta had led her hopes right to the brink and then had presented an ideal of love stripped from any context of spirituality and dedication, knocking it down to an earthly plane governed by suspicion and jealousy and indulgence, her noble sentiments had been badly wounded. Her devotion to Mehta was as jolted as though she were a disciple who had caught her master doing something wicked. She saw that Mehta's brilliance of mind was tugging his view of love in the direction of bestiality, leading him blindly away from her concept of the ideal, and her heart sank at the sight.

'Come on,' said Mehta, somewhat embarrassed. 'Let's sit here a little longer.'

'No,' Malti replied, 'we must go back. It's getting late.'

CHAPTER 31

THE Rai Sahib's star was at its height. Three great ambitions had been fulfilled. His daughter's marriage had been celebrated in grand style, he had won the lawsuit, and he had not only won the election but had been appointed Home Minister. Congratulations were pouring in from all sides and there was a stream of telegrams. By winning the case, he had reached the highest rank of zamindars. Not that he had commanded less respect than anyone else previously, but its roots were now deeper and stronger. A succession of photographs and character-sketches began appearing in the daily papers. His debts had multiplied greatly, but he was no longer concerned. He could get out of debt by just selling a small piece of the new property. The good fortune was exceeding his wildest dreams.

Previously his only house had been in Lucknow. Now it became necessary to acquire houses in three other places—Naini Tal, Mussoorie and Simla. It would detract from his new glory to visit those places and stay at a hotel or at some other raja's mansion. When Surya Pratap Singh had homes in all those cities, it was a matter of shame to the Rai Sahib not to have the same. Fortunately he was spared the bother of construction. Houses were already available and he acquired them at low cost. A gardener, a watchman, an overseer and a cook were hired for each one.

The supreme good fortune, however, came on the occasion of His Majesty's birthday, when the title of Raja was bestowed on him. His highest aspiration was now satisfied. The day was celebrated with grand festivities including a feast so magnificent that all records were shattered. At the ceremony when His Excellency the Governor officially conferred the title on him, he was drowned in such a wave of pride and patriotism that his whole body tingled. This was living! How pointless it had been to fall in with a bunch of rebels and get a bad name—going to jail and dropping out of favour with the officials. The Deputy Superintendent of Police, who had once arrested him, now stood by quietly, perhaps hoping to be forgiven for his offence.

But the greatest triumph of his life came when his vanquished enemy, Raja Surya Pratap Singh, sent a message offering his daughter in marriage to the Rai Sahib's eldest son, Rudrapal Singh. Neither winning the election nor becoming a minister had brought the Rai Sahib such delight. Those were things of which he had dreamed, whereas this was something beyond his wildest dreams. That same Surya Pratap Singh who for months had considered him lower than his dog now wanted to marry his daughter into the family! Incredible!

The Rai Sahib, in Naini Tal at the time the offer was made, almost burst with pride. Although he had no desire to apply any kind of pressure on the boy in regard to marriage, he was confident that Rudrapal would not create a fuss over any decision reached by his father. Besides, the chance to become a relative of Raja Surya Pratap Singh was such a stroke of good fortune that the possibility of his son's rejecting it never entered the Rai Sahib's mind. He immediately accepted the offer and phoned his son. Rudrapal was currently working for an M.A.—a fearless, completely idealistic, self-confident proud, passionate and lazy young man who disliked his father's greed for wealth and fame.

'I don't accept,' Rudrapal replied.

Never had the Rai Sahib been more disappointed or angry. 'There's some reason?' he asked.

'You'll find out when the time comes.'

'I want to know right now.'

'I don't wish to say.'

'You must obey my order.'

'I can't accept your order in a matter unacceptable to my conscience.'

'Son,' the Rai Sahib explained gently, 'you're only putting the axe to your own feet by pursuing this idealism. Have you stopped to realize the high position in society this union will give you? Think of it as inspired by God. I'd have thanked my lucky stars to get just a penniless girl from that family, and here this is the very daughter of Raja Surya Pratap, our prince himself. I see her every day, and you must have seen her too. I've never seen another young woman with such beauty, such talent, such character and such a disposition. My days are numbered, but your whole life lies before

N

you. I don't want to put pressure on you. You know how broad-minded I am on the question of marriage, but it's also my sacred duty to warn you if I see you making a mistake.'

'I made up my mind on this matter long ago,' Rudrapal replied. 'It can't be changed now.'

The boy's obstinancy made the Rai Sahib furious again. 'You seem to have lost your head,' he roared. 'Come and see me without delay. I've already given my word to the Raja Sahib.'

'Sorry, I have no time at present,' came the response.

The next day the Rai Sahib himself arrived in Lucknow. Both had their weapons ready as they confronted each other. On one side stood a lifetime of experience in settling disputes; on the other, raw idealism —stubborn, aggressive and unrelenting.

The Rai Sahib struck directly for the heart. 'I want to know who the girl is.'

'If you're so curious, I'll tell you,' the boy said calmly. 'It's Malti's sister, Saroj.'

'So she's the one!' The Rai Sahib fell back wounded.

'You've surely seen her, haven't you?'

'Plenty of times. Have you seen the Raja's daughter?'

'Yes, plenty of times.'

'And still. . . .'

'I don't believe looks mean a thing.'

'I pity your stupidity. You know the kind of woman Malti is? Could her sister be any different?'

Rudrapal scowled. 'I'd rather not discuss this matter any further with you; but if I get married, it will be to Saroj.'

'Not while I'm alive it won't.'

'Then it'll be after you've gone.'

'Oh, so those are your intentions!'

The Rai Sahib's eyes filled with tears. His whole life seemed devastated. The ministry, the estate and the title would be as meaningless and joyless as withered flowers. The attainments of a lifetime had become worthless. Being no more than thirty-six when his wife had passed away, he could have remarried and enjoyed the pleasures of life. Everyone had urged him to remarry, but he had looked at the faces of his children and accepted the dedication of a widower's life, sacrificing sensual pleasures for the sake of these children. All this time he'd kept pouring out his whole love on them; but now that this boy was talking as callously as though they were not even related, why should he work himself to death over property and honour and power? He'd been doing all this just for the boy's sake, but why lead a life of self-denial when the boy hadn't the slightest regard for him? He was not long for this world, and he too knew how to take things easy. Thousands of his friends just twirled their whiskers and went around enjoying themselves. Why shouldn't he do the same? He momentarily forgot that the dedicated life he'd been leading was not for the sake of the children but for himself—not just for the sake of prestige but because he was a man of action who had to work in order to live. Becoming a libertine and an idler could never have satisfied his soul, but he was unaware that some people by their very nature cannot accept the indolence of self-indulgence. They are born to work their hearts out, and they go on working their hearts out until their dying breath.

The blow produced an instantaneous response. Even if we don't look for recompense from the object of our sacrifice and devotion, we do expect to have some control over the person's feelings. That control may be intended for the welfare of the other person, but his welfare means so much to us that it becomes not his welfare but our own. The more we sacrifice, the stronger the desire for domination; and when we are suddenly faced with rebellion, we become frustrated and that dedication changes to retaliation. The Rai Sahib had resolved that Rudrapal should not be allowed to marry Saroj even if it meant taking help from the police or doing violence to his own principles.

As though drawing a sword, he said, 'Yes, it'll take place only when I'm gone and that's going to be a long time from now.'

'May God help you to live forever,' Rudrapal fired back. 'I'm already married to Saroj.'

'That's a lie.'

'Absolutely not. I have the evidence to prove it.'

The Rai Sahib fell wounded. Never had he eyed an adversary with such a thirst for blood. An enemy could at most have injured his interests or his body or his prestige, but this injury hit the vital point where his whole life-impulse was centred. It was a gale that had torn up his life by the roots. He was totally disabled and helpless, helpless though he held all the power of the police in his hands. The use of force was to have been his ultimate weapon, but that weapon had now dropped from his hand. Rudrapal was of age and so was Saroj. And Rudrapal was the owner of his own estate, so the Rai Sahib had no power over him. If he'd only known that this wretch was going to rebel against him, he'd never have fought for that new property. Over a quarter million had been wasted on the legal manoeuvring. Life itself had been wasted. Now, however, he could only spare himself humiliation by flattering the brat. The slightest opposition, and his honour would be dragged in the dust. Despite this lifetime of sacrifice, he was still not the boy's master. His whole life had been wasted. His whole life!

Rudrapal had left. The Rai Sahib ordered his car and set off to see Mehta. If Mehta were willing, he could convince Malti, and Saroj could not disregard her. Even if it took fifteen or twenty thousand rupees to stop this marriage, he was prepared to pay it. Obsessed with his own stake in the matter, it never occurred to him that he was about to make a proposal to Mehta in which the man's sympathies could never be on his side.

After hearing the whole story, Mehta began to kid him along. 'Why, this is a question of your prestige,' he declared, pulling a long face.

The Rai Sahib didn't catch on. 'That's right,' he said, jumping up, 'It's a purely a matter of prestige. You know Raja Surya Pratap Singh, don't you?'

'Yes, and I've seen his daughter too. Saroj isn't equal to the dust on her feet.'

'But this stupid kid has gone off his head.'

'Then to hell with him. There's nothing you can do about it. He'll regret it himself.'

'Ah, but that's exactly what I can't bear to see, Mehtaji. One doesn't just toss away a chance for prestige. I'm prepared to sacrifice half my estate for this honour. If you convince Malti Devi, everything can be worked out. If Saroj backs out, Rudrapal will be left beating his breast and in a few days this madness will go away of its own accord. It's just a crazy fancy—has nothing to do with love.'

'But Malti won't agree without some sort of bribe.'

'I'll give her anything you say. If she wants, I'll make her head of the Dufferin Hospital here.'

'Suppose she wants you! Would you be willing? Her opinion of you must have changed now that you've become a minister.'

The Rai Sahib glanced at Mehta's face and saw the hint of a smile. Catching on, he said in a pained voice, 'So even you find this a good chance to make fun of me. The reason I came to you was that I expected you to think over my situation and give me some good advice. And instead, you go making fun of me. A person with good teeth knows nothing about toothaches.'

'Forgive me,' Mehta said soberly. 'I'd feel silly to take seriously the kind of question you've raised. You can be responsible for your own marriage, but why take responsibility for your son's marriage, especially when he's of age and can weigh the advantages and disadvantages himself? I for one don't feel that prestige has any place in matters as important as marriage. If prestige were a matter of wealth, then the Raja Sahib wouldn't stand humbly in front of that naked holyman. As it is, he even bows to the police inspector of his area. Is that what you call prestige? Mention his name to any shopkeeper, any official, any passerby in Lucknow. All they'll do is curse when they hear it. Is that what you call prestige? Just go home and relax. You'd have real trouble finding a daughter-in-law as good as Saroj.'

'But she's a sister to that Malti,' the Rai Sahib said in distress.

'And what's wrong with being a sister to Malti?' Mehta said hotly. 'You've never really known Malti nor have you cared to know her. I felt that way too, but now I realize that she's genuine gold which glows when it's put in a fire. She's one of those stalwarts who show their excellence when the occasion arises, rather than going around brandishing their swords all the time. Are you aware of Khanna's circumstances these days?'

The Rai Sahib nodded sympathetically. 'Yes, I've heard. Many a time I've wanted to go see him, but I couldn't get away. That fire in the mill has completely ruined him.'

'That's right. In a way he's living off the kindness of friends. On top of that, Govindi has been sick for months. She sacrificed herself for Khanna, that beast who was always tormenting her. Now she's dying, and Malti sits by her all night—that same Malti who wouldn't stay all night even with a raja who'd pay her a doctor's fee of five hundred rupees. She also has the burden of looking after Khanna's young children. I don't know where those motherly feelings were hiding. Seeing that side of her, I began to feel respect for her, though I'm terribly phlegmatic as you know. As she became purified inwardly, a saintly glow began brightening her face. I've been discovering at first hand how many-sided and how capable human beings really are. If you'd like to see her, come along. That'll give me an excuse to go too.'

'When even you can't understand my troubles,' the Rai Sahib said skeptically, 'how could Malti Devi? I'll just be embarrassed for no reason. But why do you need an excuse to go there? I thought she'd been caught in your spell.'

'That's become only a dream now,' Mehta said with a regretful smile. 'I never even see her any more. She doesn't have the time. I went three or four times, but I realized she wasn't happy to see me, so I've been hesitant to return. Oh, thank goodness I remembered. The ladies' gymnasium is having a programme today. Will you come along?'

'No,' the Rai Sahib said disinterestedly, 'I haven't the time. I'm preoccupied with concern over what reply to give the Raja. I already gave him my word.'

With that he got up and walked slowly toward the door. The problem he'd come to solve had become even more complicated. The gloom had grown deeper. Mehta went as far as the car and saw him off.

The Rai Sahib went straight home and had just picked up the daily paper when Mr Tankha's card was brought in. He despised Tankha and had no desire to see even his face, but in this debilitated state of mind, he was looking for someone to sympathize. The man might be incapable of anything else, but he could at least show sympathy. The Rai Sahib called him in immediately.

Tankha came tiptoeing into the room with a mournful look on his face. Bowing all the way to the floor, he said, 'I was just leaving for Naini Tal in order to see your honour. By good fortune I've met you here. Your honour is in good health?'

At that he began singing the praises of the Rai Sahib in elegant language, completely forgetting his previous behaviour. 'How could there ever be such a great Home Minister? Everyone in town is talking about your honour. The position gives fitting splendour to you, your honour.'

What a sly rascal, the Rai Sahib was thinking. Willing to call a donkey 'grandfather' in order to gain his ends, whereas previously he had been a first-class traitor with not an ounce of shame. He felt pity for the man rather than anger, however. 'What are you doing these days?' he asked.

'Nothing, your honour. I'm unemployed. That's why I was coming to wait upon you, in the hope that you might still glance with favour on your old servants. I'm in great difficulty these days, your honour. You know Raja Surya Pratap Singh of course. He thinks no one's as good as he is. He began criticizing you one day. I couldn't stand it.

I told him to stop, that you were my lord and I wouldn't hear any aspersions on you. At that he got furious. I bade him goodbye brusquely and left the house. I told him point-blank that no matter how much pomp and show he put on, he could never obtain the honour and prestige which is yours—that prestige and honour come from worth, not from ostentation, and that the whole world knows how worthy you are.'

The Rai Sahib acted amazed. 'Well, you really let him have it!'

'Your honour,' Tankha strutted, 'I always speak up plainly, whether people like it or not. Why should I be afraid of anyone when I have your feet to cling to? He gets upset just hearing your name. All the time saying nasty things about your honour. He's had a snake in his bosom ever since you became a minister. My whole source of income was completely swallowed up. He doesn't know how to give anything. I can't tell you how he mistreats his tenants. No one's honour is safe. Every day the women wail as he....'

A car roared up and Raja Surya Pratap Singh alighted. The Rai Sahib came out of the room and greeted him. 'I was just about to come pay my respects to you,' the Rai Sahib said, bowing with the weight of gratitude for this great honour. This was the first time that the Raja had graced his house with his presence. Such good fortune!

Mr Tankha sat there looking like a drowned cat. The Raja Sahib —here! Had these two somehow become friends? He'd hoped to fan the Rai Sahib's jealousy and then warm his hands on the fire. Well, it was one thing for the Raja Sahib to come; but the seething in their hearts was not going to be extinguished just by plastering over the surface like a potter would do.

Lighting a cigar, the Raja Sahib looked sternly at Tankha and said, 'You never even show your face these days, Mr Tankha. You collected all the money for that banquet from me and then never paid a single pice to the hotel people. They're getting on my neck about it. I consider this a breach of faith. If I want, I could turn you over to the police right now.'

Turning to the Rai Sahib, he declared, 'I've never seen anyone so dishonest. I'm telling you the truth—I'd never have run against you, but this devil misled me and wasted a hundred thousand rupees of mine. Bought himself a bungalow, the scoundrel, and a car too. He's even carrying on an affair with a prostitute. A regular man of wealth he's become, and now he's starting to be a double-crosser. A rich man has to have some means of support to sustain his splendour. This fellow supports himself by throwing dust in the eyes of his friends.'

The Rai Sahib looked contemptuously at Tankha. 'Why are you so quiet, Mr Tankha? Speak up. The Raja Sahib has held back the reward for all your labours, has he? Have you anything to say in defence? Please get out now, and take care you don't show your face here again. The business of instigating fights between two gentlemen to serve your own interests takes no investment of capital. But remember, either a gain or a loss endangers your life.'

Tankha, his head drooping as though he would never be able to raise it again, slipped away like a stray dog sneaking out of a house when the owner shows up.

When he had gone, the Raja Sahib said, 'He must have been talking against me. Right?'

'Yes, but I made a fool of him in the process.'

'He's a devil.'

'Absolutely.'

'He'd start trouble between a father and son or between a husband and wife. He's a past master of that game. Anyway, the wretch got a proper lesson today.'

The conversation then turned to Rudrapal's marriage. The Rai Sahib froze as though a gun were being aimed at him. There was no place to hide. How could he admit having no power over the boy any longer? The Raja Sahib had already learned the situation, though, so the Rai Sahib was spared the need to say anything.

'How did you manage to find out the news?'

'Rudrapal just recently sent my daughter a letter, which she passed on to me.'

'The young men these days have no other virtue but this craze for independence that's taken hold of them.'

'It's a craze all right, but I have the remedy for it. I'll have that slut whisked away where he'll never locate her. Just a week or ten days and the craze will wear off. Mere persuasion won't do any good.'

The Rai Sahib trembled. A similar idea had occurred to him, but he had not let it take shape. The two men had similar backgrounds and there was something of the cave dweller in them both, but the Rai Sahib kept those tendencies hidden from view while in the Raja Sahib they were completely exposed. This opportunity to prove his expansiveness was more than the Rai Sahib could resist. Acting somewhat shocked, he said, 'But this is the twentieth century, not the twelfth. I can't say how Rudrapal would react, but from the point of view of human decency. . . .'

'You get all carried away about human decency,' the Raja Sahib interrupted, 'and don't realize that in the world today man's bestiality is winning out over his humanity. Why are there wars otherwise? Why aren't matters settled through peaceful means such as village councils? As long as man exists, his bestiality will continue to express itself.'

A mild argument ensued and a stalemate was finally reached on the marriage question, at which the Raja Sahib got angry and left. The next day the Rai Sahib departed for Naini Tal, and a day later Rudrapal left for England with Saroj. The two men were no longer related as father and son but as adversaries. Mr Tankha now became Rudrapal's supporter and adviser. He filed suit on Rudrapal's behalf against the Rai Sahib for a settling of accounts, and a million-rupee judgment was issued against the Rai Sahib. What hurt the Rai Sahib was not so much the judgment as the disgrace. What hurt even more than the disgrace was the collapse of a lifetime's longings, and what hurt most of all was that his own son had double-crossed him. Any pride in having an obedient son had been snatched ruthlessly away from him.

But his cup of misery was evidently not full yet. What deficiency remained was completed by the severing of relations between his daughter and her husband. Minakshi, as mute as the average Hindu girl, had gone away with the man to whom her father had married her; but there was no love between husband and wife. Digvijay Singh was a libertine and an alcoholic. Minakshi pined inwardly and tried to divert her thoughts through books and magazines. Digvijay was not more than thirty, and educated too, but he was full of pride— always bragging about his family's status—and cruel and stingy by nature. He kept chasing after the low-caste women of the village, married or unmarried, and made alliances with the worst of them, their flattery making him all the more egotistical. Minakshi had been unable to feel any respect for such a man. In addition, her eyes had begun opening as she read in the papers about women's rights. She started attending the Women's Club, where there were so many ladies from distinguished and educated families. There was lots of talk amongst them about voting and rights, freedom and female enlightenment, as though they were creating some deadly weapon to use against the men. Most of the women were ones who didn't get along

N*

with their husbands, who had received a modern education and as a result wanted to break down ancient traditions. There were also several young ladies who had earned college degrees and now, considering married life a destroyer of self-respect, were searching for jobs. One of these was a Miss Sultana, who had returned after being admitted to the bar in England and was now employed in giving legal advice to women kept in seclusion.

At her suggestion, Minakshi filed suit against her husband for separate maintenance. She no longer wanted to live in his house. She had no real need for the money, since she could have gone to live comfortably in her family home; but she wanted to blacken the reputation of her husband before she left. Digvijay Singh in return filed charges of immorality against her. The Rai Sahib had tried his best to keep the squabble hushed up, but now Minakshi didn't ever want to see her husband's face again. Although his suit was dismissed and she was awarded separate maintenance, the insult of his charges stuck in her throat. She was living in a house of her own and taking an important part in social reform movements, but the fires of resentment continued to smoulder.

One day, whip in hand, she went in a fury to Digvijay's bungalow. A ribald bunch was gathered there and a prostitute was dancing. Descending like the warlike Kali on this assembly of filthy devils, she poured out chaos and destruction. Lashed by the whip, people ran in every direction, base creatures helpless in the face of her fury. When only Digvijay remained, she took the whip to him until he fell unconscious.

Meanwhile the prostitute had been huddling in a corner. Now it was her turn. Minakshi raised the whip and was about to strike when the girl fell weeping at her feet and cried, 'Please spare my life this once. I'll never come here again. I'm innocent.'

Minakshi eyed her with loathing. 'Sure you're innocent. Do you realize who I am? Get out and never come here again. We women are all just pawns of men's pleasure. That's no fault of yours.'

Her forehead touching Minakshi's feet, the girl said, 'God grant you happiness. Everything I've heard about you is true.'

'What do you mean by happiness?'

'Whatever you think, maharani.'

'No, you tell me.'

The prostitute's blood turned cold. Why had she gone and blessed the woman? Her life had been spared and she should have gone quietly

394

on her way, but instead she'd had the crazy idea of invoking a blessing. How could she save herself now?

'I mean,' she said fearfully, 'may your grace's good fortune increase. May your fame spread.'

Minakshi smiled. 'All right, that's fine.'

Getting in her car, she drove to the house of the district officer, reported the affair, and then returned home. Both husband and wife had been out for blood ever since. Digvijay Singh went around with a revolver, keeping an eye out for her, and she hired a couple of wrestlers to guard her wherever she went.

The Rai Sahib saw the blissful heaven he'd created tumbling now about his feet. Weary of the world, he withdrew more and more into himself. Previously his life had been inspired by dreams and ambitions. With the closing of that door, his mind leaned automatically toward devotion, toward a truth greater than personal desires. The new estate, on whose security he had been borrowing money, had slipped out of his hands without covering the loans, and these were now piled onto his head. True, he was getting a good salary as a minister, but every bit of that disappeared in just maintaining an appropriate standard of living.

In order to support his regal luxury, therefore, the Rai Sahib was forced to levy new assessments on his tenants, forfeit their holdings, and give and take bribes, much as he hated to do so. He had no desire to cause his people trouble, and he felt sorry for their condition, but he was caught up by personal necessity. The difficulty was that he found no peace even in worship and devotion. He wanted to let go of worldly desires, but worldly desires would not let go of him, and in the struggle he could not escape humiliation, remorse and unrest. And when the soul is not at peace, the body can not remain healthy. Despite all precautions against illness, one affliction or another was always getting hold of him. All kinds of delicacies were prepared in the kitchen, but for him there was only the same bland diet. He saw some of his fellows who were more indebted and disgraced and distressed than he suffering no lack of pleasures or of fancy living, but that kind of shamelessness was beyond him. The lofty traditions embedded in his mind had not been destroyed. His conscience could not satisfy itself by claiming that cruelty, deceit, effrontery and oppression were the source of a zamindar's power and glory—and this was his greatest failing.

CHAPTER 32

When Mirza Khurshed got out of the hospital, he started up a new business. It was not in his nature just to sit around idly. And what was the business? Forming a theatrical troupe of the city's prostitutes. In his better days he'd been quite a rake, and during the solitary days in the hospital, suffering from his injuries, his penitent soul had become inspired about religious obligations. Recalling that past life filled him with anguish. If he'd had more sense, how philanthropic he could have been toward others, how many people's sorrow and poverty he could have eased; but he'd thrown away his wealth in riotous living.

It's no new discovery that our souls become awakened in times of crisis. In old age everyone regrets the follies of his youth. If only that time had been spent acquiring knowledge or strength, in building up a wealth of meritorious deeds, what peace of mind there would be now. The agonizing realization had come to Mirza that he had no one in the world to call his own, no one who would even shed a tear at his death. An incident out of his distant past came slowly back to mind. . . .

In a camp at a village near Basra, where he'd been down with an attack of malaria, a village girl had looked after him with unlimited devotion. After he recovered, when he'd wanted to repay her kindness with money and jewellery, her eyes had filled with tears and, head lowered, she had refused the gifts. Hospital nurses were disciplined, systematic and sincere in their services, but where was the love, the total involvement which there had been in the unskilled ministrations of that inexperienced girl? That image of affectionate dedication had before long disappeared from his heart, and, despite his promise to return, he had never gone back to see her. Intoxicated by pleasures, he had never even thought of her again. Even now, when he did so, it was only with pity, not love. Anything might have happened to the girl since then. Recently, however, her disturbed, tender, peaceful and simple face kept appearing before his eyes. How rich his life would be if only he had married her. His regret for the wrong done to her turned all people of her social class now into objects worthy of his sympathies and services. As long as the river had been in flood, rays of light were deflected in its swift and muddy foaming current. Now that the flow was calm and peaceful, the rays were penetrating to the very bottom of the river:

One cool spring evening Mirza Sahib was sitting on the veranda of his cottage talking with two ladies of easy virtue when Mr Mehta showed up. Mirza shook hands warmly and said, 'I was just waiting for you, with everything for your entertainment.'

The two lovelies smiled. Mehta blushed.

Mirza signalled the women to leave and offered Mehta a comfortable seat. 'I was just about to come see you myself. It's been dawning on me that I can't accomplish the job I'm setting out to do unless I have your help. Just keep slapping me on the back and telling me "That's right, Mirza old man, keep going." '

Mehta laughed. 'You won't need help from a bookworm like me for anything you set out to do. You're older than I am and you've really seen the world. If I had the power to influence every single person the way you do, God knows what all I might have accomplished.'

Mirza Sahib gave a brief description of his new scheme. It was his conviction that the only women who ended up in the red-light district were either ones who for some reason could not get support and respect at home, or ones who were compelled by economic necessity. So if these two problems could be resolved, few women would stoop so low.

Mehta, like other thoughtful men, had speculated a lot about this question and it was his opinion that inborn tendencies and lustful cravings were chiefly responsible for drawing women in that direction. A lively debate on the matter broke out between the two friends, each holding firm to his position.

Mehta waved a clenched fist in the air. 'You've not reflected on this question dispassionately. There are lots of other ways to earn one's daily bread, but bread doesn't satisfy the hunger for luxury. For that you need the best the world can offer. This kind of dance troupe won't be of any value unless the social system is transformed from top to bottom.'

Mirza twirled the ends of his moustache. 'Well I still say it's purely a matter of earning a living. The problem's not the same for everyone of course. For the labourer, it's just a question of the bare necessities—flour and dal and a straw hut. For a lawyer, it's a matter of a car and a big bungalow and servants. A man doesn't want mere bread—he'd like a number of other things too. And if the question also takes different shapes in the case of women, then what fault is it of theirs?'

If Dr Mehta had reflected for a moment, he'd have realized that there was no real difference of opinion between the two of them— that they were just quibbling over words. In the heat of argument, however, there is no time for reflection. 'Excuse me, Mirza Sahib,' he said hotly, 'but as long as there are rich men in the world there'll also be prostitutes. Even if your troupe succeeds—and I doubt that very much—you won't be able to use more than a handful of women, and those only for a few days. Not all women can perform on the stage, just as not all men can become poets. And even assuming that the women stay with your company permanently, their places in the red-light district aren't going to remain empty. Trimming off the leaves won't accomplish anything. You have to put an axe to the roots. Occasionally some wealthy person turns up who sacrifices everything and devotes himself to God, but wealth goes on ruling as firmly as ever. It's not weakened one bit.'

Mirza was pained at Mehta's obstinacy. What a way for such a well-educated thinking man to talk! The social system couldn't very well be overhauled. That would take centuries. Meanwhile was this perversity to be allowed to continue? Was it to go on unhindered, leaving these helpless women at the mercy of men's lust? Why not lock up a lion in a cage so that even though he still had teeth and claws, they wouldn't bring harm to anyone? What point was there in sitting back quietly and waiting for the lion to take a vow of non-violence? Rich men could throw their money around any other way they pleased, for all Mirza cared. Let them drown themselves in drink, hang necklaces of cars around their necks, erect forts, build pilgrim resthouses or mosques—that was no concern of his, as long as they didn't corrupt the lives of defenceless women. That was the one thing he couldn't tolerate. He'd have the red-light district so cleaned out that the rich men wouldn't find anyone even to spit on their gold sovereigns. At the time the liquor shops were being picketed, hadn't even the worst drunkards contented themselves with water?

Mehta laughed at Mirza's stupidity. 'You surely know that in countries where there are no prostitutes, the wealth of the rich still creates ways of satisfying their inner cravings.'

Now it was Mirza's turn to laugh. 'I know, my good friend, I know. I've been fortunate enough to see the world. But this is India, not Europe.'

'Human nature is much the same the world over.'

'But keep in mind also that each culture has something which can be called its essence, its soul. And the soul of Indian civilization is its purity, its chastity.'

'Now that's really blowing your own horn!'

Mehta calmed down and said gently, 'I supported Khanna once he was free from the clutches of wealth, and you'd feel sorry for him too if you were to see his condition these days. Anyway, what help could I give him when I get no time away from my books and the university? The most I can give is just feeble sympathy. Miss Malti's the one who has really helped him. She's been his salvation. I never knew how much dedication and sacrifice was hidden in the depths of the human heart. You should go see Khanna some day. He'd be overjoyed. What he needs most these days is sympathy.'

'Since you say so, I'll go,' Mirza said somewhat reluctantly. 'I couldn't refuse even if you told me to go to hell. But weren't you and Miss Malti planning to get married? That was the latest news as I heard it.'

'I'm devoting myself to austerities and penance,' Mehta blushed. 'We'll have to wait and see when the blessing will come.'

'Come now. She was dying for you.'

'I was under that illusion too, but when I reached out to take her, I found her up in the clouds. I could never reach those heights, so I'm hoping and praying that she'll come down to earth again. She's not even speaking to me these days.'

At that Mehta let out a melancholy laugh and rose to his feet.

'When will I see you again?' Mirza asked.

'You'll have to take the trouble of visiting me the next time. Be sure to go see Khanna though.'

'I will.'

Mirza watched out the window as Mehta left. He was walking slowly, as though drowned in worries.

399

CHAPTER 33

DR MEHTA had now become an examinee rather than an examiner. With Malti so distant, he began to fear that he might lose her completely. For several months she had not come to see him, and when he finally got so anxious that he went to her place, he was unable to meet her. When Rudrapal and Saroj were courting, Malti had come seeking his advice once or twice a day, but she stopped coming after they left for England. It was hard to find her at home. She seemed to be avoiding him, as though wanting to force him out of her mind. The book on which he was working those days was refusing to make any progress, as he seemed to have lost all power of concentration. He'd never been very good at taking care of household matters. All together he was earning more than a thousand rupees a month, but not a pice was going into savings. All he ate was dal and chapaties. The only ostentation was his car, and he drove that himself. Some of the money went for books, some for charity, some for scholarships to needy students and some for embellishing his garden, for which he had a special passion. Ordering and raising all kinds of expensive plants and vegetables from abroad was his great indulgence—or perhaps it should be called his great lust. However, in the last few months he'd been neglecting even the garden, and his house was in worse shape than ever. Eating almost nothing and spending over a hundred on it! His achkan was wearing out but he made do with it all through the severe winter. To get a new one made would be beyond his means. At times he had to do without ghee in his dal. He couldn't even remember when he had last bought a tin of ghee, and he couldn't very well ask the cook lest he feel he was being distrusted.

When he finally managed to meet Malti on the fourth try, she observed the condition he was in and couldn't stand it. 'Are you going to spend the whole winter this way? Aren't you ashamed to wear that achkan?' Although not his wife, she felt so close to him that the question came out as naturally as though addressed to one of her own family.

'What can I do about it, Malti?' Mehta declared without embarrassment. 'There's never any money left over.'

Malti looked surprised. 'You earn over a thousand and yet you can't even afford to have some clothes made? My income's never more than four hundred, but I run the whole household on it and still have some to spare. So what do you do with it all?'

'I don't spend even a pice unnecessarily. I've no desire for luxuries anyway.'

'All right. Take some money from me and have a couple of achkans made up.'

'I'll have some made soon,' Mehta said apologetically. 'Believe me I will.'

'If you're going to come here, then come looking like a man.'

'That's a very harsh condition.'

'So it is harsh. It takes harshness to get anywhere with people like you.'

His cash box was empty, however, and he didn't have the courage to ask for credit anywhere. How could he face Malti again though? He was left in a state of agitation, and then one day a new calamity struck. For several months he had not paid the house rent, and that seventy-five rupees a month kept adding up. When the landlord, despite all his efforts, was unable to collect his money, he finally served notice. But a notice is no magic formula that can suddenly produce money. The deadline expired and there was still no payment. So the landlord was forced to file suit. He knew that Mehta was a respectable gentleman and a kind man, but how much more courtesy could he extend, having already allowed the matter to slide for six months? Mehta did not contest the case at all, an *ex parte* decree was granted, and the landlord immediately set out to have it enforced. Meanwhile the bailiff came to give Mehta advance warning, since his son was studying at the university and was one of the people to whom Mehta was giving some scholarship money.

Malti happened to be visiting Mehta at the time. 'What sort of decree is this?' she asked. 'What's the problem?'

'It's about the eviction notice that's been issued,' the bailiff explained. 'I thought I should pass on the information. It's a matter of four or five hundred rupees—no great amount. If you pay it off within ten days, there'll be no problem even now. I can stall the landlord for that long.'

When the bailiff had gone, Malti spoke up scornfully. 'Well, so it has come down to this! I'm amazed at the way you can write such fat books whereas with six months' rent overdue you're not even aware of it.'

Mehta hung his head. 'Certainly I'm aware of it, but I haven't the money—and I don't waste even a pice.'

'Do you keep any written accounts?'

'Of course I keep accounts. Everything I earn gets recorded. Otherwise the income tax people would be on my neck.'

'And what about the money you spend?'

'Well I don't keep track of that.'

'Why not?'

'Why write it down? Seems like a great nuisance.'

'And how do you turn out these volumes?'

'That takes no special effort. I just sit down with a pen. But the account book isn't lying around open all the time.'

'Then how are you going to pay the money?'

'I'll get a loan somewhere. If you have the money, please let me have some.'

'I can give it to you on one condition—that you put all your earnings in my hands and let me do all the spending too.'

'Great!' Mehta beamed. 'If you'll take that burden on yourself, who am I to refuse? I'll beat the drums in celebration.'

Malti paid off the decree and the very next day compelled Mehta to vacate his bungalow, giving him a couple of large rooms at her place. Arrangements for his food and so forth were also made with her family. Mehta didn't have much in the way of possessions, but he did have several cartloads of books which filled up his two rooms. Leaving his garden did make him unhappy, but Malti turned over her whole yard for him to put in whatever flowers and shrubs he liked.

Mehta was now carefree, but Malti was faced with great difficulty in organizing his finances. She found that the income was actually more than a thousand rupees but that it was all being taken up in secret charities. Some twenty-five students were getting scholarships to the university from him, and an equal number of widows were also getting aid. How to reduce these expenditures was more than she could figure. All the blame would fall on her head; all the infamy would be hers. Sometimes she became irritated at Mehta, sometimes at herself, and sometimes at the recipients, who felt no shame or hesitation in dumping their burdens on this simple-hearted generous person. And the irritation grew as she realized that some of the people receiving aid did not deserve it. One day she finally took Mehta to task over it.

After listening to her charges, he said casually, 'The power is all yours. Give to anyone you wish and refuse anyone you wish. There's no need to consult me. Of course you'll have to answer for it.'

'Yes of course,' she twitted. 'You take all the credit and give me all the blame. I don't understand what logic you could use to justify this practice of charity. It's this tradition which has made man so lazy and parasitic and has damaged his self-esteem more than any oppression could have. In fact I believe oppression has done society a big favour by arousing man's rebelliousness.'

'I believe that too,' Mehta nodded.

'You do not.'

'No, Malti, I'm telling you the truth.'

'Then why such a gap between belief and practice?'

The third month, Malti disappointed a lot of people. To some she gave a straight answer, to some she suggested jobs, and others she berated.

Mr Mehta's budget gradually straightened out, but he felt a certain remorse in the process. When Malti displayed a saving of three hundred rupees that third month, he said nothing, but his estimation of her certainly dropped somewhat. Women were supposed to be generous and sacrificial. That was their greatest virtue, the foundation which upheld society. He considered business acumen only a necessary evil.

When Mehta's new achkans and a new wristwatch arrived, he stayed home several days, ashamed to go out. Nothing seemed worse to him than self-indulgence.

The curious thing was that although Malti wanted to restrict him financially to close off the door of his generosity, she nevertheless gave extravagantly of herself—of her time and magnanimity. She always collected fees from the rich, but she examined the poor without charge and even gave out free medicines. The only difference between them was that Malti cared both for her home and for the outside world, whereas Mehta cared only about those outside. For him, home had no meaning. Both were trying to wipe out selfish individuality. Mehta's path was clear—he had to answer only to himself. For Malti the path was more difficult. She had responsibilities and ties which she could not break and did not wish to break. It was those ties which gave inspiration to her life. Now that she could observe Mehta at close quarters, she realized that this free spirit, accustomed to wondering loose in the jungle, could not be shut up in a cage. If she were to confine him, he'd rush around biting and scratching. Even if he were given everything for his comfort and happiness in the cage, his spirit would always keep yearning for the jungle. For Mehta, the world of home and family was an unknown world with whose forms and ceremonies he had no acquaintance.

Mehta had viewed the world as an outsider and had believed it full of hypocrisy and duplicity. No matter where he had looked, something unpleasant came to view. As he penetrated the depths of human society, however, he had come to see that below the unpleasantness there was sacrifice, there was love, there was courage and there was endurance. But he also saw that these virtues, however real, were rare; and in the midst of this doubt and suspicion, when Malti had appeared to him out of the darkness in the form of a goddess, he had lost all patience and restraint, wanting immediately to conceal her in such a way that no one else could even set eyes on her, forgetting that this fascination is the very root of destruction. Could a thing as relentless as love be kept bound by fear? It needs complete confidence, complete freedom, complete trust and responsibility. The power of germination lying within it needs light and space. It is not some kind of wall on which bricks are to be piled. There is life in it, an unlimited power to expand and unfold.

Ever since Mehta moved into this bungalow, he had been getting to see Malti several times a day. His friends assumed that this was leading up to marriage, the only delay being a deference to custom. Mehta was caught up in the same vision. If Malti had shoved him aside for good, why would she be showing him so much affection? She was probably giving him time to think things over; and after much thought, he'd reached the conclusion that without her he was only half a man. Only she could lead him to fulfillment. On the surface she was a voluptuary, and there was a core of those hedonistic feelings within her, but the situation had changed. At first Malti had been the eager one; now Mehta was dying of eagerness. Having once received an answer from her, he lacked the courage to ask her that question again, though he no longer felt any shadow of doubt about her feelings. Seeing Malti at such close range, he found himself more and more attracted to her, like the letters on a page which at a distance appear blurred and smudged but up close become clear, revealing a meaning, a message.

Meanwhile Malti had hired Gobar as a gardener. She had been driving back from seeing a patient one day when her car ran out of petrol. It was nine o'clock on a cold January night and she could think of nowhere to get petrol. The streets were silent and there was no one in sight who might push the car to a gas station. 'That lazy good-for-nothing servant!' she swore. 'Just lies around in a stupor.'

Just then Gobar happened by. Seeing Malti standing there, he realized what had occurred and pushed the car a quarter of a mile to the nearest station. Pleased, Malti asked if he'd like a job, and Gobar accepted gratefully. A salary of fifteen rupees a month was agreed on. Gardening was a job he liked and knew well. The wages at the mill had been better, but the work there had been a strain on him.

He started work at Malti's place the next day. He was also given a cubbyhole in which to live, so Jhuniya moved in too. When Malti would go into the garden, she'd find their little boy playing in the dirt. One day she gave him a sweet and from then on the child was won over. At the sight of her, he'd toddle up and keep following her until he'd been given the sweet.

One day the boy failed to show up when she went to the garden. Inquiring of Jhuniya, she found out he'd caught a fever.

'A fever!' Malti exclaimed. 'Then why didn't you bring him to me? Come, I'll take a look.'

The boy lay unconscious on a small cot. The tile-roofed room was so damp, so dark and, despite the cold weather, so full of mosquitoes that Malti could hardly endure it. She at once took his temperature and discovered that it was a hundred and four. He'd not been vaccinated and Malti feared it might be smallpox. There was a danger that the fever would get worse if he remained in this damp cell.

Suddenly the child opened his eyes. Finding Malti standing there, he stretched out his hands to her, a pathetic look in his eyes. Malti took him in her arms and patted him gently.

Being held in her arms seemed to give the boy some great pleasure. His burning fingers caught hold of the string of pearls around her neck and he began pulling it toward him. Malti took off the necklace and slipped it over his head. Even in that condition, the natural self-centredness of a child asserted itself. Having the necklace, he no longer needed to stay in her arms, where there was the danger of its being snatched away again. Jhuniya's lap would be safer now.

'He's a clever one,' Malti said playfully. 'Look how he runs off with the thing.'

'Give it back, son,' Jhuniya said. 'It belongs to the *memsahib*.'

The boy clutched the necklace in both hands and glowered at his mother.

'Keep it on, little one,' Malti said. 'I'm not asking for it.'

Returning to the bungalow, she had the living room vacated and Jhuniya installed in these new quarters.

The boy Mangal gazed wide-eyed at this paradise—with its ceiling fan, tinted bulbs, and pictures on the wall. For a long time he just kept staring at all these things.

'Mangal!' Malti called out affectionately.

He turned to her and smiled as though saying, 'I'm not up to laughing today, memsahib. I'm sorry. If there's anything you can do, please do it.'

Malti gave Jhuniya a number of instructions and finally added, 'If there's another woman available at home, tell Gobar to bring her here for a few days. I'm afraid it's smallpox. How far away is your village?'

Jhuniya mentioned the name and location of the village, estimating it to be some thirty-five or forty miles away.

Malti remembered the name Belari. 'Isn't that the village half a mile east of the river?'

'That's right, memsahib. That's the one. How do you know?'

'We went there one time. Stayed over at Hori's house. You know him?'

'He's my father-in-law, memsahib. You must have met my mother-in-law too.'

'Yes indeed. Seemed to be a very intelligent woman. She had a long talk with me. Well then, send Gobar to fetch his mother.'

'He won't go.'

'Why not?'

'Oh, for some reason or other.'

Jhuniya had to do all the cooking and cleaning for her family. During the day she and the boy managed on parched gram, but she was able to cook in the evening when Malti would come home and sit with the child. Jhuniya kept offering to take over, but Malti wouldn't hear of it. At night the boy's temperature would go up and, becoming uncomfortable, he'd raise his arms in the air. Malti would take him in her arms and walk the floor for hours.

On the fourth day, the smallpox broke out clearly. Malti had herself vaccinated and gave vaccinations to everyone else in the house including Mehta, Gobar and Jhuniya. Not even the cook was spared. At first the pocks were small and separate, and it appeared to be a light case. The next day they swelled up the size of grape seeds and then joined together until they were like cherries. Racked with fever, itching and pain, Mangal whimpered and moaned pathetically, looking toward Malti with forlorn and helpless eyes. The tone of his voice and the expression on his face were like those of an adult, as though this intolerable suffering had wiped out all innocent childishness and suddenly projected him into manhood. He seemed to realize that only Malti's care and skill could make him well.

Whenever Malti had to leave for any reason, he would cry until she returned. At night he became especially distraught, and she would have to sit up with him almost all night, but she was never irritated or resentful, although she did get angry at Jhuniya occasionally for doing things wrong out of ignorance.

Both Gobar and Jhuniya put great faith in spells and witchcraft, though they got no chance for that here. Although Jhuniya had been a mother twice, she knew nothing about raising children, and whenever Mangal annoyed her, she would curse and scold him. At the first opportunity she would fall asleep on the floor and not rise until morning. And Gobar crept into the room as though he were terrified. How could he enter with Malti sitting there! He'd ask Jhuniya how the child was getting along, eat his dinner, and then stretch out to sleep. He had not yet recovered fully from his injuries and any little work tired him out. In the days when Jhuniya was selling grass and he was taking things easy, he had been somewhat restored, but his condition had deteriorated in these last few months of carrying head loads and mixing mortar. The job here had been strenuous—drawing water from the well, watering the whole garden, hoeing the flower-beds, cutting the grass, and feeding and milking the cows. With such a kind employer, one couldn't very well shirk on the job, and this sense of obligation kept Gobar from taking even a moment's rest. Besides, when Mehta himself took up a hoe and worked in the garden for hours, how could he sit back and relax? He himself was withering, but the garden was flourishing.

Mr Mehta had also become very fond of the child. One day Malti held the boy and let him pull Mehta's moustache. The rascal took hold as though he were going to tear it out by the roots. Tears came to Mehta's eyes. 'The kid's a real devil,' he sputtered.

'Why don't you shave it off?' Malti demanded.

'My moustache is dearer to me than life itself.'

'The next time he takes hold, he won't let go until he's pulled it all out.'

'Well then I'll pull out his ears in return.'

Mangal found some special delight in pulling at the moustache. Bursting with laughter, he tugged still harder. Evidently Mehta took some pleasure in it, too, though, for he would let the boy play tug-of-war with the whiskers once or twice a day.

Ever since Mangal had come down with smallpox, Mehta had been very concerned. He periodically went into the room and eyed the boy with distress, the thought of the boy's suffering moving him deeply. If his efforts could have made the boy well, he'd have done anything in the world. If money would have done it, he'd have cured the boy even if it meant going out and begging, but he was powerless. Just to touch the boy made his hands tremble. If only the blisters would not break. . . .

The tenderness with which Malti picked him up, put him over her shoulder and walked the floor, and the affection with which she coaxed him to take his milk, reflected a motherly devotion which raised his estimation of her immeasurably. She was not just a beauty but a mother too, and not just any old mother but a woman and mother in the truest sense—a giver of life, who could consider another's child her own. It was as though she'd been storing up these motherly feelings and was now pouring them out lavishly. Every inch of her was bursting with motherliness, as though this were her true nature and all the coquetry and blandishments, the charms and embellishments, had been only a protective shield.

It was one o'clock in the morning. Hearing the boy cry, Mehta sat up with a start. Thinking that Malti must have stayed up until midnight and that it would be hard for her to get up again, he decided to go quiet the child himself if the door was open. Jumping up, he went to the door and peered through its glass panel. Malti was sitting there with the child on her lap and he was crying uncontrollably. Perhaps he'd been frightened by a bad dream or something. Malti cooed to him, patted him, pointed to the pictures and rocked him in her arms, but the sobs showed no sign of stopping. The sight of

Malti's maternal tenderness brought tears to Mehta's eyes, and he felt like going in and clasping her feet to his heart. Words soaked with passion came to mind—my dear—my angel—my queen—my darling. . . .

In a rush of affection he called out, 'Malti, would you open the door?'

Malti opened it and looked at him questioningly.

'Isn't Jhuniya up?' Mehta asked. 'He's certainly crying hard.'

'It's been eight days now,' Malti said sadly, 'and the pain must be worse. That's the reason.'

'Well let me hold him a while. You must be tired.'

Malti smiled. 'You'd get annoyed in no time.'

What she said was true, but no one wants to admit his own weakness, and Mehta persisted. 'You think I'm as petty as all that?'

Malti handed over the baby and he stopped crying as soon as he was in Mehta's arms. The child's instincts must have told him that it would do no good to cry now—that this new person was a man, not a woman, and that men are short-tempered and cruel. They're likely to lay you down on a bed somewhere, or put you outside in the dark to sleep and then go far away—and they won't even let anyone else come near.

'Look how I quieted him down,' Mehta said triumphantly.

'Oh yes, you're an expert in the art,' Malti said with a smile. 'Where did you learn it?'

'From you.'

'But I'm a woman and not to be trusted.'

Mehta looked embarrassed. 'Malti, I beg of you—forget those things I said. You can't imagine how sorry, how ashamed, how penitent I've been all these months since then.'

'Believe me, I've forgotten what you said,' she assured him.

'How can I be sure of that?'

'The proof of it is that we're both living under the same roof— eating, talking and joking together.'

'Would you allow me to ask you for something?'

He laid Mangal on the cot, where the boy went right to sleep, Mehta then looked at Malti with pleading eyes as though his whole life depended on her answer.

'You know there's no one in the world closer to me than you,' Malti said in a thick voice. 'A long time ago I dedicated myself to you. You're my guide, my god, my master. You have no need to ask me for anything. You have only to hint what you want. Before I had the good fortune of knowing you, my life was devoted to my own enjoyment. Your coming gave life inspiration and stability. I'll always be grateful to you. I was deeply struck by what you said on the river-bank that night. What pained me was that you thought of me the same way any other man would have, which I'd not expected from you. The fault is mine, I know that. But you did me an injustice in thinking that I would remain unchanged by your love. You can't realize how proud I feel now. There's nothing lacking for me now that I have your love and confidence. That gift is enough to make life rich and meaningful. It makes me complete.'

Malti felt such a burst of affection that she wanted to throw her arms around him. Bringing out her inner feelings seemed to verify them. Every pore seemed to be tingling. The happiness which she had been convinced was inaccessible was now so accessible, so close. And as the inner delight became reflected on her face, it gave her a radiance that appeared to Mehta practically divine. This was a real woman—the image of well-being, of purity and of dedication.

Just then Jhuniya woke up. Mehta went back to his room, and for two weeks there was no opportunity to talk with Malti in private. Her words kept ringing in his ears—so modest, so comforting and so intoxicating!

Within two weeks, Mangal had recovered, and the smallpox had not managed to pit his face. Malti fed the neighbourhood children all the sweets they could eat and made all the offerings promised to the gods. She was beginning to discover the joys of a life of service. Jhuniya and Gobar's happiness seemed reflected in her. In the days of self-indulgence she had never known the pleasure and delight she experienced now in relieving the suffering of others. Those desires were like flowers which had faded away as the fruit appeared. She had passed beyond the stage where people consider gross pleasure as the greatest happiness. That pleasure now seemed superficial and degrading and rather disgusting. What pleasure was there in living in that big bungalow when wails of distress seemed to be rising from the mud huts all around? Riding in a car was no longer a matter of pride. A simple child like Mangal had flooded her life with a light that opened the door to real happiness.

One day Mehta had a splitting headache. Eyes closed, he was tossing on the bed when Malti came and put a hand on his forehead. 'How long have you been having this pain?'

410

Mehta felt as though her soft touch had drawn out all the pain. Sitting up, he said, 'It's been going on since noon. I've never had such a bad headache before, but as soon as you put your hand there, my head cleared up as though there'd never been any pain. You have a magic touch.'

Malti brought him some medicine, warned him to lie still and rest, and then started to leave.

'Won't you sit down for just a couple of minutes?' Mehta urged.

She turned in the doorway. 'If you start talking now, the headache will probably return. Keep lying there and rest. I notice you're always reading or writing something these days. You'd better lay off work for three or four days.'

'Won't you sit down for even a minute?'

'I have to go see a patient.'

'All right then, go ahead.'

Such a look of misery crossed Mehta's face that Malti came back and said, 'Very well, tell me. What do you want to say?'

'Nothing special,' he murmured disconsolately. 'I was just going to ask what patient you were going to visit so late at night.'

'It's the Rai Sahib's daughter. She was really in a bad way, but she's a little better now.'

As soon as she left, Mehta lay down again, puzzled as to why the pain had eased at the touch of her hand. She really must have some magical power, a reward from the gods for her self-sacrifice and hard work. By now Malti had attained such a height of womanly perfection in his eyes that she appeared like a planet in the heavens— an object of worship rather than of love. She seemed to have passed beyond his reach. But unattainability is the charm that inspires brave souls to greater zeal. The happiness in love of which Mehta had been dreaming was made still deeper and more exhilirating in devotion. A state of love preserves a certain pride and self-importance, whereas a state of devotion destroys the self and makes one desire self-effacement. Love wants to dominate, expecting something in return for whatever is given, whereas the highest joy of devotion is a self-surrender in which egotism in completely demolished.

After three years of work, Mehta had finished writing a voluminous book synthesizing philosophical truths from all over the world. He had dedicated the book to Malti, and presented one to her the day the copies arrived from England. Finding it dedicated to herself, Malti was both astonished and unhappy.

'What's this you've done?' she protested. 'I don't feel myself worthy of this.'

'But I do,' Mehta said proudly. 'It's nothing really. If I had a hundred lives, I'd lay them all at your feet.'

'Mine? A person who's known nothing but self-seeking?'

'I'd consider myself blessed to have even a fraction of your unselfishness. You're a goddess.'

'Of stone. Why don't you add that?'

'Of sacrifice—of happiness—of holiness.'

'Then you really understand me! Me and sacrifice! Believe me, the thought of service or sacrifice has never entered my head. Everything I do is done directly or indirectly out of self-interest. When I sing, it's not in order to make any sacrifice or in order to console sad hearts, but only because it gives me pleasure. I provide medicine and treatment to the poor for the very same reason—just to please myself. Maybe it gives satisfaction to my ego. You're determined to make a goddess out of me. All that remains now is for you to bring the incense and candles and start worshipping.'

'I've been doing that for years, Malti,' he murmured, 'and I'll keep on doing it until I get the boon I've been praying for.'

'And once you got the boon, you'd probably throw the goddess out of the temple.'

'I'd have no separate existence though,' Mehta said, unshaken. 'The worshipper would be absorbed in the object of his worship.'

Malti turned serious. 'No, Mehta. I've been thinking about this question for months and I've finally decided that there's greater happiness in being friends than in being husband and wife. You love me, you believe in me, and I'm confident that, if the occasion arose, you would protect me with your life. I've found not only a guide but also a protector in you. I love you too, and I believe in you, and there's no sacrifice I couldn't make for you. And I humbly pray to God that he keep me firmly on this path the rest of my life. What more do we need for our fulfillment, for our self-development? If we set up our own small household, shutting our souls in a little cage and restricting our joys and sorrows to each other, could we ever approach the Infinite? It would just put an obstacle in our path. There are some rare souls who put themselves in these shackles and are still able to move, and I know that the love and devotion and sacrifice of marriage are very important for fulfillment, but I don't find that much strength in myself. As long as there's no selfish-

412

ness or egotism, then there's no attachment to life and no pressure of self-interest; but as soon as our hearts become charmed by worldly desires, we'll be chained down—the scope of our humanity will shrink. New responsibilities will arise and all our energies will be spent in trying to discharge them. I don't want to confine the soul of a man as intelligent and gifted as you in that dungeon. Your life so far has been one of sacrifice, in which there's been little room for selfishness. I'm not going to drag it down. The world needs dedicated men like you whose concerns reach out and embrace the whole world. Fear, injustice and terror reverberate all over the earth. The fires of blind faith, religious humbug and self-interest are raging. You've heard that cry of distress. If you won't listen, who will? But you can't turn a deaf ear the way corrupt men do. You'll shoulder the burden. You must push forward on that path with even more drive and enthusiasm in your intellect and learning, in your enlightened love of humanity—and I'll follow along behind. Make my life meaningful along with your own—that's all I ask of you. If your heart should veer toward worldliness, I'd keep a check on mine and correct your course. If I were unsuccessful—God forbid that it be so—I'd shed a few tears and let you go. I can't say what would become of me then or where my heart would find its mooring; but whatever be the refuge, it wouldn't be the refuge of captivity. Tell me—what advice do you have for me?'

Mehta had listened with head bowed. Each word had opened up his inner vision as though he had been completely blind until now. Emotions which previously had appeared to be dream fantasies now became pulsating life truths. Light and exaltation seemed to pour through him. In times of great crisis, childhood memories flash before our eyes. Mehta suddenly recalled the sweet days when he had known great happiness resting in the arms of his widowed mother. Where was that mother now? If only she would come and witness this triumph of her son, and give her blessing. That obstinate boy of hers was today taking up a new life.

Taking Malti's feet in both his hands, he trembled and said, 'I'll do as you suggest.'

Separated though they were, the two were joined in close embrace. Both were in tears.

CHAPTER 34

AFTER spending several hundred rupees, Matadin had finally been reinstated as a brahman by the Banaras pandits. An elaborate sacrificial fire had been arranged for the occasion, great numbers of brahmans were feasted, and lots of sacred verses and formulas were chanted. Matadin was also required to eat pure cowdung and drink cow's urine. The cowdung was to purify his mind, while the urine was to kill the germs of impurity in his soul.

In a way this atonement really did purify him. His humanity was cleansed and restored in the blazing sacrificial fire, and by the light of the flames he scrutinized well the pillars of religion. From that day on, the very mention of dharma became distasteful to him. He threw away his sacred thread and sank his priestliness with it in the Ganges. Now he was an ordinary peasant. He had also observed that, although the learned men accepted his restored brahmanhood, people in general would still not take water from his hands. They would ask him about auspicious days, getting his advice on the best time for marriages and other ceremonies, and they would even give him donations on festival days, but they wouldn't let him touch their cooking utensils.

On the day that Siliya's baby was born, he drank double his usual dose of bhang. His chest almost burst with pride, and his fingers kept straying up to twirl the ends of his moustache. What would the baby look like? Would it be like him? How could he get to see it? His mind kept chafing and squirming.

Three days later he ran into Rupa in the fields. 'Rupiya, have you seen Siliya's baby boy?' he inquired.

'Well of course I have,' she replied. 'He's all pink, very plump, and has curly hair and great big eyes that just stare and stare.'

Matadin felt as though the baby was right in front of him, throwing its arms and legs about. Intoxicated delight filled his eyes. Snatching Rupa up in his arms as though she were the child Krishna, he set her on his shoulder and then swung her down and kissed her on the cheek.

Brushing the hair from her eyes, Rupa said daringly, 'Come on. I'll show him to you from a distance. He's right out on the porch. I don't know why, but sister Siliya keeps crying all the time.'

Matadin averted his face. There were tears in his eyes and his lips were quivering.

That night, when the whole village was asleep and even the trees were lost in the darkness, he crept up to Siliya's door and filled his heart with the sound of the baby's crying, a sound whose joy and tenderness was like the music of the whole universe.

Siliya would put the child to sleep on a little cot in Hori's house and then go off to work. Matadin would go there on some pretext or other and find solace for his heart and eyes and soul with a furtive glance at the boy.

'What are you so shy about?' Dhaniya would say with a smile. 'Take him in your arms and cuddle him. What a wooden heart you have! He takes after you completely.'

Matadin would toss her a rupee or two for Siliya and then leave. His soul was growing along with the child—blossoming out and beginning to sparkle. His life now had purpose and dedication, and developed a new restraint, a new seriousness and a new sense of responsibility.

One day Ramu was lying on the little cot. Dhaniya had gone out somewhere and Rupa had heard the sound of children playing and gone out too, to join them. The house was deserted. Just then Matadin arrived. The baby lay gazing up at the blue sky, his arms and legs thrashing, bouncing around with the joy of life still fresh within him. At the sight of Matadin, the child started laughing. Bursting with affection, Matadin picked up the child and clasped him to his chest. A tingle ran through him like rays of light quivering through rippling water. It was as though he had found the meaning of his life in the deep, clear, joyful eyes of the child. But then a kind of fear struck him, as though the sight had pierced his heart. How could he, so impure, touch this gift from God? He apprehensively laid the boy back down on the cot. At that moment Rupa returned and he went away.

Siliya's son was almost two years old now and pattered all around the village. He had developed a peculiar language in which he always spoke whether anyone could understand or not. It was heavy with t's and l's and gh's, with s's and r's missing entirely. So 'roti' became 'oti,' 'doodh' was 'toot,' 'saag' was 'chaag' and 'kauri' came out 'tauli.'

His imitations of animal sounds made people double up with laughter. Someone would ask, 'Ramu, what does a dog say?' 'Bhau—bhau' he would reply gravely and then start snapping and biting. 'And what does a cat say?' 'Meow-meow' he would answer, eyes bulging and hands clawing. Really a spirited boy! He spent most of the time cheerfully engrossed in play, oblivious to food and drink. Being picked up and fondled annoyed him, and he spent his happiest moments playing just outside the door under the neem tree in the dust—piling it up, rolling it, pouring it over his head, and making little mud houses. He didn't get along at all with his children his own age, perhaps not considering them worthy to play with him.

'What's your name?' someone would ask.

'Lamu,' he would reply promptly.

'And your father's name?'

'Matadin.'

'And your mother's?'

'Chiliya.'

'And who's Datadin?'

'He's my chaalaa.'[1]

Someone or other had evidently taught him this answer.

Ramu and Rupa got along famously. He was Rupa's little doll, and she would massage him with oil, darken his eyelids with kohl, bathe him, comb his hair, feed him bite by bite from her own hands, and sometimes fall asleep at night with him in her arms. Dhaniya protested that she was polluting everything by associating with this low-caste boy, but Rupa listened to no one. She had learned to be a mother from rag dolls, but dolls could no longer satisfy those maternal instincts now that she'd found a real live baby.

There had once been a cowshed behind Hori's house, and Siliya set up a straw hut amongst the debris there. She certainly couldn't go on living in Hori's house forever.

One day there was a heavy hailstorm. Siliya had taken a load of grass to the bazaar and Rupa was engrossed in play. The hailstones scattered over the courtyard looked to Ramu like a shower of bataasaa sweets. He picked up several, ate them, and had a fine time playing in the courtyard. That night he developed a fever which turned into pneumonia in a couple of days. On the evening of the third, while being held in Siliya's arms, the child breathed his last.

Although the boy had died, he continued to be the centre of Siliya's

[1]saalaa—wife's brother, often used as a derogatory or abusive term.

416

existence. Milk would well up in her breasts and moisten her sari, and then the tears would flow from her eyes. Previously, when she had been freed from the day's labours, she would put the baby's mouth to her breast, and let the vigour of the child suffuse her. She would break into tender songs, dream blissful dreams, and build new worlds in which Ramu reigned as king. When she got off work now, she would weep in her empty hut, her soul yearning to fly to the regions where her dear one must still be playing. The whole village shared in her grief. Ramu had been so friendly, going to the arms of anyone who called him. Now that he was dead and out of reach, he had become still more beloved, his shadow being even more friendly and winning and attractive than he had been.

Matadin broke loose that day. Curtains are intended for breezes, but in a storm they are taken down lest they be blown away. Resting the lifeless body on his outstretched arms, he carried it himself across a mile of sand to the cremation ground on the edge of the river which had dried up to a thin stream. For eight days he was unable to straighten his arms, but he was no longer the least bit apologetic or ashamed. And no one breathed a word of criticism. On the contrary, everyone praised his courage and strength of character.

'That's how a man should behave,' Hori declared. 'Once you've taken a woman, you can't desert her.'

Dhaniya's eyes flashed. 'Cut out the praises. It makes me boil. He's a man? I call a man like that no man at all. Was he such a babe in arms as to believe Siliya a brahman at the time he got involved with her?'

A month passed. Siliya had begun working again. Night had fallen and a full moon had risen. Siliya had plucked some stray ears of barley from the harvested field. Putting them in her basket, she was about to leave when the moon caught her eye and released a flood of painful memories. Milk dampened her sari and tears her face. Bowing her head, she abandoned herself to the solace of weeping.

The sound of a footstep suddenly startled her. Matadin had come up behind and now stood facing her. 'How long are you going to keep crying, Siliya? Tears won't bring him back.' At that he himself burst into tears.

The words of reproach on Siliya's lips melted away. Steadying her voice, she said, 'What brought you here today?'

'I was just passing this way,' Matadin said timidly. 'I saw you and came over.'

'You never even had a chance to hold him.'

'No, Siliya. I did one day.'

'Honestly?'

'Honestly.'

'Where was I?'

'You had gone to the bazaar.'

'Didn't he cry when you picked him up?'

'No, Siliya, he laughed.'

'Really?'

'Really.'

'You only held him that once?'

'Yes, just once, but I came every day to see him. I'd watch him lying there happily on the cot, control my feelings, and go away.'

'He looked just like you.'

'I'm sorry—it was wrong for me to hold him even that once. What happened is the punishment for my sins.'

A gleam of forgiveness appeared in Siliya's eyes. Putting the basket on her head, she started for home, and Matadin went with her.

'I sleep on the porch of Aunt Dhaniya's house now. My own place upsets me.'

'Dhaniya was always advising me.'

'Really?'

'Yes, really. Whenever we met she would start explaining....'

As they approached the village, Siliya said, 'All right, you'd better head for your own house now so your brahman father doesn't see you.'

Matadin lifted his head and said, 'I'm not afraid of anyone now.'

'Where would you go if he threw you out of the house?'

'I have my own house.'

'You mean that?'

'Yes, it's true.'

'Where? I've never seen it.'

'Come. I'll show you.'

They walked forward, with Matadin leading the way. When they reached Hori's house, Matadin walked around back and stood at the door of Siliya's hut. 'Right here is our home.'

Siliya's voice reflected disbelief, indulgence, sarcasm and sorrow. 'This is the house of Siliya the chamar.'

Matadin opened the thatch door. 'This is the temple of my goddess.'

'If it's a temple, then you'll just pour out an offering of water and go away,' Siliya said, her eyes gleaming.

Matadin helped her take the basket off her head. His voice trembled with emotion. 'No, Siliya. As long as there's life in me, I'll take shelter with you. I'll worship you alone.'

'You're lying.'

'No, I touch your feet and swear it. I hear the patwari's brat Bhunesari was chasing you a lot and you really told him off.'

'Who told you that?'

'Bhunesari himself told me.'

'Really?'

'Yes, really.'

Siliya struck a match and lit the little oil lamp. On one side of the hut was a clay pot and on the other an earthen cooking place next to which lay a few brass and iron pots, clean and sparkling. Some straw had been spread out in the middle of the room. This was Siliya's mattress. At its head, Ramu's little cot seemed desolate and forlorn. Two or three broken clay horses and elephants were scattered about. With their master gone, who was to look after them? Matadin sat down on the straw. A great ache filled his heart and he longed for the comfort of sobs.

Siliya touched his back and asked, 'Did you ever think of me?'

Matadin took her hand and pressed it to his chest. 'The sight of you kept spinning before my eyes. And you—did you ever think of me?'

'I was mad at you.'

'And you felt no pity?'

'Never.'

'Then Bhunesari. . . .'

'All right now, no abuses. I'm afraid of what the people in the village are going to say.'

'The decent ones will say I did the right thing, and I don't care about the others.'

'And who'll cook for you?'

'My princess, Siliya.'

'Then how can you remain a brahman?'

'I want to live as a chamar, not a brahman. Besides, a true brahman is one who does his duty, who fulfills his dharma, while one who shirks it is a chamar.'

Siliya threw her arms around his neck.

CHAPTER 35

HORI'S situation was deteriorating day by day. He'd been fighting a losing battle all his life but he had never lost heart, each defeat seeming to give him new strength to fight against fate. But now he had reached that final stage where he no longer had confidence even in himself. It would have been some consolation if he had been able to remain true to his conscience and his dharma, but that was not the case. He'd violated his principles, failed in his duty, and done every kind of wrong imaginable. Despite that, not one of his ambitions in life had been fulfilled, and the prospect of better days had receded into the distance like a mirage until not even illusion remained. The lushness and glitter of false hopes had now faded away entirely. Like a vanquished ruler, he had shut himself up in the fortress of his two acres and was guarding it as though it were his life. He had endured starvation, suffered disgrace, and hired himself out as a common labourer, but he had held the fort.

Now even that fort was slipping from his hands. Three years' rent lay unpaid and Pandit Nokheram had filed eviction proceedings against him. There was no hope of getting the money anywhere. The land would be lost and he'd spend the rest of his days as a hired hand. Such was God's will. He couldn't very well blame the Rai Sahib, who had to make a living off his tenants. More than half the families in the village were facing eviction, so they were all in the same boat. If fate had ordained happiness for him, would he have lost his son that way?

Darkness had fallen and Hori was sitting brooding over these problems when Pandit Datadin appeared and spoke to him. 'What's happened about your eviction notice, Hori? I'm not on speaking terms with Nokheram these days so I don't know anything. I hear you have fifteen days left.'

Hori pulled out a cot for him to sit on. 'He's the master. He can do what he likes. If I had the money, this mess would never have happened in the first place. It's not as though I'd gobbled up the money or thrown it around. If the land doesn't yield anything, or if what it does yield sells for a pittance, what's a farmer to do?'

'But you must save the property. How else are you going to live? This is all that's left of the inheritance from your forefathers. Lose that and where would you live?'

'That's in the hands of God. What control do I have over it?'

'There is one thing you could do.'

Hori fell at his feet like a man just granted amnesty and said, 'Blessings on you, maharaj. You're my only hope. I had given up.'

'There's no question of giving up. All you have to realize is that a man's duty is one thing in times of plenty and something quite different in times of trouble. In good days he gives out charity, whereas in bad, he even takes to begging. It becomes his duty then. When we're in good health, we don't even touch water to our lips without the proper bathing and prayers, but when we're sick, we take food in bed without bathing or praying or changing clothes. It's the right thing to do at that particular time. There's a big gap between you and me here in the village, but when we go to the Jagannath temple in Puri, that distinction disappears. The high and the low sit down in the same row and eat. In a time of crisis, the lord Rama ate wild berries polluted by the touch of Shabari and hid craftily to kill Bali. In times of distress, even the greatest of the great compromise their standards, not to speak of people like ourselves. You must know the man Ramsevak, don't you?'

'Yes, of course.' Hori conceded.

'He's a patron of mine. He's very well off these days—lands on the one hand and moneylending on the other. I've never known a man with such power and influence. His wife died several months ago. They had no children. If you would be willing to marry Rupa to him, I could get him to agree. He'd never oppose my advice. The girl has come of age, and these are evil times. If anything should happen, your name would be mud. It's a very good opportunity for you. The girl will be married off and your land will be saved in the bargain. You'll be saved all the bother and expense of the wedding too.'

Ramsevak was only three or four years younger than Hori, and the proposal to marry Rupa to a man like that was insulting. His Rupa, in full bloom, marry that withered old stump? Hori had suffered a lot of blows over the years, but this one struck deepest. He had now reached the point where someone could suggest selling his daughter and he lacked the courage to refuse. His head dropped in shame.

421

'Well, what do you say?' Datadin asked after a slight pause.

Hori refused to commit himself. 'I'll have to think it over first.'

'What's there to think over?'

'I should ask Dhaniya too.'

'Are you agreeable or not?'

'Let me think a bit, maharaj. Nothing like this has ever happened in the family, and our honour has to be upheld.'

'Let me have an answer within five or six days. Otherwise the eviction is likely to go through while you're still thinking it over.'

Datadin went away. He had no worries about Hori. It was Dhaniya he was concerned about, with her nose in the air. She'd rather die than compromise the family prestige. If Hori agreed, though, she'd come around too after much weeping and wailing. After all, losing the land would damage their prestige also.

Dhaniya came and asked, 'What did the pandit come for?'

'Nothing special. We just talked about the eviction matter.'

'He must have offered only sympathy—he certainly wouldn't be offering a hundred-rupee loan.'

'And I don't have the gall to ask for one at this point.'

'Then why did he come in the first place?'

'To suggest a match for Rupiya.'

'With whom?'

'You know Ramsevak? With him.'

'How would I know him? Of course I've heard the name for a long time. But he must be an old man.'

'He's not old, but—yes, he is middle-aged.'

'And you didn't tell the pandit off? If he'd talked to me, I'd have given an answer he'd never forget.'

'I didn't tell him off, but I did turn him down. He was saying the wedding wouldn't cost us anything and that we'd save the fields besides.'

'Why don't you come right out and admit he was suggesting we sell the girl? The nerve of that old man!'

The more Hori thought about the matter, however, the more his resistance weakened. He had no less pride about family honour, but when a person is seized by an incurable disease, he stops caring about what should and what should not be eaten. Hori's attitude in front of Datadin could not have been called compliance, but inwardly he had melted. Age wasn't so important after all. Life and death were in the hands of fate, and sometimes the young pass away while the old remain. If happiness were written in Rupa's destiny, she would find happiness even there. If sorrow were ordained, she'd be unable to find happiness anywhere. And it was certainly not a question of selling his daughter. Anything he accepted from Ramsevak would be only a loan, to be repaid as soon as he got hold of some money. There was nothing shameful or humiliating about that. If he had the means, he would certainly be marrying Rupa to some young man of good family, giving a good dowry and sparing no expense to entertain the marriage party. But since God had not granted him the wherewithal for that, what could he do but marry her off with only a tuft of sacred grass for a dowry? People would jeer at him, but there was no need for him to worry about people who just made fun without offering any help. The only trouble was that Dhaniya wouldn't agree. She was a real mule and would keep hanging on to that same old pride. This was no time to worry about family prestige. It was a chance to save their lives. If she was going to be so fussy about honour, all right—let her come up with five hundred rupees. Just where was she hoarding it?'

Two days went by and no mention was made of the subject, although both of them talked about it indirectly.

'A marriage is only happy when the boy and girl are equally matched,' Dhaniya would say.

'Marriage doesn't mean happiness, you fool,' Hori would answer. 'It means self-denial.'

'Come off it. Self-denial?'

'Yes, and I'm the one to say so. What else can you call the state of being content with whatever circumstances God places you in?'

The next day Dhaniya came up with another angle on this question of marital happiness—'What fun is it to be in a husband's home with no father or mother-in-law and with no brothers or sisters-in-law? A girl should have the pleasure of being the new little bride for awhile.'

'That's not pleasure, it's punishment,' Hori retorted.

'You have such queer ideas,' Dhaniya snapped. 'How's a bride going to manage all by herself in a house with no one else around?'

'Well when you came to this house you had not one but two brothers-in-law, as well as a mother-in-law and a father-in-law. Tell me, what happiness did you get out of that?'

'You think people in all families are just like the ones who were here?'

'What else? You expect angels come down from the skies? The bride's alone in any case. The whole house orders her around. How can the poor thing please everyone? And anyone whose orders she ignores turns against her. Being alone is by far the best.'

The discussion would always stop at this point, but Dhaniya was steadily losing ground. On the fourth day, Ramsevak himself showed up, riding a big horse and accompanied by a barber and a manservant as though he was some great zamindar. Though he was over forty and his hair was turning grey, there was a certain brightness in his face and he had a sturdy physique. Hori looked really ancient alongside of him. Ramsevak was on his way to see about some court case and wanted to stop off for awhile to avoid the noon heat. The sun was so fierce today and the wind so scorching! Hori got wheat flour and ghee from Dulari's shop and special wheat-cakes were prepared. All three guests were served. Datadin also turned up to give his blessings and a conversation ensued.

'What sort of case is it, mahto?' Datadin inquired.

'Oh there's always some case or other pending, maharaj,' Ramsevak boasted. 'Being meek as a cow doesn't get you anywhere in this world. The more you cringe, the more people put you down. The law courts and police and so forth are all supposed to be for our protection, but no one really protects us. There's just looting all around. People are all ready and waiting to cut the throat of anyone poor and defenceless. God forbid that we be dishonest—that's a big sin. But not to fight for one's rights and for justice is an even bigger sin. Think about it—how long is a person to knuckle under? Everyone around here considers the farmer fair game. He can hardly stay on in the village if he doesn't pay off the patwari. If he doesn't satisfy the appetite of the zamindar's men, life is made impossible for him. The police chiefs and constables act like sons-in-law. Whenever they happen to be passing through the village, the farmers are duty-bound to entertain them royally and provide gifts and offerings lest they get the whole village arrested by filing a single report. Someone or other is always turning up—the head record-keeper or the revenue official or the deputy or the agent or the collector or the commissioner—and the farmer is supposed to attend him on bended knee. He has to make arrangements for food and fodder, for eggs and chickens, and for milk and ghee. You must know all about this yourself, maharaj. Every day some new officer is added to the list. Recently a doctor has started coming to treat the water in the wells. Another doctor comes around occasionally to look at the cattle, and then there's the inspector who tests the school children. Lord knows all the departments these officers represent—there's a separate one for towns, one for jungles, one for liquor, one for village welfare, one for agriculture. . . . You want me to keep on naming them? The padre shows up and even he has to be supplied with provisions or he'll make a complaint. And anyone who says that all these departments and officers do some good for the farmers is talking through his hat. Just the other day, the zamindar levied a tax of two rupees on every plough. He was putting on a feast for some big official. The farmers refused to pay so he just raised the rents of the whole village. And the officers always side with the zamindar. It never occurs to them that the farmer is also a human being, that he too has a wife and family, and some honour and status to maintain.

'And this is all the result of our servility. I've had a drummer announce throughout the village that no one should pay the extra rent or let his land go. We're prepared to pay the new rate if someone can convince us there's a good reason, but if the zamindar was intending just to grind up and devour the defenceless farmers, he was mistaken. The villagers went along with me and they all refused to pay. When the zamindar saw that the whole village had united, he was forced to back down. Confiscate all the land and who would work it? In this day and age you have to be tough or no one pays any attention. Even a child has to cry before he gets any milk from his mother.'

In mid-afternoon Ramsevak went on his way, having left an indelible impression on Hori and Dhaniya. Datadin's spell had worked. 'Now what do you say?' he asked.

Hori pointed to Dhaniya. 'You'd better ask her.'

'I'm asking you both.'

'Well he is much older,' Dhaniya replied, 'but if you all approve, I'm willing too. What's written in the stars will show up in time, but anyway he's a good man.'

As for Hori, he had the kind of confidence in Ramsevak which the weak feel for men of spirit and courage. He had begun building great castles in the air. With the support of a man like this, he might pull through after all.'

The date for the wedding was set. Gobar would also have to be invited. It was up to them to write; whether he came or not was up

425

O*

to him. At least he wouldn't be able to say he'd not been invited. They'd have to send for Sona too.

'Gobar was never that way,' Dhaniya said. 'Now if Jhuniya will only let him come... Since going away, he's forgotten us so completely that there's been not a word from him. No telling how they're getting along.' Tears came to her eyes as she spoke.

Gobar began preparing to leave as soon as he got the letter. Jhuniya didn't like the idea, but she couldn't object on an occasion like this. For a brother not to attend his sister's wedding would be unthinkable. Not going to Sona's had been enough of a scandal.

'It's not right to be on bad terms with one's parents.' Gobar's voice was thick with emotion. 'Now that we're on our own two feet, we can pull away from them or even fight them. But it was they who gave us birth and brought us up, so even if they give us a hard time now, we ought to put up with it. They've been in my thoughts a lot recently. I don't know why I got so angry at them that time. Because of you I've had to leave even my mother and father.'

'Don't dump the blame on my head,' Jhuniya barked. 'The quarrel was all your doing. All that time I lived with your mother, I never even breathed a harsh word.'

'The fight was over you though.'

'Well what if it was? I gave up my whole home and family for your sake.'

'No one loved you at your place anyway. Your brothers were furious and their wives were spiteful. And if your father had got hold of you, he'd have eaten you alive.'

'All because of you.'

'Well from now on let's live in such a way that they'll get some pleasure out of life too. Let's not do anything against their wishes. My father's such a good man that he's never even said an unkind word. Mother beat me a number of times, but she would always give me something special to eat afterwards. She'd thrash me, but then she'd have no peace of mind until she had made me smile.'

They both mentioned the matter to Malti. She not only allowed the time off but also gave them a spinning wheel and a bracelet for the bride. She wanted to go herself, but she was treating several patients who couldn't be left for even a day. She did promise to come for the ceremony itself, though, and brought out a pile of toys for Mangal. She kissed and fondled him as though to compensate for all the time he'd be away, but the child took no notice of her caresses in his delight at going home—the home he had never even seen. In his childish imagination, home was something better than heaven itself.

When Gobar reached home and saw its condition, however, he was so disheartened he felt like returning to the city right away. Part of the house was about to fall down. Only one bullock was tied up near the door and even it was on its last legs. Dhaniya and Hori were beside themselves with delight, but Gobar was disturbed and dejected. What hope was there of saving this home? He worked like a slave in the city but at least he ate his fill—and he served only one master. Here in the village everyone in sight was browbeating the people. This was slavery with no compensation. Struggle to raise a crop and then give its income to someone else, leaving you to console yourself repeating the name of God. Only people with hearts like his father's could put up with all this. He couldn't have tolerated it for even a day.

And Hori was not the only one in this condition. The whole village was in misery, and there was not a man but wore an expression as gloomy as though suffering had drained the life from him and was making him dance like a wooden puppet. They moved about, did their work, were crushed and suffocated only because this was written in their fate. Life held neither hope nor joy, as though the springs of life had dried up and all greenness had withered away. Being June, there was still grain in the barns, but no happiness on anyone's face. Most of the grain in the barns had been weighed out and turned over to the moneylenders and the zamindar's agents, and even what was left was owed to others.

The future loomed darkly ahead with no path in sight, and their spirits had become numbed. The mounds of garbage piled up by the doors filled the air with stench, but no odour reached their noses and no light their eyes. They ate whatever scraps came their way like engines taking in coal. Their bullocks would sniff and poke around before putting their mouths to the trough, but all the people wanted was to get something in their stomachs. Flavour made no difference, as they'd lost their sense of taste. And life had lost all flavour too. For half a pice people could be made dishonest; for a handful of grain, the sticks would fly. They had reached the limits of degradation where men forget all about dignity or shame.

The village had been in much the same state when Gobar had known it as a child, but he had been accustomed to it. In the four years away, however, he had seen a new world. Living in the midst of refined people in the city had stimulated his mind. He had stood

427

at the back of political meetings and heard the speeches until they penetrated every part of him. He had heard that men must carve out their own destiny, that they must conquer their misery through their own insight and courage. No gods, no supernatural powers, would come to their rescue. Profound sympathies had been awakened within him. Where he had been headstrong and arrogant, he was now gentle and industrious, realizing that whatever one's situation, greed and selfishness would only make it worse. Threads of suffering had bound them all together, and men would be foolish to let petty self-interest break these sacred bonds of brotherhood. The ties uniting them must be strengthened. Such feelings had given wings to his humanity, and with the magnanimity which comes to the good at heart from observing the best and the worst in the world, he seemed poised to soar into the skies.

Whenever he saw Hori working now, Gobar would take over the job and do it himself, as though trying to atone for his previous behaviour. 'Father,' he would say, 'don't worry about a thing any more. Leave it all to me. From now on I'll send money for your expenses every month. You've been working yourself to death all this time. Take a rest now for a while. A curse on me, that you've had to suffer so when I could have helped.'

Hori blessed the boy with every inch of his being, new inspiration filling his worn and aging body. How could he cripple Gobar's rising manhood with anxiety at this point by describing all his debts and obligations? Let the boy enjoy his meals in comfort and get some pleasure out of life. He, Hori, was willing to slog and slave. That had always been his life, and to sit around chanting prayers would be the death of him. He needed the axe and the hoe. Twirling a rosary would bring him no peace of mind.

'Just give the word,' Gobar said, 'and I'll arrange instalments on all the debts and pay them off month by month. How much would they add up to?'

Hori shook his head. 'No, son, why should you burden yourself down? You don't earn much yourself. I'll take care of everything. Times are bound to improve. Rupa's going away, so now all that's left is to pay off the debts. Don't you worry about it. Make sure you eat well. If you build up your body now, you'll live happily ever after. And me? Well I'm used to killing myself with work. I don't want to tie you to the fields as yet, son. You've found a good employer. Serve her for awhile and you'll become a man. She came here once, you know. A real live goddess.'

'She's promised to come again the day of the wedding.'

'We'll be happy to welcome her. Living alongside such good people may mean less money but it increases one's wisdom and opens his eyes.'

Just then Pandit Datadin beckoned to Hori. Leading him some distance away, he took two hundred-rupee notes from his waistband. 'You did well to take my advice. Both things have been taken care of. You've done your duty to the girl and you've also saved the inheritance of your ancestors. I've done all I can for you. The rest is now up to you.'

Hori's hands were trembling as they took the money and he was unable to raise his eyes or say a word. He felt as though he had fallen into a bottomless pit of shame and was still falling. After thirty years of struggling with life, he had finally been defeated, as defeated as though he had been stood up against the city gate with every passerby spitting in his face while he cried out—'I deserve your pity, my brothers. I didn't know what the wind of summer was like nor the rain of winter. Slash open this body and see for yourself how little life is left in it. Count the bruises and scars, the blows that have crushed it. Ask it if it has ever known rest and peace, if it has ever sat in the shade. And now this humiliation!' But he was still alive—cowardly, greedy, contemptible. All his faith, which had grown so infinite, so firm, so unquestioning, had been nibbled away.

'I must be leaving,' said Datadin. 'You should probably go see Nokheram right away.'

'I'll go in a moment, maharaj,' Hori murmured meekly, 'but my honour is in your hands now.'

CHAPTER 36

FOR two days the village rocked with revelry. Music rang out, songs filled the air, and finally Rupa departed with much weeping and wailing. Hori was never seen to leave the house, however, as though he were hiding in disgrace.

Malti's arrival had added to the excitement, and women had flocked in from the neighbouring villages. Gobar's warmth and courtesy had charmed the whole village, and not a house was left unimpressed with the memory of his graciousness. Even Bhola fell at his feet, and his wife offered betel, gave a parting gift of a rupee, and even asked his Lucknow address, saying she would certainly look him up if she ever got to the city. She made no reference to the money she had loaned Hori.

On the third day, as Gobar was making preparations to leave, Hori, in the presence of Dhaniya, came with tears in his eyes and confessed the guilt that had been burdening his heart for so long. 'Son,' he sobbed, 'I took this load of sin on my head out of love for the land. No telling how God will punish me for it.'

Gobar was not at all upset and his face registered no sign of irritation or anger. 'There's no need to feel guilty, father,' he said respectfully. 'True, Ramsevak's money should be repaid. But what else could you have done? I've been an unworthy son, your fields aren't producing anything, and there's no money available anywhere. There's not enough food in the house to last even a month. Under such circumstances, there was no other way out. How could you live if the land were lost? When a man is helpless he can only resign himself to fate. No telling how long this rotten state of affairs will go on. Prestige and honour have no meaning when a man can't fill his stomach. If you'd been like the others, squeezing people by the throat and making off with their money, you too could have been well-off. You stuck to your principles and this is the punishment you get for it. If I had been in your position, I'd either be in jail or I'd have been hanged.

430

I could never have tolerated my earnings going to fill up everyone else's houses while my own family sat by muzzled and starving.'

Dhaniya was unwilling to let her daughter-in-law go with him, and Jhuniya herself wanted to stay a little longer. So it had been decided that Gobar would return alone.

Early the next morning Gobar took leave of everyone and set out for Lucknow. Hori accompanied him to the outskirts of the village, feeling more love for him than ever before. When Gobar stooped to touch his feet, Hori burst into tears as though he would never see his son again. His heart swelled with pride and happiness and confidence. The boy's affection and devotion had restored his spirit and heightened his stature. The weariness and gloom that had overwhelmed him a few days before, making him lose his way, had changed to courage and light.

Rupa was happy in her new home. She had grown up in circumstances where money was the scarcest item, so all sorts of longings had remained stifled within her. Now she could begin to satisfy them. And Ramsevak, middle-aged though he was, had become young again. As far as Rupa was concerned, he was her husband. Whether he was young, middle-aged or old made no difference to her womanly feelings, which depended not on her husband's looks or age but were rooted much deeper—in a pure tradition which could have been shaken only by a major earthquake. Engrossed in her own youthfulness, she prettied herself for her own sake, for her own delight. To Ramsevak she showed another side of herself, that of a housekeeper absorbed in the duties of the home. She didn't want to upset or embarrass him by flaunting her youthfulness. To her mind, there was now nothing lacking in life. With the barn full of grain, fields extending to the horizon and rows of cattle by the door, there was no room to feel any kind of deprivation.

Her greatest desire now was to see her own people happy. How could she ease their poverty? Still fresh in her memory was that cow which had appeared like a guest and then departed leaving them weeping. The memory had become even more poignant with time. Her identification with the new household was not yet complete. The old home was still the one where she belonged and the people there were her own people. Their sorrows were her sorrows and their joys her joys. The sight of a whole herd of cattle at the door here could not make her as happy as the sight of just one cow at the door there. That longing of her father's had never been fulfilled. The day that cow had appeared, he'd been as excited as though a goddess had descended from the heavens. Since then he'd not had the means to get another, but she knew that his yearning was as strong as ever. The next time she went home, she'd take that prize one with her. Or perhaps she could have her husband send it. It was just a matter of asking him.

Ramsevak readily agreed, and the next day Rupa dispatched a herdsman with the cow, instructing him to tell Hori that she'd sent it to provide milk for Mangal.

Hori had also been concerned about getting a cow. There was really no hurry about it except that Mangal was there and he certainly had to have milk. The first thing he'd do when he got some money was buy a cow. The boy was more than his grandson and Gobar's son— he was also the favourite of Malti Devi and should be brought up accordingly. But where was the money to come from?

Fortunately a contractor just then started quarrying gravel from some barren land near the village to build a road. Hori hurried over as soon as he heard and began digging at eight annas a day. If the work lasted for even two months, he'd have enough money for the cow. After a full day's work in the scorching sun and wind, he'd come home nearly dead, but there was no hint of defeat. The next day he'd return to work as eagerly as ever. And after dinner at night, he'd sit in front of the dim lamp making twine, staying up until midnight or later. Dhaniya seemed to have gone crazy too. Instead of objecting to all this hard work, she'd sit down with him and join in the rope-making. A cow just had to be bought, and there was also Ramsevak's money to repay. Gobar had said so, and this drove her on.

It was past midnight one night and they were both still working. 'If you're getting sleepy,' Dhaniya spoke up, 'you'd better go get some rest. You have to be at work again early in the morning.'

Hori looked up at the sky. 'I'll go, but it can't be more than ten o'clock now. You go get some sleep.'

'I get a little sleep in the early afternoon.'

'After a bite of lunch, I take a nap too, under a tree.'

'The heat of the loo must be terrible.'

'I don't feel a thing—it's a good shady spot.'

'I'm afraid you might get sick.'

'Oh go on ! The people who get sick are those who have time for it. My one concern is to have half Ramsevak's money paid back by the time Gobar comes back again. He'll bring some money with him too. If we can free our necks from that debt this year, it'll give me a new lease on life.'

'I think of Gobar a lot these days. He's become so thoughtful and gentle.'

'He touched my feet when he was leaving.'

'Mangal was in such good shape when he arrived, but he's grown thin since coming here.'

'He had milk and butter and everything there. Here it's a big thing just to get chapaties. Well, just let me get enough money from the contractor and I'll buy a cow.'

'We'd have a cow now if you had listened to me. You couldn't even care for our own land and yet you took on the burden of Puniya's.

'What else could I have done? Duty counts for something too. Hira may have done us wrong but his family still had to have someone to look after them. Tell me, who was there except me? Just imagine the state they'd be in if I hadn't helped out. And in spite of all my efforts, Mangaru has sued her for his money.'

'When a person buries all her money and hoards it, creditors are bound to sue.'

'What nonsense you're talking. It's hard enough just to feed one's self off the land. As if anyone has money to bury!'

'Hira seems to have vanished off the face of the earth.'

'Something tells me he'll be back some day or other.'

They went to sleep. Early next morning Hori woke up and saw Hira standing there—hair shaggy, clothes in shreds, face withered, body shrunken to skin and bones. He ran up and fell at Hori's feet.

Hori helped him up and hugged him. 'You've melted away to nothing, Hira! When did you get back? We were just thinking about you last night! Have you been ill?'

The Hira he saw today was not the man who had soured his life but the little boy with no mother or father to whom he had given a home. The intervening twenty-five or thirty years seemed to have disappeared without a trace.

Hira stood there sobbing and said nothing.

'Why are you crying, brother?' Hori said, taking his hand. 'It's only human to make mistakes. Where have you been all this time?'

'What can I say?' Hira murmured. 'It's enough to know that I

433

was spared to see you again. The killing haunted me and I felt as though the cow were standing in front of me. It stood there every moment, waking or sleeping, and wouldn't go away. I went insane and ended up in an asylum for five years. I got out some six months ago and have been roaming around begging. I wasn't brave enough to come back here. How could I show my face to anyone? At last I couldn't stand it, though, so I mustered up my courage and returned. You've looked after my wife and . . .'

'You ran away needlessly,' Hori interrupted. 'Why, it just meant paying a few rupees to the police chief, that's all.'

'I'll be indebted to you as long as I live, dada.'

'It's not as though I'm some stranger, brother.'

Hori was exuberant. All life's misfortunes and disappointments seemed to roll away. Could anyone still say he's lost the battle of life? Was this pride, this joy, this bliss a sign of defeat? Those defeats had been his victory, and his dilapidated weapons had been banners of triumph. His chest swelled and his face grew bright. Hira's gratitude symbolized the success of his life. Even if he'd had a barn overflowing with ten tons of grain, or a thousand rupees buried in a pot, nothing could have brought him more ecstasy than this moment.

Hira looked him up and down. 'You've grown very thin too, dada.'

Hori laughed. 'Is this any time for me to be fat? The only people who get fat are those with no worries about debts or prestige or honour. To be fat these days is downright shameful. A hundred men have to grow thin for one man to get fat. What happiness would that bring? Everyone would have to be fat before one could be happy. Have you seen Shobha yet?'

'I visited him last night. To think that you not only looked after your own family but also upheld the family honour and took care of those who spited you—while he sold off all his land and everything. God only knows what he's going to live on.'

When Hori set off for work that morning, there was a heaviness in his body. He'd been unable to shake off the exhaustion of the previous day, but there was still vigour in his stride and confidence in his bearing.

The loo was already blowing by ten that morning, and as midday approached, the sun seemed to be raining down fire. Hori carried one basket of gravel after the other from the quarry to the road and loaded them on the carts there. When the noon break arrived, he could hardly catch his breath. Never had he been so exhausted—he could hardly lift his feet and he was burning up inside. Too tired to wash or eat, he spread out his shoulder-cloth beneath a tree and tried to sleep, but his throat was parched with thirst. Knowing it was bad to drink water on an empty stomach, he tried to control the thirst, but the burning inside kept growing worse. He couldn't bear it. A worker nearby had brought a bucket of water and was eating his parched gram. Hori raised himself up, drank a jugful of water, and then lay back down; but within half an hour he threw up, and a deathly pallor spread over his face.

'Are you all right?' the man asked.

Hori's head was in a whirl. 'I'm all right. It's nothing,' he said.

With that he vomited again, and his hands and feet began turning cold. Why was his head so dizzy? Darkness seemed to be engulfing him. His eyes closed, and memories of the past rose and flashed across his mind in jumbled succession—the recent mixed with the distant past—as incoherent, distorted and disconnected as pictures in a dream. That happy childhood appeared when he had played at boyish games or gone to sleep in his mother's arms. Then he saw Gobar coming and touching his feet. The scene then changed to Dhaniya as a young bride, dressed in her red wedding sari and serving him food. Then the image of a cow rose before him, just like the celestial cow which grants all wishes. He milked the cow and was giving the milk to Mangal when the cow turned into a goddess and . . .

'Time's up, Hori,' the labourer nearby called out. 'Come pick up your basket.'

There was no answer from Hori—his spirit was soaring through other worlds. His body was burning and his hands and feet were cold. He'd been struck down by the loo.

A man was sent racing to his house. An hour later Dhaniya came running. Shobha and Hira followed, carrying a cot as a litter.

When Dhaniya felt his body, her heart seemed to stop and the colour drained from her face. 'How do you feel?' she asked, her voice trembling.

Hori's eyes flickered. 'You've come, Gobar?' he murmured. 'I've bought a cow for Mangal. Look, she's standing over there.'

Dhaniya had seen the face of death and she recognized it. She had seen it creep up on tiptoe and she had seen it burst like a storm.

435

Before her eyes, her mother-in-law had died, her father-in-law had died, two of her sons had died, and scores of village people had died. A blow seemed to strike her heart. The foundation on which her life had rested seemed to be slipping away ∴ but no, this was a time for courage, and her fears were groundless. He'd only been knocked unconscious momentarily by the burning loo.

Checking the rush of tears, she said, 'Look here. It's me. Don't you recognize me?'

Hori returned to consciousness. Death had moved in close. The smoke had cleared away and the coals were about to burst into flame. He looked at Dhaniya tenderly and a tear rolled from the corner of each eye.

'Forgive my mistakes, Dhaniya. I'm going now. The longing for a cow has had to remain a longing. And now that money will go for the last rites. Don't cry, Dhaniya. How much longer could you have kept me alive anyway? I've suffered every possible misfortune. Now let me die.'

His eyes closed again. Hira and Shobha came forward with the litter. Lifting him onto it, they started back to the village.

The news had swept through the village like a great wind and everyone had assembled. Lying there on the cot, Hori perhaps saw everything and understood everything, but his lips were sealed. Only the tears flowing from his eyes spoke of the anguish of breaking the ties of worldly attachment. The sorrow of things left undone—that is the source of attachment, not the tasks completed and the duties discharged. The pain comes in making orphans of those to whom obligations could not be met, in the half-realized ambitions which could not be fulfilled.

Although she understood full well, Dhaniya clung to the dwindling shadow of hope. Tears were flowing from her eyes but she dashed around like a machine, making a mango drink one moment and massaging his body with wheat chaff the next. If only there were money, she'd have sent someone for a doctor.

'Make your heart strong, bhaabi,' Hira said, weeping. 'Make the gift of a cow. Dada is leaving us now.'

Dhaniya's eyes glowed resentfully. How much stronger could she make her heart? And did she have to be reminded of her duty to her husband? She'd been his partner in life—obviously her duty was not just to mourn over him.

'Yes, make the *godaan*,' other voices called out. 'Now is the time.'

Dhaniya rose mechanically and brought out the twenty annas earned that morning from the twine they had made. Placing the money in the cold palm of her husband's hand, she stepped forward and said to Datadin, 'Maharaj, there is no cow nor calf nor money in the house. There are only these few coins. This is his *godaan*, his gift of a cow.'

And she collapsed on the ground, unconscious.

GLOSSARY

aarti—religious ceremony in which a lamp is moved around the image of a deity and is then passed around on a tray to the worshippers, who put their hands over the flame and then to their heads in symbolic blessing, and may then place offerings on the tray

achkan— a long high-collared coat

amma—mother

anna—sixteenth part of a rupee

bhaabi—elder brother's wife

bhang—a narcotic preparation from hemp which is often mixed with food or drink

Bhavani—one of the names for the consort of Shiva

biri—a cheap country cigarette consisting of tobacco wrapped in a leaf

brahman—the highest of the four main subdivisions of Hindu society; originally composed of priests and teachers

chamar—until recently an untouchable caste, traditionally leather workers

chapati—unleavened bread, usually of wheat flour, somewhat similar to the tortilla

charas—a strong narcotic preparation from hemp for smoking

chilam—clay pipe which may be smoked either cupped in the hands or mounted on a hookah (water pipe)

chuha—rat

cowrie—a small shell, once the lowest monetary unit in India

dada—father; elder brother; grandfather

dal—pulse or lentils; somewhat similar to the split pea

Dashahra—a ten-day Hindu festival celebrating the victory of the epic hero Rama over the demon Ravana, a customary part of the celebration being an enactment of the story of the *Ramayana*

devi—literally 'goddess'; commonly used as a polite form of address for ladies

439

devta—god; deity

dharma—righteousness; sacred law; a man's sacred duty as determined by his nature and station in life

dhoti—man's lower garment or, occasionally, a cotton sari

Draupadi—wife of the five Pandu princes in the *Mahabharata*. When Duryodhana started tearing off her clothes, Krishna took pity and restored them as fast as they were torn.

Durga—consort of Shiva; usually represented as a beautiful woman in a fierce attitude riding a tiger

ekka—a horse-drawn carriage in which the riders sit on a high platform over the two wheels

ganja—a narcotic preparation from hemp for smoking

ghee—clarified butter; highly valued in the Indian diet and used in many Hindu rituals

godaan—the gift of a cow made by pious Hindus to a brahman at the time of death

gulabjamun—a sweet made from milk and soaked in syrup

hakim—a medical practitioner following the Muslim system of medicine

Hanuman—the monkey chief deified for his services to Rama

Holi—a Hindu festival in early spring celebrated with merry-making and permitting considerable licence in activities such as throwing coloured liquids and powders on people and drinking narcotic preparations.

ji—an honourific suffix for Indian personal names

kabaddi—a game in which the object is for one team to capture all the members of the other team. The player on the hunting side tries to tag opponents and return across the centre line to his own side, repeating 'kabaddi ... kabaddi ... kabaddi' while he is on enemy territory to show that he is not taking a breath. The opponents meanwhile try to tackle him so that he will have to take a breath, which would put him out of the game.

kahar—a low-caste group, traditionally water-carriers

Kali—the fierce consort of Shiva

kayastha—traditionally the writer or scribe class among Hindus

Khan—a princely title applied to all Pathans

Koran—the Muslim sacred book

Krishna—a popular Hindu deity, a manifestation of Vishnu, who is celebrated and worshipped as a mischievous child, an amorous cow-herder, and a divine charioteer kurta—a long, loose shirt

Lakshmi—goddess of wealth and good fortune; the symbol of all domestic virtues

loo—a very hot dry wind which blows during the hot season in parts of North India

Mahabharata—classical Hindu epic relating a great conflict between groups of rival cousins

maharaj—or 'maharaja'—literally 'great king'; a term of respect for people of high caste or position

maharani—'great queen'

mahto—a term of respect for farmers or peasants

maulvi—Muslim religious leader versed in the scriptures

memsahib—a term, usually respectful, applied to Western or Westernized ladies primarily

neem—a tree noted for its shade, timber and medicinal properties

pajama—man's lower garment, cut either very loose or very tight

palao—a fried rice preparation which often contains spices, raisins and nuts

pandit—literally 'learned'; a term of respect for brahmans

Pathan—a tribe from the Afghanistan-India (now Pakistan) border area, known in India as salesmen and moneylenders

patwari—local revenue official; a government agent responsible for village land records and revenue collection

pice—one-fourth of an anna

pipal—a tree having special sanctity for Hindus

Puranas—scriptural narrations in verse of the powers and works of various deities

Pushtoo—language of Afghanistan

Radha—favourite milkmaid of the god Krishna

raja—king or ruler; a title conferred in the past on Hindus of rank

Rama—hero of the Ramayana epic; considered an incarnation of Vishnu and an image of ideal manhood

Ramayana—ancient sacred Hindu epic relating the story of Rama's winning Sita by breaking a huge bow, his exile, the capture of his wife by the demon Ravana, and Rama's eventual triumph

rani—queen

rupee—sixteen annas

sahib—'master'; an honourific term applied especially to superiors

Saraswati—goddess of wisdom; patroness of the arts and sciences

sari—Indian woman's garment

Shiva—third member of the so-called Hindu triad; the deity associated with destruction and therefore also with renewal; also known as Pashupati, lord of animals

shudra—lowest of the four main subdivisions of traditional Hindu society; the class of artisans and many labourers

swayamvara—the selection, as reported in classical Indian literature, of a husband by a princess or daughter of a kshatriya at a public assembly of suitors

tantric—relating to tantra, a kind of religious sect employing magical formulae, symbols and rituals

thakur—a man of the kshatriya class, second to the brahmans in the traditional Hindu social hierarchy; traditionally devoted especially to military and ruling activities

thali—metal platter

tonga—a type of horse-drawn carriage

vaidya—a practitioner of the traditional Hindu system of medicine

Vishnu—second member of the so-called Hindu triad, considered by his devotees as the supreme being from whom all things emanate, and worshipped as a preserver and restorer

zamindar—large landowner given an estate by the British government in exchange for fixed annual revenues

Printed in the USA
CPSIA information can be obtained
at www.ICGtesting.com
CBHW061043160124
3489CB00013B/70

9 780253 215673